D1272172

SELECT EDITIONS

Selected and Edited by Reader's Digest

SELECT EDITIONS

Selected and Edited by
Reader's Digest

 New York · Montreal

FROM THE EDITORS

One of the elements we take into consideration when choosing books for Select Editions is setting. It may seem like a minor detail, but the setting of a book can be critical in creating a tone or mood. When putting together this volume, we were really excited by not only the variety of plots but also the very distinctive locale of each tale.

The first book, *The Turn of the Key* by Ruth Ware, takes place in a creepy manor house in the remote hills of Scotland. The moody mists and lonely woods really add to the nail-biting suspense. Don't read this one alone at night!

The next story—Shelley Noble's *A Beach Wish*—is set in a small New England town, where a hidden beach holds shocking secrets about a family's past. After that comes *Layover,* David Bell's adrenaline-fueled tale about a regular guy on a boring business trip whose chance encounter in an airport sends him down a very dangerous path.

To round out the volume, you'll find yourself in the small town of Branson, Missouri, with the local sheriff. In *A Deadly Turn* by Claire Booth, Sheriff Hank Worth investigates a tragic accident, a dead body, and other confounding mysteries. Small-town life isn't so quiet in Branson!

Wherever you find yourself reading this volume—at the beach, in front of a cozy fire, in your favorite armchair—we hope you enjoy the stories and all of their settings.

Inside
SELECT EDITIONS

7th September 2017
HMP Charnworth

Dear Mr. Wrexham,

You have no idea how many times I've started this letter and screwed up the resulting mess, but I've realized there is no magic formula here. There is no way I can *make* you listen to my case. So I'm just going to have to do my best to set things out. However long it takes, however much I mess this up, I'm just going to keep going and tell the truth.

My name is . . . Here I stop, wanting to tear up the page again.

Because if I tell you my name, you will know why I am writing to you. My case has been all over the papers, my name in every headline, my agonized face staring out of every front page—every single article insinuating my guilt. If I tell you my name, I have a horrible feeling you might write me off as a lost cause and throw my letter away. But please, before you do that, hear me out.

I am a young woman, twenty-seven years old, and as you'll have seen from the return address above, I am currently at the Scottish women's prison HMP Charnworth.

What you probably don't know is that I'm on remand.

7

And what you cannot know is that I'm innocent.

I know, I know. They all say that. Every person I've met here is innocent—according to them, anyway. But in my case it's true.

You may have guessed what's coming next. I'm writing to ask you to represent me as my solicitor advocate at my trial.

I realize that this is not how defendants are supposed to approach advocates. I have a solicitor already—Mr. Gates—and from what I understand, he is the person who should be appointing an advocate for the actual trial. But he is also the person who landed me here in the first place. I didn't choose him—the police picked him for me when I finally had the sense to shut up and refuse to answer questions until they found me a lawyer.

I thought that he would straighten everything out. But when he arrived, he just made everything worse. He didn't let me *speak*. Everything I tried to say, he was cutting in with "My client has no comment at this time," and it just made me look more guilty. I feel like if only I could have explained properly, it would never have got this far. But somehow the facts kept twisting in my mouth, and the police—they made everything sound so incriminating.

It's not that Mr. Gates hasn't heard my side of the story, exactly. He's sat down and talked to me, but he doesn't *listen*. And he keeps talking to me about what I said in the transcripts from that awful first night at the police station, when they grilled me and grilled me and I said— I don't know what I said.

What I said then, there's no undoing that. They have all that on tape. And it's bad. But it came out wrong. I feel like if only I could be given a chance to get my case across to someone who would really listen . . . Do you see what I'm saying?

Maybe you don't. You've never sat across a desk feeling so exhausted you want to drop, with the police asking and asking and asking, until you don't know what you're saying anymore.

I guess it comes down to this in the end.

I am the nanny in the Elincourt case, Mr. Wrexham.

And I *didn't* kill that child.

Chapter 1

12th September 2017
HMP Charnworth

Dear Mr. Wrexham,

It's been three days since I wrote to you, and I'm beginning to worry. There's not much to do in here, and there's a lot of time to think and fret and build up catastrophes inside your head.

I've spent the last few days and nights doing that. Worrying that you didn't get the letter. Worrying that the prison authorities didn't pass it on. Worrying that I didn't *explain* right.

It's the last one that has been keeping me awake. Because if it's that, then it's my fault.

I was trying to keep it short and snappy, but now I'm thinking, I shouldn't have stopped so quickly. I should have put in more of the facts, tried to show you *why* I'm innocent. Because you can't just take my word for it—I get that.

I understand if you're skeptical. I didn't manage to convince the police, after all. I'm here. Without bail. I must be guilty.

But it's not true.

To convince you, I'll just have to start at the beginning and set it all out, clearly and calmly, until I get to the end.

And the beginning was the advertisement.

WANTED: LARGE FAMILY SEEKS EXPERIENCED LIVE-IN NANNY

ABOUT US: We are a busy family of four children, living in a beautiful (but remote!) house in the Highlands. Mum and Dad co-run the family architecture practice.

ABOUT YOU: We are seeking an experienced nanny, used

to working with children of all ages, from babyhood to teens. Excellent references, background check, first-aid certificate, and clean driving license are a must.

ABOUT THE POST: Mum and Dad work mainly from home, and during those periods, you will have a simple eight-to-five post, with one night a week babysitting and weekends off. As far as possible, we arrange our schedule so that one parent is always around. However, there are times when we may both need to be away, and when this occurs, you will be in loco parentis.

In return we can offer a highly competitive remuneration package totaling £55,000 per annum (gross, including bonus), use of a car, and eight weeks' holiday a year.

Applications to Sandra and Bill Elincourt, Heatherbrae House, Carn Bridge.

I remember it nearly word for word. The funny thing was, I wasn't even looking for a job when it came up on my Google results—I was searching for . . . well, it doesn't really matter what I was looking for. But something completely different. And then there it was—like a gift thrown into my hands unexpectedly.

I was scared to look at the closing date for applications—convinced I would have missed it. But it was that very evening.

It was unbelievable. Not just the salary—though that was a pretty startling sum. But the luck of it. The whole package, just falling in my lap, right when I was in the perfect position to apply.

You see, my flatmate was away, traveling. We'd met at the Little Nippers nursery in Peckham, working side by side in the baby room, laughing about our terrible boss and the pushy, faddy parents. When she left a couple of months ago, she left her stuff in her room, and we'd agreed she'd pay half rent and I'd keep the room open for her. It seemed like a good compromise.

But when the novelty of having the whole place to myself had started to fade a little, I found I was lonely. I missed sounding off to her about Val, the owner of Little Nippers, and sharing anecdotes about the worst of the parents. When I applied for a promotion and didn't get it, I went to the pub alone to drown my sorrows, thinking how different it would have been if she had still been here.

I'm not good at being alone. And I think it was that, more than anything, that pushed me out of my comfort zone and made me scroll down that ad, imagining what lay at the other end of it.

The police made a lot out of the salary when they first questioned me. But the truth is, the money wasn't the reason I applied for the post. It wasn't even really about my flatmate. No, the real reason . . . well, you probably know what the real reason was. It was all over the papers, after all.

I CALLED in sick to Little Nippers and spent the entire day working on a CV and getting together everything that I knew I would need to convince the Elincourts that I was the person they were looking for. Background check—check. First-aid certificate—check. Spotless references—check, check, and check.

The only problem was the driving license. But I pushed the issue aside for the moment. I could cross that bridge when I came to it. Right now I wasn't thinking past the interview.

I added a note to the cover letter asking the Elincourts not to contact Little Nippers for a reference—I told them that I didn't want my current employers knowing that I was casting about for another job, which was true—and then I emailed it off to the address provided and held my breath and waited.

THOSE next few days were hard, Mr. Wrexham. Because I wanted that interview *so much*. I was only just beginning to realize how much. With every day that passed, my hopes ebbed a little more. But six days later it came, pinging into my email inbox.

To: supernanny1990@ymail.com
From: sandra.elincourt@elincourtandelincourt.com
Subject: Nanny position.

Hi, Rowan! Thank you so much for your application. Your CV was very impressive, and we would like to invite you to interview. Our house is rather remote, so we are happy to pay your train fare and can offer you a room in our house overnight, as you will not be able to make the trip from London in one day.

However, there is one thing I must make you aware of up front, in case it affects your enthusiasm for the post.

Since we bought Heatherbrae, we have become aware of various superstitions surrounding the house's history. It is an old building and has had no more than the usual number of deaths in its past, but for some reason these have resulted in local tales of hauntings. Unfortunately, this has upset some of our recent nannies, to the extent that four have resigned in the past fourteen months.

As you can imagine, this has been very disruptive for the children, not to mention awkward for myself and my husband professionally. For that reason, we are offering a generous salary in the hopes of attracting someone who can commit to staying for the long term—at least a year.

If you are still keen to attend the interview, please let me know your availability for the forthcoming week.

Best wishes, and I look forward to meeting you.

Sandra Elincourt

I closed down the email and for a moment just sat there staring at the screen. Then I got up and punched the air in jubilation.

I had done it. I had *done* it.

I should have known it was too good to be true.

ALMOST exactly one week after I had opened the email from Sandra Elincourt, I was on a train up to Scotland for the interview, doing my very best impression of Rowan the Perfect Nanny. My normally bushy hair was tamed into a neat, jaunty ponytail, and I was wearing my best "approachable yet responsible" outfit—a tweed skirt and a white cotton shirt with a cashmere cardigan.

Much to my annoyance, the train was delayed, so it took nearly six hours to get to Edinburgh instead of the time-tabled four and a half, and when I got off the train at Waverley, stiffly flexing my legs, I found it was past five o'clock and I had missed my connection by a good hour. Fortunately, there was another train due, and while I waited, I texted Mrs. Elincourt, apologizing profusely and warning her that I would be late into Carn Bridge.

At last the train arrived. I settled myself in a window seat, and as the train headed north, I watched the countryside change from rolling green fields to the smoke-blue and purples of heathered moors. It was so beautiful, it made me forget my irritation at being late. Something inside me began . . . I don't know, Mr. Wrexham. It was like I began to *hope*. To hope that this could truly be real.

I felt, in some twisted kind of way, like I was coming home.

We passed through stations with half-familiar names—Perth, Pitlochry, Aviemore—the sky growing darker all the time. At last I heard "Carn Bridge, next stop Carn Bridge," and the train pulled into a little Victorian station, and I got out. I stood on the platform, jumpy with nerves, wondering what to do.

Someone will meet you, Mrs. Elincourt's email had said. What did that mean? A taxi? Someone holding up a sign with my name?

I stood awkwardly while the other passengers dispersed to cars and waiting friends and relatives. The optimism I had felt on the train was starting to fade. What if Mrs. Elincourt hadn't got my text? She hadn't replied. Perhaps I'd been marked as a no-show.

Suddenly the butterflies were back—and badly.

It was early June, but we were pretty far north, and the night air was surprisingly cold after the summer warmth of London. I pulled my coat around me, a cool wind whipping down from the hills. The platform had emptied, and I was all alone.

Then I saw a man walking down the platform, hands in pockets.

For a moment something seemed to stutter in my chest, but then he got closer and he looked up, his eyes meeting mine, and I realized, it couldn't possibly be *him*. He was much too young. Thirty, thirty-five at the outside. He was good-looking, in an unshaven kind of way, with tangled dark hair and a tall, lean frame.

He was wearing overalls, and as he came up to me, he took his hands out of his pockets, and I saw they were grained with something—soil, or engine oil. As he drew level with me, he spoke.

"Rowan Caine?"

I nodded.

"I'm Jack Grant." He grinned, his mouth curling disarmingly

at the edges. His accent was Scottish. "I work up at Heatherbrae House. Sandra asked me to pick you up. Sorry I'm late."

"Hi," I said, suddenly shy. "Um, it's fine. No problem."

"It's why I'm in such a state." He looked ruefully down at his hands. "She didn't tell me you'd be wanting a lift until half an hour ago. I was halfway through fixing the mower, but I was worried I'd miss your train, so I set out, dirt and all. Can I take your case?"

"Honestly, it's fine." I picked up my case. "It's not heavy. Thank you for coming out."

He shrugged. "No need to thank me; it's my job."

"You work for the Elincourts?"

"For Bill and Sandra, aye. I do the gardening, fix the cars, run them in and out of Carn Bridge. You'll be the nanny?"

"Not yet," I said nervously, but he grinned sideways at me, and I smiled in spite of myself.

We were outside the station now, walking across the sparsely populated car park toward a long, black car. Jack clicked something on a fob in his pocket, and the doors shot up like bat wings, making my jaw drop involuntarily. Jack grinned again.

"It's a bit conspicuous, isn't it? It's a Tesla. Electric. Bill . . . well, you'll see. He's into technology."

Jack stood back as I put my case into the rear of the car.

"Do you want to ride in the back or up front?" he asked.

"Oh, in front, please!"

The thought of sitting regally in the back, treating him like a chauffeur, was enough to make me squirm.

"The views are better anyway," was all he said, but he clicked something that made the batwing doors at the rear of the car swing closed and then held open the front passenger door.

"After you, Rowan."

For a moment I didn't move, almost forgetting who he was speaking to. Then, with a start, I climbed into the car.

I HAD known, on some level, that the Elincourts were rich. But it wasn't until we reached Heatherbrae House that I realized quite how rich they were. The knowledge gave me a strange feeling.

The Tesla was eerily silent as we drove up the long, winding drive, the sound of the gravel beneath the wheels louder by far than the hushed electric engine.

"Wow," I muttered under my breath as we rounded yet another bend and still no house was in sight. Jack shot me a sideways look.

"Big place, isn't it?"

"Just a bit."

We bumped across a bridge over a quick-running burn, the waters dark with peat, and then drove through a cluster of pines. At last we came out of the shelter of the trees and into a clearing, and I saw Heatherbrae House for the first time.

The house was a modest Victorian, foursquare, with a black door in the center and windows on each side. It was not big, but solidly built of granite blocks, with lush Virginia creeper rambling up one side of it, and it exuded warmth and luxury and *comfort*.

I stepped out of the car and into the shelter of the covered porch. Instantly, something felt off-kilter. But what was it? The door in front of me was traditional enough, paneled wood painted a rich glossy black, but something seemed wrong—*missing*, even. It took me a second to notice what it was. There was no keyhole.

The realization was somehow unsettling.

There was no knocker, either, and I looked over my shoulder, seeking Jack's guidance as to how I should announce myself. But he was still inside the car, checking something on the controls.

I turned back, and as I did so, something embedded in the wall to the left of the door caught my eye. A ghostly illuminated icon in the shape of a bell had appeared from nowhere, shining out of what had seemed to be solid stone. I saw that what I had taken for simply part of the wall was actually a cleverly inlaid panel. I went to press it, but it must have been motion sensitive, for I had not even made contact when a chime sounded from inside the house.

"Rowan! Hello!" The female voice seemed to come out of nowhere, and I jumped, looking around for a camera, a microphone, a grille to speak into. There was none. Or none that I could see.

"Um . . . y-yes," I said, speaking to the air, in general, feeling like a complete fool. "Hi. Is that . . . Sandra?"

"Yes! I'm just getting changed. I'll be down in ten seconds. Sorry to keep you standing around."

The panel faded back to blank, and I stood waiting.

Finally there was a sudden cacophony of barking and the front door opened. Two black Labradors shot out, followed by a slim honey-blond woman of perhaps forty, laughing and snatching at their collars as they ran rings around her, yelping joyfully.

"Hero! Claude! Get back here!"

But the dogs paid no attention, leaping up at me as I took a couple of steps backward. I found myself laughing nervously.

The woman stepped out of the shelter of the porch and toward me, holding out her hand. "You must be Rowan." She managed to clip the leads she was holding on to the dogs' collars and dragged them beside her. "Sorry, they're so friendly. Do you mind dogs?"

"Not at all," I said, though it was only partly true. I didn't mind dogs, exactly, but they triggered my asthma if I didn't take my antihistamines. I felt my chest tighten.

Behind me I heard a door slam, followed by Jack's feet crunching across the gravel, and it was with some relief that I watched the dogs turn their attention to him, woofing happily as he retrieved my case from the back of the car.

"Here's your case, Rowan. Pleasure meeting you," he said as he set it down beside me, and then, turning to Mrs. Elincourt, "I'll be getting back to fixing the mower, if it's all right, Sandra."

"What's that?" Mrs. Elincourt said distractedly, and then she nodded. "Oh, the mower. Yes, thank you, Jack."

Sandra shook her head as he walked away around the side of the building. "Honestly, that man is *such* a treasure. I don't know what we'd do without him. He and Jean have been absolute rocks—it's what makes the whole nanny business all the more inexplicable."

The whole nanny business. There it was, then. The first reference to the odd fact that had been at the back of my mind all the way up here: four women had already walked out of this post.

In the initial flush of exultation, I hadn't really worried about that part of Sandra's letter. But as I reread the emails on the way up to Carn Bridge, the remark had stuck out.

I *didn't* believe in the supernatural—I should say that up front, Mr. Wrexham. And so the legends of the house didn't bother me at all; in fact, the whole idea of nannies driven out by mysterious spooky happenings seemed ridiculous—almost Victorian.

But the fact was that four women had left the Elincourts' employment in the last year. Having the bad luck to engage one superstitious employee seemed likely. Four in a row seemed . . . less so.

Which meant that something else was going on, and all sorts of possibilities had run through my mind on the journey up to Scotland. I had been half expecting to find that Heatherbrae was a ruin of a house or that Mrs. Elincourt was a difficult employer. So far that didn't seem to be the case. But I was reserving judgment.

INSIDE Heatherbrae the dogs were, if anything, more boisterous and excited, and at last Mrs. Elincourt gave up trying to control them and dragged them to a room at the back to shut them up.

As she disappeared, I hastily fumbled my inhaler out of my pocket and took a surreptitious puff, then waited for her inside the front door, feeling the atmosphere of the house settle around me.

It wasn't a big house, just a family home. But there was a sense of . . . of *money*. From the slow, sure tick of a beautiful grandfather clock beside the window to the deep patina of age on the refectory table against the wall, everything conspired into an almost overwhelming sense of luxury. Even the *smell* was right—beeswax polish, woodsmoke, and the faintest hint of dried rose petals.

I was just thinking all this when I heard a door shut and saw Sandra coming back from the far side of the hallway, shaking her heavy, honey-colored hair out of her face and smiling.

"Oh, dear, sorry, they do get excited when new faces appear. Let's start again. Hello, Rowan, I'm Sandra."

She held out her hand for the second time, slim and studded with expensive-looking rings. I shook it and returned her smile.

"Right, well, you must be famished and rather tired after such a long trip. You came up from London, is that right?"

I nodded.

"Let me show you to your room, and then, when you've made

yourself comfortable, come down and we'll have something to eat. I can't believe it's past nine already. Was your journey awful?"

"Not awful, no," I said. "Just slow. There was some kind of points failure at York, so I missed my connection. I'm really sorry. I'm usually very punctual."

"I got your text. So sorry I didn't reply. I didn't see it at first; I was up to my elbows in the kids' bath time when it came through, and I only just managed to rush out and tell Jack to collect you. I hope you weren't waiting at the station for ages."

"Not too long. Are the children in bed, then?"

"The three youngest, yes. Maddie is eight, Ellie is five, and the baby, Petra, is just eighteen months, so they're all in bed."

"And your other child?" I asked.

"Rhiannon is fourteen going on twenty-four. She's at boarding school over near Inverness. She comes home most weekends."

"So I won't meet her?" I asked. Sandra shook her head.

"No, unfortunately not, but to be honest, your time would be spent mostly with the little ones. Anyway, it means we can have a lovely chat now and you can get to know the kids tomorrow. Oh, and I'm afraid my husband—Bill—can't be here, either."

"Oh?" It was a surprise—a shock, even. I had been so sure that someone would want to meet the person they were considering hiring to look after their children . . . but I tried to keep my face neutral. Nonjudgmental. "Oh, that's a shame."

"Yes, he's away working. We're both architects in a two-man firm. Well, one man, one woman!" She flashed a smile. "We try to juggle it so that there's always one of us around, but with Katya leaving—she was our last nanny—it's just been chaos. I need to be honest and say that whoever does get the post isn't going to get a very smooth introductory period. Normally I try to work from home for the first month or so, but that just won't be possible this time. We need someone experienced who isn't going to be fazed by being left with the kids early on, and they need to be able to start ASAP." She looked at me, anxiously. "Do you think that describes you?"

I swallowed. Time to shed my doubts and step into the role of Rowan the Perfect Nanny.

"Definitely," I said. "I mean, you've seen my CV—"

"We were very impressed with your CV," Sandra said. "Quite frankly, it's one of the most impressive ones we've had. But what's your notice period like? I mean, *obviously* getting the *right* nanny is the most important thing. But we need someone who can start pretty much now, if I'm being completely honest."

"My notice period is four weeks." I saw Sandra's mouth twist in a little worried moue—and added hastily, "But I think I could probably negotiate an earlier finish."

I didn't miss the flash of hope and relief that crossed Sandra's face. But then she seemed to realize where we were.

"Look at me, keeping you talking in the hallway. It's hardly fair for me to be interviewing you before you've even got your coat off! Let me show you to your room, and then we can retreat to the kitchen and have a proper talk."

She turned and began to make her way up the long, curving flight of stairs. At the first landing, she stopped and put her finger to her lips. I paused, taking in the wide sweep of space, the table with a vase of blush peonies. A corridor disappeared off into semidarkness, with half a dozen doors leading off from it. The one at the far end had wooden letters stuck on it, and I made out the words PRINCESS ELLIE and QUEEN MADDIE. The door closest to the stairwell was slightly open, and I could hear a baby's soft breath.

"The kids are asleep," Sandra whispered. "At least, I hope so. Bill and I sleep on this floor, but Rhi sleeps upstairs. This way."

At the top of the second flight, three more doors led off a slightly smaller landing. The middle one was open, and inside I saw a small cupboard housing a jumble of mops and brooms.

The door to the left of it was closed and had "KEEP OUT OR YOU DIE" written across it in what looked like red lipstick.

"That's Rhiannon's room," Sandra said with a slight lift of her eyebrows. "This one"—she put her hand on the door to the far right of the stairs—"is yours. I mean—" She stopped, looking flustered. "I mean, it's where we always put the nanny, and it's where you'll be sleeping tonight. Sorry, don't want to be too presumptuous!"

She opened the door. It was dark inside, but instead of groping for a switch, Sandra pulled out her phone. She pressed something, and the lights inside the room flickered into life.

It wasn't just the main overhead light. The reading light by the bed had come on, too, as well as a standing lamp next to a table.

My surprise must have shown on my face, because Sandra gave a delighted laugh.

"Pretty cool, isn't it? This is a smart house. All the heating and lights and so on can be controlled from our phones." She swiped at something, and the main light grew suddenly much brighter and then dimmer again, and across the room a light turned on in the en suite bathroom and then flicked off again.

"It's not just lighting," Sandra said, and she tapped an icon and music started playing softly out of an invisible speaker.

"There's also a voice option, but I find that a bit creepy, so I don't often use it. Still, I can show you." She coughed, then said in a slightly artificial raised tone, "Music off!"

There was a pause, and then the Miles Davis shut off abruptly.

"Obviously, you can also control the settings from the panel." She pressed something on the wall, and a white panel lit up as the curtains on the window swished closed and then opened again.

"Wow," I said. On the one hand it was impressive. On the other hand . . . I found myself coming back to Sandra's word. *Creepy.*

"I know," Sandra said with a little laugh. "It's a bit ridiculous, I do realize. But being architects, it's a professional duty to try out all the cool gadgets. Anyway"—she looked at her phone again, checking the clock—"I *must* stop talking and get the supper out of the oven. Shall I see you downstairs in . . . fifteen minutes?"

"Sounds good," I said a little faintly, and she gave me a grin and disappeared, closing the door behind her.

After she had gone, I surveyed the room. It was an odd mixture of traditional and modern. The window was Victorian, right down to the brass latch. But the lights were twenty-first century, with a plethora of spotlights and lamps, each focused on part of the room.

The furniture was more conservative. Opposite me, facing the window, was a king-size bed, and beneath the window was a small stuffed sofa, with a little table beside it. There were chests of drawers, a desk, and an upholstered chest at the foot of the bed. Doors led off to each side, and opening one at random, I found a walk-in closet. I tried the second one, but it seemed to be locked.

The third was ajar, and I remembered it was the one that Sandra had lit up to show the bathroom inside. Venturing in, I saw a panel on the wall. I touched it, and it glowed into life, displaying a confusing configuration of icons. I pressed one, and the lights became brighter, revealing a state-of-the-art wet room with a rainwater shower and a vanity unit the size of my kitchen counter.

I thought of my bathroom at home—hair in the rusting plughole, dirty towels kicked into the corner, makeup stains on the mirror.

How I wanted this. I wanted this beautiful house and this gorgeous room, right down to the sumptuous marble-tiled shower.

More than that, I wanted to be part of this family.

For a long moment I just stood at the vanity unit, staring at myself in the mirror. Then my hand went to my necklace.

I wore it every day. It had been a present for my first birthday, and now, after more than two decades, it felt like part of myself. An ornate silver R on the end of a dangling chain.

There was no reason to take it off. It wasn't inappropriate. The chances of anyone even noticing it were very low. And yet . . .

Slowly I reached around my neck and undid the clasp.

Then I straightened my skirt, tightened my ponytail, and prepared to go back downstairs and give the interview of my life.

Chapter 2

WHEN I GOT DOWNSTAIRS, Sandra was nowhere to be seen, but I could smell some kind of delicious, savory scent coming from the far side of the hallway. When I pushed open the door, I found I had stepped into another world.

It was like the back of the house had been sliced off and grafted onto a startling modernist box. Soaring metal beams went up to a glass roof, and beneath my feet the Victorian encaustic tiles of the hall had abruptly stopped, replaced by a poured concrete floor, polished to a dull sheen. It looked like a combination of a brutalist cathedral and an industrial kitchen. In the center was a shiny metal breakfast bar, surrounded by chrome stools, dividing the room into the bright kitchen area and beyond it the dimly lit dining space, where a long concrete-topped table ran the length of the room.

In the middle was Sandra, standing in front of a monstrous stove, ladling a casserole into bowls. She looked up as I came in.

"Rowan! I forgot to ask—you're not veggie, are you?"

"No," I said. "No, I eat pretty much anything."

"Oh, phew, that's a relief, because we've got beef casserole and not a lot else! I was just frantically wondering if I had time to do a baked potato. Which reminds me." She walked across to the huge steel fridge, tapped an invisible button on the fridge door, and said, "Happy, order potatoes, please."

"Adding potatoes to your shopping list," replied a robotic voice, and a screen lit up, showing a grocery list. "Eat happy, Sandra!"

I watched as Sandra put the bowls on the table, along with a crusty loaf on a board and a dish of something like sour cream.

"There we go," Sandra said unnecessarily as she sat down and waved me to the seat opposite her. "Beef stew. Help yourself to bread to soak up the juices, and that's horseradish crème fraîche."

"It smells amazing," I said truthfully, and Sandra gave a little smile that tried to look modest but really said, *I know*.

There was a bottle of red wine already open on the table, and she poured us out two glasses and pushed one across to me.

"Now, would you rather eat first, or shall we get started?"

"I . . ." I sat up a little straighter on the metal stool. "Get started, I suppose. What would you like to know?"

"Well, your CV was very impressive. I already contacted your previous employer—what was her name? Grace Devonshire?"

"Er . . . yes, that's right," I said.

"And she couldn't say enough good things about you. I also spoke to Mrs. Grainger, and she was very complimentary as well."

"You didn't contact Little Nippers, did you?" I said slightly uneasily, but she shook her head.

"No, I understand. It's not easy job hunting in an existing post. But perhaps you could tell me about your employment there."

"Well, it's pretty much like I explained on the CV, really. I've been there for two years, in charge of the baby room. I wanted a change from one-family nannying, and a nursery seemed like a good option. It's been excellent experience having a bit more managerial responsibility and having to organize staff schedules and stuff, but quite honestly I've found I miss the family feel of nannying. I love the children, but you don't get to spend as much one-on-one time with them as you do with a private position. What was stopping me making a change was the idea of taking a step backward in terms of pay and responsibility, but your post seems like it might be the challenge I'm looking for."

My—slightly massaged—version of events seemed to have done the trick, for Mrs. Elincourt was nodding sympathetically.

"I can quite imagine."

"Plus, of course," I added, this on the spur of the moment, "I'm keen to get out of London. It's so busy and polluted, I guess I'm just looking for a change of scenery."

"That I can *quite* understand," Mrs. Elincourt said. "Bill and I had the same long night of the soul a few years back. Rhiannon was eight or nine, and Maddie was a toddler. I was so sick of pushing her around dirty parks and having to check for needles before I let her play. This seemed like the perfect chance to break away."

"And are you glad you made the move?"

"Oh, totally. We adore Scotland, although Heatherbrae House was a real project. It had been neglected for decades, lived in by an eccentric old man who went into a care home and allowed it to fall into disrepair until his death. Dry rot everywhere, burst pipes, dodgy electrics. Two years of absolute grind. But it was worth it."

I nodded.

"But that's enough about me and the house. What about yourself?" Sandra said. "What attracted you to nannying?"

Wow. That was a big question. About a dozen images flashed through my mind. My parents shouting at me for getting Play-Doh in the carpet at age six. Age nine, my mother shaking her head over my report card. At twelve, the school play no one bothered to come to. Age sixteen, "What a shame you didn't revise more for history," instead of congratulations on the A's I got in math and science. Eighteen years of not being good enough.

"Well . . ." I felt myself flounder. "Well, I suppose . . . I just like kids." It was lame. And also not completely true. But as the words left my mouth, I realized something else. Sandra was still smiling, but there was a neutrality in her expression that had not been there before, and suddenly I understood why. A woman on the cusp of her thirties, going on about how much she likes kids . . .

I hurried to repair my mistake.

"But I have to say, I'm in awe of anyone who wants to be a parent. I'm definitely not ready for that yet!"

Bingo. I could not miss the flash of relief that crossed Sandra's face, though it was quickly suppressed.

"Not that it's an option right now, anyway," I said, feeling confident enough for a little joke, "since I'm firmly single."

"So . . . no ties to London, then?"

"Not really. I have friends, of course, but my parents retired abroad a few years back. In fact, once I've sorted things out with Little Nippers, there's really nothing keeping me in London. I could take up a new post almost straightaway."

Sandra was smiling and nodding enthusiastically.

"Yes, I'd be lying if I said that wasn't a significant factor. We're coming up to the summer holidays, and we absolutely *must* get someone in the position before the schools break up. Plus, there's a really important trade fair in a few weeks, and both Bill and I need to be there. You said your notice period is four weeks?"

I nodded. "Yes, but I was figuring it out while I unpacked, and I can get it down to just over two weeks if I factor in my leave, and maybe even less. I think they'll be prepared to negotiate."

In actual fact, I had no idea how helpful they would be. Janine, my boss and current head of the baby room, wasn't my biggest fan. But I didn't say that to Sandra.

As we ate, Sandra looked through the papers I had brought with me—the background check, the first-aid certificates. They were all in order, but I still felt a flutter of nerves as she reviewed them.

"And the driving license?" she asked. I put down my fork onto the polished concrete top of the table and took a deep breath.

"Ah, right, yes. I'm afraid that's a problem. I do have a full UK driving license, and it's clean, but the actual card was stolen last month when I lost my purse. I've ordered a new one, but it's taking an age to come through. But I promise you, I *can* drive."

That last part was true, after all. To my relief she nodded and moved on to my professional ambitions. Where did I see myself in a year's time? The question really mattered; I could tell that from the way Sandra actually looked at me as I answered.

"In a year's time?" I said slowly, frantically trying to figure out what she wanted to hear from me. At last I made up my mind.

"To be honest, in a year's time I would hope to be here. I wouldn't want to uproot myself from London just for a short-term post. When I work for a family, I want to think it's a long-term relationship, both for me and the kids. I want to really get to know them, see them grow up a little bit. If you'd asked me where I saw myself in five years . . . well, that's different. I'm ambitious—I'd like to do a master's in childcare or child psychology at some point. But a year—any post I took now, I would definitely want to think of it lasting longer than a year, for all our sakes."

Sandra's face broke into a huge grin, and I knew—I just *knew* that I had given the right answer, the one she had been hoping for. But was it enough to get me the post? I didn't honestly know.

WE CHATTED for about another hour or so. Finally, Sandra looked at the clock and gave a little gulp of shock.

"Heavens, ten past eleven! You must be shattered, Rowan."

"I am a bit," I said truthfully.

"Well, look, I think we've covered everything I wanted to ask, but I was hoping you could meet the little ones tomorrow, see if you click, and then Jack will drive you back to Carn Bridge to catch your train, if that's okay? What time does it leave?"

"Eleven twenty-five, so that works fine for me."

"Great." She stood up and swept all the crockery into a stack. "Let's leave that for Jean and call it a night."

I nodded, wondering again who this mysterious Jean was, but not quite wanting to ask.

"I'll just go and let the dogs out. Good night, Rowan."

"Good night," I said back. "Thank you so much for a delicious supper, Sandra."

"My pleasure. Sleep well. The children are usually up at six, but there's no need for you to get up that early—unless you want to!"

She gave a little tinkly laugh, and I made a mental note to set my alarm for six, even while my eyes felt heavy at the thought.

As Sandra shooed the dogs into the garden, I made my way back up the staircase and to my luxurious, waiting bedroom. I washed and brushed my teeth, and then at last I was ready for bed, my alarm set, my clothes for tomorrow neatly set out on the little sofa.

Then I realized, I had not drawn the curtains.

Wrapping my dressing gown around myself, I walked across the room and tugged gently at their fabric. They didn't move.

Then I remembered—Sandra pressing something on the wall, and the curtains swishing closed, then open again.

I walked across to the panel beside the door and waved a hand in front of it. Instantly it lit up with that confusing configuration of squares and icons. None looked like curtains. There was one that might have been a window, but when I pressed it, a blast of jazz trumpet split the silence, and I hastily stabbed it with a finger.

It cut off immediately, and I returned to studying the panel. Then I remembered Sandra's comment about the voice settings.

"Shut curtains," I said in a low voice, and somewhat to my shock, the curtains whisked across with a barely audible swoosh.

Great. Okay. That only left the lights to figure out.

The bedside light had a switch, and the others I managed to figure out by trial and error, but there was one lamp by the armchair that I could not manage to extinguish.

"Turn off lights," I tried. Nothing happened. Bloody hell.

In the end I traced the cord back to a plug socket on the wall and pulled it out. The room was plunged instantly into darkness.

Slowly I groped my way back across the room to the foot of the bed and crawled into it. I was just snuggling down when I remembered, with a sigh, that I hadn't plugged my phone in to charge.

I couldn't face contending with the lights again, so instead I switched on the torch on my phone, got out of bed, and began to rummage through my case.

The charger wasn't there.

I tipped the bag upside down, letting my possessions tumble out onto the carpet, but no electrical wire came snaking out. Had I forgotten it? I stood there for a moment, chewing my lip, and then opened up one of the drawers in the bedside table, hoping against expectation that a previous guest might have left a charger behind.

And . . . bingo. Not a charger, but a charging lead. That was all I needed; there was a USB port built into the socket.

With a sigh of relief, I untangled the lead from the papers in the drawer, plugged it in, and attached my phone. I was about to lie back down when I noticed that a piece of paper had fallen out of the drawer. I glanced at it. It was a child's drawing.

It was hardly a work of art, just stick figures and crayoned lines. It showed a house with four windows and a shiny black front door, not unlike Heatherbrae. The windows were black, all except for one, which showed a tiny pale face peeping out of the darkness.

It was oddly disconcerting, but there was no name signed to it and no way of knowing why it was in the bedside drawer. I turned it over, looking for clues. There was writing on the other side. It wasn't a child's but an adult's—sloped and looping.

To the new nanny, it read. *My name is Katya. I am writing you this note because I wanted to tell you to please be*

And then it stopped.

I frowned. Who was Katya? The name rang a bell, and then I remembered Sandra's voice at dinner saying, *but with Katya leaving—she was our last nanny . . .*

So Katya had lived here. Slept here, even. But what had she wanted to say to her successor?

Please be . . . *kind to the children?* Please be . . . *happy here?*

It could have been anything. So why was the phrase that kept hovering on the tip of my tongue *please be careful?*

Well, whatever she had wanted to say, it was too late now.

I folded the drawing and slipped it back into the drawer. Then I switched off my phone, pulled the covers up to my chin, and tried to forget everything that hung in the balance.

WHEN I woke, it was to the insistent shrill beep of my alarm, and for a moment I could not think where I was or why I was so tired. Then I remembered: I was in Scotland. And it was six a.m.

I sat up, smoothing my rumpled hair and rubbing the sleep from my eyes. Downstairs I could hear thumps and shrill sounds of excitement. It sounded as though the children were probably up.

After showering, I ventured downstairs, and the first thing that greeted me was the smell of toast and the sound of children laughing. I made my way to the kitchen, where Sandra was standing in front of a chrome toaster holding a piece of brown bread and waving it at the two little girls in bright red pajamas sitting at the metal breakfast bar. Their curly heads—one dark, the other white-blond—were tousled with sleep, and they were both giggling helplessly.

"Don't encourage her! She'll only do it again."

"Do what again?" I said, and Sandra turned.

"Oh, Rowan! Gosh, you're up early. I hope the girls didn't wake you. We're still trying to train certain members of the family to stay in bed past six a.m." She nodded pointedly at the younger of the two girls, the one with white-blond hair.

"It's fine," I said truthfully as I sat at the table to eat a piece of toast and marmalade.

"Petra threw her porridge," said the girl with a gurgling laugh, pointing at the pink-cheeked baby sitting in the high chair at the corner, and I saw that she was right. There was a dollop of porridge the size of an egg sliding down the front of the stove. Petra was crowing with delight and scooping up another spoonful.

"Peta frow!" she said.

"Uh-uh," I said with a smile, and I leaned over and took the bowl of porridge away from her. "I think you've had enough, little Miss Petra. I'll take charge of that."

"Thank you, Rowan," Sandra said with a grateful smile. Then she turned and said, "Girls, I didn't get a chance to introduce you to Rowan. She's come to have a look around our house and meet you. Say hello."

"Hi," Maddie muttered. She looked younger than her eight years, with her dark hair and a sallow little face.

"Hello, Maddie," I said, but she kept her eyes firmly down. Ellie was easier; she was looking at me with frank curiosity from beneath her white-blond fringe. "Hello, Ellie. How old are you?"

"I'm five," Ellie said. Her blue eyes were round as buttons. "Are you going to be our new nanny?"

"I—" I stopped short, not sure what to say.

"Maybe," Sandra cut in. "Rowan hasn't decided yet whether she wants to work here, so we must be well behaved to impress her!"

She gave me a little sideways wink.

"I tell you what, run upstairs and get dressed, and then we can show Rowan around."

The two girls slid off the tall stools and pattered away across the hallway and up the stairs. Sandra watched them go, fondly.

"Gosh, they're very good!" I said.

Sandra rolled her eyes. "They know not to play up in front of visitors. But let's see if they're actually doing as they're told."

She pressed a button on an iPad lying on the counter, and a picture flickered into view. It was a children's bedroom, the camera obviously sited up near the ceiling, pointing downward at two little beds. There was no sound, but the noise of a door slamming was loud enough to filter down the stairs, and a teddy bear on the mantelpiece rocked and fell. As we watched, Maddie stamped angrily into view at the bottom of the screen and sat on the left-hand bed, her arms folded. Sandra pressed something, and the camera zoomed in on Maddie's face. There was a faint crackle coming from the iPad now, as if a microphone had been switched on.

"Maddie," Sandra said, "what have I told you about slamming doors?"

"I didn't." The voice came tinny from the iPad speaker.

"You did, and I saw you. You could have hurt Ellie. Now get your clothes on and you can watch some TV."

Maddie got up, and Sandra shut down the screen.

"Wow," I said, slightly taken aback. "Impressive!"

It was not the word I was thinking. *Stalkerish* was closer to the mark.

"The whole house is wired up," Sandra said casually, dropping the iPad back onto the counter. "It's very handy, especially in a place with several floors."

"Very handy," I echoed faintly, suppressing my unease. The *whole* house? What did that mean? The bedrooms? The *bathrooms?* But no, that was beyond possibility. I put my remaining bit of toast back on the plate, my appetite suddenly gone.

THE rest of the morning seemed to pass in a blur. I spent the time making homemade Play-Doh with the children and then helping them fashion it into a variety of lumpy creations, most of which Petra mashed into shapelessness again with crows of laughter and howls of annoyance from Ellie. Maddie was the one who puzzled me most—she was stiff and unyielding, as if determined not to smile for me, but I persisted, and at last, in spite of herself, she seemed to unbend a little.

At last Sandra tapped me on the shoulder and told me that Jack was waiting to take me to the station. I stood up, washed my hands, and gave Petra a little chuck under the chin.

Jack was waiting outside with the car, his hands in his pockets, the sunshine finding specks of deep auburn in his dark hair.

"Well, it was a *total* pleasure to meet you," Sandra said, and there was a genuine warmth in her eyes as she held out her hand. "I'll need to discuss things with Bill, but I think I can say . . . well, let's just say you'll be hearing from us very soon with a final decision. *Very* soon. Thank you, Rowan, you were fabulous."

"It was lovely to meet you, too, Sandra," I said. "Your girls are lovely. I hope I get the chance to meet Rhiannon sometime." *I hope*

I get the job, that meant in code. "Goodbye, Ellie." I stuck out my hand, and she shook it gravely. "Goodbye, Maddie."

But Maddie, to my dismay, did not take my hand. Instead, she buried her face in her mother's midriff, refusing to meet my eyes. Sandra gave a little shrug as if to say, *What can you do?*

I shrugged back and turned toward the car.

I had stowed my luggage in the back seat and was just walking around the opposite side of the car when something hit me like a small, dark hurricane. Arms wrapped around my waist, a hard little skull digging into my lower ribs.

Wriggling around in the fierce embrace, I saw to my surprise that it was Maddie. Maybe I had won her over, after all?

"Maddie!" I said, but she didn't answer. I bent down to hug her back. "Thank you for showing me your lovely house. Goodbye."

I hoped that the last word might make her let go, but she only tightened her grip, squeezing me uncomfortably tight.

"Don't—" I heard her whimper into my top, though I couldn't make out the second word. *Don't go?*

"I have to," I whispered back. "But I hope I'll be able to come back very soon."

But Maddie was shaking her head, her dark hair swishing against her knobbly spine. She made a sound, almost a whimper.

"Maddie? Is something wrong?"

"Don't come here," she whispered. "It's not safe."

"It's not safe?" I gave a little laugh. "What do you mean?"

"It's not *safe*," she repeated with a little angry sob, shaking her head harder. "They wouldn't like it."

"Who wouldn't like it?"

But with that, she tore herself away, and then she was running barefoot across the grass, shouting something over her shoulder.

"Maddie!" I called after her. "Maddie, wait!"

"Don't worry," Sandra said with a laugh. She came around to my side of the car. It was plain that she had not seen anything apart from Maddie's sudden hug and her subsequent flight. "That's Maddie, I'm afraid. But she must have liked you. I'm not sure she's ever voluntarily hugged a stranger before!"

"Thank you," I said, rather unsettled, and I let Sandra see me into the car and slam the door shut.

It was only as we began to wind slowly down the drive that I found myself replaying Maddie's final remark, wondering if she had really said what I thought I'd heard.

For the thing she had called over her shoulder seemed almost too preposterous to be true, and yet the more I brooded over it, the more I was sure of what I'd heard.

The ghosts, she had sobbed. *The ghosts wouldn't like it.*

"WELL, seems it's goodbye for now," Jack said. He stood at the barrier to the station, holding my bag in one hand, his other outstretched. I took it and shook it.

"Nice to meet you," I said a little awkwardly, and then I added, a little rashly, "Sorry I didn't get to meet Bill. Or . . . or Jean."

"Jean?" Jack said, looking a little puzzled. "She's not about much in the day. Goes home to her dad."

"Is she . . . Is she young, then?"

"No!" He gave that grin again. "She's fifty, if she's a day. No, she's a—what's the word? A carer. Her father lives in the village; he has Alzheimer's. She comes up in the morning before he's awake and then again in the afternoon. Does the dishes and that."

"Oh." I felt my face flush, and I smiled.

"Well, good to meet you, Rowan."

"Good to meet you, too . . . Jack." The name came off my tongue a little awkwardly, and I blushed again. Up the valley, I heard the sound of the approaching train. "Goodbye."

"Goodbye." He held out the case, and I began to walk to the platform, giving myself a stern injunction *not* to look back. When at last the train had drawn in and I had climbed aboard and settled myself in a carriage, I did risk one last glance out the window. But he was gone. And so my last glimpse of Carn Bridge was of an empty platform, clean and sun-soaked, awaiting my return.

Chapter 3

BACK IN LONDON, I prepared myself for an agonizing wait. I had dared to hope for something on my phone by the time I got home, but there was nothing that evening, or the next day when I left for work. We had to leave our phones turned off in our lockers at Little Nippers, so I resigned myself to a long morning.

My lunch shift wasn't until one, and when the clock ticked over, I virtually ran to the staff room. There, I grabbed my bag and escaped out the back entrance into the little concrete yard that we used for phone calls. It took an age for the phone to switch on, but at last I typed in my passcode with shaking fingers.

I had a message.

I dialed into voice mail and heard Sandra's plummy accent.

"Oh, hello, Rowan. I'm delighted to say that I've discussed it with Bill, and we'd be happy to offer you the job *if* you can start on June seventeenth at the absolute latest. I realize that we didn't discuss the exact terms and the bonus. The plan would be for us to issue you with an allowance of a thousand pounds a month, with the remainder of the salary to come at year-end in the form of a completion bonus. If you could let me know as soon as possible if you'd like to accept, and oh, yes, lovely to meet you the other day. Looking forward to hearing back from you."

There was a click, and the message ended.

For a minute I just stood there, the phone in my hand, gaping at the screen. And then a rush of exhilaration raced through me, and I found I was dancing, punching the air, and grinning like a lunatic.

I HANDED in my notice to Val that same day. She tried to act pleased for me, but in truth she looked mostly pissed off, particularly when I informed her that the amount of leave I had stacked up meant that I would be finishing on the sixteenth of June rather than the first of July, as she had assumed. She tried to tell me that I needed to work my notice and take the leave as pay, but when I more or less invited her to see me in court, she caved.

The next few days passed in a whirl of activity. Sandra did all her payroll remotely through a company in Manchester and wanted me to contact them directly with payment details and ID rather than sending all the paperwork up to Scotland. I had expected the process to be a major stumbling block, but in the end it was surprisingly simple: I forwarded them Sandra's email with a reference number, and then when they replied, I sent the passport scan, utility bills, and bank details they requested. It went through without a hitch. Like it was meant to be.

The ghosts wouldn't like it.

The phrase floated through my head, spoken in Maddie's reedy little voice, its childlike quaver lending eeriness to the words.

But that was bollocks. I hadn't seen a whiff of the supernatural the whole time I was in Carn Bridge. More likely it was just a cover story seized on by homesick au pairs, girls barely out of their teens, unable to cope with the isolation and remote location.

I was considerably older and wiser than that, and I had very good reasons for wanting to make this work. No amount of alleged "haunting" was going to make me turn this chance down.

I look back, and I want to shake that smug young woman sitting in her London flat thinking she knew it all, had seen it all.

Because I was wrong, Mr. Wrexham. I was very, very wrong.

LESS than three weeks later I was standing on Carn Bridge station platform, surrounded by cases and boxes.

When Jack came striding up the platform, car keys jangling in his hand, he actually broke into a laugh.

"How did you get all that across London?"

"Slowly," I said honestly. "And painfully."

"Aye, well, you're here now," he said, and took my largest two cases. "Come on, car's this way."

The sun was beginning to sink toward the horizon as we drove silently through the wooded lanes and moorland roads toward Heatherbrae. The house, as we drove up the drive, was even more beautiful than I had remembered, basking in evening sunshine.

"Rowan!" Sandra came running out the front door, her arms outstretched, and before I was fully out of the car, she had enveloped me in a maternal hug. Then she stood back and waved her hand at a figure standing in the shadows of the porch—a tall man, balding slightly, with close-shaven hair.

"Rowan, this is my husband, Bill. Bill, meet Rowan Caine."

So this—*this* was Bill Elincourt.

He strode toward me, giving me a quick, businesslike smile.

"Rowan. Good to meet you at last. Sandra's told me all about you. You have a very impressive résumé."

You don't know the half of it, Bill, I thought as he picked up one of the cases from the trunk and made his way back to the house. I took a deep breath and prepared to follow, and as I did, my hand went nervously to my necklace. I slipped the pendant inside the neck of my shirt and hurried after them.

Inside the kitchen we had coffee, and I sat on the edge of one of the metal breakfast stools while Bill quizzed me about my qualifications. I wanted to impress him. But at the same time, as he droned on about his punishing schedule and the difficulties of recruiting staff in the Highlands and the inadequacies of his previous nannies, I increasingly wanted to shake him.

Do you know what it's like? I wanted to shout at him as he complained about their gardener who had left to take a full-time teaching job in Edinburgh, and the home help who had broken the £800 waste-disposal unit in the sink and then run away because she couldn't face telling them. *Do you understand what it's like for people who don't have your money and your privilege?*

And the realization came to me. He was *selfish*. A selfish, self-centered man who had barely asked me a single personal question—not even how my journey had been. He just didn't care.

Perhaps Sandra saw something of my discomfort, for she gave a little laugh and broke in.

"Darling, Rowan doesn't want to hear about our domestic travails.

Just make sure you don't go putting cutlery down the grinder, Rowan! Anyway, quite seriously, all the instructions are here." She patted a fat red binder at her elbow. "It's got everything from how to work the washing machine right through to the children's bedtimes. If you've got any concerns at all, you'll find the answers here. Did you download Happy?"

"I'm sorry?"

"Happy—the home-management app. I emailed you the authorization code."

"Oh, I'm sorry, the app, yes, I downloaded it."

She looked relieved.

"Well, that's the main thing. I've set up your Happy profile with all the permissions you'll need, and of course it stands in as a baby monitor, though we've got a regular one for Petra's room as well. Rhiannon will be coming home next week, and I've sorted out her lift and everything so you've nothing to worry about there. What else . . . what else . . ."

"I don't think we sorted out when you're leaving," I said tentatively. "I know you said in your email that you had the trade show next week. When does it start, exactly? Is it next Saturday?"

"Oh." Sandra looked taken aback. "Did I not say? That's the . . . um . . . well, that's the only issue, really. It is Saturday, but not next Saturday—this one. We leave tomorrow."

"What?" For a moment, I thought I hadn't heard properly. "Did you say you're leaving *tomorrow?*"

"Yeess . . ." Sandra said, her face suddenly uncertain. "I . . . Is that a problem? If you're not confident about coping straight out of the box, I can try to reschedule my early meetings . . ."

She trailed off, and I swallowed.

"It's fine," I said with a confidence I didn't completely feel.

Are you mad? a voice was screaming inside my head. *Are you crazy? You barely know these children.*

But another part of me was whispering something different: *Good.* Because in a way, this made things considerably easier.

"We can play it by ear," Sandra was saying. "I'll keep in touch by phone. If the children are too unsettled, then I can fly back midweek, perhaps. You'll only have the little ones for the first few days, so hopefully that'll make the transition a little bit easier—"

She stopped again, a little awkwardly this time, but I was nodding, my face stiff with the effort of holding in my real feelings.

"Well," Sandra said at last. "Petra's already in bed, but shall we do the girls' bedtime together so you get a feel for their routine?"

I nodded and followed her upstairs, where Sandra supervised tooth brushing while I made my way down the softly carpeted hallway to Maddie and Ellie's doorway. There they were—two little beds, each bathed in the soft glow of a bedside light. I sat on the foot of one of the beds, and at last I heard feet and whining voices, swiftly hushed by Sandra.

"Shh, Maddie, you'll wake Petra. Come on now, into bed."

Ellie jumped into hers, but Maddie stood stonily for a moment regarding me, and I realized it must be her bed I was sitting on.

"Do you want me to move?" I asked, but she said nothing, only folded her arms mutinously, got into bed, and turned her face toward the wall, as if pretending I wasn't there.

Sandra began to read a Winnie the Pooh story, her voice low and soporific, and when at last she finished the final sentence, she leaned over, checking Ellie's face. Her eyes were closed, and she was snoring very gently. Sandra kissed her cheek, clicked off the lights, and then stood and came across to me.

"Maddie," she said quietly, "do you want a story from Rowan?"

Maddie said nothing, and Sandra leaned over and peered at her face, still turned to the wall. Her eyes were shut tight.

"Out like a light!" Sandra whispered.

She kissed Maddie's cheek, too, and then clicked off her light as well, leaving just the glow of the night-light. Then she made her way to the door, with me following behind.

"Can you close the door after you," she said, and I turned, ready to do so, glancing back at the little beds and their occupants.

The night-light was too close to the floor to show much except for shadows around the girls' beds, but for a moment, in the blackness, I thought I saw the glint of two little eyes glaring at me.

Then they snapped shut, and I pulled the door closed behind me.

I COULDN'T SLEEP THAT night. It wasn't the bed, which was as comfortable as before. It wasn't the heat. The room had been oppressively warm when I first entered, but I had managed to persuade the system to switch to cooling mode, and now the air was pleasantly temperate. It wasn't even my worries over being left alone with the children the next day.

The uncomfortable end to the evening flashed through my head once more. We had been sitting in the kitchen, talking and chatting, and then at last Sandra had stretched and yawned and announced her intention to make an early night of it.

She'd kissed Bill and headed for the stairs, and just as I was thinking about following her, Bill had refilled our glasses.

"Oh," I said half-heartedly. "I was . . . I mean I shouldn't . . ."

"Come on." He pushed the glass toward me. "Just one more. This is my only chance to get to know you before I entrust my kids to your care, after all! You could be anyone, for all I know."

He gave me a grin, his tanned cheeks wrinkling. He wore rimless glasses, and his cropped hair gave him an ageless quality.

I sighed inwardly and drew the glass toward me.

"So who are you, Rowan Caine?" he asked. His voice was a little slurred, and I wondered how much he'd had to drink.

"What do you want to know?" I said, attempting lightness.

"You remind me of someone. A film star, maybe. You don't have any famous relatives, do you? A sister in Hollywood?"

I gave a smile at this rather tired line.

"No, definitely not. I'm an only child, and anyway, my family's about as ordinary as you can get."

"I definitely feel like we've met." He got up and came around the breakfast bar, sitting on the chrome stool facing me, his legs spread wide so that I couldn't easily move without rubbing his thigh. "Who did you say you worked for before this?"

I rattled off the list again, and he shook his head, dissatisfied.

"I don't know any of them. Maybe I'm imagining it. I feel like I'd remember a face . . . well, a face like yours."

Damn. Something twisted in the pit of my stomach. I had been in this situation too often not to recognize where this was heading.

Countless creeps on countless nights out, putting themselves between me and the door . . .

Bill was one of *them*.

He was my employer. He was my boss's husband. And worst of all, he was . . . I can't bring myself to say it.

I cleared my throat and tried to push my stool back, but it was wedged against the edge of the breakfast bar. Bill's meaty denim-clad thighs blocked my way, preventing me from getting down.

"Well, I'd better be heading up." My voice fluted slightly with nerves. "Early start tomorrow, right?"

"There's no hurry," he said, and he reached out and took my wineglass, filled it up, and then put out his hand toward my face. "You've just . . . you've got a little bit . . ."

His smooth, slightly sweaty thumb stroked the corner of my bottom lip, and I felt one knee nudge very gently between mine.

For a second I froze. Then something inside me seemed to snap, and I slid abruptly down off the stool, barging past him so fast that the wine slopped and spilled onto the concrete.

"Sorry," I stammered. "So sorry. Let me, I'll get a cloth . . ."

"It's fine," he said. He stayed in place, half sitting, half leaning comfortably against the barstool, as I grabbed a dishcloth and mopped at the floor between his legs. Then I stood, my face burning, and dumped the wine-stained cloth into the sink.

"Good night, Bill," I said abruptly, and I turned on my heel.

"Good night, Rowan."

I walked up the two flights of stairs to bed, not looking back.

As I shut the door of my new room behind me, I felt a sense of overwhelming relief. The intricacies of the control panels were a welcome distraction, and by the time I'd wrested control of the temperature down to something more reasonable, I was talking myself into an acceptance of the situation.

Okay, so Bill was a creep. He wasn't the first I'd encountered. Why was I so disappointed to find him here?

I knew the answer, of course. But it wasn't just who he was. It was everything he represented—all the hard work and careful planning that had brought me here, all the hopes and dreams bound up with my decision to apply. There had to be a fly in the ointment, and maybe Bill was it. It felt like a kick in the guts.

It wasn't until I had finished showering and was lying in bed that I looked up at the ceiling. At the recessed light fittings and the little blinking smoke alarm by the door and . . . something else in the corner. What *was* that? A burglar alarm sensor? A second smoke detector? Or was it . . .

I thought of Sandra's remark: *The whole house is wired up.* . . .

It *couldn't* be a camera . . . could it?

But no. That would be more than creepy. That would be illegal surveillance. I was an employee—and I had a reasonable expectation of privacy, or whatever the legal terminology was.

All the same, I got up and dragged a chair over to the carpet beneath the egg-shaped thing in the corner. One of my socks was lying on the floor, and I picked it up, climbed onto the chair, and stood on tiptoes to fit it over the sensor. It fit perfectly.

Only then did I get back into bed and let myself fall asleep.

I AWOKE in the night with a start and the vague feeling of something wrong. I lay there, my heart pounding, wondering what it was that had awakened me.

It took a minute, and then it came again—a noise. Footsteps. *Creak . . . creak . . . creak . . .* slow and measured, as though someone was pacing on a wooden floor, which made no sense at all, since all the floors up here were thickly carpeted.

Creak . . . creak . . . creeeeak . . . The sound was hollow, heavy . . . a slow tread like a man's. It sounded as though it was coming from above, which was ridiculous, as I was on the top floor.

Slowly I sat up and groped for the light, but when I turned the switch, nothing happened. I flicked it again and then realized with a curse that I must have overridden the lamp at the main panel. I couldn't face grappling with the control panel in the middle of the night, so I grabbed my phone and switched on the torch.

My chest was tight, and as I took a pull at my inhaler, I realized suddenly that the room was extremely cold. No doubt when I had changed the temperature settings I had overdone it. My dressing gown was on the foot of the bed, so I pulled it on and stood there, the thin beam of torchlight illuminating a narrow sliver of carpet.

The footsteps had stopped, and I hesitated for a moment, holding my breath, listening, wondering if they would start up again. Nothing. Pulling my dressing-gown belt tighter, I opened the door of my room a crack.

There was no one outside, but nevertheless, I peered into the broom cupboard. It was, of course, empty except for the brushes and the winking charge light of the Hoover.

Then, feeling a little like a trespasser, I tried Rhiannon's door. The handle turned without resistance, and the heavy door swung wide, shushing across the thick carpet.

Inside, it was pitch-black, but it had the indefinable feel of an empty room. Still, I held up my phone and swung the narrow torch beam from wall to wall. There was no one there.

Shivering again, I returned to my room, where I stood, listening and waiting for the sounds to come again, but they did not.

I turned off the torch, climbed back into bed, and drew the covers up. But it was a long time before I slept.

Chapter 4

"Mummy!"

The Tesla wound its way along the driveway and toward the main road, with Ellie running in its wake, the tears streaming down her face as Jack's driving speed outpaced her short legs.

"Mummy, come back!"

"Bye, darlings!" Sandra's head leaned out the rear window, her honey-colored hair whipping in the breeze. Bill did not turn around. He was bent over his phone in the back seat beside her.

"Mummy!" Ellie shouted. "Mummy, please don't go!"

"Bye, sweeties! You'll have a wonderful time with Rowan, and I'll be back very soon. Goodbye! I love you all!"

And then the car disappeared from sight among the trees.

Ellie's legs slowed, and she stumbled to a halt, letting out a wail of grief before she threw herself dramatically to the ground.

"Oh, Ellie!" I hitched Petra higher on my hip and jogged down the drive to where Ellie lay, facefirst on the gravel. "Ellie, darling, come on. Let's go and get some ice cream."

Ellie only shook her head and wailed louder.

"Come on, sweetheart." I bent down with some difficulty—as I was holding Petra—and took her wrist, trying to pull her up, but she only let out a scream and wrenched her arm out of my hand.

"Ow!" she screamed, redoubling her sobs and looking up at me with angry tear-filled eyes. "You *hurt* me!"

"I was just trying—"

"Go *away*. You *hurt* me. I'm going to tell my mummy!"

I stood for a moment, unsure what to do.

"Go *away!*" she screamed again.

At last I gave a sigh and began to walk back up the drive toward the house. It felt wrong leaving her there, in the middle of what was, basically, a road, but the gate at the foot of the drive was shut, and it would be at least half an hour before Jack returned. Hopefully she would have calmed down long before then.

On my hip Petra had begun grousing, and I suppressed another sigh. Please, not a meltdown from her as well. And where was Maddie? She had disappeared before her parents left, flitting off into the woods to the east of the house, refusing to say goodbye.

"Oh, let her go," Bill had said as Sandra flapped around trying to find her to kiss her goodbye. "You know what she's like; she prefers to lick her wounds in private."

Lick her wounds. Just a cliché, right? At the time, I hadn't dwelt on it, but now I wondered. Was Maddie wounded? If so, how?

UP IN the house, I sat Petra in her high chair, strapped her in, and checked the red binder in case it gave instructions for what to do if the children disappeared off the face of the earth. The whole thing must have been at least three inches thick, and a cursory flick-through after breakfast had told me that it contained information on everything from how much Calpol to give, to bedtime routines, favorite books, and homework schedules.

As I skimmed down the "typical weekend day," I saw that Petra was overdue for lunch, which might explain her irritability. With a sigh I took a banana from a fruit bowl, peeled it, and placed a few chunks on Petra's tray. Then I went into the playroom to see if Maddie had returned. She wasn't there, nor was she anywhere in the house, as far as I could tell. At last I went to the utility-room door, the one she had left by, and called out into the woods.

"Maddie! Ellie! Petra and I are having ice cream." I paused, listening for the sound of running feet. Nothing came.

The sun had gone in, leaving the air surprisingly chilly, and I shivered in spite of the fact that it was June.

"Okay!" I called again. "More for me!"

And I walked back into the house, leaving the side door open.

In the kitchen I did a double take.

Petra was standing up in her high chair on the far side of the breakfast bar, triumphantly waving a chunk of banana at me.

For a moment I stood, frozen, looking at her precarious stance, the concrete beneath her, her small feet on the slippery wood.

And then I ran, staggering around the corner of the breakfast bar to snatch her up, my heart in my mouth.

"Petra, you bad, bad girl. You *mustn't* do that."

She could have died. If she'd fallen and struck her head on the concrete, she would have been concussed before I could reach her.

How could I have been so stupid?

I'd supervised toddlers a million times before—I'd done all the right things: I pulled her chair away from the counter so she couldn't push herself backward with her feet, and I was sure that I'd done up those clips. So how had she got free?

I examined the clips. One side was still fastened. The other was open. I must have not pushed one home quite hard enough and Petra had worked it loose and then managed to squirm out.

So it was my fault. Thankfully it hadn't happened when Sandra was here. She would have been within her rights to sack me there and then.

Though, of course . . . she still could, if she was watching over the cameras. In spite of myself, my eyes flicked up to the ceiling, and sure enough there was one of those little white egg-shaped domes in the far corner of the room. I felt my face flush.

I could be being watched right now.

"Don't do that again," I told Petra firmly, feeling the adrenaline still pulsing through me, and then, with an effort at restoring normality, I lifted her up and took her over to the sink, where I wiped her face. Then I looked at my watch. It was just gone one.

Petra gave a tired sob.

"Come on, you," I said, and took her to her room for a nap.

Inside, I switched on the illuminated mobile as the binder had instructed and put her gently down on her back. I sat quietly beside her while the soft light show played over the ceiling and walls.

At last she seemed to be asleep. With a sigh of relief, I picked up the monitor that was hooked over the end of the crib, tucked it into my belt, and tiptoed out of the room.

The house was completely silent as I stood on the landing, listening for the sound of running feet or childish laughter.

Where the hell were they?

Sandra had seemed remarkably relaxed about the children running off into the woods, but every bone in my body was screeching discomfort with the situation. What if there was a pond within the grounds? Or a steep fall? What if a dog—

The dogs. Surely they would be able to find the children.

Downstairs the dogs were lying in the kitchen, though they both looked up hopefully as I walked in carrying their leads.

"Walkies!" I said brightly. They bounded over, and I found the right attachment on their collars. I had them both on leads, and I set off, out the utility-room door, across the graveled yard, into the woods.

The dogs seemed to have a definite idea of where they were going, and I let them lead. We were heading downhill toward the bottom of the drive, though I couldn't see it through the trees.

Finally we broke into a little clearing, and my stomach gave an uncomfortable lurch, for there it was—a pond. Not very deep, but plenty deep enough for a small child to drown. Walking around the far side, I saw the imprints of small shoes on the bank. The prints led down the bank and then turned and went away again, back into the forest. I followed them until the ground became too hard to take a print, but there were two sets of shoes, and at least I knew that they were probably together and almost certainly safe.

There was no path up through the woods in the direction the footsteps had been leading, but I followed in as near an approximation as I could, when suddenly a crackling scream split the air. I stopped dead, my heart thumping erratically in my chest, the dogs barking hysterically and leaping at the end of their leashes.

I stood, looking wildly around. The scream had sounded close at hand, but I could see no one. Then it came again, long and high pitched, and with a stomach-lurching realization I understood.

I pulled the baby monitor out of my pocket and watched as the lights flared and dipped in time with the long shriek of pure fear.

For a moment I just stood there paralyzed. Then I began to run.

I was a long way from the house, and my breath was tearing in my throat by the time I saw the house in front of me. The dogs had broken away from me some way back, and now they were leaping in front and behind me, convinced that this was all a game.

When I reached the front door, it was standing ajar, in spite of the fact that I knew it had been closed when I left—I had used the utility-room door, leaving it open for Maddie and Ellie in case they returned, and for a second I thought I might be sick. What had I done? What had happened to poor little Petra?

I was almost too frightened to stumble the last few steps up the flight of stairs to the nursery, but at last I was outside Petra's door, sick with fear about what I was about to find.

It was closed, just as I'd left it, and I pushed down a sob in my throat as I turned the knob—but what I found there made me stop short on the threshold, trying to fight down my gasping breath.

Petra was asleep in her crib, arms flung out to either side. She had plainly not stirred since I had put her down.

It didn't make sense.

I backed out of the room, closing the door quietly behind me, and sank to the floor in the hallway outside, my face in my hands.

What had happened? Had the sound *not* come from the monitor? But that was impossible; it was equipped with lights that illuminated to show when the baby was crying. I had *seen* the lights. And the noise had been coming from the speaker.

Had Petra had a nightmare and cried out? But when I thought back, it was not a baby's cry. That was part of what had frightened me so much. The sound I'd heard was not the fretful wail I knew so well from the nursery but a long, throbbing shriek of terror, one made by a much older child or even an adult.

"Hello?"

The voice came from downstairs, making me jump again, and I stood, my pulse racing, and leaned over the bannisters.

"Hello? Who's there?" It had been a woman's voice, and now I heard footsteps in the hall and saw a face below, peering up at me.

"You'll be the new nanny, I dare say?"

It was a woman, perhaps fifty or sixty years old. She looked plump and motherly, but there was something in her voice and in her expression that wasn't welcoming.

I began to make my way down the flight of steps.

"Um, hello. Yes. Yes, I'm Rowan. And you must be . . ."

"I'm Jean. Jean McKenzie." She looked me up and down, not troubling to conceal her disapproval, and then shook her head. "It's up to you, miss, but I don't approve of keeping children locked out, and I dare say Mrs. Elincourt wouldna like it either."

"Locked out?" I was puzzled. "What do you mean?"

"I found the poor bairns shivering on the step in their sundresses when I came to clean."

"But wait"—I put out a hand—"hang on a second. I didn't lock anyone out. They ran away from *me*. I was out looking for them. I left the back door open for them."

"It was *locked* when I arrived" was all she said, with a touch of stubbornness.

Anger flared inside me. Was she accusing me of lying?

"Well . . . maybe it came off the latch or something," I said at last. "Are the girls okay?"

"Aye, they're having a bite in the kitchen wi' me."

"Were you—" I stopped, trying to figure out how to phrase this without placing myself even lower in her estimation. "I heard a sound from Petra on the baby monitor. Did you hear her?"

"She's not let out a peep," Jean said firmly. "I've been keeping my eye on them all"—*Unlike you* was the unspoken subtext—"and I'd have heard her if she was greeting."

"Greeting?"

"Crying," Jean said impatiently.

"Maddie, then? Or Ellie? Did either of them come up?"

"They've been in the kitchen wi' me, miss," Jean said, crossness in her voice. "Now, if you'll excuse me, I need to be getting back to them. They're too wee to be left alone wi' the stove."

"Of course." I felt my cheeks flush with the implied criticism. "But please, that's my job. I'll give them lunch."

"I've given it to them already. The poor wee mites were ravenous; they needed something hot in them."

I felt my temper begin to break.

"Look, Mrs. McKenzie, I've already explained, the girls ran away from me; I didn't lock them out. Now, if you don't mind, I've got work to do."

I pushed past her and stalked into the kitchen. Maddie and Ellie were sitting at the breakfast bar eating chocolate-chip cookies.

I pushed down my irritation and made myself smile pleasantly.

"Hello, girls. Were you playing hide-and-seek?"

"Yes," Ellie said with a giggle, but then she remembered our earlier quarrel and frowned. "You hurt my wrist."

She held it out, and there, to my chagrin, was a ring of bruises on the pale skin of her stick-thin wrist.

I felt my cheeks color.

"I'm ever so sorry, Ellie." I bent down beside her. "I truly didn't mean to. I was just worried you'd hurt yourself on the drive, but I apologize if I was holding your arm too hard. Can we be friends?"

For a second I thought I saw Ellie wavering; then she jerked and gave a little whimper. Beneath the breakfast bar, I saw Maddie's hand whip back into her lap.

"Maddie," I said quietly, "what just happened?"

"Nothing," Maddie said, speaking to her plate more than me.

"Ellie?"

"N-nothing," Ellie said, but she was rubbing her arm, and there were tears in her bright blue eyes.

"I don't believe you. Let me see your arm."

"Nothing!" Ellie said more fiercely. She pulled down her cardigan and gave me a look of betrayal. "I said nothing. Go away!"

"Okay."

I stood up. Whatever chance I had had there with Ellie, I'd blown it for the moment. Or rather Maddie had.

Mrs. McKenzie was standing against the counter, her arms crossed, watching us.

"Well, I'll be away now, girls," she said, dropping a kiss on top of each head. "You give your wee sister a kiss from me now."

"Yes, Mrs. M," Ellie said obediently. Maddie said nothing, but she squeezed Mrs. McKenzie's waist, and I thought I saw a wistful look in her eye as her gaze followed the woman to the door.

"Goodbye now, girls," Mrs. McKenzie said, and then she was gone. Outside I heard a car start up and bump down to the road.

The last thing I could cope with was losing the children on the grounds again, so while they finished up their cookies, I crossed into the hallway and examined the inside of the big front door. There was no keyhole, as I'd observed the first time I had arrived. Instead, the white panel I had noticed contained a thumb sensor— Sandra had programmed my thumbprint into her phone app.

I touched it, watching as a series of illuminated icons sprang into life. One of them was a big key. I tapped it and heard a grinding click as the deadlocks inside the door slid home.

Then I went into the utility room. The door there operated with just a regular lock and key. I twisted the key in the lock and then tucked it away on the doorframe above, just as the binder had instructed. *We keep all keys for the doors operated by traditional locks on the doorframe above the corresponding door so that they are handy in case of emergency but out of reach of the children*, the paragraph had read. There was something comforting about seeing it up there, far away from little fingers.

Mission accomplished, I went back into the kitchen.

"Girls, what do you say we watch a movie. *Frozen? Moana?*"

"Yay, *Frozen!*" Ellie said, but Maddie butted in.

"We hate *Frozen.*"

Behind Maddie I could see Ellie looking desperate but too scared to contradict her sister.

"We *hate Frozen,*" Maddie repeated stubbornly. "Come on, Ellie, let's go play in our room."

I watched as she slid down from her stool and stomped into the hallway. In the doorway she paused and jerked her head meaningfully at her sister. Ellie's bottom lip quivered.

"We can still watch it if you want, Ellie," I said. "We could watch it together, just you and me. I could make popcorn."

For a minute I thought I saw Ellie hesitate. But then she shook her head, slid from her stool, and turned to follow her sister.

As the sound of their footsteps faded away up the stairs, I sighed and then turned to put on the kettle to make myself a pot of tea. At least I would have half an hour to myself.

But before I had even finished filling the kettle, the baby monitor gave a crackle, telling me that Petra had woken up.

No rest for the wicked, then.

What had I taken on?

I KNOW I'm going on. And I know you must be wondering when the hell I'm going to get to the point—to the reason I'm here. And I promise you, it's coming. But to explain properly, I have to tell you how it happened. Piece by piece.

Only that sounds as if I'm building something—a house, perhaps. Or a picture in a jigsaw. Piece by piece. And the truth is, it was the other way around. Piece by piece I was being torn apart.

And the first piece was that night.

Petra woke up from her nap cranky and fretful, and Maddie and Ellie refused to come out of their room all afternoon, even for supper, no matter how much I pleaded.

In the end I capitulated and took pasta up to their bedroom. I knocked on the door and heard Maddie's fierce "Go away!"

"It's me," I said meekly. "I've got your pasta. I'll leave it here outside the door. But me and Petra will be downstairs having ice cream if you want some pudding."

And then I left. It was all I could do.

After supper I bathed Petra, and then I put her to bed, or rather tried to. I did exactly as the binder said, following the instructions to the letter, just as I had at lunchtime, but this time it wasn't working. Petra groused and ripped off her nappy, and then when I put her back into it, she began to wail, loudly and persistently.

For more than an hour I followed the binder's instructions and sat there, with my hand patiently on her back, listening to the soothingly repetitive jingle of the mobile, but it wasn't helping. Petra was getting more and more upset, and her cries were rising in pitch from irritated to angry to borderline hysterical.

I picked her up and put her over my shoulder, walking her up and down the room, but she wailed angrily in my arms. So I put her back in the crib, and she stood, sobbing furiously.

At last, with a final, guilty glance at the camera, I gave up.

"Good night, Petra," I said aloud, and then stood and left the room, closing the door firmly behind me and listening as the sound of her cries diminished as I walked down the corridor.

It was past nine p.m. I thought about going straight downstairs for a glass of wine, but I had to check on Maddie and Ellie.

I could hear nothing coming from behind their bedroom door, and when I peered through the keyhole, everything inside seemed to be dark. I turned the knob and pushed and then gingerly slid through the gap. Swinging my phone torch around the room, I saw them, curled together in Maddie's bed, looking for all the world like two little cherubs. Then I left them, turning on Happy's listening function on my phone so I could hear if they woke up.

Petra was still sobbing as I tiptoed quietly past her room, but the volume had decreased, and I hardened my heart and didn't look in. I told myself she would settle faster if I left her to it. And besides, I'd had nothing to eat or drink since noon. I was suddenly ravenous, light-headed, and desperate for food.

DOWNSTAIRS, IN THE KITCHEN, I walked over to the fridge. Right at the back I saw a cardboard pizza box, and with some difficulty I inveigled it out and opened it up. I was just sliding the baking tray into the oven when there was a sharp rap from the glass wall on the far side of the kitchen table.

I jumped and swung around, scanning the room. It was getting dark, rain spattering the glass, and I could see very little outside except the jeweled droplets running down the enormous glass pane. I was just beginning to think I might have imagined it, when a dark shape moved against the gloaming, black against gray. Something—some*one*—was out there.

"Who is it?" I called out. There was no answer, and I marched toward the glass wall, shrouded in darkness.

There was no panel over here—or none that I could see—but then I remembered the voice commands.

"Lights on," I said sharply, and somewhat to my surprise it worked—the huge chandelier above my head illuminating suddenly into a blaze of LED bulbs. As soon as my eyes adjusted, I realized my mistake. With the lights on, I could see absolutely nothing outside now apart from my own reflection in the glass. Whereas whoever was out there could see me plainly.

"Lights off," I said. Every light in the entire room went out immediately, plunging the kitchen into inky darkness.

"Damn," I said under my breath, and began to feel my way back across the kitchen, toward the panel by the door, to try to restore the settings to something between retina-burning brilliance and total darkness. As my fingers sought out the control panel, I looked back toward the window and thought, though I could not be sure, that I saw something whisk away around the side of the house.

I SPENT the rest of the time while the pizza was cooking glancing nervously over my shoulder into the dark shadows at the far side of the room. Petra's sobs still filtered faintly down the stairs.

It was maybe ten or fifteen minutes later that I heard a knock, this time from the side of the house.

When I went to the utility room, I could see a dark shape silhouetted outside the rain-spattered glass panes in the door. The figure spoke, his voice almost drowned by the hiss of the rain.

"It's me. Jack."

Relief flooded through me.

"Jack!" I wrenched the door open, and there he was, standing just under the threshold, hunched in a raincoat, hands in pockets.

"Jack, was that you before?"

"Before when?" he asked, looking puzzled, and I opened my mouth to explain and then thought better of it.

"Never mind, it doesn't matter. What can I help with?"

"I won't keep you," he said. "I just wanted to check you were all right, with it being your first day and all."

"Thanks," I said awkwardly, thinking of the awful afternoon. Then, on an impulse, I added, "Will you . . . Do you want to come in? The kids are in bed. I was just getting myself some supper."

"Are you sure?" He looked at his watch. "It's pretty late."

"I'm sure," I said, standing back to let him inside the utility room. He dripped onto the mat, then stepped out of his boots.

"I'm sorry it's so late," he said as he followed me into the kitchen. "I was meaning to come over before, but I had to take that mower over to Inverness to be serviced."

"You couldn't fix it?"

"Oh, I got it running. It clapped out again yesterday. But I didn't come to moan about my troubles. How was it with the kids?"

"It was—" I stopped, feeling with horror my bottom lip quiver. I wanted to put on a brave face. But I just couldn't do it.

"Who am I kidding?" I said wretchedly. "It was awful. The girls ran away from me, and I went to look for them in the woods, and then that woman—what's her name? Mrs. McKinty?"

"Jean McKenzie," Jack said. He pulled his raincoat off and sat at the long table, and I found myself sinking into a chair opposite.

"Well, she turned up and found the girls sitting on the doorstep claiming I'd locked them out, which I absolutely *didn't*. They hate me, Jack, and Petra's been screaming for like an hour and—"

The wail came again, and I felt my stress level rise.

"Sit down," Jack said firmly as I made to rise. "I'll see if I can settle her. She's just not used to your face. It'll be better tomorrow."

As the sound of his steps receded up the stairs, I listened on the baby monitor to the door of Petra's room swish gently open and her cries subside as her body was lifted from the crib.

"There, there, my little love," I heard, a low, intimate croon that made my cheeks flush. "There, there, ma poor wee lassie. Shh . . . shh now, Petra. . . . There, there . . . what a fuss over nothing."

Petra's cries were lower now, and I could hear the creak of the boards as Jack paced softly up and down, soothing the baby with a surprisingly practiced touch. At last she fell silent, and I heard the rattle of the crib as he lowered her gently to the mattress.

There was a long pause, and then the shush of the door against the carpet, and Jack's feet on the stairs again.

"Success?" I said, hardly daring to believe it as he entered the kitchen, and he nodded and gave a little wry smile.

"Aye, I think the poor wee thing was knackered. She fell asleep almost as soon as I picked her up."

"Jack, you must think I'm a complete—" I stopped, not sure what to say. "I mean, *I'm* the nanny. I'm supposed to be good at this kind of stuff."

"Don't be silly." He sat again at the table, opposite me. "They're testing you. They've had enough nannies this past year to make them a bit mistrustful of a new one waltzing in and taking over. Once they see you're here to stay, it'll get better."

"Jack . . ." It was the opening I'd been waiting for. "What *did* happen with those other nannies? Sandra said they left because they thought the house was haunted, but I can't believe . . . It just seems preposterous. Have you ever seen anything?"

"Well . . ." Jack said rather slowly. "I wouldn't say—"

But whatever he had been about to say was cut short by a loud, rather peremptory female voice saying, "Rowan?"

Jack broke off, but I jumped and swung around, looking wildly for the source of the voice. Was someone in the *house?*

"Rowan," the voice repeated, "are you there?"

"He-hello?" I managed.

"Ah, hi, Rowan! It's Sandra."

With a rush of mingled relief and fury, I realized the voice was coming out of the speakers. Sandra had somehow dialed in to the house system and was using the app to talk to us.

"Sandra." I tried to restore my voice to a cheerful, upbeat tone. "Hi. Gosh, how are you?"

"Good!" Her voice echoed around the kitchen. "But more to the point, how are *you?* How's everything on the home front?"

I felt my eyes flicker to Jack, sitting at the table, thinking of how he had been the one to get Petra down. Had Sandra seen?

"Well . . . calm right now," I said at last. "They're all in bed. Though I have to admit, Petra was a bit of a struggle."

"But she's asleep now? Well done."

"Yes, she's asleep. And the other two went down quiet as mice. I let them have supper in their room, as they seemed really tired. I hope that was okay."

"Fine, fine," Sandra said as though dismissing the question. "And they behaved okay the rest of the day?"

"They—" I pursed my lips, wondering how truthful to be. "They were a bit upset after you left, especially Ellie. But they calmed down in the afternoon. I offered to let them watch *Frozen,* but they didn't want to. They ended up playing in their room." Well, that part was true enough. The problem was that they hadn't come *out* of their room. "Listen, Sandra, are there rules about the grounds?"

"How do you mean?"

"I mean, are they really allowed to just roam around or should I be keeping them in? I know you and Bill are relaxed about it, but there's that pond . . . I'm just . . . It's making me a bit nervous."

"Oh, that," Sandra said, laughing. "It's barely six inches deep. Honestly, it's the reason Bill and I bought a place with big grounds—to give the children a bit of freedom to run wild."

"I-I'm—" I stopped, struggling with how to put my concerns without sounding like I was criticizing her parenting. "Look, you know them better than I do, of course, but I'm just—I'm used to a closer level of supervision, if you know what I mean. Particularly around water. I know the water isn't that deep, but the mud—"

"Well, look," Sandra said. She sounded a little defensive now, and I cursed myself. "You must use your common sense, of course. If you see them doing something stupid, step in. But I don't see the point of having children stuck in front of the TV all afternoon when there's a big, beautiful sunny garden outside."

I was taken aback. Was this a dig about the fact that I had tried to bribe them with a film?

"Well," I said at last. "I totally take that point, Sandra, and obviously I'm very keen to take advantage of the beautiful grounds for myself as well. I'll—" I stopped, groping for what to say. "I'll use my common sense, as you suggest. Anyway, we had a pretty good day. Would you like me to check in with you tomorrow?"

"I'll be in meetings all day, but I'll call before bedtime," Sandra said, her voice softer now. "Good night, Rowan. Sleep tight. I'm sure you will. You'll have an early start tomorrow, I'm afraid!"

"Yes, I'm sure I will," I said. "Good night, Sandra."

I waited, but there was no sign that she had hung up.

"S-Sandra?" I said uncertainly, but she seemed to be gone. I slumped back in my chair and ran my hand over my face.

"I should be going," Jack said awkwardly, evidently taking my gesture as a hint. He stood, pushing back his chair.

"No, stay." I looked up at him, suddenly desperate not to be left alone in this house of hidden eyes and ears and speakers. "Please. I'd rather have someone to eat with." I suddenly remembered the pizza. "Have you eaten?"

"No, but I won't take your supper."

"Of course you will. I put a pizza in the oven just before you arrived. I won't manage it all myself. Please, give me a hand."

"Well . . ." He glanced at the utility-room door, toward the garage, and, I assumed, his little flat above. "Well . . . if you insist."

"I do." I put on oven gloves and opened the door of the hot oven. "And I don't know about you, but I need a glass of wine. You?"

"I wouldn't say no."

He watched as I chopped the pizza into slices and found two glasses in the cupboard.

There was silence for a few minutes as we both worked our way through a greasy, delicious slice each and then another. At last

Jack picked up his third and spoke, balancing it on his fingertips.

"So . . . about what you were asking earlier."

"The . . . the supernatural thing?"

"Aye. Well, the truth is, I've not seen anything myself, but Jean, she's . . . well, not superstitious, exactly. But she loves a good yarn. She's always filling the kids' heads with folktales. And this house is very old—or parts of it are, anyway. There's been the usual amount of deaths and violence, I suppose."

"So . . . you think Jean's been telling the girls stuff and they've been passing it on to the nannies?"

"Maybe. I wouldn't want to say for sure either way. But look, those other nannies were very young. It's not everyone who's cut out to live in a place like this, miles away from a town or a pub."

"Yeah." I looked out the window. It was too dark to see anything, but in my mind's eye I saw the road, stretching away into darkness. Not a car, not a passerby. "I can understand that."

We sat in silence for a moment. I was filled with strange emotions—stress, tiredness, and something else, even more unsettling. Something that was more about Jack and his presence and the way his muscles moved beneath the skin of his forearm as he folded the final pizza slice and finished it off in two quick bites.

"Well, I'd best be away to my bed." He stood, stretching. "Thanks for the meal. It was nice to have someone to talk to."

"Same." I stood, suddenly self-conscious.

"I'm just over the garage in the old stable block if anything happens in the night—"

"What would happen?" I broke in, and he gave a laugh.

"That came out wrong. I just meant, if you need me for anything, you know where I am. Just in case."

"Thanks," I said, feeling a little awkward, and he grinned again, shrugged himself into his wet coat, and then opened the utility-room door, put on his boots, and ducked out into the rain.

AFTER he had gone, I made my way into the utility room to lock up. The house felt very still and quiet, and I sighed as I reached above the top of the doorframe for the key. But it wasn't there.

I patted my way along the doorframe, feeling with my fingertips, but there was nothing there. It wasn't on the floor, either.

Could Jean have moved it? Or knocked it down while dusting?

Except I had a clear memory of putting the key up there after Jean left, just as Sandra had instructed. Could it have fallen down?

I got down on my hands and knees and shone my phone's torch under the washing machine and dryer but could see nothing. I scoured the kitchen and even checked the bin—nothing there.

What would I do? I'd have to barricade the door with something. At last, after a lot of searching, I found a wedge-shaped door stopper in the Hoover cupboard. I rammed it firmly into the gap beneath the door and then turned the doorknob to test it.

Somewhat to my surprise it held. It wouldn't stop a determined burglar, but it did give the impression that the door was locked, and I knew I would sleep more soundly because of it.

When I went back into the kitchen to clear away the pizza box, the clock above the stove read 11:36. I could not suppress a groan. The girls would be up at six. I should have been in bed hours ago.

Well, it was too late to undo that. I'd just have to forgo a shower and get to sleep as quickly as possible.

"Lights off," I said aloud.

The room was plunged into blackness. I made my way up the stairs to bed and was asleep almost before I had undressed.

Chapter 5

WHEN I WOKE, it was with a start, to complete darkness.

My phone on the bedside table said it was 3:16 a.m., and I groaned and let it fall back to the wood with a clunk. No wonder it was still dark; it was the middle of the night.

But what had woken me? Was it Petra? One of the girls?

I lay for a moment, listening. I could hear nothing. At last I got up, wrapped my dressing gown around myself, and went out onto the landing. The house was quiet. But something felt . . . wrong.

When the realization came, it was in the shape of two things. The first was the shadow on the wall in front of me, cast by the wilting peonies on the table downstairs.

Someone had turned the hall lights on downstairs. Lights that I was sure I had *not* left on when I went to bed.

The second came as I began to tiptoe down the stairs, and it made my heart almost stop.

It was the sound of footsteps on a wooden floor, slow and deliberate, exactly like the other night.

Creak. Creak. Creak.

I froze, two steps down, looking at where the noise seemed to be coming from. Was someone in the house?

The light I could have understood. Perhaps Maddie or Ellie had got up to use the loo and left it on. But the footsteps?

I could hear them start on one side of the ceiling and move slowly and implacably to the other. Then they paused and reversed. It sounded . . . well . . . as if there was someone pacing in the room above my head. But that made no sense. Because there *was* no room up there. There was not so much as a loft hatch.

An image suddenly flashed into my head. The locked door in my room. Where did it lead to? *Was* there an attic?

Shivering, I tiptoed back into my own room and flicked the switch on the lamp by my bed. It didn't turn on.

I mashed my hand against the panel on the wall, bashing randomly at the squares and dials as they illuminated beneath my palm. Lights flickered on and off in closets; a brief burst of classical music filled the air. But finally the overhead light came on.

I let my hand fall to my side, breathing heavily but triumphant. Then I set about trying to open the locked door.

First I tried the key to my bedroom door, tucked away on the doorframe above the door, like the others. It didn't fit.

Then I tried the key to the wardrobe. It didn't fit, either.

There was nothing above the doorframe except a little dust.

Finally I resorted to kneeling down and peering through the keyhole, my heart like a drum in my breast.

I could see nothing at all—just unending blackness. But I could *feel* something. A cool breeze that made me blink and draw back from the keyhole, my eye watering.

It was not just a cupboard inside that space. *Something* else was there. An attic, perhaps. At the very least, a space big enough to have a draft and a source of air.

The footsteps had stopped, but I knew that I would not sleep again tonight, and at last I wrapped my duvet around myself and sat, my phone in my hand, watching the locked door.

I don't know what I was expecting. To see the handle turn? For someone—some*thing*—to emerge?

Whatever it was, it didn't happen. I just sat there as the sky outside my window began to lighten and a thin streak of dawn crept across the carpet, mixing with the artificial light from above.

At last, when I heard a low wail come from downstairs, I loosened my grip on my phone and saw that the display said 5:57 a.m.

It was morning. The children were waking up.

As I crawled from my bed, my hand went up involuntarily to touch my necklace—but my fingers grazed only my collarbone, and I remembered that I had taken it off that first night, spooling it on the bedside table, just as I had done before the interview.

Now I turned to pick it up, and it wasn't there. I frowned and looked down the back of the little nightstand. Nothing. Had Jean McKenzie tidied it away?

The wail from downstairs came again, louder this time, and I sighed and abandoned the hunt. I would look for it later.

But first I had to get through another day.

I HAD confined myself mostly to tea since getting here, mainly because the coffeemaker was so intimidating. However, after my sleepless night, I had decided coffee was the only thing that was going to make me feel halfway normal, and while Petra chewed her way through a dish of rice cakes, I resolved to figure it out.

I hadn't even switched it on when a voice behind me said, "Knock, knock..."

I jumped and swung around, my nerves still jangling.

It was Jack, standing in the open doorway to the utility room, jacket on and dog leashes in hand.

"Sorry, I didn't mean to make you jump. I've come to collect the dogs for their walk."

"No problem," I said. Claude and Hero were gamboling around, and Jack hushed them sharply. They fell silent at once. He grabbed the collar of the largest one and began clipping on its lead.

"Sleep well?" he asked casually as the lead slipped into place.

"Not particularly well, actually," I said. "I couldn't find the key to the back door last night. Do you know where it's gone?"

"This door?" He jerked his head toward the utility room, one eyebrow raised, and I nodded.

"There's no bolt on it, either. In the end I wedged it with a bit of wood." Though much good it had done. Presumably Jack had simply shoved the wedge aside without even noticing when he opened the door. "It didn't make for a very comfortable night."

That and the sound of footsteps, I thought, but I couldn't quite bring myself to tell him about that.

Jack was frowning now.

"Sandra usually keeps the key on the doorframe above."

"I know that. And I put it up there yesterday, but it's not there now. Do you think Jean could have taken it?"

"Jean?" He looked surprised and then gave a short laugh and shook his head. "Why would she? She has her own keys."

"Someone else, then?"

But he was shaking his head.

"No one comes up here without me knowing about it. They couldn't get through the gate, for a start."

I didn't remind him that Jean had found the door locked when I came back from looking for Maddie and Ellie. I hadn't locked it. So who had?

"Maybe it fell somewhere," he said, and went back through to the utility room to look, the dogs following and sniffing around as he pushed aside the dryer and peered under the washing machine.

"I already looked," I said. "I checked everywhere, even the bin."

But he was shifting the washing machine aside, grunting a little with the effort, the castors screeching on the tiled floor.

"Jack? Did you hear me? I said I *already* . . ."

He ignored me, leaning over the counter, one long arm stretched down the back of the unit.

"Got it."

He straightened triumphantly, a dusty brass key in his fingers. I let my mouth snap shut.

I had looked. I had *looked*. I had a clear memory of peering under that washing machine and seeing nothing but dust.

"But . . ."

He came across, dropped it into my palm.

"It was tucked behind the wheel. I expect you wouldn't have seen. Probably fell out when the door slammed shut and skidded under there. All's well that ends well. Isn't that what they say?"

I let my hand close around the key, feeling the brass ridges bite into my palm. I had looked carefully. There was no way I could have missed seeing that key if it was there. Which meant that maybe . . . it *wasn't* there. Until someone dropped it down there.

I looked up and met Jack's guileless hazel eyes.

You went straight to the washing machine, I wanted to say. *How did you know?*

But I could not bring myself to voice my suspicions aloud.

What I actually said was, "Thank you." But my voice in my own ears sounded subdued.

Jack didn't reply; he was already dusting off his hands and turning for the door, the dogs wheeling and yelping around his feet.

"See you in an hour or so?" he said, but this time when he smiled it no longer made my heart leap.

"Sure," I said quietly.

As he turned and made his way across the courtyard, dogs at heel, I watched him go, trying to figure out what had happened.

Suddenly there was an impatient noise from the kitchen, and I turned to see Petra kicking irritably against her high chair. I hurried back into the room, undid her straps, and dumped her into the play-pen in the corner of the kitchen. Then I plastered on my best smile and began looking for Maddie and Ellie.

They were in the playroom, huddled in a corner whispering something, but both heads turned when I clapped my hands.

"Right! Come on, girls, we're going to go for a picnic. We can take sandwiches, crisps, rice cakes . . ."

I had more than half expected them to refuse, but to my surprise Maddie got up, dusting down her leggings.

"Where are we going?"

"Just the grounds. Will you show me around? I heard from Jack you have a secret den." That was completely untrue, but I'd never met a child who didn't have some kind of hidey-hole.

"You can't see our den," Ellie said instantly. "It's secret. I mean—" She stopped at a glaring, furious look from Maddie. "I mean, we don't have one," she added miserably.

"Oh, what a shame," I said breezily. "Well, never mind. I'm sure there's lots of other interesting places. I'm going to put Petra in the pushchair so she doesn't wander off, but then let's set off."

It took a surprisingly long time to make the picnic and get everyone out of the house, but at last we were heading off around the back of the house along a bumpy pebbled path.

We wound our way through a rather overgrown vegetable garden, where Maddie helpfully showed me the raspberry canes and herb beds. There was a set of swings tucked behind a dilapidated kitchen greenhouse, and Ellie and Maddie leapt on them and began competing to go higher. For a moment I just stood and watched them, and then something in my pocket gave a buzzing, jangling leap, and I realized my phone was ringing.

When I pulled it out, my heart gave a funny little jolt as I read the caller ID. It was the last person I'd been expecting, and I had to take a deep breath before I swiped the screen to accept the call.

"Hello?"

"Heeeeey!" she shrieked, her familiar voice loud. "It's me, Rowan! How are you? Long time no speak!"

"I'm good! Where are you? This must be costing you a fortune."

"It is. I'm in a commune in India. Mate, it's amazing here. And sooo cheap! You should totally resign and come and join me."

"I-I did resign," I said with a slightly awkward laugh.

"*What?*"

"Yup," I said. "Handed my notice in at Little Nippers. I left a few days ago. The look on Janine's face when I told her she could stick her stupid job was almost worth all the hours there."

"I bet. She was such a cow. I still can't believe Val didn't give you that job when I left."

"Me, too. Listen, I've moved out of the flat."

"What?" The line was crackly. "I didn't hear you. I thought you said you'd left the flat."

"Yeah, I did. The post I've taken up—it's a residential one. But don't worry, I'm still paying the rent. Your stuff is still there, and you'll have a place to come back to when you finish traveling."

"You can afford that?" Her tinny, faraway voice was impressed. "Wow! This post must pay really well. How did you swing that?"

I skated around that one.

"They really needed someone," I said. It was the truth, at least. "But anyway, how are you? Any plans to come back?" I tried to keep my voice casual, not letting on how important her answer was to me.

"Yeah, of course." Her laugh echoed. "But not yet. I've still got seven months left on my ticket. But oh, mate, it's good to hear your voice. I miss you!"

"I miss you, too."

Ellie and Maddie had got down off the swing and were walking away from me now, down a winding brick path between overgrown heathers. I tucked the phone under my ear and began pushing the buggy across the rough ground, following.

"Listen, I'm working right now, so . . . I should probably . . ."

"Yeah, sure. And I should go, too. But you're okay, yeah?"

"Yeah, I'm okay."

There was an awkward pause.

"Well, bye, Rowan."

"Bye, Rach."

And then she hung up.

"Who was that?" said a little voice at my elbow, and I jumped and looked down to see Maddie scowling up at me.

"Oh . . . just a friend I used to work with. We were flatmates back in London, but then she went traveling."

"Did you like her?"

It was such a funny question I laughed.

"What? Yes, yes, of course I liked her."

"You sounded like you didn't want to talk to her."

"I don't know where you got that idea." We walked farther, the buggy bumping over the path, while I considered her remark. Was there a grain of truth in it? "She was calling from abroad," I said at last. "I just didn't want to cost her too much money."

Maddie looked up at me, and then she turned and scampered after Ellie, crying out, "Follow me!"

The path led down and down, away from the house, growing more uneven by the second. In the distance, I could see a brick wall, about six feet high, with a wrought-iron metal gate, which seemed to be where the children were heading.

"Is that the edge of the grounds?" I called after them. "Hold up. I don't want you going out onto the moors."

They stopped and waited for me; Ellie had her hands on her hips and was panting, her little face flushed.

"It's a garden," she said. "It's got a wall around it but no roof."

"That sounds exciting," I said. "Like the Secret Garden. Have you ever read that?"

"Of course she hasn't. She's not old enough to read chapter books," Maddie said repressively. "But we watched it on TV."

We had drawn level with the wall now. It was slightly taller than I was, and seemed to be enclosing one corner of the grounds.

I tried the handle of the gate.

"It's locked." Through the metalwork, I could see an overgrown mass of bushes and creepers, some kind of statue partly obscured by greenery. "What a shame; it looks very exciting in there."

"It *looks* locked," Ellie said eagerly, "but Maddie and I know a secret way of getting inside."

"I'm not sure—" I began, but before I could finish, she wound her hand through the intricate metal fretwork and did something I could not see to the far side of the lock. The gate sprang open.

"Wow!" I said, genuinely impressed. "How did you do that?"

"It's not very hard." Ellie was flushed with pride. "There's a catch on the inside."

Gently I pushed the gate open and pushed Petra inside, thrusting aside the trailing fronds of some creeper that was hanging overhead. The leaves brushed my face, tickling my skin with an almost nettlish sensation. Maddie ducked in behind me, trying not to let the leaves trail in her face, and Ellie came in, too. There was something mischievous about her expression.

Inside, there were lush evergreen bushes studded with berries, overgrown tangled creepers, and a few flowers struggling to survive beneath the onslaught. As we turned a corner, we passed underneath an ancient-looking yew so old it formed a tunnel over the path, its strange berries crunching underfoot.

Four brick paths quartered the garden, meeting in a circle in the center where a statue stood. As I drew nearer, I saw that it was a woman, thin and emaciated, her clothes ragged, her face skull-like. The nails on her skeletal hands were long and pointed.

"What a horrible statue," I said, taken aback. "Who on earth would put up something like that?" But there was no answer. The two little girls had disappeared into the thicket of greenery, and I could not see them. Peering closer, I saw that there was a name on the pedestal she crouched on: ACHLYS.

All of a sudden, I felt a violent desire to get out of this nightmarish tangle of plants, out to the open air of the grounds.

"Maddie!" I called sharply. "Ellie, where are you?" No answer came, and I suppressed a momentary unease. "Maddie! We're going to have lunch now. Let's go find a spot."

There was a burst of giggles, and both children pelted down the path in front of me, toward the gate and the cool, clean air outside.

"Come on," Maddie shouted. "We'll show you the burn."

THE rest of the morning passed without incident. We had a quiet—even a nice—lunch on the shores of the peat-dark burn that cut through the corner of the grounds, and then afterward the girls took off their shoes and paddled in the tea-colored waters.

Only marring the general contentment was the prickling of my forehead, where the creeper had brushed me. It was now properly itching, like a nettle sting, but more painful.

All in all I was glad when the sky clouded over and I could suggest packing up and starting home. Petra fell asleep on the way back to the house, and I parked her buggy in the utility room. To my surprise both Maddie and Ellie fell in with my suggestion of a film, and we were cuddled up in the media room, when there was a crackle and Sandra's voice came over the speakers.

"Rowan? Is now a good time to chat?"

"Oh, hi, Sandra." I found myself glancing up at the cameras, wondering how she knew which room I was in. The girls were both absorbed in the film and didn't seem to have noticed their mother's voice coming over the speakers. "Hang on, I'll go to the kitchen so we can chat without disturbing the girls."

"You can divert the call to your phone if that's easier." Sandra's disembodied voice followed me as I walked to the kitchen. "Just open the Happy app and click on the phone icon."

I did as she said, then lifted the phone to my ear. To my relief her voice sounded again, this time from the phone speaker.

"How's today going?" Sandra said briskly.

"It's going great, thanks. We had a really good morning exploring the grounds. Petra's asleep, and the girls are—" I hesitated, thinking of her remark yesterday, but then forged on. "The girls are watching a film. I thought you wouldn't mind, as they were out in the fresh air this morning. I think they needed some downtime."

"Mind?" Sandra gave a little laugh. "Heavens, no. I'm not one of those helicopter parents."

"Would you like to speak to them?"

"Absolutely—it's why I called, really. Well, and to check how you were coping, of course. Do you want to put Ellie on first?"

I went back to the den and handed Ellie the phone.

"It's Mummy."

She broke into smiles as she heard her mother's voice, and I went back into the kitchen. At some point Sandra must have asked to be put across to Maddie, for there was a short whining complaint from Ellie, and then I heard Maddie's voice and Ellie came padding disconsolately through to me.

"I miss Mummy." Her bottom lip was wobbling.

"Of course you do." I crouched down, not wanting to risk a hug. "And she misses you, too. But we'll have lots of—"

But my remark was cut off by Maddie, coming through with the phone held out and a strange expression in her black eyes. I was not sure what it was—a mix of trepidation and glee, it looked like.

"Mummy wants to talk to you," she said. I took the phone.

"Rowan." Sandra's voice was clipped and annoyed. "What's this I hear about you taking them into the locked garden?"

"I . . . Well . . ." I was taken aback. Sandra hadn't said anything about the garden being out of bounds. "Well, I did, but—"

"How dare you force your way into an area that we keep locked for the children's safety. I can't believe how irresponsible—"

"Hang on a minute. I'm very sorry if I've made a mistake, Sandra, but I had no idea the walled garden was out of bounds. And I didn't force my way in anywhere. Ellie and Maddie—"

Ellie and Maddie seemed to know how to open the gate was what I had been going to say, but Sandra didn't let me finish.

"I told you to use your common sense, Rowan. If breaking into a poison garden is your idea of common—"

"*What?*" I butted in. "What did you say?"

"It is a *poison* garden," Sandra spat. "The previous owner of Heatherbrae was an analytical chemist with a specialty in biological toxins, and this was his personal testing ground. Every single plant in that garden is toxic in some degree. Many of them you don't need to ingest; brushing past them is enough."

Oh. My hand went up to the blistering rash on my forehead, which made a sudden kind of sense.

"We're trying to find the best way to deal with it, but it has heritage status. In the meantime, we keep it locked up, and it never occurred to me that you would take the children for a stroll—"

It was my turn to butt in now.

"Sandra." I made my voice level. "It wasn't my idea to go in there. Maddie and Ellie suggested it, and they know how to open the lock. There's some kind of override on the inside, and Ellie can reach it. They've clearly been in there before."

That shut Sandra up. There was silence on the other end of the phone while I waited for her response. Then she coughed.

"Well. We'll say no more about it for the moment. Can you put me back on to Maddie, please?"

I passed the phone back to Maddie, who gave me a little smile as I handed it over, her dark eyes full of malice.

She took it back to the media room, Ellie padding after her, and as Maddie's end of the conversation grew fainter, I picked up the tablet on the counter and opened Google. Then I typed in *Achlys*.

A series of terrifying images popped up across the top of the screen—a variety of white, skull-like female faces, some pale and beautiful, others rotting and putrefying. Beneath them were various search entries, and I clicked one at random. "Achlys—(pronounced *ACK-liss*)—Greek goddess of death, misery, and poison," it read.

I shut the screen down. Well, I couldn't say I hadn't been warned. It had been right there, written on the base of the statue. I just hadn't understood the message.

It was much later, over supper, that I said casually, "Girls, did you know that the plants in that garden were dangerous?"

Ellie's eyes flicked to Maddie, who seemed to be wavering.

"What garden?" Maddie said at last.

"The poison garden," I said. "The one with the statue. Your mum said we weren't supposed to go in there. Did you know?"

"We're not allowed in without a grown-up," Maddie said.

"Ellie, did you know?" I turned to her, but she refused to meet my eyes, and at last I took her chin, forcing her to look at me.

"Ow!"

"Ellie, look at me. Did you know those plants were dangerous?" She said nothing, just tried to twist her chin away.

"Did you know?"

"Yes," she whispered at last. "Another girl died."

I stopped, letting her chin go in my surprise.

"What did you say?"

"There was another little girl," Ellie repeated, still not meeting my eyes. "She died. Jean told us."

"What happened? When?"

"A long time ago," Maddie said. "She was the little girl of the man who lived here before us. It's why he went saft."

For a moment I didn't understand the last word, but then it came to me. She was saying the word *soft* but with a Scottish accent, repeating whatever Jean McKenzie had said to her.

"He went soft? Soft in the head, you mean?"

"Yes, he had to be put away. Not straightaway, but after a while. Living here with her ghost," Maddie said, matter-of-factly. "She used to wake him in the middle of the night with her crying. After she was gone. Jean told us. So after a while he stopped sleeping. He just used to pace backward and forward all night long. Then he went mad. People do go mad, you know, if you stop them from sleeping for long enough. They go mad, and then they *die*."

Pacing. The word gave me a sharp jolt, and for a second I didn't know what to say. Then I remembered something else.

"Maddie." I swallowed. "Maddie . . . is . . . is that what you meant? Before? When you said the ghosts wouldn't like it?"

"I don't know what you mean." Her face was stiff and expressionless, and she had pushed her plate away.

"When you hugged me, that day I first came. You said, 'the ghosts wouldn't like it.'"

"No, I didn't," she said stonily. "I didn't hug you. I don't hug people." But there was no way I could forget that stiff, desperate little hug. I shook my head.

"You know there's no such thing as ghosts, right? No matter what Jean has told you—it's just rubbish, Maddie. It's just people who are sad about other people who have died, so they make up stories, and they imagine they see them. But it's all nonsense."

"I don't know what you're talking about," Maddie said.

"There *aren't* any ghosts, Maddie. I promise you that."

"Can I get down now?" she asked flatly, and I sighed.

"Go on, then."

She slid from her chair, and Ellie followed.

I put a yogurt in front of Petra and then went around to clear the girls' plates. I was about to scrape Maddie's into the compost bin when I stopped, turning the plate.

She had eaten most of her supper, but a dozen or so letters from her Alphabetti Spaghetti had been left, and now I saw that the letters seemed to be arranged into words.

WE H
AT
E U

We hate you.

I scraped the plate with a violence that made the spaghetti ricochet off the inside of the compost bin lid.

I hate you, too! I wanted to scream after their retreating backs.

But it wasn't true. Not completely.

I did hate them—in that moment. But I saw myself, too. A prickly little girl, full of emotions too big for her small frame.

When Maddie looked at me, with that touch of triumph in her dark eyes, I had recognized a flash of myself in those eyes. A flicker of my own determination. Maddie was a woman with a plan, just like I was. The question was, what was it?

Chapter 6

I WAS SO TIRED AFTER my near sleepless night the night before that I bundled the girls upstairs to bed early. Petra went down with no more than a token protest, and when I went to check on Maddie and Ellie, they were in their pajamas.

"Do you want a story?" I asked as I tucked them into their little beds, and I saw Ellie's eyes flicker to Maddie, looking for permission to speak. But Maddie shook her head.

"No. We're too big for stories."

"I know that's not true," I said with a little laugh. "Everyone likes bedtime stories."

Any other night I might have sat myself down, cracked open a book, and begun anyway. But I was tired. I was *so* tired.

"I tell you what," I said at last, seeing Ellie's chin wobble. "How about I put on an audiobook?"

Pulling out my phone, I managed to navigate to the Happy media system and then to the audio files. The organization was confusing, but as I scrolled, I felt a little warm head thrust up under my arm, and Ellie's small hand took the phone.

"I can show you," she said, and pressed an icon that looked like a stylized panda bear. A list of children's audiobooks flashed up.

"Do you know which one you want?" I asked, but she shook her head, and I selected one at random—*The Sheep Pig*, which seemed nice and wholesome. I pressed PLAY, and then I tucked Ellie in.

"Do you want a kiss?" I said. She didn't reply, but I thought I saw a little nod, and I bent and kissed her baby-soft cheek.

Next, I went across to Maddie. She was lying there with her eyes tightly shut, though I could tell she was nowhere near asleep.

"Do you want a good night kiss, Maddie?" I asked.

She said nothing. I stood for a moment and then said, "Good night, girls. Sweet dreams, and sleep well for school tomorrow," and then I left, shutting the door behind me.

Out in the hallway, I breathed a sigh of relief.

Could it be true? Were they really all safely in bed and no one screaming? Perhaps I had turned a corner with them.

Up in my room, I closed the door. As the curtains drew themselves over the windowpane, my last glimpse of the outside world was of the far-off peaks of the Cairngorms and of a light in Jack's window shining across the darkening courtyard.

I WOKE to the sound of screams and a confusion so loud that my first instinct was to clap my hands over my ears, even as I bolted upright in my bed, staring wildly around, shivering with cold.

The lights were on—all of them, turned up to eye-searing maximum. And the room was icy cold. But the noise—the *noise*.

It was music, or at least I supposed so. But so loud and distorted that the tune was unrecognizable, the howling coming from the speakers in the ceiling turning it into a formless din.

I ran to the panel on the wall and began pushing buttons, my pulse pounding in my ears. Nothing happened, except that the lights in the closets turned on to join the rest.

"Music off!" I shouted. "Speakers off! Volume down!"

Nothing, nothing.

From downstairs I could hear furious barking and terrified shrieks coming from Petra's room, and at last, abandoning my attempts with the panel, I grabbed my dressing gown and fled.

The music was just as loud outside the children's rooms. Petra stood up in her crib, her hair tousled on end, screaming in fear.

I snatched her up and ran to the girls' room, shoving the door open to find Maddie curled in a fetal position in her bed, her hands over her ears, and Ellie nowhere to be seen.

"Where's Ellie?" I bellowed. Maddie looked up, her face blank, and then she fled down the stairs, with me following.

There, in the middle of the Persian rug at the foot of the stairs, was Ellie, crouched into a little ball. All about her leapt the terrified dogs, adding their frantic barks to the cacophony.

"Ellie!" I shouted. "Did you press something?"

She looked up at me, uncomprehending, and I shook my head and ran over to the tablet sitting on the metal breakfast bar. I opened up the home-management app, but when I tapped in my access code, nothing happened. I tapped it in again. Still nothing. You ARE LOCKED I had time to read before the screen died. A red battery warning flashed for an instant before it went black.

I was staring around, wondering what on earth I was going to do, when I felt a touch on my shoulder. I swung around to find Jack Grant standing behind me. He was naked from the waist up and had plainly been asleep, judging by his rumpled hair. He came close, cupping his hands around my ears.

"What's happening? I could hear the din from the stables."

"I have no idea!" I yelled back. "I was asleep. Maybe one of the girls touched something. I can't get it to turn off."

"Can I try?" he shouted. Could he? I would kiss him if he succeeded. I shoved the tablet at him, almost aggressively.

"Be my guest!"

He tried to turn the tablet on and then realized, as I had, that it was out of power. Then he went to the utility room and opened up a cupboard there, the one where the Wi-Fi router was kept, along with the electricity meter. I'm not completely sure what he did in there, but all of a sudden everything went pitch-black and the sound stopped with an abruptness that was disorienting.

Then there was a click and the lights came back on—less brightly this time, and fewer of them.

"There," Jack said. He came back, wiping his forehead, the dogs padding in his wake, suddenly calm again. "It's gone back to default settings now. Bloody hell. Okay."

When he sat down at the kitchen counter, the tablet in his hands, I could see his hands were shaking.

Mine, as I set Petra beside Maddie, were trembling, too.

"Th-thank you," I said shakily. Ellie was still sobbing in the hallway. "Ellie, there's no need to cry, sweetie. It's okay now."

Jack plugged the tablet in and waited until it had enough charge to turn on. After a minute he said, "Okay, we're up and running again. I've got the app open. Try your PIN first."

I took the tablet from him, selected my username from the little drop-down menu, and put in the PIN Sandra had given me.

You ARE LOCKED OUT flashed on the screen, and then when I tapped the little I button next to the message: Sorry, you have entered your Happy number incorrectly too many times and are now locked out. Please enter an admin password to override this or wait 4 hours.

"Ah," Jack said. "Easy mistake to make in the circumstances."

"But wait," I said, annoyed. "Hang on, that makes no sense. I only entered my pass code once. How can it lock me out for that?"

"It doesn't," Jack said. "You get three goes and it warns you. But I suppose with all the noise—"

"I only entered it once," I repeated, and then, when he didn't reply, I said more forcefully, "Once!"

"Okay, okay," Jack said mildly, but he looked at me sideways. "Let me try." I handed him the tablet.

As I watched, Jack switched users and entered his own PIN. The screen lit up briefly, and then he was inside the app.

His screen was laid out differently than mine, I saw. He had some permissions that I didn't—access to the cameras in the garage and outside—but not to those in the children's bedroom and playroom, as I did. But when he clicked on the kitchen, he was able to dim the lights by tapping on the controls on the app.

The realization was like a little shock.

"Hang on. You can control the lights in here from the app?"

"Only if I'm here," he said, clicking through to another screen. "If you're a master user—that's Sandra and Bill—you can control everything remotely, but the rest of us can only control the rooms we're in. It's some sort of geolocation thing. If you're close enough to the panel in the room, you get access to that system."

It made sense. If you were close enough to reach a light switch, why not give you access to the rest of the room's controls. But on the other hand, how close was close? We were directly beneath Maddie and Ellie's room here. Could he control the lights in there from his phone down here? What about from outside in the yard?

But I caught myself. This was pointless. He didn't need to access the controls from the yard. He had a set of keys.

Except . . . what better way to make someone think you weren't involved . . . when really you were?

I became suddenly aware that Jack was watching me, his arms folded across his chest. I caught a glimpse of myself reflected in the glass wall of the kitchen—my face pillow-crumpled, my hair like I'd been dragged through a bush. I felt my cheeks grow hot.

"I'm so sorry, Jack. You didn't have to—" I ground to a halt.

He looked down at himself in turn, seeming to realize his own state of half dress, and gave an awkward laugh.

"I should have put something on. I thought you were all being murdered in your beds, so I didn't really stop to dress . . . Listen, you get the girls to sleep, I'll put a shirt on, settle the dogs, and then I'll run some antivirus software on the app."

"You don't have to do that," I protested, but he shook his head.

"No, I want to. I'll not have you all out of your beds a second time in one night. But you don't need to wait up for me. I can lock up after myself. Or I can sleep here if you're worried."

"No!" It came out sharper and more emphatic than I had meant. "No, I mean . . . you don't have to do that. Honestly. I'll—"

Shut up, you stupid girl.

I swallowed.

"I'll get the girls to bed and come back down. I won't be long."

At least, I hoped not. Petra was looking worryingly wide awake.

It was maybe an hour later, after I'd tucked the girls back into bed for the second time that night, that I made my way back down to the kitchen. Jack was waiting for me, a checked flannel shirt on this time and a cup of tea in his hand.

"Do you want one?" he asked. I shook my head.

"No, thanks. I won't sleep if I have anything caffeinated now."

"Fair enough. Are you okay?"

I don't know why it was that simple question that did it. Maybe it was the genuine concern in his voice. Maybe it was just the shock of what happened, finally setting in. But I burst into tears.

"Hey." He put an arm around me, and I buried my face against his shoulder, feeling my whole body shake with sobs. "Hey, hey there," he said again. "Rowan, it's going to be okay."

It was that one word, *Rowan*, that brought me back to my senses, reminded me of who I was and who *he* was and what I was doing here. I took a step back, wiping my eyes on my sleeve.

"Jack, I'm so s-sorry," I managed at last. "You must think I'm a complete idiot."

"I think you're a woman who's had a bad scare and was keeping it together for the bairns. And I also think—" He stopped, biting his lip at that.

I frowned. "What? Tell me," I pressed, and he sighed.

"I shouldn't say it. I don't bad-mouth my employers."

"But?"

"But . . ." He broke off, chewing his lip, and then seemed to make up his mind. "Ah, hell. I think that Sandra and Bill should never have put you in this position. It's not fair."

"I knew what I signed up for," I said.

"Aye, but did you?" He sat down beside me. "I bet they weren't one hundred percent honest about yon one, eh?"

"Who, Maddie?"

He nodded, and I sighed.

"Okay, no, you're right, they weren't. But I'm a childcare professional, Jack. It's nothing I haven't encountered before."

"Really?"

"Okay. I maybe haven't encountered anyone quite like Maddie, but she's just a little girl, Jack. We're getting to know each other, that's all. We had a good day today."

It wasn't quite true, though, was it? She had tried to get me sacked, first by luring me into that poison garden and second by tattling on me to her mother.

"Jack, is there any way it could have been one of the kids who set all that stuff off? They were playing with the tablet earlier. Is there any way they could have . . . preprogrammed it by accident?"

Or *deliberately*, I thought but did not say.

But he shook his head.

"I don't think so. There'd be a record of a log-in. And anyway, from what you said, it overrode every single speaker and lighting system in the house. None of the users on this tablet have access rights to do that. You'd need an admin password for that."

"So . . . you'd have to be Bill or Sandra, basically." The thought was odd. "Could the kids have got hold of their PIN somehow?"

"Maybe, but they're not even down as users on this tablet. Look." He clicked the little drop-down menu on the home-management app that listed the possible users for this device. Me, Jack, Jean, and a final one marked "Guest." That was it.

"So what you're saying is . . ." I spoke slowly, trying to think it through, "to get an admin level of access, you wouldn't just need Sandra's PIN, you'd need her phone?"

"Pretty much, yeah."

It made no sense. Had Sandra or Bill done this somehow? It wasn't beyond the bounds of possibility. From what I could make out, the whole point of the system was that you could control it from anywhere with internet access. But why would they?

"And the virus scans?" I asked.

He shook his head.

"Nothing on the tablet, at any rate. It's clean as a whistle."

"Damn." I ran my hands through my hair, and he put his hand on my shoulder, touching me again, lightly, but I felt a kind of static charge run between us, and I shivered lightly.

Jack made a rueful face, misinterpreting my reaction. "Look at me, blathering away. You must be cold and tired. I'll let you get to bed."

Suddenly I was very far from tired. What I wanted was a drink, with him. It was on the tip of my tongue to mention the bottle of Scotch in the cupboard in the kitchen. But I knew that if I did, I would be starting something I might not be able to stop.

"Okay," I said at last. "That's good advice. Thank you, Jack."

I stood up, and he did, too, setting down his tea and stretching.

And then I did something that surprised even myself.

I stood on tiptoes, and pulling his shoulder down toward me, I kissed his cheek. I felt the leanness of his skin, the roughness of a day-old beard beneath my lips, and the warmth of him.

When I stepped back, his expression was blank surprise, and for a moment I thought I had made a horrible mistake. But then his mouth widened into a broad grin, and he bent and kissed me back, very gently, his lips warm and very soft against my cheek.

"Good night, Rowan. You're sure you'll be all right now? You don't need me to . . . stay?"

There was an infinitesimal pause before the last word.

"I'm sure."

He nodded. Then he turned and left by the utility-room door.

I locked it after him, and then I stood, watching his silhouette against the light streaming from the stable windows as he walked back to his flat. As he mounted the stairs to his front door, he turned and lifted a hand in farewell, and I raised mine in return.

Then he was gone, the door closed behind him. And I was left standing there, fighting the urge to touch the tips of my fingers to the place on my cheek where his lips had been.

I KNOW what you're thinking, Mr. Wrexham. None of this is helping my case. And that's what Mr. Gates thought, too.

Because we know where this leads, you and I, don't we?

To me slipping out of the house on a rainy summer night, running across the courtyard and up the stairs to the stable-block flat.

And to a child's body lying— No. I can't think about that or I'll start crying again. And if you lose it in here, you really lose it.

But I *have* to be honest with you, that's what Mr. Gates didn't understand. It was acting a part that got me here in the first place. Rowan the Perfect Nanny with her buttoned-up cardigans and her perfect CV—she never existed. Behind that neat façade was someone very different. And where did that pretense get me? Here.

I have to tell the truth. And to leave out these parts would be less than the whole truth. To tell you only the parts that exonerate me would make me slip back into the old trap. Because it was the lies that got me here in the first place. And I have to believe that it's the truth that will get me out.

I HAD forgotten what day it was when I awoke. When my alarm went off, I listened blearily for the sound of childish voices, and then, when only silence greeted me, I hit SNOOZE and went back to sleep. It recurred ten minutes later, and I stood uncertainly, dizzy with lack of sleep. Then I went down into the kitchen to find Jean McKenzie scrubbing the dishes and looking disapproving.

"Are the bairns not up yet?" she said as I came into the room.

"No, we had a"—what should I say?—"a bit of a disturbed night," I finished at last. "I thought I'd let them sleep in."

"Well, that's all very well on a weekend, but it's seven twenty-five and they need to be dressed and in that car by eight fifteen."

Eight fifteen? I did a mental double take and then realized.

"Oh, it's Monday."

"Aye, and you'll need to be getting a move on if you're to make it in time."

"I'm not going." Maddie was lying facedown on her bed with her hands over her ears.

"You're going, and that's that."

"I'm not, and you can't make me."

What could I say to that? It was true, after all.

"Maddie, unless you want me to take you to school in your nightie, then I suggest you get your uniform on."

She said nothing, and at last I sighed.

"Okay, well, if you want to behave like a baby, I'll have to treat you like one and get you dressed the way I do with Petra."

I picked up her clothes and advanced slowly toward the bed. She just lay there, making herself as limp and heavy as possible as I manhandled her into her clothes. At last I stepped back. Her skirt was askew, but she was more or less dressed.

"There," I said. "You're dressed. Well done, Maddie. Now I'll be downstairs eating Coco Pops with Ellie if you want to join us. Otherwise, I'll see you in the car in fifteen minutes."

"I haven't done my teeth," she said woodenly.

I went to the bathroom in the hallway and put some toothpaste on the tip of the brush. When I came back holding the brush, she was sitting up on her bed.

"Will you brush for me?" she said, her voice almost normal. I frowned. Wasn't eight a bit old to be having her teeth brushed?

"Um . . . okay," I said at last.

She opened her mouth, and I popped the toothbrush in, but I hadn't been brushing for more than a few seconds when she twisted her head away from the brush and spat full in my face, a gob of minty white phlegm sliding down my cheek.

For a minute I couldn't speak, and then, before I had time to think what I was doing, my hand shot out to slap her face.

She flinched, and with what felt like a superhuman effort, I stopped myself, my hand inches from her face.

Her eyes met mine, and she began to laugh, totally without mirth, a kind of joyless, cackling glee that made me want to shake her.

My whole body was shuddering with adrenaline, and I knew how close I had come to really letting go.

But I had stopped myself. I *had* stopped.

I got up and walked to the bathroom and wiped my face and chest. Then I let the tap run as I shook with pent-up sobs.

"Rowan?" The call came from downstairs, faint over the sound of running water and my own weeping gasps. It was Jean McKenzie. "Jack Grant's outside wi' the car."

"I'm—I'm coming," I managed back. Then I walked back into the bedroom, where Maddie was waiting.

"Okay, Maddie," I said, keeping my voice as level as I could. "Time for school. Jack's outside with the car."

And to my unending shock, she got up calmly, picked up her schoolbag, and headed for the stairs.

"Can I have a banana in the car?" she said over her shoulder, and I found myself nodding, as if nothing had happened.

"Yes," I said, my voice flat and emotionless. Then I thought, I have to say something, I can't let this go. "Maddie, about what just happened. You *cannot* spit at people like that; it's disgusting."

"What?" She turned to look at me, her face a picture of injured innocence. "What? I sneezed. I couldn't help it."

And then she ran down the rest of the flight of stairs and out to the waiting car, as if the bitter struggle of the last twenty minutes had been nothing but a figment of my own imagination.

Chapter 7

As THE SCHOOL GATE clanged shut, I felt a kind of weak relief.

I had done it. I had *done* it. And now my reward was five hours of something close to relaxation. I still had Petra, of course—but five hours with her was nothing compared to Ellie's uncomfortable misery and Maddie's bitter campaign of vengeance.

I walked back around the corner to the side road, where Jack was waiting in the car, with Petra.

"Success?" he asked as I opened the car door and slid in beside him, and I felt a grin crack my face wide.

"Yes. They're behind bars for the next few hours, anyway."

"See? You're doing a great job," he said comfortably, pressing on the accelerator so that we slid away from the curb.

"I don't know about that," I said a little bitterly. "But I've survived another morning, which is probably the main thing."

"Now what do you want to do?" Jack asked. "We can go straight back to the house, or we can stop off for a coffee, if you like, and I can show you a wee bit of Carn Bridge."

"A tour would be lovely. I've not really had a chance to see anything much apart from Heatherbrae yet, and Carn Bridge looked really pretty as we were coming through."

"Aye, it's a bonny little place. We can walk down along the high street, and I'll show you what there is to see."

Ten minutes later I had wrestled Petra into her pram and we were walking down the main street of Carn Bridge, with Jack pointing out shops and nodding at the occasional passerby.

At the bottom of the high street was the Parritch Pot, a Victorian tea shop with a brass bell that jangled as Jack opened the door and held it for me to maneuver Petra across the threshold.

Inside, a motherly-looking woman came out from behind the counter to welcome us.

"Jackie Grant! Well, and it's a good while since you were in here for a piece of cake. How are you doing, my dear?"

"I'm well, Mrs. Andrews, thank you. And how are you?"

"Och, well, I cannae complain. And who's your lady friend?"

"Oh, this is Rowan," Jack said. "Rowan, this is Mrs. Andrews, who runs the tea shop. Rowan is the new nanny up at Heatherbrae, Mrs. Andrews."

"Oh, so you are, my dear," Mrs. Andrews said, smiling. "Jean McKenzie did tell me, and it slipped clean out my head. Well, it's a pleasure to meet you. Let's hope you've more staying power than the other lassies."

"I hear they didn't last long," I ventured. Mrs. Andrews laughed and shook her head.

"No. But you don't look like the type to be easily scared."

I pondered her words as I unclipped Petra from her pram and slid her into the high chair Jack had fetched from the back of the tea shop. Was it true? A few days ago I would have said so. But now I was not so sure.

"Jack," I said at last, after we'd placed our order and were waiting for our drinks. "Do you know what's above my bedroom?"

He looked surprised. "I didn't know there was another floor up there. Is it a storage loft or a proper attic?"

"I don't know. I've never been up there. But there's a locked door in my room that I'm assuming leads up there, and . . . well, I heard some odd noises up there a couple of nights ago."

"Rats?" he asked, one eyebrow cocked, and I shrugged.

"I don't know. It sounded . . ." I swallowed, trying not to say the word that hovered on the tip of my tongue—*human*. "Bigger."

"They make an awful racket in the night. I've a bunch of keys somewhere. Do you want me to have a try this afternoon?"

"Thanks. That's really kind."

"There you go, now." The voice came from behind us, and I turned to see Mrs. Andrews holding two coffees. I set mine to my lips and took a long, hot gulp, feeling it heat me from within.

"This is great, thank you," I said to her.

"Och, you're welcome. I don't suppose it's a patch on Mr. and Mrs. Elincourt's fancy machine, but we do our best."

"Not at all," I said with a laugh. "Actually, their coffeemaker is a bit *too* fancy for me; I can't get to grips with it."

"Jean McKenzie says the whole house is like that, no? She says you take your life in your hands trying to turn on the light."

I smiled, exchanging a quick glance with Jack, but said nothing.

"Well, it's nice that they took the place on, at least," she said at last. "There's not many here that would have, with that history."

"What history?" I looked up, startled.

"Och, don't listen to me. I'm just a gossipy old woman. But there's something about that house. It's claimed more than one child. The doctor's little girl wasn't the first, by all accounts."

"What do you mean?"

"Back when it was Struan House," Mrs. Andrews said. She lowered her voice. "The Struans were an old family and not quite"—she pursed her lips—"well, not quite right in the head. One of them killed his wife and child, drowned them both in the bath, and another came back from the war and shot himself with his own rifle."

"I heard there was . . . a poisoning," I said uncomfortably.

"Aye, that was the doctor, Dr. Grant. He came to the house in the fifties, after the last Struan sold up. He poisoned his little girl, or so they say. Some'll tell you by accident, others—"

But she broke off. Another customer had come in. "But listen to me rattling on. It's just idle gossip and superstition. You shouldn't pay any heed." Mrs. Andrews smoothed her apron and turned away with a smile. "Well, hello, Caroline. What can I get for you this morning?"

I watched her go, wondering what she had meant. But then I shook myself. She was right. It *was* just superstition.

Still, though, Ellie's words rang in my head as I tied Petra's bib more firmly under her chin and dug out her pot of rice cakes.

There was another little girl.

WE TOOK the long way around back to Heatherbrae House. Petra snoozed in the back as Jack pointed out local landmarks. In the distance the mountains loomed, and I tried to keep track of the peaks that Jack named.

Suddenly his phone gave a little chirp, and he glanced down at it and then frowned and handed it across to me.

"Sorry, Rowan, that text's from Bill. D'you mind telling me what he says? I don't want to read it while I'm driving."

I pressed the text on the home screen and a preview flashed up—all I could see without unlocking the phone, but it was enough.

"'Jack, urgently need the hard copies of the Pemberton files by tonight. Please drop everything and bring them—' And that's where it cuts off."

"Damn," Jack said. "That's my afternoon and evening gone and most of tomorrow, too. I had plans."

I didn't ask what his plans were. I felt only a sudden sort of unease at the realization that he would be gone and I would be quite alone with the children for the best part of twenty-four hours.

It meant something else, too, I realized: no possibility of trying the attic door until he got back.

JACK left almost as soon as we got back, and although I had gratefully accepted his offer to take the dogs with him, the house had an unfamiliar, quiet feeling to it after they had gone. I fed Petra and put her down for her nap, and then I sat in the kitchen.

For want of anything else to do, I opened up my phone and typed in *Heatherbrae House, child's death, poison garden*.

Most of the early results were irrelevant, but as I scrolled down, I came to a local-interest blog, written by an amateur historian.

"STRUAN—Struan House (now renamed Heatherbrae), near Carn Bridge in Scotland, is another curiosity for garden historians, being one of the few remaining poison gardens in the United Kingdom. Originally planted in the 1950s by the analytical chemist Kenwick Grant, it is thought to feature some of the rarest and most poisonous examples of domestic plants, with a particular focus on varieties native to Scotland. Sadly, the garden was allowed to fall into disrepair after the death of Grant's young daughter, Elspeth, who died in 1973, age eleven, having, according to local legend, accidentally ingested one of the plants in the garden. Dr. Grant closed the garden after his daughter's death, and after he himself passed away in 2009, the house was sold to a private buyer."

I returned to Google and typed in *Dr. Kenwick Grant*. There were few results. The first was a black-and-white picture of a man age perhaps forty, with a neatly clipped goatlike beard and small wire-framed spectacles, standing in front of what looked like the wrought-iron gate of the walled garden. He was not smiling, but there was a kind of pride in his stance.

The next photograph made a sad contrast. It was another black-and-white shot, but this time Dr. Grant was likely in his fifties.

His expression was totally different, a distorted mask of emotion that could have been grief, or fear, or anger. He seemed to be running toward an unseen photographer, his hand outstretched, either to push the camera away or shield his own face. His mouth was twisted into a snarling grimace that made me flinch.

The final photograph was in color, and it seemed to have been taken through the bars of a gate. It showed an elderly man, stooped and bent. He was extremely thin and leaning on a stick. He was staring fiercely at the person taking the photo, his free hand upraised in a bony fist. *Dr. Kenwick Grant*, the caption read, *2002*.

As I closed down the phone, my overwhelming emotion was a kind of desperate sadness—for Dr. Grant, for his daughter, and for this house, where it had all happened.

Unable to sit in silence with my thoughts any longer, I got up and put the baby monitor in my pocket. Grabbing a ball of string from the drawer by the stove, I left the house by the utility-room door and traced the path the girls had shown me the day before.

THE sun of the morning had gone in, and I was cold by the time I reached the cobbled path that led to the poison garden. When I reached the gate, I slipped my hand through the metalwork to trip the catch, as Ellie had done. The gate opened with a clang.

It was hard to believe that I had ever mistaken it for a regular garden. Now that I knew its history, the warning signs were everywhere. Laurel berries, yew needles, patches of self-seeded foxglove, clumps of nettles. And others, too, that I did not recognize.

I hugged my arms around my body as I walked, but the garden was so overgrown that it was impossible to avoid brushing up against the plants completely. I was unable to tell anymore which plants were toxic to touch or whether it was pure paranoia on my part that sent my skin itching and tingling when I brushed past.

It was only when I turned to leave that I noticed something else—a set of pruning shears, sitting on the low brick wall holding back one of the beds. They were new and bright, and looking up, I saw that the bush above my head had been pruned—not much, but enough to clear the path. And farther up I saw that a piece of garden twine had been used to hold back a swag of creeper.

In fact, the more I looked, the more I was sure—this garden was not as neglected as it appeared. Someone had been tending to it— and not Maddie or Ellie. No child would have thought of neatly cutting back that hanging branch.

So who, then? Jean McKenzie? Jack Grant? The name sounded in my head with a curious chime. Jack . . . Grant.

It wasn't an uncommon surname, particularly around here, but . . . still. Dr. Kenwick Grant. Could it really be coincidence?

As I stood, wondering, the baby monitor in my pocket gave a little grumbling squawk, recalling me to reality, and I remembered what I had come here to do.

Picking up the shears, I hurried back to the gate and pulled it firmly shut behind myself. Taking the string out of my pocket, I clipped off a generous length, and then I stood on tiptoes and be-gan to wind it around and around the top of the gate, above the height of my own head, where no child could possibly reach, until the gate was totally secure. Then I tied it in a granny knot. I was sure now that nothing short of a ladder would enable Maddie and Ellie to break in this time. Dropping the shears into my pocket, I picked up my phone and pressed the Happy app icon.

"Coming, Petra. No need to cry. I'm coming."

And I ran up the cobbled path to the house.

THE next few hours were taken up with Petra and then figuring out how to drive the Tesla to collect the girls from school. Jack had taken the Elincourts' second car, a Land Rover, with him.

The girls were both tired after their day at school. They said nothing as we drove home, and the afternoon and evening passed without incident. They ate supper, played on the tablet, and then got into their pajamas and climbed into bed with barely a peep. By nine p.m. the house was silent, and I locked up and went to bed.

After I had done my teeth and turned out the lights, I lay down in bed, my phone in my hand. But instead of going straight to sleep, I found myself Googling Dr. Grant again.

I stared at his photo for a long time, thinking of Mrs. Andrews's words in the café. There was something about the contrast between that first picture and the last that was almost shocking, something that spoke of long nights of grief and agony—perhaps even in this very room. What had it been like to live here all those years, with the memories of his daughter so stark and painful?

Returning to the search screen, I typed in *Elspeth Grant death Carn Bridge* and waited as the links came up.

A brief piece in the *Inverness Gazette* recorded the results of a postmortem on Elspeth's death. It seemed she had died from eating *Prunus laurocerasus*, or cherry laurel berries, which had been accidentally made into jam. The berries were apparently easily mistaken for cherries, and it was thought that the child had gathered them herself and brought them to the housekeeper, who simply had tipped them into the pan without checking. Dr. Grant never ate jam, the housekeeper took her meals at her own house, and Elspeth's nanny had resigned from her post two months before the incident, so Elspeth was the only person to ingest the poison. She had died of multiple organ failure in spite of efforts to save her.

A verdict of misadventure was brought, and no charges were filed as a result of her death.

I could see why gossip had arisen—though why it had settled on Dr. Grant and not the housekeeper was unclear. And what of the nanny? She had resigned "just two months before," according to the writer of the piece, who managed to put the simple phrase in such a way as to make it sound both innocent and suggestive.

Rereading the piece, I felt a sudden surge of sympathy for the nanny, the missing link in the case. She was not interviewed. Whatever had become of her was not stated. But she had missed, by just a few weeks, the possibility of being embroiled in scandal. What future was there for a nanny whose child had died in her care, after all? A very bleak one, indeed.

I'M NOT sure when I finally drifted off, my phone still in my hand, but I know that it was very late when a sudden sound jerked me from sleep. It was a ding-dong noise, like a doorbell. I sat up, rubbing my eyes, and then realized the noise was coming from my

phone. I stared at the screen. The Happy app was flashing. DOOR-
BELL SOUNDING read the screen. When I pressed the icon, a message flashed up: OPEN DOOR? CONFIRM / CANCEL.

I hastily pressed CANCEL and clicked through to the camera icon.
The screen showed me a view of the front door, but I could see
nothing but grainy darkness. Had Jack come back? Had he forgotten his keys? Either way, as the doorbell sounded for the third
time, I knew I had to answer it before the noise woke the girls.

The room was unnaturally cold, and I pulled on my dressing
gown before padding quietly downstairs, picking my way in the
semidarkness. In the hallway, I had a moment's struggle with the
thumb panel, and then the door swung open to reveal . . . nothing.

It was quite dark. The Land Rover's parking space was still
empty, and none of the motion-sensitive security lights around the
yard were on. I peered across the yard and down the drive. Nothing. Had something triggered it by mistake?

Closing the door, I made my way slowly back up toward my bedroom, but I was barely halfway up the second flight when the bell
sounded again.

Damn. With a sigh I made my way back downstairs.

But when I wrenched open the door, again no one was there.

I slammed the door. This time, instead of setting back upstairs to
my own room, I stopped and peered into Maddie and Ellie's room.
In the soft glow of their night-light, I could see both of them lying
fast asleep, their cherubic little mouths open. It was clearly not one
of them playing with the doorbell, and I shut the door softly and
made my way back upstairs to my room.

It was still very cold, and as I closed the door behind me, the
curtains billowed out, and I realized why. The window was open.

I frowned as I walked across to it. It was completely open, the
bottom sash pushed up as high as it would go.

No wonder the room was cold. I yanked the sash down, drew
the brass catch across, and then scampered back into the still warm
sanctuary of the feather duvet.

I was drifting back off to sleep when I heard it . . . not the doorbell this time but a single, solitary *creeeeak*.

I sat up in bed, my phone clutched to my breast.

But the next sound did not come. Had I misheard? Was it not the footsteps that had woken me the night before, but something else? Just a branch in the wind, perhaps?

At last I lay slowly back down, still clutching my phone in my hand, and shut my eyes against the darkness.

But my senses were on high alert, and sleep seemed impossible. For more than forty minutes I lay there, feeling my thoughts race.

And then, as I'd been waiting for, it came again.

Creeeeak . . .

And after the smallest of pauses, *creak . . . creak . . . creak . . .*

This time there was no doubt—it was pacing.

I jumped out of bed and ran to the locked door in the corner of the room, where I knelt, peering through the keyhole, my heart like a drum in my chest.

But there was nothing there. Just the unending blackness and the cool, dust-laden breeze of stale attic air.

Creak . . . creak . . . creak . . . it came again, unbearable in its regularity. Then a pause, and again *creak . . . creak . . . creak . . .*

Suddenly I understood what dark terrors had driven those four previous nannies out of their post and away. To lie here, night after night, listening, waiting, staring into the darkness at that locked door, that open keyhole gaping into blackness. . . .

I would not sleep again tonight; I knew that now.

Instead, I wrapped myself in the duvet, turned on the light, and sat, listening to the steady, rhythmic sound of feet pacing above me. I thought of Dr. Grant, and I heard Maddie's cold little voice. *After a while he stopped sleeping. He just used to pace backward and forward all night long. Then he went mad. People do go mad, you know, if you stop them from sleeping for long enough. . . .*

Was I going mad? Was that what this was?

As the footsteps passed above me again, I felt a panic rise up inside me, and I could not stop my eyes turning toward the locked door, imagining it opening and that cadaverous hollow face coming toward me in the darkness, the bony arm outstretched.

Elspeth . . .

It was a sound not coming from above, but in my own mind—a death cry of a grief-stricken father for his lost child. *Elspeth* . . .

But the door did not open. And yet still above me, hour after hour, those steps continued. *Creak . . . creak . . . creak . . .*

I lay there facing the locked door, watching, waiting, until the floor beneath the window began to lighten with the coming of dawn, and at last I got up, nauseous with tiredness, and made my way down to the warmth of the kitchen to try to face the day.

Chapter 8

DOWNSTAIRS WAS EMPTY and echoing, eerily quiet without the dogs. As I made my way across the hall to the kitchen, I found I was picking up a treasure trail of the girls' possessions—a scatter of crayons on the hall rug, a My Little Pony abandoned beneath the breakfast bar, and then—oddly—a single purple flower, wilting, in the middle of the kitchen floor. I bent down, wondering where it had come from. Had one of the girls picked it?

It seemed a shame to let it die, so I filled a coffee mug with water and stuck the stem into it and then put it on the kitchen table. Perhaps it would revive.

I was quietly nursing my second cup of coffee and watching the sun rise when the voice came, seemingly from nowhere.

"Rowan . . ."

It was a reedy quaver, barely audible, and yet somehow loud enough to echo around the silent kitchen, and it made me jump so that scalding coffee slopped over the sleeve of my dressing gown.

Mopping up, I twisted to see the source of the voice. There was no one there—at least, no one visible.

"Who's there?" I called, and strode angrily out into the hallway.

Above me a small figure hesitated at the top of the stairs. Ellie. Her face was worried, her lip trembling.

"Oh, sweetheart . . ." I felt instantly contrite. "I'm sorry. You scared me. I didn't mean to snap. Come on down and we'll have a hot chocolate together."

Down in the kitchen, Ellie sat on one of the high stools while I made hot chocolate. As Ellie drank, we talked—about school, about her best friend, about missing the dogs—and at last I ventured to ask about whether she missed her parents. Her face crumpled at that.

"Can we phone Mummy again tonight?"

"Yes, of course. We can try, anyway. She's been very busy."

Ellie nodded. Then, looking out the window, she said, "He's gone, hasn't he?"

"Who?" I was confused. Was she talking about her father or Jack? Or perhaps . . . perhaps someone else? "Who's gone?"

She didn't answer, only kicked her legs against the stool.

"I like it better when he's gone. He makes them do things they don't want to do."

I don't know why, but the words gave me a sharp flashback to that crumpled, unfinished note from Katya. The words sounded inside my head. *I wanted to tell you to please be—*

Suddenly it felt more like a warning than ever.

"Who?" I said more urgently this time. "Who are you talking about, Ellie?"

But she misunderstood my question, or perhaps deliberately chose to misinterpret it.

"The girls." And then she put down her hot chocolate and slid from the stool. "Can I go and watch some TV?"

"Ellie, wait," I said, standing, too. "Who are you talking about? Who's gone? Who makes the girls do things?"

But I was too urgent, and as my hand closed on her wrist, she pulled away, suddenly frightened by my intensity.

"Nothing. I don't remember. I made it up." She twisted her small hand out of my grip and slipped from the room.

I was still staring after her, biting at the edge of my nail, when a noise from the hallway made me jump, and I turned to see the door opening and Jean McKenzie standing on the doorstep, taking off her coat.

"Mrs. McKenzie," I said. She was neatly dressed in a woolen skirt and a white cotton blouse, and I suddenly felt very conscious of my own state of undress, in a dressing gown.

"You're up early" was all she said, and I felt the prickle of her disapproval. My temper suddenly boiled up.

"Why don't you like me?" I demanded.

She turned to look at me from stashing her coat in the cupboard.

"I beg your pardon?"

"You heard me. You've been completely off with me ever since I arrived. Why?"

"I think you're imagining things, miss."

"You know full well I'm not. If it's about that business on the first day, I *didn't* lock the children out. Why would I?"

"Kindness is as kindness does," she said cryptically. She turned to go into the utility room, but I ran after her, grabbing her arm.

"What the hell does that even mean?"

She pulled herself out of my grip, and suddenly her eyes blazed.

"I'll thank you not to handle me like that, miss, and not to swear in front of the bairns, either."

"I asked you a perfectly reasonable question," I retorted, but she ignored me, stalking off to the utility room. "And stop calling me *miss*," I called after her. "We're not in bloody Downton Abbey."

"What would you prefer me to call you, then?" she snapped over her shoulder.

I had turned on my heel, preparing to go and wake up Maddie, but her words stopped me in my tracks, and I swung around to stare at her expressionless back, bent over the utility-room sink.

"Wh-what did you say?"

But she did not answer, only turned on the taps, drowning out my voice.

"Goodbye, girls!" I called, watching them through the school gate as they traipsed into their classrooms. Maddie said nothing, but Ellie looked up from her conversation with a little redheaded girl and waved. Her smile was sweet and cheerful, and I felt myself smile back and then down at Petra, jiggling and gurgling on my hip. The sun was shining, and the fears of last night all seemed suddenly preposterous in the light of day.

I was just strapping Petra back into her car seat when my phone pinged, and I glanced at it. It was an email from Sandra, with the subject header *Update*. I clicked to open.

Hi, Rowan.

Sorry to email, but I'm in a meeting and can't talk, and I wanted to send you a quick update. Bill has been called away to Dubai, which means I'm going to have to take over on the Kensington project—not ideal, as it means I will be away for longer than I had hoped. I should be back by next Tuesday (i.e., a week from today). Does that sound doable?

In terms of the children, Rhiannon finishes school today. Elise's mum has kindly volunteered to collect both girls, and Rhi will be back at Heatherbrae any time from about twelve onward. I have texted her, and she's excited to meet you.

Do call if you have any concerns.

Sandra x

I shut down the email. I had not realized until I read Sandra's words how much I had been counting on her arrival back this Friday, ticking off the days in my head like a prison sentence.

And now . . . four more days added onto my term. And not just with the little ones but with Rhiannon, too.

As I started up the Tesla, an image flashed through my head—that scarlet scrawl across the bedroom door: *KEEP OUT OR YOU DIE*. There was something there. Something very close to Maddie's furious, wordless anger.

Perhaps, whatever it was, I would be able to get to the bottom of it with Rhiannon.

THE school run back to Heatherbrae took longer than the previous morning, because there was a van on the road ahead of me. I followed it slowly from Carn Bridge, sure that it would turn off at every junction we came to, but inexplicably it seemed to be going the same way. At the turn off to Heatherbrae House, the van drew up over the drive, forcing me to stamp on the brakes.

As I waited, the Tesla silently idling, the passenger door opened and a girl jumped out. She said something to the driver, and the back door of the van popped open. She dragged a huge case out and then slammed the door as the driver pulled away from the curb. I was just about to lean out and ask her who she was, when she pulled her phone out of her pocket and held it up to the proximity sensor of the gates and they swung open.

It couldn't be Rhiannon, surely—she wasn't due back until the afternoon, and that disreputable van certainly didn't look like it belonged to anyone's mother.

I waited a few minutes for her to clear the gates and then pressed on the accelerator. The Tesla slid smoothly up the drive behind the girl, who turned with a look of surprise on her face. I braked again and wound down the window.

"Can I help you?"

"I should be asking you that," the girl said. She had long blond hair and a clipped accent without a trace of Scots in it. "Who the hell are you, and what are you doing in my parents' car?"

So it *was* Rhiannon.

"Oh, hello, you must be Rhiannon. I'm Rowan."

The girl was still looking at me blankly, and I added, "The new nanny? I thought your mum told you."

I put the car into park and got out, holding out my hand.

"Nice to meet you. Sorry not to be expecting you; your mum said you wouldn't be here until twelve."

"Rowan? But you're—" the girl began, a furrow between her brows. Then something cleared and she shook her head. There was a smile on her lips, and it was not a very nice one. "Never mind."

"I'm what?" I dropped my hand.

"I said, never mind," Rhiannon said. "And don't pay any attention to what my mum told you; she hasn't got a clue." She looked me up and down and then said, "Well, what are you waiting for?"

"What?"

"Give me a hand with my case."

I was getting more and more irritated, but I swallowed my anger and wheeled the case around to the back of the Tesla. Rhiannon climbed into the back seat, beside Petra.

"Hello, brat," she said, though there was an undertone of affection in her voice. And then to me, as I slid into the driver's seat, "Well, let's not sit here all day admiring the view."

I gritted my teeth, swallowed my pride, and pressed down so hard on the accelerator that gravel spat from behind the wheels as we began to move up the drive toward Heatherbrae House.

INSIDE the house, Rhiannon stalked into the kitchen, leaving me to unload both Petra and the huge trunk. When I finally made it inside, Petra in tow, I saw that Rhiannon had already installed herself at the metal breakfast bar and was eating a sandwich.

"Sooooo." Her voice came out like a drawl. "You're Rowan? I must say, you don't look anything like what I was expecting."

I frowned. "What were you expecting?"

"Oh . . . I don't know. Just someone . . . different. You don't look like a Rowan, somehow." She grinned and then took another bite of sandwich and said, "By the way, it's Elise's birthday tonight. Her mum's invited me over for a sleepover. Is that okay?"

I nodded. "I'd better text your mum and check, but of course, that's fine by me. Where does she live?"

"Pitlochry. Elise's brother will give me a lift."

I nodded, pulled out my phone, and texted a message to Sandra:

Rhiannon safely back. Wants to go to a sleepover with Elise tonight. Assume that's okay but please confirm.

The message pinged back almost straightaway.

No problem. Will call 6pm. Give my love to Rhi.

"Your mum sends love and says it's fine," I reported back to Rhiannon. "What time are you getting picked up?"

"After lunch," Rhiannon said. She swung her legs over the stool and shoved the dirty plate across the counter, toward me. "Laters."

I watched her as she made her way up the stairs, long legs in school uniform stalking up the graceful curve of the staircase and then disappearing around the bend.

LATER, AS I WAS SPOONING yogurt into Petra's mouth, I heard footsteps on the stairs and peered into the hallway to see Rhiannon holding a small bag in one hand and her phone in the other.

"Elise's brother's here," she said abruptly.

"At the door?" I glanced at my phone. "I didn't hear the bell."

"Duh. At the gates." She pressed her thumb to the panel and swung open the front door. "He's waiting for me by the road."

"Wait." I moved the yogurt out of Petra's reach and then ran hastily after Rhiannon. "I need a number for Elise's mum."

"Uh . . . why?" Rhiannon said, heavy with sarcasm.

"Because you're fourteen years old and I've never met the woman, and I just do. Do you have it? If not, I'll ask your mum."

"Yeah, I've got it." She rolled her eyes but pulled out her phone and then cast around for a bit of paper. One of Maddie's drawings was lying on the stairs, and she picked it up and scribbled a number on the back. "There. Happy?"

"Yes," I said. She slammed the door behind her, and I watched through the window as she disappeared around the curve in the drive, and then I looked down at the piece of paper. The number was scribbled across one corner along with the name Cass, and I tapped it into the messenger app on my phone.

> Hi, Cass, it's Rowan here. I'm the Elincourts' new nanny. I just wanted to say thank you for having Rhiannon tonight and if there's any problems, please call or text this number. If you could let me know what time you'll be dropping her off, that would be great. Thanks. Rowan.

The reply came back reassuringly quickly while I was spooning the last of the yogurt into Petra.

> Hi! Nice to "meet" you. Pleasure, it's always nice to have Rhi over. I imagine we'll have her back by lunchtime tomorrow but let's play it by ear. Cass.

It was only when I went to put Maddie's drawing back on the stairs that I finally looked at it.

At the center of the page was a crude figure—a little girl with curly hair—and she seemed to be locked inside some kind of prison cell. But when I peered at it more closely, I realized, it must be meant to represent the poison garden. The thick black bars of the iron gate were scored across her figure, and she was clutching at them with one hand and holding something in the other—a branch, I thought, covered in green leaves and red berries. Tears were streaming down her face, her mouth was open in a despairing wail, and there were red scribbles of blood on her face and on her dress. The whole image was encircled in thick black spiraling lines, as if I were staring down the wrong end of a telescope into some kind of nightmarish tunnel into the past.

I stood there and stared at the picture. If I were Sandra, I was pretty sure that I would want to know about this. Feeling more disturbed than I wanted to admit, I slid the drawing carefully into one of the drawers in the study. Then I returned to the kitchen and set about cleaning Petra up and putting her down for her nap.

I HADN'T meant to fall asleep in Petra's room, but I woke with a start in the armchair, my heart pounding for reasons I could not put my finger on. Petra was still slumbering in her crib as I struggled upright trying to figure out what had woken me so abruptly.

I must have drifted off while waiting for her to fall asleep. Had I slept through school pickup? But no. When I checked my phone, it was only one thirty.

Then it came again, the noise that had woken me from sleep. The doorbell. A jolt of dread flooded through me. At last I stood up, left Petra sleeping peacefully in her crib, and made my way down the stairs to the hallway, where I pressed my thumb to the panel and watched as the door swung silently open.

For a second it seemed like a continuation of last night—there was no one there. But then I saw the Land Rover parked across the driveway, heard the retreating crunch of gravel, and peering around the side of the house, I saw a tall, broad figure disappearing toward the stables, two dogs bounding at his heels.

"Jack?" I called, my voice croaky with sleep.

"Rowan!" He turned at the sound of my voice and came striding back across the yard, grinning widely. "I was going to ask if you fancied a cup of tea. But I thought you must have gone out."

"No, I was . . ." I paused, unsure what to say. "I'd fallen asleep, actually. Petra's down for her nap, and I must have drifted off. I . . . well, I didn't get a very good night's rest last night."

"Oh . . . were the girls playing up?"

"No, no, it's not that. It's . . ." I paused again. "It's those noises I was talking about. From the attic. I got woken up again. Jack, you know those keys you mentioned . . ."

He was nodding.

"Aye, sure, no problem. Want to try it now?"

Why not. The girls were at school; Petra would probably nap for at least an hour longer. It was as good a time as any.

"Yes, please."

"I'll have to hunt them out. Give me ten minutes."

HE WAS back sooner than ten, a tangle of rusty keys in one hand and a tool kit in the other, a bottle of WD-40 sticking out the top.

Up in my bedroom, the bed was rumpled and my worn clothes were still scattered across the carpet. I felt my cheeks flush.

"Sorry," I said. "I'm not normally such a slob."

Jack, however, didn't seem bothered and was already trying the door in the corner of the room.

"It's this one, is it?"

"Yes, that's right."

"And you've tried all the other cupboard keys?"

"Yes, I tried all the ones I could find."

"Well, let's see if any of these match."

The ring he was holding held maybe twenty or thirty keys, all of varying sizes. Jack tried a medium-size one that fit through the hole but rattled around loosely inside, and then a slightly larger one, which fit but did not turn all the way.

He squirted the can of lubricant inside the lock and tried again, but it still turned only a quarter of the way and then stopped.

"Hmm . . . it could be jammed, but if it's the wrong key, I don't want to risk breaking the shank in the lock. I'll try a few more."

I watched as he tried maybe four or five others of the same size, but they were worse. At last he seemed to make up his mind and returned to the second key he'd picked out.

"This is the only key on the bunch that has any give at all, so I'll try it again with a bit more force. Wish me luck."

"Good luck," I said, and he began to force the key.

I found I was wincing preemptively as I watched him apply pressure, first gently and then harder, and at last so hard that I could see the shaft of the key bending slightly.

"Stop!" I cried, just as Jack gave an exclamation of satisfaction, and there was a noisy click and the key completed the full turn.

"Got it!" He stood, twisted the handle, and the door opened.

Whatever I expected, it wasn't what was there. It was just another closet. Very dusty and badly finished so that you could see the gaps in the plasterboard, but a closet nonetheless.

"Huh," Jack said, looking thoughtful. "Well, that's weird."

"Weird? You mean, why lock up a perfectly usable closet?"

"Well, I suppose so, but what I really meant is, the draught."

"The draught?" I echoed stupidly, and he nodded.

"Look at the floor."

I looked where he pointed. Across the floorboards were streaks where a breeze had plainly forced dust through the narrow gaps, and looking more closely at the dusty plasterboard, I could see the same thing. When I put my hand to the gap, there was a faint cool breeze and the same dank smell that I had noticed coming from the keyhole last night when I had peered through into darkness.

"You mean . . ."

"There *is* something back there. But someone boarded it up."

He moved past me and began rummaging in his tool kit, and suddenly I was not at all sure that I wanted to do this.

"Jack, I don't think— I mean, Sandra might—"

"She won't mind. I'll board it back up more neatly if it comes to it, and she'll have a working closet instead of a locked door."

He took out a small crowbar. There was a crunching noise, and a slab of plasterboard toppled forward into the room. He propped it against the side of the closet and let out a satisfied "Ah . . ."

"Ah, what?" I said anxiously, trying to peer past him.

"Have a look," he said, stepping back. "You were right."

And there it was. Just as I had imagined. The wooden treads. The swags of cobwebs. The staircase winding up into darkness.

My throat clicked as I swallowed.

"Do you have a torch?" Jack asked, and I shook my head.

"Nor me. We'll have to make do with phones. Mind your feet on those nails." And he stepped forward into the blackness.

For a moment I was completely frozen, watching him disappear up the narrow stairs, the beam of his phone a thin glimmer in the black, his footsteps echoing . . . *creak* . . . *creak* . . .

The sound was so close to the noise of last night, and yet there was something different about it, too. It was more . . . solid.

"Holy crap," I heard from above, and then, "Rowan, get up here; you've got to see this."

I switched on my phone torch with fingers that shook and followed him into the darkness.

JACK was standing in the middle of the attic staring open-mouthed at his surroundings. There was light coming from somewhere, a thin, gray light I couldn't immediately locate. There must be a window somewhere, but that wasn't what I was looking at. What I was looking at were the walls, the furniture, the *feathers*.

They were everywhere. Strewn across the broken rocking chair in the corner, over the rickety doll's house, across the pile of smashed china dolls piled up against the wall. Flight feathers from a crow or a raven, I thought. And there was a stench of death, too.

But that wasn't all of it. It wasn't even the worst of it. The strangest thing was the walls—or rather, what was written on them.

Scribbled on all of them, in childish crayon letters, were words. It took me a minute or two to make them out, for they were badly spelled. But the one right in front of me, over the small fireplace in the center of the room, was unmistakable: *WE HATE YOU.*

It was exactly the same phrase Maddie had spelled out in her Alphabetti Spaghetti, and seeing it here, in a locked, boarded-up room she could not possibly have entered, gave me a jolt to the stomach as if I had been punched. It was with a kind of sick dread that I held up my phone torch to some of the other phrases.

The goasts donet like you.

They hate yu.

We want you too go awa.

The gosts are angrie.

They haite you.

Get out.

GO AWAY.

Again and again, small and large, from tiny letters etched with concentrated hate in a corner by the door to the giant sprawling scrawl above the fireplace that I had seen when I first entered.

In my head I heard Maddie's little sobbing voice again—*the ghosts wouldn't like it.* It was too close to be coincidence. But at the same time, it was totally impossible. This room was not just locked, it was boarded up, and the only entrance was through my own bedroom. And I had heard those relentless pacing footsteps just moments after staring down at Maddie's sleeping form.

Maddie had not written those words. But she had repeated them to me. Which meant . . . was she repeating what someone had whispered to *her?*

"Rowan." I felt a hand on my arm. "Rowan. *Rowan*, are you okay? You look a bit strange."

"I'm . . . I'm okay," I managed. "It's just . . . who *wrote* that?"

"Kids messing about, don't you think? And, well, there's your explanation for the noise."

He nudged with his foot at something in the corner, and I looked to see a pile of moldering feathers and bones.

"Poor wee bastard must have got in through that window and couldn't get out, battered himself half to death trying to escape."

He pointed to the opposite wall, to a minute window, only a little bigger than a sheet of paper. It was gray with dirt and partway open. Jack strode over and slammed it shut.

"Oh." I found I couldn't catch my breath. Was I having some kind of panic attack? I let out a strangled sob.

"Look," Jack said, "let's get out of here, get you a drink. I'll come back in a bit, clear up the bird."

He led me toward the stairs. But then something inside me rebelled. Whatever the truth of this attic, Jack was not my white knight. And I was not some terrified child who needed protecting from the reality of what lay behind this locked door.

As Jack disappeared down the stairs toward the floor below, I made myself stop and turn, taking a last, long look back at that dust-shrouded room filled with smashed dolls and toys, broken furniture, and the spoiled debris of a lost childhood.

"Rowan?" Jack's voice came from down the stairs, hollow and echoing up the narrow corridor. "Are you coming?"

"Yes." I coughed, feeling my chest tighten. "I'm coming!"

I moved quickly to follow him. But my foot must have caught on something, for as I reached the top of the stairs, there was a sudden clatter and the pile of dolls shifted and collapsed, china limbs cracking against one another with ominous chinks.

I watched, horrified, as the little avalanche subsided.

At last all was quiet, except for one single decapitated china head rolling toward the center of the room. For a crazy second I had the illusion that it was pursuing me and would chase me down the stairs, its cherubic smile and empty eyes hunting me down.

A few seconds later it came to a rocking halt, facing the door.

One eye had been punched out, and there was a crack across one pink cheek that gave its smile a curiously mocking appearance.

We hate you, I heard in the corner of my mind.

And then I heard Jack's voice again, calling me from the bottom of the stairs. I turned and followed him down the wooden steps.

Stepping out into the warmth and light of the rest of the house felt like returning from another world. Jack stood aside to let me out and then locked the door behind us. Then we turned and made our way down to the bright comfort of the kitchen.

I FOUND my hands were shaking as I tried to rinse out the teacups and put the kettle on to boil, and at last, after a few minutes of watching me, Jack stood up and walked over to me.

"Sit down and let me make you a cup for a change. Or would you prefer something a wee bit stronger? A dram, maybe?"

"Whiskey, you mean?" I said, and he grinned and nodded. I gave a shaky laugh. "Hell, Jack. It's barely lunch."

"All right, then, just tea. But you sit there while I make it."

I shook my head, stubborn. I would not be that woman. I would not be one of those other four nannies . . .

"No, I'll make the tea. But it would be great if you could—" I paused, trying to think of a job he could do, to soften the refusal of help. "If you could find some biscuits."

I'm not normally like this, I wanted to say, and it was true. I wasn't superstitious. But for three nights now I'd had little or no sleep, and no matter what I tried to tell myself, I *had* heard those noises, loud and clear, and they were not a bird, whatever Jack thought. And besides, that bird was dead—long dead. There was no way it could have been making noises last night. In fact, judging by the smell, it had probably been up there for several weeks.

I carried the tea across to the sofa, and Jack sat beside me, handing me a rich tea biscuit. I dipped it into my tea.

"Jack," I said, "what are we going to tell Sandra and Bill? Do you think they know?"

"I'm not sure," Jack said thoughtfully. "They're sort of perfectionists; the way that cupboard was boarded up inside didn't look like their work. And I can't imagine they'd leave all that crap up there. No, my best bet is that they didn't know the attic was there."

"But . . . the poison garden," I said slowly. "They did just ignore that, right?"

"The poison garden?" He looked at me, startled. "How do you know about that?"

"The girls took me in," I said shortly. "I didn't know what it was at the time. But my point is, they've done the same thing there, haven't they? Shut the door, forgotten about it?"

"Well," Jack said slowly. "I . . . well, I think that's a bit different. They've never been as hands on in the grounds. There's nothing up there to harm anyone, though."

"What about the writing?"

"Aye, that's a bit weird, I'll give you that." He took a long gulp of tea and frowned. "It looked like a child, didn't you think?"

"It did look like a child." My thoughts flickered to Maddie, then Elspeth, and then to the heavy manlike tread I'd heard, night after night. That had not been the step of a child. "Or . . . like someone pretending to be a child," I added slowly, and he nodded.

"Could be vandals, I suppose, trying to creep people out. But then . . . vandals would hardly have boarded up behind themselves. It must have been the previous owners who did that."

"Dr. Grant . . ." I paused, trying to think how to phrase the question. "Did you . . . I mean, are you . . ."

"Related?" Jack said, and laughed. "No. Grants are ten a penny up here. I'd never even heard of the man until I began working here. Poor bastard killed his daughter, isn't that the story?"

"She ate poison berries, according to the inquest."

"I heard he fed her some experiment from his dabblings. The folks here would have you believe he was—" He stopped. "Well, never mind. Not a pretty story, either way." He drained his cup and asked, "What d'you want me to do about it, then?"

"Me?" I asked, startled. "Why do I need to decide?"

"Well, it's your bedroom it opens onto. I'm not a superstitious man, but I wouldn't fancy sleeping next to that lot myself."

I shuddered. "What are my options?"

"Well, I suppose I can board it up, leave it for Sandra and Bill to decide. Or I could try to . . . tidy the attic up a wee bit."

"Tidy it up?"

"Paint over some of that writing," he said. "But that would mean leaving it open. I mean, I could lock the door, but it wouldn't be worth boarding over the inside again if we were planning to go back in. I don't know how you feel about that."

I nodded, biting my lip. The thought of lying in that bed with that demented writing just feet away from me behind nothing more sturdy than a locked door . . . well, it creeped me out. But the idea of boarding the room back up didn't seem much better, either.

"I think we should paint it," I said at last. "If Sandra and Bill agree, of course. We can't just *leave* it. It's too horrible."

Jack nodded. Then he pulled the bunch of keys out of his back pocket and began winkling the long black attic key off the bunch.

"What are you doing?" I asked, just as it came clear with a little click. He held it out.

"Take it."

"Me? But I don't want—" I swallowed, trying not to show the depth of revulsion I felt. "I don't want to *go* up there."

"I know that. But if it were me, I'd feel better knowing that I had the key in my own hands."

I took the key from him. To my surprise he was right. There was at least an illusion of control in holding the key in my hands. That door was locked. And only I had the power to unlock it.

I pushed it into my jeans pocket. I was just trying to work out what to say when Jack nodded again, but this time at his watch.

"Have you seen the time?"

I looked down at my phone. I was late to pick up the girls.

"I'd better go, but . . . but thank you, Jack. For taking me seriously and not making me feel like an idiot for being freaked out."

"Listen." His face softened. "That writing freaked me out, too. But it's over, okay? No more mysterious noises, no more wondering what's behind that door. We know now, and it's done, okay?"

"Okay," I said. I should have known it was too good to be true.

Chapter 9

I HAVE BEEN SCARED in prison, Mr. Wrexham. But I have never been quite as scared as I was that night in Heatherbrae House.

The girls flaked out early, thankfully, and all three of them were out for the count by half past eight.

And so at quarter to nine, I climbed the stairs to the bedroom—I could no longer think of it as *my* bedroom—on the top floor.

I found I was holding my breath as I touched the door handle. I could not help imagining something horrible flying out and ambushing me—a bird, clawing at my face, or perhaps for the writing to have spread like a cancer out from behind the locked door and across the bedroom walls. But when at last I forced myself to turn the knob, there was nothing there.

Still, I knew I couldn't possibly sleep here, so I changed into my pajamas and carried my duvet downstairs to the media room.

I knew if I just lay down and waited for sleep, I would be waiting a long time. Drugging myself into oblivion with television seemed like a better option. And so I put *Friends* on the wide-screen TV, pulled the duvet up to my chin . . . and slept.

WHEN I woke, it was with a sense of complete disorientation. The TV had gone onto standby in the night, and there was daylight streaming underneath the blackout blinds in the media room.

There was a hot, heavy weight on my legs . . . No . . . *two* heavy weights. Hauling myself into a sitting position, I looked down, expecting to see the two dogs, but there was only one black hairy monster sprawled across the sofa. The other little body was Ellie.

"Ellie. Sweetheart, what are you doing here?"

She woke up, blinking and confused, and then realized where she was and smiled up at me.

"Good morning, Rowan."

"Good morning to you, too." I rubbed the sleep out of my eyes and stood up. As I did, something fell out of the folds of the duvet and hit the floor with a dull ceramic-sounding crack.

The sound made me jump. Had I knocked over a coffee mug or something? I'd had hot milk last night, but I could have sworn I'd left the cup safely on the coffee table. In fact, yes, there was the mug still sitting on its coaster. So what had made the noise?

It was only when I pulled up the blind and folded the duvet that I saw it. It had rolled halfway under the sofa before coming to a halt, facing me, so that its wicked little eyes and cracked grin seemed to be laughing at me.

It was the doll's head from the attic.

The feeling that washed over me was . . . it was like someone had poured a bucket of ice water over my head and shoulders, a drenching, paralyzing deluge of pure fear that left me unable to do anything but stand there, shaking and gasping and shivering.

I heard, as if from a long way away, Ellie's reedy little voice saying, "Rowan, are you all right? You look funny."

It took a huge effort for me to drag myself back from the brink of panic and realize that she was talking to me.

"Rowan!" She tugged at my nightshirt. *"Rowan!"*

"I— I'm okay, honey," I managed. My voice was strange in my ears, and I wanted to sit down, but I couldn't bring myself to go anywhere near that . . . that *thing*, with its mocking little grin.

How? How had it gotten there? Jack had locked the door; I had *seen* him do it. And he had preceded me down the stairs. And I had the key in my pocket. Had *I* . . . Could I have possibly . . . ?

But no. That was absurd. Impossible.

And yet, there it was.

While I was standing there trying to get a hold of myself, Ellie bent down to see what I was staring at and gave a little squeal.

"A dolly!"

She crouched and reached, and I heard my own voice shouting, "Ellie, don't touch it!" and felt myself snatching her up.

There was a long moment of silence, Ellie hanging limp and heavy in my arms, and then her whole body stiffened and she let out a wail of indignant shock and began to cry.

"Ellie," I began, but she was struggling in my arms, her face contorted with upset and anger. "Ellie, wait, I didn't mean—"

"Let me go!" she howled. She was thrashing like a cat, digging her nails into my arms.

"Ellie . . . Ellie, calm *down*. You're hurting me."

"I don't care! Let me go!"

Kneeling, painfully, trying to keep my face away from her thrashing hands, I let her slide to the floor.

"You're mean! You shouted!"

"Ellie, I didn't mean to scare you, but that doll—"

"Go away!" she wailed. "I hate you!"

And then she scrambled to her feet and ran from the room,

leaving me ruefully rubbing the scratches on my arms. I heard her feet on the stairs and then the slam of the door of her room.

Damn. I had thought we were making a breakthrough. And now I had screwed it up. Again.

And it was all because of that vile little doll's head.

I had to get rid of it, but somehow I could not bring myself to touch it, and in the end I went to the utility room and got a plastic bin liner. I slid it over my hand, inside out, like a makeshift glove and then knelt, reached under the sofa, and closed my hand over it in one swift movement, like scooping up a dead rat.

As I stood, I felt something twinge in my index finger: a shard of glass. It had pierced the bag and driven into my finger, drawing blood, which now dripped with a steady rhythm onto the wooden floor. The head was not china, I realized, but painted glass.

At the sink I pulled the glass out of my finger and then wound my hand in a piece of kitchen paper before wrapping the head in a tea towel and then another bin bag. I tied the top and stuffed it deep into the rubbish bin, feeling like I were burying a corpse. My finger throbbed as I pressed down on it, making myself wince.

"What happened to Ellie?"

The voice made me jump, and swinging around, I saw Maddie standing in the doorway.

"Oh . . . it's my fault," I said ruefully. "I'm afraid I shouted at her. She was about to touch some broken glass, and I scared her, trying to stop her. I didn't want her to hurt herself."

"She said you found a doll and wouldn't let her play with it."

"Just a head. But it was made of glass and sharp where it had got cracked. I cut myself clearing it up."

I held out my hand like evidence, and she nodded, somberly, seemingly satisfied with my incomplete explanation.

"Okay. Can I have Coco Pops for breakfast?"

"Maybe. But Maddie—" I was not quite sure how to phrase what I wanted to ask. "Do you know where the doll came from?"

"What do you mean?" Her face was puzzled, guileless. "We've got lots of dolls."

"I know, but this is a special, old-fashioned doll."

I couldn't bring myself to fish the nightmarish broken head out of the bin, so instead I pulled out my phone and searched on Google Images for "Victorian doll," scrolling down until I found one that was a slightly less malevolent version of the doll from the attic. Maddie stared at it, frowning.

"There was one like that on TV one time. It was a program about selling ankeets."

"Ankeets?" I blinked.

"Yes, old things that are worth a lot of money."

"Oh . . . antiques. I know the show you mean. But you've never seen one in real life?"

"I don't think so," Maddie said. She turned away, and I tried to read her expression. Was she being *too* casual?

I was just trying to formulate a way of bringing the conversation back to the writing on the wall and Maddie's Alphabetti Spaghetti, when she changed the subject abruptly, bringing it back to her original question.

"So *can* I have Coco Pops for breakfast?"

"Yes, I guess so, just for today. Go up and get your school uniform on and I'll have it ready by the time you get down. Oh, and will you tell Ellie there's a bowl for her, too, if she wants it?"

She nodded, and as she disappeared, I reached for the kettle.

I was spooning some porridge into Petra's mouth when a little face appeared at the kitchen door and then just as quickly slipped away, leaving a piece of paper scudding across the floor.

"Ellie?" I called, but there was no answer, only the sound of feet disappearing. Sighing, I went to pick up the piece of paper.

To my surprise it was a typed letter, formatted like an email, though with no subject, and nothing in the "To" field. Under the Gmail header was a single line of text with no punctuation.

Dave Owen I am very sorry for scratching and waning away from you and saying that I hate you please don't be angry and don't go away like the others I am sorry love Ellie p. S. I got dressed by myself

Dave Owen? The words made my brow furrow, but there was no mistaking the intent of the rest of the message, and I unclipped Petra, put her in the playpen, and picked up the letter again.

"Ellie?"

Silence.

"Ellie, I got your letter. I'm really sorry for shouting. Can I say sorry to you, too?"

There was a long pause; then a little voice said, "I'm in here."

I made my way through the media room to the living room. She was wedged in between the end of the sofa and the wall.

"Ellie." I held out the letter. "Did you write this?"

She nodded.

"It's really good. How did you know all the spellings? Did Maddie help you?"

"I did it myself. Only . . . the acorn helped me."

"The acorn?" I was puzzled, and she nodded.

"You push the acorn and you tell it what you want to write and it writes it down for you."

"What acorn?" I was bewildered now. "Can you show me?" Ellie flushed with shy pleasure at demonstrating her own cleverness and squeezed out of the little corner. I followed her to the kitchen, where she picked up the tablet, opened up Gmail, and pressed the microphone symbol above the keyboard. Light dawned. It did look a little bit like a stylized acorn.

Now she spoke into the tablet.

"Dear Rowan, this is a letter to say I am very sorry, love Ellie."

Dave Owen . . . The letters unfurled on the screen, as if by magic. *This is a letter to say I am fairy—*

There was an infinitesimal pause and the app self-corrected.

very sorry love Ellie

"And then you press the dots here and it prints on the printer in Daddy's study," she said proudly.

"I see." I crouched down and hugged her. "Well, you're very clever, and it's a lovely letter. And I'm very sorry, too. I shouldn't have shouted, and I promise I'm not going anywhere."

She hung on to me, her chubby cheek warm against mine.

"Ellie," I said softly, "can I ask you something?"

She didn't say anything, but I felt her nod.

"Did you . . . Did you put that dolly head on my lap?"

"No!" She pulled back and shook her head vehemently. I could see in her eyes a kind of desperation to be believed.

"Are you sure? I promise I won't be angry. I just . . . I wondered how it got there, that's all."

"It wasn't *me*," she said, stamping her foot.

"It's okay, it's okay," I backpedaled. "I believe you." There was a pause, and she slipped her hand in mine. "So . . ." I was treading carefully now. "Do you . . . Do you know who did?"

She looked away at that, not meeting my eyes.

"It was another little girl," she said. And somehow I knew that was all I would ever get out of her.

"Maddie, Ellie, come on!" I was standing in the hallway, keys in hand as Maddie came flying down the stairs with her coat and shoes on. "Oh, well done, sweetie. You did your shoes yourself!" She slipped past, avoiding my outstretched arms, but Ellie, coming out of the downstairs toilet, was less quick and I caught her up, growling like a bear, kissed her little tummy, then set her laughing back onto the floor and watched as she scampered out of the front door after her sister to clamber into the car.

I turned back to pick up their schoolbags, and as I did, I almost collided with Mrs. McKenzie, standing with her arms folded in the archway that led to the kitchen.

"Crap!" The word slipped out, and I flushed. "I mean, gosh, I didn't hear you come in, Mrs. McKenzie. Sorry, you startled me."

"I came in the back way" was all she said, but there was something a little bit softer than usual in her face. "You're . . ." She stopped and then shook her head. "Never mind."

"No, what?" I said, feeling annoyed. "Come on, if you've got something to say . . ."

She pursed her lips, and I folded my arms, waiting. Then, quite unexpectedly, she smiled, transforming her rather grim face.

"I was just going to say, you're doing very well with those girls. Now you'd best be getting a move on or you'll be late."

IT WAS gray and drizzling as I drove back from Carn Bridge Primary School, Petra strapped into the car seat behind me. The gate swung inward, and we climbed the winding drive up to the house. There was no sign of Jean McKenzie's car in the drive, and both Jack and the dogs were nowhere to be seen.

Somehow I could not bring myself to enter the house alone.

"Come on," I said to Petra. Her buggy was in the trunk of the car, and I opened it up and slid her in, clipping the rain cover over her. "Let's go for a walk."

"Puggle!" Petra said, pointing through the plastic. "Jumpin muggy puggle!" I followed her gaze to the huge pool of water that had collected on the gravel, and understanding clicked.

Muddy puddles. She wanted to jump in muddy puddles.

"You haven't got your Wellies on, but look—"

I began to jog, and then with an enormous splash I ran, buggy and all, through the puddle, feeling the water spray all around us.

Petra screamed with laughter.

"Again! More puggle!"

There was another puddle farther around the side of the house, and obligingly I ran through that, too, and then another on the graveled path down toward the shrubbery.

By the time we reached the kitchen garden, I was soaked and laughing, but also getting surprisingly cold, and the house was beginning to seem a little bit more welcoming.

"Puggle!" Petra shouted. "More puggle!"

But I shook my head, laughing, too.

"No, that's enough, sweetie. I'm wet! Look!" I showed her my soaked jeans, and she laughed again, her little face scrunched up.

"Woan wet!"

Woan. It was the first time she had made an attempt at my name, and I felt my heart contract with love, and a kind of sadness, too—for everything I could not tell her.

"Yes!" I said, a lump in my throat. "Yes, Rowan is wet!"

As I was turning the buggy around to start the climb back up to the house, I realized how far we had come—almost all the way to the poison garden. I glanced over my shoulder at the garden as I began to push the buggy up the steep path—and then stopped.

Something had changed since my last visit. Something was missing. It took me a minute to put my finger on it, and then I realized. The string tying up the gate had gone.

"Just a second, Petra," I said. I put the brake on the buggy and ran back down the path to the iron gate—the gate I had tied up securely in a knot too high for little hands to reach.

The thick white string had gone. Not just untied or snipped, but gone completely. Someone had undone my careful precautions.

But who? And why?

The thought nagged at me as I walked slowly back up the hill to where Petra was still sitting, and it continued to nag as I pushed the buggy back up the hill to where the house was waiting.

By the time I reached the front door, Petra was cross, and looking at my watch, I saw that it was getting on for lunch. Holding her against my hip, I pressed my thumb to the white glowing panel and stood back as the door swung silently open.

The smell of frying bacon hit me instantly.

"Hello? Who's there?"

"Oh, it's you." The voice was Rhiannon's, and as I began to make my way to the kitchen, she came out of the doorway, holding a dripping bacon sandwich in one hand. She looked terrible, green around the gills and with dark shadows under her eyes.

"Oh, you're back," I said, and she rolled her eyes and stalked past me to the stairs, taking a great bite of sandwich as she did.

"Hey," I called after her. "Hey! Take a plate, can't you?"

But she was already gone, loping up the stairs toward her room.

As she passed, though, I caught a whiff of something—the cherry-ripe reek of cheap alcohol leaching out of someone's skin the morning after it's been drunk.

Part of me wanted to mutter that it was none of my business— that I was a nanny and had been hired for my expertise with younger children, that I had no idea of what Sandra and Bill would consider appropriate. But the other part of me knew that I was in loco parentis here. Whether or not Sandra would be concerned, *I* had seen enough to worry me. But the question was, what should I do about it? What *could* I do about it?

The questions nagged at me as I made myself and Petra a sandwich and then put her down for her nap. I could go and question Rhiannon, but I was pretty sure she'd have a ready excuse.

Then I remembered. Cass. If nothing else, she would be able to explain the exact sequence of the night's events to me.

Cass's return text was still in my list of messages, and I found it and pulled out the number. Then I waited while it rang.

"Yup?" The voice was rough and Scottish and very male.

I blinked, looked at the phone to check I had dialed the right number, and then put it back to my ear.

"Hello?" I said cautiously. "Who is this?"

"I'm Craig," said the voice. The voice had to be someone at least twenty. And it definitely didn't sound like anyone's mum, or dad for that matter. "More to the point, who are you?"

I was too shocked to reply.

"Hello?" Craig said irritably. "Hellooo?"

And then he hung up.

I walked slowly to the kitchen, trying to figure out what had just happened. Plainly, whoever that number belonged to, it wasn't Elise's mum. Which meant Rhiannon had been lying to me.

Which also meant that very probably, she hadn't been out with Elise at all. Instead, she had very likely been with Craig.

The tablet was lying on the kitchen island, and I picked it up and tried to compose an email to Sandra and Bill.

The problem was, I didn't know what to begin with. There was too much to say. Should I start with Rhiannon? Or Maddie's behavior? Or should I lead with my concerns about the attic?

The subject line first, then: *An update from Heatherbrae.*

Calm and factual. Now for the body of the email.

Dear Sandra and Bill, I wrote, and then sat back, trying to think what to put next. *First of all, I should tell you that Rhiannon arrived back this morning safe and sound, but I have a few concerns about her account of her trip to Elise's.*

Okay, that was good. But then how to segue from that into

we hate you

There angry

GO AWAY

In the end I just sat there staring at the screen, and it was only when I heard Petra's cranky wail and looked at the clock that I realized it was time to pick up Maddie and Ellie from school.

Gone to get the girls I tapped out on the messaging screen to Rhiannon, *we need to talk when I get back.* Then, leaving the email unsent on the tablet, I ran upstairs to change Petra and bundle her into the car.

I DIDN'T think of the email again until nearly nine p.m. The afternoon had been a good one—Maddie and Ellie had both been delighted to see Rhiannon, and she'd been touchingly sweet with them. She was visibly hungover, but she played Barbies with them in the playroom for a couple of hours, ate some pizza, and then disappeared upstairs while I did battle with baths and bed.

When I came downstairs, I was gearing myself up for the promised discussion, trying to imagine what Rowan the Perfect Nanny would have done. Firm but clear. Get her to talk.

But Rhiannon was waiting in the kitchen, and I did a double take at what she was wearing. Full makeup, heels, miniskirt, and a midriff-baring top that showed off a pierced navel.

"Um," I began, but Rhiannon forestalled me.

"I'm going out."

For a second I had no idea what to say. Then I pulled myself together. "I don't think so."

"Well, I do."

"Rhiannon, you know there's absolutely no way I can let you do that. I'll have to call your parents. I have to tell them—" I had to say something to make her realize she'd been rumbled. "I have to tell them you came home stinking of alcohol."

"I don't think you should do that" was all she said.

But I had already picked up my phone.

I hadn't checked it since before supper, and to my surprise there was an email icon flashing. It was from Sandra.

I pressed it and then blinked as the subject header came up.

Re: An update from Heatherbrae

What? Had I sent the email without meaning to? I had logged into my personal Gmail on the children's tablet, the one they used for playing games, and had a horrible feeling I had forgotten to log out. Could Petra or one of the girls have accidentally pressed SEND? Panic-stricken, I opened up Sandra's reply.

> Thanks for the update Rowan, sounds good. Glad Rhiannon had a fun time with Elise. Bill is off to Dubai tonight, and I'm at a client dinner, but do text if anything urgent. X

It didn't make sense. At least, it didn't until I scrolled down farther and looked at the email I had supposedly sent, at 2:48 p.m., a good twenty minutes after I'd left to collect Maddie and Ellie.

> Dear Bill and Sandra, just an update from home. All is good, Rhiannon is back safe and sound from Elise's house, and she seems to have had a great time. We've had a very nice afternoon and she's a credit to you both. Maddie and Ellie both send love.
> Rowan.

There was total silence, and then I turned to Rhiannon.

"You little bitch."

"Charming," she drawled. "Is that the kind of language they expected at Little Nippers?"

"Little—what?" How did she know where I'd worked? But I refused to be derailed. "Look, don't try to change the subject. This is utterly unacceptable. First of all, I know about Craig." A look of shock flickered across Rhiannon's face, and I couldn't stop a triumphant smile from spreading across my own. "Oh, yes, didn't he tell you that? I rang 'Cass.' Obviously, the first thing I'm going to do is call your mum and explain that you sent that email, and then I'm going to tell her about this Craig person."

Rhiannon smiled. "Oh, I don't think you'll do that."

"Give me one good reason why not!"

"I'll give you two," she said. "Rachel. Gerhardt."

The silence in the kitchen was absolute.

For a second I thought my knees were about to give way, and I groped my way for a barstool and slumped down on it.

I was cornered. I realized that now. I just didn't know quite how tight that corner was going to get.

Because this is where it gets very, very bad for me, doesn't it, Mr. Wrexham?

This is where the police case on me shifted from being someone in the wrong place at the wrong time to someone with a motive.

Because she was right. I couldn't ring Sandra and Bill.

I couldn't do that, because Rhiannon knew the truth.

Chapter 10

IT WILL BE NO SURPRISE to you, Mr. Wrexham—not if you've read the newspaper pieces. Because you will have known right from the outset that the nanny arrested in the Elincourt case was not Rowan Caine but Rachel Gerhardt.

But to the police it was like a bombshell.

Afterward they focused very hard on how I managed to do it, as if I were some kind of criminal mastermind. But what they couldn't seem to understand was how temptingly, laughably simple it had been. There had been no forgery, no elaborate identity theft or manufactured papers. All I had done was pick up my friend Rowan's nannying paperwork from her bedroom in our shared flat and show it to Sandra. Background check, first-aid certificate, CV—none of it had any photographs. There was absolutely no way of Sandra knowing that the woman standing in front of her was not the person named on the certificates she was holding out.

And, I tried to tell myself, it wasn't much of a deception. After all, I really did have those credentials—most of them, anyway. I had a background check and a first-aid certificate. Like Rowan, I had worked in the baby room at Little Nippers, albeit not as supervisor. And I had done nannying beforehand, though not as much. But the basics were all there. The name thing was just a . . . technicality. I even had a clean driving license, just as I had told Sandra. The only problem was that I couldn't show it to her because of the photo. But everything I had told her—every qualification I had claimed—it was all true.

Everything except for my name.

There was luck involved, of course, too. It had been lucky that Sandra had agreed to my request and hadn't contacted Little Nippers themselves for a reference. If she had, they would have told her that Rowan Caine had left a couple of months back. Lucky that she never pushed me on the driving license.

And it had been lucky, too, that she used a remote payroll service so that I never had to present Rowan's passport in person and could simply forward the scan she had left on her computer desktop along with our shared bills.

The biggest piece of good fortune was that banks, slightly incredibly, didn't seem to care whose name was on a bank transfer, as long as the account number and sort code matched up. If you paid by transfer, you could put Donald Duck in the payee box and it would go through. It seemed unbelievably careless.

But the truth was, to begin with I hadn't even looked past that first stage. All I had focused on was getting that interview, standing in Heatherbrae House, looking Sandra and Bill in the eye. That was the only reason I had answered the ad. And yet somehow the opportunities had kept presenting themselves.

I shouldn't have done it, I know that now, Mr. Wrexham. But can't you see—can't you see what it must have been like?

Now, standing in the kitchen with Rhiannon laughing in my face, I felt a great wave of panic break over me, followed by a strange sense of relief to have this moment over and done with.

"How did you find out?" I asked.

"Because, unlike my dear parents, I bother to do a little digging when a new girl turns up out of the blue," Rhiannon said. "It didn't take me long to track down Rowan Caine. She's pretty boring. Not much ammunition."

Ammunition. So that was what this was about. Rhiannon had been digging around online for any little indiscretion she could use as leverage. Only she had stumbled on something much bigger.

"I couldn't understand it," she said, a little smile tugging at the corner of her mouth. "It all matched up—the name, the date of birth, the time at that nursery with the stupid name—*Little Nippers*," she said mockingly. "But then suddenly there were all these pictures from Thailand and Vietnam. And when I saw you on the driveway, I began to think that maybe I *did* have the wrong person. It took me a few hours to track down the real you. Must be losing my touch. Shame for you she doesn't keep her friend list private. Or that you didn't bother to delete your Facebook profile."

So it had been as simple as that. As simple as scrolling down a list of Rowan's Facebook friends and picking out the face I had so obligingly posted up for all the world to see. How could I have been so stupid? But truthfully, it had never occurred to me that anyone would join the dots so assiduously. And I hadn't been setting out to deceive, that's the thing. That's what I tried to explain to the police. If I had really been setting up a fraudulent second life, wouldn't I have bothered to cover my tracks?

Because this *wasn't* fraud, not really. Not in the way the police meant. I never meant for all this to happen.

The problem was, the thing I couldn't tell the police was *why* I had come to Heatherbrae under an assumed name. I think at first they thought I must have some deep, dark professional secret—a lapsed registration or a conviction as a sex offender or something. And of course none of that was the case, and as hard as they tried to find something, there was nothing wrong with my own papers.

It took them some time. But eventually they came into the room holding a piece of paper and they were smiling like Cheshire cats.

And I knew. I knew that they knew.

And I knew that I was sunk.

But that was afterward. And I'm getting ahead of myself.

I have to tell the other part. The hardest part.

I have to tell you about that night.

AFTER Rhiannon walked out, I stood for a long moment in the hallway watching the lights of the van disappear down the drive and trying to figure out what I should do. Should I phone Sandra? And say what? Confess? Brazen it out?

I looked at my watch. It was just half past nine. The line from Sandra's email floated into my head—*Bill is off to Dubai tonight, and I'm at a client dinner, but do text if anything urgent.*

There was no way I could ambush her with all this in the middle of a client dinner, still less, text it through. I owed her a call—to explain myself. But what the hell could I say?

The bottle of wine was there on the kitchen counter, like an invitation, and I poured out a glass, trying to steady my nerves, and then another. By the time there was only one glass left in the bottle, I knew the truth—I was too drunk to call Sandra now, too drunk to do anything sensible at all, except go to bed.

UP ON the top landing, I stood for a long time, my hand on the rounded knob to my bedroom, summoning up the courage to enter. But I could not do it. There was a dark crack at the bottom of the door, and I had a sudden image of something loathsome slithering out from beneath it, enveloping me in its darkness. . . .

I turned resolutely and ran back downstairs to the warmth of the kitchen, ashamed of myself, of my cowardice, of everything.

The kitchen was cozy and bright. As I stood, irresolute, wondering whether to make up a bed on the sofa or try to stay awake for Rhiannon's return, I could feel the throb of my finger where I had sliced it on that vile doll's head. The skin beneath the bandage felt swollen, as if infection was setting in.

Walking over to the sink, I pulled off the dressing and then jumped, convulsively, as there was a thud at the back door.

"Wh-who is it?" I called out, trying not to let my voice shake.

"It's me, Jack." The voice came from outside, muffled by the wind. "I've got the dogs."

"Come in, I'm just—"

The door opened, letting in a gust of cold air, and I heard his footsteps in the utility room and the barking of the dogs as they capered around him while he tried to hush them. At last they settled into their baskets, and he came into the kitchen.

"I don't normally walk them so late, but I got caught up. I'm surprised you're still awake. Good day?"

"Not really," I said. My head was swimming.

"No?" Jack raised an eyebrow. "What happened?"

"I had a . . . bit of a run-in with Rhiannon."

"What kind of a run-in?"

"She came back and we—" I stopped, unsure how to put this. "We argued," I said at last. "And I threatened to call Sandra and she . . . she just . . ." But I couldn't finish.

"What happened?" Jack pulled out a chair, and I sank into it.

"She's gone. She's gone out by herself—with some awful unsuitable friend. I don't know what to do, what to tell Sandra."

"Look, don't worry about Rhiannon. She's a canny wee thing, pretty independent, and I highly doubt she'll come to any harm."

"But what if she does? What if something happens to her?"

"You're a nanny, not a jailer. What were you supposed to do, chain her to her bed?"

"You're right," I said at last. "It's just—" the words burst out of me of their own accord. "I'm so *tired*, Jack. I can't think, and it doesn't help that my hand hurts every time I touch anything."

"What happened to your hand?"

I looked down at it, cradled in my lap, feeling it throb.

"I cut it."

Jack frowned. "Can I take a look?"

I said nothing, just nodded, and held out my hand, and he took it very gently, angling it toward the light.

"It doesn't look too good, if you don't mind me saying. Did you put any antiseptic on it when you cut it?"

"Just a bandage. Do you think it really needs it?"

He nodded. "It's deep, and it looks like it could be getting infected. Let me go and see what Sandra's got."

He stood, pushing back his chair, and walked to the utility room, where there was a small medicine cabinet on the wall.

"Nothing," Jack said, coming back through into the kitchen. "Or at least, nothing except six different flavors of Calpol. Come back to mine. I've got a proper first-aid kit in the flat."

"I—I can't." I straightened up. "I can't leave the kids."

"You're not leaving anyone," Jack said patiently. "You're right across the courtyard; you can take the baby monitor. If you hear a peep, you can be back there before they even wake up."

"Well . . ." I said slowly. Thoughts flickered through the back of my head. I could ask him to bring the first-aid supplies back here, couldn't I? But part of me was curious. I wanted to go with Jack. I wanted to see inside his flat.

I picked up the monitor and the tablet, and I followed Jack as he crossed the kitchen and held open the back door for me. I felt the warmth of his skin as he shepherded me across the dark courtyard to the stairs up to his flat. I mounted the stairs after him.

At the top he pulled a key out of his pocket, twisted it in the lock, and then stood back to let me pass inside.

INSIDE, Jack flicked on a light, and I saw a small, bright sitting room, furnished with good basics and a faded cotton sofa. The remains of a log fire smoldered in the little stove in the corner.

"Right, sit here," he said, pointing at the sofa, "and I'll be back with a proper dressing for that cut."

I nodded, content to sit there, feeling the warmth of the fire while Jack rummaged in the kitchen cupboards behind me.

There was something endearing about this place. Everything was reassuringly homey, from the mug stains on the coffee table to the medley of photos on the mantelpiece—friends and their kids or maybe nieces and nephews. One little boy cropped up more than once, clearly a relative from the family resemblance.

I felt my eyes closing . . . and then I heard a cough and Jack was standing in front of me, a dressing and some disinfectant in one hand and two glasses in the other.

"D'you want a drink?" he asked, and I looked up, puzzled.

"A drink? No, I'm fine, thanks."

"Are you sure? You might need something to take the edge off when I put this stuff on. It's going to sting. And I think there's a wee bit of glass or something still in there."

I shook my head, but he was right. It did sting, first when he dabbed it with antiseptic and then again when he pushed a pair of tweezers deep inside the cut.

"Got it." Jack was grinning, holding a shard of glass at the end of his tweezers. "Well done. That must have hurt like a bastard."

My hand was shaking as he sat down beside me.

"You know, you've stuck it out longer than the last few," he said.

"What do you mean?"

"The last couple of nannies. Actually, Katya made it to three weeks. But since Holly, they've come and gone like butterflies."

"Who was Holly?"

"She was the first one. Looked after Maddie and Ellie when they were wee. She stayed for nearly three years, until—" He stopped, seeming to think better of what he had been about to say. "Well, never mind that. And number two, Lauren—she stayed nearly eight months. But the one after her didn't last a week. And the one before Katya, Maja her name was, she left the first night."

"The first *night?* What happened?"

"She called a taxi, left in the middle of the night. Left half her things, too. Sandra had to send them on."

"I don't mean that. I mean, what happened to make her leave?"

"Oh, well . . . that I don't really know. I always thought—" He flushed, his neck red as he looked down at his empty glass.

"Go on," I prompted, and he shook his head.

"Damn it, I said I wouldna do this," Jack said. "I don't bad-mouth my employers, Rowan. I told you that on the first day."

"Jack, listen," I said, putting a hand on his arm. "It's not disloyalty. I'm their employee, too, remember? You're allowed to talk about work stuff to a colleague. It's what keeps you sane."

"Aye?" He looked up and gave me a little wry smile, rather bitter. "Is that so? Well . . . you've maybe a right to know, anyway. I always thought what scared them off was maybe . . . Bill."

"Bill? In . . . in what way?"

But the words were no sooner out of my mouth than I knew. I remembered his spread thighs, the persistent offerings of wine, his knee insinuating itself, unwanted, between my own. . . .

"No, you don't need to say," I said. "I can imagine."

"Maja . . . she was on the young side," Jack said reluctantly. "And very pretty. And it crossed my mind that maybe he'd . . . well . . . come onto her and she'd not known what to do. I'd wondered before . . . Bill had a black eye one time, when Lauren was here, and I did think maybe she'd . . . you know . . ."

"Belted him one?"

"Aye."

Suddenly Ellie's voice filtered through my head. *I like it better when he's gone. He makes them do things they don't want to do.*

Was it possible she had been talking about her father, predating the women his wife had picked out to look after his children?

"Listen." Jack sounded uncomfortable. "I could be wrong . . . I don't have any proof of this . . . it's just—"

"You don't need proof," I said wretchedly. "He tried it on with me the first night."

"What?"

"Yup." I swallowed. "All vague remarks and *accidentally* blocking my way. But I know when I'm being harassed."

"Rowan, I'm so— I'm so sorry . . . I'm just—"

"It's not your fault, don't apologize."

"I should have bloody said something! No wonder you've been a bag of nerves, hearing blokes creeping about in—"

"No," I said forcefully. "That's nothing to do with it. Jack, I'm a grown woman; it's nothing I couldn't handle. The attic stuff is completely unrelated. This is— It's something else."

"It's disgusting is what it is." His cheeks were flushed, and he stood, his fists clenched. "I'd like to—"

"Jack, leave it," I said urgently. I stood up, too, and put my hand on his arms, pulling him around to face me, and then—

I don't have the words for it without writing it like a trashy novel.

Melting into each other's arms. Lips coming together like a crash of waves. All those stupid clichés.

I was kissing and being kissed, and then my fingers were in his hair, and— I can't write this to you. I can't write this, but I can't stop remembering it. I don't know how to stop.

AFTERWARD we lay in each other's arms in front of the wood fire, and he fell asleep. For a while I just watched him, the dark sweep of his lashes, the curl of his hand around my shoulder. At last, when I could feel I was beginning to slip into sleep myself, I knew that I had to get up or risk lying there all night.

I had my jeans almost on when I heard the noise. It was not over the baby monitor but coming from somewhere outside the house, a noise halfway between a crack and a thud, as if a branch had fallen from a tree. I stopped, listening, but there were no more sounds and no squawking wail from the baby monitor to indicate that whatever it was had woken Petra and the others.

Still, I pulled out my phone and checked the app. The camera icon marked PETRA'S ROOM showed her flung on her back with her usual abandon. The camera in the girls' room showed nothing. I'd forgotten to switch their night-light on when I tucked them in, and the resolution was too poor to show anything except grainy black.

Shaking my head, I bent and very softly kissed Jack on the cheek. He said nothing, just rolled over and murmured something indistinct that might have been "'Night, Lynn."

For a moment my heart stilled, but then I shook myself. It could have been anything. *'Night, love. 'Night, then.* And even if it was *'Night, Lynn* or *Liz* or any other name, so what? I had a past. Maybe Jack did, too. I had too many secrets of my own to hold someone else's up to the light to condemn them.

Chapter 11

I SHOULD HAVE JUST LEFT.

I should have walked to the door and let myself out.

But before I returned to the house, I could not resist one final look back at Jack, lying there, his skin golden in the firelight.

And as I glanced back, I saw something else.

It was a purple flower, lying on the countertop. For a minute I couldn't work out why it looked familiar. And then I realized: It was the same as the flower I had found the other morning in the kitchen. Had *Jack* left the flower on the kitchen floor? But no, he had been away, running errands for Bill. . . . Hadn't he?

As I stood there trying to remember, I noticed something else. Something that made me stop in my tracks, my stomach lurching with unease. It was a little coil of string.

I walked back across the room and picked it up.

It was a hank of white string, tied with a granny knot that was suddenly horribly familiar. And it had been cleanly severed— snipped in half by a very sharp knife or perhaps the very pair of pruning shears I had rescued from the poison garden.

Whichever it was, it didn't really matter now.

What mattered was that it was the hank of string I had wound around the poison garden gate—the string I had put there to keep the girls safe. But what was it doing in Jack's kitchen? And why was it lying next to that innocent-looking flower?

As I pulled out my phone and opened up Google, there was a sick fluttering feeling in my chest, as if I already knew what I was going to find. *Purple flower poisonous* I typed into the search bar, and there it was, its strange drooping shape and bright purple color unmistakable. *Aconitum napellus (monkshood)*, I read. *One of the most toxic flowers native to the UK. Aconitine is a potent heart and nerve toxin, and any part of the plant, including stems, leaves, petals, or roots, can be deadly. Most deaths result from ingesting A. napellus, but even skin contact can cause symptoms.*

I shut down the phone and turned to look at Jack, unable to believe it. Had it really been him all along?

Him in the locked garden, pruning the poisonous plants, keeping that horrible place alive.

Him undoing the safety measures I had set up to try to protect the children.

Him, carefully selecting the most poisonous blossom he could find and leaving it lying in the middle of the kitchen floor.

But why would he do it? And what else was he responsible for?

Had he been the person who hacked into the system to jolt us all out of our beds with deafening music and terrified screams?

Was he the one who had been setting off the doorbell and keeping me awake with the terrifying creak of stealthy footsteps?

And worst of all, had he been the one who wrote those horrible things in the locked attic room and then boarded up after himself, only to "rediscover" it when the time was right?

My hands shaking, I shoved the phone back into my pocket. Suddenly I had to get out, get away from him at all costs.

I flung open the door to the flat and stepped out into the night, slamming it behind me. It had started to rain again, and I ran, feeling the rain on my cheeks and the blurring of my eyes.

The utility-room door was still unlocked, and I let myself in, leaning back against the door and trying to get ahold of myself.

I wiped my eyes, peeled off my shoes, and walked slowly to the kitchen. Sitting at the breakfast bar, I tried to decide what to do.

I could not go to bed. No matter what Jack had said, Rhiannon was still missing, and I couldn't just forget that fact. What I should do—what I *needed* to do, in fact—was write an email to Sandra. A proper one, explaining everything that had happened.

But there was something else I had to do first.

For the more I thought about it, the more Jack's behavior did not add up. It wasn't just the poison garden—it was everything. The way he was always hanging around when things went wrong. The fact that he seemed to have keys to every room in the house and access to parts of the home-management system that he shouldn't. How had he known how to override the app that night when the music came screaming out of the speakers? How had he just happened to have a key to the locked attic door?

And whatever he said, he was, after all, a Grant. Could he be some long-lost relative of Dr. Kenwick Grant, come back to drive the Elincourts out from his ancestral home?

But no, that last what-if was too much. This wasn't some nineteenth-century peasant's revenge drama. Besides, it wasn't the Elincourts who seemed to be targeted. It was me.

Because the fact was that four nannies—five if you counted Holly—had left the Elincourts. No, not left; they had been systematically driven away, one by one. Someone in this house, someone or some*thing*, was driving the nannies away. I just didn't know who.

Slowly, unsteadily, I slid from the breakfast barstool, walked over to the sink, and splashed my face, trying to clear my head.

But as I stood, hands braced on either side of the sink, I saw something. Something that had not been there when I left.

To the right of the sink was my almost-empty wine bottle. Only now it was totally empty. What should have had a glass left in it was now completely drained. And in the groove around the edge of the waste-disposal unit was a single crushed berry.

My heart was thumping as I reached, very slowly, into the waste-disposal unit.

Deep, deep into the metal mouth I reached, until my fingers touched something at the bottom. Something soft and hard by turns, into which my fingers sank as I clawed up the mass.

It was a mush of berries. Yew. Holly. Cherry laurel.

And in spite of the water I'd sluiced down the drain, I could smell, quite clearly, the dregs of wine still clinging to them.

It didn't make sense. *None* of it made sense. Those berries had not been in the wine when I left. How could they have been? I had opened the bottle myself.

Which meant someone had put them in there when I was not looking. Someone who had been in this kitchen tonight.

But then . . . But then someone else had tipped them out.

It was like there were two forces in the house—one fighting to drive me away, another to protect me. But *who* was doing this?

I didn't know. But if there were answers to be found, I knew where I had to look.

I made my way to the stairs and climbed into the darkness.

As I got closer and closer to the top landing, I couldn't help remembering the last time I had stood there, hand on the rounded knob, unable to face whatever darkness lay behind that door.

Now, though, I was beginning to suspect that whatever haunted Heatherbrae was very human. And I was determined that this time I would turn the knob, open the door, and find evidence to that effect.

But when I got to the landing, I found I didn't need to open it at all. For the door to my room was open. And I had left it closed.

It was very cold again, and I could feel a breeze. Where was it coming from? Was it the attic door? If it was open again—in spite of the key in my pocket and in spite of Jack lying asleep in his flat across the courtyard—I thought I would scream.

Then I got ahold of myself.

There was no such thing as ghosts. There was nothing in that attic but dust and the relics of bored children, fifty years dead.

I walked into the room and pressed the button on the panel.

Nothing happened. I tried a different square. Still nothing. For a long moment I stood in the dark, trying to figure out what to do. I could smell the cold, dusty air that blew through the attic keyhole, and I could hear something, too—not the *creak creak* of before, but a low, mechanical buzzing that puzzled me.

And then, out of nowhere, a wave of anger washed over me.

Whatever it was, whatever was up there, I would *not* let myself be scared like this. I took my phone out of my pocket, switched on the torch, and strode across the bedroom to the attic door.

I felt in my jeans pocket for the key and drew it out. Softly, very softly, I put the key into the closet door and turned it.

Then I set my hand to the door and opened it.

THE SMELL WAS JUST AS I remembered from last time—dank, musty, the smell of death and abandonment.

But there *was* something up there; I could see that now—something casting a low white glow that illuminated the cobwebs the spiders had woven across the attic steps. At the top of the stairs, I drew a silent breath, steeling myself, and then I stepped into the attic.

I saw two things straightaway.

The first was that the attic was just as I had last seen it.

The second was that the moon was shining into the attic, and surprisingly brightly, for the window—the window that Jack had shut—was open again. He had evidently not latched it properly, and it had blown open in the night.

I turned back to the stairs, and then I noticed something else. There was another light. A fainter, bluer one this time, and it was coming from a corner of the attic opposite the window.

My heart was thudding as I crossed the floor. Whatever the source of the light was, it was hidden behind a trunk, and I pulled it roughly aside, no longer trying to be quiet.

What I saw made me draw back, astonished, and kneel down in the dust to look closer.

Hidden behind the old trunk was a small pile of belongings. A book. Some chocolate bar wrappers. A bracelet.

And a mobile phone.

It was the light from the phone that I had seen from across the attic, and as I picked it up, it buzzed again, and I realized that was the source of the odd noise I had heard earlier. It had evidently updated and was stuck in a loop of trying to turn itself back on, failing, and restarting, buzzing each time.

It was an old model, similar to one I'd had myself a few years ago, and I tried a trick that had sometimes worked when my own phone was dying, holding the volume-up and power buttons simultaneously for a long press. It hung for a moment, the screen whirling, and then went black, and I pressed RESTART.

But as I waited for it to reload, something caught my eye. A silvery glint, coming from the pile of rubbish I had pushed aside.

And there it was, strewn innocently across the floorboards among the rest of that pathetic pile of detritus.

My necklace.

My heart was beating fast in my throat as I picked it up, unable to believe it. What was it doing here in the darkness?

I DON'T know how long I sat in the kitchen, my fingers wrapped around a mug of tea, letting the thin links of my necklace chain trickle through my fingers and trying to make sense of it all.

I had brought the phone down, too, but without a PIN, I couldn't open it to see who it belonged to. All I could tell was that it was old and that it appeared to be connected to the Wi-Fi.

It wasn't the phone that bothered me, though. That was strange, yes, but there was something personal about finding my necklace hidden up there. I tried to work out how it could have disappeared inside a locked room, behind a door to which the only key lay in my pocket.

Had it been up there before, when Jack and I first broke in? But that explained nothing. That cupboard had been boarded up for months, *years*. The dust, the thick swags of cobwebs . . . No one had entered via the stairs for a long, long time. And the window was barely large enough for me to get my head and shoulders through.

After I found the necklace, I had scoured every inch of the room looking for trapdoors, loft hatches, hidden doors, but there was nothing. I was certain there was no way in or out, apart from the flight of stairs leading up from my room.

The clock above the stove had ticked through three and four a.m. when I at last heard tires on the gravel of the drive, whispered laughter outside the porch, and the sound of the front door swinging automatically open. The door closed stealthily as the van drove off, and I heard cautious footsteps and then a stumble.

My stomach flipped, but I forced myself to stay calm.

"Hello, Rhiannon." I kept my voice level, and I heard an exclamation of disgust as Rhiannon realized she had been busted.

"Damnit."

She walked unsteadily to the kitchen. Her makeup was halfway down her face, and she smelled strongly of alcohol.

"You're drunk," I said, and she gave a nasty laugh.

"Kettle, black. I can see the wine bottles in the recycling."

I shrugged.

"Fair point, but you know I can't let you get away with this, Rhiannon. I have to tell your parents. You can't just walk out like that. You're fourteen. What if something happened?"

"Okay," she said, slumping down at the kitchen island and pulling the biscuit tin toward her. "You do that, *Rachel*. And good luck with the fallout."

"It doesn't matter," I said.

As she picked out a biscuit and pushed the tin away, I took a biscuit, too, dunking it calmly in my tea. "I've made up my mind. I'm going to tell your mum. If I lose my job, so be it."

"*If* you lose your job?" She snorted derisively. "*If?* You're delusional. You're here under a fake name, probably with fake qualifications. You'll be lucky if you don't end up getting sued."

"Maybe," I said, "but I'll take that risk. Now get upstairs and wipe that stuff off your face."

"Screw you," she said through a mouthful of biscuit, her words accompanied by an explosion of crumbs that spattered across my face, making me recoil, brushing fragments out of my eyes.

"What is wrong with you?" My temper, so carefully held, was suddenly fraying fast.

"What's wrong with *me?*"

"Yes, you. All of you, actually. Why do you hate me so much? Do you actually want to be left here alone? Because that's what's going to happen if you keep being such a jerk to the staff."

"What the hell do you know about it?" she spat, and suddenly she was as angry as me. "We don't want you. We don't *need* you."

There was a biting retort on the tip of my tongue, but somehow, as she stood there, her face twisted into a grimace of rage and pain, she looked so like Maddie, so like *me*, that my heart gave a skip.

"Rhiannon." I stepped forward, trying to keep the pity out of my voice. "Rhiannon, I know that since Holly—"

"Don't you dare say her name," she growled. She took a step

backward, stumbling on her high heels. "Don't you *dare* talk about that slut-faced witch here."

"Who, Holly?" I was taken aback. There was something here, something different from generalized world-hating hostility. This was *personal*, and Rhiannon's voice shook with it.

"What? What happened? Is this because she abandoned you?"

"Abandoned us?" Rhiannon gave a kind of derisive, hooting laugh. "Hell no. She didn't abandon us."

"Then what?"

"*Then what?*" she imitated, cruelly mocking my south London accent. "She stole my father, if you must know."

"*What?*"

"Yes, my dear darling daddy. Carried on with him for two years and had Maddie and Ellie covering up for them both, telling my mother lies. I didn't even realize what was going on until my friend came to stay and pointed it out. I didn't believe her at first, so I set them up to find out the truth. My dad doesn't have cameras in his study. Did you ever notice that?" She gave a bitter laugh. "Funny that. I got Petra's baby monitor, and I plugged it in under his desk and I *heard* them. I heard him telling Holly that he loved her, that he was going to leave my mum, just like he'd promised."

I wanted to put my arms around her, hug her, tell her it was okay, that it was not her fault, but I couldn't move.

"And I heard her, too, begging, telling him she just couldn't wait, that she wanted them to be together—" She stopped, choking with disgust for a moment. "So I framed the bitch."

"What—" I couldn't finish. I could barely even form the word.

Rhiannon smiled, but her face was twisted. "I got her in front of the cameras, and I wound her up until she hit me."

Oh, God. So this was where Maddie had learned it.

"Then I told her to get out or I'd put the footage on YouTube and ensure she never worked in this country again."

"Rhiannon." I stepped toward her. "I swear, there is no way in a million years I'd ever sleep with your father."

"You can't promise that." There were tears running down her

cheeks. "That's what they all think when they come here. But he keeps on and on and they can't afford to lose their jobs."

"No." I was shaking my head. "No. Rhiannon, listen, I . . . I can't explain, but just . . . no. There's no way I'd ever do that."

"I don't believe you," she said. "He's done it before, you know. Before Holly. And that time, he *did* leave. He had another family. Another child. A *baby*. I heard my mother talking one day. And he *left* them. It's who he is, and if I hadn't stopped him—"

But she couldn't finish. Her voice dissolved into sobs. I put my hands on her arms, trying to steady us.

"Rhiannon, listen, I can promise you this. I swear on . . . on my *grave*, I am never, never going to sleep with your father."

Because.

It was on the tip of my tongue.

I am never, never going to sleep with your father because—

I wish I had finished the sentence, Mr. Wrexham. I wish I had just said it, explained. But I was still clinging to the idea of explaining my deception to Sandra the next day, and I couldn't tell Rhiannon the truth before I confessed to her mother.

But you don't need me to finish the sentence, do you, Mr. Wrexham? You know why. At least, I imagine you do if you've read the papers. *You* know that the reason I would never sleep with Bill Elincourt was because he was my father, too.

Chapter 12

I told you, Mr. Wrexham, didn't I, that I wasn't even looking for a job when I stumbled upon the ad? I was doing something totally different, something I'd done many times before.

I was Googling my father's name.

I'd always known who he was, and for a while I'd even known

where he was—a fancy house in Crouch End, with electric gates and a shiny BMW. I had been there once in my mid-teens, under the cover of a pretended shopping trip with a friend.

I stood outside that gate for a long time, consumed with a strange mix of fear and anger, too afraid to ring the bell and face up to the man I'd never met, the man who had walked out when my mother was nine months pregnant.

He sent checks for a while, but he wasn't on my birth certificate, and I suppose my mother was too proud to force him to pay.

Instead, she picked herself up, got a job in an insurer's firm, and met the man she eventually married. The man—the message was very clear—that she *should* have been with all along.

And so when I was six, we moved into his boxy little house.

It was their home, but I—I was always there to spoil it for them. This constant reminder of my mother's past. Of the man who had left her. And every day, she had to look at me staring at her over the breakfast cereal with *his* eyes. When she brushed my thick, wiry hair into a ponytail, it was *his* hair she brushed.

For that was all I had from him. That, and the necklace he had sent me on my first birthday, the last contact I had from him. A necklace with my initial on it—R for *Rachel*.

I was working as a nanny in Highgate when she rang me up and told me. She and my stepfather were selling the house and retiring to Spain. Just like that. It wasn't that I had any particular affection for that house—I had never been happy there.

But it had been . . . well, if not my home, at any rate, the only place I could call home. "Of course, you're welcome to come and visit," she said, her voice slightly defensive, and I think it was that, more than anything, that made me lose it. *You're welcome to come and visit.* It was the kind of thing you say to a distant relative, hoping they won't take you up on the offer.

I told her to screw off. I'm not proud of that. I told her that I hated her, that I never wanted to hear from her again.

It wasn't true. Even now, even here, at Charnworth, she was the first person I put on my prison call list. But she's never called.

Two days after her announcement I went back to Crouch End.

I was twenty-two. And I wasn't angry this time. I was just . . . I was terribly, terribly sad. I had lost the only parent I'd ever known, and my need to replace her with *something*, however poor and inadequate, was consuming me.

My heart was thudding in my chest as I walked up to the gate and rang the bell. Eventually the front door opened, and a small woman holding a duster came out across the shingled drive.

"Hello?" She was in her forties or fifties, and her voice was heavily accented—Polish, I thought. "I can help you?"

"Oh . . . hello. I'm looking for Mr.—" I swallowed. "Mr. Elincourt. Bill Elincourt. Is he here?"

"He is not here."

"Oh, well, will he be back later?"

"He gone. He and his wife moved last year. Different country. Scotland. New family is here now. Mr. and Mrs. Cartwright."

It was like a punch to the gut.

"Do you . . . Do you have an address?" I asked, my voice faltering, and she shook her head. There was pity in her eyes.

"Sorry, I do not have. I am just cleaning."

"You—" I swallowed hard. "You mentioned a wife. Mrs. Elincourt. Can I ask what's her name?"

The cleaner looked at me sadly.

"She called Sandra," she said at last, very quietly. "I must go now." And then she turned and made her way back into the house.

I turned, too, and began the walk back to Highgate. As I started up the hill, it began to rain, and I knew I had lost my chance.

AFTER that, I didn't try looking again in earnest for a few years. And then one day when I was idly typing *Bill Elincourt* into Google, there it was. The ad. With a house in Scotland. And a wife called Sandra. And suddenly I couldn't *not*.

It was like the universe had set this up for me.

I didn't want him to be my dad, not now, not after all these years. I just wanted to . . . well, just to *see*, I suppose. But obviously, I couldn't travel up to Scotland under my own name without telling him who I was and setting up a whole weight of expectation and potential rejection. Gerhardt was unusual enough as a surname for him to register it as that of the mother of his child.

But I didn't need to go under my own name. In fact, I had a better name, a better identity, just ready and waiting for me. And so I picked up the papers that Rowan had left so temptingly lying around in her bedroom. The papers so very, very close to my own that, really, it didn't seem like much of a deception at all.

And I applied.

I didn't expect to get the job. I didn't even want it. I just wanted to meet the man who had abandoned me all those years before. But when I saw Heatherbrae, I knew, Mr. Wrexham. I knew that one visit was never going to be enough for me. I wanted to be a part of all this, to sleep in the softness of those feather beds, to bask under the rainwater showers—to be a part of this family.

And I wanted very, *very* badly to meet Bill.

And when he didn't appear at the interview, I could see only one way to make that happen. I had to get the job.

But when I did . . . and when I met Bill and realized the kind of man he was—it's like a metaphor for this whole thing, Mr. Wrexham. The beauty of this house and the seeping poison underneath. The solid Victorian wood of a closet door, and the cold smell of death that breathes out of the hole.

Don't look for him. That was one of the few things my mother had said to me about him before she shut off the subject. *Don't look for him, Rachel. Nothing good will come of it.*

She was right. And how I wish I'd listened to her.

"Come on," I said at last. "Up to bed, Rhiannon. You're tired, I'm tired . . . We'll talk about all this in the morning."

I climbed the stairs, Rhiannon in front of me. When we got to the second-floor landing, she turned the handle on her graffitied bedroom door and flung her shoes in with total unconcern.

"Good night," she said, as if nothing had happened.

"Good night," I said, and I took a deep breath and opened the door to the bedroom. The strange phone was hard in my pocket, and my necklace—the necklace I had feared Bill Elincourt might recognize—lay warm around my neck.

Inside, the door to the attic was shut and locked, as I had left it. I was about to grab my night things when there was a sudden gust of wind, making the trees outside groan.

The room was still painfully cold, just as it had been earlier that night, and suddenly I realized. The cold had never come from the attic—it must have been the window, open all along.

But the problem was, I had not opened that window.

Turning, I ran out of the room and down the stairs, my heart hammering in my chest. I opened Petra's bedroom door. She was there, quite asleep, and I felt my pulse rate calm, just a little, but I had to check on the others before I could relax.

Down the corridor then, to the door marked PRINCESS ELLIE and QUEEN MADDIE.

It was shut, and I turned the handle very softly, pushing gently. It was pitch-black inside, and I tiptoed across the thick carpet and felt along the wall for the night-light and switched it on. And there they were, Ellie scrunched into a tight little ball as though trying to hide from something, Maddie scooched down under the duvet so that I could see nothing except her shape beneath the covers.

My panic calmed as I turned back to the door, laughing at myself for my paranoia.

And then . . . I stopped.

It was ridiculous, I knew that, but I just had to *see*. . . .

I tiptoed across the carpet and drew back the cover. To find . . .

. . . a pillow, pushed into the curved shape of a sleeping child.

My heart began to race sickeningly hard.

THE first thing I did was check under the bed. Then all the cupboards in the room.

"Maddie," I whispered, not wanting to wake Ellie but hearing the panicked urgency in my own voice. "Maddie?"

But there was no answering sound, not even a stifled giggle.

I ran out of the room.

"Maddie?" I called louder this time. I rattled the handle of the bathroom, but it was unlocked, and when the door swung open, I saw its emptiness, the moonlight streaming across the bare tiles.

"Maddie?"

Nothing in Sandra and Bill's bedroom, either.

"What is it?" Rhiannon's sleepy voice came from upstairs. "What's going on?"

"It's Maddie," I called up, trying to keep the panic out of my voice. "She's not in bed. Can you look upstairs? Maddie!"

Petra was stirring now, and I heard her crotchety grumble, but I didn't stop to comfort her. I *had* to find Maddie. Had she come downstairs to find me when I was with Jack? The thought gave me an unpleasant lurch, followed by another, even more unpleasant.

Had she possibly *followed* me?

I ran down the stairs, shoved my feet into the first pair of Wellingtons I found at the back door, and ran out into the moonlight.

The cobbled yard was empty.

"Maddie!" I called, full-throated, desperate now.

There was no answer, and I had an even more horrible thought.

The poison garden.

The poison garden left unlocked and unguarded by Jack Grant.

It had already killed one little girl.

Dear God, I prayed as I began to sprint toward the back of the house, toward the path down through the shrubbery, my feet slipping in the too-big Wellingtons. Please let it not claim another.

But as I rounded the corner of the house, I found her.

She was lying crumpled facedown below my bedroom window, sprawled across the cobblestones in her nightdress, the white cotton soaked through and through with blood.

I knelt and picked her up, cradling her, feeling the birdlike fragility of her little bones, begging her to be okay.

But she would never be okay again. Nothing would.

She was quite, quite dead.

The next few hours are the ones that the police have made me go over again and again. And yet, even after all their questions, the memories only come in snatches.

I remember screaming, holding Maddie's body for what felt like the longest time, until first Jack came and then Rhiannon, holding a wailing Petra in her arms, almost dropping her when she saw the horror of what had happened.

I remember Jack taking Rhiannon inside and then trying to pull me away, saying, *She's dead, Rowan, we have to leave her for the police*, and I couldn't let her go. I could only weep and cry.

I remember the flashing blue lights of the police at the gate and Rhiannon's face, white and stricken, as she tried to comprehend.

And I remember sitting there, covered in blood on the velvet sofa, as they asked me what happened.

And I still don't know.

I still don't know, Mr. Wrexham, and that's the truth.

I know what the police think. They think that Maddie went up to my room to find me missing and that she saw something incriminating up there—perhaps she went to the window and saw me creeping back from Jack's flat. Or perhaps she found something in my belongings, something to do with my true identity.

I don't know. I had so much to hide, after all.

And they think that I came back to find her there and realized what she had seen and that I opened the window and that—

I can't say it. It's hard even to write it. But I have to.

They think that I threw her out. They think that I stood there, with the curtains blowing wide, and watched her bleed to death on the cobblestones and then went back downstairs to drink tea and wait calmly for Rhiannon to come home.

They think that I left the window open deliberately, to try to make it seem like she could have fallen. But they are sure that she didn't. I am not certain why—I think it's something to do with the position of where she landed—with an arc that could only have been caused by a push or a jump.

Would Maddie have jumped? That's a question I have asked myself a thousand, maybe a million, times.

And the truth is, I just don't know.

We may never know. Because the irony is, Mr. Wrexham, in a

house filled with cameras, there are none that show what happened to Maddie that night. The camera in her room shows nothing but darkness. And as for my room, that is one of the bricks in the edifice of evidence the police built against me.

"Why did you cover the security camera in your room if you had nothing to hide?" they kept asking me again and again.

And I tried to tell them—to explain what it's like to be a young woman alone in a strange house, with strangers watching you.

"Would you want a camera in your bedroom?" I asked the detective, but he just shrugged as if to say, *It's not me on trial, love.*

But the truth is, I did cover up that camera. And if I hadn't, we might know what happened to Maddie.

Because I *didn't* kill her, Mr. Wrexham. I didn't kill her, and you have to believe me, because it's the truth.

If you didn't kill her, who did? Help us out here, Rachel. Tell us what you think happened, the police asked, again and again, and I could only shake my head. Because the truth is, Mr. Wrexham, I don't know. I have constructed a thousand theories—each wilder than the other. Jean McKenzie, hiding in the attic; Jack Grant, creeping past me while I was waiting downstairs for Rhiannon.

Because Jack turned out to have secrets, too. Did you know that? Nothing as grand as what I had imagined—he wasn't related to Dr. Kenwick Grant. And when I told the police about the string in his kitchen and the *Aconitum napellus* blossom, he had a reasonable explanation. Jack, it seemed, had recognized the purple flower sitting in the coffee cup on the kitchen table—or thought he had. And so he had taken it with him to compare it to the plants in the poison garden. When he discovered that he was correct, that the flower was deadly, he had removed my string barrier and replaced it with a padlock and chain.

No, Jack's deep, dark secret was much more mundane than that. Jack was married.

When they realized I didn't know, the police delighted in ramming the fact home. But I was beyond caring. What did it matter if Jack had a wife and a two-year-old back in Edinburgh? In the face of Maddie's death, none of it seemed important.

I never saw him again after I was taken down to the station for questioning. He never wrote. He never phoned. He never visited.

The last time I saw him was as I stumbled into the back of a police car, feeling his hands gripping mine, strong and steady.

"It'll be all right, Rowan." It was the last thing he said to me, the last words I heard as the car door slammed shut behind me.

It was a lie. A lie from first to last. I was not Rowan. And nothing was ever going to be all right again.

But the thing I keep coming back to is what Maddie said to me that very first time I met her, her arms wrapped around me.

Don't come here, she had said. *It's not safe.*

And then those last words, sobbed in parting and later denied, words that I am still certain I heard months later.

The ghosts wouldn't like it.

I don't believe in ghosts, Mr. Wrexham. I never have. I'm not a superstitious person.

But it was not superstition that I heard pacing the attic above me, night after night. It was not superstition that made me wake in the night, shivering, my room cold as an icebox. That doll's head—that was real, Mr. Wrexham. Real as you and me. Real as the writing on the walls of the attic, real as my writing to you now.

Because I know—I know that's when I really sealed my fate with the police. It wasn't just the fake name. It wasn't just the fact that I was Bill's estranged daughter, come back to exact some sort of twisted revenge on his new family. It wasn't any of that.

It was what I told them on that first awful night, sitting there in my bloodstained clothes, shaking with grief and terror. Because that first night, I broke down and told them everything that had happened. From the footsteps in the night, to the deep, seeping sense of evil I felt when I opened the attic door and stepped inside.

That was the moment the key turned in the lock.

That was when they *knew*.

I'VE had a lot of time to think in here, Mr. Wrexham. I told the police the truth, and the truth undid me. I know what they saw—a crazed woman with a backstory more full of holes than a bullet-pocked signpost. They saw a woman with a motive. A woman so estranged from her family that she had come to their house under false pretenses to enact some terrible, unhinged vengeance.

I know what I think happened. I have had a long time to put pieces together—the open window, the footsteps in the attic, the father who loved his daughter so much that it killed her, and the father who walked away from his children again and again.

And most of all, two pieces I never connected right up until the very end—the phone, and Maddie's pleading little face that very first day as I drove away, and her whispered, anguished *the ghosts wouldn't like it*. And those two things were what did it for me with the police. My fingerprints on the phone and my account of what Maddie had said to me, and the domino effects of her words began.

But at the end of the day, it doesn't matter what I think or what my theories are. It's what the jury thinks that matters. I picked you, Mr. Wrexham, because when I asked the other women in here who I should get to represent me, your name came up more than any other lawyer. Apparently, you've got a reputation for getting even no-hopers off the hook.

And I know that's what I am. I have no hope anymore.

A child is dead, and the police and the public and the press—they all want someone to pay. And that someone must be me.

But I didn't kill that girl, Mr. Wrexham. I didn't kill Maddie. I loved her. And I don't want to rot in jail for something I didn't do.

Please, *please* believe me.

Yours truly,

Rachel Gerhardt.

8th July 2019

Richard McAdams

Ashdown Construction Services, internal post

Rich, bit of a funny one. One of the guys working on the Charn-worth redevelopment found this pile of old papers when he was ripping out a wall. Looks like one of the prisoners hid them. I've only glanced at the top few, but looks to be a bunch of letters from an inmate to her solicitor before her trial—don't know why they were never posted. The guy who found them leafed through and says it was quite a well-known case.

Anyway, he felt a bit awkward chucking them in case they were evidence or something. I don't imagine it matters now—but to put his mind at rest, I said I'd see it was properly dealt with.

The top part is her letters to the lawyer, but she'd also hidden a few letters written to her in the same place. They seem to be just family stuff, but I'm sticking them in the packet as well.

Anyway, be very grateful if I could leave it with you to decide what to do, if anything.

Cheers,

Phil

1st November 2017

Dear Rachel,

It feels strange addressing you by that name, but here we are.

I must start by saying how sorry I am about what happened. I imagine that's not what you expected me to say, but I am, and I'm not ashamed to say it.

What you must understand is that I have watched over those children for five years now—and I've watched more nannies come and go than I've had hot dinners. I was the one who had to sit and watch while that baggage Holly carried on with Mr. Elincourt under his wife's nose, and I was the one who patched everything up when she walked out and left the girls in bits. And since then, I've had to sit there and watch as nanny after nanny came and went and broke those poor bairns' hearts.

And every time they came, and they were another pretty young lass, I felt it like a cold hand around my heart and I lay awake at night and I wondered—should I tell Mrs. Elincourt what kind of a man her husband was, and what kind of a woman that Holly was, and why she really left? And every time, I found I couldn't do it.

So I confess, when I met you and found out that Mrs. Elincourt had hired yet another pretty young girl, my heart sank. Because I knew what he would be up to, and I knew those poor children would be the ones to suffer again when you upped and left. And that made me angry. But I should not have taken my anger out on you like that, and I feel heart sorry when I think back on some of the things I said to you. Because whatever the police say, I know that you would have walked a mile over glass before you hurt one of those little lassies, and I told the officer who interviewed me so.

So anyway, that is partly why I am writing. To say all of that to you and get it off my chest.

But the other reason is because Ellie has written you a letter. She put it in an envelope and sealed it up before she gave it to me, and she made me promise not to read it, and I said I would not. I have kept that promise, but I must ask you, if there is anything in that letter you think her mother or I should know, you must tell us.

There is no point in writing to the house, for it is shut up. Mrs. Elincourt has left her husband, taken the children, and moved down south to her own family. And Mr. Elincourt has moved away, too—there is some sort of lawsuit against him connected with an intern at his firm, and the rumor is that the house will have to be sold to pay for the legal fees.

But I am putting my address at the bottom of this letter, and I ask that if you have any concerns, you write to me there. I have faith that you will do that, for I believe that you loved those children, as I did and do. I don't believe you will let any harm come to Ellie, will you? I am trusting you on this, Rachel. I pray that you won't let me down.

Yours very sincerely,
Jean McKenzie
15a High Street
Carn Bridge

From:
To:
Subject:
Dave Owen only they said that your name is Rachel is that true

I miss you a lot and I am fairy very sorry about what happened especially because it's all my fault but I can't tell anyone especially not mummy or Daddy because they will be so angry and then daddy will go away like he tried to before like Maddie always said he would

it was me Rowan I pushed mad he because she was going to

make you go away like the others she made all the others go away by playing tricks with Mummy's old phone she took their things and she kind into the Attic window up the roof from your room the Attic was her secret den where she always went but she said I was too little to climb up and the she made the happy wake them up in the night and she took a YouTube video and played it on the speakers on the happy to make it sound like there was people in the Attic walking around but it wasn't it was just the video and she took the dollies head out of the attic and she made me put the doggies head on your lap and I am so sorry because I said it wasn't true and it was it was me who did that

she woke up and you weren't there and mad he was going to poison you with you berries but I poured the wine down the sink and then Maddie was fairy angry and she said she was going to climb into the attic window again and get you into trouble with Mummy by setting off all the alarms because you had gone and I ran after her an eye asked not to do it and she said no I will do it or she will take Daddy away and I said no don't Rowan with nice and I don't want her to go she wouldn't do that and mad he said I'm going to a new can't stop me and she kind up and I pushed her I didn't mean for 2 happen and I am so sorry

please don't tell the police Rowan I don't want to go to prison and I am so sorry but it isn't fair for you to get told off for a thing I did so can you just say that it wasn't you and that you know who did it but you can't say who because it's a secret but it wasn't you

we are going away tomorrow to a new house daddy can't come right now but I hope you can I love you please come back soon love Ellie elancourt age 5 goodbye

AfterWords

While Ruth Ware's latest novel may invite comparisons to Henry James's *The Turn of the Screw*, the truth is, Ware hadn't actually read James's classic ghost story when she began writing *The Turn of the Key*. Rather, she drew inspiration from much more contemporary material: smart-home abuse.

"There have been a number of articles in the press in the past couple of years about the phenomenon of smart-home abuse," she explains, "where one person is digitally savvy and uses home technology to control or even in some cases terrorize their partner."

Ware wanted to explore this "creepy" side of technology, focusing on our fears of manipulation and surveillance. "As our homes become more linked up," she notes, "the potential for control goes well beyond covert listening and into every aspect of the home environment, from the temperature of the rooms to whether the inhabitants are locked out . . . or in."

Of course, technology isn't the only danger lurking around the novel's Heatherbrae House. "I've always been fascinated by poison gardens," she says, referring to gardens in the United Kingdom that collect toxic plants. "Because so much of the book was about the power of technology, I wanted to show that the natural world can be quite as deadly as anything humans can dream up."

Ware currently lives with her family near Brighton, England.

NEW YORK TIMES BESTSELLING AUTHOR

SHELLEY
NOBLE

AUTHOR OF *LIGHTHOUSE BEACH*

a beach
wish

A NOVEL

Prologue

Zoe Bascombe graduated in marketing because, according to her family, she'd never make a real career out of music. What they meant was that she wouldn't climb a corporate ladder with hard work and smart investments—the only success they understood—but what she heard was, You don't have the talent to be a rock star.

She didn't want to be a rock star. She didn't want to be any kind of star. She wanted to write music. She'd studied piano—all well-heeled girls did—and tried her hand at composing; she even received a guitar one Christmas from her brother Chris. But when it came time to audition for Juilliard, she choked. She aced the entrance exam to Wharton. So . . .

After graduation, she landed a job at MAX4, a cutting-edge New York music event organizer, which put her close to music as she tackled exposure—marketing and physical. She arranged transportation for temperamental VIPs, synced schedules, and herded staff members, hoping, praying, that somehow this would lead her to what she actually loved. Music.

And then she was downsized.

"Due to a restructuring of the company . . ."

"It isn't your fault," she was assured by her superiors, all long-haired, jeans-wearing corporate types. "We hate to see you go. But . . . seniority. You'll land on your feet. Hang in. Good luck."

She gathered up her personal items and left, no closer to music than when she'd been doodling in the margins of her marketing strategy textbook as she sat in class on the Wharton campus.

She spent three months looking for jobs by day and writing music and going to clubs by night. It didn't take long to know she couldn't afford to keep her apartment. So, leaving a month's rent with her two roommates, she returned home to live in her old room with her mother as her only companion.

Home. That day, home seemed like a failure, and family was just a bunch of people to make happy and all too ready to complain about how you were doing your job.

Or they would have been if she hadn't walked into the kitchen three days later to find her mother dead on the floor.

A blood clot, they said. Jenny Bascombe had been living on borrowed time. Had known she was. And like the consummate organizer she was, she had planned her own funeral. Or, in Jenny's case, the lack thereof.

She wanted her ashes spread on Wind Chime Beach, a place none of her family had ever heard of. She'd left it to Zoe to arrange.

Chapter 1

ZOE BASCOMBE SHOT BOTH hands through her hair, leaving it in short, dark spikes. "I don't know why they're all angry at me."

She looked back at the porch steps, where her family stood framed by her mother's perennial border. Her two eldest brothers, Errol and Robert, tall and blondish like their father. Their wives, suitably thin and coiffed. Their children, fidgety with that glazed look that said they'd been away from their iPhones too long.

There were also an aunt and two uncles on her father's side. No father—he had left them years ago for his new secretary. And her mother's attorney, the one person who looked back sympathetically at Zoe where she stood by the door of her SUV.

They were still in a state of angry denial. Zoe was, too.

Her youngest brother, Chris, also blond, the most handsome of the three and her only ally, opened the driver's door. "You better get going if you want to miss rush hour."

Zoe tried to smile. "It's always rush hour on Long Island."

"It'll be okay."

Easy for him to say. He didn't have to drive to the back of beyond with their mother's ashes strapped into the passenger seat.

Chris choked back a laugh. "Check out Errol. He looks like he'd happily toss her into the perennial border and be done with it."

"She'd be happy there," Zoe said. Her mother's garden was famous, appeared every spring in all the local magazines. "So why does she want to go to this Wind Chime place? She's never even been there. And why—"

"Just go. Call me when you get to the hotel." He gave her a hug.

Zoe slid into the car. Chris shut the door and stepped back. She took a last look in her rearview mirror, where her family appeared for a bare second before dispersing. Then she drove straight down the driveway and onto the street, cutting off life as she knew it.

It was a hot day, and she turned on the air-conditioning. She'd rather lower the windows and let the air blast in to ruffle her hair—brunette like her mother's—but she was afraid of disturbing the simple celadon urn that her mother had bought for the purpose.

Putting the urn in the passenger seat had been Chris's idea. His idea of humor . . . Humor was Chris's way of coping. But Zoe knew it was because neither of them could stand the idea of their mom smothered in the darkness of a tote bag on the floor.

Zoe glanced at the urn. "It's not like you're going to want to chat." Was sarcasm a stage of grief? Because she'd been feeling really sarcastic lately.

"Why didn't you tell us? Why didn't you let me help? Why?"

She didn't expect an answer. Her mother wouldn't be answering ever again. She'd already said her last word on the subject—any subject.

Zoe reached for the radio, pulled her hand back. Her mother didn't really like music. Never let her or Chris play the car radio as kids. He was her closest brother, seven years older. Zoe had been the "surprise baby," not that anybody but her mother had seemed to welcome the surprise.

In her own way, Mrs. Jennifer Campbell Bascombe had been a stranger. Not that she let it show. But now that Zoe looked back on it, there had been moments when her mother seemed . . . remote.

Chris called it passive aggressive. Zoe wasn't so sure.

She merged onto the highway. Made her way into the left lane. The sooner she got there, the sooner she could . . . get back home? The boys were probably already putting up the FOR SALE sign on the mid-century ranch where they'd all grown up.

Look for a job? The will had been read. As always, her mother had left no loopholes. She'd been wealthier than Zoe realized, and she'd divided her estate equally among her children. Now Zoe would have time to find the job she really wanted.

Not as a songwriter. That would seem like a betrayal. Still . . . a melodic line wove through her head, a few notes; she'd been working on it before . . . but it had been silent since her mother's death.

Why hadn't she talked to her mother more? After Chris left for college and her father moved out, it had been just the two of them. She could tell her mother almost anything, but now it occurred to her that her mother had never talked about herself. She'd expressed concern over her rose bushes, wondered if she should make petits fours for the library fund-raiser. But nothing about *her*.

"Why was that, Mom?"

It didn't feel odd, Zoe doing the talking and her mother, if not listening, at least not interrupting. The way it had always been.

"Looks like it's just you and me . . . babe." She smiled. *"Babe. I've got you, babe,"* she sang, knowing that if her mother were hanging about in the afterlife, it would piss her off.

A song in a stack of old LPs on a turntable she and Chris had found in the attic one rainy Sunday afternoon. They'd taken them downstairs and were singing along to Sonny and Cher.

Their mother had burst into the bedroom, her face a livid red, her body shaking with wrath from her cultured pearl necklace to the razor crease on her linen slacks. She snatched the arm off the record, sending the needle scratching across the surface.

Without a word, she gathered up the albums and the turntable, yanked the cord out of the socket, and left the room. They never saw them again. Only in their most outrageous moments did they dare recall the "S-and-C incident."

Now they would never know what had set her off. And at this moment, nothing seemed more important than to know why their suburban garden-club mother had revealed that one brief glimpse into whatever was lurking deep inside her manicured façade.

"I've got you, babe," Zoe sang at the top of her lungs, then burst into tears.

It took Zoe an hour just to get to the Whitestone Bridge, which would connect her to I-95 north, where the real trip would begin. Traffic didn't let up when she eased onto the interstate. So she hunkered down for the long haul and did what she always did when she could snatch time to herself. Wrote lyrics in her head. Hummed a tune to go with them . . . the same elusive melody that kept pushing at her mind since she'd turned onto the highway.

She tested the tune out loud, glanced at the urn. "You can blame Sonny and Cher." Though except for that one time, her mother had never discouraged her interest in music. Had driven her to her piano lesson once a week even though it was twenty minutes away.

Zoe had even caught her occasionally wearing earbuds while she gardened, though Zoe had assumed she was listening to a recorded book. Now she wondered. Had her mother been a closet heavy metal fan? Country and western? Bach?

Zoe's stomach growled. At New Haven, she pulled into a drive-through. No way was she going to leave her mother unattended or take her inside a restaurant. She got a hamburger and a drink, texted Chris with an update, and ate as she drove.

Only a few times had Zoe glimpsed moments of the other woman she'd begun to suspect lived inside her mother. Her mother had been . . . contained. Going about life as if it had been preor-dained. She was never late for car pool, belonged to committees, spearheaded food drives, had the best perennial border in town. She loved her children and her husband—until twelve years ago, when he left them for his secretary and became "that lousy rat bas-tard." It was the only swear word Zoe ever heard her mother say.

The silence stretched to an hour, then two. Connecticut passed into Rhode Island, Massachusetts, and at last New Hampshire. Zoe welcomed the voice of "the girl"—she refused to give her GPS a name—when she said to turn off at the next exit.

She turned onto an access road. Gas stations, restaurants, drug-stores, traffic lights. One town melted into another. Zoe wondered why "the girl" hadn't just kept her on the highway.

The sun began to set. The restaurants and gas stations fell away, leaving only trees and fields. The road became narrow, the trees dense, the houses sporadic. It was rapidly becoming dark.

"Turn right in three-quarters of a mile."

She made the turn onto an even narrower road covered by low-hanging trees that managed to cut out what little light was left. The few buildings that appeared in clearings were closed for the night—or forever. She began to doubt the reliability of her GPS.

It should be only another half hour to the inn where she'd re-served a room. She stretched her back, turned on her high beams, only to have the light bounce back.

Fog. Great.

"Turn right at the next—"

Zoe turned right onto a rutted road that might have been paved at one time but had long ago lost most of its surface. Surely this wasn't the way to the spa. She slowed, swerved to miss a huge rut, and came face-to-face with a tree. She slammed on the brakes. The road forked to either side; two signs appeared in her headlights. One with an arrow pointing to the right bore the word PRIVATE.

Okay, she wouldn't be going there. The other sign announced TOWN to the left. She turned left. This had to be one of those GPS decisions to take her on the route with no tolls or no traffic jams.

The Solana Inn and Spa had a great website. Had looked very

upscale. Zoe had stayed in a lot of great hotels because of her work,
but she would never personally consider staying in a place that
expensive, that healthy, or that trendy, but she was glad she had
this time. A nice Jacuzzi tub, room service, and glass—or two—of
white wine sounded really good.

She eased the SUV ahead. She was barely going ten miles an
hour. "This is taking forever," she told the disembodied, now quiet
voice in her dashboard.

She saw a light up in the distance. A single light that winked in
and out from behind the trees.

The road curved slightly, then widened onto a ghost town of
shadowy debris that maybe had been buildings a long time and
several storms ago. Then the one light in the woods winked out
completely and didn't come back on. She was surrounded by total
darkness and encroaching mist.

"That's it. I'm turning around." There had to be a better way to
the inn. She stopped, looked over her shoulder to start the turn.

An apparition stepped out of the shadows behind her, unearthly
tall with long white hair and wearing a flowing robe. And by his
side was an animal, a beast, not a dog or anything else from this
world. *His familiar.* He raised his hand.

"Or not." Zoe floored the accelerator. The SUV shot forward
into the night. For better or worse, there was no going back now.

TEN minutes—hours, eons—later, the SUV bumped onto pavement. Pavement, glorious pavement. Up ahead were lights, lots of
lights, a whole town of them. And though it was late, places were
open, and people strolled along the sidewalk. Music wafted out of
bars. Ahead, the sign for Solana Inn and Spa rose from the lawn
of a several-storied white clapboard inn, complete with turret that,
according to the website, overlooked the sea.

"You have reached your destination."

Zoe pulled into the circular drive and stopped beneath the porte
cochere, where wide steps led up to a porch bathed in light from
hanging frosted globes.

Now, this was more like it. She unbuckled the urn from the seat belt and slipped it into a carryall, grabbed her purse, and turned over her keys to a strapping young man wearing khaki pants and a polo shirt with the hotel's name embroidered across the pocket.

"Welcome to Solana. May I help you with your luggage?"

"Just the computer case and bag in the back," she said. She handed him two dollars and, clutching the carryall tightly against her side, climbed the steps to the entrance.

The lobby was everything she'd pictured. Bright, clean, minimal, and pristine. Music sounded from a doorway that led to the bar. And the band sounded pretty good. Always a plus.

The receptionist looked up from the screen of a sleek computer. She was a little younger than Zoe—late teens, early twenties—and wholesome. Her light blond hair was pulled back in a high ponytail, but the polo shirt and khakis of the outside staff had morphed into a flowing off-white gauze blouse and harem pants.

"Welcome to Solana."

Zoe smiled and handed over her credit card and driver's license.

"Ah, Ms. Bascombe. We were beginning to think you weren't coming."

"I must have taken a wrong turn. Tell me the only way into town is not down a rutted road through a ghost town."

"GPS, right?" The receptionist sighed. "We've been trying to get the state to put up a better sign. Most people turn around and go back to the main road."

The girl handed her a plastic key card. "We have you on the third floor. It has one of our best views. The elevator is down the hall to your left, next to the stairs. And if you're hungry, the bar is open, and the grill serves until eleven."

"Sounds good."

"I'll have your luggage sent to your room. Bon appétit." The receptionist went back to her computer screen.

Zoe headed straight for the bar. As she reached the doorway, the singer moaned, *Jenny, oh, Jenny.*

Zoe stopped, slightly unnerved. She recovered quickly; it was just a coincidence. Still . . . ghosts and a singer with her mother's name on his lips. It was too weird.

The bar was crowded, the lighting dim except for the small raised stage in the far corner, where a spotlight cast an uneven glow over the performers. Four of them—a guitar, a fiddle, a bass, and a piano. Three of the musicians were pretty young, but the guitarist was an older dude with a long ponytail.

At the back of the room, French doors opened onto a softly lit patio. A long wooden bar ran across the opposite wall, where a muscular, bearded bartender served beers and cocktails with a grace that sat incongruously on his mountain-man appearance.

The guitarist crooned on. He had a good voice. *And a deep soul,* thought Zoe. She stepped into the room.

He looked up. His fingers froze, and the guitar pick fell to the floor. He looked straight at Zoe. She took an involuntary step backward. The band played on without him.

A moment later, he stood, the pick retrieved, and joined in on the next verse, but his eyes were still on the doorway.

Zoe backed out of the room. In the lobby light, the spell was broken. The singer had recovered and was singing his "lonely sad song," followed by something about trembling leaves.

Maybe she wasn't hungry after all; maybe there was a fruit basket in her room. An apple would be fine, a granola bar.

She cast a last longing look as a waitress passed by carrying a tray of burgers and onion rings. But the band had geared up for another song, and no way could she face that penetrating stare or the man's gravelly, mournful voice.

As soon as Zoe reached her room, she took the urn out of the carryall and placed it on the dresser. The urn's smooth curved surface, the delicate green glaze, fit right in with the decor.

A fruit basket was sitting on the table. Zoe found the mini fridge hidden in the wardrobe, sighed with relief when she saw it held mini bottles of—she took one out—organic Chardonnay.

She unscrewed the top and poured the contents into one of the two wineglasses on a tray. She took a sip. Full-bodied yet smooth.

She walked over to the drapes and drew them aside, revealing glass doors that opened onto a small balcony. She slid them open and stepped outside to a light breeze and a clear, star-studded sky. Below her, a lawn was surrounded by shadowed shrubs and flowers. Tiny pagoda-shaped lamps picked out a brick path that led to the sea. She could hear waves in the distance, punctuated by a gentle echo of the band that was still playing in the bar.

She walked back inside, downed the rest of her wine, and turned to face her mother. "Why am I here? We should have talked about this before—all of us. Together. The boys are angry and terribly hurt. Why just me? You don't want friends and family to see you off? It doesn't make sense."

Zoe stared at the urn, swaying slightly from the wine.

Well, tomorrow Zoe would do her duty—find this Wind Chime Beach and spread the ashes. She'd go home and hope that someday her brothers would forgive her for fulfilling her mother's wishes instead of theirs.

She started to open another bottle of wine, then opted for a granola bar from the basket instead. She chewed while she texted the only brother still speaking to her. *Arrived at hotel. Safe for now.*

Her phone pinged. *K.*

Just one letter. The granola bar turned to gravel, and she spit it in the trash. She didn't bother to unpack but pulled a nightshirt out of her suitcase and took it into the bathroom to change.

She brushed her teeth and climbed into bed. She tried not to look at the urn sitting so alone on the dresser.

"I've got you, babe," she whispered.

And tomorrow, she would have to let her go.

It was after one when Eve Gordon peeked into the silent lobby of the Solana. Seeing it empty, she stepped inside. She always made a point to mingle with her guests, but not when she was dressed in a pair of wet, baggy jeans and an overlarge T-shirt. Being the proprietor of an upscale inn and spa didn't mean you didn't have to sometimes get down and get dirty.

She'd spent the past hour and a half removing a plastic bag from the laundry pipes. How or why it got there still eluded her.

The lobby lights had been dimmed, leaving just enough light

for late-returning guests. There was no one behind the reception desk, so the last guest must have arrived. Eve fought the urge to check the registration list. Mel wouldn't leave her post early, even though Eve knew she was not happy about having to work a double shift.

Well, that was family for you. Noelle had been called out of town for a job interview. *Out of town.* It's what she'd always planned for her girls. Make a good home for them and give them the means to fly on their own. Harmony had flown to California and stayed. She had a good job and a growing family. Noelle had yet to settle, but she had her sights on New York, Boston, Chicago. Only Mel showed signs of sticking around—for all the wrong reasons.

There was still a work light on in the bar, though the patrons and band would have departed an hour or so ago. She wandered inside. Mike McGill was standing behind the bar doing a final inventory for the night.

He looked up, nodded, and poured her a glass of Chardonnay. She perched on a bar stool in front of him.

"Get the pipe cleared?"

Eve savored the crisp white wine. "Yes—a plastic bag. Go figure. Good crowd tonight?"

"Pretty good, but . . ."

Eve put down her glass. "But?"

"I'm not sure, but Lee was . . . something happened during the last set. He just kind of looked out the door and stopped playing. I was afraid he might be having a mini stroke or something."

"Is he okay?"

Mike frowned, rubbed the bar with a white cloth. "He seemed okay after that. But he had two bourbons when the set was over."

Eve shook her head. "He hardly ever drinks." *Anymore.*

"I know, but he closed the place down. I didn't want him driving home. So I put him on the couch in the office. Hope that's okay."

"Of course. I wonder what could have set him off."

Mike's large hand closed over hers. "How many years have you been trying to figure out what makes your father tick?"

"Too many."

"So you probably won't figure it out tonight. Go get some sleep. I'll close up."

Eve finished her wine and pushed the glass over to Mike. "Thanks," she said with a yawn. "See you tomorrow."

He raised his hand in farewell and went back to his inventory.

Eve headed across the lobby. She intended to call it a night, but as she passed the reception desk, she couldn't stop herself. She went behind the desk and into the office. Lying as if dead on the leather couch was her father, Lee Gordon, once lead guitarist and singer of Night Chill. *What are you dreaming, Dad? Of glory? Of fame? Of just getting through tomorrow?*

She lifted the edge of the cotton quilt that Mike had draped over him. Tucked it beneath his shoulder. She kissed his cheek, sunken from years of hard living and scruffy from not shaving. A look that had driven his fans wild in his younger years.

"Night, Dad," she whispered, then tiptoed out. She let herself out the side door and walked down the path to the cottage where she lived with Mel—and Noelle, when she was in town. The porch light was on. Either Mel was inside asleep or had been and gone.

Chapter 2

IT WAS STILL DARK when Zoe woke up. In her dream she was playing a lullaby on the baby grand in the living room. Her mother stood at her shoulder, singing. Zoe sat up, disoriented. She shot out of bed, padded across the room, and pulled the cord to the drapes, then stepped back, blinking against the sudden brightness.

Talk about your light-blocking curtains. It was dazzling outside. And later than she'd thought. She opened the glass doors, stepped onto the balcony, and stretched, letting the sun warm her face.

She peered over the balcony rail. Below her, a swath of lawn spread out like a carpet. And flowers, and shrubs, and grasses with their feathered tops riffling in the breeze. The waves a distant, steady rhythm above the staccato of human activity below her.

A perfect place for saying goodbye.

Somewhere below her, the quiet hum of conversation was punctuated by the clink of . . . silverware. The aroma of breakfast. She went inside and headed straight to the shower.

Twenty minutes later, armed with her laptop but not the urn—which she'd replaced in the carryall and hidden in the closet behind her suitcase—Zoe went downstairs in search of sustenance.

She found it at the end of a short hallway: an airy restaurant with a patio eating area. She stopped at the PLEASE WAIT TO BE SEATED sign, then opted for an outside table and followed the hostess—another wholesome-looking young woman—across the room.

She was seated at a table next to a bush heavy with red flowers, with a view of the lawn and a vee of blue ocean in the distance.

The hostess handed her a menu. "Elena will be with you shortly. Would you care for coffee while you decide?"

"Please." The woman left, and Zoe bent her head over the menu. She was deliberating when the waitress returned with her coffee.

Zoe decided to stick to eggs, sausage, and toast and gave her order. As soon as Elena smiled herself away, Zoe took a sip of coffee, hesitated only long enough to savor the rich, heady roast, then pulled out her laptop. Which was ridiculous. She had no work to do here. None that needed a laptop.

She opened it anyway. And that's how the waitress found her when she returned with her breakfast.

"How do I get to the beach?" Zoe asked.

"You can take the path through the garden over there, or there is a direct elevator to the beach access road."

Zoe considered asking the girl if it was called Wind Chime Beach. It seemed just like something a chic spa would name its beach. But if it was, they might not like ashes being spread where the clientele worked on their tans.

She closed her laptop and dug in. Her breakfast was delicious, every fried, eggy, porky morsel. She ate it all and agreed to a refill of the rich coffee. She reopened her laptop, but a shadow momentarily blocked out the sun. She looked up.

A tall, buxom, thirtysomething woman dressed in yoga pants and a bright yellow off-the-shoulder tee was standing over her.

"I hate to bother you, but would you mind awfully if I sat in your extra chair? I'm dying for a cup of coffee, and they won't seat me until the rest of my party arrives." She made a goofy face, and Zoe immediately liked her.

"Please." Zoe gestured to the empty chair.

"Thanks."

Elena appeared to fill the newcomer's cup and top off Zoe's.

The woman took a sip. "Ah. Heaven. I'm Karen, by the way."

"Zoe."

"This spa really is wonderful. You should try some of the specialties while you're here," Karen said.

A woman, possibly the activities hostess, had been making her way around the tables, and she stopped at Zoe's. She was fortyish, maybe a little older, but tall and fit, with wavy reddish-blond hair, and seemed slightly familiar. The mark of a good hostess.

"Good morning, Karen. And you must be Zoe Bascombe. I'm Eve Gordon, proprietor of Solana. Glad you made it in last night."

"Nice to meet you. It was an adventure."

"Oh, I love adventures," Karen said. "What happened?"

"Just a little fog. And a few potholes."

"We'll be sure to give better directions at the end of your stay. Meanwhile, anything you need, just ask." Eve moved on to the next table of patrons. It was a nice touch—no hard sell, and she hadn't stayed long enough to incur an awkward silence.

"Isn't she the sweetest? The spa is family run. Everyone is really friendly. Oh, there's Elaine and Brandy." Karen waved at the two women who had just stepped into the sunlight.

The women hurried over, and Zoe slipped her laptop into its case. Introductions were made. Elaine, curvy, with light brown hair, and Brandy, thin and muscular, the athlete of the three.

Zoe stood. "You guys sit down. I have to get going. I'm here on business, and it's way past time I got to it."

"Thanks for the seat. It was nice meeting you," Karen said. "Maybe we'll see you tonight at the bar."

"Maybe," Zoe said, then headed inside.

Maybe she *would* meet them at the bar tonight. Maybe she'd stay for a few extra days. That would be a change—a weekend when she did nothing but get pampered. But first she needed to find Wind Chime Beach and do her duty to her mother. Then she could take a few days before she had to get back to her life.

The thought stopped her midstep. Just what was her life? Would she return to Manhattan and land another hair-tearing job as an events coordinator? She couldn't go back home—she'd given up her apartment. Chris would take her in. But she couldn't camp out at his place while she looked for a job. Chris was an actor, but he'd had the good sense to hook up with a real estate developer, Timothy. They lived in a beautiful apartment on the Upper West Side. She wouldn't intrude.

She rode up the elevator in a fog more debilitating than the one she'd driven through the night before.

The maid had already been. The bed was made; there were fresh flowers on the dresser. The whole room smelled clean and peaceful, and she would have been happy just to relax there, except for what she knew was waiting for her in the closet.

She forced herself to take out the carryall and place the urn back on the dresser. "I'm not taking you with me. This is purely a recce. The idea of searching through town for Wind Chime Beach—a place that, by the way, isn't even mentioned on the town website—with you slung over my shoulder is just too depressing."

Zoe grabbed her purse and went downstairs. She stopped by the desk on her way out and was surprised to see the same girl as the night before. "Doing double duty?" Zoe asked her.

"Huh?" The girl looked up. "Oh, hi. Yeah, the morning shift person called in sick. And my sister Noelle is in New York interviewing for a job, so I'm here until the afternoon shift comes on."

"Instead of going to the beach?"

The girl grinned. "Yeah."

"Well, I'm looking for a beach, too—a specific place called Wind Chime Beach."

The girl frowned. "Wind Chime . . . I don't think I know of a beach . . . well, there is Wind Chime House. But it's just an old house that used to be a hippie commune."

"A hippie commune? And people still live there?"

"Oh, sure. Floret and Henry and Eli and his uncle David live there. He's kind of the caretaker. He's really a photographer, but . . . well, it's a long story. And Eli—he's, like, my best friend."

"They won't mind if I visit them?"

"Oh, no. People are always coming to visit and reminisce or to see where their parents or grandparents used to live. Only don't mention that you're staying here."

"Why?"

She leaned over the counter. "Floret and my great-grandmother have been at it for years. Nobody knows why, at least not that they tell me. It would be funny if it didn't upset Mom so much. How did you hear about it?"

"My mother." It slipped out without Zoe thinking.

"Wow! My mother was raised there. Maybe yours hung out there, too. Maybe they know each other."

Zoe shook her head. "I doubt it. I'm not sure my mother was ever here. Does this commune have a beach?"

"It does. It abuts ours." She rolled her eyes. "Mom's been trying to buy it forever. But Floret and Henry won't sell."

"So I can just walk from your beach to theirs?"

"Not really." The receptionist made a face. "It's barricaded. We—actually, my great-grandma—built a jetty across the sand to keep our people from wandering too close, and they put up a sign saying not to climb on the rocks because it's dangerous. But it's really because their people like to sunbathe nude. I don't know what the big deal is—our people are *practically* nude." She slapped her hand to her mouth.

Zoe laughed. It had been a while.

"I'm Mel."

"Let me guess. Short for Melody."

"Have you ever heard anything so dorky?"

"Zoe?"

Mel laughed.

"I think Mel is a great name."

"Thanks."

"So if I want to get to Wind Chime Beach, how would I go?"

"Just go right out the door. Two blocks, then on the next block you'll see two white houses, then a smaller cottage with one of those little wishing wells out front. That's the Kellys' house. They own the diner if you get in the mood for good and greasy. Just go down their driveway. Their house is on your left, and Little Woods will be on your right. Go all the way to the end. And you'll see it."

"Well, thanks, Mel. I think I'll go over now and take a look."

A faint flush spread over Mel's face. "Sorry. I talk too much. Everyone says so."

"I don't think so," Zoe said. "I've enjoyed talking to you."

"Thanks."

Zoe started out the door, but as she opened it, a man stepped in.

"Oh, excuse me."

"I beg your pard—" He stopped cold, and Zoe recognized the singer from the bar.

She smiled perfunctorily and tried to slide past him. He didn't move; his expression didn't change. He stood blocking her way, staring at her in a way that made a chill run up her spine.

"I'm so sorry." She ducked under his arm and fled.

LEE Gordon stared after the girl who'd just left the inn. So he wasn't losing his mind. *She was here.* She couldn't be here. Why had he drunk that bourbon last night? He couldn't do that stuff anymore. Not booze, not drugs, not women, not any of it.

He spun around and marched over to the reception desk, where his youngest granddaughter was minding the store.

"Hi, Granddad. How was breakfast?"

"Huh? Good and greasy. Who was that?"

"The woman who just left? One of our guests. Why?"

He pulled himself together. "No reason. Where's your mother?"

"In the office. Granddad, what's the matter?"

"Nothing."

EVE STEPPED OUT OF THE office. "I thought I heard your voice. I guess you went to the diner for breakfast instead of enjoying our four-star fare."

"Of course I did. Who is that woman who just left here?"

Eve raised her eyebrows. She looked at Mel.

"It was Zoe. Ms. Bascombe."

"Bascombe." Lee spat out the name.

"Yeah," Mel said, then bit her lip. "Why are you angry?"

"I'm not angry. Where was she going?"

Mel looked uncertainly at Eve.

Oh, Lord, thought Eve. Her father had his turns, as her grandmother called them. It came from his years of fast living. They were all used to it, but he'd never been interested in a guest before.

Her father's eyes locked with hers. "She's a guest, Dad," Eve said, "here to have a nice weekend."

"She was asking about a beach called Wind Chime," Mel said, her voice tentative. "I sent her down to Floret and Henry's."

Eve stiffened. But her father softened. "Sorry. I'm just a grumpy old man." He turned toward the door.

"Where are you going?"

"Home. I'll be back for the early set." He strode out the door.

"That was weird," Mel said as soon as he was gone.

"It was," Eve agreed. "Granddad has a lot of . . ."

Mel rolled her eyes. "Issues."

"Yes. I've never been able to figure him out."

"Just have to love him the way he is," Mel said.

"How did I get such a wise daughter?" Eve knew in that split second she shouldn't have said it. She could see Mel gearing up for battle. Eve cut her off before she could begin. "And that's why it's important for you to go to college. So you can continue to make wise choices."

"You don't understand."

Oh, but she did. She'd been young and headstrong once. And gotten pregnant at the end of her senior year. Of course there had never been a mother who could convince her children that it was her job to make sure they didn't make the same mistakes she had.

She'd never known her own mother. And her father never tried to give advice. He'd been too busy wrestling with his own demons.

She thought he'd mellowed, gotten over his disappointments. But she'd seen something in him just now that frightened her.

And it had been set off by Zoe Bascombe.

Chapter 3

ZOE WALKED DOWN THE sidewalk, away from the inn, and stopped at the corner to regroup and take a look around. The town was as charming in daylight as it had been busy the night before. A jumble of row houses and stand-alones had been built, or repurposed, as the business district. Not an empty storefront that she could see.

She crossed the street and walked past a boutique that displayed colorful beachwear. An antiques store, a gourmet deli, a cigar store, a pub featuring live music. That was tempting—in Manhattan, she sat in with the house band at her favorite bar at least once a week when she wasn't traveling.

She came to Kelly's Diner—presumably the same Kelly whose driveway she'd be using—wedged between a store named Babykins and a beach accessories shop. At the end of the block, a bookstore named Book Nook was housed in a white frame cottage.

She passed a big white house on the corner that had been converted into offices. Then another large house, also white. A third house was the stone cottage with the wishing well that Mel had told her about. It looked out of place next to the stately old homes.

Beyond it was the undeveloped lot Mel called Little Woods. Zoe turned down the drive, hugging the far side, where the trees sheltered her from the sun. The drive was paved as far as the Kellys' garage; then the pavement gave way to a stony, rutted car path.

It was a pleasant walk in spite of whatever might be facing her, but she wasn't prepared for the sight that met her at the end of the drive. The yard was an open space of knee-high weeds and hard dirt, with a rusted station wagon—probably left over from the hippie era—sitting idle off to one side. Straight ahead, a few straggly shrubs tangled against a sagging picket fence across the front of a three-story leaning tower of dilapidation.

WIND CHIME HOUSE. The name was painted on a white wooden sign on the gate. She had reached her destination.

EVE leaned back in her desk chair. Curiosity had driven her to the office computer. Not just curiosity but also unease. Her father's agitation had settled in her. And she didn't like it. She'd spent a childhood trying to hold him to the earth, to family, to her.

She didn't miss her mother—most of the time. She'd never known her, so she didn't see how she could miss her. Maybe it was just the idea of a mother that left a piece of Eve always longing.

Eve had lived with her grandmother at the commune until she was thirteen. It was a lonely time. Her father was usually away on tour. Her grandmother was busy building her real estate empire: meetings and travel kept her away almost as often as Eve's father was. It fell on Floret and Henry to nurture Eve as best they could, though they had no children themselves.

Eve loved them for it. Henry was a scientist who taught her about the stars and the mysteries of the universe. Floret was a mystery herself, but she loved plants and animals, and she knew how to make hurt—of knees and stomachs and hearts—go away.

Then one day, Hannah—or Granna, as Eve called her—returned home. There was an argument with Floret, then Granna told Eve to pack her things. They'd moved into town that very afternoon. No explanation.

It was because of the fight. But Eve didn't learn that until much later. And to this day she didn't know what the fight was about.

That was the beginning of the end of the commune. Hippies looking for a life where they could flourish in peace were replaced by yuppies looking for weekend houses where they could chill, which Hannah Gordon was happy to sell them. There hadn't been a new kid at the commune until David Merrick returned eight years ago to raise his nephew, Eli.

A godsend for David, a rejuvenation for Floret and Henry, but the beginning of the unraveling of Eve's plans for Mel.

Eli was a nice boy, in love with Mel, and she was nuts in love with him. But they were so young. Had no way to provide for themselves except by working at the inn.

Eve had made the inn her dream. She'd had no choice.

But Mel and Eli had options—if only they'd take them. In another month they would go off to their respective colleges. Problem solved. Right now, she had another possible situation on her hands.

Eve leaned on her elbows and peered at the computer screen. Zoe Bascombe had made a reservation online. Her driver's license and credit card were on file. Her answer to the website's "How did you hear about Solana?" question was "Other."

She Googled Zoe's name and was surprised at the number of hits. She clicked on Zoe's Facebook profile. New York City. Great Neck. The Wharton School. The usual social posts: party photos, beaches, snowboarding. Loves music. Nothing odd about that. Most young people like music, and Zoe worked for an events firm—a firm that caters to music business clients. A good job.

She kept searching. Parents: George and Jennifer Bascombe. *Jenny?* Eve's mother was named Jenny. Jenny Campbell. It was a common enough name. George was a prominent Long Island attorney. Jennifer was a member of the Great Neck Garden Club.

Eve's fingers hovered over the computer mouse, trembling slightly. She clicked on "Images."

A head shot of George Bascombe. George and his wife, Jennifer, at a fund-raising ball. Eve clicked to enlarge the photo. Zeroed in on Jenny. She was in profile, but even so, Eve could see the resemblance to Zoe. She clicked back on Zoe's Facebook photos and found one of Zoe and her mother—and stopped.

The photo was in color. The two women were strikingly similar. No mistaking them for anything but mother and daughter. The eye color was the same. Almost a lilac blue.

There were no photos of Eve's mother, but she'd seen those eyes before. On her own daughter Mel.

But eye color didn't mean anything. A coincidence. She kept scrolling back until she came to a photo: *Me getting ready for Julia's Sweet Sixteen*. The hair was dark, had obviously just been blow-dried. But it wasn't the hair that had arrested Eve's attention.

It was the face. They could have been sisters, Zoe and Mel. It was uncanny. And it wasn't coincidence.

Zoe stood where she was, waiting to see a sign of life, but no one appeared to greet her. The place looked deserted.

She took a few steps over the weeds. Hesitated. Hippies were peace-loving, right? She opened the gate and stepped inside.

The house, unpainted eyesore that it was, was surrounded by flowers. Reds, blues, yellows, oranges, and lavenders growing randomly, as if someone had cast handfuls of seed into the wind. Above them, giant yellow sunflowers swayed on their stems like drunken sentinels. Jenny Bascombe might have been appalled at the craziness of the planting, but she would have loved the color.

And the scent. One whiff dissolved into another against a pervasive smell of lavender . . . *blue, dilly dilly*. A lullaby her mother used to sing.

"Hello?" Zoe called. Getting no response, she walked down the flagstone path toward the house. "Is anyone here?"

"Ma-a-a-a-a." The voice didn't sound human.

And it wasn't. It was a beast, a little beast, galloping toward her.

Zoe looked wildly around. She was cut off from retreat. Her only hope was the house. She sprinted up the walk, took the wooden steps to the porch two at a time, and banged on the door.

"Hello!" she called, her voice rising in panic.

"I'm out here."

She turned around, looking for the source of the voice and keeping a wary eye on the animal that had stopped at the bottom of the steps and was eyeing her curiously.

It wasn't a dog, she realized with relief. It was a . . . goat, brown flecked with white hairs. The goat lifted a hoof onto the front step.

"Dulcie! Cut that out." The voice, high and lilting, came from a large vegetable garden fenced in with chicken wire. "Dulcie, let the lady come down."

After a beady-eyed look at Zoe, the goat trotted to the garden.

Zoe slowly went down the steps to the yard. The gardener came out in the open, reached back to close the gate, and—putting a protective or perhaps controlling hand on the goat—came to meet her.

Zoe guessed the gardener was a she from her high voice and diminutive size. Her face was completely hidden by the floppy wide brim of her hat, revealing only a long gray braid that draped over one shoulder. Baggy overalls were rolled to just below the knee. The shoes were old, scuffed leather work boots.

The woman stopped and pushed the hat back, revealing a sun-wrinkled face and a welcoming smile.

The smile broadened. "My sweet Lord. You've come back—"

Dulcie butted her side, and she staggered several steps.

"Oh," the gardener said, and righted herself. Her head tilted one way then the other. "You're not . . . Oh my . . ."

Oh dear, thought Zoe. "I'm just visiting," she said, smiling.

"Well . . . So glad you've come. . . ." The woman started forward. Stopped again. Frowned at Zoe and shook her head.

Well, thought Zoe. Mel had said this had once been a hippie commune. Maybe the old folks were still getting high.

"I came to see your beach," Zoe prompted.

"Ah." The woman turned and looked over her shoulder.

Zoe followed her gaze to a grassy lawn that sloped down to a white beach and the sea. To the right, she could see the back of the Solana and the patio. The inn's vibrant green lawn sloped down to a longer white beach. The two beaches met at a rock jetty that sliced through the stretch of sand, dividing one from the other.

"I'm Floret."

"Zoe," said Zoe.

"Well, there is the beach." Floret made a vague gesture with her hand. "We're not selling."

"I don't blame you," Zoe said. "But why is it called Wind Chime Beach? I don't see any wind chimes."

Floret smiled her vague smile. "The chimes are in the woods."

Zoe quickly looked around, saw a cluster of trees on the far side of the old house.

"You can hear them sometimes . . . when the wind blows."

"On the beach?"

"Oh, not on the beach. Only on Wind Chime Beach."

Zoe clenched her hands behind her back. This poor woman couldn't be living here alone. Surely there was someone who was more "in touch" who could give Zoe some straight answers.

"There's a different beach called Wind Chime?" Zoe asked.

"Oh, yes." Floret broke into a happy smile. "Only now we call it Old Beach. It's lovely." She frowned. "But no one goes there anymore. The stairs rotted out after Hurricane Gloria."

"I see."

"Is that why you came? To remember? It was always your favorite place. Yours and—"

Dulcie bleated, a grating sound that hurt Zoe's ears.

Definitely two tokes short of a doobie.

"Well . . . yes," Zoe said. "To remember . . . in a way. Would you mind terribly if I just took a look? I won't touch anything."

Floret looked toward the trees on the far side of the house. Her gloved hand lifted slowly. "Over there."

"Thank you so much." Zoe hurried toward the woods before Floret could change her mind or Dulcie decided to follow her.

The path was easy enough to find, and Zoe didn't stop until she was out of sight of the house. Beneath the trees, the sun was almost totally blocked except for dapples of light that slipped through the heavy foliage.

She was enveloped in stillness. No breeze ruffled the trees, and Zoe became aware of her own footfalls. They were answered by the counterpoint of a bird call, the scurry of animals in the brush.

It was magical. And a little frightening.

And then she heard something different, like a knife against a champagne glass. She stopped. But there was nothing. She waited, then started walking again; she'd seen a wedge of blue ahead.

Was this the place? She took the final steps into the sunlight.

Only she wasn't at the beach but standing on a ledge at a set of rotted wooden steps that led downward and out of sight.

She gingerly looked over. A secluded crescent of white sand lay below. Probably once charming, it was now cluttered by driftwood, seaweed, and other detritus—a plastic bag, several cans and bottles. This was not how she'd envisioned her mother's last resting place.

She reached for the splintered handrail of the stairs. They didn't look stable, but it wasn't very far down. She put her foot on the first step. Tried the second step. Another step, then another. She'd almost reached the bottom when the wood gave way. She grabbed the rail with both hands, getting several splinters. There she stayed, crouching, clinging on for dear life. What had she been thinking?

Slowly, she pulled her foot back, then swung her body forward and jumped. She landed on the sand with a thud.

She spent the next few seconds picking the biggest slivers of wood from her palms. The rest would have to be extricated when she was back at the hotel with her tweezers and travel sewing kit.

She looked back at the steps and the trees that formed a semicircle behind the beach, closing off the outer world. Very private. And to her relief she saw that the woods sloped off to each side until they met the sand. The undergrowth was thick, but she'd be able to find a way to the path without having to risk the stairs again.

She lifted her face to the sun. A breeze ruffled the air.

And she heard it, a tinkling of glass. A soft solo, joined by another and another until the sound disappeared into the woods.

She waited, but the breeze died, and so did the sound. But she found its origin. A nearby tree branch bent over the sand. And from it, little rectangles of glass, orange and blue and purple, hung by thin threads from a medallion of tin. *Wind chimes.*

They were still but almost alive, as if waiting for the next breeze.

Zoe was waiting, too. And she was ready when she felt the first murmur of breeze in her hair, heard the first clear ring, and she laughed silently as the woods filled with the sound of the chimes.

Good one, Mom. I don't know how you found out about this place or why, but I get it.

Tears filled her eyes. This was where she would have to let go.

"Hey! You shouldn't be down there!"

Zoe looked around and saw a man standing at the top of the stairs, feet squared, body poised aggressively forward.

"Floret said it was okay."

"Floret made a mistake. It's very dangerous, and if you used these stairs going down, don't use them trying to get back up."

"What do you suggest?"

She thought he growled. Then he moved away and disappeared.

To hell with it. She'd made it down; she could get back up again. She was nothing if not resilient. Besides, now that she was finally here, she wasn't quite ready to leave.

One thing she knew, she'd have to sneak back when no one was about or they'd have her arrested, either for trespassing or for going against whatever private burial code she was about to violate.

Finally, she knew what she had to do. Her mother would lie in rest here among the wind chimes.

But not on a beach strewn with garbage. She walked over to the largest piece of driftwood. A plastic bag was caught beneath it, and a soda can lay on its side in the sand. Zoe started to pick it up.

"Now what are you doing?"

The voice was so close that she whirled around, tripped over the log, and fell on her butt in the sand.

"Jeez, what is it with you?" Zoe looked back at the man standing on the other side of the driftwood. Tall, dark hair, jeans, T-shirt. Kind of good-looking. He leaned over and stuck out his hand.

She took it, and he pulled her to her feet.

"Ow." She pulled her hand away.

"Are you hurt?"

"I picked up a few splinters on the way down."

"It could be worse. You could have really hurt yourself."

"How did you know I was down here?"

"Floret told Henry, and Henry told me. Now come on; you're trespassing. Don't make me call the cops."

"I thought Floret owned Wind Chime."

"She does, but she doesn't always know what's best." He gestured to a bank of shrubs. "This way."

He guided her to the far edge of the beach, where a scree of large rocks led to a crevice between the trees and a gnarled mass of bared roots. The man slipped ahead, stepped onto one of the roots and then another until he'd climbed to solid ground.

He reached back to help her, but Zoe defiantly and stupidly refused to take his hand. She stepped onto the same root, looked quickly around for a handhold, and in spite of the pain in her palms pulled herself up until the root was holding her weight.

He waited for her on the path with an outstretched "after you" gesture. She was acutely aware of him walking behind her. Then she became aware of something else. A tiny refraction of light, a pinpoint of color appearing in the branches ahead of her.

And another off to the left. They were everywhere. Hanging from branches high and low. One, made of coral shells, was close enough to touch. A little farther away, bronze tubes hung like a waterfall from a leafless branch. Some were only silhouettes in the play of light and dark; some were broken and hanging by a thread.

She stopped, turning slowly, just taking it all in, waiting for the next breeze to set the chimes off again. Then she heard a distant note, a faint *ting* behind her. Felt the first ruffle of a breeze.

And suddenly she was surrounded by . . . fairy sound. It whirled around her ears, then moved on as it made its way through the woods, gradually retreating as softly as it had come.

The man was listening, too. They stood not two feet apart until the breeze had gone and the sound was a mere memory.

"Can we go now?"

"Sorry," she said, then started up the path, faster this time. For a second she'd been swept up in something magical.

She was both relieved and disappointed when they reached the sunlight and the untended outer yard of Wind Chime House.

She started to go up to the house, but the man stopped her.

"Main Street is that way, down the drive."

"I wanted to thank Floret."

"Floret's busy right now."

"Okay, what's the deal? At least Floret was friendly. You're downright"—she searched for a word—"off-putting."

"And you've got an attitude."

"What's wrong with that?"

He didn't answer right away.

"Well?"

"Well, I'm thinking."

"Don't strain anything."

He raised both eyebrows. "You can't do better than that?"

She blushed. It had been the most childish thing to say.

She'd discovered a door into her mother and to music that she hadn't expected. And he was throwing her out.

Her eyes filled. She blinked desperately; she'd made enough of a fool of herself already. She hurried blindly down the drive.

A booming voice yelled, "David, go after her."

His name was David. Zoe broke into a run.

She heard feet pounding behind her. "Wait a minute." He caught up and jogged alongside her. "Henry wants to talk to you."

Henry? Of Henry and Floret. She didn't slow down but risked a glance over her shoulder. Saw the figure standing on the porch.

It was a man. Tall, with long white hair. Long flowing robe. Her apparition in the fog. And by his side, Dulcie, the beady-eyed goat.

"Thanks anyway. Sorry to have bothered you," Zoe mumbled, then fled down the drive to the street.

DAVID crossed his arms and watched her. "Don't mention it," he muttered under his breath. Just what they needed—some oversensitive nitwit full of neuroses standing in the middle of the woods like a nutcase. And why on earth did Henry want to see her?

He turned and walked back to the house, where Henry stood on the porch. "She wouldn't stay?"

"I never got that far. I think I scared her."

"Perhaps." Henry stepped aside to let him pass. It was all very solemn, whatever was going on. David didn't have a clue; he usually didn't with Henry and Floret, but they were good people, with kind and generous hearts, and he was thankful for them.

The two of them went inside, leaving Dulcie standing guard over the porch. Floret was on the back veranda, setting out drinks and cookies. Elevenses in the British tradition.

He smiled and took his place at the table.

"Tea or lemonade?" Floret asked.

"Lemonade, thanks." David reached for a cookie.

Henry stood with his back to them, his hands clasped behind him, staring out to the sea. David sat back and munched his cookie.

What was it about this young woman that had thrown them off-kilter? She'd seemed like a flake to him. Picking up trash, then stopping to listen to the chimes. Well, that was understandable. They always stopped him, too. And he would have picked up the trash if he'd known it was there.

Floret finished pouring and sat down. Henry joined them. "She's afraid of us," he said, as if they were in the middle of a conversation.

Henry often began that way. David was used to it. He'd known Henry for more than thirty years, since David was four and he and his brother, Andy, and their parents had come to live at Wind Chime. Henry, the physicist turned dropout, and his lovely botanist hippie partner for life, Floret, and the other members of the commune had made them welcome and kept them safe.

"You sent me to stop her," David said patiently.

Floret put down her cup and folded her hands. "Don't be silly. She can't be stopped. She couldn't then, and she won't now."

David shook his head. "Floret, give us earthlings some context."

She was trying to suppress a smile. "I saw her and I thought . . . impossible, of course. I don't know what came over me."

"She's not Jenny." Henry sat down and reached for a cookie.

"I know that. Her name is Zoe." Floret frowned. "But . . ."

David leaned forward. "Who's Jenny? What's this all about?"

"It's a long story, many decades old. But about six months ago, we received a letter from an old friend. It was accompanied by a package. The letter asked us to give it to the person who came looking for Wind Chime Beach and to welcome her."

Wind Chime Beach? It had always been called Old Beach as long as David could remember.

"At first we didn't know what to make of it," Floret added. "A lot of people *could* be asking about the beach. It was a very special place in its day. Many found love there." She smiled at Henry.

David nodded. "And sometimes more than they bargained for."

The two of them got those faraway looks they often got when thinking about life, and David waited patiently for the moment to pass and for them to come back.

"But this friend was very dear to our hearts," Henry said.

"Very dear," Floret echoed. "But I wasn't expecting . . . I had no idea. She looks just like Jenny."

"Obviously her daughter," Henry said.

"Who, exactly, is Jenny?" David asked.

The sound of the front screen door banging shut and a backpack being dumped on the floor stopped the conversation.

"We're out here, Eli," Floret called.

Footsteps thudded across the wooden floor, and David's nephew exploded onto the veranda. The eighteen-year-old lived a life of high energy tempered only slightly by having spent the past eight years living with Henry and Floret at Wind Chime.

He snatched a cookie and stood looking at the adults while he munched. "What's up? You all look a little mind-blown."

"Well, we are, rather," Floret explained.

"Have anything to do with the girl who was running down the drive like her life depended on it?"

David bit back a smile. She talked tough, but it was all a façade.

"The girl is . . ." Henry seemed stuck for a word. "A Pandora."

"Like 'open the box and free the evil of the world' Pandora?"

Floret patted Eli's hand. "Not evil, just discomfort and maybe some unhappiness, but in the end, it will be . . ." She trailed off.

Eli looked at David, gave him his they're-at-it-again eye roll. "You three'll figure it out. Thanks for the cookies." He leaned over and kissed Floret's cheek, then trotted back into the house.

They were all silent as they listened to him bound up the stairs.

"It will all work out," Floret said. "It always does."

Eve stood in the shade of the oak tree outside her grandmother's white frame house. Looking at it, you'd never know that it contained not only her grandmother's home but also the inner workings of her small but consolidated real estate empire. Hannah Gordon owned a third of the buildings in town and, at eighty-eight, showed no signs of backing off.

She was respected by the locals—not always liked, but she'd been the only mother Eve had ever known. Granna and Floret. They'd both been mothers to her until the fight that ended their friendship and began the struggle for the Wind Chime property.

Eve knew she had to go inside. The old woman would be home. She did most of her work from there these days. Surgery had renewed her eyesight, but she despised having to wear her state-of-the-art hearing aids in public. It was a sign of weakness, and Hannah Gordon did not show weakness.

Eve's insides were churning. But she had to know.

She couldn't go to Floret. Eve was never totally sure about the state of Floret's mind. And Eve didn't dare ask her father. The few times she'd tried to ask him about her mother, he retreated inside himself to the dark place that so often controlled his life.

But there was no mistaking it. Zoe Bascombe's mother was Jenny Campbell. That made her Eve's half sister. All the doppelgängers in the world couldn't be more alike than Mel and Zoe. Eve had printed out photos of both of them as teens, and they were in her shoulder bag. Evidence. Let Hannah try to deny the resemblance.

She took a fortifying breath, then strode up the driveway, across the grass, and up the steps to the rectangular porch. She knocked on the door, opened it, and stuck her head inside. "Granna?"

There was no answer, but she could hear sounds from the office.

Eve went in and closed the door behind her. No going back now. She walked through the living room, where a breeze lifted the organza curtains of the open windows. Past the dark Victorian furniture, and through the archway into the office. Her grandmother sat behind her desk, almost hidden by the screen of her computer.

Hannah looked up, a vague expression on her face. "What brings you here at this time of day?" Her voice was surprisingly light, only slightly raspy with age. She'd let her hair go white and kept it short, because she was convinced it made her look younger.

Eve came around the desk until she was standing at Hannah's shoulder. She pulled out the two photos and set them on the desk.

Hannah aligned them with her index fingers. "What's this?"

"You tell me."

Her grandmother pursed her lips. "It's pictures of Mel. I remember this—she was ten or twelve, right? I don't remember this." She pointed to the photo of Zoe Bascombe. "Her hair is darker."

Eve pointed to the photo nearest to her. "This is Mel." She pointed to the next. "This is Zoe Bascombe at sixteen."

Her grandmother stilled. And that infinitesimal moment of reaction telegraphed all Eve needed to know. "Who is she?"

Hannah sighed. "I don't know—why should I? Just some girl who looks a little like Mel. Where did you come up with this?"

"It's from a Google search I did on one of my guests. Something I don't normally do, but Dad had such a strange reaction to her that it made me curious. Want to know who her mother is?"

"Not really."

"It's a woman named Jenny Bascombe, née Campbell."

"Two very common names. Must be thousands of them."

"But not with a daughter the spitting image of Mel."

Hannah pushed the photos onto the floor. "What are you doing? You're just going to upset everyone."

"I'm already upset. So is Dad."

"You didn't tell him this crock of bull, did you?"

"I didn't have to."

"Let it drop. This girl is no more related to you than Sam Hill."

Eve crossed her arms. "I don't believe you. I'm forty-eight years old, and you've never told me the truth about my mother. I want to know. Now—or I'm going to ask Zoe Bascombe."

Hannah closed her eyes. "I told you. She was young. Got pregnant. Her parents took her away. We adopted you. End of story."

It was all Eve ever got. But now it wasn't enough.

"I need more. Zoe was asking about Wind Chime Beach."

Her grandmother slumped back with a long sigh.

"Go back to the inn, Eve. You're making too much out of this."

It was over—for today, anyway. Her grandmother had spoken, and nobody ever won against Hannah Gordon when she'd made a stand.

"Did I tell you I'm thinking about buying the Kelly place?"

It took Eve a minute to catch up. "They're selling?"

"Not yet, but they will."

"They won't. They love that cottage, and Jim can walk to the diner and back every day."

"Not if the diner is closed down." Hannah smiled briefly, showing a row of capped white teeth. "I understand that there have been some serious safety and sanitary violations."

Eve narrowed her eyes. "I never heard . . ." It hit her in one great wave of understanding and disappointment. Hannah was warning her to back off. "The whole town will fight you if you try to sabotage their favorite diner."

Hannah shrugged. "I'm just a citizen trying to do my duty."

Eve didn't think her grandmother cared that people feared and despised her. And her explanation didn't fool Eve, nor anybody else, once they'd heard what she was up to. "You want the easement on their property so that Henry and Floret won't have access to the street."

"Perhaps. Is there anything else?"

Eve reached down to pick up the photos, but a thin, bony hand stopped her.

"Leave them."

Eve pulled her hand back and left without her habitual kiss on the cheek. It wasn't until she was on the street that the tears fell. Tears of anger, not hurt. Those tears had dried up a long time ago.

Chapter 4

ZOE DIDN'T GO BACK to the inn immediately but wandered through town, alternating between trying to recapture the sound of the wind chimes and wondering how she'd gotten here. It bothered and intrigued her that her mother had chosen this place to rest. How did she even know about Wind Chime? Zoe had scoured the Internet for information. Nothing had popped up. It was virtually unknown.

What was she going to do? What if she went back and explained things to Henry and Floret? They might refuse, and then where would she be? She couldn't sneak around like some thief.

She wanted to call Chris for advice, but it wasn't fair to put him between her and Errol and Robert. If her mother had wanted Chris to do this, she would have asked him, not Zoe. But she'd asked Zoe.

Zoe found herself standing in front of the corner bookstore, absently perusing the titles in the window. One half of the window was taken up by a large display. A coffee table–type book of photography, opened to show two full-page color photographs of . . .

Zoe leaned into the glass to get a closer look.

Wind chimes. Beautiful in their simplicity. Nuanced in sun and shadow, translucence and darkness, intriguing.

On the cover, *Light* was spelled out in amber letters across a dark landscape. And the photographer was David Merrick.

David Merrick. David. Wind chimes. The man from the commune? She went inside and bought it.

When she came out again, she saw Mel from the inn, head bent, striding down the sidewalk. It took a second for Zoe to recognize her: she'd changed out of her gauze uniform and into jeans shorts and a pink T-shirt, and her ponytail had been tied up in an unconstructed bun on the top of her head.

Even from where she stood, Zoe could tell Mel was upset. Should Zoe smile and keep walking? Duck back into the store and avoid her? Really, it was none of her business, but . . .

Mel's head suddenly snapped toward the street as a big silver Cadillac drove past.

Zoe had no idea what was up with Mel. But quite frankly she was more interested in the Cadillac, especially when it turned into the drive that she'd just left.

DAVID and Henry had just finished rehanging one of the freshly painted shutters when David saw a late-model Cadillac coming up the drive. He knew who it was; everyone in town recognized that symbol of wealth and power. He was just surprised. Hannah Gordon didn't venture this way much.

"Here comes trouble," he said to Henry.

Henry looked up. "It was inevitable," he said, then went into the house.

David was used to Floret and Henry's cryptic statements, but today's unexpected visit from their archenemy—though Henry and Floret would deny that they felt any animosity toward Hannah—sent a ripple of unease up his spine.

A minute later, Hannah came to a stop inches from the place where David was standing. He refused to jump out of the way.

How stupid was that? It wasn't his fight. He didn't even know what it was about, except that Hannah and Floret had had a falling-out years ago. When he was much too young to remember.

He opened the car door for her. "Good morning, Hannah."

"David." The old woman eased herself from the car, nodded minutely to him. Hannah had to be close to ninety, tall still, but frail-looking, and so thin that it didn't seem she'd be able to balance on all that height. "Where are Henry and Floret?"

"I imagine they're in the house."

He followed her inside. She was wearing a navy blue pantsuit. Her cap of white hair clutched her head like a helmet.

Henry was waiting in the foyer. "Welcome," he said. "To what do we owe the pleasure—calling a truce?"

"When hell freezes over." The old woman scowled and looked around. "This place looks shabbier than the last time I was here."

Henry smiled. "Then you should come more often, and you wouldn't notice it so much."

Hannah turned her scowl on him.

Jeez, she was a bitter old woman. David knew she'd lost a son in the war; her surviving son, Lee, was a local music legend, though a bit of a recluse. She had two daughters living nearby. She had several grandchildren—one of whom was Eve Gordon—and great-grandchildren. She should be enjoying her twilight years. Yet she seemed miserable.

"Where is Floret?"

"Making tea."

Without a word, Hannah turned and tottered toward the kitchen. David and Henry both hurried after her.

Floret was just pouring water into the teapot, and the aroma of chamomile filled the air around them.

"Don't bother," Hannah said. "I won't be staying that long. I'm here to warn you that you may be getting a visitor."

"Already came," Henry said, then pulled out a chair for Hannah.

"Damn." She sank into the chair but straightened quickly.

Floret brought the teapot to the table, followed by a plate of the cookies they'd been eating earlier out on the veranda. Hannah didn't take one or reach for the cup of tea Floret had poured her.

"Will you please sit down, Henry? You're very distracting hovering like that in—that getup."

Henry looked down at his white caftan. "This getup is what I choose to wear. In fact you used to say that—"

"I know what I used to say. Sit down and pay attention."

Henry walked around the table, seated Floret with the formality of a butler, and sat down opposite Hannah.

The energy between Hannah and Henry arced across the table.

"What did you tell her?" Hannah demanded.

Henry reached for a cookie. "What was there to tell?"

"I hate it when you answer a question with another question."

"There are only questions."

Hannah banged her knobby fist on the table. "Just don't talk to her. And don't let Floret say a word; she'll spill the beans for sure."

Floret was staring into the distance, but at the mention of her name she turned to Hannah and said dreamily, "She was lovely. She looked just like Jenny . . . at first I thought she was Jenny."

David froze. What was going on here? Who the hell was Jenny?

"Not to worry," Henry said. "David chased her off."

David shrugged. He wasn't about to show any other reaction. And he really hated the way Hannah treated her once-closest friends. All over some slight years ago, and now over money and property—and power.

Hannah gobbled up real estate like a hen on corn. She ostensibly wanted Wind Chime so the inn could use the beach that abutted the spa. But Hannah couldn't be satisfied just leasing the beach. She had to own the entire property. She'd probably raze the house to build banquet pavilions or something, but not if he could help it. This was Floret and Henry's home. And his and Eli's.

David had grown up here. He had returned eight years ago, when his brother and sister-in-law were killed in an accident and he became the guardian of ten-year-old Eli. He was only twenty-seven then and clueless about how to raise a grieving boy. But Eli had thrived living with Henry and Floret. And living here gave David the freedom to accept the occasional assignment that required travel.

Hannah pushed her chair back and stood, looking more awkward than powerful, and for a second David felt sorry for her.

She raised a crooked finger. "Don't talk to her again."

"Hannah," said Henry patiently. "Will you never learn that some things are inescapable?"

"Let me tell you what's inescapable. If you encourage that little witch, I'll make sure you lose this place. I will stop at nothing."

Henry smiled. "Hannah, sometimes I see the girl in you. And I don't know what happened to make you so not your true self."

Hannah cut a vicious look toward Floret, but it was wasted on Floret, whose attention was rapt on her life partner.

"Do not cross me in this." Hannah turned and walked determinedly to the door. A look from Henry, and David rushed to see her to her car. But she stopped him at the kitchen door.

"I know the way. Don't bother to see me out."

He returned to the kitchen and watched from the window until he saw the Cadillac drive away. Then he turned to Floret and Henry. "What's going on here?"

"All in good time, my boy. Shall we finish our tea? Then we'll get the rest of those shutters hung."

MEL ducked into the trees just as the silver Cadillac came down the drive from Wind Chime House and turned onto the road. She'd doubled back through the woods, or else she'd be sitting in that car right now, being treated like some idiot who didn't have a mind of her own. It was like the world was against her—her and Eli.

She peered out from behind the tree until she was sure the car was gone, then sank back against the rough bark and let out a huge sigh of relief. It wasn't fair. They didn't understand. Her mom, since her dad left, was finished looking for love, and David Merrick had never wanted it in the first place. At least that's what Eli said. Who didn't want love? That was crazy.

No wonder they were all against her and Eli being in love. Well, in three months, Mel would be eighteen. Then she'd be legal, and no one could boss her around anymore.

"Gotcha!"

Mel jumped about a hundred feet. And turned into Eli's arms. "You scared me. Where did you come from?"

"I saw you walking back from town and was coming out to meet you, but I had to wait until Hannah left." He pulled her closer. Kissed her.

She gave in to the feelings of safety and love and wanting to be with him forever. "What was she doing here?"

"I don't know. They all went into the kitchen. And I couldn't really hear without putting my ear to the door."

Mel sighed. "What are we going to do?"

Eli grinned, and she loved him all the way to her toes. He pulled the backpack off his shoulder and held it up. "Everything we need for a getaway picnic." He frowned. "One thing I did hear was that someone came to the house today asking about our beach."

Mel grabbed his arm. "The woman from the hotel. I thought it was called Old Beach. It's really called Wind Chime Beach."

"First I ever heard of it. I was just coming back from town when I saw her running down the driveway like ghosts were after her. But it wasn't a ghost; it was Uncle David."

"He was chasing her away?"

"I think so. Henry called her Pandora."

"Pandora? Do you think something bad is going to happen?"

Eli shrugged. "Nah. I hope not."

ZOE TOSSED HER BOOKSTORE package onto the bed and headed for the bathroom and her sewing kit. She spent the next ten minutes digging slivers out of her palms and smearing them with antibacterial cream. Then she took her new book to the balcony, where she stretched out on the chaise and opened it to the back flap.

And there was the face of the man who had thrown her off the Wind Chime property.

He looked dashing in the photo—artistic, with sensitive brown eyes looking back at the camera. *False advertising,* she thought. She turned the book over and flipped through the pages.

The first photograph was . . . a beach? A desert? It was sand, contoured into dunes. After the desert photo, there was a close-up of something that might be an orchid, but she couldn't be sure.

Then came two pages of wind chimes. They were the first of several wind chime photos, as she was to discover. Sometimes they were hanging from a branch; sometimes they were hidden among the trees. Some photos were so delicate that she was afraid to breathe on the page.

The guy could take pictures. She'd been sucked into them in the same way she was with a beautiful song, a symphony, or when the wind chimes today had passed through her world and opened a new one. There was something about David Merrick's photos. Beautiful—but solitary. She knew how that felt.

Zoe closed the book.

It was a sunny day, high clouds floating through a blue sky. A heady breeze blew cooler than the air around it. Below her on the lawn, a yoga class was just ending. Spirits renewed, the participants would soon be sunbathing on the hotel beach.

Suddenly she wanted to be down there with them. Not here alone, hands raw, heart sore, holding on to her mother even after her mom was clearly gone.

She turned back into the room, marched over to the phone, and booked her room for another five days. Then she turned to the urn, ran her finger along its cool, hard contours. "I found Wind Chime Beach. I heard the chimes. I get it. The peace, the magic, the specialness. What I don't get is how you got it."

There was no answer from the urn. There never would be.

The phone rang, and her first thought was that Chris was calling at last. But it was the house phone.

"Hello?"

"Hi, Zoe? This is Karen. We met this morning at breakfast. We're all headed downstairs to the bar for happy hour; they have great appetizers. Would you like to meet us there?"

"I—" She stopped her usual reply—that she'd love to but was just too busy. She wasn't too busy. "Sure. I'd love to."

"Great. About fifteen minutes? See you."

Karen ended the call. Zoe changed into slacks and a silk T-shirt, dumped essentials into her purse, then met them in the lobby.

"Hope you don't mind eating here," Karen said as they went into the bar. "Elaine has something going with the fiddle player."

Brandy rolled her eyes.

"It was the clarinetist in a New Orleans jazz band last time," Karen explained.

"Hey," Elaine said, then gave Karen a playful punch. "I'm legally divorced after the longest-running court case of the century."

The hostess showed them to a table near the bandstand. They ordered drinks, then headed for the hot buffet bar, where they loaded plates with wings, sausages, quesadilla wedges, and a pile of other happy-hour food—all organic.

The bar began to fill up. Brandy kept them in stitches with stories about her recent honeymoon. Her new husband was an ex-basketball player, now an announcer with a sports television affiliate in Philadelphia.

The three friends ordered another round of drinks, but Zoe began to think about going upstairs. The band was setting up, and she'd caught the eye of the guitarist several times as he climbed back and forth among the amps. She supposed that angry look of his was part of his persona. It had probably been sexy a few decades ago. But the "bad boy" appeal was nonexistent in this old guy.

"I really have to do some work." Zoe started to stand.

"You're kidding, right?" Karen said. "The night is young."

"Sorry. But I'm behind as it is. Let me get the tab," she said on impulse, then took the check the waitress had been adding to throughout the evening.

"No," Brandy said. "We go dutch all the way."

The guitarist was staring at her, and it was beginning to creep her out. "No, really. My treat." Zoe backed away.

"Then tomorrow we treat you," Karen said.

Zoe hurried to the bar, where the bartender was talking to the woman she'd met that morning—the proprietress, Eve. "Making it an early evening?" he asked as he took her credit card.

"Work to do." She smiled her too-busy-to-talk-now smile.

People usually got the message. Eve didn't.

"Do you have business locally?" Eve asked.

"No. I'm working remotely." Just a little white lie. She smiled and signed the check, adding a big tip, something her mother taught her. *Tip big the first time: they'll treat you right after that.*

"Night." Zoe turned to the door just as the band started to play.

"Jenny," crooned the singer, as if calling Zoe back. But Zoe barely slowed down. Eve's penetrating gaze on her back propelled her through the door.

Eve watched Zoe Bascombe hurry from the room. The girl was definitely spooked. She knew. She must know. That must be the reason she'd come here, to return to Wind Chime Beach. Her mother must have sent her. Her mother—and Eve's mother.

Did Lee know? The way he'd been acting, he must have a suspicion that Zoe's mother was Jenny Campbell. Why else start the set with his "signature" song? He usually didn't sing it until the end of the evening.

There could be no mistake. Eve had a half sister. They didn't know about each other—at least Eve hadn't known. And Zoe still seemed clueless. Was it fear or knowledge that made her act so furtively? Was she checking Eve out?

Eve stopped herself, horrified at her own suspicions. She'd spent years undoing the mistrust of people that exuded from her grandmother, which Hannah had wittingly or unwittingly taught Eve to expect in life. It hadn't always been that way. When they'd lived at Wind Chime with Floret and Henry and the others, Eve had seen the good in people every day. Had trusted them, depended on them.

Her grandmother had been born and raised nearby. The family had worked hard just to survive. Then she'd lost a husband and a son. Her daughters had married local boys who turned out to be lazy, ready to blame everyone but themselves for their lack of success. And they blamed Hannah for not doing more for them, when she'd actually been very generous. She loaned them money she knew she would never see again; then one day she stopped.

The daughters cried and cajoled, and when she didn't cave, they turned their backs on her. Hannah knew they were just waiting for her to die so they could claim their part of her self-made empire.

But not Eve. Eve loved her as a mother, even as she watched her grandmother turn from bitter to toxic to destructive. Hannah had bought the inn for Eve and turned it over to her. Eve had made good. She had a legacy to leave her own daughters, who were all hardworking and caring people.

And never once would Hannah tell Eve about her mother.

"Deep thoughts," Mike intoned softly.

Eve jumped, not realizing he'd leaned all the way across the bar to whisper in her ear. "What?"

He frowned at her, jerked his head toward the door to the storeroom. Eve slid off the barstool and went around the bar, waited while he told Gary, the barman, to take over for him, and then let him trundle her through the door.

As it shut behind him, Mike turned her around and took her by the shoulders. "What's up?"

At first Eve just shook her head. The whole thing was too strange. Her father was acting crazy, her grandmother was being secretive, and a woman had checked into her inn asking about a local commune. It sounded ridiculous.

"Out with it."

"Zoe Bascombe."

"What about her?"

Eve shook her head again. She could tell Mike anything, everything. He was more than a bartender, a right-hand man. He was her best friend. He was always there for her.

He'd been there at her wedding ceremony to Walter Flannigan and kept her going when Walter left them for the promise of wealth in the oil fields of Alaska. Had stood by her when the call came that Walter had died on the job.

They were on-again, off-again lovers. Friends with benefits who led their own lives.

"I think she's my half sister," Eve blurted out.

"Whoa."

"Possibly," she added. "I looked her up. Her mother's name is Jenny Bascombe, née Campbell. My mother is Jenny Campbell."

"There must be a lot of Jenny Campbells out there."

"That's what I tried telling myself, but then . . . I found this." She unfolded the copies of the two photos of Zoe and Mel she'd made as soon as she returned to the hotel and had been carrying around all day.

Mike took them, moved over to the desk, and turned on a lamp. Set the two photos down side by side. Let out a low whistle.

Eve leaned against his back. "This is Mel." She pointed to the one on the right. "And that is Zoe at sixteen. They're practically identical except for the hair color."

"Huh."

"You don't seem surprised. Do you think it's a coincidence?"

"No. I noticed it last night. She checked in late and took a look in at the bar. For a second I thought she *was* Mel. I didn't think that much about it until Lee started acting so crazy."

"Do you think he suspects?"

"How could he not? But whether he's willing to confront it is a whole 'nother other."

Mike turned off the work lamp and opened the door. Lee's song hit them like a blow to the solar plexus.

> *"I saw you last night in a dream*
> *You were young, but I wasn't*
> *You wanted to stay but I scared you away . . ."*

"You're going to have to face him," Mike said.

Eve nodded. "And he's going to have to face her."

He went back to the bar, and Eve headed for the door and home.

Chapter 5

THE COTTAGE WAS LIT UP, and for a moment Eve hoped Mel would be there instead of out with Eli. But it was Noelle, home earlier than expected. She was curled up on the couch, a bowl of popcorn on the coffee table next to her, a movie streaming on her open laptop. She was fast asleep.

Eve tiptoed past and went into the kitchen, made herself a cup of tea. Why was Noelle home so early, and why was Mel so late?

She sat until her tea grew cold. Poured it out and rinsed the cup. Then, with nothing left to do but worry, she went to bed.

But not to sleep.

Her brain was a jumble of moving parts, none of which made sense and all of which were accelerating out of control. She'd known at an early age that you couldn't control most things. If she could, she'd have had one of those nuclear families the kids in town had. A father who went to work in the morning and came home at night in time for dinner. A mother who'd shop for school clothes with her and sing her to sleep.

Her father had sung her to sleep: *Lavender's blue, dilly dilly* . . . Then Floret did, or sometimes even Henry tried, though he couldn't, as everyone knew, "carry a tune in a bucket."

Eve turned over, tried to empty her mind, heard the movie go silent, then heard Noelle go off to bed. She hadn't checked to see if Mel had come home. Was that an omen?

Eve rolled onto her back, looked at the time. One o'clock.

She pulled the pillow over her head. Threw it off again.

She had a half sister. What did that mean, half sister?

For nearly fifty years, Eve had been an only child. So what if Zoe's mother might also be Eve's? They shared a mother, but family? Memories? Kinship? They had no common background.

Eve heard the front door open and close. Mel was home. She went straight to her room.

Eve's eyes closed. *I have a half sister.*

DAVID paced the floor of his room at Wind Chime. Heard Henry go downstairs for his late-night snack. David was tempted to join him, but he didn't want to be standing in the foyer like an irate parent when Eli finally returned. It was after one, but Eli had turned eighteen two months ago. He was an adult.

He had his big exam for the pre-semester science program on Sunday, and he needed his sleep. He'd been looking forward to it for months. He'd studied like crazy, but now he seemed distracted. And David knew why.

Mel. Wherever Eli was, Mel would be with him.

David stopped at the window, leaned on the sill. Not that he had anything against Mel. She was a good kid. Had a good heart. But at seventeen, she was immature for her age. Didn't seem to have any drive. They might be happy together one day. But not yet.

And what would happen when David left? Which he had to do soon. He couldn't make a living without working in the field. He needed outside assignments to fill the coffers.

And he needed to breathe, to feel the exhilaration of discovery. He'd been able to keep working because he had Henry and Floret to look after Eli while he was gone. But they couldn't anymore.

David saw Eli before he heard him, walking up the drive in the moonlight. He looked as if he didn't have a care in the world.

David went downstairs and was caught standing in the foyer when Eli came through the front door.

"Oh, man," Eli said, and closed the door. "I'm a little late."

"Where were you?"

"Just around. Hanging out. We lost track of time."

"Who is we? Mel?"

"So? You sound just like Mel's mother. It's because of that stupid feud, isn't it? That's so last century."

"It has nothing to do with any feud. It has to do with your future— and Mel's."

"Mel wants to get married."

David had been expecting this, but hearing it out loud . . .

"What about university, the pre-semester science program? The entrance exam is this weekend."

"I don't know."

Well, David did. He knew that he had a responsibility to his brother to raise his child the best he could. And not going to school to marry a girl, neither of them with any way to support themselves, was no future.

"Our future is together."

"It may be, but right now—"

Henry stepped out of the kitchen, holding a bowl of yogurt and granola. Eli brushed past him and ran up the stairs.

David followed slowly. Eli was teetering on a life decision, and David had made a hash of trying to help. As he usually did.

"The future is the future," Henry said and put his free hand on David's shoulder. Then they walked up the flight of stairs together.

NOELLE was up and sitting at the table staring into her coffee mug when Eve wandered into the kitchen the next morning.

"Hey," she said. "Coffee's fresh."

Eve nodded, got another mug down from the cabinet. She had a headache from lack of sleep, from stress, from worry, and from the recognition that her world was about to change drastically.

She sat down across from Noelle.

"Guess you're wondering why I'm home two days early."

"You're always welcome."

"I didn't get the job," Noelle said.

"I kinda figured that might be the case. What happened?"

Noelle toyed with her mug. "I don't know. I thought I did a great interview. But at the end of the day, they called and said I wouldn't need to come back for the next round."

"That sucks, but there are other jobs."

"Just not in graphic arts."

Eve took her coffee and moved around to sit next to her middle daughter. "You've been out of school two months. It's not a race."

"I know. It's just really disappointing."

Mel appeared in the doorway; her hair was a rat's nest. She walked straight to the coffeepot without looking at either of them.

Eve tried not to ask the question. So she formed it as a statement. "I heard you come in last night."

Mel shrugged and started to take her coffee out of the room.

"Aren't you going to say hello to your sister?"

"Hi. Guess you didn't get the job."

"Mel," Eve began.

"So much for your fancy college education."

Eve's mouth dropped open. "Mel, what's gotten into you? If this is what hanging out with Eli Merrick is doing to your—"

"Why does everyone hate Eli? He wants to marry me."

"No!" The word exploded from Eve's mouth before she could stop it. "Look, honey, we all like Eli, and if you still want to get married in a year or so, that's great. But first you need to—"

"Get an education," Mel said in a high-pitched voice.

Eve smoothed her face. Took slow breaths. "I'm just saying that marriage and education aren't mutually exclusive."

"You don't want me to get married because you never loved Dad."

"I did love your father," Eve said. She'd never gone to college because she'd loved him too well. Harmony had been born eight months after she graduated from high school. No college, no travel to foreign countries. All the plans she'd made had fallen by the wayside. She didn't begrudge the loss; she had her girls and Walter Flannigan for a good twelve years before he left. And then he died. And Eve became a widow with three little girls and no degree. She'd be damned if she let Mel throw her chance away.

"Well, we're getting married. You can't stop me."

Something in Eve snapped. "As long as you live in my house I can." She whirled around, then stormed out of the house.

EVE had gone out the back and down the path several hundred feet before she stopped for breath. What had she just done? She never lost her cool. But she wouldn't go back and apologize. Because right now, she didn't feel like relenting.

She marched down the path toward the inn but turned onto the walkway that led to Main Street. Mike's house was three blocks away, set back on a wooded lot. She went there automatically, not wondering if he'd be awake.

She stopped outside the craftsman-style house. Why had she come here? She could probably just sneak away before she was tempted to whine out the whole story to him, her long-suffering friend. She turned to go.

"Hey. You made the walk. Now come make the coffee."

She turned and smiled at Mike waving from his doorway, as burly as a spring bear. But much more good-natured.

She walked back to his door, said thanks with downcast eyes, and slipped past him.

"Oh, brother," he said before closing the door on the world.

ZOE spent the morning pacing in her room. She practiced several scenarios for talking to Henry and Floret, most of which began with stopping to listen to the chimes and hoping for inspiration. But what she would do after hearing the chimes was sketchier. Walk up to the house and declare her intentions of spreading her mother's ashes on Wind Chime Beach? Ease into it?

She couldn't put it off any longer. She'd just go and hope for the best. She grabbed her purse and strode to the elevator. Well, maybe she should have breakfast first. But not at the inn. She'd seen the diner on her way to Wind Chime yesterday. It would be faster. Then she'd go straight to the commune.

She peeked down the hall before she stepped out of the elevator on the ground floor, then tucked her head in preparation for scooting past the reception desk. She didn't get far.

"Hey! Wait."

She didn't look around but kept going. She heard the receptionist come from behind the desk.

"Good grief, Mel. What did you do to your hair? Mom's gonna kill you. No wonder you crept out of the cottage without saying goodbye."

A hand clamped around Zoe's arm and spun her around.

A woman about Zoe's age, with light brown hair that waved past her shoulders, stared open-mouthed at her.

"Oh, I'm so sorry. I thought you were my sister."

Right. She'd called Zoe Mel. A case of mistaken identity.

"Your hair looks great. It's just . . . I'm Noelle, Mel's sister."

"Nice to meet you." Zoe began to ease away.

"I'm sorry," Noelle said. "It's a great style. Perfect for your face."

"Thanks. Listen, I've got to run."

Noelle nodded. "Have a nice day," she said as Zoe hurried through the lobby door to the street.

KELLY'S Diner was pretty busy, so Zoe sat at the counter between an old guy who hunched over his coffee cup and a hipster couple who kept asking questions about which was the best beach.

According to Jim, the short, happy-with-his-own-food man behind the counter, there were several. He mentioned a few, none of which were named Wind Chime.

The breakfast was good and greasy. And Jim, who turned out to be the Mr. Kelly who owned the driveway to Wind Chime House, was a jovial conversationalist as he filled coffee cups and gave directions in an efficient but unhurried way.

Zoe turned down a second cup. And, metaphorically girded for battle with a stack of pancakes and a side of bacon, she continued on her way to Wind Chime.

She had second thoughts as she neared the house. But she hadn't made contingency plans for running into David Merrick, who was hammering new pickets onto the sagging fence. Bent over his work, shirtless, his skin glistening in the sun, he looked more like a manual laborer than the creator of those amazing photographs.

There was no way to get to Henry and Floret without passing him. She strode ahead.

He straightened and turned around just as Dulcie appeared from the woods. The goat did a funny hop and trotted over to him.

Zoe scooted toward the gate with her hand outstretched, as if that could ward off attacking goats. "Do you think I could talk to Henry and Floret this morning?"

"Sure." David shoved the hammer he'd been holding into the loop of his jeans and started toward the gate, Dulcie by his side.

He grabbed a T-shirt off one of the pickets, then leaned past her to pull the gate open. Dulcie bumped her head against his leg, and he shut the gate against her indignant bleating.

David turned toward the house and called out, "Company!"

The door opened, and the tallest man Zoe had ever seen stepped onto the porch. A chill ran up her spine. There was no doubt in her mind. Henry was her ghost. And Dulcie the terrifying demon from hell. They must have been taking an evening walk in the fog.

Zoe climbed the steps and stopped in front of him. He was wearing a blue-and-white-striped caftan. His long white hair was pulled back in a ponytail. There was a calm about him that was seductive.

"Welcome. Come in." He turned to precede them, and Zoe saw there was a daisy stuck in the band of his hair.

It was dark and cool inside. She followed him down a short corridor hung with handwoven tapestries past a door that led to a country kitchen. The hall ended in a staircase and opened to a large room filled with light and comfortable-looking furniture. Beyond that room was an enclosed veranda that overlooked the sea. This was a long-established and well-loved home—Zoe could feel it.

"Have a seat," Henry said.

Zoe sat on the couch. David sat in a chair across from her.

She frowned. She hadn't planned for him to be around when she made her request. He leaned back in the chair and crossed a foot over one knee. A move that said he wasn't going anywhere.

Henry left the room and soon returned with a tray of glasses and what appeared to be iced tea, followed by Floret carrying a plate of cookies. Today she had forgone her gardening overalls for a long dress printed with smiling owls.

Henry poured tea. Floret passed the cookies, and David Merrick sat staring out to sea.

After a nerve-racking display of manners, Henry sat in a big wing chair. Floret sat down on the couch next to Zoe. Even though she perched on the edge of the cushion, her feet didn't quite reach the floor.

"I have a confession to make," Zoe began. "I'm not just a sight-seer. I have a reason for being here."

"Oh, we know, dear. You don't have to explain," Floret said, leaning over to pat her hand. She turned it over and looked at Zoe's palm. "Good heavens."

"It's nothing, just some splinters." Zoe pulled her hand away. She was losing her train of thought.

She clasped her hands in her lap, took a breath. "I came be-cause . . ." Her voice gave out, and she realized that so far she hadn't said the words out loud. She reached for the glass of tea, took a sip. It was light and naturally sweet. Henry took the glass from her and placed it on the table.

"It's all right, Zoe. We know why you've come."

Zoe eyed him warily, then cut a look toward Floret, but they both looked perfectly benign.

She looked across at David, who seemed a thousand miles away.

Henry laughed. "You're safe here. We're not psychics."

"Then how do you know why I've come?"

"She sent us a letter."

"Who?" blurted Zoe.

Floret leaned toward her. "Jenny, of course. She said you'd be coming and . . ." Her words trailed off.

"She sent you something," Henry said. "She asked us to keep it until you arrived, but you ran off so quickly yesterday, I didn't have a chance to give it to you." Henry stood and left the room.

No one moved or spoke until he returned holding a flat, wrapped package. He placed the package on the table, then retrieved a pen-knife from a nearby writing table and handed it to Zoe.

Zoe stared at the package. It had all the trademark neatness and tape overkill that were—had been—her mother's.

"When? When did she send this?"

Henry looked at Floret. "Months ago. She sent us a letter along with it, asking us to keep it. That you would be here . . ."

"I didn't expect it to be so soon," Floret said. "When I first saw you, I thought . . . but it's no matter."

"It looks rather difficult to open," Henry said. "Would you like me to take off the outer wrappings?"

Zoe nodded; she was shaking so much she didn't think she could use the little knife without injuring her hands.

It only took a few graceful swipes to reveal a box about the size of a shirt box. Henry handed it to her.

She placed it in her lap and pulled the top off. Whatever was inside was covered with tissue paper. She peeled it back to find a layer of bubble wrap.

She touched it, her smile wavering. It was so her mother—this overkill of protection. She unrolled the bubble wrap and finally came to the object. Lifted it out.

She held up a delicate piece of hammered bronze formed into the shape of a heart. The action set off a cascade of sound as five smaller glass hearts danced on thin silver threads. *Wind chimes.*

Panic chased wonder into Zoe's throat. "I don't understand. She wants me to hang these at the beach?"

Floret nodded and touched the metal heart, a gesture as soft as a caress. Zoe could see all the wrinkles in her face now. A tear ran down her cheek. "That's exactly what she wants."

Wanted. What she wanted. "But why? How did she know about this place? Did you know her? What am I doing here?"

"You've brought her home," Floret said, still fingering the heart.

Home? "Home? She's from Long Island."

Henry exhaled. "The heart can have many homes."

"I have to go." Zoe tried to get up, but a small, gentle hand on her arm prevented her. Floret.

Henry leaned over the table and brushed the last piece of tissue paper from the box. A legal-size envelope was taped to the bottom. Across the front, Zoe's name was written in her mother's hand.

Zoe's fingers were trembling so much that she couldn't even pull the tape away. Henry took the envelope from the box, used his penknife to slit it open. When he handed it to her, she swore there were tears in his eyes, or maybe the tears were in her own eyes.

At last the letter was open in her hands.

Dear Dilly. Her mother's pet name for her. It soothed her.

You were my life, Zoe. I knew you would be. And you've never disappointed me. I'm so proud of you. Something I could never feel about myself. Your mother is and has always been a coward. And because I couldn't stand up for what I wanted, I made some tragic, tragic mistakes. I'm going to try to rectify some of them now that I am dead. I know you will fulfill my wishes about my remains. But there are other things I wish—I need—you to do.

It's a long story, and Henry and Floret can tell it better than I ever could.

Zoe looked up. Henry smiled encouragingly, but Floret had succumbed to tears and sat still as they streamed down her cheeks.

I hope you and the boys know I love you all with my entire being. A mother couldn't have had better children. And I hope I did well enough that you know this. But I didn't do so well for another. In fact, I made an unforgivable choice. I'm afraid it's too late to rectify what I did, but I hope with all my heart that you will do it for me.

Henry handed her a large white handkerchief, which she took and wiped her eyes and nose.

Look closely at my wind chimes, which I hope you will hang in the glen above Wind Chime Beach. All my children together at last.

Zoe frowned. There were five little hearts. What? *You had four children, Mom. Me and Chris and Robert and Errol.*

There is one whom I never acknowledged in life except in my heart. But she never left my heart, and I hope you can see your way to letting her know, since I can't.

You have a sister. Her name is Eve. You've probably met her by now. She runs the local inn. I was certain that one day you would find your way there. I don't know how many years have passed or if it has only been days. I wish I could see my two daughters together. I should have insisted on it. Maybe I will before I die, but just in case, I wanted you to know.

Zoe reached the end of the page and moved on to the next.

When I was young I met my soul mate. Are you laughing, dear Dilly, to hear your suburban mom say things like "soul mate"? Sometimes I thought you guessed at the things I tried to hide. But perhaps that was just my hope.

I was a coward. I gave in to my parents and gave away the child we created—Eve. She was adopted by his family.

But I didn't leave her in spirit, and I tried to stay in touch with her, wrote her so many letters. At first I was desperate for news of her. Later I wanted to share so many motherly things with her. At first it nearly drove me crazy because I never got a reply. Year after year I wrote, only to get no reply. But then I began to hope she never received them, because if she had and never tried to get in touch with me, it would break my heart beyond repair.

Please let her know that I loved her and it ripped a part of my heart out when I had to leave her. Let her know I'm proud of her. I came to her high school graduation. I wanted to tell her how much I loved her, but I didn't want to cause a scene. Hannah and Lee must hate me so much.

I'm more afraid of what I must say now than I have ever been in my life. I saw Eve's father once after I was taken away. It was years later. He was still angry. And so was I because our bond was stronger than ever even after all the years apart.

He was performing at Nassau Coliseum. I went and was let backstage. The rest, as they say, is history. And you became my beloved surprise baby. Lee Gordon is your biological father. I never told him about you. I'd caused him too much heartache as it was.

I'd lost one daughter, and I refused to have the other stigmatized by my weakness. You became my precious secret. My wonderful, precious secret.

I told no one. I suspect George knew. We weren't so happy in those days as we had been. But he was a good father to you in spite of it all. And I hope I was a good mother.

So there you have it. I hope you will forgive me and grow to love your sister as I have loved the both of you. Introduce her to her half brothers, and beg her to forgive me. I hope the two of you can be friends and sisters, my beautiful daughters.

Love,
Mom

Lee Gordon was her father. Could it be true—that bitter old man? No. George Bascombe was her father—the same father who had left his family for another woman and another family.

Eve Gordon was her sister. Her sister. And Eve's children . . .

"No." Zoe pushed herself up. "No."

Floret smiled at her. "There is so much she wants you to know."

Zoe looked wildly around. She had to get out. Henry and Floret's acceptance and serenity were suffocating her.

But Henry stood. "We'll tell you everything we remember, and you can catch us up on the rest, but later. First you need to see Eve and tell her about the letter. She's been waiting a long time to hear those words."

Chapter 6

Eve came back from Mike's feeling a bit calmer. She was still undecided about what to tell Noelle and Mel about Zoe Bascombe, but when she entered the cottage, she was granted a mini reprieve. No one was there. She changed clothes and hurried over to the office.

Noelle was waiting for her. She jumped up from the desk chair. "I thought you'd never get back. The strangest thing happened after you left. I came out to the lobby, and I saw, or thought I saw, Mel. She'd cut her hair and dyed it. I thought she'd gone out and done it just to be rebellious, you know?"

Eve nodded, but she had a dreaded idea of where this was going.

"And I went right up to her and told her so. But it wasn't Mel. It was one of the guests. I apologized the best I could, but, Mom, from the back she looked just like Mel, and then when she turned around, for a split second she still looked like Mel. Then she was just this nice-looking young woman I'd never seen before."

"Zoe Bascombe," Eve said. "She does look a little like—" Oh, hell, best just to come out and say it. Eve shut the door. "I think she might be my half sister."

Noelle's mouth dropped open. "Wow. You have a half sister? Why didn't you tell us?"

"I didn't know."

Noelle frowned. "Wait. What do you mean she *might* be? Aren't you sure? Did you Google her?"

"Of course I Googled her. We have the same mother. Jenny Bascombe, née Campbell. And between her resemblance to Mel and the way your grandfather has been acting—"

"Granddad recognized her?"

"Actually, I think Granddad thought she *was* Jenny Bascombe."

Eve reached into her pocket, pulled out the photos of Mel and a younger Zoe, and placed them on the desk.

"Holy cow," Noelle said. "They could be sisters. Have you talked to her?"

"I will. I'm just waiting for the right time. And Noelle, let's just keep this between us for now."

"You'd better go after her, David," Henry said as he watched Zoe Bascombe walk away from the house.

"Me? And do what?"

"Just make sure she gets back to the inn safely. I don't think she was prepared for all this news at once."

"And take her this," Floret said, coming to stand beside him. She handed him a small jar. "It's for her hands. Some of those cuts looked angry. This salve will heal them nicely."

David took the jar and caught up to Zoe at the end of the drive.

"Go away."

"Gladly," he said. "But Henry is worried about you."

"Tell him I'm fine."

"And Floret sent this for your hands." He thrust the jar at her.

She cut him a sideways glance and took the jar. "Tell her—"

"You're fine. Yeah. I get it. If you're going to be defensive, why don't I just walk by your side and make sure you don't walk into a bus?"

She didn't bother to answer, and two silent blocks later they stopped on the sidewalk in front of the inn. He felt only a ripple of satisfied amusement when she tripped on the first step. He made an automatic grab for her arm but stopped himself just in time to avoid getting reamed for his concern.

As soon as she was up the stairs, he wiped his hands of the whole situation and decided to treat himself to lunch at Kelly's. He strode down the street thinking about what he would order. You could tell the days of the week by the diner's specials.

He'd barely walked through the door before Jim Kelly called him over to the counter. He sat down, and Jim leaned over.

He lowered his voice. "What's been going on at your place?"

"Not much," David said. "Started repairing the fence today."

"You know what I mean."

"Actually, I don't." No way Jim could have heard about their visit from Zoe Bascombe that morning.

"Well, it must be something. Hannah Gordon's on my case to sell her the right-of-way back to their house."

"Again? Aw, Jim, you know she gets out her tentacles whenever the market is slow. She'll crawl off when something more interesting comes up for sale."

"This time she offered to buy me out completely."

A cup of coffee appeared at his elbow. "Thanks, Leeann," he said to the waitress.

"What do you mean, completely?"

"My whole property—house, land, everything. Lock, stock, and barrel. And she offered a decent deal. Why would she do that unless Henry and Floret had done something to set her off again?"

That was a distinct possibility, considering what had happened in the past two days.

Jim shook his head and snatched the menu out of the hovering Leeann's hand. "That old witch is gonna get her comeuppance one day." He handed David the menu.

"I'll have the special," David said.

Zoe stepped into the inn's lobby—right into Eve Gordon. *Gordon.* Zoe Gordon. She licked incredibly dry lips.

For the longest time, neither of them moved.

"Ms. Bascombe?"

Zoe looked at her. "We need to talk."

"I know," Eve said serenely. "My mother was Jenny Campbell, who married your father and became Jenny Bascombe. We're half sisters, aren't we?"

"Rather more than that," Zoe said, then laughed. She clamped her hand over her mouth, trying to stop herself.

Eve frowned, but Zoe was seeing her through a fractured lens of disbelief and hysteria, and it made her sister—*her sister*—look unreal.

"I don't understand. More than half?"

Zoe gulped in air. She felt so odd, like maybe she was going to faint. She nodded. "We're sisters. Whole sisters."

Eve stilled, suddenly coming back into focus. "Noelle!"

The young woman who had mistaken Zoe for Mel stuck her head out of the office door. "Oh." She grinned. Why was she grinning? Zoe tried to breathe.

"Can you watch the desk for a while?"

"Sure. Take your time." Noelle smiled broadly at Zoe.

She knew? Did they all know? What was happening here?

Zoe was being led down the hall. But instead of stopping at the elevator to Zoe's room, Eve kept going, out the side door, to a cottage surrounded by grass. Zoe thought it was a pretty cottage.

Eve opened the door. It seemed to Zoe that she was like a dream person. A sleepwalker. A glass of water was thrust into her hand, and she drank half of it before putting it down on the coffee table in front of the couch where she was sitting. She glanced up at Eve, who was standing over her.

"Did she send you? Is she coming here?"

How did Zoe answer that one? It was hard to watch a woman, her sister, old enough to be her mother, so dreading the answer. Zoe couldn't begin to understand how that must feel.

She touched her purse, where the letter was concealed. "My—our—mother is dead." There; she'd said it.

Eve started, swayed for a perilous moment, while Zoe sat watching, unable to help her. Eve stuck out her hand, found the arm of a chair, and eased herself down onto the cushion.

"I'm sorry, Eve." She meant sorry for everything. *For our loss, for the years you didn't have a mother and neither of us had a sister.*

Eve stared into her hands, and Zoe stared at her.

She and Eve didn't look at all alike. Zoe had always taken after her mother. Eve was taller and larger boned than Jenny. She had lighter hair than Zoe. But the immaculate pants and tunic that Eve wore were spot on, and though the silver and turquoise in her necklace weren't Jenny's trademark pearls, there was no mistaking the traits that Eve and Jenny shared. And Eve was the owner of a high-end spa. Successful, self-assured, organized.

Had running the inn been Eve's first choice for her life? Or had she, like Zoe, had other dreams?

There was so much she wanted to know.

"She loved you." Zoe opened her purse, looked inside. The letter was still there. "Before we get any further, I think you should read this. It was waiting for me at Floret and Henry's. She sent it months ago. She didn't know she was going to die. Or maybe she suspected. I don't know."

Zoe thrust the letter at Eve.

Eve stared at it. Then she began to read.

Zoe watched her, looking for the first sign of recognition, of anger or denial. Something that would make her world make sense again. Perfectly still, Eve's face showed no emotion as one tear after the other fell onto the paper. Finally, she looked up.

"She loved you," Zoe said again. She moved from the couch to sit on the arm of Eve's chair. Then slid down to squeeze onto the cushion next to her. Her sister.

"She loved me," said Eve. And Zoe let her own tears flow.

Eve read the letter again, then went to make tea. Zoe went to use her bathroom. She splashed water on her face until her mascara ran, then tried to rub the smudges off. It only made it worse.

She looked around for a bottle of makeup remover. She'd never seen so much stuff packed into such a tiny room.

Beauty products were balanced on the windowsill, the side of the tub, the back of the toilet. Zoe was amazed that they could get in and out of the room without setting off an avalanche of bottles.

She found lavender hand cream on the sink. She rubbed a drop under her eyes and blotted it off. She looked better, but the scent set off memories that surprised her. *Lavender's blue, dilly dilly.* It was her mother's favorite scent—and evidently Eve Gordon's, too.

It was hard to reconcile this bathroom with the minimalist, Zen-like feeling of the inn. And it was so not like Jenny Bascombe. She was the only person Zoe knew who could get out of a tub and not drip water on the floor.

"Are you okay in there?" Eve asked through the door.

Zoe opened the door. "Yes. I wasn't snooping or anything, just amazed at how much stuff you have."

"It kind of sneaks up on you. Noelle graduated from college, so she's home while she's looking for a job. And Mel—she's our free spirit, and her surroundings reflect that. Most of my toiletries are in the cabinet."

Zoe smiled. Why was she not surprised?

She followed Eve back to the living room, where a pottery teapot and two mugs were placed on a tray. Zoe sat while Eve poured the tea. It was the first time she'd been calm enough to notice her surroundings. A combination of pastels and rich, deep jewel tones. A bookcase crammed with books. The walls shared space with posters of the Eiffel Tower, the Grand Canyon, and tropical islands.

"Have you been to all these places?"

Eve glanced up. "None of them. But someday . . ." She handed Zoe one of the mugs. "So what do we do now?"

For the next two hours, Zoe told Eve about her mother. It was a slippery slope, trying to balance things that would give Eve a picture of their mother without making her feel slighted or that Zoe was somehow bragging. She told her about the perennial border, her committees, and her charity organizations. The good things.

They were both exhausted when Zoe said, "You know about her life with me, but do you know what happened before that?"

"I'm not sure," Eve said. "No one talks about it, not even Floret and Henry. Hannah—that's our grandmother, Dad's mother; we all call her Granna—and I used to live at Wind Chime until I was about thirteen. You'll meet her. She can be tough, but she started out with nothing and ended up a millionaire from local real estate."

Zoe nodded.

"Hannah traveled a lot in those days, was busy building her empire, so Floret and Henry became my surrogate parents."

"Why did you leave?"

"All I know is Hannah and Floret and Henry had a big fight. I remember it vividly, because people didn't have screaming fights in those days, not at Wind Chime, anyway. They've been enemies ever since. Well, at least Hannah has been."

"Didn't you ask?" Zoe said.

Eve shrugged. "I think I need to process this before we ask Henry and Floret about the past. Can you wait until the morning?"

Zoe nodded. "Right now I just need to eat. I know that sounds pedestrian, but I ate early this morning. And we missed lunch."

"Want some company? It'll have to be the bar, since my cupboard is bare. But it's early, so there won't be many people there."

"Sounds like a plan."

They carried the tea things to the kitchen and went out the side door. "I wonder what happened to the letters," Eve said, then locked the door.

As they walked across the lobby, Zoe heard piano music coming from the bar. She stopped and cocked her head. "It can't be."

"What?" Eve said, looking around the room.

"That's my song. I wrote that song. How is that possible?" Zoe hurried across the tiled floor, Eve right behind her.

The bar was dimly lit, and the sun coming through the French doors turned the two people at the piano into silhouette.

"Dilly!" The pianist swiveled his legs around the bench and made a beeline toward her.

"Dilly?" Eve said beside her.

"Chris?" Zoe said.

"Hey, baby sister." Chris wrapped her in a hug that lifted her off the ground. She loved his hugs; he was only a few inches taller than she was, but his hugs could encompass her whole world.

He put her down. "Surprised to see me?"

"Yes. What are you doing here?"

"I thought you might need some moral support."

"What about your play? Don't you have a matinee?"

"Another story. But you're in luck. I was noodling around at the piano waiting for you, and . . ." He lowered his voice. "Lee Gordon came in. Can you imagine? He toured with Night Chill. Great group, a little before our time, but one of the classic rock bands. He came over, and he liked what he heard. Hey, Lee," he said louder. "Come meet my sister, the composer and lyricist."

He turned to the man who had been leaning on the baby grand but now stood facing the three others—but only for an instant.

"You!" he spat, then strode past them out the door.

"What the—" Chris looked from Eve to Zoe. "Sorry. I don't know what set him off."

"We do," Eve said. "He's my father."

"Wow."

"Chris, meet your half sister, Eve."

Chris's eyes narrowed. He glanced at the door, then back to Zoe. "Say again? You mean Lee Gordon and our mother, uh . . ."

Zoe tried to nod, but she seemed incapable of moving.

"They did," Eve said.

"You're, like, our half sister?"

"Yes."

"So am I," Zoe said.

He beetled his eyebrows. "Okay, lost me. She's my half sister and you're . . ." He looked at Zoe.

"Promise you won't freak out."

"I'm an actor. It's what I do best. Hit me with it."

"Lee Gordon is my father, too."

"Wait," said Chris. "You gotta give me context, Dil."

"I will, but I have to eat."

Chris spun a full 360-degree pirouette, stopping at the bartender, who was at the bar, watching them intently. "Hey, Mike!"

"Have a seat," the bartender called back. "That table near the window, where it's quiet. I'll bring menus."

Zoe held on to Chris's arm with both hands, as she had as a kid anytime she felt insecure. Chris veered toward the piano and snagged his drink from the top. They sat down, then he took a sip.

"Okay. Our mother, Jenny Bascombe, got it on with Lee Gordon at least twice and, if I'm not mistaken, several years apart."

Eve snorted a laugh.

Chris leaned forward. "How long have you known this?"

Zoe could hear the hurt in his voice, and she quickly blurted, "Just since this morning. I swear."

Chris turned on Eve. "Did you tell her?"

"She told me."

"Okay, I'm having a hard time processing this."

"It's true. I'm not your full sister," Zoe said. "I feel like I am, but we're only half. Not yours, not Errol's, not Robert's."

"Are you sure? Where did you get this?"

Zoe fumbled in her bag. Realized the letter wasn't there. Had she left it at the cottage? Eve reached into her own pocket, pulled it out, and smoothed it against the table before handing it to Chris.

"I didn't want to leave it in the cottage for anyone to find."

Chris reached into his shirt pocket and retrieved a pair of reading glasses. He began to read while Zoe and Eve watched. When he reached the end, he folded the letter and placed it on the table.

He looked at the two women, blew out a long exhale. Pushed his hand through his hair. Sandy and wavy, not like Zoe's.

"So I have a half sister," he said.

"Chris. I'm only your half sister, too," Zoe said tentatively.

"Nah. You'll always be my one-and-a-half sister."

He always knew the right thing to say. She wanted to throw her arms around him and cling there forever, but she didn't.

"You're not upset?"

"Upset? No. But I am in need of another drink."

Another drink appeared on the table next to him, along with glasses of white wine for Eve and Zoe.

"Man, you and I could take this on the road," he told Mike. "You got great timing."

"He gets a little silly when he's nervous," Zoe explained.

"I'm not nervous, I'm gobsmacked." He turned the full wattage of his smile on all of them.

"To our mother." He raised his glass. "I always suspected she had a secret life. Though I gotta admit, I never expected this."

"I don't think Errol and Robert will be amused."

"No," he said. "Not at all. But we'll cross that bridge."

Mike cleared his throat.

"Sorry. What shall we eat?" Chris said, opening his menu.

WHEN the bar began to fill up, they stopped at the desk to find Chris a room for the night. The inn was booked, but they usually saved a couple of rooms for last-minute favors.

"It doesn't have a view except of the garden," Eve said.

"Not a problem," Chris said, then took his key card.

They retrieved his suitcase from behind the reception desk. "That's a big suitcase for overnight," Zoe said suspiciously.

Chris smiled. "Show closed."

"Oh, no," Zoe said. "I'm so sorry."

"Good reviews, decent box office," Chris said. "But the theater was booked with another show. It's been down for several weeks."

"So can you stay and see where Mom . . ." Zoe glanced at Eve.

"Sure, Dil. No problem."

"Why do you call her Dil?" Eve asked, knowing the answer.

"Short for Dilly. Our mother always sang that song 'Lavender's Blue' to her when she was little. It drove us all crazy."

"My father—our father—used to sing it to me when he was home from tour," Eve said.

"How weird is that?" Chris said. "I mean in a good way."

"Maybe Timothy will come up and you can make it a long weekend," Zoe said.

"Tim's in Chicago."

Eve thought she detected a sudden coolness in his voice. Roommate? Boyfriend? Husband?

"Actually, he's thinking about moving there. He's in pretty deep with this development firm there." Chris ended with a shrug.

Zoe seemed at a loss for words, so Eve stepped in.

"Why don't we meet after breakfast tomorrow? Give us all a chance to assimilate the changes."

"Sure you don't want a nightcap?" Chris asked.

"Not for me," Eve said. "I'm pretty wiped out, and I still have to close out tonight's books."

"How 'bout you, Dil?" Chris asked.

"Right now, I think I have to go to bed."

"Lord, girl, it's not even eight o'clock."

"I know, but I'm beat. How about a cup of tea in your room while you unpack?"

Chris rolled his eyes. "Okay, tea, then bed for you. Then maybe I'll take a walk around the town. Night, Eve, sister mine." He gave Eve a peck on the cheek.

Zoe gave her a long, sisterly hug. Then she took Chris's arm, and the two of them walked toward the elevator.

"I got you, Dil," Chris sang.

"I got you, Chris," Zoe sang back.

They stepped into the elevator and stuck their heads out long enough to sing, "And we got you, Eve," before the doors closed.

"I've got you, too," Eve said quietly. "I've got you."

EVE walked past the empty reception desk and into the office. She'd barely sat down before the door opened.

She swiveled her chair around. Her father stood in the doorway.

He seemed unsteady on his feet, and at first she thought he was drunk. God knows she had vivid memories of those times when he'd come home in the middle of the night, out of his mind with booze and bitterness. Eve didn't know which was more frightening—the alcohol or the emotions it unleashed.

"Come in," Eve said. "Is the band here?"

"No. Not yet."

He stood there looking at her. Finally he took one step forward, just far enough to close the door.

"She's Jenny's daughter, isn't she?"

Eve was not ready for this conversation. She wanted to savor her newfound status. But it would just postpone the inevitable.

"Yes."

"I could tell the minute I saw her. Why did she come here?"

"Why don't you ask her?"

Eve watched her father's fists tighten, release, tighten.

"Sit down. You'll give yourself a heart attack." Her voice sounded cold, but she didn't want to be the one to tell him that Jenny Bascombe, née Campbell, was dead.

He lowered himself onto the couch. His long legs set at a perfect right angle to the floor. His back straight. But his head was bent. "Did Jenny send her? What does she want?"

Eve took a breath. "She wants to meet her father."

Lee's head jerked up. He narrowed his eyes. She could see the confusion and the slow grasp of understanding transform his expression. He shook his head.

"She's your daughter. Zoe Bascombe is your daughter, too."

"No." Lee unfolded himself from the couch but didn't make it to his feet. He fell back onto the seat. "No. It's not possible."

Eve gave him a nudge. "Remember backstage at Nassau Coliseum? Jenny came back after the show. Must have been a big surprise after all that time, huh?"

His expression changed in a moment of recognition, a sad, reminiscent smile. "I remember." His voice was so distant that Eve wasn't sure if he was speaking to her or to himself.

"You must have been glad to see her. Really glad."

"Don't use that tone of voice about your mother."

Eve flinched. "Then tell me the truth."

"The truth? She was the only woman I ever loved. She walked out on me. Gave you up. That's the truth. But she can forget about walking back into our lives now. And I don't believe that girl is my daughter. So if she's thinking about getting money out of me, she can forget it. They won't get anything from me or your grandmother. Not one dime."

"You arrogant bastard. You think after all this time she would suddenly need something from you?" Eve said. "What on earth could you give her but a bucketful of bitterness?"

He flinched.

"You're just like Hannah. You two are so poisoned. I used to think it was because of what my mother did, but I think you did it to each other. Well, you can stop worrying. Jenny will never want anything from you. She's dead. That's why Zoe's here."

Lee sat for a long time, not speaking.

"Jenny has been dead to me for a long time. I don't want anything more to do with her or her daughter."

"Does that include me, Dad?"

He opened his mouth. Closed it.

"What did you do with the letters? Read them? Burn them?"

"What the hell are you talking about?"

"The letters my mother sent me."

"She never sent you any letters. Is that what this girl told you? She made it up. Lies, just like her mother's lies."

Eve fumbled in her pocket for the letter. Thrust it at him. "Read it. But so help me, if you try to tear it up, I'll kill you."

His eyes rounded; his jaw went slack. He mechanically reached for the letter, but his eyes never left hers. Slowly he unfolded the paper. Read. His eyes rested on the second page for a long time.

At length he looked up. "She came to your graduation? Why didn't she—no. It can't be true. It's just like her to lie. Your mother was a liar, Eve. It's time you dealt with it."

He sounded so certain that for a brief instant Eve almost believed him. But why would her mother lie, knowing she would be dead by the time Eve saw the letter?

"What happened to the letters, Dad?"

Lee thrust the one he was holding back at her and stood.

"I don't know anything about any letters. There were none. Not a letter, not a postcard, not a phone call, nothing ever, until she walked into my dressing room and I fell for her lies all over again."

She didn't want to hurt him, push him into that dark place where he'd spent so much of his life. But she had to know.

"Promise me there were no letters," she said.

The only answer she got was the door closing behind him.

Chapter 7

ZOE WAS THE FIRST ONE downstairs the next morning. The young woman who had mistaken her for Mel was at the desk. *Noelle.* She waved, and Zoe knew she had to go over and introduce herself.

She looked more like Eve than Mel did. The reddish-blond hair was the same, slightly wavy, only longer and parted on the side.

"I've been dying to meet you since yesterday. I hope you don't mind. Mom told me. I think it's so cool. To have an aunt, I mean. Are you going to stay for a while? Mom would love that. Especially since Mel is going to college. I'm looking for a job and—"

"What kind of job?" Zoe broke in, attempting to stanch the unending stream of enthusiasm.

"Graphic arts." Noelle made a face. "I know. I should have gone into business, but I like art. What can I say?"

Zoe could relate. "Good for you. Where do you want to be?"

"Anywhere interesting. I interviewed in Boston a couple of weeks ago." She named a big marketing firm Zoe was familiar with. "I made it through a couple of rounds."

"With a big company like that, you might have to start with an internship. Think you'd be interested in moving to New York?"

"Would I ever. Actually, I was just there." She shrugged. "They liked me, just not enough to hire me."

This is when Zoe Bascombe, scheduler of travel, mover of VIPs, organizer of promo dates, looked at her niece and said, "Why don't you show me some of your work later? Maybe we can zero in on some appropriate avenues to pursue."

"Oh, man, would you? That would be so incredible."

"I see you've met Noelle."

Zoe turned to find Eve standing beside her. "Yep."

"Zoe's going to help me find a job," Noelle said. "I mean, point me in the right direction."

"Just give advice," Zoe amended. "If it's okay with you. I'm not even sure I can help." She got her first good look at her sister. *Her sister.* Eve looked like she hadn't slept much.

Unlike Zoe, who had zonked out as soon as she'd left Chris. She'd gone upstairs, turned on the television, and the next thing she knew a Sunday church service was flickering on the screen.

"Fine by me. Do you want to have breakfast? Floret said she'd have muffins and coffee if we just wanted to come straight there."

"Coffee and muffins work," Zoe said. "Chris is coming, too, if that's okay. And he never eats breakfast at all."

"He's part of the family. Speaking of whom. Here he comes."

Chris stepped out of the elevator and sauntered toward the lobby.

Zoe smiled. "How late were you out last night?"

"The better question is, how early was I back this morning? There is some amazing music in this town."

"We're going over to Wind Chime House if you're up for it."

"Wouldn't miss it. After coffee."

Zoe him took by the arm. "They'll give you coffee there."

Chris slowly turned his head, giving them a deadpan face.

Noelle laughed. "Please, please tell me he's my uncle."

Chris flourished one of his most ridiculous bows. Straightened up with a groan, and Eve and Zoe hustled him out the door.

"Okay, I'm a little slow this morning," Chris said, edging himself between Zoe and Eve as they walked down Main Street. "But give me the lowdown on Wind Chime. Floret and Henry, right?"

"Yes," Eve said. "Maybe I should give you a brief history before we get there."

"Good idea," said Chris, and gave her his full attention.

"Floret inherited the house from her mother when she was a little girl. It was uninhabited for years until one day she and Henry came to live here, bringing an assorted group of flower children with them. I was raised there by my grandmother and dad, whom you met yesterday. And Hannah—well, maybe you won't have to have the pleasure."

"That bad?"

"Depends. She got me started when I wanted to buy the inn, but she's been carrying on a feud with Floret and Henry for years. We lived here until I was thirteen. Now it's just Floret and Henry and David, who's raising his nephew, Eli, who is in love with Mel."

She shook herself. "One day there was a shouting match. All the shouting was on my grandmother's side. She packed us up, and we moved into town. She's always refused to talk about it. But it came to a head a few years ago when I suggested that I wanted to lease their beach for hotel use. We had come to an agreement until Hannah got wind of it. The next day she had a backhoe come in with a load of rocks and built the wall, as the locals call it."

"And you all just caved?" asked Chris.

"Wait until you meet Hannah, and you'll understand."

Before long they turned down the drive to Wind Chime House and soon came to the gate.

Chris stopped to survey the vista. "Whoa. I'm loving this visual. Is that the border-wall beach over there?"

"One and the same," Eve said and pushed open the gate. It moved more easily than it had the day before, Zoe noticed. The whole fence was standing a little straighter.

"Oh, and there's Dulcie," Zoe said as they stepped into the yard and the goat raced toward them. Chris did a flying leap back through the gate and pushed it shut.

"What is that?" He lifted his chin in Dulcie's direction. Dulcie gave Eve and Zoe a welcoming butt, then zeroed in on Chris.

"You might as well come in and say your hellos," Henry called from the porch. "She's not violent, just a little needy."

Chris raised an eyebrow but opened the gate. Dulcie gamboled and butted and pushed Chris the rest of the way into the yard, then trotted along by his side.

"You've made a friend," said Henry as they reached the porch.

"Great," Chris said. "You're my favorite goat. Now go away." He climbed the steps and stuck out his hand. "Chris Bascombe, Zoe's brother. Oh, and Eve's, too. Hope you don't mind me—ignore the pun—butting in."

Henry smiled in his all-will-be-well way, and Zoe immediately felt better. And to think she'd thought he was some kind of evil spirit just three nights ago in the fog.

"Floret has muffins and coffee out on the porch," Henry said, ushering them inside.

Floret waved to them from the archway. She was wearing a long dress, soft and flowing, its pattern of blues and greens and yellows seeming to mix with the ocean and sky behind her. "Come in, come in," she said in her high, tinkling voice.

It took some time to get them all situated around the table with muffins and fruit and coffee served in mismatched china. Once they got past their first cups of strong pressed coffee, Henry's voice caught them by surprise, changing from conversational to story-teller without transition.

"Eve."

Eve jumped.

"Your mother—and Zoe's . . . and Chris's here—was a joy. Not your typical groupie, just a young girl who went to a concert and fell in love. And Lee. He was transformed . . . he brought her back here after his tour. He and Hannah and his sisters had been living here for a while. His brother had been killed in the war, and Hannah was desperate to keep Lee from getting called up.

"He'd always been deep. Talented but flawed. It was like a little hole to darkness that hadn't been completely closed. So it dogged him, even that summer, when happiness ruled the days."

There was something in his voice that foreshadowed a much sadder story, and Zoe braced herself.

"Then one day Jenny's parents came. None of us ever knew how they found her. They just appeared one day and took her away."

"Just like that?" Eve blurted out. "She just walked away?"

"So it appeared. But no one knows what's in someone else's soul."

Eve let out a slow, tortured breath.

"Lee was distraught, as you can imagine. To have no warning. We didn't know about the baby until later. Lee went back on the road, tried to drown his sorrows in drugs and alcohol and music. It was Hannah who found out that Jenny was pregnant and arranged to adopt you, Eve. Don't doubt what you meant to her."

Eve broke down. Zoe didn't bother to hide her own tears. Chris sniffed and blinked and finally pulled out his handkerchief.

"Then why didn't you tell me about the letters?"

"We didn't receive any letters until the one she sent several months ago telling us to expect Zoe."

Eve fumbled in the pocket of her slacks. "But Jenny says here that she wrote, but I never answered her letters. I never got any."

Henry and Floret exchanged looks.

"Hannah." Eve stood, nearly knocking over her chair. She started toward the front door, but Henry was there before her.

"Don't go in anger."

Floret had moved beside Henry, and they formed a calming wall between Eve and the door. But it didn't last.

"I'll never forgive her."

"Oh, Eve." Floret stretched out her arms.

But Eve swept past her down the hall and out the front door.

Zoe started to stand. "Should I—?"

"No," said Henry. "If it has to be done, it's best done quickly."

Silence fell around the table.

Chris stood abruptly. "Thanks for having us. But I think we should be going."

Zoe frowned at him. She had a hundred questions, wanted to hear stories about their mother, maybe understand what made her run away. Had Jenny's parents really forced her to go home? The Campbells were sweet, doted on their grandchildren. Zoe couldn't imagine them dragging a heartbroken, pregnant Jenny away.

She started to tell Chris to go without her, but Henry stood, too.

"I'm glad you're here," he said to Chris. "You and Zoe are part of the family now."

Chris nodded gravely. "Thank you. It's an honor."

Henry walked them to the door. "Come back anytime."

And then somehow they were down the steps and standing in the yard. Chris kept moving her toward the gate.

"What's the hurry? Don't you want to see Wind Chime Beach?"

"Yes," Chris said, looking behind them. "But right now you look like underdone pastry. You barely touched your coffee, and that poor muffin was nothing but crumbs. I know there's a big cheese-burger and a Coke with your name on it at that diner I saw in town. Now, let's get out of here. Dulcie the goat cometh."

They reached the street, and Chris had managed to take her mind off the meeting they'd just had and what they'd learned. There would be time to hear every tidbit. But for now, she could use the time to get used to her new family.

"So what's on your agenda?" Zoe asked once they'd been seated in a booth at Kelly's.

Chris looked over the edge of the oversize menu. "Audition? Give up my life and move to Chicago, where I'll freeze my tail off waiting for Timothy to build apartment complexes that I'll never be able to afford to live in?"

They ordered New Hampshire burgers and two Cokes.

"A long-distance relationship, maybe?"

Chris shrugged. "It's that age-old question. The thea-tah or the relationship. I'm leaning toward the theater. That can't be good."

"Does Timothy know?"

"Frankly, I'm not sure he cares."

"I'm so sorry."

Chris sighed. "The sad part is I'm not sure I do, either."

"Are you in a hurry to get back?"

Chris leaned back while the waitress deposited plates and glasses on the table.

"Only if my agent calls. Now eat."

Eve didn't bother to knock but walked right into her grand-mother's house. She'd tried to talk herself into slowing down, tak-ing time to get control of her anger. But it was a losing battle.

Why had she never seen any of her mother's letters? If Flo-ret and Henry only knew about one, what had happened to the others?

Hannah had to have intercepted them. It was the only word for it. Which meant chances were she still had them.

Eve marched across the parlor and went straight to her grand-mother's desk.

She hesitated. Searching someone else's desk was something her grandmother might do. But not Eve. No. She'd wait and—

The door to the kitchen opened, and Hannah came through carrying a mug of tea with the string of the tea bag hanging over the side. With all the money she'd made in her life, Hannah Gordon was still just a working-class girl from the poor side of town.

"Good Lord, you nearly scared me to death. What is it now?" She put the tea down and sat behind her desk.

Eve reached in her pocket for the envelope and letter. She stuck it under her grandmother's nose.

"And what is this?" Hannah said dismissively, uninterested.

"It's from my mother to Zoe. It was waiting for her at Wind Chime House."

"Let me see it."

Eve shook her head. "I don't trust you. But listen to this." She read the part about Jenny's letters. "Year after year she wrote me, but she never heard back. Because I never got those letters. Not one. What did you do with them, Hannah? Run to the mailbox every day to make sure you were always the first one to see the mail? Did you throw them in the trash? Burn them?"

Hannah heaved a sigh. "They're in the drawer of the credenza," she said in the same way she might say, "The napkins are in the cupboard."

Eve stared. In the drawer, all these years? She whirled around, practically lunged at the old curved credenza against the wall.

"The middle drawer, in the back corner."

Eve stumbled over to the middle drawer. It was locked.

"Give me the key. Give it to me or I swear I'll take an axe to it."

"Oh, Eve, don't be so dramatic." Hannah reached bony fingers inside her blouse and pulled out a key on a chain. She carefully unclasped the chain and let the key slide down into her palm. She held out her hand, fingers open.

Eve reached out slowly. She didn't breathe until the key was between her fingers and she'd turned back to the credenza drawer.

It was one of those old, thick brass keys, and it took several tries before she felt the latch give. She pulled the drawer open.

She found them almost immediately. A stack of envelopes, tied up with a lavender ribbon. It seemed like the final slap. A mean-spirited, vindictive joke. *Lavender's blue, dilly dilly . . .*

She pulled the ribbon off, turned them over. The first envelope hadn't been opened. Nor had the second or the third. Just as tightly sealed as the day they'd been sent.

She looked up. "You never read them? Why?"

"She broke my son's heart. The only son I have left. She didn't deserve a second chance."

Eve didn't know if she was going to be sick or yell a string of obscenities at the woman who had raised her.

Hannah's expression didn't change, but she seemed to have grown smaller during the last few seconds, as if the holes left inside her by so much loss had sucked the life out of her very soul.

Eve cared about souls. But right now, she only wanted to get home and read the letters she'd been waiting for her entire life.

Eve woke with a start. Blinked against the lamplight. And bolted upright. She had fallen asleep. She'd come to Mike's to read the letters in peace.

She took in the bottle of wine, half empty, the letters spread out on the coffee table before her.

A door opened. The sound of footsteps across the oak floor.

Eve hurriedly checked the time on the cable box. It was almost ten o'clock. Mike must be home. What if he wasn't alone?

She didn't ordinarily take advantage of their open relationship. But she'd been so upset that she hadn't thought to ask him if she could use his house. Hadn't even told her daughters where she was. She hadn't meant to stay.

She bolted to her feet, and her knees buckled, stiff from the couch and the fetal position she'd been lying in. She quickly ran her fingers through tangled hair and turned to face the door.

"Mike," she called. "It's me. I just had to borrow your living room for a bit. Sorry."

A shadow appeared in the doorway. Followed by Mike and a beer. He came into the room.

"Who else would it be? No one else leaves all the lights on."

"Are you alone?"

He chuckled. "Just me and this microbabe." He held up a bottle from a local brewery.

Eve sank back onto the couch. "Thank goodness. I fell asleep. And I was afraid I might have interrupted—"

"It's Sunday night. Restock night. Order night. Ain't-got-time-for-love night."

"I forgot."

"I can see you've had other things on your mind," he said, taking in the littered table and the open wine bottle. His gaze moved up to her face.

She didn't need a mirror to know what she looked like. She could barely open her eyes, swollen and raw from crying.

He glanced at the table. "Taking up scrapbooking?"

Eve shook her head.

He came over to sit beside her. He ignored the letters, though anybody else would have at least been tempted to take a peek.

"From my mother," she said.

"Wow. I take it you just got them tonight?"

"This afternoon."

"Zoe bring them?"

She shook her head, couldn't make herself say the truth. She sorted through the envelopes, found one of the square ones. Handed it to him. Watched as he opened it.

"'Happy first birthday,'" he read aloud.

The card had pink balloons on the front. "Open it."

She watched as he read the printed greeting, then squinted as he reached the lines her mother had written in a neat, sloping script.

He gently slid the card back into the envelope, set it on the table, then leaned back and put his arm around her shoulders.

She leaned into him. "I don't think I'll be able to forgive her."

He pulled away to look a question at her. "Jenny?"

"Hannah. She took every one my mother sent and hid them. Henry and Floret didn't even know about them. She must have waited every day at the mailbox to intercept them."

Just to prevent what? Eve's knowing that her mother had loved her even though she couldn't or wouldn't keep her? Eve had cried herself to sleep more nights than she could count.

"She thought I didn't want to know her because I never wrote back." Eve buried her face in Mike's shoulder. "I never knew."

Mike wrapped her up in his bear arms, and she felt safe. Safe to cry, to let her nose run, to not be in control.

And Mike just held her. Occasionally he'd lean forward to reach for his beer, carrying her with him, then settle back onto the couch.

After a while, Mike took her phone. Texted someone—Noelle, probably. Put it down. A responding *ping*. Mike ignored it.

"She saw me graduate, Mike. She came to see me graduate."

Chapter 8

IT WAS BARELY LIGHT when Zoe left her hotel room the next morning, her tote stuffed not with the celadon urn but with two plastic laundry bags from the hotel. She didn't think anyone would question where she was going. She doubted Mel or Noelle would be manning the desk.

The lobby was empty this early. Zoe tucked her tote under her arm and hit the streets. Her first stop was the coffee bar. A double-shot latte, and she was on her way.

She didn't follow the drive all the way to the house but cut through the woods that surrounded the property. She didn't want to run into Dulcie and have her alert the household to her presence. She just needed some time to herself to clean up the trash from the beach—and to think. Then she would go up to the house.

But first she needed to make some decisions. Alone, without everyone and their memories and advice and opinions. She just needed to hear the wind chimes in the breeze and try to recapture the magic she had felt in those few seconds, when she'd felt as if everything made sense. Before her whole world had gone haywire.

The undergrowth was thick, and she tried to move quietly as she made her way to the path that led to the beach. She was alert, waiting for the first breaths of wind, the faint tinkle of the first chime.

She'd almost reached the path when she felt it, the slight shifting in the air. She stopped to listen.

And was startled by the whack of a hammer.

She knew where it was coming from. She hurried along, the music forgotten, until she stepped off the path into the sunlight and saw David Merrick in jeans and T-shirt, hands protected by thick work gloves. He raised a heavy sledgehammer over his head, then swung it downward.

Whack. The left side of the rotten stair handrail creaked, swayed, and then a piece broke apart and dropped out of sight below the ledge. But the stairs held. He dropped the hammer to the ground and stood back, his hands fisted on his hips.

"I hope this isn't about me," she said in the sudden quiet. "Because I wouldn't think of suing."

Slowly he turned around, gave her a resigned look. "Floret and Henry are up at the house." He picked up the sledgehammer and turned away from her.

Zoe started down the path toward the beach.

"Where are you going?"

She stopped, turned back to him. "Well, I do want to see Henry and Floret, but first I want to clean up the debris on the beach."

"Why?"

"Because it's an eyesore."

He didn't react, so she slid down the boulders and jumped onto the sand. She was surprised to see even more garbage than there was the last time she was here. She set the tote down, pulled out one of the plastic bags she'd brought, and began to pick up pieces of garbage. Soggy cardboard. Two bottles of kombucha, half empty. She poured out the contents and went back for the second plastic bag. No reason not to recycle what she could.

She looked up to the ledge, where David had stopped and was watching her. "Could you wait until I get these stairs down? I don't want you to get injured by flying debris."

He was right, she knew. But she was driven to get this done.

"Thanks for the warning." She knelt down and lifted up something that looked like pillow stuffing and slid it into her bag.

"Stand back, Zoe. It's unstable."

She stopped, not because of his warning but because he had called her by name. That was a first. "I'll be careful."

He looked down at her. Zeroed in on the bag. Then he threw down the hammer and started down the path toward the beach.

Once there, he let out an exasperated sigh. "Come on. I'll take you up to Floret. She'll give you a cup of something and make you believe everything will work out fine. Then I'll come back and clean up the garbage."

He took her elbow, steered her toward the rocks, then reached down to help her up the boulders. This time, she accepted his help. When they were back on the path, he grabbed the hammer and waited for her to precede him. Soon they stepped into the sunlight.

Floret and Henry were outside, looking past David and Zoe and into the woods behind them.

"I'm going to take some stuff upstairs," David said.

Zoe, Henry, and Floret were alone.

"I WANTED to talk to you," Zoe blurted before Floret could suggest tea. There was much she wanted to know about her mother and the days she'd spent with them, but Zoe didn't feel it was fair to ask without Eve being present. And she did need to get their approval for spreading her mother's ashes.

"I came here because . . ." She started again. It was hard to say the words. "My mother . . ." *Asked me? Told me?* "Requested that . . ." She swallowed. Blew out a long stream of air.

"Take a walk with us," Henry said. He and Floret turned, and Zoe could do nothing but follow.

As soon as they stepped onto the path through the trees, the chimes began to play. Henry kept them walking while the music surrounded them, sending chills up Zoe's arms and down her back. The sound ebbed away, but before the last tinkle had faded, a new wave began, then another, until the woods rang with the sound.

Zoe knew it was a coincidence, but it was hard not to think Henry—or Floret, or both—had summoned them.

And that's when Zoe realized that they weren't on the path to Wind Chime Beach but on the fork that led past the beach. She could feel the breeze now, more steady than it had been before. Ahead of them, a keyhole of light beckoned through the trees.

Floret sighed. "Lovely, isn't it?"

They both turned to Zoe. And she knew it was time to begin the letting go. "My mother sent me here to spread her ashes."

They didn't interrupt.

"In a letter she left with her lawyer." Saying it aloud stabbed at her. It sounded so impersonal. And so like her mother.

She'd wanted Zoe to meet her other family, to be the messenger to Eve. Had she been afraid to tell her in advance? Afraid that Zoe would hate her for lying to her all these years? Was that why her mother kept her secret life a secret?

She cleared her throat. "She wanted to rest here at Wind Chime Beach. If that's okay."

"We've known this day would come," Henry said. "Hoping she would want to return to us. She won't be alone, Zoe."

"She'll join the others." Floret laid her hand on Zoe's back. It was a brief gesture, but Zoe felt a warmth spread within her.

Henry stepped beside Floret. She smiled up at him, and their love for each other was palpable, so intimate it made Zoe want to pretend she didn't see.

Floret gestured to the woods. "Many lives began here, flowered here, then left to discover other things. Now they've begun to come back—the ill at ease, the displaced, the lonely, the old. Our once-thriving commune of free love, joy, and self-discovery has become a house of memory, of refuge, of hospice." Floret walked a little away from them. Turned back. "She'll be among friends."

"Other people are buried here?"

Floret laughed. "They aren't buried. They've merely returned to the earth. They've become the earth. Supporting life. Supporting us. They celebrate us. And we celebrate them.

"Everything will work out fine," she continued. "We'll have a grand celebration for our Jenny." She darted a look at Zoe. "Unless you would rather it be private."

Zoe shook her head. "I don't know."

"There's no hurry. Take time to decide. Unless *you* have to be back somewhere."

Zoe thought about it. Shook her head. "I guess not."

"Well, then, here comes Dulcie. Let's get some lunch."

Bewildered, she let them lead her back toward the house while she fought the swell of the song "Circle of Life" in her head. But that's what it was, birth, life, death, birth, life . . .

"I'll make an omelet," she heard Floret say. "I picked some lovely mushrooms this morning."

In the circle of life.

Eve wiped sweat from her forehead. It wasn't that hot inside the basement laundry room, but her back hurt, her head hurt, and her eyes were still swollen and gritty from crying. She'd slept late at Mike's, had been tempted to spend the rest of the day there, but he worked at the local brewery on Mondays helping with their books, and she didn't want to be alone.

She tried not to think. To just concentrate on the rhythmic folding of hotel linen as the dryers thump-thumped in the background. It wasn't easy. She hadn't had to fold laundry for thirty-six rooms in a long time. She was getting soft. But two of her usual laundry ladies had had family emergencies. Another was on vacation.

Eve thought she and Mel and Noelle could handle the extra work, but it was not going well. None of them wanted to be here today. Mel was on towel duty and was going about her task as if she were the only person in the room.

Chris Bascombe stuck his head in the door. "Thought I might find you guys down here."

"Am I needed upstairs?" Eve asked. He didn't look at all like Zoe. He was blond and wiry. His personality was a lot more outgoing than Zoe's. He must take after his father, George Bascombe.

"Nope—everything's fine. Seen my sister?"

None of them had.

Noelle placed a folded sheet on the stack. "Maybe she went down to Wind Chime House."

"Probably. She's on a mission." Chris abstractedly took a towel and began folding it. "I know she's anxious to get the whole thing over with, but . . ." He placed a perfectly folded towel on the stack.

Chris looked up to see the three women watching him. "I'm an actor. It's Monday. It must be laundry day. What can I say?"

"Are you saying she didn't want to come?" Eve asked.

"What? Well, not at first." He took another towel from the pile. "I mean, it's cool she found a whole other family we didn't know she had. I say the more the merrier."

"Then what?" Mel asked.

He stopped midfold and looked at her. "Oh, it's not you. She's over the moon about having a sister and nieces. So am I. It's the other family." He frowned at them. "You know. Over the ashes."

"What ashes?" Mel asked, growing pale.

Chris shot a panicked look at Eve. "Sorry—she didn't tell you? That's how she found you. Mom designated her as the one to bring her ashes to Wind Chime Beach. None of us had ever heard of the place. That's why I came. I figured she could use the support."

"Who could use the support?" Zoe walked into the room and looked at the others, who had all stopped in a freeze-frame.

"You," said Chris. "I told them about Mom's ashes. I didn't realize they didn't know."

Zoe's eyes widened.

Eve hurried toward her. "It's okay. Just kind of a shock."

"I was going to tell you. But I thought there was so much else to say, and take in, and . . . well."

"It doesn't matter. I'm glad you brought them."

"But what are you going to do with them?" Mel asked.

Zoe leaned her elbows on the folding table. "She didn't give me specific instructions. Just to take her ashes to Wind Chime Beach. Floret and Henry want to do a big ceremony with you all there."

"Are you going to ask the bros to come?" Chris said.

"I don't know. I want them to. But first I have to tell them I'm not even their whole sister."

"Nah. You're their sister. But it may take some time for them to get used to the new development." Chris turned to the others. "Very straitlaced, our brothers. Beautiful wives. Two point nine children. McMansions on cul-de-sacs. The whole nine yards. But nice people."

"I guess I have to tell them," Zoe said. "But what if they don't want me in the family anymore? And what about Dad?" Her eyes widened. "My dad isn't even my dad. What will I say to him?"

No one spoke.

"Come on," Chris said. "Let's text them and schedule a conference call." He gently pulled her out the door. "No procrastinating."

ZOE and Chris sat on the bed in her hotel room, heads together, Zoe too upset to cry.

"Don't worry about it, Dil. They'll come around."

But he didn't sound convinced.

"It was almost like they'd been waiting for my call," she said.

"It was the fastest text to conference call I've witnessed in years," Chris agreed. He pushed off the bed and went over to the mini fridge. Took out a bottle of wine and a can of beer.

Zoe shook her head. "I think I'll be sick if I drink that."

"Because you probably haven't eaten today. Have you?"

Zoe shrugged. "I . . . don't remember."

"Well, I'm calling room service." He picked up the phone. "Then we'll go out on the town. You can sit in with the local band. I'll check out the scene. It'll be like the good old days in Manhattan."

She tried to smile. She'd loved making the rounds of the music clubs and bars with Chris. But trying to talk to Errol had been hard. Hands down the hardest phone call she'd ever made. It started out okay. They'd been concerned for her. Though no one had tried calling or texting her to see if she'd made it.

And then she hit them with the news. Her mother had sent her to Wind Chime Beach because she had another daughter there. That had been met with total silence. Then she hit them with the rest. That she was only their half sister.

"Jeez, that was awful," she said after Chris hung up the phone.

"When Errol refused to believe you were only a half sister, or when Robert screamed, 'They're after your inheritance'?"

She laughed. "I don't know how Laura puts up with him."

"He'll be calling to apologize before the night is out."

"I didn't get a chance to invite them to the ceremony."

"Plenty of time. They'll come around."

"And what about you?"

"Me?" He grinned. "I'll provide moral support and handle the guest list." He walked out to the balcony and leaned over the rail.

She followed him out.

"I mean what about your life? I love having you here, but aren't you getting antsy to get back to auditioning? Or have you decided to go to Chicago?"

He lifted his beer can. "Hey, isn't that Mel out on the lawn?"

"Yeah," Zoe said as Mel broke into a run down the path to the beach.

"Uh-oh. Trouble in Laundry City."

Zoe turned to look at him. "What should I do?"

"What you do best. Fix things."

Zoe had already started for the door. The last thing she heard before it closed behind her was Chris's voice. "Can you put a hold on that room-service order?"

Zoe found Mel sitting on the top of the jetty, her arms clasped tight around her knees, her head buried. One unhappy teenager.

Zoe took off her shoes and trudged over the sand. Climbed up the rocks and out to the place where her niece sat.

Teenagerdom was a decade behind Zoe, but she remembered wishing she could talk to someone who would just listen. Her mother had listened but never really heard. Zoe would be different with her niece. She hoped.

She sat down on the rock next to Mel. "Hey."

"Go away."

Zoe didn't move. "I know this is unsettling. At least you've always known who your family was. Imagine my surprise."

Mel's head rose a little. "You mean you really had no idea?"

"None."

"What are you going to do?"

"Spread my mom's ashes. Look for a new job. Get on with my life. Like the rest of the world."

"You make it sound easy."

"Do I? It isn't."

Mel frowned at her. "At least you know what you want to do."

"Do I? Glad I fooled somebody."

Mel turned to face her. "I wish I knew what to do. But it seems like even if you want to do something, it doesn't work out. Harmony wanted to be a teacher. Noelle wants to be a graphic artist. Harmony is always pregnant, and Noelle can't get a job."

"She will. What about you?"

"I don't know. Eli came over last night to tell me he thought he'd done well on his exam. He was excited about going away. More excited than he was about staying with me." Mel shrugged. "I just want to marry Eli and stay home and raise our children."

"That's cool. If you have enough money."

"I guess I would have to get a part-time job. Except Mom is so set about me going to college. It's just . . . everyone seems to know what they want to do, and I don't. I'm such a loser."

Zoe laughed. "Sorry—not laughing at you but at how much you sound like me."

"No, I don't. You're a successful event planner."

"I wanted to be a songwriter."

"You did? What happened?"

"I blew my audition at Juilliard, so I went into business."

"That sucks."

"It turned out that I liked my job. And now that I think about it, I could have been writing music as well. You don't need an office to do that." *You just have to have the guts.*

"I think Mom wanted to travel, but that's not a profession."

"It could be. Do you want to travel?"

"I don't think so. I like being here, where everything is . . ."

"Safe?"

Mel hesitated, bit her lip, then slowly nodded.

"Home will always be here."

Mel frowned, as if that hadn't occurred to her.

"But what about Eli? He might go and not want to come back."

"I don't know much, but I do know better than to depend on another person for my own happiness. You kind of have to find your own place, and once you've done that, other people make it better. But you have to make it for yourself first."

Zoe was tempted to say, *You'll understand when you're older.* But she was older, and she didn't have a clue.

She stood up. "Come on."

"Where to?"

"To the nude-beach side. We're going skinny-dipping." Zoe scrambled off the jetty and ran across the sand to the private beach.

"Wait, Zoe, you can't. We'll be in so much trouble."

"Try and stop me," Zoe called over her shoulder, then started pulling her T-shirt over her head.

Mel caught up to her and grabbed Zoe's shirt. Zoe spun around, and they both fell fully clothed into the surf, laughing.

In the end they didn't go skinny-dipping. Zoe hadn't really planned to. But they had a little fun before they finally staggered out of the water, holding on to each other and giggling.

Mel turned suddenly serious again. "I left Noelle to do all the laundry by herself. I gotta go."

She took off over the sand and was soon sprinting up the path.

Zoe gathered up their shoes and her cell phone and followed more slowly, texting as she went. *Forget room service. Put on your high-heeled sneakers, bro, 'cause we're going out tonight.*

Chapter 9

DAVID AND HENRY SAT stretched out on two chaises on the front lawn, drinking beer and watching the ocean sky go through its pyrotechnics of sunset. The smell of fresh-mowed grass mixed with salt air. David was half thinking about going to get his camera, but tonight there were more important things on his mind.

He glanced back to the house and Eli's window. Eli was inside studying. He'd been studying for weeks whenever he wasn't with Mel. Even more since returning from taking his exam. David didn't know what that meant. Did he think he was accepted?

"I got a gig offer today," he said into space.

Henry made a "go on" sound but kept looking at the sky.

"September through most of October."

"Where is it?"

"Patagonia."

Henry chuckled. "Had enough of civilization?"

"Not really. Well, yeah, sort of. It's a travel shoot, but there are also some interesting caves and . . . I don't know."

"What's stopping you?"

David tapped his beer bottle with one finger. He wasn't sure why he was worried about leaving. He'd done it plenty of times before. "First of all, there's Eli."

"I have no doubt he'll be accepted into the pre-semester program, and then he'll start college. Floret and I will make sure he gets settled." Henry turned his head on the chair cushion. "I'll even wear jeans and a button-down shirt." He grinned.

David grinned back and was struck with a wave of love. He'd known Henry for most of his life; he'd been like a grandfather, uncle, mentor, and friend all rolled into one. He trusted him completely, with Eli and anything else.

"I know, but I'm worried about him. He's been remote lately. I don't think he's seen Mel since he got back from the exam."

"Well, if you're worried about him, go talk to him."

David glanced back at the house. "I'm not worried. Not exactly. But he doesn't seem to want to talk to me lately."

"It's what kids do when they make a break from their parents." Henry sat up to face David. "It's best that truth come to light . . ."

"Oh, hell, don't quote Shakespeare at me." David pushed himself out of the chair. "I'm going."

Henry gave him a thumbs-up and took a swig of his beer.

DAVID didn't normally hesitate to talk to his nephew. They got along pretty well. But lately, everything around them seemed so volatile. They'd already had a couple of run-ins about Mel. David had nothing against the girl. He just didn't want them doing something stupid just to prove they were in love.

Eli's door was open. He was sitting at his desk in the dusky room, his desk lamp shining on his bent head.

He was so engrossed in whatever he was studying that he didn't hear David coming to the door. And David stood watching him, remembering. He was looking more like his father every day.

David had always looked up to his big brother. Strong, confident, adventurous. He traveled the world taking risks, reveled in it. Then one day he fell in love, settled down to have a family. Play it safe in the suburbs, he'd say ruefully. Then lost his life on the way home from the movies, some drunk driver . . . David had thought he'd never get over his grief or the panic of suddenly finding himself guardian of a ten-year-old boy.

Henry and Floret had taken them in, soothed them, kept them safe. Henry introduced the confused, angry young boy to the thing he loved most besides Floret. Science. And Eli had blossomed.

It had taken a long time for David to accept his role of caretaker of his nephew; he had no experience, no understanding. He couldn't have done it without Henry and Floret. But he had ignored his own . . . what? Personal life? This was his personal life. His private life? Photography was his private life.

He knocked on the door frame. "Busy?"

"Just studying. What's up?"

David came into the bedroom. A teenager's room. Dirty socks on the floor, a Nerf basketball hoop suctioned to the closet door. It could be a bedroom anywhere in the country.

"We didn't get a chance to talk about your day at the exam."

Eli glanced over his shoulder. "Yeah, we did. It was fine." He swiveled his chair around. "I met some cool people. The exam seemed fair. I think I did okay. We'll just have to wait and see."

So it wasn't that.

"How's Mel? I haven't seen her much lately."

Eli shrugged. "You know."

No, I don't know.

Eli turned back to his desk. It was a cue that he was finished with the conversation, but David wasn't.

"Hey, talk to me."

"About what?"

"Whatever's going on."

"I'm studying. I realized that I'm behind in several areas, so I have to bone up to not look like a total jerk when—if—I get into the program. Henry got me into the Stanford library online."

"Good thinking. Everything else okay?"

"Yeah."

"Okay. I'll yell when dinner's ready."

David got as far as the door.

"Uncle David?"

He came back into the room and sat on the bed. There was a long, drawn-out silence while he waited for the worst.

"You think Mel and I should cool it. I know you do."

"I just want you to follow your dream."

"That's such a nerdy thing to say."

"Yeah, well, that's me. The all-supreme and magnificent nerd."

Eli laughed, then his expression fell. "Mel's afraid that when we go to college we won't . . . you know. Stay together. She doesn't want to go to college. There's nothing she's excited to learn. You know? Like, she'd just be going to get a general education."

"That's how most people start."

"I guess, but it's hard for her. I think she wants me to stay here."

"Instead of going to school?"

Eli nodded.

"But you still want to go, right?"

"Yeah, but I don't want to leave her here alone."

"She's not alone, and plus, she's supposed to go to college, too."

"But she feels alone. What am I going to do?"

"You're going to catch up with your studies."

IT WAS nine o'clock the next morning when Zoe's cell phone rang. She was awake but hadn't ventured out of bed. She was pretty sure she was going to have a hangover.

She and Chris had hit several music bars the night before. She vaguely remembered sitting in with a couple of the bands. In fact, she had written down email addresses of several musicians on a napkin. She could see the napkin on the table across the room, where her phone buzzed away.

She eased back the covers. Slowly sat up. Blinked. *Hmm.* Definitely a little pounding on the left side of her head. She padded across the room and picked up the phone. *Chris.*

"Hello?"

"Oh, man, don't tell me I woke you up."

"No. But what are you doing up? You got an audition?"

"I got something better than that. A callback for our niece."

"Huh?"

"You know Noelle interviewed last week in the city? Well, they called her back this morning. They want her to come in again."

"That's great," Zoe said.

"And I thought, why don't I drive her down? I can check in with my agent, show her the sights, and drive her back. If I can borrow your car. You aren't using it, are you?"

Zoe eased herself down into the closest chair. *He's leaving?* "My car? Sure, you're welcome to take it. You're coming back?"

"Of course. We'll be back as soon as Noelle knows something."

"And if *you* get work?"

"I'm coming back for the ashes thing definitely. Anyway, you never just get a part—you know that."

She pulled herself together. "That's great about Noelle. When are you leaving?"

"Not until after breakfast, if you can get your slugabed body downstairs in the next few minutes."

"I'll hurry." She hung up, her hangover forgotten, then threw on some clothes and hurried downstairs.

FOUR hours later, Zoe, Eve, and Mel stood outside the inn saying goodbye to Chris and Noelle.

"I know you'll ace the interview," Eve said.

"Thanks," Noelle said, and gave Eve a big hug.

Chris waved when he got into the driver's side of the car. "Ready when you are," he called.

"I'm ready," Noelle said, then got in and closed the door.

"They'll be great together," Zoe said.

"Looks like it," Eve agreed. "Well, just us girls. What shall we do? Tuesday is a slow day compared to the weekend."

Zoe smiled, but she noticed that Mel didn't. "What are you up to today?" she asked her.

"I . . . I think I'll go out for a while."

"Fine. Maybe we'll all have dinner together later."

Mel hesitated. "I'll see what's going on." Her gaze slid past Zoe and Eve, and she hurried off.

"I didn't think our last summer together would be like this."

"Cutting those apron strings," Zoe said. "I'm not sure I ever did. Maybe it would have been better, but water under the bridge."

"I wish you'd tell her that."

They walked into the hotel.

"Maybe you could show me around the inn," Zoe said. "I've hardly had a chance to see any of it."

"I'd love to. I'll give you the tour. You've seen the dining room and the bar. There are also two meeting rooms on this floor and a small ballroom that we use for yoga and tai chi during the winter."

They walked down the hall and into a large room with a shining wooden floor. The ceilings were high, and French doors let in a stream of sunlight and a view of the lawn and the ocean beyond.

"Wow," Zoe said. "It seems like every room has an ocean view."

"It was a real beauty in its day. Actually, we've only restored part of it. The whole third floor is still unfinished."

"You're kidding. Why?" Zoe clamped her mouth shut. "If I get too snoopy, just tell me. I'm used to butting in and taking over. Kind of have to in my business."

"Ask anything. You're family. And I feel stupid, but what exactly is your business?"

As they toured the second floor, Zoe explained what a project manager does. "You know, setting up events for clients, arranging transpo, accommodations, food for guests, coordinating vendors, managing event teams. Stuff like that."

"It sounds mind-boggling."

"You just have to be efficient and have a thick skin."

Eve used a key to open the elevator doors on the third floor.

"Yikes, it's a little like *The Shining*," Zoe said as they stepped out into a hallway of wall sconces and faded fleur-de-lis wallpaper.

Eve laughed. "I know."

Zoe looked up and down the hall. "All guest rooms?"

"Actually, no. And if I had a bigger operation . . . well, come and see." She led Zoe to the left and opened a set of double doors.

Zoe stopped in her tracks. "Wow." She stepped onto the dusty wooden floor of a huge dining room. The old tables and chairs were still stacked along the walls. Heavy brocade drapes hung from ornate, patina-covered rods.

Eve walked across the room. She pulled open a pair of drapes, revealing the most spectacular view Zoe had ever seen.

She joined Eve at the window. "I can't believe you left this to last. It's an incredible venue."

"It is," Eve agreed. "But just a little beyond my ability. I'd need to grow the staff, and it would cost a lot. I'm not sure I could maintain everything without going corporate, which I refuse to do. The thought of taking it to the next level is just a little overwhelming."

Eve closed the drapes, and they returned to the hallway. All in all, Eve had done a wonderful job with the renovation and the ambience. And, from what she said and Zoe could see, she had made Solana a success. "You're pretty amazing," Zoe said.

"Thanks. What do you say we walk down to the beach?"

"Sounds great."

Zoe and Eve didn't talk on their way down the path. They stopped at the edge of the sand. A few guests were relaxing in chaises set up beneath brightly colored umbrellas. Ahead of them, the refreshment cabana looked more like an open-front beach house. Lively blue-and-white-striped canvas curtains were pulled back from lattice columns across the front.

The concessioner saw them coming and waved.

Eve waved back. "At ease," she called. "Just us chickens."

Zoe stared at her. "Mom used to say that. That's just weird."

"Not really," Eve said. "Floret used to say it all the time. We probably picked it up from her. Come on." Eve struck off across the sand in the direction of Wind Chime House.

Zoe hurried after her. "Doesn't Floret say it anymore?"

Eve stopped. "No . . . she doesn't. At least . . ."

They both looked at the black rocks of the jetty that tumbled across the width of the beach like a poorly healed scar.

A sign posted where the rocks met the lawn read PRIVATE. KEEP OUT. And the image of Mel sitting on the jetty rose in Zoe's mind. Half in one world, half in the other, and not belonging to either.

"I hate that it's cut the beach in two," Eve said.

"Then why does it? Does anybody on their side go down there?"

"Not really. It was Hannah's doing. I was thinking about expanding the inn and asked Henry and Floret if they'd be willing to rent me their portion of the beach, with the stipulation they could use it, just not nude. After all, they have Old Beach, which I guess they used to call Wind Chime Beach. I offered decent money, and all was on its way, until Hannah decided we should buy the beach and the land behind it outright, for expansion. Then things fell apart. Hannah threatened, they withdrew their acceptance of my offer, and the next day, trucks arrived to build the jetty. Floret and Henry were forced to put up the sign to protect themselves legally. Actually, it was David who put up the sign."

They began walking toward the jetty.

"Do you ever talk to David about Mel and Eli?" Zoe asked.

Eve shrugged. "David doesn't share his thoughts too much. I don't think he really gets close to people beyond Floret and Henry. He wants Eli to go to school, feels responsible for his future.

"He was only twenty-seven when he was called home to raise his nephew. I remember that day . . . he was devastated over his brother's death—and he didn't know anything about children.

"He's worried about Eli giving up too soon. I worry the same for Mel. I just hope we're not putting too much pressure on them."

Zoe thought it was very likely they were.

Eve stood across from Zoe, watching her, noticing how the vivacious young woman who had arrived at the inn less than a week ago was looking tired. Was she thinking about how soon she could leave? Eve wanted to ask but was afraid of the answer.

It was odd. She'd never lacked for the company of sisters and brothers when they lived at the commune. But now that she had a sister of her own, she was loath to let her go.

"I meant to tell you . . . but so much has been happening. You know how Jenny said she wrote me letters? I went to my grandmother's Sunday. Jeez, has it only been two days?"

"I know. It seems like decades."

"I asked her about the letters. What had happened to them." Eve still couldn't wrap her mind around Hannah's reaction. "She'd kept them all these years, tied up like love letters. She didn't bother to deny it. Just said she'd known this day would come and pointed to a drawer in the credenza. And there they were."

"I'm glad Hannah, for whatever reason, kept them," Zoe said.

"You can read them."

"Someday, if you want. But not now. For now, they're yours, just yours. Something that belongs only to you."

"Thanks," Eve said.

THE room was dark when Zoe awoke the next morning. She knew it was morning because there was a sliver of light dancing along the wall next to the blackout curtains. Another sunny day.

She got out of bed, stumbled over to the desk. Powered up the phone. Messages and calls pinged on the screen. She scrolled through a list of calls—Errol, Errol, Robert, Chris, Errol—which she ignored. Texts—Errol, Chris.

She wanted coffee, but she needed to deal with Errol first. And where was Robert in all this? He, of course, would defer to Errol; they all did. When their father had packed his suitcase and walked out the door, Errol had become head of the family.

She pressed CALL.

Errol picked up immediately. "Why didn't you call me?"

"I went to bed early." *And I'm tired, and I couldn't face any more incriminations.*

"Are you still in whatever that town is? Have you done it yet?"

"I—no. Not yet."

"Well, don't."

"I have to. It was her last wish."

"I don't understand you. To throw us over for people who made her an outcast. She was obviously not in her right mind."

"Errol, don't. You're not helping."

"Don't do a thing. I'm getting a court order to stop you."

A court order? Is he nuts? "You can't do that. These are her final wishes. She wrote them down long before she died."

"It's no longer up to her. Or you. You're not even a Bascombe."

His words knocked the breath out of her lungs.

"Do you hear me?"

"Yes. Errol. Please don't do this. It's hard enough losing her."

"Too late. You'll be hearing from my lawyer. Until then, don't do anything with those ashes. You'll be in contempt if you do."

"Errol! No!"

He ended the call. She held the phone while her stomach heaved and a searing anger passed through her. *You're not even a Bascombe.* Maybe she wasn't a part of their family anymore. But she was still her mother's daughter.

And what was "contempt," anyway? Could they put her in jail if she spread the ashes? Would they go through a lengthy court battle over who had custody of their mother's remains?

The whole thing was ludicrous. She stood, then dressed in jeans, a T-shirt, and sneakers. Not exactly funeral clothes, but she still wasn't sure what she planned to do. And if she had to run for her life on the way, she'd be prepared.

Besides, she couldn't sit here waiting for some police officer to come and wrest the urn from her hands. Jenny Bascombe would be mortified, though Jenny Campbell, rock-star paramour, might be willing to fight for her right to be buried where she chose.

Where did Zoe's duty lie? *Henry and Floret.* She grabbed the tote and slid the urn inside. She'd come back later for the rest of her things.

Eve poured herself a cup of coffee and wandered into the living room. It seemed too quiet. Mel was at Wind Chime with Eli. Noelle was in New York with Chris Bascombe. She wanted to call Zoe and see if she wanted to come over for coffee. But she didn't want to wake her.

Her phone rang.

Noelle. Eve mentally crossed her fingers. *Please be good news,* she thought, while suddenly wanting to keep her close.

"Mom!"

Good news. You could always tell with Noelle.

"I got the job! They have this new project that sounds perfect, but they want me to start in two weeks. I told them I had to clear it with my current employer."

"Wow. That soon? What current employer?"

"You, Mom. I don't want to leave you in the lurch."

"Honey, this is just what you wanted. Go for it. But you'll have to find a place to live, pack your stuff."

"Mom, chill. I'll figure it out. And Chris said he will help."

"That's great, honey. When are you coming home? We'll have a celebratory dinner."

"Tomorrow night. It'll be a quick turnaround."

She already sounded like a New Yorker.

"And maybe . . . should we invite Granddad? He hasn't really met Zoe, officially."

No, thought Eve, he hadn't, but he'd made his feelings clear. "It might be a little too early for him. But we'll see."

"Oh, and tell Zoe to call Chris. He's been trying to call her. I guess their brothers are being weird about the whole burial thing."

"Oh, dear. I'll tell her."

"Gotta run."

"Congratulations. I'm so happy for you. Love you."

"Thanks. Love you, too."

Eve sipped her coffee and walked back into the kitchen. Her phone rang. Noelle again?

"Eve, this is David. Kelly's Diner has just been shut down by the health department. This is Hannah's doing. Call her off before this gets really nasty. There are a lot of pissed-off people outside. I think they've had enough of Hannah Gordon."

Eve's mouth went dry. "I'm on my way."

Chapter 10

ZOE HAD BARELY LEFT the hotel when she saw people hurrying down the sidewalk, all heading in the same direction. Something was going on: maybe one of the locals had a new truck.

A crowd was gathered. People spilled into the street, and as more people joined them, Zoe got a terrible sinking feeling. They were surrounding the doorway to Kelly's Diner.

Please let it be a false fire alarm . . .

She crossed the street and saw an old guy in a T-shirt with a DINKINS' HARDWARE logo stretched over his belly standing on the fringes of the group.

Zoe hurried toward him. "What happened?"

"The health department just closed down Kelly's. I've been eating there for twenty years and never had a bout of indigestion."

"Damn straight," agreed a man next to him. Zoe pushed to the front of the crowd.

Jim Kelly stood at the door of the diner arguing with two men, both in khaki slacks, ties, and short-sleeved shirts. Summer official wear. "You can't do this!" Jim yelled. "You can't just walk into a place and close it down. You didn't even identify yourselves."

The two men ignored his protestations while one of them posted a notice on the window and the other put a lockbox on the door.

"I need to get back in there. The grill is still on. You wanna burn down the town?"

A woman—his wife, Zoe guessed—clung to his arm, trying to restrain him. "Stop, Jim. You can't talk sense into them. You know who's behind this."

Zoe was pretty sure she did, too.

"You haven't heard the last from me," Jim yelled as the two men pushed their way through the crowd, which was getting louder.

"Where are we supposed to eat?"

"How long is this going to last?"

"You can't lock him out of his own establishment."

The two men looked straight ahead and kept walking across the street to a white Chevy with COUNTY HEALTH DEPARTMENT imprinted on the door.

"We know who put you up to this! Hannah Gordon!" yelled the man in the hardware T-shirt.

"Yeah!" cried several other people. "And we've had enough."

The two men got in their car and drove away.

Kelly stood at his front door, his wife clinging to him. The jovial, friendly man who'd greeted Zoe her first day in town was slumped forward, beaten and dejected.

David Merrick appeared out of the crowd and took Jim Kelly's elbow. "Come on, Jim. Floret and Henry will meet you back at Wind Chime."

Jim tried to pull away. "It's all we got. This and the cottage. What will we do? She won't be satisfied until she's ruined us."

His wife burst into tears. David started to lead the Kellys away.

The crowd had broken into pockets, and now they began to disperse, giving one man who stood off to the side a wide berth.

Lee Gordon. Their eyes met, and he turned away; he was leaving. But not before she had her say. Gripping the tote, she stepped in front of him, barring his way.

He stepped to the side; she stepped with him. He moved the other way; she did, too. It was like a bizarre dance.

Finally, he stopped. But he looked over her head, gazing down the street as if she wasn't there.

"I know what you and your mother are doing. And I know why. I don't care for myself. But you're wrecking your family and these good people for no reason. Stop it. I'm leaving. You can go back to your hate and your greed and all the unhappiness you people spread wherever you go. I'd like to say it was nice meeting my father. But it wasn't. Go make yourself miserable. I don't care. But leave the Kellys and Floret and Henry alone."

She spun around and hurried down the street. She never wanted to see him again. She had one thing to do, and then she would go.

She reached the drive to Wind Chime and saw Floret and Henry hurrying toward the Kellys. She stepped into the shadows of a tree, held still, hoping they wouldn't see her. Hoping that Dulcie had stayed back at the house. Hoping until her chest ached.

Once they'd gone into the house, she crossed the drive and cut through the woods to the glen.

The glen was dark, as if the trees had closed over themselves, intentionally blocking the sun. Not the faintest breeze disturbed their branches. Not one faint tinkle of a wind chime. They weren't singing today. Not for her or Jenny Bascombe. Fine. She never wanted to hear another wind chime as long as she lived.

She lifted the urn out of the tote, let the bag drop to the ground.

The urn felt cool in her hands. Cool and dead. She gulped back the sob that had found its way up her throat.

"I'm doing this because you asked me to. I hope you're happy. The feud that started with you is tearing this town apart, all because you wanted to come back. So you're here. Hope you enjoy your life in eternity." She twisted the top to the urn. It didn't budge.

She dug her fingernail along the rim and broke the seal. Yanked off the top of the urn. Dropped the top on the ground. She wouldn't be saying any inspiring words at this ceremony.

"This is what you wanted. This is what you get. Alone with the ashes of strangers."

The tears dropped off her chin. "You left Lee and Eve and lived a lie your whole life. Then sprang the truth on your unsuspecting family after you were gone. Did you ever wonder how we would feel?" Her voice cracked; her throat was on fire, and she realized she was screaming at someone who wasn't there.

She turned the urn over. Nothing happened. She shook it and stared incredulously. The ashes were sealed in a plastic bag.

She dug her fingernails into the plastic. It stretched but refused to break. Why couldn't she get the thing open? It was the most ludicrous thing in the world. She raised the urn over her head.

It was snatched from her hands.

"Not in anger."

The voice was low, gravelly, not Henry's.

She turned. And stared up at the stern face of her father.

"Give that back. This is none of your business." She grabbed for the urn, but he held it out of reach.

"Don't send her into the afterlife in anger."

"Why do you care? And where do you get off lecturing me about anger? You're the most bitter man I've ever met. Give me the urn."

"You're right. I've lived most of my life in anger. Once anger gets you, it won't let go. You think you've bested it, then it rears its ugly head when you least expect it."

Her arms dropped to her sides. "Like the night you saw me in the doorway of the bar."

"Yeah, like that."

"Thanks for sharing." Zoe wiped her face with both hands.

"I was angry at her, not you."

"It doesn't matter. After seeing you and Hannah in action, I don't want anything to do with you."

Lee swayed slightly.

Zoe fought the reflexive stretch of her hand. Snatched it back.

"What about Eve?" he asked, looking around as if he was going to sit down. "It will break her heart if you leave so soon."

"She managed her whole life without me, she'll manage now."

"You don't mean that."

"Don't presume to know what I mean or not. Give me the urn."

He turned from her, searched the ground, then carried the urn and top over to a fallen tree, motioned to it.

"Sit down."

Zoe shook her head.

"Please."

"It's because that girl came here. Isn't it?" Jim Kelly said. "The reason Hannah's doing this now. There are rumors all over town that she's Lee's daughter."

David looked at Floret and Henry, who sat on either side of Jim like a pair of benevolent guardian figures.

Floret took his hand gently in hers.

His wife, Sheila, turned to David. "Isn't there anything you can do?" She cast a look toward her husband, then lowered her voice. "It will kill him to lose the diner. And the house. We'll lose it, too."

"Don't you have some . . . I don't know . . . savings?"

Jim shook his head. "We lost a bundle in the market, and I've never been able to get ahead since."

"They can't just close you down." David frowned. "What were the violations?"

"Damned if I know. Everything was the same as it ever was. They never complained before. They just came in, posted a bunch of gobbledygook on the door, and closed us down."

"They can't do that unless it's life-threatening. They have to give you time to fix the offenses."

"It's Hannah's doing, I tell you. She's forcing us out of our house and business."

"Where will we go?" Sheila said.

"You'll not go anywhere," Henry said. "Sell her the right-of-way. We can keep the station wagon somewhere else or David can sell it. We can walk when we need to get to town."

"It's a little late for compromise," David said. "I think the old broad has gone over the brink."

"What did any of us ever do to her?" asked Sheila.

Three pairs of eyes turned toward Floret and Henry.

"We don't know," said Henry. "We've never known. One day she came home from one of her real estate conferences, said, 'I know what you're up to,' told Eve to pack, and they moved out that afternoon."

"We were never up to anything," Floret said. "We've asked, guessed, racked our brains to no avail. We still haven't learned why she was so upset with us. I don't even think she remembers."

Henry sighed. "Perhaps . . . it's time for us to go," he said.

Both the Kellys and David stared in disbelief.

"No," David said. It was a pure knee-jerk reaction on his part. "Sorry, Jim, Sheila, but that's not an option."

"No, of course not," said Jim.

"It will not end until the source of her pain is removed," Henry said. "And we must be that source."

David stood. "What does that mean? If you leave, she'll just find another victim. Some people are like that. Besides, maybe it isn't about Zoe Bascombe at all. She's also angry about her great-granddaughter Mel seeing my nephew."

"That's crazy," Sheila said. "Eli's a lovely young man. They're just children. They shouldn't be dragged into this."

"No, they shouldn't." Henry stood. So did Floret. "I believe I may be able to end this once and for all."

"It's time," Floret agreed.

Jim pushed to his feet. "You're not going to sell because of us. I'd never be able to show my face in town again."

"Not to Hannah, no. But I have an idea." He walked calmly toward the door.

Floret cast her calming smile over the other three.

David bolted from his chair. "Wait—what's he going to do?"

Floret turned her smile to him. "I have no idea. But all will be fine." And she followed Henry out.

KEEPING her eyes on the urn, Zoe walked over to the log, sat down beside her father, and turned so she could see his face, even though he was looking down at the urn he held in both hands.

The air was so still that Zoe began to wonder if the chimes had been a dream. She was tempted to look into the trees, catch sight of them, but she didn't take her eyes off her father.

She waited. She wanted to leave. But he had the ashes.

"Why didn't you follow your music?"

Zoe shot him a glance. "I don't know what you mean."

"You were going to be a musician."

"How do you know?"

"Your brother told me."

"Did he tell you I blew my Juilliard audition?"

"Juilliard isn't the only place to learn music; you gave up."

Of all the things they could be talking about, this was the last she expected. "I didn't give up. It was a deal I made with myself. If I failed, I would study something useful."

Lee carefully placed the urn beside him. The side farthest from her, Zoe noted. "Music *is* useful. You got shouted down by your family, just like your mother did."

"No, I didn't." She could have stood up to her family—she could have, but she didn't. "You don't know what I'm like. You don't even know what my mother was like."

"I know she gave in to her parents. She didn't give us a chance."

"Maybe. But my mother loved order above everything. Do you really think she could have been happy sharing the life you led?"

"Why not? You only know her after the spirit was taken out of her. She wasn't like that before."

For the first time, Zoe felt a pang of sympathy for this man.

"Did you go after her?"

"I was on tour. Then it was too late. Her parents wouldn't let me see her. When Hannah told me about the baby, I couldn't believe it. At least they let her bring the baby home."

He hadn't known about Eve before Jenny left? Maybe Lee Gordon deserved a little more understanding than she'd thought. But she wasn't ready to let him off the hook yet.

"So you blamed her for your unhappiness and let that wreck your life. Everyone says you succumbed to drugs and alcohol."

He looked out into the distance, through the keyhole of trees to the sea. They were perfectly positioned, as if the log had been placed there so people could admire the view. Maybe it had been.

"At least she knew where Eve was. I never knew about you."

"And if you had?"

"I would have told her to send you to me."

"What? You don't even like me."

"I would have raised you right. With music."

"Oh, give me a break. You had Eve, and she hasn't mentioned music once since I came."

"Music isn't in Eve's soul. That's okay. Something else is. The inn, the spa—she's a nurturer. But you . . . music is in your soul."

"You don't know me."

"I heard your song."

Zoe looked away. Afraid of the burning in her throat, the feel of tears welling up in her eyes.

She found herself drawn to this old, gaunt, ponytailed rock-and-roller. She had to pull back; to care about him would be a betrayal of the woman who had nurtured her for her entire life.

The urn appeared below her downcast eyes. The smooth celadon cradled in long, leathery fingers.

"Take her."

Zoe took the urn. Watched as Lee Gordon pushed himself slowly up from the log and walked into the woods.

Zoe sat in the quiet, listening for footsteps, but there was nothing. Why had he just left like that? *Take her?* Take her where?

She wanted to run after him. Say, *Not so fast. You can't just unload on me and leave.* But it was just what he'd done.

She felt the breeze before she heard the first tinkle of sound.

This time she didn't welcome it. It sounded like it was mocking her as it echoed through the trees. She stood, snatched up the tote, returned the urn inside, and got out.

MEL watched as Eli nervously tore open the envelope from the university. She kind of felt like she was going to throw up. Because she was sure it was his acceptance to his big pre-semester program.

"Yes!" he said, and pumped the letter in the air.

She smiled. It wasn't a real smile. But it was the best she could do. "That's great. Congratulations."

He picked her up and twirled her around. "I made it." He set her down and wrapped his arms around her. She clung to him.

"Mel, be happy for me."

"I am. When do you leave?"

He let go of her abruptly. "In three weeks. But we'll see each other all the time. I'll only be in Boston. It's not so far away. Can't you be a little happy for me?"

"I said I am. I think it's great."

"I'll come home every weekend. Well, not at first, but once regular term begins."

"You're already talking like a college student."

Eli's face fell. "Please be happy for me, Mel."

She wanted him. To stay. Here. She'd been thinking of nothing else for the past few months. Eli had a plan. All her friends had plans. She didn't have a clue. What was wrong with her?

"I am happy for you. I really am." She had to turn away. She looked out the window to keep from crying. Saw Zoe Bascombe running down the drive.

Why was she running like somebody was chasing her? Mel peered into the woods but didn't see anything.

Eli came up behind her and put his arms around her, nestling his chin into her shoulder. "I love you, Mel."

"I love you, too."

"But I don't want to get married. Not yet. I want to be a scientist. If we're meant to be together, a few years won't matter."

"They matter to—" Mel sucked in her breath. Her grandfather

stepped out of the trees, looked toward the house. Mel pulled back from the window, pushing Eli backward.

"Mel, don't."

Mel peeked around the window frame. He had turned from the house. He was going down the drive after Zoe.

"I have to go."

"Mel. Don't be like that. It's for the best. You know it is."

"It's not that. Something else." She rushed out the door and ran outside, letting the door slam behind her. She didn't know what was going on, but she had to stop him from doing something awful.

Zoe wasn't sure what she planned to do. She'd meant to go straight to her room, but when she reached the Solana lobby, she changed her mind. Instead of going down the hall to the elevator, she turned right, stopped at the closed doors of the bar.

It was early still, and the bar wouldn't be open for several hours. The door was probably locked. She tried it anyway. It opened; she slipped inside.

The room was dark. The rectangle of sunlight framed by the French doors cast everything else into shadow. Everything but the edge of the bandstand.

She didn't know why she'd come. She was on autopilot; something beyond her moved her closer until she was standing in the sun, staring at the shining ebony wood of the piano.

She stepped onto the bandstand, placed the tote carefully on the floor. Pulled the piano bench out and sat down.

Lifted the fallboard. The sun cast a swath of light across the keyboard, and she sat looking at the pattern of light and dark.

There had been a time in her life—most of her life—when she would rush home from school, wash her hands, and sit down at the piano. She dutifully practiced her scales, her études, learned her first Scarlatti, then Beethoven and Mozart, but it was her free time she cherished most. When tunes came into her head, then to her fingers—sometimes words, sometimes just a harmony.

She thought about what Lee Gordon had said in the glen. Had

she given up too easily? What did that say about her? It seemed the decisions were all black and white, like the unplayed keys of the piano. Until they were joined in music.

Zoe saw it now. The reason for her mother's award-winning flowers. It was the color—the underlying harmony—she was missing in her life.

Jenny's life was ordered by black and white, down to whether pearls or gold looked better with whatever outfit she wore on a particular night. Pearls with the black de la Renta cocktail dress and the gold mesh chain with the blue Anne Klein. Never once did the pearls make their way to the blue dress or the gold to the black.

Zoe had left that painstakingly precise family and fallen into this messy, angsty alter family. They were complicated and unreliable; they caused too much heartache, sometimes catching onlookers like the Kellys in the crossfire. She'd left a life where she had a place, even if it wasn't the place she had chosen, and now she was afraid she couldn't go back—if she even wanted to go back.

She certainly couldn't stay here. As much as she wanted to get to know her family, it was a relationship that was rife with emotional land mines. She didn't want to live that way twenty-four/seven.

But when she left, she'd take one thing with her. She wouldn't forsake it again.

She lowered her right hand, fingers curved; her index finger gently touched the keys, and a deep current surged through her, filling every empty place inside her. She lifted her wrist, lowered another finger to the keys, the faint hint of a sound, the left hand quietly joining the first, the individual notes moving closer and closer until they tumbled together. Separating, interweaving, running along the scale, then exploding in pure little bits of sound.

The song of the chimes she had been carrying in her head. Now it was all around her in the air, and she relished it, lost herself in it, and she played, alone with her music. Where she belonged.

"What are you doing?" Mel whispered, coming up behind her grandfather.

He was standing at the doorway to the Solana bar. The double doors were ajar. The bar should be closed at this time of day. She didn't see Zoe anywhere. She hoped he wasn't after the bourbon.

He glanced back at her. "Shhh. Listen." He motioned her to stand beside him.

She did, straining her ears to hear what he was talking about. Then she heard it. Someone was playing the piano.

Not their house piano player; maybe one of the guests. She started to tell him to ask them to leave, but she saw his face. It had a strange expression. She couldn't tell if he was mad or sad or what. His mouth was slightly open, and his eyes seemed too bright.

She started to open the door. He grabbed her arm and held her back. "Just listen."

She listened, watching his face, feeling the energy in him. So they stood there, grandfather, granddaughter, one rapt, the other wondering what was going on and whether she should go find her mom before he did something crazy.

Eve knew things had gotten out of hand. She'd let Hannah run her life all these years, but whatever was driving Hannah, it was killing her family and turning the town into an angry mob.

She'd missed the confrontation with the health department, but she wondered if Hannah had finally gone too far by closing down Kelly's. She'd overheard Ralph Perkins, who owned the three laundromats in town, telling a group of store owners that it was time someone did something about Hannah. He had breakfast at Kelly's every day. And he was not happy about this turn of events.

Eve couldn't help worrying. Would the anger spill over to her own family? The inn? It was not something she wanted to test.

But could she turn on her grandmother, who had given her a good life and a start in business? And what about her own family? They needed a secure future.

Eve wandered around the empty cottage. Mel would be gone soon. The last of her three girls to leave the nest. She was resisting, but Eve couldn't let her stay. There was more in the world for her daughters than Eve had managed to find for herself, and she was determined that they would at least get a taste of another life.

Not that her life had been bad. She loved the inn—at least she'd learned to love the inn. And she'd grown to love Walter. A foolish teenage mistake could have ended much worse. He stuck by her, even though it was hard being under Hannah's thumb and not able to support his family the way Hannah constantly reminded them he should. So he took off to the Alaskan oil fields. The money was good; he sent it home every month, but he rarely returned. They got used to living without him. Then one day, Eve received a phone call saying he had died on the job, and that was that.

Would she have been happier if she had gone to college, traveled the world like she'd dreamed of? Maybe not. Especially knowing now what joy her girls would bring her. Maybe Mel wouldn't be happier either. But at least she would have the chance to find out.

And now Noelle had a job in New York City.

And Eve had a celebratory dinner to prepare. She walked over to the bookshelf and reached for her favorite cookbook.

She'd just opened it when there was a knock at the kitchen door. She went to answer it.

Henry Gladstone stood in the doorway. "Let's take a walk."

Chapter 11

ZOE WAS STILL PLAYING when the lights to the bar suddenly popped on and Mike walked through the door.

She stood and hastily covered the keys.

"Hello. I thought I heard music."

"Sorry. The door was open, and I—I shouldn't have come in."

"Don't apologize. It sounded nice. And after all, you're one of the family."

"I guess everybody knows."

"Is it supposed to be a secret? I hope you're not upset."

"No. I've always wanted a sister."

"Come over here. You like white wine, right?"

She nodded.

He reached under the counter and took out a bottle of Chardonnay. He poured a glass for Zoe.

"I keep this for Eve. The house wine is good, but this . . ."

He kissed his fingers, a gesture so incongruous to his burliness that Zoe laughed.

"That's better," he said. "Have you seen Eve lately?"

"No. I saw her this morning. Kelly's got closed down. She was there, but I didn't get to talk to her."

"I'm thinking this time Hannah may have overplayed her hand."

"What do you mean?" Zoe asked. She took a sip of wine. "Oh, that is good."

"Stick around, kid. You'll get an education in the fine wines of New England."

"So how did Hannah overplay her hand?"

"She's been jerking this town around ever since I can remember, but you don't get between folks and their favorite diner. They're already planning a pushback. I wouldn't want to be Hannah if they follow up on the talk I was hearing this morning."

"They won't hurt her, will they?"

"Just where it hurts her most—in her purse and her ego."

He took out a white cloth and wiped the scrupulously clean bar. Zoe watched him while she sipped the delicate, crisp wine. She liked it here. She'd really like it here if things would just calm down. The inn's guests went back to their homes refreshed and revitalized. But Zoe was wound as tight as an E string.

"There's the boss lady," Mike said, looking past Zoe.

Eve came in and sat down next to Zoe. Mike poured her a glass of wine.

"The oddest thing just happened."

Mike handed her the glass, and he and Zoe gave her their undivided attention.

"Henry just offered to sell me Wind Chime—house, grounds, beach, everything."

Her announcement was met with a minute of total silence. She was pretty gobsmacked herself. Henry and Floret were willing to give up their lifelong home to get the Kellys out of Hannah's sights. It was more than she could bear.

"You can't," Zoe said, at the same time Mike said, "It's worth a fortune. Can you afford it?"

"As it turns out, I could. He was offering it for a song, the dear man. He hoped to save the Kellys from losing everything. He didn't see any other way. And, quite frankly, I don't either."

"So he's giving in to Hannah?" asked Zoe.

"Or making it so that Eve has to deal with her," Mike said. "Selling to you is not going to solve the problem. It will just roll over the problem to you."

"Would it? With Floret and Henry gone, what more could she want?"

"Gone?" Zoe blurted. "But where would they go?"

"Henry suggested one of the old cottages on the old road."

Mike snorted. "Where Lee lives? They're barely standing."

"I know. And there were certain caveats."

"For instance?" Mike asked.

"Mainly that I'd keep the glen as a memorial garden and let others continue to be buried there."

Mike put his hand over hers. "Is this what you really want?"

"No, it's not what I want. It's a lot of land, but I'm not sure I want to expand. Ever. Besides, I'm full to the gills. We're already booked solid into the New Year. Totally unfeasible."

"What did you tell him?"

"I turned him down, of course."

"So the Kellys are still in danger of losing everything," Zoe said.

"Maybe not," Mike said.

Eve and Zoe both looked at him.

Mike shrugged. "Evidently, after the closure this morning, there was an impromptu meeting at the lodge house. Some of the local businessmen—and women—have called for a general boycotting of your grandmother. Mr. Paxton at the market already canceled her account and refused to deliver groceries."

"No. Where did you hear this?" Eve asked.

Mike laughed. "I'm a bartender. Actually, I was in the barbershop. The only place you hear more gossip than behind the bar. If everyone sticks to their guns, the cleaners, the landscapers, and all the other services she uses will no longer have her as a client."

"She can't say she hasn't been asking for it," Eve said.

Zoe put down her glass. "Do you think they'll all really stand together?"

"Yeah, I think they will," Mike said.

THE bar began to fill up, and Zoe and Eve returned to Eve's cottage to make plans for Noelle's celebration dinner.

"I guess we should invite my—our—father. If that's okay," Eve said as they pored over recipes. "He probably won't come."

"It's okay. I guess. Actually, we kind of talked this morning. I'm not sure how it went."

"You met him? How did this happen?"

"It wasn't exactly planned. I sort of told him to call Hannah off. I'm afraid I wasn't very nice."

Eve sat down at the table. "You want to share?"

Zoe started with the call from Errol and his threats to sue. "Then I was going to dump the ashes and go back to Long Island. But the things were enclosed in indestructible plastic, so while I was fighting to get them open, Lee sneaks up on me and grabs them out of my hands. He told me I couldn't scatter her ashes in anger, then gave me a lecture on my life. Then he got up and left without a word. I waited a few minutes and came back here."

"That's what he does when he has to think about stuff. He just leaves. Then he'll come back and give you his reaction. That's when the fun begins."

"Oh, goody. I can hardly wait."

CHRIS and Noelle rolled into the inn the next afternoon, loaded down with Noelle's suitcase and several large shopping bags.

"Presents and some updated wardrobe for me," Noelle announced, dropping everything on the cottage couch and giving Eve a big hug. "I've got a job." She hugged Zoe. "I've got a job." She danced around the room singing, "I've got a job. I've got a job."

"She has a job," Chris said drily. "In case you're wondering."

"How about you?" Zoe asked.

"Nothing. The only thing on my dance card at the moment is brokering the 'what to do with the ashes' deal."

"I thought the bros might have called you."

"Not to worry. After Errol's first call, I called back and got the lovely Allison on the phone. She's tired of the whole rigmarole— her word, not mine. Errol is putty in her hands. She promised to dissuade him and Robert from suing. So I don't think we'll be visiting you in the slammer quite yet. You still have the ashes?"

"Yep," Zoe said, suddenly glad that Lee had stopped her.

Noelle took a deep breath. "What's that divine smell?"

"Your favorite," Eve said. "Boeuf bourguignon. The kitchen is sending over lobster patties. And I have asparagus and homemade hollandaise. And pineapple upside-down cake for dessert."

"I won't be able to fit into my new clothes."

"It may just be us," Eve said apologetically. "I asked your grandfather. And I left a message for Hannah . . ."

"They're both being buttheads. It's okay. We'll have a feast."

MEL and Eli arrived just as Zoe and Noelle finished setting the table. Mel was wearing a bright red baseball cap with the university's logo across the front.

Noelle gave Mel a hug. "Like the cap," she said.

"It's Eli's. He's letting me break it in."

"Congratulations on the new job," Eli said. He held out a bouquet of flowers. "Floret sent them."

Noelle took them. "Thanks. I'll just go put them in a vase. Park it with Chris. You've met, right?"

"Yo," said Eli.

"Yo-ho," said Chris. "Try one of these cheese puffs."

Eli laughed and sat down on the couch.

Eve was serving the main course when there was a knock at the front door. A moment passed when they all looked at each other, then Eve went to answer it. "I'll just get some more plates," Noelle said, then slipped into the kitchen.

Eve opened the door, and Lee Gordon stepped into the room. "Dad. Glad you could make it. We're just getting started."

Lee nodded toward the people at the table.

Chris popped out of his chair. "Sit here. I'll get another chair."

Zoe watched her father walk across the floor. He was freshly shaved; his hair was pulled back in his usual ponytail, but he was wearing black jeans and a button-down shirt. He was kind of handsome, something Zoe hadn't noticed in their few brief encounters.

He nodded to Chris and sat down without looking at the others.

Chris returned with the extra chair, and the unease was covered over by the passing of dishes, the pouring of wine. Eve raised her glass. "To Noelle's new job and a bright future."

They all drank, then dug into their meals.

Conversation gradually began once the initial bites and compliments subsided. It reminded Zoe of the scene where Scrooge comes to dine with his nephew. She hoped their dinner tonight would have as happy an outcome.

After dessert, Chris and Zoe cleared the table, and Eve made coffee. When they returned from the kitchen, Mel and Eli were getting ready to leave.

"Sorry to eat and run, but I have studying to do," Eli said.

"So glad you came," Eve said and walked them to the door.

"I'm just going to walk him home," Mel said.

Zoe turned and caught Lee watching her. She smiled tentatively, but when Eve came back in, he stood and took her aside.

She looked startled, then nodded and took him into her bedroom. A few minutes later she came out alone.

"He apologizes, but he wants to read Jenny's letters." Eve's mouth worked. She looked at Zoe.

Suddenly, it was all happening fast, maybe too fast. Noelle's job; Lee making an overture to both daughters. Now if Zoe could just resolve the problem of her mother's ashes. She immediately felt contrite. It wasn't a problem. It was an honor that her mother chose her to send her on her final journey.

And she realized with a jolt of blinding clarity that she wanted her brothers to join her for the ceremony. Jenny should get her wish, but her family should be there to send her off.

"We'll leave you two alone," Zoe said. "Call if you need us."

"Where's Noelle?" Chris asked, looking around. "I'll tell her to meet us in the bar downstairs." He pulled out his phone to text her.

Noelle stepped out of the kitchen. "What's up?"

"We're going out," Chris said, and trundled both her and Zoe toward the door.

Eve watched them go. When the door closed behind them, she tiptoed over to the hallway and listened for any sound coming from her bedroom. Nothing. The only thing she could hear was the hum of the dishwasher.

She went into the kitchen, poured herself half a glass of wine, then went back into the living room to wait. She began to wonder if he was ever coming out. She imagined dozens of things as time dragged by: that he'd managed to sneak out of the cottage while she'd been in the kitchen. Or climbed out the window, too angry—too sad, too humiliated—to face her.

The last thought had her up and knocking on her bedroom door. When he didn't answer, she turned the knob and peeked inside.

He was sitting on the bed, her mother's cards and letters spread out across the coverlet. His head was bent, and she saw that the hair on the top of his head had begun to thin. It was a heart-melting realization. Her father was getting older. They'd wasted too many years caught in a web of regret and blame.

Eve stepped inside and closed the door.

He looked up, and she realized that his cheeks were wet with tears. "I'm sorry," he said.

She rushed to the bed and sat down beside him, wrapped her arms around him. "I'm sorry, too."

"You? You have nothing to be sorry about."

"I do. Don't be sad. I shouldn't have told you about them." She reached for them, meaning to put them away, but he stopped her.

He picked up a card with pink and green balloons on the front: HAPPY BIRTHDAY, SIX-YEAR-OLD!

"Pink and green were your favorite colors. Every cake had pink icing with pink roses and big green leaves."

"I always thought that was Floret and Granna's doing."

"They made the cakes. But she knew. She was your mother."

Eve wasn't sure she believed that, but if it made Lee feel better, so be it. "And you didn't know about these?" she asked.

"No. Never. I would have tried one more time. Even though I knew it was too late. She chose the life she knew instead of giving the one with me a chance. I loved your mother with all my heart, and when she left I kind of went crazy. I went on a self-destructive binge. Hannah bullied me through, and she brought me the best gift she could . . . you."

Eve's throat felt about to burst. Her dad had never opened his heart in all these years, had never shared anything with her.

"But she didn't show you the letters. Why?"

She felt her father's hand on her hair. A soft touch.

"She never approved of Jenny. She warned me against her. Said she'd never leave her comfy life for the erratic life of a musician. She was right, as it turned out."

"People split up all the time. It doesn't have to be a fight to the death."

"For your grandmother it did."

"But why?"

"It was just Hannah's way. I think she did it for me at first. At least I hope she did. But Hannah doesn't understand love. She can only love what she can own. It started long before you or me."

Eve pulled away to see his face. "I don't understand."

"She married my father when she was fourteen. She'd grown up on the poor side of town in a house full of hate, with parents who blamed others for their own failures. You know the type. I'm one of them," he added more quietly.

"No, Dad, you're not a failure. But it wasn't Jenny's fault, either. Hannah manipulated you both just like she does everyone."

"It's the only way she knows how to act. She thought she escaped all the poverty and hopelessness when she married your grandfather. He was a handsome guy, a big talker. He swept her off her feet. She took what little love she'd kept alive through her childhood and placed it on him, but he was just as bad.

"He cheated on her, spent all the money she meticulously saved. They lost the house, and we had to move in with Henry and Floret.

"When he died, she was determined to make her life a success. And she did. She went to night school. Learned real estate and gradually turned nothing into a lucrative business. Along the way she lost my brother, and my sisters married deadbeat moochers just like our father. I pretty much screwed up the rest for her. I let myself turn into a disillusioned, bitter old man. And I'm sorry."

Eve shook her head. "It's because Hannah kept Jenny away from you."

He coughed out air. "Jenny could have tried harder."

"So could you."

"I guess I could have. And I could have done better by you, and I'm sorry for that."

"Don't be. We'll just do better from here on out. Deal?"

"I don't know if I can. I'm old, with a lot of ingrained bad habits. But I need you to know that I love you. Hannah at least gave me that—my most precious gift of all."

"And what about your other daughter? Will you love her, too?"

Eve was shocked to see tears in his eyes. "I don't know if I can."

Mel wasn't in a hurry to say good night to Eli, so she'd been stopping to look in shop windows of stores she never went in and would never buy anything from just to keep what she had for as long as she could.

Eli put his arm around her shoulders, but Mel thought it might be just to move her faster down the street. She could tell he was anxious to get home because he wanted to read about some process they were going to work on at his science program. He made it sound like something out of *Star Wars*.

They turned down the drive to Eli's house much too soon. Dulcie was waiting for them at the gate.

"How come you're still out?" Eli said. "It's past your bedtime."

"That's why," Mel said, and pointed down to the beach, where a couple was standing on the sand looking out to sea. Moonlight washed down on them. "It's Henry and Floret," Mel said. "They're holding hands. It's so romantic."

The silhouetted figures raised their arms. Fabric waved above their heads before dropping to the sand, and they walked toward the waves. "They're skinny-dipping," Mel said and giggled. "You don't think about old people . . . you know."

"Why not?"

"I don't know. It's nice. Growing old together. Like that." Mel leaned into him. "That's what I thought we would be."

"Come on, Mel."

"No, really. But we're not like Henry and Floret. Not two halves of the same thing."

Mel looked out to the spot where Floret and Henry floated on the waves. *Soul mates.* "I'd better get back."

"You sure you don't want to stay here tonight?"

"Yeah. Thanks, but it's time for me to go home."

A fleeting shadow was all the warning they got before Dulcie careered out of the darkness and butted Mel backward.

"Dulcie, get off." Laughing, Eli pulled the goat away.

"She is so lame," Mel said.

"See you tomorrow?" Eli asked.

"Yeah, probably. See ya"—she kissed him, but already it felt different—"mañana." She turned and walked quickly down to the drive. First Noelle, now Eli. Who would be next?

She felt something at her leg. Dulcie.

"Go home," Mel hissed at her. "I don't want you. Go away."

A car turned into the drive. A Cadillac. She recognized it even at this distance. Granna was probably coming to ream out Henry and Floret and drag Mel home.

Why couldn't she just leave things alone? Hadn't she done enough damage for one day?

Mel looked back at the house, but Eli had already gone inside. And she didn't want to face her granna alone.

She raced into the woods. Hid there while she waited for the Cadillac to pass. But the car slowed.

"I saw you, Mel! Come out and get in this car. I won't have you running around in the middle of the night."

Mel held her breath and plastered herself against a tree.

"Mel!"

Finally the Cadillac drove on. But instead of stopping at the house, it turned and stopped at the edge of the woods.

The door opened. Hannah got out of the car and reached back in for her cane. "Mel, come out of there!"

Mel eased back and nearly fell over Dulcie.

Granna was coming down the path. She'd pass right by Mel. Mel grabbed Dulcie around the neck and dragged her into the trees.

"Shh," she said as she held the goat close.

Hannah moved slowly past them, almost close enough to touch. "I'm not going to ask you again," she called.

Mel buried her face in Dulcie's rough coat.

Hannah disappeared for a minute, and at first Mel thought she had given up and gone back to the car. Then she heard Hannah's voice from the opposite direction.

"I know where you're going. To meet that boy—on the beach."

She wasn't going back to her car; she was going to Mel and Eli's beach. Because she thought Mel was going there. Then Mel remembered the steps. Granna didn't know they were rotten.

"Granna, no!" Mel ran toward the path. "Granna, I'm back here. Behind you! Stop!"

Mel ran, crashing through the trees until she reached the path. She saw her great-grandmother looking over the caution rope at the beach below. "I know you're down there."

"Granna, I'm back here!"

Hannah reached out to grasp the balustrade.

"Granna! No!" Why didn't she stop? Because she couldn't hear her. She must have her hearing aids off. "Granna!" she screamed.

Hannah stepped on the first step. Mel raced toward the stairs.

Just as she reached the steps, they gave way; Hannah swayed with the motion.

Mel threw herself at her great-grandmother and managed to grab her as the steps sagged and broke into pieces. She swung Hannah to the ground, but her own momentum carried her forward. She grabbed for the closest thing—the last standing piece of wooden support. The post teetered, groaned. And it gave way in her hand.

The whole stairway collapsed, carrying her downward.

She heard Hannah cry out above her, then nothing but the rumble and splintering of wood.

It only lasted seconds. Somehow, the wood ended up on top, with Mel underneath. But she was still alive.

She moved slightly, setting off a small rain of splinters and wood pieces. She gingerly lifted her head. Saw that the whole frame and risers were crisscrossed like pickup sticks, and she was on the bottom.

"Granna," she croaked. "Are you okay? Granna?"

Hannah didn't answer. Mel tried to look around but saw only dark, jagged pieces of wood.

"Granna!" Mel had to get out. She moved her leg, gently so she didn't pull the whole mess down any more. She tried the other leg. One arm, then the— "Ow." She grabbed the arm. That really hurt.

She turned her head. There was a small rectangle nearby where she could see some sand. She tried scooting on her back toward it.

She managed to get close enough to see out to the beach. But the opening was way too small for her to escape through. *Man, my arm really hurts.*

"Granna, are you up there? Are you okay? Can you go for help?"

The reply she got was the last one she expected to hear. One ear-grating bleat. Dulcie stuck her head in the opening and grabbed Mel's cap in her teeth. One tug and she backed out of the opening, sending another shower of sticks down on Mel's now bare head.

"Stupid goat."

Though . . . maybe she would go home, and when Henry came out to put her in the shed for the night, he'd see the cap and wonder where it came from . . . only what if Dulcie dropped the hat? What if she didn't go back to the house?

Dulcie had stopped just out of reach, the hat dangling from her mouth. "Go get Henry, Dulcie. Please."

She just had to be patient. Henry or David would come looking for Dulcie before long. They never let her stay out all night. There were wild animals that might hurt her.

"Dulcie, you gotta help. Please! I'll never call you stupid again."

Chapter 12

DAVID SET DOWN HIS BEER on the table and listened. "Is that Dulcie? Why isn't she in the shed for the night?"

Eli looked up from his iPad. "Because Henry and Floret are out swimming in the raw. Mel and I saw them."

David hid his smile. "Crazy old folks." He dragged his body from his chair. "I'll go bed her down. Let them have their fun."

Eli went back to his reading.

David opened the front door and trotted down the porch steps. Dulcie was standing at the bottom. She let out a lengthy bleat and ducked her head. She came up with something in her mouth.

"What have you found now? You'd better not be raiding the Daltons' laundry line again." He walked over to her and pried whatever it was out of her mouth. Eli's new university cap. That didn't take long. "Okay, it's bed for you, Dulcie."

He started toward her pen, but Dulcie didn't budge. He went to urge her toward the shed, but she danced away and took off into the woods.

"Suit yourself, but there are wild animals out there."

But not this early, he thought, and went back into the house.

"Dulcie had your cap," he told Eli, tossing it toward him.

Eli picked it up. "How did she get it?"

"I dunno. Where did you leave it?"

"I gave it to Mel."

David felt a frisson of unease skitter up his spine. "You better text her and tell her you found it."

Eli was already on the phone texting. They both waited, staring at the phone.

Eli fired off another text. They waited.

Eli stood up. "I'm going to look for her."

"She's probably in the shower and can't hear the phone." On the other hand . . . "When did you last see her?"

"She walked me home from dinner, then she left."

"Let's just check to make sure she didn't step in a pothole and sprain an ankle or something."

Without a word, they both headed for the front door.

They met Henry and Floret coming back from the beach, their robes clinging to wet bodies.

"What's afoot?" Henry asked.

"Dulcie found Eli's cap. Mel was wearing it when she left here a while ago, and she's not answering her phone."

"Oh, dear," Floret said. "Look."

David and Henry followed her outstretched hand to the place where Hannah's Cadillac was parked at the edge of the woods.

"Is she inside?" Henry asked.

David made sure no one was in the car. "Not here. The beach." He shoved his cell phone at Henry, and he and Eli ran for the path.

"Mel!" Eli called. "Mel! Mel!"

They ran headlong into Dulcie, bleating her head off. Behind her, Hannah Gordon, bent nearly double, gripped her cane with both hands. David just managed to catch her before she collapsed.

"There." Hannah waved her finger in the air, not pointing to anything, but Dulcie let out an unearthly wail and bounded away.

Henry caught up; David transferred Hannah to him, and he and Eli ran on.

Dulcie had stopped where the steps to the beach had been. The treads, the risers, the posts, the warning rope were gone.

"Mel!" Eli called.

"Eli? Down here," came the faint reply. "Help me."

"We're coming. Hold on. Uncle David?" Eli pleaded before he took off to the rocks, where he could climb down to the sand.

David followed him down and just managed to grab him before he ran headlong into the crumpled structure.

"You don't want it to collapse any more." He moved Eli out of the way and crouched down to try to ascertain how severe the collapse was and how badly Mel was injured.

He found a small opening near the bottom. "Phone," he ordered Eli, then reached out behind him. The phone was pressed into his palm. He opened the flashlight app and shone it into the opening.

Mel's scared, dirty face looked back at him.

"Are you hurt?" he asked.

"I don't think so. Just my arm. The rest of me can move."

David could have laughed with relief. "Well, don't. We're going to take some time to get this debris off you safely, so be patient."

"Okay." An answer rife with fear.

Henry appeared above them. "We called the EMTs. I left Hannah sitting on a rock with Floret. Do we need beach rescue?"

"I think the three of us can manage," David called back. "Mel, hold still until I tell you."

"Okay. Is Granna okay?"

David looked over to Henry.

"I think so," Henry said. "And as ungrateful as ever."

"It was an accident."

"It's all right. You're not in trouble," David said.

It took some time and several false starts, but at last they opened a hole wide enough for Mel to wiggle through.

She sat on the ground and burst into tears. Eli sat down beside her. "You're okay. You're safe now."

Henry and David made Mel wait where she was until the EMTs arrived. The hardest part was getting the EMTs past Dulcie, who was guarding the way to their patient. Even after Henry pulled her away, she insisted on staying close and walked beside them all the way back to the house.

Hannah was sitting up on a gurney while an EMT monitored her blood pressure.

Floret met them in the yard. "She refuses to go to the hospital." David rolled his eyes.

"I called Eve. I didn't think I should wait."

"Do I have to go to the hospital?" Mel asked. "I can move my fingers and everything."

Henry looked at the EMT who was wrapping her wrist in ice.

"She should have an X-ray to make sure her arm isn't broken," the EMT said.

"I have to talk to Granna first," Mel said.

"When your mother comes. Until then, you sit right there with the EMTs," Henry said.

The squad began packing their things. Once again Hannah refused to go into the ambulance.

"Well, then you'll have to come inside," Henry said. "Until someone can drive you home."

"I can drive myself."

"No, you can't," Floret said. "Come in and have some tea." She helped Hannah to stand.

They were interrupted by a car careering down the drive. It screeched to a halt next to the ambulance, and Eve jumped out and rushed to Mel's side. Lee and Noelle were right behind her.

Zoe's brother climbed out of the driver's seat at the same moment Zoe got out of the back.

Eve consulted with the EMTs. "I've promised to take her to the doctor first thing tomorrow." She tried to lead Mel to the car, but Mel hung back.

"I have to make sure Granna is okay." Her voice sounded on its way to hysterical. "It was my fault. She was looking for me, and I hid in the trees. By the time I figured out what she was doing, she was going down the path to the beach. She didn't know about the steps. I called but she didn't hear me, and then I got there and she was looking down and she fell. She's not hurt, is she?"

Eve looked to David.

He shook his head. "It wasn't your fault," David said. "I put a rope across the stairs. She had no business getting that close. And you saved her from a serious fall. So don't blame yourself."

Eli looked up at him, so grateful that it squeezed David's heart.

"That's right, Mel. You're a hero," Eli said.

"No, I'm not," Mel said, then fell into Eve's arms.

"We'll go see Granna, and she'll tell you herself." Eve walked her up the stairs and into the house. Everyone else followed.

"MAYBE we should wait outside," Zoe told Chris as they started up after the others.

"Not on your life. I wouldn't miss this for the world."

They walked into the living room on Hannah's "Don't make a fuss, girl."

Mel recoiled as if she'd been slapped.

Lee stood with his arms crossed. "Mother, Mel wanted to make sure you were okay before she went to get treated. You could at least be grateful that she kept you from a nasty spill."

"Huh," the old woman said. "Is that what she said?"

A cry was wrenched from Mel. "Why did you go after me, Granna? What were you going to do? Tell me I couldn't see Eli anymore? He's going to college in a few weeks. You didn't have to come after me."

Lee took a step forward. "Get up. I'll drive you home."

"I can drive myself."

"She can't stay alone tonight," Floret said. "What if she takes a turn during the night?"

"You'd be happy to see me go, I expect," Hannah snapped.

Floret didn't react. "We'll make up the daybed on the porch for you. It's quite comfortable."

"So you can poison me in my sleep. I won't stay here."

"Why not?" Floret asked in her sweetly modulated voice. "You made this your home for twenty years. What's one more night?"

"Why would I stay in the house of betrayers? You've turned the whole town against me. The laundry returned my clothes without cleaning them. The grocers refused to deliver my groceries."

Henry sighed. "When will you learn, Hannah? It's *your* doing. We had nothing to do with any of this. Everything that happens is because of you and your relentless greed and vendetta against Wind Chime and everything it stands for."

"I think it's time for you to explain," Floret said. "This has been going on for too, too long. So tell us all why, because I don't know. I don't think you even know why you're so angry."

Hannah's eyes narrowed. "You. You conniving witch."

Floret moved away from Henry as if she were afraid he might get caught in the crossfire of Hannah's venom.

"Tell me. Get it all out, and let's settle this."

"You and my husband."

"What?" The question was pure gut level. "Your husband? What on earth does he have to do with anything? He's been dead for a good forty years."

"But not before you tried to steal him away."

Floret laughed. Clapped her hand over her mouth. "I beg your pardon, Hannah. But you'll have to explain yourself."

"You seduced him."

"Actually, Hannah, that's an insult," said Henry. "Stop this nonsense. We're tired to death of it. Surely you are, too."

"Don't play innocent with me, Floret. He came to you day after day. Night after night. With your salves and your massages and your—I knew what the two of you were doing. I hated him even then, but he was mine."

Floret smiled. "Good heavens." She made a quiet purring sound. A laugh maybe. "My dear Hannah. Free love is one thing, but I would never commit adultery. Especially not with Ed Gordon. Where are your wits? He cheated on you—that was common knowledge—but not with me. He came to me because he was sick. He came for treatment for pain, and for a little understanding. You were too angry about what was happening to give him the strength he needed to die. So he came here. There was nothing else to it."

"I don't believe you."

"Believe it. He was dying, and I tried to ease his way out because you were our friend. You needed our support and were too stubborn, even then, to ask for it."

"You took in Eve's mother, and look what it did to my son." Hannah turned on Zoe. "And now this one shows up. Trying to take advantage. What will it take to get you to leave?"

"I don't know. What did it take to get my mother to leave?"

The room dropped into silence.

Zoe tried to swallow. Why had she said that? She had wanted to hurt Hannah, but she was afraid that it had hit her sister instead.

Eve stood immobile in the sudden vacuum that Zoe's words had created. And Zoe didn't dare look up to see her face.

She turned on Hannah instead. "You can't answer, can you? Because I know my mother would never have given Eve away to you. She loved her children—all her children—above everything. What did you do to her?"

"How dare you." The old woman struggled to get out of the chair.

"What *did* you do, Mother?" A voice hardly recognizable as her father's.

"I merely informed her parents of her whereabouts, and they did the rest. Did you honestly think they would let their precious daughter give up all they had planned for her? Marry a drugged-out musician, always on the road? Is that any life for a pampered rich girl with the whole world at her feet?"

Hannah pointed a palsied finger toward her son. "Did you think she would travel with you, she and the baby? Were you so bewitched that you couldn't see there was no future for the two of you? The Campbells had no illusions as to where that would lead. So they came and got her. And they could have her, but by God they wouldn't get my granddaughter."

Eve sucked in a raw, ragged breath.

"They agreed to let me adopt her with the understanding that they would keep their daughter away from her. They were only too happy to agree. They thought they were saving their precious Jenny from a terrible future. I was saving my son." Hannah coughed out a dry, raspy laugh. "It was the best deal I ever made."

For a long moment no one moved; then Lee crossed the floor and took his mother's arm. Hauled her out of her chair. "Come on, Mother, I'll take you home. You've caused quite enough trouble for a lifetime." He steered her out of the room.

Several minutes later they heard the Cadillac drive away.

The whole room exhaled.

Henry squeezed Floret's hand. "I think some tea would be in order, dear. Spiked with something a little stronger."

"That's exactly what I was thinking. Valerian for Mel, then off to bed with her."

Half an hour later, they were all piling into Zoe's car. David carried a sleeping Mel to the backseat. Eve sat with her, and Noelle, Zoe, and Chris squeezed into the front.

"I'll never complain about our boring Long Island family again," Chris said as Zoe turned into the drive.

Zoe smiled. "Yes, you will."

AT NINE the next morning, Eve stood across from her grandmother's house staring at the scene before her. A dozen townspeople lined the sidewalk in front of the house, carrying placards. REOPEN KELLY'S. DON'T MESS WITH OUR DINER. IT WORKS BOTH WAYS. Hannah was being picketed.

Eve wondered if the backlash would include her and her family. There was only one way to find out. She headed across the street.

"Morning, Eve," said Bobby Pritchard, owner of the Cadillac dealership.

"Morning, Bobby," Eve returned, then raised her eyebrows in question.

"Like we told Lee this morning when he came out to get the paper, there won't be any paper this morning, or tomorrow, or the next morning. Not until Kelly's reopens. We've had enough. Tell Hannah that until she backs off from Kelly's, she won't get any more services from us. Nothing personal to you or yours."

Eve nodded. She agreed with them, but for all her faults, Hannah was her grandmother, and she wouldn't side against her. Not yet.

She walked up to the front door. Lee opened it as she reached for the bell. "When did this happen?" she asked, coming inside.

"They were there when I got up this morning."

"You stayed here all night?"

Lee shrugged. "I couldn't really leave her alone, could I?"

Eve sighed. "Is she okay? Is she awake yet?"

"Yep. Already planning her attack. The woman's incorrigible."

"She can't go on like this. You know that."

"Yes, and I don't intend to let her. I've enabled her behavior all these years because . . . well, I didn't see the harm it was doing to my family, much less the town."

Eve gave him an impulsive hug. He patted her back, stiff and awkward, and she loved him in spite of it—all the more for it.

"We'd best go get it over with."

Hannah was sitting in a wing chair in the parlor, fully dressed and made up, though it didn't hide the bruises on her cheek and forehead; her pantsuit probably hid a few more.

She sat up when she saw Lee and Eve. "Well? Did you get rid of them?"

Eve hesitated. Lee stepped ahead of her, and a thrill of love coursed through her.

"No, I didn't," he said. "It's no more than you deserve."

"So you turn against your own mother. I gave you everything." She lifted her head at Eve. "I gave you your daughter."

Lee's whole body tightened, and for a long moment Eve didn't know whether he would back off or go for the old woman's throat.

"No, Mother. While I appreciate what you did, it was Jenny who gave me Eve, for which I'll ever be grateful, though I didn't always show it to my daughter, and for that I'm sorry."

Eve gulped back a cry.

Lee plowed on. "We let you run roughshod over us—over the whole town—all these years. And I turned my back on what you were doing. Told myself that it had nothing to do with me.

"But I was wrong." He stopped as if the words had stuck in his throat. "Mel, my granddaughter, your own flesh and blood, could have been killed last night because you couldn't stand to let her be free. And for what? All for your wounded pride over things that you thought happened years before she was born."

Hannah glared at him. "I gave you everything. And this is how you repay me?"

"You didn't give—you bought. Our love, our lives. And you didn't have to. We loved you, but that wasn't enough, was it? I made excuses for your vindictiveness because I thought you were doing it for the family. But it was all done in revenge. For your upbringing, for an affair that never happened, for affection you mistook for a power play. You've been punishing us for nothing.

"I'm sorry for your unhappy childhood, for your disappointment in adulthood. I admire your courage, but not how you used it. This vendetta against Henry and Floret is tearing the whole town apart. Is that what you want?"

Hannah lifted a shoulder. "I don't care about this town. They never gave me anything I didn't take."

"Maybe because you never asked."

Hannah turned on Eve. "I suppose you feel the same way."

"Granna, we love you. We always will. But we love you too much to let you go on this way. You went too far by dragging the Kellys into this. We're going to appeal the condemnation to the council. I'll tell them you're not in your right mind if I have to."

"Get out, then. Go on and do your worst."

"I'm going to call Vicky Rogers and ask her to send someone over to help until you're feeling up to par," Lee said.

"Don't bother. I can do for myself."

"I know, Mother." Lee's voice cracked on the word. "But you don't have to. You never had to."

"You ungrateful—"

Eve burst forward. "Stop it, Granna. We have never been ungrateful. Just the opposite. Why would you think that? Is that what your family said to you? That you were ungrateful, when they barely gave you enough to exist?"

"Go." Hannah barely croaked out the word.

Lee took Eve's arm and guided her out of the room. She glanced back as Lee opened the door. Hannah sat in her chair, chin against her chest, just an old woman who had chosen anger over everything else and whose bitterness had almost consumed them all.

She stopped. "I should go back."

"No going back." Lee put an arm around her and pulled her close, and they stood on the porch looking out at the throng of people that seemed to have grown since Eve had gone inside.

"We can't leave her alone," Eve said.

"Nope, but I don't have the patience right now." Lee took out his phone. Keyed in a number. "Vicky. Glad I caught you . . ."

Vicky Rogers agreed to come herself until they could find a caregiver. She was on her way over.

"Hannah won't take this lying down."

"Vicky is used to ornery patients. And she's a good friend. She'll be patient but won't be bullied."

They stood arm in arm on the porch until Vicky arrived, bearing a tote bag filled with food. They explained what happened while Vicky nodded her head, asked a few questions, then persuaded them not to accompany her inside.

"I know what to do. Sometimes it's better not to push the issue."

Still, they waited a few minutes more, then, with a wave to the picketers, walked back to the inn.

ZOE overslept and had to rush to get downstairs, where she'd agreed to meet Chris before going to Eve's cottage for coffee. Mel was up and relishing the attention from Noelle, who seemed to have designated herself her sister's personal assistant.

There was no sign of Eve.

"She went over to Granna's," Mel said. "I think she was worried about her." She lifted her arm, which this morning had a thick soft cast covering her wrist and most of her forearm.

"Yikes," Zoe said. "When did you get that?"

"This morning Mom took me over to Dr. White's. It isn't broken, just sprained."

"I smell coffee," Chris said. He wandered off to the kitchen to help himself.

"Mom just called," Noelle said. "They're headed home. I told her to stop at the bakery on their way."

"They?"

"She and Granddad. And don't even think about escaping."

Chris came back into the room carrying two mugs of coffee. He handed one to Zoe. "You good?" he asked Noelle.

"Yeah. Who needs caffeine when I'm rushing on Manhattan?"

Chris rolled his eyes. "We need to work on your sparkle technique."

"We?" Zoe said. "You decided to stay in the city?"

"Yep." He took a sip of coffee, savored the taste. "Timothy decided to take the job in Chicago. It's a great career opportunity. But not for me. My life is in the city. Anyway, now I have to keep an eye on my niece. And if Eve doesn't think it looks too weird for an old gay uncle to share his apartment with her daughter until she finds some happening young millennial to live with, I won't have to look for a roommate right away."

"She won't," Noelle said. "She was raised in a commune."

The front door opened, and Eve walked in. Lee followed her, carrying a big bakery bag. "I'll just take these things to the kitchen," he said, not catching anyone's eye.

"How's Granna?" Noelle asked.

"Same as she always is, but we called Vicky Rogers to sit with her until we're sure she's back to normal."

"What did you say to her?"

"I'm gonna tell you," Lee said, coming back into the room. "But first I got something to say."

He turned toward Zoe. She braced herself.

"Zoe." Lee opened his hands.

She shook her head. "It's okay. You don't have to accept me. It was not your fault or your responsibility." But she felt the cold ache of disappointment anyway. A week ago she hadn't known of his existence, of any of them, but now she wanted more than anything to be accepted by them.

"I'm not easy," said Lee. "But I loved your mother. I was a fool then. I'm gonna try to be a little less of a fool from now on. So we play it by ear." His voice rose a half note on the last word.

"Sure," Zoe said, her stomach rebounding back from defeat. "That's fine. I was always good at improv."

Eve chose that minute to return with a tray of pastries. "I've got a fresh pot brewing."

"Everything okay, Mom?" Noelle asked.

Eve exchanged a look with Lee. "Well, there's a picket line in front of Hannah's house."

Noelle snorted. "What? Over Kelly's?"

Eve nodded. "Already the cleaners, grocers, the paper, and the Cadillac dealer are boycotting her. Others are bound to follow."

"Shows you what can happen when you get between a man and his eggs and bacon," Chris quipped.

Eve sighed. "I feel a little sorry for her."

"Maybe if she gets a taste of her own medicine, she'll lay off everyone else," said Noelle. "Oh, by the way, Uncle Chris said I could live with him until I find a place."

Lee opened his mouth.

Zoe jumped in. "I can vouch for him. He's very responsible."

"Thanks, Dil." Chris beamed at her. "You can come visit whenever you want. You too, Lee."

"Uh, thanks, but right now, I need to go."

"Dad, sit down and have some coffee and a pastry," Eve said.

"Thanks, but there are things that need to be done, and it's time I did them."

"Later, then," she said.

"Later." He nodded to the room and walked out the front door.

They all watched him go. No one moved.

"Now, that's an exit," Chris said. "What are those flaky things with the jelly oozing out?"

Chapter 13

"Now, for our afternoon entertainment," Chris announced when they'd boxed up the leftover pastries, "we're all going to the beach. The hotel beach. No naysayers."

There was immediately a round of excuses. "I can't get my hand wet." "I have to pack." "I have to do next week's schedule."

"We'll put a plastic bag on Mel's cast," Chris said. "Noelle, you can wait a couple of hours to come to more indecisions on what not to wear. Zoe can help with next week's schedule."

"What about—" Zoe began.

"Mom?" he finished. "Well, heaven can wait. Get your stuff, everybody. I can't believe you have this beautiful beach and never enjoy it. Now, chop-chop."

"You're right," Eve said. "Let's all go. I'll have Mike hand over the bar to whoever is on duty and tell him to join us. Noelle, call your grandfather and tell him to come down to the beach when he gets back. We'll have a picnic. I have an announcement to make."

After that, they all agreed to change into beachwear and meet again half an hour later.

It was a family affair. At first they just swam and watched the beach yoga class twist themselves into one asana after another. Then Mike arrived, accompanied by two busboys carrying two large coolers and a picnic basket.

"I figured since the beach officially closes for the evening soon . . ." Mike opened the lid of one of the coolers to reveal several wine bottles, beers, gin, vodka, and mixers.

Chris peered in. "S'all right. S'all right." He grinned at Mike.

The busboys went off to store the food in the cabana, then returned to the inn. Mike sat down in the sand next to Eve's chair, his arm stretched comfortably along her bare leg.

They drank; they swam. They did cartwheels on the sand. The day grew long, and the sun began to arc toward the horizon. They were all back in their chairs, sighing over fruit and wine, when Chris said, "He makes great entrances, too."

They all turned to see Lee walking toward them, silhouetted by the setting sun and surrounded by a blaze of red and orange.

"You said to meet you here," he said.

"Yes, Dad. Sit down. Noelle, get your granddad a beer."

Noelle reached into the cooler and handed him a bottle.

When everyone was settled, they all turned expectantly to Eve.

"Now that everybody's here, I have something I want to say." She took a breath. "I want to travel."

The statement was met with silence.

"That's your big announcement?" Lee said.

Mel stood up. "But what about the inn?"

"I have a capable staff. I just need to start looking for a manager who could run things while I'm gone."

"But why?" Mel's question was almost a wail.

Noelle said, "She's always wanted to travel. Haven't you, Mom?"

"Yes. Since I was a little girl. But I never went anywhere. So much has changed this summer. I don't want to wait any longer."

"You're not going to sell the inn," Mel said.

"No, Mel. I'm just thinking about taking a few weeks off to see someplace I've never seen before. Gradually turn over the day-to-day running of the inn to give me more free time."

"But for how long?" Mel asked. "Where would you go?"

Eve smiled. "Well, to start with, the Grand Canyon, or maybe Paris, then Easter Island, London, the redwood forests. China. I've never seen the Statue of Liberty. I've never been anywhere."

Noelle clapped her hands together. "Good for you, Mom. I think it's great."

"Thank you." She turned to Mel. "What about you, Mel?"

"I guess. I mean, you should go if you want to."

"I was thinking that maybe you'd like to go with me."

"Instead of going to college?"

"You could postpone until second semester."

Mel ran her toes across the sand. Back and forth, back and forth.

"You can study hotel management in school, and when you graduate you can come back to run the inn if that's what you want. But only if it's what *you* want. It's just something to think about. But I will be taking a few weeks off. As soon as I find someone to keep things going."

"That won't be easy," Mike said. "I can try, but needless to say, I don't have your charm."

The girls laughed, and Eve hugged him. "You don't, but you could be the point man for whoever comes in. It's a family business. It would have to be someone special who knows how we do things, who understands that the inn's soul is what keeps it safe from becoming some corporate octopus."

"Well, you can count on me," Mike said.

"I always have, my dear." He slipped his arm around her.

"So now we have to go about finding the perfect replacement. Any suggestions?"

Silence ensued while Mike, Lee, Noelle, and Mel considered.

"I could." Everyone turned to look at Zoe.

She swallowed. What was she thinking? She'd just gotten here. "Not take over. But I bet I could run front end for a few weeks. I know how to move people, book flights and hotels, synchronize transportation and meals. It would be a learning curve. And I'd need help. I can't do orders for a restaurant or stock a bar, but I can schedule work shifts and events. I mean, I can do it until you get back. You are coming back, right?"

"Of course," Eve said. "That would be perfect. I could take a few weeks to show you the ropes. Then I could take off for a few weeks, and you'd still be here when I got back."

"I could show you the reception things," Mel volunteered. "If you think I could help."

"Of course I do," Zoe said. "I checked out your hospitality skills the first time I met you. And let me tell you, girl, you crushed it."

Mel beamed. "And, Mom, maybe if you schedule your vacations around school breaks, I could come and help Zoe out then, too."

"Wait!" Zoe said. "I can juggle front end for a few weeks. I don't know anything about long-term management."

"Ahem," Chris said. "Not to mention this in the midst of all this exuberance, but, Mel, does this mean you're going to college?"

Mel flicked sand at him. "Maybe." She looked over at Eve. "I've kind of been thinking. Eli always says that in science you have to have more than one option to make an informed hypothesis. That if there's only one, it doesn't prove anything."

"Whoa, Eli," said Noelle.

"Well, he's right, isn't he?"

Zoe realized she wasn't the only person having a lightbulb moment. She let out a long breath. "Why don't we take a test run and see if it will work? If you're up for it. Just say no if you're not."

"I think it's great," Eve said. "But are you sure you want to?"

"It's like Eli said: You need more than one choice. I could put my experience to work in a different field, and I . . ." She hesitated. "And . . . I could learn music somewhere besides Juilliard." Zoe risked a tentative look at Lee.

Slowly his expression changed. He pointed to his chest.

She nodded.

He frowned for a bit, then stood. Zoe's heart slipped. She'd pushed him too fast.

"Dad, where are you going?" Eve said, alarmed.

He patted her on the shoulder. "You girls work it out. I'm just gonna make sure the piano's tuned."

THE next day, David, Henry, and a group of volunteers showed up at Kelly's to begin the minor cosmetic changes that would put the diner in compliance with the health department regulations. Eve and Lee had called each of the commissioners and made them an offer they couldn't refuse. Zoe guessed it had something to do with their reelection.

Whatever the cause, two men showed up on Monday morning, did a cursory inspection, and declared Kelly's back up to code. There was general celebration and free coffee while diners waited in line for a place inside.

And Eve knew what she had to do. That afternoon, she drew up a formal agreement and took it to Wind Chime. Henry and Floret read it over, and all three of them signed a lease agreement allowing the inn to use Wind Chime House's adjacent beach. Henry and Floret agreed to restrict nude sunbathing to the secluded beach on the opposite side of the property during the day. What happened after dark was left to the occupants. Eve promised that no further attempts to cut off the right-of-way to the house would be made by her family. She'd have to get Hannah to sign off on it. She had every intention of making that happen.

She headed straight to Hannah's house and with some trepidation told her of the arrangement. But Hannah didn't seem interested. She was more concerned that the cleaners had twice returned her dry cleaning uncleaned.

"They're doing this on purpose."

Yes, they most likely were, thought Eve, but at least it would give Hannah something to keep her mind off Kelly's and Wind Chime House. And the Zukowskis, who owned the only dry cleaners in town, also owned almost as much real estate as Hannah did.

Hannah signed the contract with "Who cares about them anyway? But if that low-down Sam Zukowski thinks he can give me the cold shoulder . . ."

Eve, amazed at how easily she'd acquiesced, left with Hannah mumbling about the nerve of some people. She must enjoy the constant confrontation, the chaos. She could have it. All to herself.

Two days later, they all watched as a dump truck and backhoe arrived to tear down and cart away the jetty that had separated them for several years.

And Errol still hadn't called.

Zoe left Chris and Noelle arguing over how much stuff she really needed for the first weeks of work in Manhattan. She ran back to the hotel and up to her room to use her phone in private.

She keyed in her brother's landline. On the fourth ring, she was about to hang up when he picked up.

"Hi. It's Zoe."

"Zoe," he began.

"Please, Errol, just let me have my say." She heard him sigh, and she hurried on. "I want to have a ceremony here. Nothing extravagant, just a few friends and family." She crossed her fingers. "I understand how you feel; I really do. I wasn't happy about this, either, not until I got here. *She* was happy here. This is what she wanted. I think we owe her this much."

"Well, I can't say I blame her totally," Errol said. "Not after what our father did. But who's going to look after the grave?"

Zoe heard a click, and for a second she was afraid he'd hung up.

"Honey, there's not going to be a grave."

He hadn't hung up; someone had picked up. Allison was on the line. "We talked about this."

"It's just . . . she'll just be floating around out there."

"She'll be in good company," Zoe said. "It's a memorial garden. There are others here. Not really a garden but a glen with a window through the trees where you can see the ocean. It's beautiful."

"And there's someone to take care of her?"

"Yes. Her friends who, um, take care of the garden."

She heard a sound and realized that her brother was sobbing.

Tears filled her own eyes. She couldn't remember seeing him cry. "I want you all to come to the ceremony. Rob and Laura, too."

"Of course we will. When is it?" Allison asked.

"Whenever you can make it. I was hoping next weekend or the next. Does that give you enough time?"

"I'll check with Laura and get back to you, but we'll be free one of those weekends. The sooner the better, I say."

"Thanks, Allison. Am I still one of the family?"

"Of course you are. What a thing to say. And don't worry about Errol. He'll come around."

Zoe hung up. Dropped the phone on the bed. Whew. Now to consult with Floret and Henry about what to do. She pulled herself together and walked down to Wind Chime House.

Henry and Floret didn't appear to be at home, but she heard hammering from the woods. Now what was he doing?

She walked down the path until she saw David standing between two new posts where the old stairs had been.

"Déjà vu," she said, walking up behind him.

He nodded in her direction. "I should have finished tearing these down the day I started. I just got busy and—"

"Stop. You cordoned them off. It was an accident. Everyone's okay." She frowned. "So you're building them back?"

"Yeah. Henry and Floret said the commune will be using this beach, since they're leasing Eve the other beach, so I decided to make life easy for them."

"You take care of them."

"It's the other way around. But I need to do this before I leave."

"You're leaving?"

"As soon as I get Eli to college. An assignment in Patagonia."

"Sounds exciting."

He cocked his head as if considering. "It is sometimes. Mainly it's just waiting for the right shot. I like it."

"You're coming back?" She was beginning to sound like Mel.

"Yeah, but I'll have freedom to take more work—for a while, anyway."

Until Henry and Floret need you again, she thought.

"Listen." He stopped. "I just want to say that we got off to a rocky start. I'm sorry I didn't get to know you better."

Zoe tried not to smile. "Thanks. But if you're only going to be gone a couple of months, I'll still be here when you get back."

"You're staying?"

"At least to help run the inn while Eve is gone."

"Eve? Where is she going?"

"She, like you, wants to travel. I told her I'd keep the home fires burning while she's away." She laughed. "It's funny. I just got here, and everybody's leaving."

"Do you have any idea how to run an inn?"

"Not really, but I know how to deal with people at major music festivals. How hard can it be?"

THE celebration of the life of Jenny Bascombe was held the following weekend. It was a clear morning. The sky was blue, the clouds were high, and the day was hot. They'd decided on a simple gathering, with a few short prayers in deference to the Long Island family. There would be a feast afterward at Wind Chime House.

Errol and Robert and their wives drove up the night before. They arrived late, with only time for a nightcap at the bar before going off to bed in the two rooms Eve had reserved for them.

The next morning, they drove to Wind Chime House.

The others—Eve and Mike and Noelle and Mel—had walked ahead. Chris had chosen to walk with them. They were all dressed for a celebration.

They parked at the house, and Zoe was glad to see that David and Eli had joined Henry and Floret, both dressed in full robes and flowers, in greeting the Bascombes. Floret held the wind chimes they would hang in the woods, wrapped in a prayer shawl of brilliant colors.

Zoe carried the urn, her fingers molding to the cool ceramic, reluctant to let go. Henry gave her a calming smile and patted the robe pocket that held the penknife that would cut the ashes free.

Lee wasn't there. She'd invited him but hadn't pushed him to attend. She didn't know how her brothers would take him as a stand-in for their own father, whom they had decided not to invite.

Zoe began the procession down the path, feeling a little queasy and hoping she wouldn't embarrass herself by bursting into tears.

They reached the glen and formed a semicircle facing the keyhole in the trees, where the brilliant blue of the sea shone through like a pathway to the sky.

Henry stepped forward and faced the group, his robes outlined by the sea. "We are here today to welcome our dear friend Jenny home. We promise to love her and keep her soul safe."

He looked to Errol and then Robert, who both lowered their heads. Zoe knew that beneath their stoic demeanor, they were saying goodbye in their own way.

She handed the urn to Chris, who held it while Henry cut the plastic. That was when she saw Lee standing in the trees, near the group but not part of it.

She was glad he'd come. Henry cut the ashes free, and she began to sprinkle them in an arc until she completed a full circle.

And then it was done. Henry took the bag from the urn and held it in the air until the last vestiges of Jenny Bascombe were set free. Together he and Floret hung the wind chime Jenny had sent to them for safekeeping.

"Welcome home, dear friend," said Floret, and the two of them started toward the house. Everyone else followed. Zoe lingered, but only to let David and Eli get a head start.

As she stepped out of the trees, the breeze lifted the leaves behind her, and the first faint tinkle of the chimes teased her ears. She stopped to listen as it swept gently through the woods, knowing her mother's chime would join the others. And as the clear sound grew, another melody wove in counterpoint to the chimes. A melody she knew well and a voice she was growing to love. *Lavender's blue, dilly dilly. Lavender's green* . . .

Zoe smiled, knowing her mother was at peace and she would never be alone.

THE Long Island family left about an hour later, pleading a five-hour drive and wanting to miss the Sunday night exodus from the beach. When Eve and Zoe left, about an hour after that, the music had changed to reggae, friends and townspeople had joined the party, and things were rocking. A perfect end to a day that could have been steeped in sorrow.

Zoe and Eve were walking back to town when a car turned into the drive and came to a stop. The window lowered, and a young woman with curly red hair stuck her head out.

"I'm sorry to bother you, but our family is vacationing nearby, and I'm out with my grandmother today. She wants to go to this place where she had seen some wind chimes, I think. It was a long time ago. It might not even be here still." She looked over to the older woman seated in the passenger seat, who looked straight ahead. "She thought it might be down this road."

"You're perfectly right," said Eve. She leaned in toward the old woman. "Wind Chime House is straight down the drive."

The old lady turned, smiled. "Wind Chime House," she whispered, and looked ahead in anticipation.

"Thank you. Do you think the owners would mind if we drove by? We'll try not to bother them. It would mean so much."

"Not at all," said Zoe. "They'd be delighted to see you. In fact, I think they're expecting you."

AfterWords

Shelley Noble has been a self-professed "closet fiction writer" since childhood. But prior to her career as a *New York Times* bestselling author, Noble danced for a living. After receiving her BFA and MFA in dance from the University of Utah, she performed with greats such as Louis Falco and Twyla Tharp, appeared on the PBS series "Great Performances," and performed with American Ballroom Theatre. Additionally, Noble consulted on Broadway shows and worked on movie choreography for films, including *Amadeus, Mona Lisa Smile,* and *The Game Plan.*

After all this, says Noble, "I retired, sort of, to raise two children in the suburbs." As her children grew up, however, she began thinking about her next chapter. At a friend's suggestion, she began writing mysteries, drawing on her knowledge of the dance world. The Linda Haggerty mystery series, published under Noble's real name, Shelley Freydont, is set amidst the drama of a dance company.

Despite her success with mysteries, Noble decided to switch gears and try penning women's fiction. "What really interested me [about mysteries] besides the whodunit aspect was how people reacted to murder and how it changes their lives," she says. "And I wanted to try my hand at writing about people without murder and really be able to get inside their skin without having to sprinkle clues and bodies around."

LAYOVER

DAVID BELL

Prologue

THE NURSE OPENED the curtain around my bed and said there was somebody who wanted to see me.

I tried to read the look on her face. She cut her eyes away from mine, busying herself with the chart on the wall and then asking me to lean forward so she could examine the back of my head. She wore a colorful smock decorated with Disney characters.

"Everything looks good," she said, her voice flat. Her shoes squeaked against the floor. "How's the pain?"

"Throbbing mostly," I said.

"That's not surprising," she said. "You have a mild concussion. You're lucky it wasn't worse. Most people who get hit the way you were end up with staples in their scalp."

"Who wants to see me?" I asked. Each word required effort, like I was pushing it out of my mouth.

I pieced together the previous few hours from the fragments of my concussed memory. The amusement park. My face in the rich, damp earth. A cop standing over me, shining a light in my eyes. And then the ambulance ride to the hospital, winding through the county roads, nausea rising with each turn and bump.

I knew I was in Wyckoff, Kentucky, the little college town

ninety minutes northwest of Nashville. And I knew what I'd come there for.

And *whom* I'd come there for.

And I knew no one else in town, so if someone wanted to see me . . .

Could it be . . . Morgan? Coming to check on me?

The nurse slipped out through the privacy curtain. I heard the sounds of the emergency room around me. The chatter of doctors and nurses. A machine beeping nearby. The lights above me were bright, making me squint. And a wave of nausea swept through me again, roiling my stomach like a rising tide.

Then a woman pushed aside the curtain. She wore a business suit, with a gold badge clipped to her belt.

"Mr. Fields," she said. "How are you feeling?" She had a friendly face with sympathetic eyes, but her voice was strong.

"My head hurts." I looked down. The blanket came up to my chest, and I appeared to be wearing a flimsy hospital gown. "And I don't know where my clothes are."

"They'll give those back when the time comes," she said. "I'm Detective Kimberly Givens with the Laurel Falls police. We spoke on the phone earlier. You remember that, right? I need to ask you some questions. Do you think you're up for that right now?"

My heart started to race at a rate that matched the thumping in my head. Detective Givens lifted one eyebrow, and that gesture served as a repetition of her question.

Was I up for that right now?

Did I have a choice?

"Yes." My mouth felt like I'd been chewing felt. I looked around for a drink but saw none.

"Do you know how you ended up here?" Givens asked.

I closed my eyes, saw a replay of the same images. The amusement park . . . my face in the dirt . . . the cop shining a flashlight in my face . . . the ambulance ride . . .

"Somebody hit me," I said. "I think."

"There was another man on the ground near you. Someone had hit him. Likely more than once. Do you remember that?"

I looked down. I could see that the knuckles on my right hand were scraped raw like they'd been dragged across concrete. Givens followed my gaze; then her eyebrows rose again.

"Is he okay?" I asked.

Givens held my gaze for a moment, and then she said, "Who else was out there with you?"

My lips were as cracked as crumbling plaster. I ran my tongue over them, trying to generate some moisture.

"Mr. Fields? Who else was out there with you?"

I returned her gaze and didn't blink. "You must know who."

"Tell me where she went," she said.

"I don't know."

"Here's what happened," she said. "The police arrive at the scene. We find two unconscious men. Both with hands that look like they've been in a fight. Oh, and did I mention . . ." She paused, drawing out the moment, letting me stew. "We found other evidence out there as well. Very interesting evidence."

"What kind of evidence?" I asked.

She chose not to tell me. "So, what can we conclude, Joshua? You're the only one left to explain it all."

The machine kept beeping. A siren rose and fell in the distance.

"You're not going to tell me how that man is doing?" I asked.

"I really don't know. But if you answer my questions, I can see what I can find out." She took a step closer to the bed. "I bet you're the kind of guy who cares how that man is doing. Especially if you're the one who hurt him. You're a nice guy, right? Not the kind who gets involved in crimes like this. Right?"

The pain at the back of my head came back in a rush. I felt the need to squint. But I couldn't pull the covers over my head. I couldn't walk out, not with a detective standing over me. Not without any clothes. I had no idea where my car was.

I was very far from home. And alone.

"Morgan Reynolds, Joshua," Givens said. "Tell me how you met her. Tell me the whole story."

I sighed. I was tired. And I hurt.

"It began at the airport, during a layover. . . ."

Chapter 1

WE ENDED UP NEXT TO each other in the airport gift shop.

Fate. Chance. Randomness.

I passed through Atlanta almost every week, heading for another city to take care of the same customers I'd been working with for five years. I arrived and left on the same flights. One week I might fly to St. Louis, the next to Dallas or Little Rock.

On that Tuesday I was headed to Tampa.

I traveled all over the country. There was a never-ending blandness to the concourses and planes. On more than one occasion I'd found myself in an airport, walking through the terminal, and couldn't recall which city I was in or where I was heading.

But that Tuesday, the day I met Morgan, something different happened. Something put the two of us right next to each other.

I'd been working in commercial real estate development for five years, ever since I graduated from college. My life felt like an endless merry-go-round. I'd hopped on when my dad helped me get the job, and the carousel had been spinning since then. Everything around me had blurred.

My apartment. My friends. My life.

I passed through airport gates across the country, handed over boarding passes, thanked flight attendants. I didn't notice faces anymore. I didn't connect with the people I passed in my travels. We transacted things. Business. I bounced along with the rest of them like cattle in a chute.

My dad always told me to keep my cards close to the vest when negotiating. I'd taken that advice too much to heart. I'd started doing it everywhere.

But then she ended up in line next to me in the gift shop.

I wouldn't have noticed except she almost dropped her purse.

Something rustled and shuffled behind me. When I turned to look, she made a sudden movement, lunging to catch the leather bag before it fell, but her iPhone tumbled to the floor, bouncing up next to my shoe. I bent down and picked up the phone.

"Good thing you have a case," I said.

Her left hand shook as she took the phone back.

Nervous flier?

But she didn't thank me. I couldn't say I blamed her, since I'd been tuning my fellow travelers out for years. I'd adopted a glassy-eyed stare that warded off conversation.

But when she took her phone back, I noticed her. The shaking hand—the vulnerability—somehow slipped past my defenses.

I looked right at her.

She wore her dark brown hair in a ponytail that hung below a tan bucket hat. Her eyes were covered by oversized sunglasses.

She was almost as tall as I am—a couple of inches under six feet—and wore black leggings, black running shoes, and a gray Lycra hoodie. She had a carry-on over one shoulder and clutched a purse against her body. Her flushed cheeks looked delicate, the skin flawless. We appeared to be the same age, mid-twenties.

She looked away from me as I studied her. At least she seemed to, as much as I could tell with the sunglasses on.

A holdup occurred ahead of us, drawing my attention to the front of the line. A man was arguing about the price of his newspaper. The cashier listened with a strained look on her face.

I turned to the woman behind me again. The one who had dropped her phone and taken it back without thanking me. The one with the shaking hand. The one who had managed to pierce the stoic determination I adopted when I traveled.

"We might be here a while," I said, nodding toward the man in front of us.

The woman ignored me. She opened her purse and started rooting around frantically, as though she'd lost something.

"I don't think anything else fell out," I said.

She whipped her head up toward me. "What did you say?"

"I'm sorry," I said. "I was just saying . . . you look like you thought you lost something. When the purse fell."

She considered me for a moment from behind the glasses. Her mouth was small. A tiny beauty mark sat on her left cheek. A silly thought crossed my mind: *She's a celebrity. After all, we are in Atlanta, and they film a lot of movies here. I occasionally spot celebrities in the airport. That explains the sunglasses. That's why she's so pretty.*

It looked as if she was going to say something, but then she tucked her purse against her body and turned and walked away.

THAT should have been it. I should have gone on with my Tuesday layover routine—paid for the paperback thriller I'd picked up off the rack, stopped in the bathroom and swallowed a Xanax, headed to the bar for my preflight drink.

But it didn't work out that way.

I did buy the book. It bore an embossed foil cover and the black, shadowy outline of a man who carried a gun and appeared to be running away, turning slightly to look over his shoulder. And I did head toward the bathroom near my gate. My flight boarded in ninety minutes, so I had plenty of time to kill. I moved through the crowds, dodging my fellow travelers and their bags.

It was all the same. Everywhere I went, always the same . . .

Except . . .

I found myself thinking about *her* as I walked. Her face—those delicate cheeks, the beauty mark, the brown hair. Her shaking hand. Her coldness toward me before she walked away. What did she think she'd lost that made her so frantic?

My love life had been floundering recently. Six months earlier, I'd broken up with Renee, who'd been my girlfriend for almost a year. I liked her, but I'm not sure I loved her. We broke up because of that. And because I traveled so much.

Renee and I had been talking off and on again, but neither one of us seemed ready to jump into a full-on reconciliation. At least not yet. But the thought of being with Renee back in Chicago had become more and more appealing. I was tired of being on the road, of sleeping in hotels. The thought of being home seven nights a week, of having someone to come home to, of sharing a meal and conversation, made my heart swell with anticipation.

And then Renee texted me as I walked to the bathroom:

Hey, guy, have a great trip!

Was that all marriage was? A lifetime spent with someone who cared about whether you had a good flight? Someone who'd notice if you didn't check in when you were supposed to?

It was starting to sound pretty good.

I stopped outside the bathroom door and started to write back.

Thanks! At the airport but

Then *she* came out of the bathroom. The woman from the gift shop.

She still wore the hat and sunglasses, had the carry-on over one shoulder, the purse in her hand. She froze in her tracks when she saw me. I stopped mid-text. It felt like our gazes locked, but I couldn't be certain because I couldn't see her eyes. But I saw the brown hair and the beauty mark and the long, athletic body.

And what must she have thought of me? I wore a sport coat and a button-down shirt. Khaki pants and oxford shoes. I looked like any other young guy going off to some boring job. Airports and offices were full of them. What made me stand out?

She took two steps toward me. I put my phone away, sliding it into my inside jacket pocket. I'd get back to Renee later.

Rather than scare her off again, I waited, making what I hoped was something close to eye contact.

Finally she spoke. "I'm sorry about before. I . . . was distracted. When you spoke to me, I was lost in my own head."

Her voice carried a trace of a southern accent.

I nodded, relieved to see she didn't seem to think I was a total creep who harassed strange women in airport gift shops.

"I get it," I said. "I get lost in my thoughts sometimes too. Especially before noon and especially in airports."

She nodded as though she understood.

I relaxed. We'd connected, even if only to a small degree.

We could have gone our separate ways. But then I saw something in her hand, something that hadn't been there before.

"That's a good one," I said, pointing to it.

She looked down, saw the book in her hand. "Oh, this. Yeah, I was looking for something to pass the time."

"I read it last week while I was flying." Some details about the story came back to me. A woman who used to be a spy was being pressed into service after a terrorist attack. "It moved really fast."

"Good. That's what I need. Distraction."

She stopped speaking but didn't rush off.

And I wanted to know what was behind those sunglasses.

Maybe I wasn't aware back then of how desperate I was to connect with someone, to share something on a deep level. To be surprised by what someone else was thinking or doing. Or feeling.

In the gift shop, the door had opened a crack. I wanted to kick it open farther. I needed the fresh air, the bright light.

"It's early," I said, "but I always get a drink before my flight or when I have a layover. Would you like to join me?"

I pointed to a bar, the Keg 'n Craft. I'd stopped there many times. I'd started thinking about a career change when one of the bartenders recognized me and began calling me by name.

I thought I'd overstepped. I'd pushed harder than I should.

She glanced down at the Fitbit on her wrist.

"You know what?" she said. "I shouldn't, but I could really use a drink." She nodded, confirming her decision. "Let's do it."

I WENT to take a seat at the front of the Keg 'n Craft, on the side closest to the concourse, which afforded a view of the flight boards and a better chance to hear the announcements.

But she kept walking. She didn't say anything or look back as she went to the other side of the bar where no one sat.

I followed her.

She hopped up on a barstool, and I slid onto the one next to her. She put the carry-on bag on the bar in front of her and then placed her purse next to it. She seemed to want to keep those things close to her at all times.

Although she'd agreed to the drink, she seemed to have regressed. When I sat down, she kept her face straight ahead, as though I wasn't there. And she still wore the sunglasses.

The bartender made drinks for travelers near the front, giving us a few moments to sit next to each other without any distraction except the muted TV above the bar.

My phone dinged in my pocket. Twice in quick succession.

"You better get that," she said without looking at me. "Someone really wants to talk to you."

I reached in my pocket and pulled the phone out. It was Renee.

Just worried your flight was delayed and you'll miss your connection.

I wrote back quickly, finishing the thought from earlier.

Thanks! Made it to Atlanta. More later.

I silenced the ringer.

"Sorry," I said, putting the phone away.

"It's okay," she said. But her voice became lighter, almost flirtatious, when she said, "Somebody cares about you."

Emboldened by the new tone in her voice, I decided to seize the moment. "I'm Joshua," I said. "Joshua Fields."

I held my hand out.

She nodded but still didn't look at me. "Right," she said. "We're going to have to do this, aren't we?"

"Do what?" I asked.

She turned, the sunglasses still on. She reached out and took my hand. "I'm . . . Morgan. Nice to meet you."

"Where are you headed?" I asked, ignoring the strange pause before she told me her name.

She reached up and took her sunglasses off, revealing eyes that were a cool blue and tired-looking. "You're awfully curious."

"It's ask about you or watch television. And there's no sound. Actually, I was worried you couldn't hear me in the gift shop."

She smiled, and some of the weariness left her eyes. "Well, it's been a long few days. I've been dealing with . . . family complications." She paused. "But now I'm going to a friendlier place."

"And where would that be?" I asked.

"Where I went to college. In Kentucky. About an hour and a half from Nashville. Henry Clay University in Wyckoff."

I nodded. "I live in Chicago now, but I grew up in Indiana. I got brochures from Henry Clay when I was looking at colleges."

"I grew up in Wyckoff," she said. "It was easy for me to decide to go there." She pressed her lips together. "Yeah, that's home, more or less. A lot of memories."

"Are you going for a reunion or something?" I asked. It was early October, the time of year for homecoming weekends.

"I wish it were that simple." She smiled without showing her teeth, and beneath the smile I detected a strain. She seemed eager to turn the question back on me. "What about you? This is work travel for you?"

"Is it that obvious?" I asked, holding my arms out. "How do you know this isn't my beachwear?"

"Not quite," she said with a little laugh. "Not even close."

"Okay, you got it. I'm traveling for work. Again. I'm in the air about two hundred thousand miles a year."

Her eyebrows rose, and her mouth opened. "Wow. Now, that's exciting. I'd love to travel that much."

"It's not as glamorous as it sounds," I said. "All I see are airports and planes and hotels. It's the same, over and over again. I look in the mirror, and I feel like I'm turning into my dad."

"Is that a bad thing?" she asked.

"No, not really. He's a good man. But maybe . . . Here." I reached into my pants pocket. I brought out a small, round plastic case and held it in my palm. "Do you want to know a secret?"

She moved ever so slightly toward me. "I'd love to. Everybody has a secret. And here in an airport bar is the perfect place to spill it. Everything here is temporary, isn't it? We're all just passing through on the way to somewhere else."

Her words brought me up short. "Yes, that's exactly how I feel. Like I'm a tourist, except the thing I'm observing is my own life. And I'm just buzzing through it without absorbing anything."

"That's pretty existential for the Keg 'n Craft," she said, with a real smile this time. "So, what's that in your hand?"

I twisted off the lid of the pill case. "Do you know what it is?"

"Viagra?"

"Really?"

"Just having fun. It looks like it might be Xanax."

"Exactly. I hate to fly. I have nightmares about a plane crashing and being trapped on board. I take one of these and then head to the bar because it's the only way I can get on a plane. I took one this morning to get on my first flight. And now that I'm on my layover, I'm going to take another so I can get on the next flight."

"And yet you do it that much?" she asked. "You're afraid that much of the time?"

Hearing someone else say it made it seem even more absurd. "Yeah. Crazy, right?"

"Then why do you do it?" she asked. She seemed genuinely curious about my answer.

"That's what my job requires, and I make good money," I answered honestly. "I really don't like the work, but I keep doing it. It's not exactly what I envisioned for myself when I was in college. I thought . . . it would all be more exciting, you know?"

Morgan nodded as if she understood. But then she said, "I feel for you. I do. But I'd trade my problems for yours any day."

I started to ask what she meant, but the bartender showed up and asked what we wanted. Before she placed her order, Morgan slipped her sunglasses back on.

AFTER the drinks came—a Bloody Mary for her, a bourbon for me—I asked her about the sunglasses.

"Why did you put them back on before you ordered?"

She pinched her straw between her thumb and index finger and jabbed it into the drink. The ice rattled against the glass.

Then she turned to me and asked, "Why do you work a job that makes you miserable? Why are you turning into your dad?"

I noted how she evaded my question. I also felt disarmed by the directness of her response. On a couple of occasions I'd tried to talk to Renee about my job, about feeling unfulfilled. But no matter how hard I tried to explain my dissatisfaction, I couldn't seem to make it clear to her. She just couldn't hear me. Really hear me.

"Everyone feels this way in their twenties," Renee told me. "You have a good job. Who knows where it will lead?"

I couldn't argue with her. I knew how fortunate I was. Most people didn't have a dad like mine, who greased the wheels for me to start working as soon as I walked off the campus of Indiana University, diploma in hand. And Renee was focused on her career too, working for an architectural firm. We were perfect for each other in every way . . . except the way that mattered most.

Morgan was still staring at me.

"I'd like to quit," I said. "But it's tough. Especially when your dad's the boss. He made a lot of sacrifices, worked his butt off raising me and building a business. It's not easy to walk away."

"I quit my job." She turned back around, facing forward. "I understand about things not going the way you planned."

"How so?"

"I thought working would be different. That my coworkers would be more mature, more courageous than the kids I went to college with. That there'd be a higher purpose, something more meaningful. But I learned that people in the workforce are just like the college kids I knew. Scared. Impulsive. Deceitful."

She sounded cynical, jaded. Almost bitter.

"Maybe not all places are like that," I said. "Maybe we just haven't found the right place yet."

"Maybe. It's a complicated situation, but my mother is sick too. Very sick with cancer."

I let out a small, involuntary gasp. "I'm sorry," I said.

"Thank you." She looked genuinely touched by my words, although I wished I'd found something more meaningful to say. "She needs someone to care for her as things get closer to the end. That's part of why I quit my job. Not all of it, but some."

Things grew quiet between us, but I kept my eyes on her. The directness of Morgan's words, the unvarnished bluntness of a stranger I'd likely never see again, made the hairs on my arms stand up. I had the sense that the conversation could be going anywhere and could touch on anything. How different it was from the prescribed work conversations I always had, the same sales pitch and negotiation I went through over and over again.

Morgan was right about the airport—it was all temporary. Maybe that freed me too. Or maybe I just liked her, felt a spark I hadn't experienced in a while. My guard dropped further. I spread the cards I'd always clutched so tightly on the table.

"My mother left me when I was seven," I said as I turned away from her. "My dad handled both roles. The older I get, the more I realize how tough it was for him. And how well he did it all."

"I'm sorry," she said. A silence lingered. Then she said, "You know what I think?"

"What?"

She smiled a broad, genuine smile. The spark I'd felt grew hotter, the embers flaring.

"I think I need another drink. And so do you."

I usually stuck to one drink before each flight. That and the Xanax allowed me to doze off—but kept me from being so out of commission I couldn't work once I reached my destination.

But Morgan left little room for argument. When she called the bartender over, I ordered a refill.

"You're hard to say no to," I said when the glass of bourbon was placed in front of me. "Are you like this with everyone?"

She considered her answer before she spoke. "You're special. You're trying to figure things out. Most people don't even bother to ask these questions." She took a drink, then said, "What would you do if you quit your job? What do you dream of being?"

Again, her question took me off guard. I stared into the amber liquid in my glass. "Promise not to laugh."

"Do I seem like the kind of person to laugh at another person's dreams?"

"I guess not." I felt any remaining inhibitions coming down. She smiled. Her teeth were perfectly straight and white.

"I've always thought about being an illustrator." It felt strange to give voice to my dreams. I hadn't mentioned them to anyone in a long time. "I like to draw. I took a few classes in college. But I had to be practical. My mom left us the same year my dad started his business. There were some tough times for my dad and me. So we adopted a 'you and me against the world' mentality. We were going to make it no matter what."

"Sure."

"And my mom leaving taught me a lesson. I just didn't want to be . . . unprepared for the world. I wanted to know where I was going. I wanted certainty. Or I thought I did."

"I hear you," she said. "Money, parents . . . It's complicated."

"It must be for you, if your mom is sick. Is your dad—"

She started to answer but then held her index finger up in the air. "Can you hold that thought? I have to run to the bathroom."

"Sure."

She gathered up her purse and carry-on. Then she walked out to the concourse.

I looked at my phone. I saw a text from my dad. I was meeting him in Tampa to see a new project he was developing—a small strip mall in an up-and-coming neighborhood. He hoped to get a couple of restaurants and maybe a craft brewery to go in there, and he thought he needed me along to offer the "young person's perspective." His text message was typically short and didactic:

See you at 2. Don't be late. Remember, don't oversell these properties. They speak for themselves.

I wanted to write back and remind him how many deals I'd handled on my own. But I kept my response to myself.

When I looked up from the phone, I expected to see Morgan returning from the bathroom. Instead, I saw two airport police officers. A week earlier there'd been a security scare—a suitcase left unattended. It ended up being nothing, but it unnerved me to think of all the things that could go wrong—bombs, terrorists, pilot error. The cops served as a reminder of how much I disliked flying.

And Morgan still hadn't come back.

Maybe she'd walked off, left me at the bar while she boarded her plane. Or maybe she'd stopped to make a phone call, reaching out to her own version of Renee in some faraway city. *I'll be there soon. . . . I can't wait to see you. . . . I miss you. . . .*

And as I thought about that, an unreasonable jealousy crept through me. What did I care if she had someone else? What claim did I have on someone I'd known for just an hour?

The truth was that her life, despite the problems she'd told me about, sounded better than mine. I was trapped by work and obligation. She was going somewhere she associated with happy memories. Her travels sounded uncomplicated and easy.

But then she was there, walking toward me. Still wearing the sunglasses. She came close but kept standing. "I have to go now."

The corners of her mouth dropped.

"I thought you had more time," I said, looking at my watch. I tried to sound light and carefree, but I felt desperate. I didn't want her to go yet. I'd imagined the time we shared would stretch out forever, that the bubble would never pop.

But she was wielding a giant pin, ending our time together and sending me back to my mundane life. Florida. Real estate. Dad.

She put her bags on the bar, and my heart lifted. She was going to stay. But she ignored the drink and took off her sunglasses. She moved in close to me, placed her arms around the back of my neck, and leaned in. Her soft skin brushed against mine, cheek against cheek. I couldn't believe it was happening.

"I wish I could stay, but I can't," she said. "I've got to go."

"I don't even know your last name."

We stayed frozen for a moment before she said anything.

"My name's Morgan Reynolds."

And then her mouth brushed across my cheek and pressed, soft and smooth, against my lips.

I lost myself in the kiss. I gave in, slipping away from the airport as everything around us disappeared.

Long seconds passed, and I placed my hands on her hips—

But then she abruptly pulled back.

She was smiling, and I didn't want to let her go.

"I like you," she said. "I really do. And I loved that kiss."

"You know, you don't have to—"

But she was shaking her head, her eyes weary again.

"I do," she said. "I really have to go." She pulled away from me and picked up her bags and her sunglasses, which she slid back onto her face. "And you know what else?"

"What?"

"I'm sorry. But we're never going to see each other again."

Chapter 2

KIMBERLY GIVENS WAS running late.

As always.

She ran down the steps of her town house, carrying her laptop bag in one hand, her gun and badge in the other. Kimberly had no time to waste that Tuesday since her daughter, Maria, was waiting, soccer gear in hand, her face scrunched by the kind of impatience only a twelve-year-old could muster. The Laurel Falls, Kentucky, city sedan with municipal plates sat outside in the carport. Kimberly found the key fob, hitting the button.

"There, it's open," she said to Maria. "Go on."

Kimberly checked the clock above the stove: 9:55. She was meeting with the mayor of Laurel Falls at eleven. She couldn't be late. She had to deliver an update on the case.

The case. The case.

It had landed in Kimberly's lap just the day before, Monday, when prominent businessman Giles Caldwell hadn't shown up for work after not being seen or heard from all weekend.

Maria tossed her things into the back seat of the car. Kimberly climbed in and jabbed the "Start" button.

"We're going to be late," Maria said.

"We'll be fine," Kimberly said. "It's practice, not a game. Plus, I'm allowed to speed."

"Don't. Everyone will look at us."

"I was kidding," Kimberly said as she backed out of the driveway into the street, heading to the soccer field. "I'll get you there in time."

They rode in silence for several blocks, Maria's breath going in and out through her nostrils like a cartoon bull's. Kimberly rolled her eyes internally, recognizing behavior her daughter had gotten from her ex-husband and Maria's father, Peter. Maria had always fumed when things didn't go her way. When Kimberly and Peter were married, Kimberly had jokingly called her "Peter Junior."

"So I'm not going to see you tonight," Kimberly said.

"What do you mean?"

"I'm working late." Kimberly felt the guilt rising like high tide in her chest. "Dad's picking you up after soccer."

Maria let out a sigh. "The stupid case you got yesterday?"

"Yes, it is. We don't usually solve them in a day."

"This is the missing old guy? What's his name? Miles?"

"Giles. And he's not that old. He's fifty."

"How long has he been gone?"

"Since Thursday. That's when he last showed up at work."

"So he's dead," Maria said.

"Why would you say that?" Kimberly asked.

"The first forty-eight hours matter most. You always say that."

Kimberly tried to change the subject. She didn't want to dwell on what had happened to Giles Caldwell. "You know my job can be unpredictable. You'll have plenty of things to do with Dad."

No response. Maria was looking out the window.

"You know," Kimberly said, as if she were just thinking out loud, "if I get promoted, my work hours will be more regular. My boss is retiring, and the job is available."

And I have to see him this morning and tell him we don't have any leads in the town's biggest case in years. He'll be thrilled.

"You said they don't promote women," Maria said.

"I might have said that, yes. But I don't want you to worry. You can do anything you want, anything a man can do."

"I know, Mom. You tell me this all the time. So does Dad."

"Does he?"

"Yes."

Kimberly placed a mental check in Peter's "good" column.

"Well, I'm going to go for the promotion. And this case might make it happen." *If I can solve it* . . . Kimberly gripped the wheel tighter as the field came into view. "We're waiting on a crime scene report. I'm hoping there's something in there. It looks like this guy just disappeared into thin air. Or maybe he ran away."

Maria sat up. "Pull over. Right here."

"I know the drill," Kimberly said. She stopped the car and waited patiently while Maria dragged her things out the back. Her task complete, she came by Kimberly's window.

"So Dad's picking me up after practice?" she asked.

"He is. I texted him last night."

Maria sighed. "How long before you find out what happened with this missing man?"

Kimberly didn't believe in giving false hope. "I don't know, pumpkin. When people disappear . . . It can be slow work."

Maria shivered, and the corner of her mouth lifted in discomfort. "A man really disappeared? A grown man?"

"He did."

"But grown men don't disappear," she said, suddenly interested. "You say women are vulnerable. And kids. But a man. Someone that old. I mean . . . who would want to take him?"

"We don't know. We just know he's missing, and his brother is worried," Kimberly said. "He might just be out of town and forgot to tell anyone. He might have other problems."

"Like, he owes money to the mob?" Maria asked dramatically.

"We don't have that here."

"Yes, we do. I read about it online. The Dixie Mafia."

"I don't think he's mixed up with the Dixie Mafia." But then Kimberly wondered . . . How did she know what he was mixed up with? "Whatever it is, you don't have to worry about it. Your school is safe. The soccer field is safe. The coaches are here."

"You *are* coming to my match tomorrow night, right?"

"I wouldn't miss it. My calendar's highlighted. In bold letters."

"Okay." Maria sighed again. "Bye."

She walked away, cutting off Kimberly's farewell.

"Bye-bye. I love you."

AFTER MORGAN WAS GONE, I finished my drink.

The feel of her lips, the touch of her hips—the sensations lingered, like waking from a vivid dream. My head swirled with the effects of the alcohol and the intoxication of being so close to Morgan, of kissing her so intensely for those brief moments.

The bartender came my way, a slender, middle-aged woman. She wiped up a spill but looked at me from the corner of her eye.

"Did you want another one?" she asked.

"I have to stop," I said.

She took our glasses away and then handed me an ice water. I felt the curiosity coming off of her body in waves.

"Thanks," I said.

"You two seemed to be having an intense conversation."

"That was one of the strangest things that's ever happened to me," I said. "I just met her in the gift shop. We started talking about our lives, and then she just kissed me like that."

She nodded. "Not your average Tuesday morning. Do you want something to eat? You look a little pale."

I knew I needed to eat, so I asked for a club sandwich. I checked my phone again. My dad had written two more messages. He reminded me not to have a drink before I boarded my flight, to make sure I didn't show up smelling like alcohol.

Too late.

My dad could summon little sympathy for weaknesses or phobias. He thought I let my fear of flying control my life. *Control it?* I flew all the time despite it, but I couldn't tell the old man that. *Close to the vest. Keep it close to the vest.*

I started thinking of what was to come. The long, tense flight to Florida. The rental car pickup. The sterility of the highways, the never-ending stream of fast-food restaurants, gas stations, and toll plazas. All of it leading to a meeting with my dad and a few strangers who wanted to talk about zoning ordinances and profit and loss.

A cold sweat broke out on my forehead. I felt like a guy staring down a long, narrow tunnel with the light at the end flickering.

Nashville . . .

I reached for my wallet and found a fifty. I figured that should cover the drinks as well as the sandwich that hadn't yet come.

I grabbed my carry-on and headed for the concourse.

I CHECKED the board as I left the Keg 'n Craft. I found the flight—the only one in that terminal—departing for Nashville. It was boarding. My heart thumped against my rib cage.

When I reached the Nashville gate, a line of people moved slowly into the retractable jet bridge. I looked for Morgan. A fantasy came to my mind. She'd see me. She'd smile. She'd beckon me to her.

But I saw no sign of her.

She must have already boarded. Or maybe she was on a different flight. That thought brought me to a stop. What if Morgan wasn't even on that plane? If she'd lied . . .

"Can I help you, sir?"

A middle-aged man stood behind the counter.

"Can I get on this flight?" I asked.

"I can check," he said, although he didn't look happy about it.

He started tapping away. And while he did, I looked out at the plane, the long silver tube that probably—likely—held Morgan.

Then I realized I hadn't taken my second Xanax yet. Air escaped my lungs. "How's it looking?"

"We have nothing in coach. I can get you in first class."

I didn't hesitate. Not the way I felt. Not with the memory of the kiss and everything else. I had to gamble.

"I'll take it."

"Oh, wait," the man said. He started shaking his head. "Our computers have been glitchy all morning."

I looked over, and the entire line of people had passed through the jet bridge.

"Am I on or not?" I asked. "They're closing the door."

The man seemed too casual, too relaxed. Didn't he know I was dancing on the edge of a knife? That I was changing the course of my life based on a brief but intense conversation in a bar?

And a kiss. I could not, would not, forget that kiss.

"Ah," he said. "Got it."

Then something started printing—my boarding pass. It came out, and the man handed it to me.

"There you go."

"Thanks."

I hustled down the jet bridge, my carry-on banging against my side. An image of my dad flashed in my mind. I wouldn't ever be able to explain this to him. But I also felt a secret rush that I was doing something I knew would piss him off. It was a juvenile way to think, of course, but I couldn't help myself.

The flight attendant checked my boarding pass as I entered the plane. I was in the third row, aisle seat. I looked through the passageway to the coach section, where a few stragglers were blocking the aisle, stowing their bags overhead. I scanned the faces quickly, of those sitting and standing, but I couldn't see her.

The flight attendant came along beside me, gently placing her hand on my shoulder. "If you'd just settle in now, sir."

"I have to go back there. I have to see someone."

As if on cue, another flight attendant stepped through the passageway from coach and pulled the curtain shut behind her.

"We're close to takeoff, sir," the attendant by my side said. "We need everyone to buckle in."

"It won't take long—"

"You'll be able to do that once we're in the air," she said.

I stood frozen in place. I contemplated ignoring the flight attendant's wishes and just going back there to find Morgan. *If she was even there.* But I knew they wouldn't let me.

I had no choice. "Okay, okay," I said, and finally sat down.

I buckled up and pulled out my phone to text my dad, trying to tell him . . . but I didn't know what to say.

As the plane rolled back from the gate, I started to dread the fallout from my impulsive choice. I didn't regret it. But I knew how unpleasant it would be with my dad. I hated to disappoint him.

I'd rarely acted out as a teenager. I'd sensed intuitively how overwhelmed my dad was playing the role of single father while also trying to run a business. I knew the sacrifices he'd made, the opportunities he'd afforded me over the years. It made it basically impossible to contemplate telling him I wanted to quit and do something else. So I wrote quickly, trying not to overthink.

Dad, long story. Problem with flight. I won't make the meeting on time. Call you later.

Then the flight attendant was next to me, asking me to turn the phone off. We were taxiing down the runway, the pilot's tinny voice over the speaker telling the crew to prepare for takeoff.

The Xanax rattled in my pocket like dice. Too late to help.

I gripped my armrests. We sped down the runway, and my stomach dropped as we lifted into the air.

KIMBERLY ate a sandwich at her desk, losing herself in the process of reading a report about Giles Caldwell's business dealings.

The meeting with the mayor that morning had been short and decidedly unsweet. Mayor Robbins had enumerated Giles Caldwell's contributions to the town, in both business and philanthropy. She reminded the police they had a funding measure on the ballot next month to hire more officers and upgrade their equipment.

"Voters won't vote for it if you can't find a grown man in a town of sixty thousand people," Mayor Robbins told them.

Kimberly wanted to say, *Maybe he doesn't want to be found,* but she held her tongue. The cops were in the room to listen. To get their marching orders from the mayor.

Find Giles Caldwell. *Soon.*

Kimberly knew finding him meant more time away from Maria. The chance at the promotion . . . or the chance to fail spectacularly in the biggest case in years. How long would this take?

Kimberly told the voices in her head to knock it off.

She'd spend time with Maria next week. Once Giles Caldwell was found. Alive, she hoped. Peter, for all his faults, was an excellent father, and he'd see that Maria ate right and brushed her teeth and finished her homework. The girl was in good hands.

Just do your job, she told herself. *Wrap this up as soon as you can, but do it right.*

Her spirits lifted when she saw Brandon Ehrlich, one of her

fellow detectives. He'd promised to come see her as soon as he heard from the state crime lab.

"Brandon," she said, "tell me something good."

Brandon Ehrlich was thirty, ten years younger than Kimberly. He and his wife had a newborn son at home, and just the thought of a newborn made Kimberly feel tired. Even more tired than dealing with an intensely driven, smarter-than-average preteen.

"I've got the report."

"Okay. Any hits on fingerprints?"

Brandon shook his head. "There were a lot of prints in the house. They ran them through all the databases. Nothing."

"Figures. What about blood?" Kimberly asked.

"Nothing. They're still working on the hair and fiber analysis, but we need a suspect to match it to. That's about all we've got. What about Giles's ex-wife? Anything there?"

"I just got off the phone with her half an hour ago," Kimberly said. "Nothing useful. They divorced years ago. She lives in Idaho."

"Kids?" Brandon asked.

"None."

"And we've talked to his brother, Simon. He was a piece of work."

"Yeah," Kimberly said, "like we really needed his theories on what happened to Giles. What were they? Central American gangs? The neighbor who complained because Giles left his trash cans out too long once?"

"Don't forget a neighborhood kid selling candy. Have we had a rash of Girl Scouts murdering grown men?"

"Not that I'm aware of," Kimberly said. "He's worse than the nuts who send us notes with the letters they cut out of magazines."

Brandon tapped the report against his knee. "So what was he doing this past weekend when his brother supposedly disappeared?"

"We're piecing it all together," Kimberly said. "He says he went to a lecture on campus one night. A poker game with friends another. He lives alone too, so he has a lot of time unaccounted for."

"Hmm," Brandon said.

"Yeah. Yesterday he comes in here and pitches a fit about his brother being missing. But something seems off about the guy."

"He's pushy. And he has the two assaults on his record."

"He seemed more concerned about chewing us out than the fact that his brother might be in danger. Did you notice that?"

"Sure," Brandon said. "That could just be his way. Some people respond to grief with anger."

"Or maybe he protests too much. I told him we'll call when we know anything. But I'm not ruling anything out about him."

A phone rang on another desk. A door opened and closed.

"It doesn't look like Giles has a lot of friends," Kimberly continued. "He just works a lot. His business partner is out of the country but is flying back soon."

"Nothing at the office?"

"We've started talking to the employees. It's one of those hippy-dippy places. Ping-pong in the cafeteria. People bringing dogs to work. Everyone seems to show up when they want, so we've only talked to some of them. They give the impression that Giles was distant, hands-off. A little odd. Cold. He founded the company, but his partner . . ."

"Steven Hatfield," Brandon said.

"He handles the people side of things. He's the guy who's on the news touting the company's achievements, giving checks to charity. It doesn't sound like Giles's thing, although a lot of it is Giles's money. That's why the mayor cares so much. Giles donated to her campaign. Big-time."

"And Hatfield's out of town?" Brandon asked.

"Coming back tonight or tomorrow. He cut his vacation short."

"And the only thing missing is the ring. Giles's mother's engagement ring."

"No electronics," Kimberly said. "TV's there. Computers."

"His car too. A junkie would have taken something else."

"Hmm. It's odd. The place was ransacked, but only the ring was missing."

"And the ransacking . . ." Brandon said. "Is it possible for ransacking to be half-hearted? Stuff was thrown around, but some drawers were untouched. It almost looked . . . fake. Like someone didn't really want to trash the place. Could Giles Caldwell have wanted to disappear and make it look like a robbery?"

"Is it possible Giles Caldwell staged his own disappearance? We haven't found any reason for him to do that."

"I'm just thinking out loud. About everything," Brandon said.

"And the ring was sitting out in that creepy display dedicated to his mother. It didn't take much effort to find. So we have a criminal who only takes antique jewelry and ransacks half-heartedly. I'll say this—it's original," Kimberly said.

Brandon tapped the file folder against his knee a few more times. "What do you want to do now?"

Kimberly reached out and took the file. "I'm going to look this over and then make more calls. But you have other work to do. There's more happening than just Giles Caldwell."

"That's not how the mayor feels."

"We've got plenty of eyes. I'll let you know if I need you."

Brandon stayed in his seat.

"What?" Kimberly asked.

"I hope you get promoted to lieutenant. I really do."

"Thanks, Brandon. I hope so too."

She watched Brandon go and opened the manila folder.

MY HANDS remained locked on the armrests until we reached our cruising altitude and the seat belt sign dinged off. I hadn't even bothered to open the book I'd purchased in the gift shop, the one meant to take my mind off flying.

So what did I think was going to happen when she saw me? Were we going to fall into each other's arms and then run off together? I didn't even know if Morgan was on the plane. Maybe I'd boarded the wrong flight, fouling up things for nothing.

I unbuckled the metal clasp and stood up. The curtain to the rest of the plane had been opened, affording me a view of coach, but people were up and milling around, so I couldn't see much.

A low hum of conversation filled the confined space. My ears had popped on the way up, so everything sounded like we were underwater. I started back, excusing myself around my fellow travelers. As soon as I passed the curtain to coach, I scanned the seats, looking for the telltale hat and glasses.

Some people looked up as I moved by. Others were lost in their own worlds. They wore headphones, read books, whispered to their partners. Two flight attendants pushed a drink cart my way. I felt like a man swimming against the tide.

But then I saw Morgan, sitting on my left near the rear of the plane, the hat and sunglasses appearing among the sea of faces.

I squeezed around the drink cart. Then I rushed down the aisle.

I thought she'd sense me coming, that she'd automatically look up and see me, but she kept her head down. My mouth went dry, and I tried to think of what I was going to say.

Before I could formulate anything brilliant, I was next to her, standing over her and looking down.

She was staring at her iPad, headphones in her ears. She still hadn't noticed me. So I reached out and tapped her shoulder.

Her head whipped up so fast it startled me, and I took a step back. The plane hit an air pocket, and I lost my balance for a moment, stumbling back one step before regaining my footing.

Not the most graceful approach.

"It's me," I said. "I didn't mean to startle you."

Her facial expression didn't change, though her cheeks flushed. She removed her earbuds, but her face showed no joy or surprise at seeing me. She simply looked put out.

"I changed my flight," I said in a rush. "I'm in first class. That's all they had left. I know this is nuts. . . ."

Morgan still hadn't spoken, but a couple of the people around her—the gray-haired woman in the middle seat, the college student right in front of her—stared up at me.

Morgan said nothing, so I looked around, desperate for my next move. A guy about my age sat across the aisle from Morgan. He too had turned his head our way.

"Do you want to sit in first class?" I asked him. "We could trade seats so I can sit by her."

The guy looked confused. He seemed eager to sit in first class, but when he glanced Morgan's way, his face grew uncertain.

"Don't do this," Morgan said. "I don't want to sit by you."

The guy turned his head away. I felt my mouth drop open. I wasn't even sure what to say. I sensed more eyes turn to me.

I leaned toward Morgan, speaking in a lower voice. "I know this is crazy, changing my flight. I didn't even know for sure if you were on board. But we had a real connection back there, and I just . . . I couldn't stand the thought of never seeing you again. When you said that, Morgan, that we'd never see each other—"

"I don't know what you're talking about," she said in the coldest voice I'd ever heard. "I've never seen you before in my life. That's not even my name."

"But—"

"You don't even know me."

The woman next to Morgan gasped, then stared at me in disapproval. I noticed the same disapproving look rippling across the faces of our other fellow passengers. With those few words, Morgan had transformed me into an aggressive creep, a stalker.

I couldn't understand her behavior. Why speak so intimately, why kiss me that way in the bar, if she wanted to send me away?

"Morgan, I don't—"

But instead of listening, she stuck her hand straight up and hit the call button, summoning a flight attendant.

The woman next to her leaned over and said, "You're fine, honey. We won't let him bother you this way."

My mind raced. None of this was going the way I pictured.

A flight attendant materialized, asking what Morgan needed.

"This man," Morgan said, nodding my way. "This man thinks I'm someone else. He's bothering me."

The gray-haired woman joined her, all too eager to participate in my execution. "She's right. He's being very rude. He tried to make that gentleman move so he could sit down."

"Where is your seat, sir?" the flight attendant asked me.

"First class," I said.

"Would you like to go back and sit down? You can get a beverage up there and something to eat." She sounded firm and calm.

I looked down at Morgan, at her soft lips, her sunglasses and hat. I saw the indifference on her face. Her jaw was set firm.

The flight attendant placed her hand on my shoulder, gently guiding me away and to my seat.

But I resisted, turning back. "She's wrong," I said loudly, trying to explain the injustice of it all to a preoccupied jury. For some reason, I held my hands out as if I really thought I could convince them. "I do know her. She's wrong."

The flight attendant spoke low so only I could hear, her face close to mine. "Sir, I don't want to have to get the pilot involved."

I dropped my arms and let the flight attendant lead me back to first class.

I STAYED in my seat the rest of the way to Nashville. The image of Morgan—if that was even her name—reaching for the call button, the memory of the flight attendant threatening to summon the pilot, the realization that everyone thought I was a stalker . . . It all brought a flush of embarrassment to my cheeks.

It was an hour-long flight, but the time in the air dragged interminably. I tried to read the book with the running man on the cover. I learned about his drinking problem brought on by the loss of his wife and child in a tragic accident. And how that tragedy turned the man into a loner who killed for hire.

The woman next to me paged through a photo album. I envied her—she seemed to have a safe, fulfilling life. She looked over and smiled at me, and I nodded back. But we didn't speak.

When the plane rolled to a stop and reached the gate, I grabbed my bag and got out as soon as possible. If I never saw Morgan, the flight attendants, or the passengers around her again, it would be too soon. Surely they'd all go home and tell the story about the weird guy creeping after the beautiful woman on the plane.

I knew when I turned my phone back on that a blast of texts and voice mails from my dad would be waiting. I couldn't make the meeting in Tampa, no way, but he'd likely scheduled a dinner, and I could swoop in and present the united front of father and son working side by side. I could never mention that I'd been chasing a woman in the wrong direction. If I did, he'd shake his head, asking himself what kind of idiot child he had raised.

I beelined to the nearest ticket counter and asked about flights to Tampa. One was leaving, direct, in two hours. And it still had room for me. The ticket agent, a middle-aged woman with a pencil stuck in her hair, started tapping away to make it happen.

The effects of the alcohol were abating, and I was starting to feel more like myself. Feet on the ground. Plans to be made.

And mercifully out of the sky for a short time.

I leaned against the counter, trying not to look at the passengers from the Atlanta flight as they deplaned. I knew Morgan would be among them. She'd have to walk right past me.

Don't look. Don't look for the hat and glasses. Just let her go.

The ticket agent worked everything out and booked my seat. She printed a boarding pass, my third of the day.

"Thanks," I said.

I lingered for a moment. Would it be so wrong to take one last look? I scanned the people exiting the jet bridge. Maybe she'd already gone past me, or maybe she'd walked another way.

But then I saw the bucket hat, the bobbing ponytail, the large sunglasses. She walked with purpose, her head never turning.

I watched her go, holding back the impulse to approach or say anything else. I didn't need to have a long conversation with her. I just wanted to ask: *What's going on? Is there something wrong?*

But I squashed the desire. And she passed me and left my life forever.

WITH two hours to kill, I headed for the nearest bar.

I skipped the alcohol and opted for water and a sandwich, to prepare me for what was sure to be an onslaught of voice mails from Dad—although I figured a scolding from the old man wouldn't be nearly as humiliating as the events on the plane.

So I held the phone up to my ear and listened.

But people can surprise you. Morgan did.

And so did my dad.

His familiar, permanently raspy voice came through.

"Hey, kid, what's going on? Did something happen? I'm worried about you. Give me a call, okay? Love you."

My eyes burned. I needed a moment to collect myself. Somehow he knew I needed a pick-me-up, a show of support. Yes, people can surprise you in all kinds of ways.

I called him, and he answered right away.

"Are you okay, Joshua? That's all I want to know. You've never been late; you've never missed a meeting."

"I know. I got sidetracked. I'm in Nashville."

"Nashville? What are you doing there?"

"I've booked a flight to Tampa for later this afternoon. I can catch you for dinner, okay? We won't miss a beat."

"That's fine." He'd adopted the soothing voice he used in crises. "I don't care about the deal. The deal will happen. I want to know what's going on with you."

"I told you, I'm good."

"Look," he said, "we don't have to talk about this now, but I can tell things aren't right. I can tell you aren't happy. Why don't we talk when you get to Tampa? We can find the time."

I thought of all the work we had to do. I thought of Dad staying up late, doing paperwork and studying reports. If it meant I had to put up with the occasional gruff text or short-tempered call, I could handle it. It seemed like a small price to have financial security and someone I could always count on.

"Dad, I just . . . I've been a little lost lately, a little distracted. But I'm back on board. I am. I'll see you in Tampa."

"Is it Renee?" he asked, gently probing. "She always seemed like a nice girl. She's levelheaded, has a good job."

"It's not Renee, Dad. I've got to go." I had nowhere to be for two hours, but I didn't want to keep dodging his questions.

"Travel safe, kid. Love you."

"I love you too. Talk soon."

I hadn't paid any attention to the TV screen above the bar until that moment, but my eye caught a flash of something. A face.

A woman's face, a still photograph.

And it looked like Morgan.

But it was gone. I told myself my mind had been warped by her touch, by the kiss. I thought I was seeing her everywhere.

My food came, and I brought out my computer and started looking over the files relevant to the trip to Tampa.

I also texted Renee, leaving out where I was. But I told her I was fine and we could talk that night when I got to my hotel.

I went back to the files but couldn't concentrate. I opened Facebook and typed in: "Morgan Reynolds."

I scrolled through the results until I saw her face. Without sunglasses. I hesitated before opening her page. What would I see? Pictures of a boyfriend? Or . . . even a husband? But I couldn't stop myself from looking.

Her picture filled my screen. She looked beautiful. And happy. And it looked like her name really was Morgan Reynolds. Why she said it wasn't on the plane, I had no idea.

I thought I'd seen enough. We'd brushed up against each other; then we'd parted. That was that. She'd blown me off. It was just that simple. Still, I took a quick scroll through her timeline, and what I saw there almost sent me tumbling back off the barstool.

HAVE YOU SEEN MORGAN? Missing Person. Believed Endangered.
MORGAN REYNOLDS Age 25

I stared at the words, not entirely processing them. When I shook myself loose, the gears in my mind finally unlocking and moving forward again, I scrolled through the rest of her timeline.

The words and images went past. *Hasn't been seen in several days . . . not answering her phone . . . not at her apartment . . .*

It explained so many things. The sunglasses, the hat. Her refusal to speak to me on the plane. Her farewell delivered with such certainty: *We're never going to see each other again.*

Had that been her face on the TV? On the local news there in Nashville, reporting her disappearance?

It all led to the question: *Why?*

And could I very well travel to Tampa and continue with my day if I'd just seen a missing person?

Then it hit me—maybe she hadn't even left the airport yet.

I picked up my bag and made my way back to the concourse,

feeling a strong sense of purpose. I had to find the airport police. I went up to the ticket agent, the one with the pencil in her hair.

"Excuse me," I said. "I need the police. How do I find them?"

The woman's face fell. "Is something wrong?"

How could I explain the situation? "I just need to talk to them."

The woman picked up a phone and pressed a few buttons. Scenarios ran through my mind. Morgan was being chased. She owed money. A relationship had ended poorly.

I stood off to the side, staring out the huge windows at the planes. Then two police officers came up to me. I reported what I'd seen, realizing how far-fetched my story sounded. I met a stranger in Atlanta and changed all my plans to follow her to Nashville. And now I thought she was a missing person.

When I finished, they both studied me, their eyes opaque.

"Why don't you come with us, sir?" one of them said.

WE PASSED through heavy steel doors into a small station. Only then did they start to ask me questions. I directed them to Morgan's Facebook page and waited while they called it up on a desktop computer. They both studied it, their brows furrowed.

"It says she lives in Nashville," one said. He was older, likely in his fifties. His name was Officer Travis. "So if she flew here, maybe she was heading home?"

"I guess that's possible. Yes."

"But she told you she was going up to Wyckoff, across the state line into Kentucky?"

"She said she grew up and went to college there," I said.

"This is social media. Has she been reported to the police?"

"I think I saw her face on TV," I said. "The local news."

"Really. Why don't you give Metro Nashville a call and see what's going on there?" Travis said to his partner, about my age, with hair cut in a military-style buzz. His name tag said JANSEN.

Jansen left the room while Travis picked up the phone and pressed a few buttons. "I'm going to need to look at a passenger list. And CCTV footage from Concourse B, near gate thirteen." He provided the flight number and the airline, then hung up.

He turned to me. "So you just met this woman at the gift shop in Atlanta? And then decided to follow her here to Nashville?"

"Yeah. I know it sounds crazy. You know how sometimes you just connect with someone right away?"

I could clearly see he was skeptical. Apparently, his uniform didn't conceal the beating heart of a romantic.

"What was she wearing?" he asked.

I described everything I remembered—the sunglasses and hat.

"So you didn't really see her face?" Travis asked.

I hesitated. But then I figured the cops had heard it all. "She took the glasses off. We kissed. At the bar. And then she left."

I filled him in on the rest—changing flights, the seat in first class. Approaching her at the rear of the plane.

"She said her name wasn't Morgan?" he asked, his brow furrowing with even more skepticism. "And she didn't know you?"

"That's right. But it was her. I know it was. Same hat. Same beauty mark. But I don't know why she said she wasn't Morgan. Or why she acted like she didn't know me."

"Maybe she's married and regretted getting you all stirred up."

"She didn't have a ring on," I said. Then I pointed at his computer. "People are worried about her. I didn't make this up. If someone is in danger, then we have to help, don't we?"

"Easy, chief," he said, leaning back.

Jansen came back into the room and nodded at Travis, who asked me to wait in an outer office, which I did. I sat in an uncomfortable chair while other cops came and went, ignoring my presence.

About twenty minutes passed, and then Jansen opened the door and summoned me back with a quick wave of his hand.

"Have a seat, Joshua," Travis said. I did what he asked, and he sat behind the desk. "We talked to the Metro Nashville Police Department. Morgan Reynolds was reported as a missing person just yesterday. That's why she was probably showing up on the news, and why her friends are concerned. Nobody's heard from her for a few days. I looked it up and saw the alert."

A chill ran up my back, oppressive and clammy.

"But she is an adult," Travis said, "and if she doesn't want to answer her phone or talk to her friends, she really doesn't have to. There's no evidence of a crime. Yet."

"But the police think she is missing."

"Sure. But you say you just saw her. So maybe she's back."

"Yeah, but— So we do nothing? The police do nothing?"

"Nashville PD are on it. She's in their system, and you saw her on the news. They're taking care of *that* missing persons case."

I didn't like the way Travis sounded. He suddenly had the demeanor of a guy who wanted to wash his hands of the problem.

"Why are you saying 'that case'?" I asked. "Isn't it the same case? I met Morgan Reynolds in the airport. She's missing."

"We looked at the CCTV footage," Travis continued. "We saw a woman matching your description get off the flight. She walked right past you without even turning her head to look your way."

I felt a little needle stick me in the heart when he told me that.

"So what does it mean?" I asked. "Are you saying I'm crazy?"

Travis looked over at his partner; then his eyes settled on me.

"Here's the thing. We checked the passenger list. I'm not sure who you saw, but there was no one named Morgan Reynolds on that flight. According to the airline, she was never on that plane."

I GIVE the police officers credit—they were patient. Maybe they felt bad for me because I might have been led up the garden path by the Keg 'n Craft's version of a femme fatale. They put up with me for another fifteen minutes as I threw progressively less believable theories at them to explain Morgan's behavior.

Finally Travis stood up, hitching his pants as he did. He gave me a patient look, one that was almost fatherly and served only to remind me of the clock ticking against my flight to Tampa.

"Look, Joshua," Travis said. "We don't know what's going on with this woman. I have no doubt you met someone in Atlanta and kissed her and followed her here. Maybe she gave you a fake name to throw you off her trail. Maybe she had heard of Morgan Reynolds the missing person and decided to say that's who she was, like a woman handing out a fake phone number in a bar. Why she chose to blow you off or say she didn't know who you were . . . Well, I think you just need to chalk this one up to a strange, brief encounter."

"But if she's missing—"

"Like I said, Nashville PD is searching," he said. "And we're going to file a report right here as well."

Travis failed to make me feel any better. In fact, he made me feel worse, since he was suggesting I'd been an amiable stooge who'd fallen for the whimsical games of a manipulative woman.

I hated to be taken for a fool, in business or in love.

Cards close to the vest.

I hated even more that Travis might be right.

I stood up and shook both of the officers' hands.

"If we need anything else, we'll give you a call," Travis said.

I trudged down the concourse and found a quiet place near my gate and sat staring into space. None of it made sense. A strange woman had taken me for a ride. Maybe she was laughing at me.

Except . . .

Why had she left town in a way that alarmed her friends and caused someone to go to the police? That didn't fit with what Travis said, unless she simply wanted to take everyone for a ride.

I wasn't sure how many times the PA announcer called my name before I heard it. The sound of my own name seemed to reach me through a fog. It had to be the cops. Travis and Jansen, they wanted something else from me.

I asked the first ticket agent I saw where the courtesy phone was. She pointed me across the concourse. When I picked up the phone, an operator waited. I gave my name, and she told me to hold one moment. Then I remembered that I'd given the police my phone number. If they'd wanted to reach me, they could have called my cell, so . . .

"Hello?" I said.

"It's me." The voice was unmistakable. "Don't hang up."

It was Morgan.

I LOOKED around the concourse before I said anything. No one was paying any attention to me.

"Are you calling to tell me what's going on with you?" I asked.

"I don't have much time," she said.

I shook my head even though she couldn't see me. "Your friends think you've disappeared. The police are looking for you. I think I saw you on TV."

Morgan sighed. "I know. I'll take care of it as soon as I can."

"So what did you call me for?" I asked.

"I wanted to apologize. I acted like . . . I don't know what. A total weirdo. But there's a reason why I blew you off on the plane and then walked past you in the airport. I told you we'd never see each other again. I had every intention of honoring that."

"My plane's leaving soon," I said. "My plane to Tampa for the meeting I already missed because of you. If you have something more to say, you should spit it out."

"That's just it," she said. "Your job, all the things we talked about at the bar. I'm glad we said those things about having a larger purpose in life. I've been struggling with that a lot lately. It was good to find someone else who felt the same way I feel."

I agreed with her—it *had* felt good to talk about those things.

She continued, "I don't know what else there is to say. I needed a little lift, and you gave it to me. That's why I kissed you. That's why . . . I'll always remember you. And that moment."

Something shifted inside me. The ice had cracked. It was floating away. Her voice—the southern flavor, the soothing tone. The unvarnished honesty. No one talked to me like that. No one.

"Why are you traveling under another name?" I asked. "Why are you hiding? Are you in trouble?"

"How do you know . . . Oh, you've been to the cops?"

"I had to. I saw everything online about you being missing."

"Word spreads fast. Okay, then. I have to get moving."

"Where are you?" I asked. "Are you really going to Wyckoff?"

"Just remember what we talked about. Don't go to that stupid meeting in Tampa if you don't want to. I know it's with your dad, and that makes it complicated. But, believe me, it can all get much more complicated if you stay involved with something that isn't working. I know all about that."

"That's easy for you to say. You quit your job. You're free."

She laughed, and I sensed a combination of frustration and humor. "Look," she said, "if you have to take Xanax in order to do your job, maybe it isn't the right one."

"You should call your friends. Let them know you're okay."

"Yeah. I don't know. I'm trying . . ."

"Morgan, if you're in trouble . . . if you need someone to help you, let me do it. I can go back to the cops; I can call someone."

"I meant what I said about never seeing you again," she said. "Forget that job, Joshua. Have a good life. A meaningful one."

The line went dead. She was gone.

Again.

Chapter 3

KIMBERLY SPENT NINETY minutes at Giles Caldwell's house. She met the crime scene tech there and walked through the premises. She hoped they'd stumble across something they'd missed, some breakthrough. A blood spatter. A note. A shell casing.

But she knew she was dreaming. If one of those things had been there to discover, it would have already been found.

"What do you think about the way this place is ransacked?" she asked the tech, echoing Brandon's theory.

The tech pushed her glasses up on her nose. "Incomplete."

"Meaning . . . staged?"

"Maybe. It's odd nothing is missing but that ring."

After Kimberly finished with the crime scene, she joined the other officers as they fanned out through the neighborhood again, in case they had missed something the first time. Kimberly felt her frustration grow with each dead end. It had been twenty-four hours since Giles Caldwell had been reported missing by his brother, Simon. Twenty-four hours, and nothing to go on.

When she returned to the station, she checked the landline on her desk and saw five calls from Simon Caldwell.

"What now?" she said out loud. "Did he see Jack the Ripper fleeing his brother's house?"

Then she received a text from Peter.

You're going to be at the soccer match tomorrow, right?

Kimberly wrote back, feigning a confidence that was starting to slip away.

Of course. See you there.

An anger rose inside her. Why did he think he needed to ask her? *Let it go*, she told herself. *Think about Maria. Think about the great child the two of you managed to create.* That was her world. She had a great kid and a job she loved. Even if the job was pushing her to the edge.

Kimberly knew her nights wouldn't return to normal until they knew what had happened to Giles Caldwell. She wished they had just one decent working theory. He'd run off with a woman. He owed a mobster money. His brother killed him in a fit of rage. . . .

You never knew what family members would do.

She'd already told Peter to prepare for more nights with Maria, more unpredictability. Fortunately, they worked better as a divorced couple than they had when they were married.

Her cell phone rang. She rolled her eyes when she saw the name on the caller ID, but she answered.

"Hey, Nelson," she said. "To what do I owe the pleasure?"

Detective Ben Nelson worked for the Nashville Police Department, an hour away from Laurel Falls. They'd met on a handful of occasions, working regional cases. He was divorced, and asked every unmarried woman he came across to dinner. And kept asking. Kimberly felt thankful for the sixty-mile buffer between them.

"Well, I suspect you're expecting an invitation to dinner, aren't you?" Nelson asked.

"I'd hate for you to disappoint me. I like saying no for the ninety-ninth time."

"Then prepare to be disappointed," he said, his voice buoyant. "I have something that might be important."

"Okay. I'm listening."

"I've got a friend who works for the airport police in Nashville. His name's Travis. I was talking to him about another case, and then he tells me about this thing that just happened at the airport."

Kimberly looked back at her desk, expecting Nelson to share some diverting story about a terrorist scare or someone smuggling something bizarre. She listened with one ear and half her mind. . . .

". . . meets this woman . . . shares a kiss with her . . . then she ignores him when they're on the plane. . . . He finds her on Facebook. . . . She's missing . . . used to live in Laurel Falls. . . ."

"What was that?" Kimberly said.

"My friend looked her up on social media. She lived and worked in Laurel Falls until she moved down here to Nashville a few months ago. No one knows what's going on. A friend filed a police report, and there's a lot of chatter on Facebook. Travis took all the information down and let the man who smooched her go. They're not even sure if he saw this woman or if he was just kind of lovestruck. She didn't show up on the passenger list."

"Sure, okay. So you're calling me because this woman lived in Laurel Falls at one time?" Kimberly asked. "Are you saying you want me to do some legwork for you? I'm kind of buried right now."

"I know. You've got a missing adult in Laurel Falls. Prominent businessman, friend of the mayor. Clock's ticking, right?"

"Even as we speak."

"I'm not calling about him. Not exactly." His voice brimmed with excitement. "When Travis told me about it, I checked out this woman's Facebook page too."

Kimberly tried to organize her thoughts. What did this guy kissing a woman in the airport have to do with her?

"I just sent you the link," he said. "I figured I'd let you check it out for yourself. You can thank me later."

And then he hung up.

Kimberly sighed as she accessed her email. The message from Nelson popped up. She clicked on the link, which took her to the

Facebook page for someone named Morgan Reynolds, apparently the woman in the airport who had been reported missing. Kimberly scanned the page. A pretty girl. Athletic, slender.

But why had Nelson sent it? What did it have to do with her?

Then she read what he'd written above the link.

"Check out where she worked."

Kimberly clicked the "About" button on Morgan's page. The name of the company where she'd been employed popped up.

She read it once. And then twice. For it to really sink in.

"Holy crap," she said, even though no one was listening.

I WENT as far as standing in line, getting ready to board the flight to Tampa. But I kept thinking about Morgan. An undercurrent of desperation had run beneath her words when we spoke on the courtesy phone. She'd sounded like a person who wanted to say more, *needed* to say more, but couldn't.

The rush to get away from me, the failure to explain it all.

The alias, the sunglasses.

How could I just stand by and do nothing?

I couldn't go back to the airport police. They weren't even convinced I'd seen Morgan on that plane. And wasn't it possible involving the police would make things more difficult for Morgan?

I faced the prospect of squeezing into a long metal tube, or I could turn around and try to help someone who really needed it.

What choice did I have?

I headed for the rental car counter, where I acquired a large sedan. Once my carry-on and my computer were stowed in the trunk, I started out, the dashboard-mounted GPS pointing me north on I-65 toward the Tennessee-Kentucky border.

Then I remembered my dad.

What would I tell him about this excursion to Wyckoff?

I checked the clock on the dash: 4:33. He wouldn't expect me until seven or so. I decided to get to Wyckoff and look around, and then decide what to tell Dad. I hoped to know something, and then give him as much information as possible. He'd still think I was nuts, but at least I could provide the whole story.

I wasn't sure what I expected. How would I find a person who didn't want to be found? How did I know she'd even gone to Wyckoff after she'd bobbed and weaved around the other facts?

But what did I have to lose? If I went there and struck out, then I could return to my life knowing I'd done everything I could to help Morgan. If I'd taken the plane to Tampa, and faked it through a series of meetings and dinners, I'd always wonder.

I crossed the state line from Tennessee into Kentucky, and then the GPS took me off the interstate, sending me northwest toward Wyckoff on a two-lane state road. I cracked the window, letting the fresh air wash over me.

Then my phone rang. I saw the caller's name. Renee.

I answered. "Hey."

"Hey, guy. Are you in Florida yet?"

I thought about lying. But that felt wrong. I might not have been in love with Renee, *really in love,* but I didn't want to lie.

"A change of plans," I said. "I'm not going to Florida."

"Oh. Does your dad have you doing something else?"

"No, I'm doing something on my own," I said.

"You are? What do you mean? Your own deal?"

The scenery looked peaceful. The open fields and white farmhouses reminded me of growing up in Indiana. I'd lived in Chicago for five years, but it never felt much like home.

"It's not work," I said.

And I told her the story. Meeting Morgan in the gift shop. The drinks at the bar. The Facebook posts about her disappearance.

I left out the kiss. Of course. And I left out the awkward exchange on the flight to Nashville.

But Renee was smart. She could figure out I wouldn't be following a woman across state lines unless I felt something for her.

Maybe I was an idiot, but I didn't feel like lying. I didn't feel like living a life I didn't want to live anymore.

When I was finished, she stayed quiet. Then finally she said, "That's quite a story."

"You understand, right, that I can't just turn my back on someone who might be in trouble?"

The question sounded foolish even as I asked it.

"Someone in trouble who happens to be a woman," she said. "What if it's some scam? She could be crazy, and you're running off to chase her like you're some chivalrous knight."

"It's not like that, Renee. It's about . . ."

But I couldn't finish the sentence. It *was* about her being a woman. A beautiful woman. And it was about that kiss. It was about how connected I already felt to her.

"It's fine, Joshua," Renee said. "Go on and do what you have to do. You're a good guy—I know you are. But the last six months we dated, I couldn't get you to tell me the most basic thing about your life. Getting you to tell me how your day went felt like pulling teeth. And heaven forbid I asked you about your mother. But this stranger . . . You were able to talk to a stranger in a bar? Wow. Maybe all of this running around will bring you some clarity."

"I . . ." She was right. I did want clarity. Not about Renee. More about myself, my life. About everything. "I hope so too."

"Good," she said. "But when you get back, don't expect to find me waiting again. Because we are as over as over can be."

I ENTERED Wyckoff, Kentucky, the college town Morgan said she was heading to, and drove along the edge of the campus.

Nostalgia sank its hooks into me. I was far enough away from college to remember it fondly, close enough to believe I could easily go back. For a moment, I allowed myself to wonder how I would do things differently if that mythical time machine existed.

Would I major in illustration? Would I spend more time having fun? Would I find the guts to say no to my dad when he offered me the chance to start a career in his company?

It hurt in a sweetly painful way to think about. I pushed the thoughts away, tried to accept a past that couldn't be changed.

I followed the road around the north end of campus into a small downtown. I passed dive bars advertising cheap beer and sandwich places with overly hip names. Students milled on the sidewalks, and I scanned the faces, looking for Morgan. Futility landed on me like a heavy cloak. Needle in a haystack much?

I made several circuits of downtown and went through campus twice. I needed to make a plan, so when I ended up in the downtown again, I pulled over and looked up hotels on my phone. Would Morgan even stay in a hotel? Or was she crashing with a friend or lover or family member? But I had to start somewhere.

Two moderately priced hotels sat within a block of each other—a Best Western and a Hampton Inn. They were in a commercial area just south of campus, so I headed that way. I pulled into the Best Western lot and circled the building, hoping . . . what exactly? That I'd find Morgan standing outside, one hand on her hip, eagerly awaiting my arrival?

I took another turn around the building. I knew I couldn't just walk in and ask if a woman was staying there. And if Morgan had purchased her plane ticket under an assumed name, why would she stay in the hotel using her real one?

I guided the car over to the Hampton Inn. I circled once and then one more time. A hotel employee, a young guy, pushed a bin of trash out the back door, heading for the Dumpster. I pulled my car alongside him and got out. He turned and looked at me.

"Help you with something, sir?" He was thin and wiry with floppy hair that fell over his forehead. His name tag read BILLY.

"I'm looking for someone."

"A hotel guest? You can ask at the front desk," he said. "But they aren't at liberty to give much information out."

I brought out my phone and showed him the picture of Morgan from her Facebook page. "Have you seen her?"

Billy finished dumping the trash. He leaned over, studying the picture. "I don't know. I don't interact with the guests much."

"The hotel is pretty empty, right? Could you go in and look around? Or ask at the desk if they've seen someone like her?"

He stared at me.

I reached into my pocket and brought out two twenties. "She's a friend of mine. I'm not going to hurt her. I'm here to help her. Just let me know if she's here."

Billy studied the two bills in my hand. Then he reached out, took them, and tucked the bills into his shirt pocket.

"You've got to give me a minute, okay?" He shrugged. "I need to take this back in and dump another load."

I got back into my rental car and waited.

It took fifteen minutes for the security guard to come out the same door Billy had gone in with his trash bin, his floppy hair, and my forty bucks. He made a beeline for my car.

"Thanks, Billy, you little bastard," I said to myself. Apparently, forty bucks wasn't the going rate for buying off a garbage boy.

The guard came along the driver's-side window.

"Are you looking for someone, sir?" he asked.

He had a shaved head that could have been used as a battering ram and wore a dark suit two sizes too big.

"Just a friend," I said. "She told me she'd be here."

"The police might like to know that you're here bribing hotel employees for information about one of our guests."

"I didn't really think of it as a bribe. I thought of it more as a donation to his college fund. You know, helping a working kid out."

"You need to leave, sir," the guard said. "I've taken down the plate number on your car. If I see you back, I will call the police."

I drove out under his watchful eye and left.

I didn't know where to go. But three blocks from the Hampton Inn and Best Western, I saw a figure trudging along the side of the street. I recognized his floppy hair. I pulled over, powering down the passenger-side window. He turned to look at me.

"Thanks for ratting me out."

Billy stepped over to my car. "I didn't rat you out. Sean overheard me talking to the desk clerk." Billy dug in his pocket, bringing out the two twenties. "You can have this back if you want."

"It's okay," I said. "I didn't mean to get you in trouble. You didn't get fired or anything, did you?"

"No, I'm off now. The last thing I do is take the trash out."

"Do you need a ride?" I asked.

"I'm cool. My girlfriend lives up here." He nodded toward the next block.

"Well, have fun," I said.

Billy looked like he wanted to say more. He leaned down, casting his eyes both ways before resting his hands on the windowsill.

"My friend who works the desk. Sometimes she works at the hotel next door. The Best Western. We all get moved back and forth between the two places if they need us."

"Okay," I said. "Go on."

"She was over there earlier today, helping out. She says a lady checked in there who might be the one you're looking for."

"The clerk thinks this woman who checked in was my friend?"

"Might be. She couldn't remember the room number, but it's on the third floor. Three ten? Fourteen? Something like that."

"Okay." I felt better. At least I had something. "Thanks."

"She remembered her because she seemed kind of jumpy," he said. "And she was crying the whole time she checked in."

I WALKED through the lobby of the Best Western like I belonged there. The desk clerk, who was busy talking on the phone, barely looked my way. I hopped on the elevator and pressed "3."

It had to be her.

But what happens when I get to her room? Would she be alone? Why was she holed up in this hotel? Why was she crying?

The doors opened, and I stepped onto the third floor. The room numbers Billy had mentioned were to the left, so I went that way.

Room 310 came in sight, the first possibility Billy had given me. I stopped and listened but heard nothing. Then I knocked.

It took a minute, and then the door opened, revealing a massive guy who wore only a white towel.

"I'm sorry," I said. "I'm looking for Morgan."

"You're barking up the wrong tree, bud."

"Yeah, maybe I am." But I still looked past him into the room.

"Need something else?" he asked.

"Not really—"

He closed the door in my face. So I went to the next room Billy mentioned, hoping for better results. I knocked, but no one answered. I moved on and knocked on yet another door, with no answer. Then I came to room 306.

With sore knuckles and fading hopes, I knocked.

A light glowed from behind the peephole, and then something blocked it for a moment, meaning someone was looking out. But the door didn't open, and no one said anything. The person remained at the peephole a long time.

For all I knew, the person was calling the front desk.

Then I heard the lock being undone. The door came open, and it was her. Morgan. No hat, no sunglasses, but wearing the same clothes she'd worn in the airport. The hallway light struck her face, catching her eyes, and the breath stuck in my throat.

She was as beautiful as I remembered.

She stared at me, her lips pressed together. Her eyes darted to either side of me, up the hallway and down. When they settled on me again, they narrowed. "What are you doing here?"

"I followed you," I said. "I was worried."

She let out a long sigh, the sound of a punctured tire rapidly losing air. "Get in here," she said, waving me into the room.

I went in, and she bolted the door shut behind me. I looked around the room. Two beds, the carry-on bag next to the hat and sunglasses on one of them.

"You shouldn't be here," she told me. "You should leave. Go back to wherever you have to go."

"You told me to quit my job," I said.

"Fine. Go do that. But you can't do it here. Really, Joshua."

"You're using another name, traveling in disguise. Your friends think you've disappeared."

"Those are my problems. Not yours."

"You agreed to have a drink with me. You kissed me, and then you called me at the airport."

"And told you to leave me alone," she said.

"I couldn't," I said. "Not when it seems like you're in danger. If you tell me everything is okay, I'll go. But I think there's something bad going on, and you're dealing with it alone."

She continued to stare at me. Her eyes were red and raw.

"So why don't you tell me what's going on?" I asked.

She turned away, paced to the door, and then came back.

"You don't want to know," she said.

"I do, Morgan. Look how far I've come."

"You're an idiot. You'll be implicated. Do you know that?"

"Implicated? In what?"

"I'm not trying to be cruel. . . . I just . . ."

"Look, try me. Okay? Just try me."

"Okay," she said after a long pause. "I haven't told anybody, so I might as well tell you."

We sat across from each other on opposite beds, and I waited for her to begin.

"Do you know anything about the way women can be treated in tech companies?" she asked.

"I've heard stories," I said. "Is that what happened to you? Were you . . . harassed or something?"

She shook her head. "No, nothing like that. I'm talking about the way women get taken advantage of in terms of their work. We get shut out and overlooked. Or ignored."

I told her I understood, trying to keep calm and patient.

"Remember this morning, how we talked about how we come out of college all idealistic and hoping to make a difference?"

"Sure."

"That's what I thought I was doing." She paused. "I went to work for a tech company called TechGreen. They make apps and do Web design. In Laurel Falls, a town about thirty minutes east of here. I got the job a year after I finished college at Henry Clay. It sounded like a good place to work. They were trying to help the environment through tech, and they said they treated their employees differently. You know, healthy, catered lunches in the break room. Massages. Yoga. That kind of thing."

I compared her experience to working for my dad. I spent my time cramped in airplanes. Dad didn't know what yoga was, and the closest thing I came to a catered meal was when he took me to a diner and regaled me with stories of his early days in business. . . . Although to be honest, I liked hearing the old man talk.

"I've heard of companies like that," I said.

"It was great. I met people I liked. We all wanted to create technology that helped the planet. Things that reduced our impact on the environment. Make a difference." She met my eye. "So I get involved in some projects, make some decent money. I'm moving along the way I'm supposed to. Then it was time for me to take the lead on an app instead of just helping other people."

"That sounds like progress."

"Moving on up. Becoming a big girl."

She sounded cynical and disappointed. Maybe we'd both seen what was behind the curtain of adulthood and found it wanting.

"I came up with an app, something the company could really run with. It allowed you to enter products you found in the store— clothes, food, cleaning supplies, whatever—and it would tell you the product's environmental impact. You know, are there poisons in the product? Or was pollution generated as it was made? Were workers being mistreated somewhere in the world? We called it LifeShoppe with an 'e' on the end, and, damn, it was good."

"I'm sure they were happy," I said.

"Oh, yeah. The app was a smash. It sold and sold. And got written up in industry magazines. It did better than anything else TechGreen had ever done. It was . . . really just great. Not only had I come up with something that made the world a better place, but I'd also done something to help the company."

"So, what happened after that?"

She heaved a big sigh. "They'd had successful apps before. Not quite this big, but things that had done well. Every time—*every time*—the owner of the company would give the person or team who came up with the idea a bonus—enough to say that the company valued what those people had accomplished."

A troubled look came over her face. Tears filled her eyes.

"I'm sorry," I said.

"This is way more than you bargained for, isn't it?" she asked.

"We can stop talking if—"

"No," she said. "I want to tell you. It feels good to have someone listening. So you can guess. I didn't get the damn bonus. Nothing." She shook her head. "And here's the kicker. The other developers, the ones who had received bonuses? They were all men. I was the first woman to make them this much money, and when it came time to get the bonus, there was nothing for me. Nothing at all."

Morgan rushed to the bathroom, closed the door behind her, and locked it. I heard running water and then coughing.

"Are you okay?" I asked. "Do you need anything?"

"Just leave me alone," she said.

A pretty clear answer. I checked the bedside clock: 7:21. It was getting late. I had to call Dad. I couldn't avoid him forever.

"I'm going to step out and make a phone call," I said through the closed door, hoping Morgan heard me.

I went out and took the stairs down to the first floor. I found a small sitting area in the lobby and sat at a small table in a corner. I took a deep breath and called Dad.

When Dad answered, he sounded cheery. His tone told me the afternoon meetings had gone well.

"Hey. Did you just land? Was the plane late?"

"I haven't landed. I'm not coming to Tampa."

A pause. "Joshua, what's going on?"

His voice sounded uncertain, bordering on disapproval.

"Dad, a friend of mine is going through a crisis. It's a long story, and I don't have time to tell it now. But I'm not going to make it to Tampa tonight. I have to be here. It's the best thing, and I know you can handle what's going on down there."

"I don't like this, Joshua. First you tell me one thing, and then you decide to do something else. Are you in trouble?"

"No, I'm not." But I wasn't sure. I remembered the word Morgan had used. *Implicated.* Not a pretty word, not at all. "Dad, remember earlier today when we talked, and you said you could sense that I was a little dissatisfied?"

"Sure. We said we'd talk about it when you got here."

"I know. I appreciate that. But you were right, so I'm trying to take care of something, with this friend, because it seems more important at the moment than work does. Does that make sense?"

A man in khaki pants and a sweatshirt came through the swooshing automatic doors and into the lobby. He looked around, then went to the desk. I couldn't say why, but I wondered if he was looking for Morgan. It seemed like an irrational thought, not backed up by anything he'd done, but might someone be looking for her?

"Is this *friend* a woman?" Dad asked.

Could I lie? "Yes, she is."

"Oh, Joshua," he said. "A woman?" He let out a rough sigh. "Look, Joshua, I understand. . . . But you need to be smart here."

"It's not like that, Dad. It's not some . . ." I couldn't find the words. What did I have with Morgan beyond a—potential—one-night stand? All started by that kiss in the airport bar. Was I thinking with anything more than the lower regions of my body?

The man at the counter seemed unhappy with whatever he and the clerk were discussing. He shook his head disgustedly, looked around the lobby, then walked down the hall.

"If I'm making a mistake, Dad, then I'm making a mistake. I'll call you tomorrow and give you an update."

"Okay, okay."

I heard the impatience in his voice.

"What's this woman's name?" he asked. "And where are you? If something goes wrong, I want to know where you are."

I hesitated. I wasn't a little kid. I didn't need to check in with my father. But I knew so little about her. . . .

"I'm in Wyckoff, Kentucky," I said. "A little town ninety minutes northwest of Nashville. Her name is Morgan Reynolds."

Dad muttered to himself, then said, "We'll talk tomorrow. I have more work to do tonight. But if you wake up in the bathtub missing a kidney, don't say I didn't warn you."

Chapter 4

I KNOCKED ON MORGAN'S door. A DO NOT DISTURB sign hung from the knob, and I tried to remember if it had been there before. I didn't think it had. I waited and knocked again, but still received no response. I'd gone to the car and retrieved my bags, and their weight on my shoulder tilted me to one side.

I leaned in close, pressing my ear against the wood. I thought I heard the sound of running water and maybe more coughing.

I knocked again, harder and faster.

"Morgan?" I waited. "Just let me know you're okay."

And then the door swung open. Her eyes were red. She stayed back in the doorway, and I stepped into her room.

She closed the door. "Are you trying to make a scene? That's the last thing I need. Somebody might call security."

"I was worried. You didn't answer. And it sounded like you were crying or something."

"I'm fine."

Morgan went to sit on her bed. I remained standing, uncertain of what I should do.

"I'm sorry you went through all that," I said.

"Thanks. It's life in the big, grown-up world, I guess."

"It sounds like a lousy work environment. But now you have enough experience to move on to something else."

Morgan remained silent, staring at the carpet. I wondered if she wanted me to leave. But I wasn't finished asking questions.

"If all of that happened, why are you traveling this way? Under another name and keeping such a low profile?"

Her eyes remained fixed on the carpet, her face stony. "I'm not perfect, Joshua," she finally said. "Yes, I was treated poorly by my company, but I didn't handle myself well either."

I waited.

"My mom is sick. She needed help, and I was so fed up with work that I just quit. I decided to spend time with her in Nashville, trying to figure out what to do next." She paused. "But it didn't help. I just thought about what happened more and more."

She reached up and scratched her cheek with a trembling hand.

"My mom needed money for her care. And I kept getting notices about my student loan. I made a dent in it while I worked at TechGreen, but without a steady income, I couldn't keep up." She looked at me. "Did you take out a loan for school?"

"No. My dad . . . He had enough money."

She said one word. "Lucky."

"So what did you do? About getting your mom help?"

"I tried to make an appointment to see my boss, but he kept putting me off. So one night I went to his house." She shifted her weight on the bed. "I felt like I didn't have anything to lose. I just rang the doorbell and waited for him to answer."

"Did it work?" I asked.

"He opened the door and let me in, but nothing changed. He told me the company was in a cash crunch because they were opening another office. He said he valued my work and offered me my job back. He said a lot of things . . . but none of it amounted to anything. And then . . ." She shook her head, her cheeks flushed. "I hate to say it. I cried. Like a stupid little girl, I broke down. I cried in his living room. I hate that. But everything had built up inside. My mom, the job, the money."

I knew that couldn't be the whole story.

"There's got to be more," I said. "You still haven't told me why you used a fake name."

For a second, she acted again like I wasn't there. Then she went over to the luggage stand and undid the zipper on her carry-on bag. She rummaged around in the bag and then drew her hand out. Something small was clutched inside.

"This is the problem. This complicates everything."

I squinted, trying to see the object in her hand. She was cupping a small bundle of red tissue paper.

"Go ahead and unwrap it," she said.

I lifted it and peeled back the paper. Had my dad been correct? Was I about to unwrap a stolen human kidney? Had she cut off her former boss's finger?

Instead, I found an antique ring with a large diamond in the middle and two smaller diamonds on either side.

"It's someone's ring," I said. "Did this come from your boss?"

"It belongs to him, yes, or it belongs to his family."

I still didn't follow. I felt like I was one step behind.

"I stole it," she said. "From his house. It belonged to his mother."

"Oh," I said, wrapping the ring back in the tissue paper and handing it over to Morgan. "I assume his mother is deceased."

"Within the last year." Morgan slid the ring back into her bag. "It was weird. He had an urn with his mother's ashes in the entryway. It was like a shrine, with a picture of her on display on a shelf." She shook her head. "The ring was there. I wish I'd kept my hands to myself, but I wanted to do something that would hurt him, that would feel like a reward for my work."

"Were you planning to pawn it?" I asked.

"I don't know. Once you have something like that, once it's done, you realize . . . well, you realize how stupid it is. What am I going to do with the damn ring? And then . . . there's my boss.

"What about him?"

"They're going to know I took it. They're going to know everything. And . . . I just know none of this is ever going to stop."

I paced back and forth in the room. I'd come this far because I'd felt a connection with Morgan in the airport. And because her behavior made her seem like a person who needed help.

But I'd be lying if I said I wasn't hoping, wishing, that she and I would follow through on that kiss. Having watched Morgan sit on the bed, her long legs folded under her body . . . Yes, I hoped for more than just conversation. I felt it in every cell in my body.

But I also wanted to help her, even if I didn't know how.

"Okay," I said as I stopped pacing and tried to sound practical. Strangely, I reminded myself of my dad in that kind of situation. He always remained calm in a crisis. "You made a mistake. You acted impulsively and took a ring. How valuable is it?"

"I don't know. Twenty thousand? Maybe more."

"Really? That much?"

"Rings like this are worth a lot. Hell, I've committed larceny."

"Grand larceny, probably."

She gasped. "Really?"

"Could be," I said, remembering my business law class. I went over to the bed where she sat and eased myself down next to her. Our thighs touched. "Look, why don't you just go home? Take the thing back to your boss. Apologize and—"

"I won't apologize," she said, suddenly scooting back, moving her body away from mine. "I won't."

"Okay, don't apologize. But then . . . do you think he's going to press charges against you?"

"He loved his mother," she said. "Hence the creepy shrine."

No surprise there. Most people love their parents. I felt an intense bond with my dad.

Morgan looked at me straight on. "I mean, he *really* loved her. Really. When she died, he was a wreck. For weeks."

"This is why you ran? Because you took a ring worth a lot of money, and you think this guy is going to the police?"

She nodded. Then she reached over and placed her hand on my knee. Her touch hit me like a shock. "It's good to tell someone about this. Finally. You know, it's not the police so much. And it's not me I'm worried about. It's my mom."

"Right. Cancer?"

"Yes. And I'm the only one who can take care of her. If anything happens to me . . . if I get in trouble . . ."

"Who's with her now?" I asked.

"She's being cared for. My mom and I . . . We've had a complicated relationship. But we're working on it now. I don't want that to slip away. But if I go back . . ."

"You might get in trouble."

"I *will* get in trouble. Or . . . there's something else."

"Okay, what is it?" I asked.

"After I took the ring and left the house . . . Well, my boss has this brother. I'd met him at a couple of work functions. He was kind of weird, like my boss, but so what. Right?"

"What does he have to do with this?"

"Yesterday the brother showed up at the hospice where my mom is staying. He was looking for me, but I wasn't there."

"Where were you?" I asked. "Why were you flying through Atlanta?"

She sighed. "I have an aunt who lives in Norfolk, Virginia. My mom's sister. They've been estranged, but I flew there to tell her about my mom's condition. I wanted her to come and help. You know, as things get near the end. Since I might be in trouble . . . I wanted to make sure Mom wouldn't be alone."

"Sounds like it didn't work."

"It didn't. Aunt Linda . . . Well, she's not budging."

"So what about your boss's brother?" I asked.

"He came to the hospice, and he wanted the ring. He told my mom that it belonged to his mother and I needed to give it back."

"If you'd been there, you could have done it right then," I said.

"If I'd been there . . . who knows what he would have done? The guy scares me. He told my mom if I didn't give the ring back, something bad would happen to me. And to her." She lifted her hand to her head. The strain, the fear, was etched on her face.

"You didn't tell the police?" I asked. Then I figured it out. "If you'd told the police, you'd be admitting the crime. But if you don't tell the police, you worry your mom is in jeopardy."

"I *am* worried about her," she said. "That's why I'm here. The brother scared the hell out of me. I'm worried about what he might do. To me. Or to Mom. That's why . . . I'm trying to take care of things." Morgan groaned, then shook her head. "I came to Wyckoff because I thought I could make it right."

"Make it right here?" I asked. "How?"

"I want to end it, once and for all."

"But I don't understand. . . . What's here?"

I looked down. Her hand had inched halfway up my thigh. I swallowed hard, my mind unable to think about much else.

I reached down, placed my hand on top of hers. She smiled at me, then adjusted her grip so our fingers intertwined.

"I think if you go home and come clean," I said, "then nothing too bad will happen. Talk to a lawyer. Tell them about the stress and strain of caring for your mother. Say you need to help her."

Her grip tightened. "They have money. *He* does. And power. I just don't know if any of it can go the right way for me."

"It can. Call the police or a lawyer and explain everything."

She shook her head. "No, no." She reached out and placed her long index finger over my lips. "Let's just . . . let's just not think about that tonight." She stopped shaking her head, and her eyes bored in on mine. "Tomorrow, okay? It will be okay until tomorrow."

She leaned toward me. We moved closer to each other. Then we were kissing again. Our lips pressed. Our hands explored.

Tomorrow.

Morgan was right.

It could all wait until tomorrow.

KIMBERLY parked in front of the brick house in Laurel Falls. She checked the clock on the dash before turning the car off: 7:43. She tried not to think about what she could have been doing with Maria. Cooking a meal, talking about school . . .

Maria would do all of those things, and she'd have a perfectly pleasant evening. She would just do them with Peter instead of with her. And that was fine. Absolutely fine.

Kimberly told herself that over and over. She was still trying to convince herself when the phone rang before she could get out of the car. "Hello, Brandon. Aren't you supposed to be at home?"

"I'm on my way," he said. "But I wanted to give you an update on our mystery man, Joshua Fields."

"What about him?" she asked as she silently thanked the officers of the Nashville airport for taking the man's information. The man who kissed and then followed Morgan Reynolds.

"Clean record. Twenty-six years old. Works in commercial real estate. His dad's company. He lives in Chicago."

"You haven't been able to get hold of him?" Kimberly asked.

"Not yet."

"Anything on social media?" she asked.

"No connection to Morgan Reynolds."

"So why is this guy running around with her?"

"You don't believe his story, that he met her in the airport?"

"I don't know." The wheels turned in Kimberly's mind. "It's weird. You think Giles Caldwell and Morgan Reynolds could have been involved? A boss and an employee running off together? Older man, younger woman? It happens."

"Kind of gross. But, yes, it happens."

"He's not that old," Kimberly said. "Well, keep trying. Thanks, Brandon. Now you really should head home."

"You don't need help with these interviews?"

"Only a few more left. Kiss the baby for me."

She hung up and stepped into the cool evening air. The sun had disappeared, leaving the sky dark, the stars popping into view.

The neighborhood was a recently built subdivision for the upper middle class. The yards were all neat, the bushes trimmed.

She walked up the drive to the front door and rang the bell.

It didn't take long for a figure to emerge. Kimberly had called, asked if she could come by. The door swung inward, and a young, smiling face greeted her. Pretty, blond hair pulled back.

"Hi. Detective Givens?"

Kimberly flashed her badge. "Ashley Clarke?"

"Come on in."

Kimberly followed her into an entryway. "Thanks for making time for me," Kimberly said.

"I just put the baby down," Ashley said. "So this is great."

They left the foyer for a sitting room. Ashley took a spot on the couch, and Kimberly settled into a love seat.

"You wanted to know something about Morgan?" Ashley confidently held Kimberly's gaze as she asked the question.

"You're friends with her. Right?"

"Well, used to be," Ashley said. "She moved away. And Brianna is nine months old. She doesn't allow me time for much else."

"I remember those days. I have a daughter too. Twelve." Kimberly projected a smile. "So, Morgan Reynolds. You're not as close as you were. But you were friends at one time?"

"Oh, yeah. We met a couple of years ago. We went to the same gym." Ashley leaned forward. "Is what they're saying on Facebook true? Is she really missing?"

"We're trying to figure all that out. So tell me, did anything unusual happen before she moved away?"

"Not really. I only saw her once right before she moved. I ran into her at the grocery store. I hadn't seen her in a while. And when I said she could come out to the house and see Brianna, she told me she'd quit her job and was moving to Nashville. She said her mom was sick."

Ashley's face scrunched.

"What is it?" Kimberly asked.

"I guess I don't know when or why her mom moved to Nashville. Morgan's from Wyckoff, right?"

"She is. Originally. Did she talk about her job at all? Why she was quitting?"

"No. She said she just needed a change."

"Did she ever talk about her boss? Giles Caldwell?"

"Not that I can remember." Then recognition spread across Ashley's face. Her mouth formed a small, perfect O. "He's the guy who's missing, right? And Morgan . . . you think . . ."

"I don't know if there's any connection," Kimberly said. "Did she ever talk about her boss's brother? Simon Caldwell?"

"I don't know that name."

"Ever mention a boyfriend?" Kimberly asked. "A girlfriend?"

"No one serious. Just, you know, guys. A date here or there."

"How about a man named Joshua Fields? Did she mention him?"

Ashley shook her head. "I don't think so. Is he a suspect?"

"Just a name right now," Kimberly said. "So you're the fifth friend of hers I've talked with. None of them have really stayed in touch with her. Why do you think that is?"

"I guess she was kind of closed off. She had a rough childhood. Her mom had some issues. That's why it was weird when she told me she was moving to Nashville to be close to her mother. I guess . . . well, I guess something changed."

Kimberly checked her watch. She didn't want to keep Ashley.

"And that's pretty much it for you and Morgan?" she said.

"Until a few days ago. I saw her one more time."

"You saw her here? In Laurel Falls? Where?"

"In a gas station. On my way home from yoga class." Ashley's face scrunched again. "Thursday. Five days ago. I'm at the gas station, watching the pump, and I look up and see Morgan."

"What did she say?" Kimberly asked, keeping her voice level.

"Nothing. I waved, but she turned away, jumped in her car, and sped out of there." She shrugged.

Morgan Reynolds had been back in Laurel Falls five days ago. And that very morning she'd been on a plane from Atlanta to Nashville, where she was supposed to be living with her sick mother. And on that plane she'd ignored a guy she'd kissed in the airport. Just like she'd ignored Ashley at the gas station.

The baby started crying in the other room.

"I've heard everything I need to," Kimberly said. "I can show myself out. If you hear from Morgan, will you call me?"

"Of course." Ashley looked at the floor. "Detective? Do you think she's in trouble? Maybe someone was trying to hurt her."

"We don't know what's happening with Morgan just yet," Kimberly said. "She's missing from Nashville, so the police down there are in the lead on that case. I'm investigating Giles Caldwell's disappearance. But they might be related since they're connected through work. So we have to check everything."

Ashley shivered. "Do you think it's normal, what happened with Morgan?"

"You mean disappearing? No—"

"I don't mean that," Ashley said. "I mean . . . Well, my mom is my best friend, so I couldn't imagine living away from her. But some people do. Like Morgan. And she moved back to be close to her, so they must have patched things up. Do you think that always happens? Do people work things like that out?"

"It certainly happens, Ashley," she said. "Yes, it does."

Ashley smiled as the baby cried louder. "Duty calls," she said. And she slipped away as Kimberly turned to the door.

I woke up sometime during the night.

I didn't know where I was. I'd been dreaming about flying, about being on a plane, high in the air, but the flight never landed.

When I awoke, I was naked and sweating. The sheets felt cool against my damp skin. Everything came back to me. The daylong quest to find Morgan, the drive to Wyckoff. Our night in the hotel.

I stumbled through the dark and found the bathroom. When I came back to bed, Morgan was facing the wall. I heard her sniffle. I propped myself up on my elbow and looked at her face. Tears glistened against her skin. She reached up and wiped them away.

"What's wrong?" I asked. "Can I do anything?"

"Go back to sleep. I'm fine."

"You're crying."

"I just . . . I started thinking about my childhood in Wyckoff. My mom used to take me to an amusement park near here. It was expensive to get in, but she always scrounged up the money."

"That's what parents do. Good ones, anyway."

"I don't know about the good part."

"What do you mean?" I asked.

"My mom . . . Let's just say they served beer at the amusement park. Fantasy Farm, it was called. My mom . . . She couldn't handle drinking so well. It could get ugly."

"I'm sorry."

She took my hand and squeezed it. "I remember the petting zoo. There were goats and sheep. You could bring them little pellets of food, and they'd eat out of your hand. I loved that."

"That sounds like a great memory."

"No, it isn't." She turned to face me. "We went there one summer when I was about nine. My mom was drinking. I went to the petting zoo to feed the animals, and all of a sudden there's a commotion. Some people gasp. It's my mom. Down on the ground. She passed out. They had to call security. The police came."

"It sounds terrifying."

"The place is closed now," she said. "It's kind of satisfying to drive by and see that part of my childhood boarded up and shut down. That memory of my mom . . . I wish I could forget."

"So why are you here if the memories are so bad?" I asked.

"I have other things to do, things to resolve."

"Should you go back to Laurel Falls?" I asked. "Turn in the ring? It's what—thirty minutes east of here? That's not far."

She nodded in the dark.

"I mean it when I say I think it will be okay," I said.

"I know." She reached over and brushed her hand along my cheek. "You're sweet. But we both need to go back to sleep."

"I'll go with you to the police if you want."

"Really, let's just sleep on it."

She was right. We were both tired. I turned away. The night was quiet, not a sound except the hum of air-conditioning.

When I woke again, there was bright sunlight coming through the window. My head hurt. I needed food. And water.

The clock read 9:02. The combination of travel, Xanax, and alcohol had made me sleep late. It occurred to me I had no idea what I was going to do. Was I going to go back to work? Hop on a plane to Tampa? Catch up with everything I'd let go?

Or would I go with Morgan? Help her return the ring and make all of that right? I liked the sound of that much more than I liked the sound of going back to work.

I rolled over. Her side of the bed was empty. I heard water running in the bathroom. The shower.

I picked up my phone. There were a number of missed calls, all from numbers I didn't recognize. I had no idea why.

And a voice mail from Renee as well.

I'd told her what was going on. But I knew she'd worry and check in. I sent her a text without listening to the voice mail.

Just got your message. I'm fine. In hotel. Will call later when I can. Everything fine.

I felt like a jerk writing those words. I wasn't really lying, but I wasn't exactly telling the truth either.

Renee's calls and texts told me that I couldn't stay in limbo without making some kind of decision. Unlike in my dream, I couldn't stay in the air forever, living in a bubble and not touching the ground. People were waiting for me. They expected things from me.

I pulled on my boxers and T-shirt and walked over to the bathroom door. It stood ajar an inch or two, so I leaned my head in.

"Hey. Are you almost done in there?"

No response.

"I just want to know what you're thinking. I can go with you if you want."

Still nothing. The water ran and ran.

"Morgan?"

I opened the bathroom door and pushed the shower curtain aside. Empty. I went back out to the room and looked around. I hadn't seen it before. But her bags were gone. Her clothes. Her shoes. Everything. I searched for a note. For anything.

But I knew it was a lost cause. She was gone.

MORGAN had left her room key on the nightstand. I grabbed it, threw on clothes, bolted out the door, and went down the stairs. In the lobby I saw no sign of Morgan. I approached the desk and asked if anyone had seen her.

The clerk stifled a yawn before answering me. "I just came on a few minutes ago. Is something wrong?"

"No," I said, before dashing out the sliding doors and stopping under the front portico. It was a bright morning, the sun sparkling like diamonds on the dew in the grass. I thought of the ring.

She was gone. And not waking me was intentional.

I trudged back into the hotel. What had I expected? If she'd wanted me to help, she would have waited. Twice she'd ditched me.

The lobby smelled of coffee and waffles. A few people sat eating, their small plates full of pastries and fruit. I headed back for the stairs. I needed to shower and eat. And then after that . . .

Who knew what I'd do next?

I entered the stairwell and was halfway to my floor when the door below me opened. I looked down but saw no one. When I reached my floor, I pushed through the door and into my hallway. As I took out the key card, the door from the stairwell opened.

I froze. Had Morgan returned? Had she seen me outside?

Instead, I saw a man. Middle-aged. Taller than me. The guy from the lobby the night before.

Why was he there?

"Excuse me," he said, waving at me.

Was he hotel security?

"Can I talk to you for a moment?" he asked.

He looked to be in his mid-forties, trim and fit. His knuckles were large, his hands giant.

"Can I help you?" I asked.

"Yes, I think you can," he said. He nodded to the room. "Maybe we want to talk in there. It's more private."

"What do we need to talk about?" I asked. "I don't know you."

But I should have guessed.

He said simply, "Her."

THE man followed me into the room. I stood as he looked around, like he expected to find someone else inside, and when he saw nothing, he sighed, his disappointment heavy.

He sat on the bed with his knees spread, his giant hands resting on his thighs. "Do you know where she went?" he asked.

I almost laughed. "Hold it. I don't even know who you are."

He stood up and held out his huge hand. "Simon Caldwell."

I reached out, and we shook. "Joshua Fields."

"Nice to meet you, Joshua. And I'm sorry to barge in on you like this." He returned to the bed and sat. "Well, not really sorry. I think you can help me. And maybe I can help you."

His voice was deep and commanding. He looked like a guy used to getting his way.

And he'd said the magic word: "Her."

"So, Morgan," he said. "Where is she? Did she leave town?"

His smug entitlement irritated me, and I regretted letting him in, though I wasn't sure I would have been able to keep him out.

"What do you want?" I asked. "And how do you know her?"

Simon tilted his head. "You don't know what you're dealing with, do you?" He rubbed his chin. "I'm sure she told you quite a tale. How did you meet her anyway? Are you her boyfriend? It looks like . . ." His eyes traveled over the bed, the mussed covers. "Oh, jeez, don't tell me you love her. Is that it?"

"Okay, I've had enough of this." I took out my phone. "I can call the front desk. Or the police. I want you out of here."

Simon spread his hands, a calming gesture that failed to put me at ease. "Okay. You want to know the truth? I'm sure she told you all about her job, right? About the app and the way she didn't get her bonus or whatever she thought she was entitled to."

Then I understood. She felt cheated by the company. She told me she'd confronted the owner. And now this guy wanted to talk to her. To reach an agreement? To apologize?

"So are you a lawyer?" I asked. "Someone here to pay her off?"

"My brother owned the company. He's the reason I'm here."

"Owned? He sold it?"

Simon paused, and took a deep breath. Then he looked at me.

"Owned, as in my brother is missing. And I think Morgan knows where he is."

Chapter 5

KIMBERLY ENTERED THE STATION on Wednesday morning carrying her bag, which was stuffed full of the reports and crime scene photographs she'd been studying the night before.

A tired-looking Brandon stood by his desk. She guessed he'd been kept awake by an unhappy baby, and that brought Kimberly's mind back to Ashley Clarke. Kimberly wasn't sure where to fit the information Ashley had provided into the grand scheme of things. Two missing people—boss and former employee. And they'd both disappeared over the same weekend. Except one of them—*the employee*—had been seen back in Laurel Falls around the time of her boss's disappearance. And that had happened when she was supposed to be living an hour away in Nashville.

Maybe she was just passing through, stopping to get gas?

So then why not talk to her friend? Why run off?

Kimberly filled Brandon in on what Ashley Clarke saw at the gas station.

"And Morgan just drove off?" Brandon asked. "Without saying anything?"

"Not a word."

"And this was Thursday night she was at the gas station?"

"Yup."

"And the last time Giles was seen at work was . . ."

"Thursday afternoon."

Brandon whistled. "Did this Ashley know of any, um, deeper connection between Morgan and Giles?"

"Nope." Kimberly started to sit at her desk.

"Don't settle in," Brandon said. "Steven Hatfield called. He's back in town, eager to talk. He said he'd come here if we want."

"No, that's okay," she said. "I'm happy to go to his office again. You never know what else might come up there."

"Want me to tag along?" he asked.

"No, I'm good."

Kimberly went outside, enjoying the chance to have the sun on her face again. She drove her city sedan ten blocks to the Tech-Green offices, which occupied the top floor of a complex south of downtown. TechGreen had started gaining national attention, occasionally getting written up as a company to watch.

She stepped off the elevator into an open-concept office. No walls separated the coworkers. No cubicles.

She introduced herself to the young man at the reception desk. His eyebrows rose. She was apparently expected.

"I can take you right back to Steven," he said.

Steven Hatfield stood up when Kimberly walked through his open door. His curly salt-and-pepper hair and loose sweater gave him the air of a college professor. She pegged him at about the same age as Giles Caldwell, around fifty. He held out his hand, which felt smooth as Kimberly shook it.

"I got back to town last night," he said. He resumed his seat, and she sat down as well. "Everyone is shaken. Is Giles really missing?"

"It looks that way," Kimberly said. "He didn't come into the office on Friday. But that's not unusual for him, is it?"

"He doesn't come in every day, no. He goes his own way sometimes. Did something happen to alert you to his absence? How did the police get involved?"

"His brother contacted us on Monday. He hadn't been able to

reach Giles over the weekend, and then he wasn't at work again. The brother called us, so we went to the house. No sign of a break-in, but some things were out of place. Do you have any reason to think someone would harm him?"

Hatfield looked perplexed. He lifted his hands, then dropped them. The creases in his brow grew deeper. "I've got nothing."

"Disgruntled employees?"

"No one who would hurt him. I don't think."

"Competitors? Your company is doing pretty well."

"We have a lot of competitors. None who would . . . Are you thinking someone . . . I mean, could it be that someone . . ."

Steven Hatfield couldn't bring himself to say the awful words. His features trembled at the thought. *Murder. Death. Killing.*

"We're trying not to speculate," Kimberly said. "Do you think something else might be going on?"

"No, I don't. Sometimes he talked about retiring. He wants to travel. But just disappearing would be odd, even for Giles."

"Even for him?"

"He's an unusual guy. With a sharp mind and his own way of doing things." Hatfield clasped his hands together on the top of the table. "I'm better with people, and Giles is better . . . behind the scenes. He can be short. He doesn't understand social cues. If an employee made a mistake, he'd tell them. Directly. Harshly. He didn't take the time for the social niceties the rest of us use."

"That's an easy way to piss people off, right?"

Hatfield pressed his lips tight. "Okay, yes, he pissed people off. I'm reluctant to talk about these things because they make Giles look bad. But he hasn't committed a crime, has he?"

"What things are you reluctant to talk about?" Kimberly asked.

Hatfield rubbed his hands together. "A couple of female employees have complained about Giles. Not sexual. They complained that Giles could be aggressive."

"Aggressive how? Yelling?"

"Yes. But more than that. Almost . . . physically abusive. No one ever said he hit them. But he seemed almost out of control."

"What did the company do about it?"

"I talked to Giles," Hatfield said. "We dialed back his inter-actions with people. We didn't want to make it a big deal."

"How about Morgan Reynolds? Did she get abused?"

"Oh, no." Hatfield leaned forward, letting his forehead rest in the palm of one of his hands. "I saw that on Facebook. And the news. Her being missing. Do you think there's a connection?"

"What was her departure from the company like?"

Hatfield looked pained. "Morgan and her bonus. She thinks she wasn't paid for an app. It's not true. She got paid the way she was supposed to be paid. Nothing more, nothing less."

"But no bonus? Did other employees receive bonuses?"

"Sometimes."

"Other employees who were men?" Kimberly asked. "Giles acted aggressively toward women. Did that extend to bonuses? Did men receive bonuses that Morgan Reynolds didn't?"

"We're expanding now. It's hard. It's about cash flow. We're a very fair company. We treat everyone . . . The company's diverse. You can see that, can't you? Look around."

He was right. Kimberly saw that when she looked around the room. She also knew being diverse wasn't the same as being fair.

"Morgan would have gotten the bonus. Probably. But she quit. Months ago. As far as we knew, she wasn't even in the business anymore. I haven't heard anything from her."

"Did she make any threats?" Kimberly asked.

"Morgan? No. Not to me." He scratched his head.

"Morgan Reynolds called Giles three times in the last few weeks. They exchanged emails. She wanted to meet with him."

Kimberly withheld the information about Morgan being seen in town right before Giles disappeared.

"He didn't tell me. Like I said, Giles has his own mind." Hat-field looked confused, uncertain. "Do you really think those two things might be related? The two of them disappearing?"

"Were Giles and Morgan . . . involved in any way?"

"Oh, no," he said. "I can't imagine anything like that."

"Did you know about Giles's personal life? Or Morgan's?"

"Giles? He was divorced. For years. I never knew him to have a date." He shook his head. "Morgan? Who knows? You think they're connected in some way? Even if it wasn't romantic?"

"Giles's brother thinks the two things are connected."

"Oh. Him." Hatfield slumped in his seat. "Simon. Oh, Simon."

"You know him? Is there something we should know?"

"There's so much. Where do you want me to start?" Hatfield rubbed his forehead. "Do you know him?"

"He's come to the station," Kimberly said. "He's called on the phone. He's . . . intense. Understandable. He's worried about his brother. It's distressing when a loved one is unaccounted for."

Hatfield shook his head. He looked weary. "I met Simon and Giles in college. We all went to Vanderbilt together. Giles is older by a year. They're very different on the surface. Simon can be warm. Affable. That's the impression he can make on people."

"But he's not part of the business."

"No. He wanted to be in on it when we founded the company. He was around, offering ideas. But his presence concerned me."

"Because?"

"Simon didn't seem like someone who would work well in a company like the one we envisioned. We were in college when the Gulf War started. The first one. He quit Vanderbilt and enlisted, got sent to Iraq for a year. He finished his degree later and works for a financial firm now."

"You still haven't told me the problem with him. A Vanderbilt graduate who volunteered for the Gulf War? What's the issue?"

"In college, Simon had a girlfriend. We went to a party one night, and some frat boy started hitting on her. Simon didn't do anything. He acted like he didn't care. The girlfriend was mad at him, telling him she felt uncomfortable and he should have done something. About a month later, we hear that the guy, the one from the party, had dropped out of school. Someone had been harassing him. Systematically. Flat tires on his car. A stolen bike. Things missing from his apartment. The guy became really anxious. Not sleeping. Struggling in classes. Then the guy's stuff showed up on his doorstep one night. All of it. And . . . with his stuff was a dead rat. *That* was it for the guy."

"And you think Simon did this?" Kimberly asked.

"I know he did. I mentioned it to him one day. I told him about the guy leaving. I just wanted to see how he reacted."

"And?"

"Simon just . . . smiled. Then he said it sounded like justice."

Hatfield let his story hang in the air.

"So one brother acts aggressively toward females. The other acts aggressively toward . . . everyone?" Kimberly said.

Hatfield's words settled like a stone in her gut. Everything he said about Simon Caldwell fit with her impressions of the man.

"Does Simon know who Morgan is?" Kimberly asked.

"I have no idea."

"But it's possible that Giles told Simon about the issues with Morgan, right?"

"It's possible. And if that's true, then I think you should find Morgan, wherever she is."

"Because she might know where Giles is?" Kimberly asked.

"Because she might need your help if Simon is looking for her."

IN THE hotel room with Simon, I felt like I'd been invaded by something I couldn't predict or fully understand.

"I think you better go," I said. "I have a plane to catch and—"

Simon wore a smug, self-satisfied look. "You're taken in by her. Hey, I get it. She's a pretty girl."

"I'm calling the police if you don't go."

Simon wasn't put off. "You're not going to make that call." He pointed at me, punctuating his words. "Because you've been asking yourself all of these questions. What is she up to, running all around the country from flight to flight? You know she's missing?"

"I do."

My eyes trailed past him in the direction of the door. If I made a quick move, I could get out. He had superior size, but I was faster and more agile. But did I really want to turn tail and run?

I gave Simon credit for being right about something. He knew how much I wanted to know about Morgan.

"You know what?" he said. "Google my brother. Go ahead."

I didn't move. I hated being ordered around.

"What did she tell you about him?" Simon asked. "Did she say he refused to pay her bonus? That she got cheated out of money from that app she helped develop?"

"If you know, why are you asking me?"

"Go ahead and Google him. Giles Caldwell."

I wanted to search, but a part of me feared what I might learn.

"Look, Joshua, my brother was a bastard." Simon pursed his lips and turned toward the window. "*Is* a bastard. I hope he still is a bastard." He gave his attention back to me. "How do you think he made all that money? How do you think he built that company? Not by giving money away when he didn't have to."

But something about his words stood out to me.

"Hold on," I said. "You said your brother is missing. Maybe Morgan had nothing to do with it. Maybe he's alive and well somewhere. Maybe he's on a fishing trip."

"Sure, I'm trying to be optimistic."

My thoughts raced. What had Morgan not told me?

"Google Giles. It's important, Joshua. For both of us."

I brought my phone up. I saw the missed calls and messages from earlier. I needed to check them. Maybe Morgan had called. But I couldn't check in front of Simon.

So I tapped in "Giles Caldwell" and waited for the results.

I clicked on the most recent story from the *Laurel Falls Times*. Simon was right. Giles hadn't been seen since Thursday evening.

I scrolled through the information on my phone as fast as I could. Giles Caldwell, owner and founder of TechGreen, had not been seen or heard from in five days. Police had declared him a missing person on Monday, two days earlier.

"You see what the issue is?" Simon asked.

I did. Clearly.

Morgan admitted to me she'd been to Giles Caldwell's house to talk about the bonus. And she'd admitted to stealing the ring from him. But the information online added a disturbing element—the man had disappeared. Without a trace.

"This doesn't mean Morgan did it," I said. But my voice was low. I was unconvinced.

Simon laughed. "Like I said, I don't know what kind of story she told you. What matters is she held a grudge against Giles. Maybe frustration set in. Maybe anger. And rage."

"But how could Morgan have killed or kidnapped a grown man?" I asked.

"Where there's a will, there's a way."

"The police have no evidence. They don't mention Morgan as a suspect in any of these stories. You're grasping."

"I'm not. I went by my brother's office yesterday and chatted with a few employees. Morgan was emailing and calling my brother. Asking about this bonus. She was hounding him. She wanted to meet with him. And now they're both gone."

"Maybe it's just a coincidence."

"Yeah, right." Simon stood up. It felt like his shoulders filled the room. He walked back and forth. "I tried to tell the cops Morgan should be a suspect. But they're not returning my calls. Giles is gone, and then *she's* gone. What else can you conclude?"

He asked the question in a reasonable tone of voice, making it seem as if no normal person could fail to agree.

If Morgan had done something to Giles Caldwell, if she was responsible for his disappearance—or worse—then it explained her secretive behavior. The not wanting to talk or be followed.

Her taking off before I woke up without the benefit of a note.

It explained everything.

Morgan had done something to Giles.

Simon resumed his perch on the edge of the bed. He forced a smile. "I'm sure you're a nice, normal guy," he said. "Good job. Clean-cut. Now you got yourself wrapped up in something you didn't understand when it started. It happens. To everybody."

I wanted to say, *No, it doesn't. Not every guy finds himself with a strange man accusing the woman he slept with of murder.*

"I don't even care about this Morgan," Simon said. "The police will find her and arrest her. She'll be taken care of the way she needs to be taken care of. You know what I mean?"

I fought off a shiver.

"There are other considerations," he said. "Now that the deed is done, that Giles is . . . Well, what are the odds he's alive?"

"There's no body or evidence of foul play. Maybe—"

Simon shook his head. "We both know the odds, okay? After a couple of days . . . forget about it."

"Maybe he ran off? Maybe he owed someone else money?"

"No. No way. Our mother died about a year ago. And she left something very valuable behind, something meant for me that's been in the safekeeping of my brother. It's a family heirloom, something I want to pass on to *my* daughter when she gets married. It has sentimental value as well as . . . financial value."

My heart rate accelerated.

"It's a ring," he said. "My mother's ring. A ring she wore for fifty years. Until the day she died. It was supposed to come to me. But it didn't. I think Giles convinced her to give him the ring before she died, to keep me from having it. Like he needed the money. My brother had that ring in his house. And I want it back. It's supposed to be mine. Not his. Mine."

"How do you know your brother doesn't have it in a safe-deposit box? Or somewhere else—"

"He doesn't," Simon said. "I know where he kept it. I was there a few days before he disappeared. I saw the ring in its place. He hadn't moved it since he got his greedy hands on it."

"Maybe you took it," I said.

"Don't be simple. It's gone. And I want it back. Plus, I want my brother's mortal remains, assuming he's dead. He deserves a proper rest, next to my mother. Even if he is a bastard."

I had to hand it to Simon. He possessed a rare gift. He managed to seem off-kilter and perfectly reasonable at the same time. Who wouldn't want to give his loved one a proper burial? Who wouldn't want a missing family heirloom? And something else turned over in my mind. Morgan had lied to me more than once, and she'd bolted more than once. Was I supposed to defend someone who'd been so dishonest?

"It sounds to me," I said, "like you need to let the police track her down. And if you want me to call them, or even go to the cops right here in Wyckoff, I will. I have no problem with that."

But Simon's head was shaking. "The Laurel Falls cops are slow-witted. They didn't know where she was. I did."

"How did you find out she was here?" I asked. "You were here last night. I saw you in the lobby. But you didn't say anything to Morgan."

Simon kept shaking his head. "If I'd just put it all together sooner . . ." He thumped one meaty fist into the other palm. "I talked to people where she worked. And I went down to Nashville too. A consensus emerged—if she was in trouble, she would retreat here to Wyckoff, where she grew up, where she went to college. No one had any better guess. I had to take a chance."

"So how did you choose the right hotel?" I asked.

"I didn't. I just checked into a hotel. This hotel. I'd been looking all over town, not finding a damn thing. I was going to leave this morning. Then *you* came into the lobby, asking the clerk about a woman, describing Morgan to the letter."

"So you followed me up here?"

"And what do you know? I was right. I found the very guy who was with her last night." He looked overly satisfied, a shark with a taste of blood. "So it's on you now. Tell me where she went."

"She left this morning without saying anything to me," I said. "All of this is new to me . . . You're telling me I spent the night with a killer. That's what you want me to believe?"

Simon considered me. "Yes, that's what I believe."

"Let's call the police, and I'll tell them the whole tale."

Simon looked pained. He lowered his head, eyes closed. He spoke without looking up. "I don't like these delays. You know the clock is ticking. She's getting farther and farther away."

"You don't really know that she's getting farther and farther away. You don't know where she is. And neither do I. But why would she come to Wyckoff if there wasn't a reason?"

"What are you driving at?" he asked.

"You should go look for her." I stood up. "I need to shower. I need to put on clean clothes. And then . . . I don't know."

"I'll wait." He folded his arms.

"No," I said. "Don't wait for me."

Simon looked up. "You're my best hope. So I'll wait."

"Look, I'm in the same boat you are. I'm trying to understand what's happening with Morgan." He continued to stare at me. "Do you think I don't want to know what's going on? You're the first person to make any sense about this whole thing."

Simon rocked a little, his arms still folded.

"Go down to the lobby," I said. "Think about calling the police. But . . . can I please just get ready alone? Seriously."

Simon waited. Then he stood up. He came close to me, took his index finger and poked me in the chest.

"I'll be in the lobby, then." He pointed to his watch. "Twenty minutes." He went to the door but looked back before he stepped through to the hallway. He pointed to his watch again. "Twenty."

Chapter 6

Kimberly looked across Steven Hatfield's uncluttered desk. No papers, no notes. No pens or paper clips. How did people work in such a sterile, organized environment?

"You're telling me Simon is dangerous," she said. "A threat to Morgan Reynolds or whoever he thinks may have harmed his brother. That's why you told me about the dead rat."

"Yes," Hatfield said.

"Do you have any reason to think that besides something that happened more than twenty years ago? Are the brothers close?"

"Giles refused to go into business with Simon. When we were starting the company, Simon was around for our initial discussions. He wanted in. I was willing to bring him on board because he was Giles's brother. I was prepared to swallow my doubts."

"But you didn't."

"I brought it up with Giles once. Casually. About Simon. He told me that Simon was to have nothing to do with the company. That was it for me. He was happy to have Simon on the outside, so I was too."

"Did that lead to bad feelings between the two of them?" Kimberly asked. "This company is doing well. So Simon missed out on a nice amount of money. That can make someone angry."

"I don't think they were ever very close. Whether Simon resented being cut out of TechGreen, I don't know."

"Okay. Did they have other problems?"

"Not that I'm aware of." Hatfield paused. "I sensed they didn't agree on everything when their mother died. Giles was very close to her . . . a little too close. He might have gotten first crack at some things Simon wanted. It's just the two of them."

"Was there a lot of money?"

"A decent amount. It put a strain on Giles when the estate was being settled. He became withdrawn, moodier than normal."

"And Giles doesn't have any kids?" Kimberly asked.

"No."

"So who gets his share of this if he's . . . if the worst happens?"

Hatfield rubbed his forehead. "I don't know. Simon?"

"Could be," Kimberly said. "No kids for Giles. No other siblings. Parents dead."

"Crap. You're not thinking . . . I mean, would he do that?"

"I don't know. But I do know somebody went in there and took the ring. And that's all they took."

"Okay. Sure. But that doesn't make sense. If Simon inherits from Giles, then he gets the ring. So why kill for it?"

"Maybe Simon doesn't inherit Giles's estate. Maybe someone else does. We'll have to get a copy of the will."

"Why did Simon come in and push you to look for his brother if he killed him?" Hatfield asked.

"It would make a good diversion. You said yourself how crafty Simon is." Something crossed her mind. "I'm just curious. You're expanding, right? Where?"

Hatfield looked cagey, like he didn't want to reveal his business plan to her. "We're thinking of a few places."

"Have you worked with a commercial real estate developer named Joshua Fields?"

"Joshua Fields?" He frowned. "I don't know him."

"Did Morgan ever mention that name?" she asked.

"Morgan? I don't know anything about her personal life."

"Fair enough." There didn't seem to be anything else to ask him, so she stood up and told Hatfield she'd be in touch.

When she stepped outside his office, she noticed something on the closest desk. "Landlines?" she asked Hatfield.

He rolled his eyes. "Giles wanted them."

"Where did Morgan Reynolds sit?" Kimberly asked.

Hatfield looked perplexed. He leaned down and asked the woman at the desk closest to them the same question.

She pointed across the room. "Where Sasha sits now."

"Do you mind?" Kimberly asked, but started walking that way before Hatfield could answer.

She came alongside Sasha's space. "Excuse me."

Sasha looked up. She was young. Her dark eyes were pretty and clear, and the tips of her hair were dyed purple. "Hi."

Kimberly didn't remember her from the first round of interviews. "Did you know Morgan Reynolds?"

"No, I sure didn't. I started here after she left."

"Did you ever get any calls for Morgan Reynolds on this line?"

Sasha reached up and started twirling her purple tips. "A few. I'd tell people she didn't work here anymore. If it was about a project, I'd refer them to the right person."

"Sure. And that's it? Anything lately?"

Sasha continued to twirl. "There was a wrong number a week or so ago. Somebody called and asked for Morgan, but they gave a different last name . . . Woodward? Woodhead? Something like that. I told them they had the wrong number. Morgan's last name is Reynolds. Anyway, it had been so long since she'd quit."

"Why would you remember a random call like that?" Kimberly asked, hoping there was more.

"I'm supposed to go to Ireland. I need to get a passport."

"So?"

"It was the passport office calling. That's why I remember. They were calling looking for this Morgan . . . whatever her name was."

I STOOD UNDER THE SHOWER for as long as I could.

I still felt the impact of Simon's index finger on my chest. I wouldn't be surprised if I ended up with a bruise right there.

Twenty minutes.

He seemed like a man who meant what he said. He'd tried to be affable, friendly. But I'd seen his type before. A man who appeared normal, until you tried to veer away from what he wanted.

I stepped out of the shower, trying to sort through what Simon had told me. I knew only one thing for certain—Morgan had admitted to stealing the ring. Had she done more?

I almost couldn't contemplate it. . . . Had she killed a man?

Then I ran through the past twenty-four hours. If that was true, it meant I'd met, fallen for, and pursued a murderer.

I started getting dressed. Simon made it all seem so certain. But why not go to the police? Was he just impatient? Or was there something else?

I wasn't sure, so I did what I do when I'm confused. I called Dad.

"Thank God," Dad said, sounding relieved. "You got everything out of your system? You met your girl and . . . Well, you don't have to tell your old man about all of that."

"Dad, I need your help."

"What is it? Are you in more trouble?"

"Not exactly. I need you to look someone up for me. I was hoping . . . you could ask your friend Jim Tuttle to do it."

A long pause. "Jim Tuttle? You can't just ask a retired cop to look somebody up for kicks, Joshua. What is going on?"

I checked the clock. I'd used thirteen of my twenty minutes.

"I can't explain," I said. "But I'm not in danger. I'm just working something out. For that friend of mine I mentioned. And Jim owes us a favor. You helped him find the location for his pet store when he retired, right? So he can do a little favor in return."

"Are you still in Kentucky?" he asked.

"I am. In Wyckoff, at the Best Western." I gave him Simon's name and a brief description. "Call me when you hear anything."

He cleared his throat. "You know . . . you're my only kid. If you're in deep here . . ."

"It's okay, Dad." I tried to sound more certain than I really was. "So you'll give the name to Tuttle?"

"I'll call him. And you're right. He does owe me one. Or two. And I think opening that pet store was a dumb idea."

Before we hung up, I asked one more thing. "Can you have Jim look up someone else? Morgan Reynolds. Nashville. Formerly of Laurel Falls, Kentucky, and Wyckoff, Kentucky."

ONCE I was off the phone, I gathered my things, zipping my carry-on and computer bag. I took a last look around the room to make sure I hadn't forgotten anything. That's when I saw my T-shirt on the floor, between the bed and the nightstand. I bent over and picked it up, and when I did, I saw something beneath it.

It was a photograph. It showed a child, unmistakably Morgan, about eight or nine years old. Her hair reached her shoulders, and she wore a red top and denim shorts. Behind her stood a woman with limp blond hair. She wore sunglasses and held a cigarette in one hand, a purse in the other. She appeared unhealthy, her skin sallow. In the lower right-hand corner I saw something else.

It was ghostly white and slightly blurry, as though whatever it was had been moving when the shot was taken. I scratched my head. Then I remembered the story Morgan had told me in the night. The petting zoo in the amusement park. A goat.

I flipped the picture over. On the back someone had written, "Morgan (7) and me at Fantasy Farm. 7/13/01."

Her mother. Her dying mother, the one she'd moved near when her job in Laurel Falls went south. The photo had likely fallen out of her bag, and she'd been in such a rush to leave—*to leave me*—she hadn't bothered to look. She'd left it behind.

Or had it even been an accident?

She'd spoken about the amusement park, sharing the pain of the memories associated with her mother. And then she just happened to leave the photograph behind when she took off?

Someone thumped on the door.

I checked the clock. My time was up. It must be Simon. Had he even gone down to the lobby?

"Come on," he said, his voice muffled by the door. "Joshua?"

He knocked again, even louder.

"I need another minute. I'm packing."

Then my phone rang. It was my dad. I answered.

"What the hell is going on up there?" Dad asked.

"Did you get that information from Jim already?"

"Jim? No. The cops called me right after I hung up with you. They're looking to talk to you. They've been trying to call you. Joshua, this woman is a missing person. And she's wanted for questioning in another case. Really. What's going on?"

Simon banged on the door again.

"Dad, what did you tell them?"

"I told them all I knew. You're in Wyckoff, Kentucky. Apparently with a young lady named Morgan Reynolds. I'd say you should be expecting a visit from the police soon—"

"Dad, I'm going to have to call you back." I hung up.

Simon pounded on the door again. "Joshua?"

KIMBERLY inhaled the familiar scent of burning coffee, which hovered over the squad room. Brandon's desk was empty, so she went to talk to her boss, Lieutenant Larry Willard.

Before she got there, Brandon stuck his head out of Willard's door and waved her over.

"I was just about to call you," he said.

She followed him in. Willard sat behind his desk, his big gut squeezed against its wooden edge. He wore a short-sleeved white shirt and a blue tie. Kimberly knew he was counting the days until his retirement in a few months.

And Kimberly wanted his job.

Three years earlier, they both had gone up for that same job, and he'd beat her out. It was her turn now. She'd earned it.

"Kimberly, Brandon was just about to share some good news," he said, pointing to the two chairs across the desk from him.

They sat like obedient children. She noticed Brandon's grip tighten on the armrests. He grew nervous around Willard.

"So?" Willard asked. "What did you want to share?"

"We've got a lead on Morgan Reynolds," Brandon said. "This guy Joshua Fields, the one who saw her on the plane and followed her? We've been trying to reach him on his cell, but he hasn't answered. This morning he called his father and told him he was in a hotel in Wyckoff with Morgan. I guess Fields skipped out on a big meeting to run off with Morgan Reynolds."

"And this guy, this Fields, decided to do all that after meeting her in the airport?" Willard asked.

"That's right," Brandon said.

"So, he's there. And she's there," Kimberly said. "Did we—"

"We called Wyckoff PD," Willard said. "They're heading to the hotel right now. We'll hear from them soon."

"Do we *know* Morgan Reynolds and Joshua Fields just met in the airport?" Kimberly asked. "They weren't friends before?"

"We haven't found any connection," Brandon said.

"What else did the father say?" Willard asked.

"It took a while to get this information out of him. You could tell he didn't want to get his son in any deeper. It's obvious the guy loves his kid. But here's the news. Fields called his dad, asking him to have a cop friend look into *two* people for him. One was Morgan Reynolds. The other? Simon Caldwell."

Kimberly felt a burst of energy. "Simon is there, then. Thirty minutes away, in Wyckoff."

Willard raised a cautioning hand. "We don't know for sure."

"Why else would Fields ask to have the police check on him?"

"It's possible," Willard said. "Of course."

"We haven't seen Simon in almost forty-eight hours," she said. "When Giles was first reported missing, he was all over us."

"Maybe he's laying low because we learned about the two assaults on his record," Willard said.

"Not to mention the one in college Hatfield just told me about."

"Assault?" Willard asked.

"Intimidation, maybe," Kimberly said. "But there's more."

Brandon and Willard both edged forward in their seats.

"It turns out Giles also had some issues with his temper." She told them about the run-ins with two female employees, the ones she'd heard about from Steven Hatfield. "We know Morgan Reynolds and Giles Caldwell had a beef over money. Could it have blown up into something more?"

"We don't know," Willard said. "But it's a theory."

"But we do know Fields and Reynolds are together in Wyckoff," Brandon said. "At least they were as of last night."

"And Morgan grew up in Wyckoff?" Kimberly asked.

"Yup," Brandon said. "She went to Henry Clay."

Willard shifted his weight. "So we have a missing person here, Giles Caldwell. Meanwhile, that man's brother, his former employee, and a random stranger may all be together in Wyckoff, where the former employee grew up and went to college. And the stranger is getting his dad to call in favors with the police to dig up dirt on the other two. What a wonderful world we live in."

"I just got back from TechGreen," Kimberly said. "Hatfield didn't have any insights about Morgan Reynolds, except he didn't think the company did anything wrong in not paying Morgan the bonus. But everyone else who made an app got a bonus."

Willard nodded. "It's a leap from disappointment to murder."

"What else do people kill for?" Kimberly asked. "Love and money. Right?"

"We need a body, though," Willard said directly to Kimberly. "Or some kind of evidence. Is that all?"

"No, it's not," Kimberly said. "I learned something about our brothers. Apparently, Simon feels like he got the shaft when their mother died, that certain things went to Giles in a way that wasn't fair. If you're looking for a motive, that's money right there."

"But to kill his brother over it?" Willard asked. "He came in here pitching a fit, saying we weren't doing enough."

"That's a big risk," Kimberly said.

"This guy doesn't seem like one for the safe bet," Willard said. "He's over in Wyckoff chasing down leads on his own. He's not shy. Or completely stable. Was that it at TechGreen?"

Kimberly shook her head. "Get this: TechGreen still has landlines. Turns out the desk where Morgan Reynolds used to work got a call from the passport office. Except they didn't ask for Morgan

Reynolds. They asked for Morgan something else. The woman who has Morgan's desk now couldn't remember the name. Thought it began with a 'W.'"

"Maybe it was a wrong number," Brandon said.

"What are the odds?" Kimberly said. "She used another name on the plane. She probably used another one for the passport."

"It's starting to sound like premeditation," Willard said. "She planned to do something to Giles and then leave the country."

"Exactly," Kimberly said. "And she's right over in Wyckoff. You want me to take a little road trip?"

IT TURNED out to be one of those rare hotels with windows that open, and I managed to slide the pane over, creating a three-inch space. Unless I could lose fifty pounds in two minutes, I wasn't going out that way. Not to mention that I was on the third floor.

But then I saw something useful.

Simon banged again. I called to him: "Give me one more minute. I have to use the bathroom."

"You better not be screwing with me," he said.

"Just wait for me in the lobby. I'll be down soon."

I looked down and saw Billy, the garbage boy, pushing a cart full of clean laundry across the parking lot. I gave a soft whistle, hoping Simon couldn't hear me. Billy looked up.

"Oh," he said, recognizing me.

I dug in my wallet and pulled out a twenty. It fluttered in the breeze two stories above Billy's head. "I need your help. Bring that cart to my room. Three oh six. Right now."

Billy blinked a few times. "But my manager—"

I pulled out another twenty. "Just get up here. Fast."

Billy pushed the cart into the building. I went over to the door and looked through the peephole. No sign of Simon. Maybe I'd put him off just long enough.

And then I waited.

I'd like to say I waited calmly. But I didn't. Instead, I paced. Back and forth, back and forth.

Finally a gentle knock sounded. Through the peephole I saw

Billy. I undid the chain and pulled the door open. I looked up and down the hall. I didn't see Simon or anyone else.

"Do you know what I want you to do?" I asked.

"I'm guessing you don't want a bunch of clean towels."

I grabbed my bags and came back to the door. Billy was already moving laundry aside, making space for me. Before I got in, I handed him three twenties, a big raise from the night before. A trip in the laundry cart past a maniac seemed like a more expensive job.

"There's a man in the lobby. Big guy, light jacket, edgy."

"I saw him. He looked at me like he wanted to choke me."

"He wants to choke me, I think. For sure he wants to choke the woman I was looking for last night. He can't see me. My car's on the north side of the building. A black Charger. Just get me there."

"We'll have to go right past him."

"Don't look at him," I said. "Roll me past."

Billy moved some of the laundry aside. "You're crazy, man."

"Think of the story you can tell your friends. Or your girl."

He nodded. "Okay," he said, pointing at the cart. "Get in."

KIMBERLY called Peter while her city-issued sedan hummed against the two-lane state highway, heading to Wyckoff.

"What's up?" he asked. "Is something wrong?"

"No. Nothing's wrong. Not really. It's just work. I'm not going to make the soccer game tonight."

"Oh, okay. I'm going. No worries."

"I know you're going. It's not you I'm concerned about. We have a touchy, judgmental preteen to deal with."

"Yes, her," Peter said with a sigh. "She'll have to deal. It's nothing you can get out of, is it? Is it about Giles Caldwell?"

"Who else could it be but Giles Caldwell? He's taking over my life. Or at least the people who knew him are. And the mayor."

"Did you find him?" Peter asked.

"No. We have a couple of leads, so I'm driving to Wyckoff right now to check on it all in person."

"It's a nice drive," he said. "Always makes me think of taking Maria to Fantasy Farm when she was little. Remember that?"

"Of course I do."

"You must have a good lead if you're going in person."

"You forget, Giles Caldwell is a prominent citizen in our little burg. He employs people, pays a lot of taxes. And he and the mayor are friends. The mayor wants this wiped away as soon as possible."

Kimberly felt wired, edgy. And she was frustrated over missing the soccer game after promising she'd attend.

"Do you want me to break it to Maria?" Peter asked. "After the game we'll go for pizza. That usually soothes her preteen angst."

"Yes, and tell her I'll call her when I get the chance."

"Isn't it good for her to learn she's not the center of the world?" Peter asked. "Sometimes work comes first, right?"

"Right. And it is kind of important to find a missing person." Kimberly sighed. "I'll let you know when I'm coming back. Maybe we'll learn something big in Wyckoff and wrap this up."

"Be safe," Peter said.

"I will." She hung up and continued driving.

THE laundry was warm. It smelled fresh and clean. I jostled around a little as Billy pushed the cart into the elevator and we descended to the lobby. My frazzled nerves made me sweat, and I swiped at my forehead. The cart rumbled and rattled as we exited the elevator onto the lobby's tiled floor.

Then the cart stopped. I heard a sharp voice, muffled by the towels. "Where are you going?" It didn't sound like Simon.

"I have to take this outside."

A long pause. I hoped Billy had a good poker face.

"They need those on four," the voice said.

"I'll go right up there after this," Billy said.

We started moving again but stopped almost immediately.

A familiar voice spoke. I could almost see the smug look on his face. "What floor were you on?" Simon asked.

Billy seemed stuck for an answer. An eternity passed. "I was outside," he finally said.

"You were upstairs," Simon said. "You just got off the elevator. What floor were you on?"

Another long pause. Billy had no future as a poker player.

"Five," he said.

Had Simon been watching the numbers move?

"Five? You didn't see anyone up there?" Simon asked.

"No, sir."

I heard Billy say something else, and then the cart started moving again, rumbling over the tiles. We hit a large bump; then I sensed a change in the light. We were outside.

We stopped, and Billy said, "Okay, it's clear." He reached in to help me out. I swung one leg and then the other over the side of the cart, grabbing my bags in the process. I threw my stuff in the back seat and opened the driver's door of the rental car.

"The guy you told me about, he talked to me," Billy said.

"I heard. Where did he go when you left?"

"I think he went upstairs. He seemed pissed."

"Stay away from him," I said. "And don't tell him anything."

"Got it."

"Hey, you ever hear of a place called Fantasy Farm?" I asked. "You know, the old amusement park? It's closed now."

"I've never heard of it," Billy said.

"Okay." I closed the door. "Thanks, Billy. Be safe."

I started the car and drove off.

KIMBERLY reached Wyckoff around noon. Willard had spoken to the Wyckoff PD, letting them know one of his detectives was coming to town, but still she went to the police station first. No police department liked having cops from other jurisdictions showing up and nosing around without them knowing about it.

But before Kimberly pulled open the front door of the station, a woman in her thirties, wearing a business suit, stepped out.

"Detective Givens?"

"That's me."

"I'm Detective Alicia Hughes," she said. "That hotel we told your lieutenant about? There's been a disturbance there. I think you'll want to check it out."

"I think I do," Kimberly said.

"I'll drive," said Hughes. "I can fill you in on the way."

They climbed into a dark sedan, and Hughes backed out of the parking space. "When Willard called," she said, "we sent an officer over to the hotel, hoping we could catch one of these folks, but none of them were around. That was a couple of hours ago. By the way, I've met Willard before. He's a good cop."

"He's retiring."

"That's what he said. Anyway, after our officer was gone, something else went down—we just got a call."

Kimberly felt tense as they drove, distracting herself with the passing scenery, the buildings on campus, the kids strolling by.

They came in sight of the hotel. Hughes pulled to a stop near a squad car in the parking lot. They jumped out, the sliding doors whooshed open as they approached, and a uniformed officer greeted them.

"What have you got?" Hughes asked.

"It's an assault," the young officer said. "One of the guests roughed up a hotel employee. He's telling a pretty wild story."

Hughes nodded, and she and Kimberly went back to the small, cluttered office. A kid sat in a desk chair with an ice pack on the back of his neck and another one pressed to his lip.

An officer explained, "This is Billy Newcomb. He's a maintenance worker here. Why don't you tell them what happened?"

Billy kept the ice pack pressed against his lip as he started talking about a guy who showed up at the hotel the previous evening, looking for a woman. He didn't know which room she was staying in or how to contact her. Billy admitted that he took the guy's money and asked the desk clerk if she'd seen the woman.

"The clerk remembered her," Billy said.

"So you revealed her location to this guy?" Kimberly asked. "What if he'd wanted to hurt her?"

"No, no, it was nothing like that. He liked her; I could tell."

"So this guy went to look for this woman?" Hughes asked.

"He was still here this morning. I don't know about the woman."

Billy then told a whole story about the guy asking to be wheeled out of the hotel in a laundry cart so he wouldn't be seen leaving.

"And who did he want to avoid?" Kimberly asked, but then she went on. "Let me guess. . . ."

"Yeah, the guy who did this to me."

"And why did he do that?" Kimberly asked.

"He wanted to know where the first guy went. Or where the woman went. Either one. When I pushed the laundry cart out to the parking lot, he went upstairs. But he came back."

"And he just jumped you here?" Hughes asked. "At work?"

"Out back. About half an hour ago."

"Do you know where this first guy went?" Kimberly asked. "The one you . . . the one you pushed out in a laundry cart?"

"I have no clue." But then he mumbled, "Fantasy Farm."

Hughes held up her hand. "Billy, what about Fantasy Farm?"

"The laundry guy asked about Fantasy Farm . . . so I told the crazy guy. I told him laundry guy asked me that. I didn't want my ass kicked, but he did it anyway."

"You told the guy who beat you up that Mr. Laundry Cart was interested in Fantasy Farm?" Hughes asked.

"Mmm . . . yeah."

Kimberly and Hughes walked out. "Is he talking about the old amusement park?" Kimberly asked.

"Fantasy Farm. Yeah. It's about thirty minutes outside of town."

"Looks like he got thumped pretty hard," Kimberly said. "He could be spouting nonsense. But it might be worth checking out."

Chapter 7

I ATE AS SOON AS I drove away from the Best Western, fast food from a drive-through window. I'd barely eaten the day before, but I'd had plenty to drink and two Xanax.

Stomach full, I considered my options. Then I remembered the missed calls from that morning. Who had been calling and why?

I listened to my voice mails. Two were from a cop who told me the police in Laurel Falls, Kentucky, wanted to speak to me.

Laurel Falls? Where Morgan worked at that tech company.

Where her boss disappeared, according to my stalker Simon.

Then a detective, Kimberly Givens, left me a series of messages. She knew I was in Wyckoff. Would I talk to her there? She was coming to town to look for Morgan Reynolds. . . .

"Damn," I said. But I called her back.

"Mr. Fields?" she said. "You're a tough man to get hold of."

"I'm traveling. And my phone was off for a while."

"Are you still in Wyckoff?"

"How did you know I was here?" I asked.

"You told your father. So. Are you?"

"I was thinking of leaving, actually."

"Is Morgan Reynolds with you?" she asked.

"No, she isn't."

"Do you know where she is?"

"I don't. She took off without saying a thing."

"You spent the night together, then?"

"We did."

"Did you already know each other?"

"What? No, we met yesterday. At the Atlanta airport."

"Mr. Fields, what do you say we meet in person? I'm worried you've gotten in over your head, and the longer you stay out there, the deeper you get. It could start to look suspicious."

"Suspicious?"

"Or maybe dangerous. I know you had to run away from Simon Caldwell this morning. I don't know where he is either."

"He's not with me."

"When can we meet, Mr. Fields?"

I didn't like the suspicion being cast on me. And I didn't know whom to believe—Simon or Morgan. Or neither.

"Detective, do you think Morgan Reynolds harmed her boss?"

"I'm trying to figure that out. Did she say anything to you?"

"No, she didn't," I said. "But I don't think she hurt anyone."

"Where can I meet you? I can come to you if you'd like."

I watched people coming and going at the fast-food restaurant. Elderly couples. College students. Their lives looked safe and predictable. Did I want to be one of them? Wasn't I already?

"Give me some time, Detective. Morgan, she's . . . skittish. I think if I can talk to her . . ."

"You're not a police officer. Let us handle it, Mr. Fields."

"Give me just a few hours," I said. "Then I promise I'll call."

I hung up, cutting off any reply she might make.

My hands were shaking. I'd never disrespected authority that way in my life. How deep was I digging the hole for myself?

And I faced the prospect of looking for a human-size needle in a small-college-town haystack. A human-size needle who'd run out on me, leaving me to face her pursuer.

I checked my phone. There were lots of flights from Nashville to Chicago. I'd have no problem getting home and away from everything. My real life waited for me there. Predictable. Boring. Safe.

No cops. No Simon.

It sounded better than it had in months. Maybe years.

And then I remembered Renee. I texted her.

> *Just wanted you to know I'm leaving Kentucky today. Coming home. We can talk when I get there. If you want.*

I hit SEND. Renee wrote back instantly.

> *Sure, let's talk. Are you safe?*

I wrote back. *Perfectly.*

I didn't like the word. Or the sentiment. *Perfectly safe.* Is that all I wanted out of life—to be perfectly safe?

I put the phone down and looked out the window. Students passed by, all looking happy. I thought about the gap between them and me. The five years that had passed had turned into a lockstep march toward . . . what? A mortgage and kids and a minivan?

I decided not to call Detective Givens back. She and I wanted the same thing—to find Morgan and convince her to turn herself in. Admit she stole the ring. It wouldn't be too bad, would it?

And who was going to have a better chance of convincing her to turn herself in? Me? Or a cop?

Well, I wasn't really sure. But I really wanted to try. And I meant what I told Detective Givens—I'd look for a little while, and then, if I saw no sign of Morgan, I'd call Givens and head to the airport when she was finished with me. So I started looking.

I drove through town, working my way past the edge of campus. As the day passed, I grew more and more frustrated and tired, feeling very much like a man on a pointless mission.

It was getting close to five o'clock. I was ready to throw in the towel and drive to the airport when my phone rang.

I expected it to be the police. Or my dad.

But the number on the car's display was unknown to me. My hand shook as I reached out and answered the call.

"Don't hang up," Morgan said. Her voice sounded tinged with a nervous edge. But was it because she was talking to me, or because she was on the run from the police and a crazy man?

"Oh, I won't," I said, shaking my head even though she couldn't see me. "I have a ninety-minute drive to the airport, and I forgot to bring an audiobook. You should provide plenty of entertainment as I go. I like mysteries and thrillers, the crazier the better. I'm sure you've come up with something good."

"Don't be such a baby," she said. "You know I had to leave. You know I have to keep moving."

"Yeah, I guess so. You're Lucy, and I'm Charlie Brown. And I keep missing that football."

"I'm guessing you got away from Simon," she said.

"Did you know he was in the hotel?" I asked.

"I saw him this morning. I knew I had to go. And go fast."

"You could have called," I said. "Clearly you had my number. And how did you get that, by the way?"

"I got it off your phone while you were asleep. And, yes, I thought about calling you and warning you. But, to be honest, I knew if Simon was occupied with you, then I'd be able to get away. I don't know how long I can be here."

"You're still in Wyckoff?" I asked.

"Kind of," she said. "I want you to meet me somewhere. I want to show you something. It will explain everything."

I gritted my teeth. I looked at the horizon.

"I need your help," she said. "And you're the only person I can trust right now. And after that, if you want to call the police, you can. I think it will all make sense if you come and meet me."

"Where are you?"

"I think I left something in the hotel room. Did you find it?"

The photo. "Why did you leave that there? Did you want me to find it and guess where you are?"

"Not really. I had the picture out . . . just to think about things. When I drove away, I realized I'd left it. Maybe, on some level, I wanted you to find it. I don't know. So . . . do you have it?"

"I do," I said. "You want it?"

I thought about my perfectly safe life again.

A long, perfectly safe Chicago winter with Renee. Deiced planes and dirty snow in the gutters. Making money with Dad.

"Is that where you are?" I asked. "Fantasy Farm? Why?"

Before she answered, I was already turning the car around.

KIMBERLY spent the afternoon in Wyckoff, using a desk at the police station. She spoke to Willard about what she'd learned at the Best Western. Then she took a phone call from the mayor.

Hughes, the Wyckoff detective, came by and told her that she'd asked the county to send an officer to Fantasy Farm.

"And?" Kimberly asked.

"He didn't see anything. It's abandoned, kind of a dump."

Kimberly turned back to her laptop and checked Morgan Reynolds's Facebook page again, looking for more friends. She got a few names and phone numbers, but all the women Kimberly reached told a similar story. They'd moved away from Wyckoff and maintained only sporadic contact with Morgan.

Kimberly had stood up to stretch, contemplating heading back to Laurel Falls, when Hughes stopped by her desk.

"The county cops cruised by Fantasy Farm again," Hughes said. "There's a rental car at a side entrance. They're reaching out to the company to see who rented it. We might check it out if you're game."

"Let's go."

On their way out of Wyckoff, Kimberly's phone rang with Maria's ringtone. Kimberly took the call, bracing herself for a short conversation with a disappointed child.

"Hey, baby. So? How was it?"

Maria's voice brightened. "We won. Two to nothing."

"Oh, that's great. Really, I'm happy for you."

Kimberly breathed easier, listening while Maria gave a blow-by-blow of the game, including the save she made.

"And we're on our way to get pizza now," she said.

"I'm glad you're having a good time," Kimberly said.

"How long will you be away?" Maria asked.

"I'm not sure," Kimberly said. "But we're on our way to something we hope is important."

There was a long pause. Then Maria said, "Well . . . you can go to my next match, right? Or the one after that?"

"I fully intend to."

"And then *we* can go out for pizza."

Kimberly's phone beeped. Another call coming in. She checked the screen. Brandon. "Shoot," she said.

"If you have to go, Mom, it's fine. We're almost at the restaurant. And I know you have a job. And it's important."

"Okay. I'll call you tomorrow. I love you."

"I love you too."

Kimberly's phone beeped again. She pushed a button.

"Kimberly? Sorry to bother you," Brandon said.

"That's okay. What is it?"

"I found out that . . ."

The call dropped.

"Brandon? Hello?"

She tried calling back, but the call dropped again.

"No service out here," Hughes said. "Do you want me to turn around? If we head back, service will pick up."

Kimberly thought about it. Whatever Brandon knew could wait. "No," she said, "keep going. I want to check out this place now."

I TOOK THE STATE ROAD heading east. The sun was sliding down the sky behind me, so as I drove, the sky began to darken, the first faint stars popping up ahead of me along with a bright half-moon.

I'd lived in Chicago so long, I'd forgotten what it was like to be out in the middle of nowhere at nightfall. The darkness felt heavy, like a physical presence descending on top of me.

As I drove, I thought about Morgan. I could have ended the whole thing by calling the police and letting them know where Morgan was and headed on my way, never looking back. As I'd told her, it might have been the best thing for her, to give the ring back and be protected from Simon.

But what would become of her? She'd face charges for the theft. She'd have to deal with that during her mother's final days.

And then there was the fact that I'd likely never see her again.

She'd promised some kind of answers at Fantasy Farm.

So I went to get them.

The GPS told me I was getting closer, and then I saw a battered sign, announcing the entrance to the park.

I turned left into the entrance and came face-to-face with a low, padlocked gate. The chain securing it in place looked loose, meaning that with a little effort someone could slip through.

A car sat at the entrance, a gray sedan with Kentucky plates that I parked alongside. I assumed it was Morgan's. Before I turned the headlights off, I stared through the gate and down the midway, looking for her. But I saw only a series of squat buildings and weeds growing through the cracked pavement.

I turned the car off, climbed out, and went over to the gray vehicle. I used the flashlight app on my phone and waved it over the car, trying to see if anyone was inside. There wasn't.

I hesitated. I could easily turn around and go back to town. But I'd come that far. . . .

Once I'd made up my mind, I covered the short distance to the gate, pulled it apart, and with a little effort squeezed through.

I started walking on the midway, looking for Morgan. As my eyes adjusted to the dark, I saw small, empty booths that once held games like a shooting gallery or ring toss. The booths gave way to abandoned rides—a carousel, bumper cars. I saw no sign of people.

I came to a crossroads. It took me a moment in the dark, but then I saw a signpost pointing toward the petting zoo.

I remembered Morgan's troubled memories of her mother at the zoo. The photo showed the same thing. So I turned that way.

Ahead I saw the outline of a rail fence and a small barn. When I moved closer, a tall, slender figure emerged from the shadows. She walked over to the fence and waited for me.

"I wondered if you'd remember where to find me." She leaned against the top of the weathered fence.

I came closer and leaned against the fence next to her. She reached out and placed her hand on my arm.

I wanted to pull back but didn't. Still my body tensed, which Morgan registered, her face showing surprise at my edginess.

"What did you think?" I asked. "I'd be happy to see you?"

"Okay, I guess I can see that now."

"You should have seen it when you ran out on me. Hell, you've run off several times. The only reason I'm here is because you promised to clear everything up. You said you'd explain why you were in Wyckoff. So . . . let's get to it. It's dark, and there's a crazy man and the police looking for both of us. So this better be good."

Morgan glanced down at the ground, almost as though she wanted to rest her head against the top rail. I waited until she looked up again.

"Do you want to climb over the fence and look in the barn?"

"What's in the barn?" I asked.

She stepped back. "You wanted answers. They're here."

"Okay." What choice did I really have?

I placed my foot on the rail and swung my body over the fence. Once on the other side, I followed Morgan to the barn, where two big doors stood wide open. Morgan stopped. She looked into the darkness and then back at me. She dug around in the pocket of her hoodie and came out with the tissue-wrapped object, the one I'd seen back in the hotel room.

"The ring?" I said.

She nodded. The whites of her eyes were prominent, like a scared animal. "I don't want to go in there alone."

"Why not?"

"Because I've been in there already."

I felt like I was one step behind, trying to keep up with someone who knew much more than I did. "Why do you have the ring here? You said this was going to explain everything."

"In there. It explains everything."

"Then let's go in." I tapped my phone, activating the flashlight. I sounded confident, but Morgan's anxiety infected me.

Did I have something to be afraid of? And if so, what?

I stepped past her, holding the light. It cast a glowing cone over the barn floor.

"Back there," Morgan said. "On the left."

"And do you mind telling me what we're going to see?"

She stopped and spun around, facing the entrance to the barn.

I froze in place and whispered, "What is it?"

She held up her index finger.

We both stood there, like kids playing statues. Just when I thought there was nothing going on, I heard footsteps. Heavy.

I shut off the flashlight, but it was obvious we were inside.

I moved past Morgan, back toward the open doors. When I reached the entrance, I peeked out. In the dim light I saw a large figure leaning against the fence.

"Hello, Simon," I said.

With surprising ease and deftness for a man his size, Simon swung his leg up onto the fence rail and came over it, landing on both feet. He straightened and moved toward us.

I put my hand out instinctively, placing it in front of Morgan and moving her behind me.

He stopped a few feet away from me, looming before us. "What do you know? This worked out better than I imagined."

"What do you want?" I asked.

He stared at me for a moment. "You went out in the laundry cart, right?" He wagged his finger. "You should have worked with me. You could have told me what I wanted to know, and you would have been done. Now you're tied up with her."

"Maybe the police are on their way," I said, trying a bluff.

"How would the police even know where we are? I bet they're not coming by anytime soon."

Simon looked over my shoulder. His eyes zeroed in on Morgan.

"You know what I want," he said directly to her. "I made it clear in Nashville. You understand what this is about."

The words almost sprung out of my mouth: *Give him the damn ring.* But I held back. I didn't trust the guy.

Morgan must have read my mind.

"I don't believe you'd ever leave me alone," she said. "You threatened me. You threatened my mother."

"And you killed my brother," he said. "Which is worse?"

"It's a big leap to say she's a murder suspect," I said.

"Oh, really? Hell, you're probably a suspect too. You're running around with her. Do you think that doesn't look bad?"

"Let him go, okay?" Morgan said.

"What?" I asked, looking over my shoulder at her. "No."

"Just let him go," she said. "He didn't have anything to do with this. Let him walk away; then you and I can settle things."

Simon shook his head. "How are we going to settle things out here?" he asked. "We're so far from where we started."

Morgan thrust her hand out. Simon studied what she held. I looked too. And I understood. The red tissue paper.

Simon snatched it out of her hand and started to unwrap it.

KIMBERLY quickly became disoriented as they headed down the dark state road. The sun was long gone. She wanted Hughes to drive faster, but she seemed to be going as quickly as was reasonably safe. The road wound and dipped.

"If it's really her there," Hughes said, "I hope we don't miss her."

"If it's her, I hope she's not alone. I'd like to talk to that dope Fields who's been chasing her around."

"You think he's involved?"

"I don't know what to think about him. But he's hitched his wagon to her for some reason."

Kimberly's phone rang. It was Brandon again. She answered.

"What's up?" Kimberly asked. "This call may drop."

"I just heard from one of Giles's former employees, a woman named Megan Bright. She worked for Giles for about eighteen months and then quit. She's in Memphis now."

"Yeah, yeah. What did she have to say?" Kimberly asked.

"Apparently, those two women Hatfield told us about weren't the only ones to have run-ins with Giles Caldwell."

Kimberly sat up straighter in her seat. "Yeah?"

"Yeah. This woman felt the same kind of threat from Giles. But this time he actually put his hands on her."

Simon fumbled with the paper, casting each layer aside as he pulled it off, a look of glee shining out of his face. Finally he held the ring in his giant hands, muttering, "Yes, yes, yes."

I managed to slip past him while he was distracted. I looked down the midway. There was nothing between me and my car. If I simply ran, I could be back to my car in minutes. I could drive off and call the police. But I'd be leaving Morgan in Simon's hands.

I looked at the ground. An object caught the faint light from the moon and stars. A beer bottle.

"Okay, okay," Simon said, and stepped closer to Morgan. "What about the rest?"

"What rest?" Morgan asked.

"My brother," he said. "Where is he? I want the body. I want to bury him next to our mother. So just tell me where he is."

Simon lunged forward and grabbed her arm.

Morgan tried to pull away but couldn't.

I picked up the bottle. I turned and, with one motion, brought it down on the back of Simon's head.

I'd never hit anyone with a bottle before. In the movies, the glass shatters and the guy slumps to the ground. But Simon must have had a stronger constitution. The bottle flew out of my hand. Simon remained on his feet but let go of Morgan.

He reached back and rubbed his head. Then he turned to face me. His initial movements were slow, but then he came at me, both hands clutching at my throat. I fell backward, his body landing on top of mine and crushing the air out of my lungs.

He started swinging his fists. I bucked beneath him, trying to get away. I worked my right hand loose and swung at his head.

Simon repositioned himself, pinning my right arm under his knee. He swung at me. Over and over.

I squeezed my eyes closed, strangely detached as I contemplated what an odd place this was to die.

But then the punching stopped.

I thought Simon might be winding up for one big, final blow. But it never came. I opened my eyes. Simon still loomed over me, but then, like a giant oak, he slowly tipped over.

That's when I saw Morgan. She stood there, holding the still-unbroken beer bottle. For once she hadn't run off. She'd stayed.

She'd even saved me.

BRANDON's call dropped. "I lost the call," said Kimberly.

"We're coming up on it," Hughes said. She slowed the car, and Kimberly squinted into the night. Then she saw it. A small drive-way, a gate. Two civilian cars plus a police cruiser.

"Did you call for backup?"

"I let the county boys know. They must have sent someone."

Hughes parked next to the cruiser. A uniformed officer stood by the two civilian cars, flashlight in hand. He was sweeping the beam around the vehicles, looking for something . . . anything.

They climbed out of Hughes's car. When they did, the uniformed officer came over, his flashlight pointing at the ground.

"What have you got?" Hughes asked.

"I found the first car at an entrance about a quarter mile away. Then I came over here and saw these two." The officer brought out a small spiral notebook. "The one at the other entrance is a rental, and so is this one. This other vehicle here is registered to a Simon Caldwell. Laurel Falls, Kentucky."

Hughes looked at Kimberly. "Your boy Fields is probably in one of the rentals."

"Morgan Reynolds would be in the other one," Kimberly said.

Hughes said, "Okay, you ready, Detective?"

"Sure am," Kimberly said.

Hughes pointed to the officer. "Call county for a little more help. We might need it."

The officer followed instructions, using his lapel mike to call. When he was finished, they all squeezed through the gate and started down the midway.

I PUSHED out from under Simon and to my feet.

Morgan took my arm, helping me. When I got up on two legs, I wobbled briefly as my equilibrium came back. My hands went to my face, checking for blood. I didn't see any on my hands, and all my moving parts seemed to be working.

"Are you okay?" Morgan asked.

"I think so," I said.

"I thought he was going to kill you," she said. "And me."

I looked down. Simon lay on his side, his face in a clump of hay. I bent down, took his arm, and pressed against his wrist.

I waited. Nothing.

So I placed my fingers against his throat, the way I was taught in the first aid class I took in high school.

"What is it?" Morgan asked.

"I don't think he's breathing."

"No, you can't say that."

"Morgan, I think he's dead." I pressed even harder, but I still felt nothing. "We have to call for help."

"Our phones don't work out here."

I stood up. "Then one of us has to go back to their car and drive until they do work. You do it. I'll wait here. Go."

But she just stood there in the dark, shaking her head.

"I can't," she said.

"What do you mean? He needs help. Go get the police."

"I can't." She gestured in the direction of the barn. "I've done some things I can't come back from, Joshua. Bad things."

"You took a ring. Get the cops to help this man."

"It's not just the ring," she said. Then, quickly, she took a step closer to me. "And I'm about to do another bad thing."

I didn't see the bottle. I only saw her arm make a sweeping

motion toward my head. And then I felt it. The bottle. *Thwump.*

Before I understood, I felt wobbly on my knees next to Simon, shaking my head.

I tried to get up. But then she swung again.

Chapter 8

I TRIED TO OPEN MY EYES. They felt like they were glued shut. And weighed down by lead. I opened my mouth to speak, my throat dry and cracked. I couldn't produce a sound.

Someone said my name. The words sounded distant and muffled, like they were coming from far away, down a long tunnel.

I had no idea what was going on. Had hours passed? Days?

Someone said my name again. The voice sounded closer, and like a woman's. I tried to respond, thought I made a sound.

When my eyes opened, everything was bright. Too bright.

I closed them again. It felt painful to squeeze the lids shut. The action put pressure on my brain and made my head hurt.

It didn't just hurt. It throbbed. Like a giant bass drum.

A presence came close to me and said my name. "Mr. Fields?"

I groaned, keeping my eyes shut.

"Mr. Fields? Do you know where you are?"

I opened my eyes ever so slightly. The light came rushing in. I saw a curtain. A woman wearing a colorful shirt, so intense it hurt my eyes, leaned close to me. It wasn't hard to figure out where I was. "Hospital," I said. "Emergency room."

"That's right," she said, drawing her words out like I was a kindergartner. "And do you know why?"

"Someone hit me," I said.

"Yes, they did," she said, encouraging me.

"Am I okay?" I asked.

"The X-ray was negative. The doctor will be by in a minute. We're going to keep watching you closely."

"How long . . . ?"

"You've been here since Wednesday evening," she said. "It's Thursday morning now."

My eyes adjusted. I opened them more but didn't like the starkness of the room and promptly shut them again.

"You can rest some more," she said, "but not for long. There's someone who wants to see you."

I didn't know who she meant. Did she mean Morgan? Or someone else? I drifted back to sleep until the nurse came in again and told me I had to wake up. That's when the detective came in. That's when I started talking.

I LOST track of time. I just poured the story out, welcoming the distraction from the throbbing in my head. The detective mostly listened, interjecting with questions only when she had to.

She sat in the chair next to my bed. Dirt stained her shoes, and I imagined she'd been wandering around in the amusement park, trying to make sense of everything that had happened out there.

"That's quite a couple of days," she said.

"More than I bargained for."

"So do you know where she went?" the detective asked.

My mind still felt fuzzy. "You mean after she hit me on the head with a bottle?" I asked. "No, I don't. I have no idea."

Detective Givens stood up. I saw no jewelry. No wedding ring, just a functional digital watch.

"So you have no idea where she might go?" Givens asked. "She didn't mention anything? Places she wanted to travel to?"

I strained my mind. "No. She didn't tell me much."

The detective nodded at my scraped-up knuckles. "A pretty good struggle out there, wasn't it?"

"Yeah." I tried to read her face. I remembered kneeling over the man. "Is he okay? Simon? He wasn't . . ."

The detective studied me. "Mr. Caldwell took a pretty good knock on the head," she said, her face revealing little. "You're worried about him?"

"I am. I hit him. And then . . . then she did too. I thought . . . He looked like he might be pretty bad. Can you just tell me?"

She waited a long time. It felt like hours. "He's alive, if that's what you're wondering. He got it worse than you. Last I heard, he hadn't regained consciousness yet. That's all I know."

A trickle of relief flowed through me. He wasn't dead. Simon wasn't dead, and Morgan hadn't killed him.

I flexed my hand, felt the ache in my knuckles.

"Will you let me know when you get an update?" I asked.

Givens nodded. "Do you know what else we found out there? In the amusement park?"

Why did it feel like a trick when a cop asked a question?

"What?" I asked. "The ring?"

Givens nodded. "We did. Do you know where we found it?"

Who had the ring last? Simon. But he couldn't have held on to it while we fought. His hands were free as he swung at me.

Could he have slipped it into his pocket?

"Did Simon have it?" I asked. "Morgan wanted to give it back. She brought me out there to resolve everything, put an end to it. But we started fighting before any of that happened."

"So you don't know where we found the ring?"

"I don't."

Again, the blank look. The cool consideration of my words.

"You don't seem to know much, do you, Mr. Fields?"

"I don't know where you found the ring. You found me, and I was out cold. Right?"

She thought about that. Then she said, "We found it in the barn. It was sitting on top of a shallow grave. The one where Giles Caldwell's body was buried."

KIMBERLY watched Joshua Fields's face as she delivered the news. He closed his eyes and gritted his teeth, then lifted his hand and placed it against his forehead. He said nothing.

Kimberly asked, "Did you know the body was there?"

"No."

"How did you end up out there?"

"Like I told you, she told me to meet her there. She said she could explain everything if I went."

"What did she explain?"

He kept the hand on his forehead. "I feel sick."

"What did she explain?"

"Can you call the nurse?"

As if she'd been listening outside, the nurse appeared. She didn't look at Kimberly, but she said, "I think he needs his rest."

Kimberly left the room. She'd heard enough for the time being.

LATER that morning, Kimberly found the woman at the Spring Street Elementary School. She worked as a teacher's aide and had agreed to meet Kimberly.

Kimberly checked in at the front desk, and after she'd waited a few minutes, Elaine Adams came into the lobby, a young, slender woman who wore her curly red hair pulled back.

They shook hands and stepped through a double door, then settled on a bench just outside the main entrance of the school.

"I saw the news about Morgan on Facebook," Elaine said. "Is there any new information? Do you know what happened?"

"Have you seen or heard from her?" Kimberly asked.

"Not since high school, really. We were friends then, but I went away to college, and she went to Henry Clay. We saw each other sometimes during the summer. Then I moved back here two years ago, but she was over in Laurel Falls then."

"So you haven't seen or heard from Morgan recently?"

"No. We're friends on Facebook. I wish her happy birthday and all that. She seemed to have a good job."

"You knew her in high school?"

"And junior high."

"We've heard she had a rough childhood. Is that true?"

Elaine nodded. "Her mom had a lot of problems when we were growing up. Her parents got divorced before I knew her. And her mom . . . She never got her head on straight after the divorce. She was an irresponsible parent."

"How so?"

"She drank. Then drugs. She wasn't abusive . . ." Elaine lifted her hand to her mouth, considering what to say next.

"Was she neglectful?"

"Yeah. That's the word for it. Neglectful . . . She'd be out, and Morgan would be home alone. She'd have to wake up and get herself off to school because her mom was sleeping it off. My parents used to have Morgan over for dinner; then my mom would send her home with leftovers. That kind of thing."

"She must have been grateful for that."

Elaine shook her head. "You don't know how prideful Morgan is. All that time, while all of this was going on, she never talked about it. I almost never went inside her house. I almost never saw her mom. Morgan always said everything was fine. I could tell it wasn't, but I respected that she didn't want to talk about it."

"But you knew?"

"I heard things." Elaine raised her arms, gesturing to everything around them. "Wyckoff is a small town. When Morgan went into foster care, we all heard about it."

"She went into foster care? When was that?"

"You didn't know that?" Elaine asked. "You're the police."

Kimberly wanted to explain how tough it is to know everything about everyone, but she held her tongue. "We're just starting to learn about Morgan. We've been looking for her. You know about that, right?"

"Right. I heard." Elaine looked sad as she thought about it. "This was in high school. When we were about fifteen. And then . . . maybe another time, when we were seventeen. The second time she came back and seemed happy about her experience. She raved about her foster mother, about how caring she was. She told me it had been a long time since someone paid so much attention to her, and she was sad that she couldn't stay with her permanently. I guess compared to her own mother, the foster care families must have looked amazing."

"So you knew her mother then?" Kimberly asked.

"Better when we were younger. Like I said, once the big problems started, she became withdrawn. She'd be holed up in the house. Drunk. Or who knows what." Elaine rubbed her hands together. "It's a shame. She was nice to me when we were younger. I liked talking to her. My own parents were so boring . . . and she seemed so full of life. At least back then. Ava. Ava Reynolds."

Kimberly looked out to the parking lot. "Well, for what it's worth, Morgan and her mother seem to have patched things up recently."

Elaine stared at Kimberly like she'd started speaking in tongues. "That's not possible."

"What's not?" Kimberly asked.

"It's not possible. About Ava. About Morgan's mother."

"Why not? Morgan moved to Nashville to live near her."

Elaine shook her head. "That's just not possible. Not Morgan's mom. Not Ava. That just can't be."

THEY kept me a whole day for observation. They said I had a concussion, and the neurologist wanted to observe me more closely, so I spent the day lounging around my room.

On a few occasions I dozed off and slept fitfully.

I dreamed about the events in the amusement park. I dreamed about Simon, swinging at him, bashing him. I dreamed about being chased through the dark, prey to some unknown predator.

When I woke, I stared at the ceiling, listening to the ambient noises of the hospital. Beeping machines, wheeling carts. The low voices of nurses and orderlies in the hallway.

Morgan.

Why was that body in the park? Why did she lead me there?

Around eight thirty that evening, Friday, Detective Givens came back and grilled me about Morgan all over again. She asked the same questions several times. *Where did she go? Did she say anything about where she might be heading?*

Over and over, I said I didn't know.

Givens nodded a few times. She became quiet, but I knew she had more to say. So I waited.

Finally she said, "Morgan told you her mother was sick?"

"She did."

"And that's why she moved to Nashville?"

"Yes, to take care of her. After she quit her job."

"Did she say what was wrong with her mom?" Givens asked.

I tried to remember. "I think so. Cancer? She gave the impression it was terminal."

Givens reached into her jacket pocket and brought out a folded sheet of paper. She unfolded it and then passed it to me.

It was an obituary, printed from a newspaper website. My brain must have still been moving slowly, because it took a moment for the name to register. Then it clicked.

"Ava Reynolds," I said.

"Do you know who that is?" Givens asked.

I scanned the paper again. I saw one relative mentioned as a survivor. Morgan Reynolds, loving daughter.

"This is from when?" I asked.

"See the date?"

I found it. Three years earlier. Morgan's mother had been dead three years.

My head immediately started to throb again. Even worse than earlier. Had Morgan told me a single thing that was true?

"Is this supposed to make me feel better?" I asked.

"I thought if you knew the truth, you might remember more details," she said.

I handed the paper to her. "It's not like that. I'm not holding anything back."

But I finally asked a few questions of my own.

"Do you think Morgan killed Giles Caldwell?"

Givens stared down at me in my hospital bed. She looked sympathetic, kind even. But her apparent lack of judgment concerning my actions made me feel like a sap, a sucker who had stumbled into something bigger and more complicated than he could handle.

"We're not jumping to any conclusions," she said. "We're going to examine the crime scene. We're going to do an autopsy."

"I know, Detective. I know. But . . . did she kill him?"

She cleared her throat. "You tell me, Joshua. *She* knew where the body was. *She* brought you to the body, saying it would explain everything. *She* took off before the police arrived. *She* placed the ring on the body."

The detective lifted her hands and held them out in front of her body as if to say, *What more do you need to know?*

I shrank down into the pillows. "How did he die?"

"We can't tell yet. But we suspect foul play."

Givens leaned closer. Her phone beeped, but she ignored it.

"I'll offer you some free advice," she said. "You're not out of the woods on this yourself. You were with her. You were at the scene where the body was found. You say you just met in Atlanta, but we intend to make sure of that."

"You think I'm lying?"

"I think everybody is lying until I know they aren't. And I have an unsolved death on my hands and a woman who's run away."

I felt real fear. Had Morgan left me holding the bag? Would I face an arrest over the death of this man I didn't know?

"You can head home when they clear you to travel," Givens said. "But stay in touch. We've notified Chicago PD about you. They'll be keeping an eye. Don't leave Chicago without letting us know."

"I have a job."

"We know. We'll keep an eye on the places you travel. And we've got the word out about Morgan. She'll be brought in soon. If not, she's going to spend the rest of her life on the run. You want to stay away from that, or it's going to get even deeper."

I knew she was right. I just hated saying so.

I nodded the tiniest bit, accepting the truth in my silent way.

"But what about . . . Simon?"

"You mean are you going to be charged with anything?"

"Yes."

"Like I said, head on home, and we'll be in touch."

And that's exactly what I did, flying back to Chicago and my regular life the next afternoon.

KIMBERLY hung up the phone, ending her call with the medical examiner's office. She'd been back in Laurel Falls for two days, following every path to find Morgan Reynolds, a "person of interest" in the death of Giles Caldwell. So far they'd found nothing. She'd pulled a complete Houdini act after she smacked Joshua Fields over the head with a beer bottle at Fantasy Farm.

Yet Kimberly was happy. She'd taken Maria out for dinner the night before. And it had been exactly the distraction Kimberly needed. Maria talked about soccer and school and friends, and even let slip the name of a boy she had a crush on.

When Kimberly ended her call, Brandon plopped down in the chair next to her desk. "Was that our autopsy results?" he asked.

"It was." Kimberly looked down at her notes. "Official cause of death on Mr. Giles Caldwell—manual strangulation."

Brandon whistled. "Wow."

"No other significant injuries. Some marks on the back of his legs and torso, likely from being dragged out of the house and thrown in a car, then dumped at Fantasy Farm. Apparently, he had clogged arteries and some fluid in the lungs. He was cruising for a heart attack. That might have made it easier to strangle him."

"Could make it easier for a woman to do the deed."

"Exactly. The time of death matches what we know of Morgan Reynolds's whereabouts last Thursday night. They took hair and fiber samples, so we can match them to samples from Morgan's home and car. . . . And to her, if she ever resurfaces."

"And I guess there's no other real news?"

"Nope." Kimberly flipped her notebook shut. "I'm going to have to tell Simon Caldwell his brother's official cause of death. His concussion was pretty severe, but he's supposed to be home today."

"He's probably in a great mood."

"I'm sure." She paused. "It's weird that he hasn't been bugging us. Maybe the bottle knocked some sense into him. Or maybe he's just happy no one's pressing assault charges against him."

"Not even the kid at the hotel?"

"He doesn't want to bother. So Simon's in the clear right now."

Brandon appeared to be thinking of something.

"What?" Kimberly asked.

"Are we thinking about him as a suspect in Giles's death?"

"Who? Simon?"

Brandon nodded, and Kimberly took her time answering. After talking to Steven Hatfield about Simon, she seriously considered him a suspect in his brother's death. He had the temper and the track record. But so much pointed to Morgan Reynolds.

"I'm keeping my options open," she said. "So I'm going to go see what Simon knows. If anything."

"Do you really think he'll tell you something useful?"

Kimberly laughed. "Will anyone ever tell us anything useful? I try to keep my expectations low. That way I'm pleasantly surprised when good things happen."

SIMON Caldwell opened the door of his town house, blinked against the midday sun, and then stepped back out of the light.

"Can I come in?" Kimberly asked, stepping forward.

Simon just grunted, and she took that as assent.

Inside, the blinds were drawn. They went into the living room and sat on opposite ends of an overstuffed sofa. Simon wore sweatpants, white socks, and a loose, oversize sweatshirt.

Kimberly glanced at his knuckles. They were scabbed, healing from his battle with Joshua Fields at Fantasy Farm.

Kimberly told Simon about his brother's cause of death, as well as the information about his bad heart. Simon listened without looking at her, and she wondered if he was hearing her at all, or if the effects of the concussion were causing him to miss what she was saying. She paused, giving him a chance to speak.

Finally he said, "He ate a lousy diet. But that doesn't mitigate the cause of death. She killed him."

"I'm not ruling that out, but I was hoping you were up for a couple of questions," Kimberly said. "Specifically, did your brother ever mention an employee of his named Megan Bright?"

Simon stared at her. He seemed to have aged a decade since she'd last seen him. He shook his head.

"No. Why? Is she missing too?"

"No, it's not that. She worked for Giles. They had a disagreement over some work she had done."

Simon grunted. "My brother kept me at arm's length from his business affairs. A long arm's length."

Kimberly waited. The man across from her looked too miserable to be hiding anything.

"She says Giles grew aggressive," Kimberly said. "Physically aggressive. He grabbed her by the arm, and she had to pull away. And flee. This happened after hours one night in the office, when everyone else had gone home. She resigned from the company."

"But she never filed a lawsuit or harassment claim?"

"She was scared. Had he ever been violent with women?"

Simon reached up and rubbed his temple. "I don't know what you want me to say. I suppose you're trying to make a case that this Morgan Reynolds killed my brother in self-defense."

"I'm not making a case," she said. "I'm exploring all avenues."

He rubbed his head again.

Kimberly felt a measure of sympathy for the man. He'd lost his brother. He'd been attacked. But she also couldn't dismiss his single-minded pursuit of Morgan Reynolds, a pursuit that led to an innocent, young hotel worker getting beaten up.

"Okay, Mr. Caldwell," Kimberly said, "I'll let you rest. We may need to talk again as the investigation proceeds."

Kimberly stood up, ready to go. Simon stayed on the sofa.

"I figured you were here to read me my rights or something," he said. "I was about to call my lawyer."

"I told you the laundry guy in the hotel isn't pressing charges. And neither is Mr. Fields. Given the circumstances of your brother's death . . . and everything you've been through . . ."

"I know I didn't make your life any easier over in Wyckoff," he said. "So thanks for working out the charges. I suppose the Nashville Police will talk to me about the other thing."

"What other thing?" she asked.

"The Nashville thing? The thing with Morgan's mother?"

Kimberly sat down on the sofa again. "What about her mother?"

"Remember? She says I went down there and threatened her? The mother?"

"Yes, I remember. But her mother is dead. Has been for three years. How could we charge you with threatening a dead woman? Is there something I don't understand? I figured Morgan Reynolds was lying, trying to make Joshua Fields feel sorry for her. What are you saying?"

He picked at a thread on his shirt. "Well, maybe I'll regret being honest about this. . . . Look, I didn't threaten the woman. I went by Giles's office that Monday after he disappeared. Somebody told me he and Morgan were having a dispute over money." He pointed at Kimberly. "I called you. Five times. But you didn't answer or call back. You just brushed me off."

"Somehow you ended up talking to this woman you say is her mother."

"It was a Monday afternoon. I didn't know the woman was so sick. If I'd understood that . . . Well, I have my limits too. But I did talk to her. I asked her questions I wanted to have answered. But I never threatened anyone. Certainly not a woman who was so frail."

"Did you hear me clearly, Mr. Caldwell?" She wondered if the blow to his head had scrambled his brains. "Morgan's mother is dead. You must have talked to someone else in Nashville."

"Her mother . . ." He reached up to his head again, confused. "No, not her mother." He stared into space for a moment.

Kimberly remained quiet, letting him think.

"Her foster mother. That's who it was. Her foster mother."

Her foster mother?

Kimberly went back to the conversation with Ashley Clarke. A rough patch in Morgan's childhood. And then Elaine Adams had reported the same thing. Foster care. During high school.

And how much she liked one of the families she had stayed with. Had she reconnected with that woman?

"How did you know about this woman?" Kimberly asked.

Simon shook his head. Slowly. "I didn't. She called me up on Monday afternoon and said she wanted to talk to me about her daughter. When I got there, I didn't learn a damn thing."

"Her foster mother called you?" she asked. "Why?"

Simon leaned back against the sofa cushions. A weariness passed across his face. "Her mother or whoever she is called me because I'd been down to Nashville, trying to find Morgan. Asking her friends where she was."

"Word got back to the mother that you were looking for her?"

"Yes. And that woman got my number from someone so she could tell me to knock it off. I almost laughed. She calls me and tells me off and then hangs up. But her number comes up on my caller ID. So I look up the address and find out it's a hospice facility. River Glen in Nashville. I figured she was a nurse."

"So, what did you do with that information?" Kimberly asked.

"I went down there. Only when I arrived did I find out she was a patient. And she was pretty coherent at first. She told me how Morgan lived with her when she was in high school. Her birth mother was having trouble. Drugs? Booze?" Simon shook his head. "So Morgan goes into foster care. And really gets along with the woman. She says she felt like Morgan was her own child. Valerie Woodward. That's her name. But, of course, when the real mom gets her act straightened out, what happens to the kid?"

"She has to go back."

"Exactly. Fast-forward a few years. The real mom dies. Now Morgan wants to have a relationship with the foster mom."

Simon paused, a hint of real emotion in his eyes.

"It stinks," he said. "Now the foster mom is sick too. I know what that's like, to lose your mom."

"And a brother," Kimberly said.

He looked at her a moment before he said, "Yes, a brother too."

"Why did she say you threatened her?" Kimberly asked.

Simon gave a shrug. "Maybe I was a little overzealous. She started out clear but lost her focus while I was there, until I didn't know what she was talking about. So I left. She must have remembered, because she told her daughter I'd been there."

He leaned forward on the sofa.

"I told you all of this. Okay? I came clean. I want this over with as much as anyone else."

Kimberly agreed. She wholeheartedly agreed.

Chapter 9

I EXPECTED TO FEEL RELIEVED when I walked through the door of my apartment in Chicago. And for a moment I did.

I welcomed the familiar sights and smells. The couch shaped to my body. The window I sat by with my computer and coffee.

But I pretty quickly found myself looking at the place with a different set of eyes. Maybe it was everything I'd been through. Maybe it was giving voice to my concerns about my life to Morgan. Maybe it was coming face-to-face with a snarling, living, breathing madman who wanted to bash the life out of me.

Maybe it was all of the above.

I called Morgan a few times. But she never answered. I had no idea what I'd say if she did answer. *So, you really were a murderer. . . . Imagine that! And you lied about your mother!*

Later, Dad called. It was good to hear his voice. He was glad I'd made it home safe. He asked about the status of my head.

"It's better. Pretty much back to normal."

"Good, good. I was worried about you," he said. "To have my kid in a hospital in another state. I was ready to get on a plane and come up there when they said you could go home."

"I know. I'm sorry if I scared you."

"It's okay," he said. "You got caught up in something. It happens. Maybe you just need to get back to your real life?"

"Probably."

"Good. Look, I need you to do something. I need you to head down to Tampa. Those guys really want to meet you. It will seal things if they see your face. Just one night. Down and back."

The emptiness returned in me. Another flight. More Xanax.

"Head down there," he said, "take care of business, then come back and take a few days off, or a week. I don't care. You've earned it."

As much as I dreaded the flight and another night in a hotel, I didn't have anything keeping me at home.

"Okay," I said. "I'll do it."

I LOATHED going into the airport on Monday. But I went.

I swallowed my Xanax and found a quiet spot where I could read before my flight boarded. I'd brought the novel I'd purchased in Atlanta, the one with the grizzled loner who kills in order to forget the pain of losing his wife and child.

Then Detective Givens called.

She sounded friendly. I told her I was in the airport. A pause followed, as we both thought about how I'd met Morgan.

"I need to make sure you haven't seen Ms. Reynolds."

"No, I haven't."

"No contact of any kind? Nothing you need to tell me?"

I thought about my attempts to call her. The phone ringing and ringing. That didn't count as contact, did it? "Nothing."

"Anything else come to mind about where she might be?"

"No," I said. "Has there been any kind of break in the case?"

"There's been nothing," she said. "But we'll keep looking."

"What about the Caldwells?" I wasn't sure what I was asking.

"Mr. Caldwell is being buried in the family plot, just like his brother wanted. That part of their struggle is over. I'm hoping we bring them justice one of these days."

I wasn't sure how to respond, since I knew bringing them justice meant arresting Morgan. I hadn't yet been able to reconcile the idea that the Morgan I knew might be a murderer.

"Is that all, then?" I asked.

"Did Morgan say anything about being in foster care?"

"Foster care? No, she just told me her mom was a drunk."

"Did she ever mention the name Valerie Woodward?"

"No. Who's she?" I asked.

Givens explained that Morgan had a foster mother, a woman she lived with for a time during high school. And that woman was currently in a hospice in Nashville. "That's who she meant when she said Simon Caldwell threatened her mother. Simon did visit the woman and utilized his . . . delicate powers of persuasion. This woman goes by Valerie Woodward. We wonder if Morgan was using the last name Woodward some of the time."

I'd been holding my thumb between the pages of the novel, marking my place. But when I heard the news, the book slid off the end of my hand and onto the empty seat next to me. "So what does that mean? She wasn't lying about her mother?"

"It doesn't change anything else, but she wasn't lying about her mother," Givens said. "Her foster mother, I should say."

I let the information sink in. "So her mother, or foster mother, is in hospice in Nashville?"

"She is. The police have been watching, making sure Morgan Reynolds hasn't been to visit. If she shows up, she'll be arrested."

"I see. And that's it?" I asked.

"That's the latest," she said. "Let me know if you hear anything. Any information you provide will be favorable to you."

"I understand. Sure."

When we hung up, it was time for me to board. And I read my book all the way to Tampa.

I TOOK care of everything in Tampa. I met with the investors. We went to a nice meal, made jokes, and by the time I walked bleary-eyed back to the hotel, I felt certain the deal was sealed. The alcohol, the travel, the Xanax—they made me feel wiped.

The next morning, I was back in the airport, following my old routine. Gift shop, Xanax, breakfast. The thought of returning home brought little joy.

While I sat there in Tampa, I thought of Morgan and the first conversation we'd had. Had she been right about the airport? That it was a neutral space, the kind of place where you could say anything without consequence? If that was true, then I must not have meant anything I'd said to her that day, because I hadn't changed a damn thing in my life since then.

I wandered onto the concourse, thinking of what Detective Givens had told me the day before. Morgan's foster mother was alive in Nashville. I remembered how distraught Morgan was at the thought that something might happen to her. How she'd left town to find help from her aunt, and then learned that Simon had been by. Her fear suggested a deep bond.

Who was likely to know more about Morgan than her mother?

I could go home and continue with the routine I'd come to despise, or I could finally make the change I wanted to make. So I found myself at the gate, changing my destination once again.

Instead of returning home to Chicago, I was going to board a flight for Nashville.

KIMBERLY ordered a coffee and took it to a table near the back of the café. She waved when Trooper John Mattingly of the Gordon County Sheriff's Department came in. He ordered a drink, then carried his paper cup over and sat across from Kimberly.

"I appreciate you taking the time to meet," she told him.

"I had to be here in Laurel Falls anyway. It's nice to get out of Wyckoff and come to the big city."

Kimberly had met Mattingly before and found him to be a reliable cop. "Did you have a chance to review your notes?"

"I did." He nodded his head. "What can I tell you?"

"You got called to a dispute between Valerie Woodward and Blaine Fant. At his house. And this was . . . four years ago?"

"That's right. He called us. Said his girlfriend was getting violent. I responded. Fant answered the door. About fifty. Wearing a T-shirt and shorts. As soon as he saw me, he started trying to get rid of me. It was all a misunderstanding, he said. He loved his girlfriend. They'd had a disagreement, but they'd worked it out. I told him I had to make sure no one in the residence was injured. I went to the kitchen, and Valerie Woodward was sitting at the table. I asked her if she felt she was in any danger. She told me no. I didn't see any sign of injury, so I figured I'd leave it at that."

"Not much you could do at that point," Kimberly said.

"No reason to do anything else," Mattingly said. "Until I turned to go, and I saw a thirty-eight on the counter. Underneath a kitchen towel. I asked them about it, and Mrs. Woodward told me she was licensed and registered. She produced the paperwork. It all checked out. I ran them through the system. He'd been arrested for DUI once. She was clean. Nothing outstanding, so I left. That was that."

"Until . . ."

"Right. Until the thing with her daughter."

WHEN I got off the plane, I didn't know where Morgan's mom was. All I knew was her name, given to me by Detective Givens.

Valerie Woodward.

I called several hospice facilities, asking if they had a patient by that name. They all told me no.

Then I caught a break. I dialed a number that went to the offices of a group of hospice facilities. The receptionist could check their patient list in five locations. I waited while she put me on hold. Then she came back and informed me that Valerie Woodward was at a place called River Glen. She gave me the address.

When I hung up, I rented a car and started on my way.

River Glen sat off the road in an upper-middle-class Nashville neighborhood full of wine shops and organic grocery stores. At the reception desk, a woman looked up and smiled at me. I asked her which room Valerie Woodward was in.

She checked a list and told me room 4, down the hall. Then she asked me to sign in. I gave the names above mine a quick scan, hoping to see Morgan's, but the sheet was new.

The hallways were wide and spacious, and I heard nothing from behind the closed doors of the patients' rooms as I walked by. I came to room 4 and knocked. I waited but heard nothing. I tried the handle, which turned easily, and went in. In the middle of the room sat a hospital bed with, I presumed, Valerie Woodward under its covers. I closed the door and stepped to the side of her bed.

Valerie's eyes were closed.

"Valerie?" I whispered. She looked thin, her skin pallid. "Valerie?" I said louder. "Mrs. Woodward?"

Her eyelids fluttered. Her hands moved on top of the covers, and I noticed a slight discoloration on her left elbow, the remnant of a fading bruise. Then her eyes opened.

"Are you another social worker?" she asked.

"No. My name's Joshua Fields. I'm a friend of Morgan's."

"Oh." Her eyes were blue. Dark circles of exhaustion and pain smudged the skin beneath them. "How do you know her?"

"I haven't known her long," I said. "We met a few days ago in the Atlanta airport, while we were waiting for our flights."

"I know who you are." She smiled slightly, her eyelids fluttering.

"How do you know who I am?"

She remained perfectly still; then her eyelids came wide open. "You're the boy Morgan was telling me about this morning."

KIMBERLY finished her coffee. "So," she said, "this other thing, the one with her daughter."

"Foster daughter," Mattingly said. "This was about a year after the thing with Fant and the gun. We got called there again. Same house. Mrs. Woodward had a new boyfriend named Rick Yates."

"And this Yates got into it with the foster daughter?"

"Right. First he got into it with Valerie Woodward. When the daughter, Morgan Reynolds, tried to intervene, Yates got in her face, threatened her. That's when Valerie Woodward got out the thirty-eight. So Yates called nine-one-one, and we showed up."

"And this time the boyfriend wanted to press charges."

"He did. So we brought Mrs. Woodward in and booked her. Charged her with assault. She said she didn't care; she'd do anything to protect her child. She pled out and avoided jail time." Mattingly flushed with pride at having information about a big case. "When you found that body at Fantasy Farm and named Morgan Reynolds a person of interest, it all came back to me."

"I'm glad it did," Kimberly said.

"I hope it helps. I wish I could tell you more."

"This is very helpful," Kimberly said. "We want to know all we can about Morgan Reynolds. Anything else about her?"

Mattingly shook his head. "She was very concerned about Mrs. Woodward. Said that she'd been diagnosed with cancer, and she worried the stress of being arrested could make her take a turn for the worse." Mattingly cleared his throat. "I'm sure you've already thought of this, but—"

"We're trying to find Yates," Kimberly said. "But it's a long shot, isn't it? Why would he be tangled up in this after all this time?"

"You're right. I'm grasping there."

"No, I had the same thought," Kimberly said. "I want to talk to everybody."

And she wanted to know about that gun. She'd wondered how Morgan Reynolds would have been able to overpower Giles Caldwell. Had she taken the gun from her mother? Had she used it to force her way into Giles Caldwell's house?

Had things gone wrong, leading to Giles Caldwell's death?

I LEANED in closer to the bed, closer to Valerie Woodward. "Morgan was here?" I asked. "She was here this morning?"

"Morgan . . ." Her eyes closed and then opened a few times.

"Valerie? Did you say Morgan was here? This morning?"

"Morgan . . . She was here. She's so protective. She worries about me. About falling. About my arm getting hurt."

"Your arm? What happened?"

She didn't answer.

"Where is she now?"

The door to the room swung open then. I straightened up and turned to look. Morgan?

But it was just a nurse. She smiled, her face warm. "Hello," she said. "I just need to check Valerie's chart."

The nurse studied some information on a stapled packet of papers, gave Valerie's arm a gentle squeeze, then turned to go.

"Excuse me," I said. I spoke to the nurse in a low voice. "Has Valerie had a lot of visitors?"

"Some."

"Has her daughter Morgan been here to see her?"

"I haven't seen her." The nurse considered me. "You know the police have been here asking about her."

I nodded. "Yes, I know that." Then I glanced at Valerie. "Is she coherent when she says things?"

"Someone in her condition can be in and out of lucidity," the nurse said. "People think a hospice patient is on the brink of dying any moment, and that's not true. Sometimes they rally. Their condition can change from moment to moment. Very quickly."

"I don't have much experience with this," I said. "Thanks."

"If you want to help Valerie," the nurse said, "and if you're a friend of Morgan's, then maybe the best thing to do would be to sit with her. Just visit . . . so she's not alone."

When the nurse left, I went back to the chair by the side of Valerie's bed and sat down. Valerie turned toward me, her eyes closed, and muttered something I didn't understand.

If I ended up alone someday, dying in a hospice facility, would it matter to me if I knew the person who sat with me? Was there such a thing as the wrong kind of comfort?

I decided there wasn't. And if Morgan couldn't be there, then I would step in. I stayed the rest of the afternoon.

KIMBERLY arrived at River Glen just before ten in the morning. She'd called the day before and arranged the visit after talking to Mattingly. She'd let Nashville PD know she'd be in the city.

Kimberly introduced herself to the receptionist and asked for the administrator, Brooke Boyle, explaining they'd talked the day before. While she waited, Kimberly looked over the items on the desk. A calendar, a jar of pens, a phone, and a blue three-ring binder. She tapped the binder. "What's this?" she asked.

"That's where visitors sign in."

Kimberly picked it up and started paging through. "You didn't ask me to sign in," she said. "Should I?"

"Well, we don't ask the police to sign in."

"I see," Kimberly said. She studied the pages. If she'd come across the name "Morgan Reynolds," she would have fallen over. Morgan wouldn't have used her real name. But then she saw a name that made her eyes lock on the page. "Well, hello."

"Is something wrong?" the receptionist asked.

"Were you working yesterday? Around twelve fifteen?"

"Yesterday? Yes, I was."

"Did you see this man?" Kimberly spun the book around and tapped a name with her index finger. "Joshua Fields?"

"Oh, yes. Him. He came in yesterday."

"Was he alone?" Kimberly asked.

"Yes, he was."

"Did you see him in Mrs. Woodward's room?"

The receptionist looked around. "You should talk to Brooke."

"I will." Kimberly closed the book but didn't put it down. Joshua Fields had come to River Glen to see Valerie Woodward. Kimberly intended to talk to him about this little excursion.

BROOKE Boyle breezed through the lobby, carrying a small stack of manila folders under one arm. She approached Kimberly. "I'm sorry, Detective. It's been a crazy morning."

Kimberly smiled. "I'll try not to take too much of your time."

Brooke led her to an office, where she sat at a desk littered with papers, leaving Kimberly to take an empty chair adjacent to the desk. "Now, what can I help you with, Detective?" Brooke said.

"I was looking over the visitor log. . . ." Kimberly held it in her lap. "I see that a man named Joshua Fields visited Mrs. Woodward yesterday. Did you talk to him?"

"I didn't." She brushed a stray hair off her forehead. "He did speak to one of the nurses, who reported the conversation to me."

"What did he say?"

She cleared her throat. "He asked about this Morgan Reynolds you're looking for. He wanted to know if she'd been by, and the nurse told him no. Then she encouraged him to stay and visit. The nurse told me he sat by Valerie's bedside for several hours."

Kimberly tapped her fingers against the binder. Joshua Fields never failed to surprise.

"There's been no sign of Morgan Reynolds?" Kimberly asked.

"No sign of her besides that thing a couple of days ago."

Kimberly tightened her grip on the binder. "What thing?"

Brooke glanced at the computer, then turned back to Kimberly.

"One of our desk clerks was coming in for her shift. She'd seen the notices about Ms. Reynolds. We've all seen them. She saw a woman in the parking lot, sitting in a car, who looked like her. She called the police. They came; they looked around."

"But the woman was gone?"

"Yes. The clerk said maybe she was wrong." Brooke shrugged.

"And there was nothing else? No other sightings or anything?"

"Nothing."

"Well, thanks for telling me." Kimberly paused, then asked, "So, how is Mrs. Woodward?"

Brooke looked like she didn't know what to say. "She's in hospice care. Her condition is only moving in one direction."

"Sure. But are we talking . . . sooner? Or later?"

Brooke took a breath and said in a low voice, "When her daughter brought her in, she'd had a fall. Bruised her arm. She was very tired and weak. But she's stabilized."

Kimberly nodded. "Is she coherent? Able to talk or respond?"

"Sometimes. That's why I said to come earlier in the day. Patients tend to be more alert after a good night's sleep."

"Thanks." She handed the blue binder to Brooke. "If it's okay, I'm going to poke my head in her room. See how she's doing."

"That's fine."

Kimberly stood up, and so did Brooke. They shook hands. "If anything like that happens again, someone thinking Morgan Reynolds is around, would you let me know?"

"I will. For sure."

"Thanks."

Kimberly started down the hall to Valerie's room. When she stepped inside, she saw Valerie Woodward propped up in bed.

"Hello, Mrs. Woodward. I'm Kimberly Givens. I'm with the Laurel Falls Police Department."

Valerie nodded slightly, so Kimberly moved closer to the bed.

"Can you hear me, Mrs. Woodward?"

Valerie, her eyes slightly glassy, turned her head toward Kimberly. "Yes." Her voice came out as a hoarse whisper.

"Do you know why I'm here?" Kimberly asked. She saw the bruise on the woman's arm, remembered Brooke mentioning a fall.

"She's not here," Valerie said.

"I figured that. Do you know where she is?"

"If I did, I wouldn't tell you."

"Does she have friends or family anywhere else?"

"I'm her family," Valerie said.

"That must mean she came to see you. Or told you where she was going."

Valerie reached for the call button to summon the nurse. She held the device, running her thumb over it without pressing.

"Can you tell me about your gun?" Kimberly asked. "You know, the one you use to threaten men? Where is it now?"

Valerie closed her eyes. She looked like she'd been hit by a wave of pain. But it seemed to pass quickly.

"If you care about Morgan," Kimberly said, "if you want to protect her, then you should tell me where she is. If we can get to her, it will make things go better."

Valerie's eyelids closed a little. "Promises, promises."

"Okay," Kimberly said. "I'll leave you alone." She took a step away from the bed. "If I see Morgan, I'll tell her you said hi. Of course, I'll be arresting her at the same time."

She'd backed up to the door, and her hand rested on the handle, but Valerie still hadn't pushed the call button.

"You sure you want me to go?" Kimberly asked.

Valerie stared at her, her face displaying a trace of desperation.

"Okay," she said. "If you really want to know what happened . . ."

Chapter 10

Two weeks later

I WENT THROUGH MY USUAL routine in the Atlanta airport.

But everything seemed different. I went through the security line, went to the gift shop, grabbed another paperback. I went into the bathroom. I took out the Xanax and stared at the little orange pill. People came and went. I probably looked like a junkie, wrestling with some inner demon over whether to pop that pill.

I decided I wouldn't take it.

I needed to be sharp. A lot was at stake that day.

I went into the concourse, looking both ways when I emerged from the bathroom. I saw the usual blur of anonymity, people rushing here and there. I entered a bar called BrewFlyers and walked around to the back.

I hopped onto a barstool, dropping my carry-on to the floor and looking up at the inane morning show playing on the TV. Two talking heads were discussing disciplining children.

I thought of my dad. He'd never laid a hand on me. He'd never done anything but support me. And yet I'd told him I didn't want to work for his company anymore. That he'd be on his own.

I told myself he'd be fine. He'd adjust. He'd hire someone else.

And I wondered when—or if—I'd see him again, depending on how my time in the airport went.

The TV program shifted to a commercial, just as someone slid onto the stool next to mine.

I waited a moment before I looked, anticipation flooding my bloodstream like boiling oil. Then I turned my head.

She'd cut her hair and dyed it a dark shade of red. She wore dark glasses, but not the same ones she wore in the Keg 'n Craft. She carried one bag, which she plopped on the floor next to mine.

Our hands rested next to each other on the bar. My left and her right. I wanted to place my hand on hers. But I couldn't. Not yet.

The bartender approached us and asked us what we wanted.

I ordered a bourbon, then turned to my left to watch her.

She kept the sunglasses on but ordered in the same voice I remembered from that first day.

"Bloody Mary," Morgan said.

And it was all under way.

We didn't say anything as we waited for the drinks. Adrenaline pumped through every cell in my body.

When the bartender set our drinks in front of us, I reached for mine and took a sip. A measure of calmness worked through me.

"I'm sorry about your mom," I finally said. "About Valerie."

"Thank you."

"I saw the obituary online," I said.

"I know. Or you wouldn't be here. It's been exactly a week."

"That was the plan," I said. My mind raced along. "There are so many things I've wanted to ask you. Questions you wouldn't answer that day—"

"Like what?"

"Like the name. You started using her last name. That's why you didn't show up on the passenger list the first time we met."

She nodded. "You really want me to explain this stuff? Now?"

"I do."

"Okay. I'll try. I started the process to change my name right before I moved to Nashville. I kept using Reynolds until it became official, which was about a month before I met you. I'd always felt something special for Valerie, so I went with it. New life, new name. My own mom was gone. . . . And it came in handy when I needed to travel under the radar. I used my new name on the plane. I'm using it now."

"But you told me Reynolds in the airport that first day. Why?"

"I didn't want you to find me. I really meant to never see you again. But you found me anyway. I hadn't changed my name on Facebook yet, so the trail was right there for you."

I swallowed more of my bourbon, the ice rattling in the glass. "Did you get to see her? I mean, before she died?"

Morgan nodded. "I got in a couple of times. There was one clerk, a woman who worked nights. I knew when she slipped out to smoke. When I got in that last time . . . Valerie . . . Mom . . . wasn't doing well. I don't even think she knew I was there. But I saw her. I squeezed her hand. I kissed her cheek."

Morgan took a sip of her drink.

"I guess you couldn't go to the funeral," I said.

She shook her head. "I stayed away. I figured the police would look for me. . . . Anyway, I'd already said goodbye."

"Sure, sure. That makes sense."

She took another drink. "I went back to Wyckoff. I obviously had to leave in a hurry that night we were at Fantasy Farm."

I reached up and touched the back of my head where she'd hit me with the bottle. It was fully healed, didn't even hurt anymore. Morgan offered no comment about my injury. So I asked.

"Why did you bring me out there to Fantasy Farm and then whack me with the bottle? What good did that do?"

"You have a lot of questions, don't you?" she asked.

"Yes, I do. And time is short, so could you answer them?"

"I know time is short," she said. "Our flight for LA boards in forty minutes. We'll be on the plane for four hours."

"I'd like to talk about some things now."

She sighed. "Okay. I got scared. I brought you there because you'd been telling me to come clean, and I wanted to. I thought you'd understand and support me. I wanted to leave the ring there, with the body, and call the police. They could find everything there and give it back to Simon. Then it would be over. And I could leave when Valerie died. But when I went into that barn and came close to the body . . . it all hit me. Then Simon blew the whole thing when he arrived. I freaked out."

"You could have just told me."

"I'm sorry. I am."

"Okay. What have you been doing?" I asked.

"I went back to Wyckoff last week," she said. "I visited my mom's grave. My biological mom. I hadn't seen it in a while, and I figured I'm not going back there. I wanted to take a last look."

"That was probably a good idea."

"We can talk about all of this later," Morgan said. "Once we're on the plane and once we're away."

"Sure," I said. "But there's something you need to know." I hesitated. "Did you hear the latest about the case? About Giles?"

"No, obviously I've been lying low."

I faced Morgan directly. "Several women who worked for Giles reported feeling threatened by him. They had disputes with him, problems at work over pay or promotions, and he became physically aggressive. Do you remember Megan Bright?"

"I remember her. Barely. But, yeah, I remember her."

"She told the police that Giles grabbed her by the arm when they had a dispute. She feared for her safety—she thought he might hit her. She quit her job. She didn't want to be around him. Apparently, the company just overlooked these things."

Morgan nodded a couple of times but didn't say anything.

"You see where I'm going with this?" I asked. "These women have said they felt threatened by Giles. In danger. So maybe *you* felt threatened by Giles. Maybe that's why everything that happened in his house that night happened. Maybe it was all an act of self-defense. Is that it? Is that what went down that night?"

She reached over and put her hand on mine.

"That's not what happened," she said.

And then my phone rang. Insistently.

I knew who it was.

THE phone rang and rang. Kimberly muttered under her breath, "Come on. Come on. Answer."

"Nothing?" Brandon asked.

Kimberly looked around at the uniformed airport cops. They were all looking to her, seeking her guidance. She ended the call when it went to voice mail and then immediately hit REDIAL.

The phone started its endless, annoying ringing again.

Kimberly replayed everything with Joshua Fields. . . .

They trusted him. They made a deal with him. He was supposed to be at the Keg 'n Craft in Concourse B. He was supposed to call and let them know once he met her. But he hadn't called. . . .

And now no answer . . . Was he backing out?

Would they be able to find him in the giant Atlanta airport?

The phone kept ringing.

"Come on," she said. "Come on."

THE phone stopped ringing. Then it started again.

"I have to take this," I said.

She looked at me over her sunglasses. "Who is it?" she asked.

"I just have to take it."

I took the phone out to the concourse before she could say anything else. I looked back once to make sure Morgan wasn't following me. I took the call.

"Mr. Fields?" Detective Givens said. "You were going to be in Concourse B. You were going to call us when you found her."

"I did say that, yes. But you need to give me a minute."

"Where are you? Really?" Givens asked. "More importantly, where is *she*? We took a big risk letting this happen this way. Now you have to give us something. We agreed to that."

"I need time to talk to her," I said. "You promised me that."

"Where are you?"

"I'm in a bar," I said. Then I hung up.

It felt bold. A little crazy. But Morgan had that effect on me.

And the cops could wait just a little longer.

I took a deep breath and went back. When I arrived, Morgan asked, "What's going on? Who was that?"

I sat and faced her. She was nervous. Uneasy.

"We don't have much time."

"Why?" Then recognition spread across her face. "Who was on the phone?" She studied my face. "Joshua? Is it the police?"

I took a moment to answer, her laser glare boring in on me.

"They came to me," I said. "After I got back from Nashville."

"Why are you doing this?"

"Hold on," I said. "*They* told me about these women who Giles was rough with. They don't know what happened in his house that night. They really don't have much to go on." I leaned forward. "They wanted me to wear a wire, to get you to spill everything when we met here. But I refused." I put my hand on her knee. "I wouldn't do that to you. It's too dirty, too underhanded."

"They're bastards. They're—"

I stopped her. "I wouldn't do that to you."

She reached for her glass and took a drink. She studied me, her eyes moving over my chest. "You're really not wearing one?"

"Of course not. Do you want to check?"

Her eyes studied my shirt for any bump that would give things away. There was nothing there, nothing to see.

"Okay, fine."

I checked my watch. I didn't know how far away the police were, but they would be coming. Soon enough they'd be coming.

"Listen, the cops told me something Valerie said."

A change passed over her when I mentioned Valerie and the police. Her cheeks flushed. She clenched her teeth.

"What is it?" she asked through her pressed lips.

"If it's true, then maybe . . . maybe it can help you out as well."

"What exactly did she say?"

"Valerie said she's the one who killed Giles Caldwell. She went to see him when you needed the money, and when he wouldn't come around to her way of thinking, she killed him. She said *she* took the ring and hid the body."

Morgan turned away.

"The cops seemed pretty skeptical of that story," I said. "But they have no way to prove or disprove it. And they have no way to prove or disprove whether Giles tried to hurt you."

Morgan reached up with both hands, rubbing at her temples. "So what you're saying is I have a couple of options here. I can claim self-defense because Giles has a documented history of threatening women. Or I can back my mother's claim that she did it. That she killed Giles. Since she's gone now, she's out of their reach."

"She is, yes."

Morgan turned to face me again. "And what is your interest in all of this now?" Her words carried an undercurrent of anger. "You're here. And the police are here too? In the airport?"

"They are. I told them we were meeting here, but I didn't tell them where. I gave them the wrong concourse. I put them off. But they're going to be looking, so we have to talk fast."

As if on cue, my phone rang again. Givens. I silenced it.

"I don't want to have to relive what happened in Giles's house that night."

"But you didn't tell the whole truth. You said you went there to demand your bonus, and when he balked, you took the ring. But if you didn't have anything to do with his death, how did you know where the body was? In a park near where you grew up?"

"You shouldn't worry about this," she said, not looking at me.

"The cops aren't going to let it go. So I am worried. We can't move ahead if we can't trust each other."

She stared into the distance before heaving a deep sigh. "Okay," she said. "Okay. What do you want to know?"

I hesitated before I spoke. I needed to hear it all.

"Valerie had a gun," I said. "The police know that. So how did you get into Giles's house? How did you get him to listen to you? He could have made you leave. But you had something to control him . . . something like a gun."

She leaned forward and spoke in a low voice. "Why do you want to know this? When we ran into each other that day at River Glen, you didn't have any questions. I was so moved by the fact you were visiting Valerie. Then when we talked in the car, and we made these plans to go away once . . . once she was gone. I thought we'd figured it all out. Are you having second thoughts? If you are, you can just leave. We can go our own ways now."

"I'm asking *because* we're going away together," I said. "If we're going to do this, if we're starting over together somewhere, then I need to know what happened that night. We need to trust each other. I quit my job, Morgan. I'm giving everything up. We need to begin on the right foot. No secrets. Nothing hidden."

"And that's what you want to know?" Morgan asked. "If it was my mother or if it was me who killed Giles?"

"Yes. Because I find it hard to believe that a woman who was dying of cancer would drive an hour from Nashville to Laurel Falls and still have the strength to kill a man. Gun or no gun."

Morgan smiled a little. "You underestimate her, Joshua. You don't know how strong she was, how fiercely protective. Yes, she did go there. She had the strength to make that drive, and she went there to confront Giles. But that's not all of it."

KIMBERLY and Brandon walked down Concourse B with a uniformed officer on either side of them. Word had gone out to police, along with photographs and descriptions of Joshua Fields and Morgan Reynolds, aka Morgan Woodward.

They checked every restaurant, every store.

Just get to them before they get on a damn plane.

"What's wrong with Fields?" Kimberly said. "Why isn't he doing what we asked him to do?"

"We asked him to get the story if he could," Brandon said. "Maybe that's what he's doing."

"Or maybe they're on their way to Belize or Timbuktu."

"We knew it was a risk, letting them meet. . . ."

Kimberly tried not to think of any mistakes she might have made. She tried not to think of the promotion she'd just earned, the one she might lose if things in the airport went sideways. And Maria. She wanted to make her daughter proud.

Kimberly tried to focus on the task at hand—finding Joshua Fields and Morgan Reynolds.

"Valerie went there to defend me," Morgan said. "I wasn't getting the money I deserved, and Giles wasn't budging."

"And you needed the money," I said. "She was sick, and you hadn't been working."

"Yes, we needed the money. She had doctors' bills. Prescriptions and tests. Even with insurance it was way too expensive."

"How did she manage?" I asked. "I mean, she was so sick. She must have gone into hospice right after she went to Laurel Falls."

Morgan looked into her glass.

"Valerie had her moments," Morgan said. "Even when she was getting sicker, she'd have some days when she seemed perfectly fine. She'd get out of bed. She'd cook. She'd shower and put on makeup. Those days were fewer and farther between. . . ."

"So I'm guessing she was having one of these good days when she decided to go see Giles. With her gun," I said.

"She'd been talking about it, saying she was going to Laurel Falls to set things straight with Giles before it was too late. I didn't take her seriously. The day she got in her car and drove off, I was meeting with the hospice people, ironically, because I knew that was getting close. I came home and couldn't find her. She didn't answer her phone. I checked her bedside table and saw her gun was gone.

I remembered all her talk about going to see Giles. So I jumped in my car and drove off after her."

"She made it to Laurel Falls?" I asked.

"She did. And when I got there, Giles let me in."

"He was still alive?"

"Yes. He looked almost happy to see me. Valerie had told him who she was, and he hoped I was there to get this crazy lady out of his house so he could get back to his normal, entitled life."

I started to feel a dull ache growing in my chest. If Giles Caldwell was alive and well when Morgan showed up . . .

"What happened then?" I asked. "What went wrong?"

"Giles had taken the gun away from her. It was sitting on an end table. Valerie was in a chair in the living room. She looked tired and spent. Driving up there must have taken a lot out of her. And it scared me seeing her like that. I thought we were going to have to call an ambulance. And if we did, how was I going to explain what we were doing there confronting a guy over money I couldn't really prove I was owed? And Valerie had brought her gun to do it. How did that sound?"

"Why didn't you just leave?" I asked. "You could have put your mom in the car, apologized, and left."

Morgan flared. "Apologize? To him?" She shook her head from side to side. "Never. I was never going to do that."

"Valerie could have. She was the one who brought the gun."

"No. Never. I'd take her out of there, but I wouldn't apologize. And I wouldn't let her either."

"So then what happened?" I asked. I didn't say it out loud, but it was there between us. At some point, Giles ended up dead.

Morgan looked away, out toward the concourse and then up at the TV. Her hands were clenched into tight fists.

She turned back to me but didn't say anything.

I said, "I'm not going to go away and uproot my whole life unless I know what happened in that house."

"I told you in the hotel that night. In Wyckoff."

"No," I said. "You didn't tell me how a woman with cancer, who had collapsed in a chair, could strangle a grown man."

"He was out of shape—"

"And you didn't tell me how the body got out of the house and from Laurel Falls to Wyckoff. And ended up buried in Fantasy Farm. If it was Valerie, tell me. Or if you thought your life was in danger. If he tried to hurt you . . ."

She shifted on the stool a little. She looked at her watch and let out a deep breath. "Is that what you want to hear?" she asked. "You want to hear that I did it? Would that make you feel better?"

"At least I'd know what I was getting into," I said.

I couldn't believe I was about to ask the question I needed to ask. But I had to do it.

"Who killed him? Who strangled him?"

Morgan studied me for a long time, then resumed her story.

"Did you see Valerie's arm?" she asked.

The bruise. Valerie had said something about falling.

"What happened?" I asked.

"I was going to take Valerie out of there. Just get her up and in the car and away. And hope nothing else came of it." She shook her head. "Valerie . . . Mom . . . she couldn't leave well enough alone. She couldn't concede we'd lost. She pushed herself out of the chair and reached for the gun. When she did, Giles grabbed her by the arm, then pushed her back into the chair. Hard. It was a breaking point for me. I got so sick of being told no. Of Giles's absolute certainty that he could do anything and get away with it. That he could hurt her. I had a sick mom, and we needed money. It was too much." She laid her hand flat on the bar. "Joshua, he saw my mom, how desperate she was . . . and still he said no. Just like that. One word over and over. *No.*"

"And you just . . ." My words came out low.

"I was behind him," she said. "I got the advantage on him. It was like a choke hold, and I squeezed and held on. I felt like I was outside of my body, looking down on myself choking the life out of this man. And I couldn't stop."

I suddenly felt cold. I sat there facing Morgan, letting everything she'd said to me sink in.

"And you took the body . . . out to Fantasy Farm."

"I took the ring, and I messed the place up so it looked like a robbery. I just wanted to get rid of him, to never see him again."

"You drove thirty minutes with a dead man in your trunk?"

"I obeyed the speed limit. But I had to stop and get gas. I ran right into an old friend. . . . I was scared, and I just wanted to get rid of him. I tried to think of a place that nobody went anymore."

"An abandoned amusement park."

"I remembered my mom passing out there. Why not dump a body there? Why not bury another memory in that place?"

"Morgan," I said, "this sounds insane."

"It was. Valerie left for home when I left with Giles. She made it okay, but when I came back, she was out of it. That was late Thursday night. I couldn't keep up with caring for her. I told hospice she fell—that's why her arm was bruised. They didn't question any of it. They had a bed open, so she went in on Friday."

"You must have been terrified you'd be caught."

"Mom told me to leave. She said I could just leave the country. I had my passport with the different name. I could go, but I didn't want to. She'd die alone in that hospice room. It was Mom's idea to send me to Virginia, to talk to Aunt Linda. I made a deal with Mom. If Aunt Linda agreed to come and stay until the end, I would leave. But Aunt Linda didn't go along, and that was when you saw me in the airport flying back that Tuesday morning."

"People thought you'd disappeared?"

"They did. When the police asked Mom where I was, she said she didn't know. That's when they all reported me missing. But I should never have gone to Virginia. . . ."

"Because?"

"That's when Simon came and threatened her. He came to Nashville and started asking about me. He'd heard about me from someone at TechGreen. He figured I was his best lead. Word got back to Mom from a friend of mine that he was asking about me, and she called him, telling him to knock it off. But instead, he went to River Glen and confronted her. Threatened her. And me. I felt such enormous pressure. I wanted to make it right . . . if I could. That's why I went back to Wyckoff."

"What were you going to do there? Leave the ring with the body . . . and what?"

"Call the police once Valerie was gone. Tell them where everything was. I'd be gone, and so would she. But you know what happened."

Indeed I did.

I finally turned away from her and looked for something, anything, to distract me. But there was nothing. Just the two of us. With all the truth laid bare between us.

Nowhere to hide. Nothing to hide behind.

"We should go," Morgan said, looking at her watch. "We should head to our gate. It's time."

I didn't say anything. I couldn't. Everything she had just told me swirled in my head.

"Joshua?"

I shook my head. "I don't know if I can do it, Morgan," I said. "I just don't know."

KIMBERLY's radio crackled.

"I think we have eyes on them," the voice said.

Her heart jumped out of her chest.

"Where?"

"Concourse A. Some bar. BrewFlyers. Back by the window."

"Concourse A is one over," Brandon said. "Let's go. Fast."

They started running.

"Keep an eye on them," she said.

Please, please, please . . .

MORGAN slid off her stool and picked up her bag. She slung it over her shoulder.

"What are you saying?" she asked. "We need to go."

"I just wanted to know the truth," I said. "And I thought . . . I hoped the truth would be different from what you just told me."

"I'm not lying to you, Joshua," she said. "I told you exactly what happened that night in Giles's house."

"I know," I said. "That's the problem. Your mom threatened him with a gun. Can you blame him for grabbing her? For defending himself?"

"Did you want me to lie?"

"No, I didn't. You had a lifeline. Self-defense or Valerie's confession, but neither of those is true," I said. I felt frozen. Stunned. "Go now. Maybe you can make it to the gate. Maybe you can get on the plane. I won't tell them anything until after you're gone."

She looked at me, confused. Then realization spread across her face. "You're not going to come, are you?"

"I wanted to prove to the cops you didn't kill Giles. I wanted to prove it to myself. I wanted to get away with you, to have a clean slate and leave the past in the past."

She continued to stare at me. Then she took a step forward, her face showing a mixture of hurt and affection.

"I'm sorry," I said.

I saw a tear on her cheek.

"Don't be," she said. "I wouldn't want you to go with me if you didn't want to. Even if in the end it means I can't have you."

She leaned in and pressed her lips against mine. For an eternal but fleeting moment, we kissed. And just as quickly it was over.

She pulled back from me. "Goodbye."

Morgan turned and started for the concourse, walking quickly.

I paused a moment, and then I jumped off the stool, leaving my bag behind, and followed her. "Morgan!"

I lost sight of her in the crowd. I ran faster. And then the crowd thinned for a moment. Or maybe it parted.

Morgan stood in the middle of the concourse twenty feet ahead of me. She clutched her bag as she turned to face me.

I froze. There was no one between us. She looked so beautiful and so, so sad. And I didn't know what to do.

"It's okay," she said. "It's over."

She looked past me. I heard rushing footsteps behind me.

"It's fine," she said. "I'll tell them everything."

Detective Givens came up behind Morgan. With three airport cops. And two more cops appeared from behind me.

They closed in on her, engulfing her.

Let her go, I thought.

But I was telling myself more than I was telling them.

She disappeared from my sight again.

For good.

IT TOOK a few hours to sort everything out. I sat in a room outside the airport police station. Waiting. Eventually Detective Givens came out. She looked worn-out, but relieved.

"You're a lucky man, Mr. Fields," she said. "Morgan is telling us everything. I think she's relieved to get it out in the open."

"How does that make me lucky?" I asked.

"She says you had nothing to do with it. Not the murder, not the cover-up. I've had my doubts about you, especially considering the fact you told us the wrong concourse and the wrong bar. We could charge you for obstruction, or aiding and abetting."

She stared me down. She wanted me to sweat.

I didn't have much left to feel. Morgan's story in the bar and her arrest had pretty much drained me. It was over.

"Maybe you should feel relieved too?" she said.

I thought about my answer. "In some ways. It's complicated."

"Most things are," she said. "You know, we took a huge risk letting you come to the airport to meet her. We figured this was the best chance of finding Morgan and getting the truth out of her. But if she hadn't shown up today . . ." She lifted her hands and then let them fall back into her lap. "I don't know where we'd be. I'm not sure where you would be either."

"I understand. But I thought she'd show up."

"I think she wanted to see you again. I really believe she wanted to go away with you. And I know you wanted to hear a different version of events. But we all know the truth now."

I felt a stabbing regret in my chest, the ache of knowing the truth. I fixed on the image of her in the middle of the concourse as the cops closed in. Defiant to the end, refusing to apologize for killing a man who cheated her out of money.

I didn't like it, but I knew the truth.

And I remembered the kiss. I'd never forget that.

"I need to get back in there," Detective Givens said. "We'll be in touch when we need to. Can I offer you some advice?"

"Sure."

"Just get back to your regular life. And don't look back."

And the swirl of emotions grew chaotic, a vibration through my body. I was sitting in an airport with nowhere to be and nothing to do. I'd quit my job, broken up with Renee once and for all.

I could go anywhere. Do anything.

And the thought scared the hell out of me.

"Goodbye, Mr. Fields," Givens said.

I WALKED out to the concourse, unsure of where to go. For so long I'd thought being free of my job and any obligation would liberate me. But I quickly learned how scary liberation felt.

I stopped in front of a departure board. The cities rolled by— East Coast, West Coast. So many options . . .

I don't know how long I had been lost in my thoughts when I heard my name being called by the PA announcer.

I was being told to head to the nearest white courtesy phone.

The police. It had to be the police.

But I flashed back to Nashville, the time when I picked up the phone and heard Morgan on the line. Could she be calling me?

I went to the phone and picked it up.

"How are you, champ?"

My dad's gravelly voice surprised me like nothing else.

"Dad?" I asked. "Why didn't you call my phone?"

"I tried. You're not answering."

Then I remembered. Ever polite, I'd turned it off when the cops were questioning me. "Sorry about that."

"Where are you?" he asked.

How did I explain it? How did I explain any of it?

"I'm in Atlanta," I said.

"I know that. I'm here too. Where are you in the airport?"

"You're here?" I asked. "What are you doing here?"

"You booked your flight using the company account," he said. "I got a notice saying you were traveling to Atlanta. And I asked myself, 'Why would my son who just quit his job be heading to Atlanta? Could it have anything to do with this girl? With the cops? Might he need moral support if it doesn't work out?'"

I didn't know what to say. I felt some of the weight lift from my shoulders. Someone else understood. . . .

"Thanks, Dad," I said.

And then I told him which terminal I was in.

I waited for him. He showed up and came right over and gave me a hug, and I welcomed being folded up in his arms.

We sat down next to each other.

"I thought after I'd quit you'd be so busy. . . ."

"Nah." He waved my words away. He considered me for a moment. "So, I'm guessing things didn't work out with the girl?"

"No, not exactly."

I gave him a quick rundown of the events, all the way up to and including Detective Givens's advice to get on with my life.

"You thought this Morgan would be innocent?"

"Yeah. I couldn't accept that I'd have these feelings for someone who had done something so awful. I thought it would turn out differently. And I'm still processing all of that."

"Let me tell you, relationships don't always work out the way we want. I know that." His eyes shone in the fluorescent lights. "Maybe I'm to blame. Your mom and I didn't set the best example. Or maybe I made you work too hard or expected too much."

"It's not that. Not you." I swallowed hard before I went on. "I've been holding things close to the vest, playing it safe. The job, the relationship with Renee. Then I let my guard down with Morgan. Because she was different. She was . . . just not like anyone else I knew. Maybe there's a lesson there. Maybe it's good I stepped off the merry-go-round."

Dad nodded. "You know," he said, "I was thinking about it, and I realized I never took you to Disney World when you were a kid. And maybe that was a deficiency in your life."

"Do you think that's why I fell for Morgan?" I asked.

"Who knows?" He shrugged. "Do you want to go?"

"No, thanks. I have no desire to go back to Florida."

"Somewhere else, then? I rearranged things, so I have the time. But maybe you just want to be on your own—"

"No," I said. "It might be nice to just get away for fun."

He looked relieved. Happy. I liked seeing him that way.

"So where, then?" he asked. "You know . . . I've never been to the Grand Canyon."

"Me neither."

"And Monument Valley is near there. We could see that too."

"I'd love to."

He smacked me on the knee and stood up. "Great. Let's go check the big board for a flight."

But I remained in my seat. He looked down at me, his face creased with concern. He looked older. The lines deeper around his eyes, his hair thinner and grayer.

"What's wrong?" he asked. "Are you still . . . I mean, are you waiting for something from her?"

"It's not that, Dad. It's just . . . I don't want to fly. I'm not sure I want to fly ever again. Can we rent a car?"

"Drive all the way to Arizona?" he asked, thinking out loud.

"We'd see a lot of the country," I said. "More than we've ever seen from the air."

He started nodding, warming to the idea. "A cross-country road trip. Sounds kind of crazy."

I stood up. "So you'll do it?"

"I'll miss more work," he said, scratching his chin. "But what the heck. I mean . . . how many more times can we do this?"

I clapped him on the shoulder. "As many as we want, Dad. As many as we want."

AfterWords

Bestselling author David Bell was inspired to write *Layover* by a scene he witnessed—where else?—in an airport.

"I saw a man and a woman having a very intimate conversation at the bar while I was waiting for a plane," he recalls. "Suddenly the woman stood up, kissed the man passionately, and left. When she was gone, I heard the man tell the bartender that he'd just met the woman in line at the gift shop, and he was never going to see her again. I had to write a story about that!"

Indeed, airports and planes provide much of the backdrop for *Layover*. For Bell, these transient spaces are filled with possibilities, as "people are freer to share secrets and take risks in those kinds of places." Bell believes that these random, brief encounters can have enormous consequences. "Everybody has a story or a secret," he says. "When you see that person sitting next to you on a plane or in an airport, you never know what's going on in their life."

A native of Cincinnati, Bell lives in Bowling Green, Kentucky, with his wife, writer Molly McCaffrey. When he's not hanging out in airport bars, he is a professor of English at Western Kentucky University, where he directs the MFA program in creative writing. He spends his free time rooting for the Reds and Bengals, watching movies, and walking in the cemetery near his house.

CLAIRE
BOOTH

A DEADLY TURN

A Sheriff Hank Worth Mystery

Chapter 1

He walked casually up to the car. They'd been going twenty-five miles an hour over the limit. It was a warm night, and all their windows were rolled down. He knew because he could hear the laughter as they sailed by his cruiser, which was hidden behind the newly installed billboard on Highway 248, a few minutes south of the Ozark Mountain Highroad.

He reached the back of the brown sedan and put on his best stern sheriff face as he took the last steps to the driver's door. There were six teenagers—two in the front and four wedged in the back. They all stared at him with the panicked look of good kids who had no experience getting into trouble. He bent down to get a better look at the driver and did a double take.

"Gabe?"

The kid in the front passenger seat froze. "Hi, Mr. Worth."

He swallowed nervously. Gabe was a quiet teen who sometimes caught a ride home with his aunt, a secretary in the county government offices next door to the sheriff's department. Hank gave him a disappointed half-smile and asked to see the license and registration of the driver. That teen dug his wallet out of his pocket with shaking fingers, and Gabe rooted frantically through the glove box until he found the correct paper. Hank calmly took both documents. And then frowned. The address of the sixteen-year-old driver didn't match the address on the registration.

"Whose car is this?"

A boy in a red-checked flannel shirt sitting directly behind the driver slowly raised his hand. "My . . . my mom's," he stuttered.

And everybody was taking turns at the wheel, Hank figured. He collected all the driver's licenses and took the stack back to his patrol car. He'd give them five minutes to sweat before he went back. He had run the plates before pulling them over, and that data matched the registration. The car wasn't stolen, the kids hadn't been called in as runaways, and no other vehicles were affected. The whole thing was nothing more than a little Saturday night joyriding.

He made a show of pretending to talk into the mic for a bit. That terrified the girl peeking at him through the back window. He decided to start with her as he walked back to the sedan.

A petite blonde, she got her license back and a stern lecture about seat belts. Then Hank watched as she buckled herself to the brunette also wedged in the middle seat. They were bookended by the car owner's son and another boy. Those two got Hank's responsible-citizens-don't-go-along-with-law-breaking-activities speech.

Then Hank returned his attention to the front seat. He had the driver step out and told back-seat boy to do the same.

"I think," Hank said, looking at the owner's son, "that your mom loaned you her car so you could drive it—not your friends."

He switched the two boys' seats, putting the car owner's son behind the wheel. He looked at Gabe and decided to cut them a break.

"You will all go straight home," he said. "If I run into any of you again, I will be talking to your parents—while you sit in a jail cell."

They all gave jerky, frightened nods, and the sedan pulled away with the speed of a tired tortoise. Hank swung the cruiser into a three-point turn and headed back toward his patrol route, chuckling at the blithe recklessness of the young.

He made his way south. Not much going on for a weekend night. He cruised along for several more miles before a call came in: Vehicle accident. He headed toward it.

IT WAS A TWISTED CRUSH OF metal that had rained bits and pieces all over the roadway. Twenty minutes ago, it had been a brown sedan.

It looked like it had rolled at least once. The roof was caved in, and the supports had buckled outward. The impact had bent the hood back and through the windshield.

Hank ran toward it, his whole body shaking. The driver's-side doors were wedged shut. He bent down but couldn't see through the shattered windows. He hurried to the other side. The front passenger door had crumpled in a way that forced it ajar an inch or two. Hank wedged his hands into the gap and pulled. He got it open about a foot before the bent framework made it impossible to go farther. He pulled the flashlight out of his duty belt and aimed the beam inside. Gabe was pinned to his seat by the air bag. His head was tilted at an impossible angle, and his lifeless eyes stared straight ahead.

Hank couldn't make out much of the driver behind his inflated air bag, except for a swatch of red-checked flannel. He turned the flashlight toward the back. The roof had collapsed so low, he couldn't see any bodies. Just blood.

There was no possibility any of them back there were still alive.

How, how, how? How had this happened?

Hank stumbled back around the car. He had to try for the driver again. The kid might still be alive. But the driver's door still wouldn't budge. He punched the already spider-webbed window glass with the butt of his flashlight and was trying to clear it out when a strong hand grabbed his shoulder.

"Hank, come on. We'll do that. We have equipment."

The hand forced Hank to turn away from the car. Larry Alcoate, his paramedic friend, stood there. There were two fire engines and an ambulance behind him. Hank hadn't even heard the sirens.

Larry stared at Hank, then pointed off to the side. "Go catch your breath. We'll take it from here."

Hank walked until he was clear of the immediate scene. He sank to his knees. He should have given them a ticket. He should have called their parents. He should never have let them go.

LARRY WIELDED THE HYDRAULIC jaws with expert ease, snipping apart the car as if it were a tin can. Two other guys started to peel back the roof. Within seconds, the red flannel shirt was visible and a gurney was wheeled close. The paramedics lifted slowly and carefully. But it didn't matter. They called it as soon as the kid was on the gurney. He was dead, too. All six, dead.

Hank dropped his head and tried to control his breathing. Then two running shoes appeared in front of him. They were small and pink. He looked up into the face of his chief deputy.

"What the hell happened, Hank? Are you hurt?" said Sheila.

He shook his head. Why would she ask that? He raised his hand to wave her away and saw the blood. Oh.

"Stand up. Let me look at you."

He obeyed. She eyed him with concern. It was not like him to lose his composure over an accident scene.

"I'm going to go check in with Larry," she said. "See if he's figured out how many victims we've got."

"There are six. I stopped them. Earlier. Gave them . . . lectured them . . . and told them to go straight home. They were just kids . . . they . . ." His voice stopped working.

All the starch went out of Sheila. "Oh," she whispered.

They stared at each other. Sheila thought for a moment and then drew herself up to her full five feet four.

"I'm going to talk to Larry and call in the Major Crash Investigation Unit from the Highway Patrol. You"—she pointed away from the crash site—"are going to go take his statement."

Hank looked over. He hadn't even noticed anyone there. A stubbled old man in a bathrobe and galoshes stood at the end of a driveway with a phone in one hand and a garden hose in the other.

Hank walked across the two-lane road, pulling himself together as he pulled his notebook out of the breast pocket of his uniform. "Sir, I need to ask you some questions."

The man nodded. "I was the one that called nine one one."

"Where were you when it happened?"

"Inside," the man said, gesturing to a little house about twenty yards off the road.

Ralph Dindleton was a wiry six-footer, with a square jaw that made his skinny neck look even thinner. He'd just turned off the TV when he heard it. For the first second, he thought it was just another speeder who hadn't done the curve in the road right. Sometimes they hit the boulder he'd put there at the bend to keep folk from driving into his garden. That made a noise when it happened, but most times there wasn't enough damage to stop 'em and they'd drive off by the time he got outside.

But this was different. Dindleton gestured helplessly at the wreck. Something awful. Too big a sound. He grabbed his cell phone and called as he ran down the driveway. He ended up with the hose, too. Not sure why.

What exactly had the impact sounded like?

"Well, now," Dindleton said slowly, "at first, I thought it was one long sound, but reflecting on it here right now, I'm pretty sure it was two." He nodded decisively. "Yep. Two sounds."

The first crunch was like what he was used to hearing. The two men walked to the large rock set at the curve in the road. On it was a smear of brown paint and black rubber.

The second sound came so quick that it ran together with the first, Dindleton said, staring down at the boulder. But it was different. It was a crack and a boom and a skid all at once.

"Like the sky fell . . . that's what it was," Dindleton said. "It fell, and I was too late to catch it."

Hank forced himself to turn back to the wreckage. He saw Sheila striding toward him and walked over to meet her.

"MCIU is on its way," she said, putting her cell back in her pocket. She was in civilian clothes—T-shirt, jeans, and tennis shoes. "They said they'd have a sergeant here within a half hour, so we need to leave everything as is until he gets here."

"We can't leave those kids in there," Hank said. "They have to get them out." He flung his arm toward the emergency workers, just in time to see them all step back from the twisted metal.

Sheila raised a calming hand. "I think that—"

"Hey, it's okay," Larry interrupted as he loped over to them. "We can wait. The rest of the county's quiet. Everything's fine."

Everything was not fine. "We should get the victims out of the car," Hank said. "They need to be . . . taken care of."

Larry nodded. "I get it. But to get to them we have to tear the car apart. And that's not going to do the Major Crash folks much good when they try to reconstruct what happened."

"You're right . . ." Hank said. "I'm just a little wound up about it because . . . because I pulled them over. That car. Earlier tonight. About twenty minutes before . . ." All three turned to look at the bloody wreckage. "I made them buckle up and promise me they'd go straight home to their parents. And this . . ."

Larry—irrepressible, wise-cracking Larry—could manage only a faint gasp. He looked at Hank and shook his head. "Man."

They all stood in silence and watched the one person who could continue working, Kurt Gatz, with his camera flash going off repeatedly. The crime scene tech moved methodically around the car as he photographed every inch of the wreck.

"All right," Sheila said. "This inaction isn't good for anybody. Here's what we're going to do. Larry, you start walking back along the road the way they came. Take some evidence markers and put them wherever you see skid marks." Larry grabbed a stack of yellow A-frame markers; then Sheila focused on Hank. "You're with me."

She pulled on plastic gloves and walked over to the boulder. She turned her flashlight toward the rock to study the scrapes. The rock was about two feet high and maybe thirty inches wide, big enough to inflict damage on the fenders of cars taking the curve too quickly. She got as close as she could without touching the surface, muttering about a dozen different colors of paint and the microscopic analysis that would be needed to figure out exactly what was from the sedan. Kurt the crime scene tech walked over, and his high-wattage flash immediately began lighting up the rock.

"What the hell are you doing?"

All three of them turned toward the road, where a Highway Patrolman stood, arm raised accusingly in their direction.

"We're photographing evidence," Hank said. "And you are?"

The man lowered his arm and stared at Hank. "Who the hell do you think I am? I'm Major Crash Investigation. And I want him to follow me, right now." He jabbed his finger toward Kurt.

Kurt froze, looking at the patrolman and then to Hank, silently asking what he should do. Hank nodded at Kurt, who rose to his feet and was hit with a torrent of orders from the investigator. He hustled away with a backward glance of trepidation.

The Highway Patrol guy spun on his heel and headed for the sedan. Hank called after him. "I didn't get your name . . . Trooper."

The man stopped and slowly turned back to Hank. He had gray hair in a crew cut, a Dudley Do-Right jaw, and Tony Soprano eyes. "I am a sergeant. You will address me as such. My name is Jenkins."

Hank knew he had to be well above the starting rank of trooper in order to be assigned to the Major Crash Unit. Out of the corner of his eye he could see Sheila grinning as Jenkins strode away.

"That's just what we need—a total jerk," she said.

Larry came jogging up the road, still clutching a full stack of evidence markers. He hadn't found any skid marks. "I did find her, though," he said with a smile, pointing at the petite woman in cargo pants walking down the road toward them.

Alice Randall, the sheriff department's other crime scene tech, rolled her eyes. "You did not 'find' me, Larry." She turned to Hank. "I heard multiple fatalities. Is Major Crash here yet?"

Sheila growled a yes as Jenkins the jerk looked over. Hank quickly stepped in front of Alice. "Larry, get over there and distract that guy," he said. "Keep him away for a while."

Larry walked back toward the wreck. Hank, still shielding Alice from view, told her what photos he wanted taken of the boulder. She quickly started as Hank stood nonchalantly in front of her.

"Whatcha doing?"

Both Hank and Alice froze, and then looked up to see another Highway Patrol official staring at them from the road side of the large rock. This one, however, did not seem to be a jerk, and certainly didn't appear to be a man.

Hank stepped clear of the evidence area. "We're just making sure everything gets recorded. Before it can possibly be altered."

"Good idea. We're going to need to analyze that rock—paint scrapings, things like that." She peered at the boulder and then turned to him. "I'm Nina DeRosia, Major Crash Investigation."

Hank introduced himself. She raised an eyebrow.

"You're the actual sheriff, and you're out here in the middle of the night fully uniformed?"

"I take a patrol shift every once in a while. That's what I was doing tonight. I was the first on scene."

Now both eyebrows rose. She was tall and slim, with what looked like blondish hair pulled back in a bun. "First on scene? We're definitely going to want to talk to you, then. But I need to start with what's going on over there. When you finish with your evidence technician, can you send her over?"

She gave him a smile and walked away.

AFTER a fierce argument they tried to pass off as only a friendly discussion, the two Major Crash sergeants agreed that the lowly sheriff's deputies could help mark the debris field that had occurred when the sedan crashed. Sheila was amused by the whole thing. Hank didn't think anything would ever amuse him again.

He combed the slope on the far side of the wreck until it was blanketed with yellow evidence markers. He was about ten yards down from the car when the yelling started. Jenkins appeared at the top of the rise and ordered him to come up. Hank complied.

The second he reached the level ground by the road, the jerk let loose. He hadn't been told that Hank pulled the car over earlier in the evening. He wasn't informed that Hank had information about the passengers in the vehicle. He didn't know that Hank was essentially a witness and shouldn't be participating in the investigation. He should've been told everything immediately.

Hank stared at him impassively. "You didn't give me a chance to tell you. You walked away."

"Oh, you need an invitation? Is that it? You need somebody to hold your hand? What kind of law enforcement officer are you?"

"I'm the sheriff of Branson County." He drew himself up to his full height, which was exactly as tall as Sergeant Jenkins. "And this might be your scene, but it's my road, and my constituents. So you're stuck with me, because I'm not going anywhere."

Sergeant DeRosia materialized at Hank's side. She somehow steered him off to the side and sent Jenkins back to the wreck without either of them throwing a punch. "Now," she said calmly, "you checked the IDs of everyone in the car?"

Hank took her through the whole traffic stop, his stomach churning. He confirmed that the driver they'd pulled from the wreckage was the registered owner's son, Alex Danzig.

"And the other names?"

Her pen and pad were ready. He took a long breath and rattled them off, starting with Gabriel. They were just kids. Doing what just kids always do on a lazy Saturday night.

DeRosia laid a hand on his arm. "Look, I'm sorry, but Jenkins is right. It's better that you don't participate anymore. Who knows how your traffic stop is going to play into this? You should just go home. I'll keep you updated, talk to you tomorrow."

Hank pointed toward the end of Dindleton's driveway. "I'll be over there. Out of the way."

DeRosia nodded. Hank certainly didn't intend to sit around doing nothing while they took their measurements and calculated their angles and bagged their evidence. He pulled out his phone as he walked over to Dindleton's driveway. There were a couple of big logs lining the drive as it got closer to the house. He had a seat and pulled up an internet browser. He'd start with the car owner's son.

Alexander Danzig was seventeen. It was his mother's brown sedan that was scattered in pieces. He lived in a neighborhood across from the Branson Events Center. Alex was a drum major for the Branson Valley High School marching band.

Gabriel Schattgen was also seventeen. A Schattgen lived on Fall Creek Drive. And another on Abbott Lane. Hank would have to narrow it down later.

Isaiah Barton had just turned sixteen. He was the original driver Hank had demoted to the back seat. His grandmother passed away last year—he was listed as a survivor in her online obituary. Now he would be getting his own. Hank's stomach lurched.

Kayla Anderson was also sixteen. She'd ended up sitting next to Isaiah. Without access to the databases on his laptop, it was impossible to figure out which of the county's many Anderson families she belonged to. From a year-old neighborhood news site, it looked like she was a marching band member, too.

Hailee Fitch was seventeen and a member of the BVHS honor society. Her parents were easy to find. There was only one Fitch in the white pages. They lived near the Strip.

Hank wrote all of his findings out carefully, using a fresh sheet in his notebook for each teen. He flipped to a new page and wrote out the name Johnny Gall. Age seventeen. The one farthest away, on the right-hand side of the back seat.

Hank couldn't picture him. Skinny, but that was it. He surfed around on his phone and couldn't come up with an address, or any information from local websites. He'd have to pull up the driver's license once he had access to a department laptop.

The area around the wreck suddenly got very quiet. He looked over. They were starting to pull the teens out of the car. Hank stood and walked over. DeRosia looked up from her clipboard and started to say something, but stopped at the look on his face.

To extract Isaiah, they needed to cut away the driver's seat he was sitting behind. It had pinned his lower body. They laid him on a gurney, and Larry closed his blue eyes. Two paramedics pulled out Johnny, who was so limp he had to have multiple broken bones.

The petite one, Kayla, barely filled half the body bag. Next, they lifted out Hailee, but Hank stopped them before they could close the bag. He took hold of the zipper and pulled it up himself.

Chapter 2

SHEILA SHOVED HANK. Hard. Four feet away, DeRosia had Jenkins by the arm and was stepping in front of him to use her body weight to force him back. She should be using her fist to shut the jerk's mouth. Hank started to say something, but it died in his throat as Sheila's palm hovered in front of his face. "Don't."

He met her gaze and nodded. She lowered her hand, and they both turned their attention to the Highway Patrol sergeants. DeRosia had succeeded in moving her colleague back several feet but wasn't yet able to stop his torrent of verbal invective. He kept yelling at Hank over her shoulder as she pushed him farther away.

The beginning of the argument had been inconspicuous enough that no one had noticed. But now, all work at the scene came to a stop and everyone stared at them as they stood off to the side.

The deep diesel rumble of an arriving flatbed tow truck finally broke Jenkins's focus on Hank. He spun around and stomped back over to the wreckage. DeRosia's shoulders slumped—whether with fatigue, resignation, or embarrassment, Hank didn't know. She slowly straightened and turned toward them.

"Sorry about that," DeRosia said as she closed the distance between them. "He doesn't like people walking away from him."

"That's ridiculous," Sheila said. "Hank is the county sheriff. He is not that man's subordinate. He doesn't have to take orders."

DeRosia pushed a strand of hair back into her bun. "That is correct. But he does need to play by the Major Crash rules. And that means he doesn't do the death notifications. We do."

Hank, annoyed that they kept referring to him as if he weren't there, said, "That's not going to happen. These are my constituents, and this is my responsibility."

DeRosia sighed. "All right. We'll go together."

Hank nodded and walked away, looking at the list of addresses in his notebook. He'd gotten them from the drivers' licenses Sheila had taken from the teens' wallets. He wasn't far when he heard the women's conversation continue.

"I don't get it," DeRosia said in a low voice to Sheila. "Usually, local authorities are more than happy to let us do the dirty work."

"Well," Sheila said, "he isn't usual. That's for sure."

SHEILA talked Hank into letting DeRosia drive in her marked Highway Patrol truck. His deputy wanted the teens' families to associate the bad news with DeRosia's agency, not the sheriff's department. Sheila should have been the politician, not him.

But it wouldn't work. It was his fault, regardless of what car they took. He snuck a glance at DeRosia, who sat stick straight behind the wheel as she carefully watched the road. He placed his hand against the window and let the cold seep into his fingers.

They'd chosen Isaiah Barton as their first stop. His parents were the only ones to have reported their child missing. They'd called Branson PD at two a.m. to say he hadn't come home.

They pulled up to the neat split-level off Bee Creek Road.

"Nice flowers," DeRosia said as they walked up the path to the porch. "What are they? Rhododendrons?"

Hank just kept walking.

"Fine. Can't say I didn't try."

A woman in a pink sweat suit stood in a doorway that had been closed seconds before. "I saw you coming up the walk." Her gaze flicked to the Highway Patrol truck parked on the street. "You'd best come in."

They obeyed, standing awkwardly in the small tiled foyer.

"Mrs. Barton?" Hank asked quietly.

She gave the kind of "yes" that wished it were a "no."

"We need to talk to you and Mr. Barton," he said. "Could we sit down?"

She waved toward the kitchen with a hand that seemed to weigh a thousand pounds.

"He's still praying. In Isaiah's bedroom. I'll go get him." She retreated down the hall.

Hank stepped into the kitchen. The sunrise was just starting to filter through the lace curtains. He crossed over to the small round dining table in the middle of the room and pulled out the chairs. He motioned DeRosia over and had her sit in the farthest seat.

Mrs. Barton entered her kitchen followed by her husband, who was wearing jeans but still had on what looked like a pajama shirt. They both wordlessly sat in the chairs Hank had readied. Only after they had settled themselves did Hank sink into the one remaining seat. He introduced himself and Sergeant DeRosia.

Mr. Barton started praying again. His wife put her hand on his, and he fell quiet. "Tell us, Sheriff," she said.

So he did. He left out the condition of the car and his attempt to save the occupants. He also left out the traffic stop. For now.

Mrs. Barton's grip on her husband's hand fell away, and she tried to stem the tears streaming down her face. "What about Gabe?" she asked when she regained her voice.

"Gabe Schattgen? Is that who Isaiah was with last night?" Hank said. "Anyone else with them?"

"No. Just them," Mrs. Barton said. "They went to a movie at the IMAX, and then Isaiah was supposed to drop Gabe off. He should have been home by midnight at the latest."

Isaiah had been dead by then. "So you called the police," Hank said. "Did you also talk to Gabe's parents?"

She shook her head. "We tried. They didn't pick up their phone. They might not have heard it. It's downstairs . . ." She started sobbing, and Mr. Barton finally moved, pulling his wife into his arms. He turned toward Hank.

"You didn't answer. What about Gabe? Is he . . ."

"Yes, sir. He was also killed in the accident."

"Oh, my Lord. Oh, Della. I've got to call her." Mrs. Barton struggled to get her feet under her.

DeRosia reached out her hand and placed it over Mrs. Barton's. "Ma'am, I'm sorry. I need to ask you not to do that just yet. We need to notify them first. We can let you know once we do."

Mrs. Barton stared at DeRosia.

"Honey, that makes sense," Mr. Barton said. "We'll . . ."

He couldn't continue. He buried his face in his wife's hair. Hank looked away.

Several minutes later, they let themselves out and walked to DeRosia's pickup truck in silence. As DeRosia pulled away, Hank gave her the Schattgen address.

Ten minutes later, they stopped in front of a neat brick house on a large lot. A rumpled man of about forty-five answered the door. Hank was in the middle of introducing themselves when they heard a woman yell inside the house and then come running.

"Stan. Edith is on the machine. She says she doesn't know where Isaiah is. He didn't come home. What's going—" She came into view at the same moment she saw the two officers on her doorstep. "Oh, God."

"We need to come in, please, Mr. and Mrs. Schattgen," DeRosia said as she started to do just that.

Worry began to cut into Mr. Schattgen's face as DeRosia's advance made him step back from the door. Della Schattgen was already on her way into the living room. She rounded on them the minute they were in the room. "What is going on?"

"Ma'am, were your son and Isaiah Barton together last night?"

"Yes. They went to the movies, and then Gabe spent the night over at Isaiah's," she said. "What. Is. Going. On."

"Why don't we all have a seat," Hank said.

Mr. Schattgen stayed standing. "They didn't make it back to the Bartons' house? Where are they?"

Hank chose an easy chair by the fireplace and across from the sofa. That left a hard-backed chair for DeRosia, who followed his lead and sat down. That left the Schattgens little choice. Della immediately settled herself on the couch, and Stan followed. Hank leaned forward, softening his stance. He began to talk.

Mrs. Schattgen swayed alarmingly, and her hands started to shake. Her husband didn't move. He sat stick straight with his hands on his knees. He didn't take his eyes off Hank.

When? Where? How? Stan Schattgen barked each question and glared furiously at Hank until satisfied with the answers.

Until the last one. "We don't know yet how it happened," Hank said. "The Missouri Highway Patrol's Major Crash Investigation Unit is investigating the accident."

DeRosia explained that such investigations took time. "It appears to be a single car accident. We don't yet know the cause."

Mr. Schattgen scowled. "It was Isaiah's car. It had to be. We never should have let him get in that bolt bucket."

Hank started to speak, but DeRosia got there first. "Sir, the car involved in the accident was not registered to the Bartons."

They both stared at her. "He was in somebody else's car?" Mr. Schattgen finally said.

"It appears so," the sergeant said. "There were a significant number of fata . . ." DeRosia stopped herself. "Six people died."

"Six people." Stan Schattgen was shouting. "Who was he with? What's going on?"

"We'll be able to give you additional details later today," DeRosia said, "but right now, we can't say anything more."

"I bet it was that blond kid," Mr. Schattgen growled. "What's his name? Matt something?" He turned to his wife. "Or that girl. The Fitch kid. She's trouble."

"Oh, no," Mrs. Schattgen said. "I . . . I'll need to call her mother." She started to wring her hands. "But I don't have her number. I don't know her, really. How can I—"

Both Hank and DeRosia leaned forward in alarm. "Ma'am, we have to ask you not to call anyone yet. We haven't yet gone through the process of notifying all of the next of kin."

"What do you mean?" Mr. Schattgen was yelling again. "You can't just come in here and forbid us from calling people."

He went on, with DeRosia trying to break in and explain. Hank had a feeling that no matter how much sense they made, the Schattgens would be on the phone the minute he and DeRosia left the house. He made a show of checking his phone and acting like he had a call, mouthing an apology as he stepped outside.

He quickly dialed Sheila. "Look, you're going to have to do the notification for Hailee Fitch. Fast. I'm afraid Gabe Schattgen's parents will call before we can get to her family."

As he hung up, he could hear Sheila already jogging to her car. He took a deep breath and went back inside.

From the glint in her eye, DeRosia knew exactly what he'd been doing. She continued her strained discussion with Mr. and Mrs. Schattgen. Everyone talked in circles until DeRosia pretended to cave in and allow them to call the Bartons. "Because I do understand your feelings," she soothed.

Stan Schattgen looked like he'd scored a victory. Probably a good time to leave. Hank rose to his feet. Schattgen walked them to the door. His wife was already on her way to the phone.

SHEILA started her 4Runner and was backing away from the crash scene when there was a pounding on the passenger window. She looked over to find Sergeant Jenkins fogging up her glass.

She jabbed at the window control button. "What?"

"Where the hell are you going? I give you special permission to assist, and now you're leaving?"

Special permission? "As you know," she said slowly, "I am not under your command. I am a sworn officer of this county, and I'm leaving to go do my job. In my county. So let go of my car."

"Look, if you're doing things relating to this investigation, you need to clear that with me."

She really did not like this man. She especially didn't like that he had a point. "I'm going to notify the Fitch family about their daughter. It needs to be done immediately, before other families get in touch with them and break the news."

Jenkins processed all that very quickly. Within seconds, he'd agreed, told her he was going, too, and insisted on driving.

"Fine." She hid her smile as they walked to his truck. She'd been a little worried about showing up at the Fitch house in civilian clothes and driving a dirty blue SUV. Now they'd arrive in a vehicle marked Missouri State Highway Patrol.

Jenkins drove like he talked, bulldozing straight through any potential interference. Sheila discreetly double-checked her seat belt and braced herself as they headed into town. As they got closer, she started to give him directions to the Fitch neighborhood. He waved her off. "I know where that is."

"You do?"

"I know all of my coverage areas."

Fine, she thought. She'd just sit back and try to survive the drive. But no, he wanted to chat.

"So, you're not in uniform. What are you at the sheriff's department? Why come out to the scene if you're off duty?"

"I'm chief deputy."

"Really?"

She leveled a look that would have made a normal human shrivel away to nothing.

"No. Um, what I meant was . . . well, one metro jurisdiction in my zone just got their first black second-in-command last year. So to have someplace way down here already have a, um . . ."

Sheila didn't bother with a response. She stayed silent for the rest of the drive, half hoping he'd get lost, and was first out of the car when they arrived at the little frame house with peeling paint and a front yard full of busted concrete.

She'd already knocked on the door by the time Jenkins caught up. She waited. And knocked again. Finally, the door opened.

"What'd she do?" The woman stood there in a T-shirt and flannel pajama pants, her curly brown hair exploding in all directions.

"Mrs. Fitch?" Sheila said.

"It's Rossetto and Ms. I ditched the Fitch when I ditched the man. Only place I haven't got rid of it is the phone book."

"Ms. Rossetto, then. Nora Rossetto? We need to speak with you. May we come in?"

The former Mrs. Fitch sighed. "Can't you just tell me what she did and get on with it? I'm not going to bail her out."

"We're here regarding Hailee," Sheila said slowly.

"What?" Nora whispered. "Hailee? Not Emily?"

Sheila held out her hands, palms up, and asked again to come inside. Nora Rossetto nodded. She showed them into the tiny front room, where there was only a couch, a beanbag seat, and a smallish TV. There was a hole in the wall by the front door.

Nora Rossetto disappeared and returned with a rickety wooden chair. She didn't sit, instead standing behind it and gripping the back until her knuckles turned as pale as her face. Sheila sank into the sofa. After a second of hesitation, Jenkins did the same.

"Is there anyone else with you here in the house? Someone who could come be with us, too?" Sheila asked.

Nora shook her head. Sheila took a breath.

"Ma'am, we need to tell you that Hailee was involved in a car accident. She was killed."

Hailee's mother started to shake. Sheila leaped to her feet and barely caught her before she collapsed. She helped her into the chair and, her eyes still on Nora's face, pointed across the little hall to the kitchen and ordered Jenkins to get a glass of water.

"Ma'am . . ." Sheila grasped both of the woman's hands to calm the trembling. "I need to ask you a few questions, okay?"

Nora Rossetto stared at her blankly. Jenkins handed over a faded plastic cup and retreated back to the couch. Sheila coaxed Hailee's mother into drinking half the water and then tried again.

"Hailee spent the night at Kayla Anderson's," Nora said. "She was so excited. She never really got invited anywhere." She took another sip. "It came up at the last minute. I thought it was because whoever Kayla really invited fell through. I didn't say anything, though . . ." She looked at Sheila with such anguish that Sheila felt her own heart break.

"Do you know who else they might've been hanging out with or what they might've planned on doing?"

The mother shook her head. "Like I said, she didn't really have a lot of friends . . . People didn't like their kids being too near to Emily. I don't think— Wait, did Kayla die, too?"

Sheila nodded. Nora moaned and looked like she might be sick. Jenkins dashed out of the room and returned with a trash can just in time. Afterward, Sheila tried to make her drink the rest of the water, but she pushed the cup away. "Was Hailee driving? Was it her fault? Oh, God, the Andersons are—"

Sheila stopped her. "No. Hailee wasn't driving."

Nora slumped back in her hard wood chair.

"Ma'am." Sheila grabbed her hands again. "Ma'am, you need to have someone here. Is there someone we can call for you?"

Nora shook her head.

"A pastor? Anybody like that? Anybody?"

Another shake. Sheila thought frantically. Who could she call?

The screen door slammed, and Jenkins stepped in from outside. Sheila hadn't realized he'd left the room. He cleared his throat. "Ms. Rossetto. A Highway Patrol chaplain is on her way to be with you. You may rely on her for anything you need."

That was surprisingly compassionate, Sheila thought. Nora didn't seem to hear. Jenkins stood there awkwardly for a minute and then disappeared with the trash can. Sheila got up and went into the kitchen to refill the water cup. The sink was full of dirty dishes, but the room was otherwise clean. The refrigerator had a yellowing photo of two little girls with their arms around each other and a 3.9 GPA report card from Branson Valley High.

Sheila returned with the water in time to see through the front window that another car had pulled up in front of the house. The woman who got out talked briefly to Jenkins, who was holding a garden hose in one hand and the trash can in the other. Then the woman came in, introduced herself, and politely held the door open for Sheila. She took the hint.

Sheila took a deep breath as she walked to the street. Jenkins finished washing the trash can and joined her. "Thanks for calling a chaplain," she said. "I can't believe she got here that fast."

He waved it off. "They automatically go on call when our unit responds to a scene with multiple fatalities. So she was close."

"Did you notice the holes in the walls?"

"There was one by the front door," he said.

"And one covered up by the TV and another in the kitchen. All at eye level. All about the size of a grapefruit. Somebody likes to throw punches. Somebody with a big fist."

As THEY drove away from the Schattgen house, Hank pulled out his cell and dialed Sam. "We've had an incident—"

"I know. I just talked to Sheila," said Sam, sounding peeved that he was only now finding out about it.

"I need you to go down to the IMAX and see if there's a white two-door Chevy hatchback in the parking lot." He read off the license plate number. "If it's there, impound it. Have Buster's Towing take it to the Branson satellite office."

Hank hung up the phone and saw DeRosia staring at him.

"What would you possibly need to do with Isaiah Barton's car?" she asked. "This isn't a criminal investigation."

He shrugged noncommittally. It never hurt to cover your bases.

THEY HAD TO DECIDE WHICH family to visit next. Hank unfolded the list, even though the names were burned into his brain.

"If we're essentially running against the clock—or the small-town grapevine, more like—we should probably go to the Anderson girl next," DeRosia said. "Fitch's mom might be more likely to call the girl before the other two boys, don't you think?"

Hank nodded, and they headed toward one of the city's older neighborhoods, Branson North.

The Anderson house was long and low with big windows. A man in his mid-fifties in shirtsleeves with still-damp hair and an untied necktie answered the door.

"Don Anderson?"

"Well, goodness, Officers. Good morning to you. Come to escort us to church?" His chuckle was deep and easy.

Hank introduced himself and DeRosia, and asked to come in. The first sign of unease flitted across Mr. Anderson's face. He swung open the door just as a woman in a carefully pressed blue cotton dress hurried across the foyer toward them.

"I've got the coffee cake right here, and . . ." She stopped and stared, the foiled platter in her hands forgotten.

Don Anderson ushered them inside, talking the whole time. "I knew I should've parked it in the garage. Did they smash the windows?" He turned to Hank, who had been trying to get in a word. "Oh, shoot. It's the business. Was it a break-in? A fire?"

"We would love to sit down, sir," Hank said, looking into the living room. "And I'm just going to hold this, ma'am, just until we get settled . . ." He gently took the coffee cake out of Cathy Anderson's hands. DeRosia stepped behind her, unobtrusively directing her forward into the living room.

They finally got the Andersons seated. Hank set the platter on the coffee table and sat next to DeRosia on the couch. "We need to talk to you about Kayla."

Dread flooded Cathy Anderson's face. Don just looked puzzled. "She slept over at her friend Lauren's house," he said. "She's going to go to church with them and then come on home."

Cathy latched on to her husband's hand and started to squeeze.

"Kayla was in a car accident last night," Hank continued. He knew from experience that the next part had to come quickly. "I'm sorry to tell you that she was killed."

They stared at him. After a long moment, Mrs. Anderson asked if Lauren had also died.

"No, ma'am. She was not in the vehicle," DeRosia said.

"Why would Kayla have been and not Lauren?" Cathy blinked rapidly. "What about Lisa and Doug? Are they okay?"

Those must be the parents. DeRosia asked for their last name. Blenkinship. Lisa and Doug Blenkinship. There was no one, DeRosia said, with that last name in the car. There were no adults—just teenagers. She gave them Hailee Fitch's name, and the Andersons scowled but said they didn't know her personally. They'd heard vaguely of the Barton family, but Alex Danzig was the only one DeRosia listed who was a friend of their daughter's. As far as they knew.

A sudden thunder came from below. It rumbled up the stairs from the basement and ended in three boys smelling of soap and dressed for church. They stood wide-eyed at the door to the living room. The youngest one looked about eight years old.

Hank felt sick. He looked at Mr. and Mrs. Anderson. Cathy shook her head and rose to her feet.

"Thank you for coming, Sheriff. Sergeant." She gestured toward the front door. Hank and DeRosia quietly let themselves out as Cathy Anderson gathered her sons around her.

IT WAS parked three rows away from the theater entrance. It was an ordinary, beat-up, secondhand teenage ride. And the only car in the lot at seven thirty on a Sunday morning.

Sam double-checked the license plate and confirmed that it was registered to Edith and Charles Barton. Must be the parents of one of the dead kids. He wouldn't know, though, would he? Because he hadn't been called out to the scene. Even when he finally got brought into things, the chief had just ordered him to go and get a car that probably wasn't important anyway.

He kicked an empty soda can around the parking lot until Buster showed up with his big ol' rig. Buster unloaded himself—the guy was as big as his truck—and hooked up the Chevy. Then they argued about whether he was allowed to stop for breakfast on the way out to the sheriff's department substation. It took some pointing at the evidence tape on the car and waving his badge around before Buster gave in and promised he wouldn't. Sam really hated when people treated him like a kid and not a deputy. He gave the soda can one last kick and climbed into his Bronco.

Buster pulled out of the lot, and Sam turned to follow. Then he sighed, slammed the Ford into park, and jogged over to a planter between parking rows. He picked up the can, threw it into the trash bag in his trunk, and hauled out after Buster's huge cloud of diesel exhaust.

Chapter 3

"WE'RE GOING TO NEED to talk to this Lauren Blenkinship girl."

DeRosia gave Hank a quick glance and then refocused on the road. "Why? We need to figure out what happened with the car. We don't need to figure out why these kids lied to their parents."

Hank ignored her and wrote Lauren's name in his notes. Maybe this girl knew something about what had gone on before the crash. Or where the group was really headed.

He put away his notepad, touched the cool window again, and decided that since it'd been Alex Danzig's mother's car, they should go there next. He rattled off the address, and ten minutes later, they pulled up to the Danzig's mobile home off Highway 248. It was not the worst Hank had seen in his year as county sheriff, but it could definitely use some new siding.

The front yard had a Dodge pickup that appeared to work and a 1980s-era Chevy Camaro that appeared to not. DeRosia knocked politely. They waited a few minutes, until a heavy tread and phlegmy cough got closer and finally opened the door. The poor guy looked like he'd stepped out of a NyQuil commercial. Mid-forties and portly, he stared at them through a decongestant haze. "Uh . . . yeah? Can I, um, help you?"

Hank confirmed that he was Mike Danzig. "Sir, we need to speak with you and your wife," Hank said. "May we come in?"

Danzig stepped away from the door and mumbled something about his wife still being asleep. They walked into the living room, which was obviously where Typhoid Mike had spent the night. There were crumpled blankets on the couch and an explosion of tissues on the coffee table. Danzig staggered down the hallway and returned with a solidly built woman in a bathrobe who grunted confirmation that she was indeed Jenny Danzig.

"We need to talk to you about Alex," Hank said.

"What'd he do?" she asked, crossing her arms over her chest.

"He was involved—" Hank started.

Mrs. Danzig cut him off. "Mike, go get him. He can stand here and look at the cops while they tell us what he did."

"Ma'am," Hank said carefully, "where do you think he is?"

"In his room."

Mr. Danzig was already halfway down the hall. He banged on a door and then tried to open it.

Like any self-respecting teenager, Alex had locked it. Likely before sneaking out the window. Mr. Danzig hollered to his wife to find the key, which was met with a roll of the eyes.

"We never had a key to any of those doors," she snapped.

Hank fished his notebook out of his shirt pocket and pulled off the paper clip that held the cover shut. It took more time to unbend the metal than it did to pick the cheap lock on the door. He pushed it open and found what he expected. An empty room.

Mr. Danzig sucked in a noisy breath as the haze of cold medication gave way to the fog of worry. DeRosia took his arm and led him back out into the main room, where Mrs. Danzig was sinking into the corduroy sofa with a panicked look on her face.

DeRosia guided him to a spot next to his wife and then pulled over a kitchen chair, sat down, and told them both. Hank remained standing, looking out the window at the Camaro as they dissolved into tears. If only he'd brought the kid home, Hank thought. Woken the parents up in the middle of the night.

And then DeRosia asked about the sedan.

"What?" both Danzigs said simultaneously.

"We don't own a sedan," Mike said.

"What?" both cops said simultaneously.

DeRosia rattled off the year, make, and model. They shook their heads. And then a thought occurred to Jenny Danzig, contorting her face. "I'm not Jennifer Danzig."

"Ma'am, we seem to be missing something here," said Hank.

"Oh, God." Mike groaned and dropped his head into his hands. "She didn't . . ."

Not-Jennifer spelled her name. G-i-n-n-y. Short for Virginia, you know? It's his ex-wife who's named Jennifer, she said, jabbing her finger toward her husband.

"But this is the address on the registration," DeRosia said.

"That bitch. She used our address."

Mr. Danzig told them where he thought Jenny was living now. They'd been divorced for eleven years. She didn't have much contact with Alex, who was their only child.

"How do you think Alex got your ex-wife's car?" Hank said.

"She probably came and picked him up," Mrs. Danzig muttered. "Helped him climb out the window, too, the lyin' little—"

Hank stopped her before she really got going. They again offered their condolences and left the trailer quietly.

"Only one more," Hank said. "Let's get it over with."

Johnny Gall lived in Bellflower Apartments, just off the Strip. They walked along the balcony until they found Unit 213. DeRosia rapped on the door. Nothing. DeRosia knocked again.

There was the suck of a weather-stripped door back the way they'd come, and an old lady appeared on the narrow concrete walkway. "Nobody's there right now," she said.

"Do you know where they might be?" said DeRosia.

She sniffed. "No, girlie, I don't. I don't keep track of people I got the bad luck to live near. None of them deserve my attention."

She gave a nod that indicated she considered the matter settled and weeble-wobbled her way down the balcony toward the stairs. Hank tried to peer in the blind-blocked window. The little he could see was completely bare. "You think there'd be at least a chair or something, right? There's nothing in there."

Ten minutes later, they were in the office of a still-sleepy building manager. He told them that a man named John Kalin had rented the place three months prior. He consulted the creased rental application. Age, twenty-two. Occupation, waiter. Currently four days late on the rent.

DeRosia was holding her phone. "There's nothing in the state databases on this Kalin guy. And there's nothing on Gall."

Hank turned to the manager. "Is there anything in the rental contract about when you can enter without permission?"

The man thought for a second. "Fire, water damage . . . ah . . . nonpayment of rent." Hank's nod was the go-ahead he needed. He unlocked the bottom desk drawer and pulled out a master key.

They walked back to the apartment. The manager—"Name's Jim"—jiggled the key around and swung the door open.

The front room and the kitchen were completely bare. They walked inside. DeRosia stayed by the door, frowning.

There was a McDonald's bag in the refrigerator with a few shriveled fries and one hardened McNugget. That was it.

Hank headed toward the bedroom door. He stopped two feet away. The barest whiff of something had him wrinkling his nose.

No.

He took another step, then ordered Jim outside at the same time he drew his Glock. DeRosia was at his side instantly, her gun in her hand. She covered him as he turned the knob and pushed.

The room was bare, except for a sleeping bag and a stack of textbooks. And a dead man in the middle. The stab wounds were obvious, even from where Hank stood. A huge, amebic pool of blood, tacky with time, lay all around him. Twenty-to-twenty-five-year-old male. Black hair. Brown eyes. Height and weight difficult to estimate due to position of the body.

Hank put away his Glock. Then he punched Sheila's number.

SHEILA WATCHED A MAN LEAN over the railing on a second-story balcony and lose his lunch. That must be where Hank was.

She didn't wait for Sergeant Jenkins to get out of the car, instead heading directly for the stairs. By the time she reached the apartment, the balcony man had hauled himself upright.

"Who're you?" she asked.

"The manager," he said. He pointed toward the apartment. "I went in to see what was taking them so long . . ." He moaned.

She stepped through the door. The living room was completely empty. That was weird. The bedroom was off to the left.

She stepped in the bedroom and eyed the body. "Well. I thought our Sunday morning was bad already."

DeRosia nodded. Hank, whose gaze was sharper than it had been all night, started issuing orders. DeRosia was told to try to find the "neighbor lady." And Sheila was instructed to take the statement of the manager, who should still be out on the balcony.

"Oh, we've met," Sheila said. "I'll go see if he's coherent yet."

"Wait," Hank said. "Are you by yourself?"

"No. I've been lucky enough to have Jenkins for company. We're in his truck."

"Great. He'll have crime scene tape. Have him get up here with it and start securing the scene."

She hid a smile. She'd be more than happy to boss that man around. She met him at the top of the stairs, gave him his marching orders, and then sat the poor little manager down on a step.

His name was Jim Chrzanowski. After he'd finished spelling that, she asked him how long the unit had been rented.

"Since July. To John Kalin. I looked that up for the tall guy. Before we went into the apartment."

"And were you able to tell, from what you saw in the bedroom, if the man on the floor was John Kalin?"

Jim shook his head. "I don't think so."

"Did you xerox the license of the guy you rented to?"

Jim slumped against the railing. He hadn't, because the copier was on the fritz. The complex had twenty-two units, all of which were currently rented. They offered three-to-six-month leases.

That worked well with all the seasonal folk who came for the peak tourist times and then left. That's why he hadn't thought anything of it when Kalin wanted a six-month lease. Although July was a little late to be coming into town for the summer season, he said with a shrug.

Jim trailed off just as Jenkins arrived on the stairs with the crime scene tape. He started to angle between the two of them as they sat on the top step, but Sheila had a sudden thought and stopped him. "We need to use the laptop in your car."

The look he gave her could have felled an elephant. But he turned on his heel and stomped back down the stairs. Sheila quickly prodded Jim down the stairs after him. She wanted to check her theory before Jenkins completely blew his stack.

Jenkins unlocked his door and stalked off with the crime scene tape. Sheila settled herself in the driver's seat, and her fingers flew over the keyboard of the computer in the center console. There was no Missouri driver's license for John Kalin.

She pulled her phone out of her pocket and opened the photo roll. She and Alice had pulled the boys' wallets out of their pockets before they were taken away from the scene. She had a photo of each of their IDs. And Alice had sent her pictures of the girls' from their purses in the wreckage.

"Yeah, that's him. That's the guy I rented to." Jim pointed at the phone screen and the DL photo of Johnny Gall, age seventeen.

"You found a murder victim in my city?"

Yes, Hank said to Ed Utley, the city of Branson police chief. That was exactly what he'd done.

"I was going to spend the day on the lake fishing, but well, dead people trump dead trout. I'll be right there." Utley hung up.

Jenkins had finished with the tape and was contemplating the corpse. "This doesn't have anything to do with my crash. Some guy rents an apartment and gets killed in it. End of story."

Actually, it's only the beginning, Hank thought. *For us, anyway.* He turned away from Jenkins before he got mad again. He started to hear the first sirens as Sheila walked back inside.

"Were you able to figure out if he's the guy who rented the apartment?" Hank asked.

"I was, and he's not," Sheila said. "The guy who rented the apartment was Johnny Gall."

Both men turned to stare at her.

"So . . . who's that guy?" Jenkins pointed toward the bedroom.

She shrugged. "No idea. But I do know that the kid who died in the crash is the same person who used an ID in the name of John Kalin to rent this place."

Well, that put a new spin on things. Hank looked again at the dead Not-Kalin. "And Jim didn't recognize this guy at all?"

"Nope. Just in case, it'd be a good idea to show him a photo once we can get a headshot of the body. But I don't think Jim had ever seen the man."

They'd need that photo to show the weeble-wobble lady as well. And the rest of the neighbors. Hank was starting to make a mental list of everything he needed to do when Jenkins cleared his throat and headed outside. DeRosia met him at the door.

"I can't find the neighbor lady," she said. "She must've gotten a ride, because she is nowhere in this complex. I did get her name from another resident. Apparently 'crotchety' was the only description necessary. And I just asked the manager to get you a list of the rest of the tenants. Figured you'd want to get started."

Sheila glared at Hank.

"This isn't our jurisdiction," she said. "You can't be—"

He tried to wave her quiet. He didn't want to do this in front of the Highway Patrol. She picked up on it. Her eyes flitted to Jenkins and DeRosia in the doorway, and she hustled them outside.

Left alone, Hank walked the length of the living room and waited for the approaching sirens to arrive. He paced as he added to his homicide to-do list. The longer the list got, the calmer he became. The pounding in his head lessened to an ignorable ache.

"Well, what'd you stumble into in my fair city, Worth?" Utley chuckled as he walked in. "You don't have enough to do in your own jurisdiction?"

The Branson city police chief was a few inches shorter than

Hank, with a potbelly his wife kept trying to shrink with wacky diets. He must be on a juice thing right now. He held a green mess of some kind in a clear plastic cup.

The men shook hands, and Hank explained how he came to be wearing a dirty patrol uniform and standing in an apartment that contained nothing except a dead body and a chicken McNugget. Utley sipped at his concoction and listened. "I saw Highway Patrol trucks in the parking lot. They're involved, too?"

Hank shook his head. "Only with the crash investigation. They were helping with the death notifications." He spread his arms wide. "But there's nobody here to notify."

Utley walked to the bedroom and looked inside. "We haven't had a homicide in three years. There goes my streak."

"Well . . . about that," Hank said. "I think it might be related to my crash. There has to be a reason Johnny Gall rented this apartment. And where did his other ID come from?"

Utley nodded. "Or . . . your crash could be related to my homicide. Clearly, this guy was dead before your crash happened."

Hank had to agree with that.

"Or . . . could be, it was an empty apartment that was getting squatted in or something. We don't know that the dead guy was connected to your guy at all." Hank certainly wasn't ready to agree with that. But he nodded anyway.

This was the delicate part. "So . . . until we figure out what's really going on, you think it'd be better to work together on this?" Hank said. "It seems like all sorts of things could overlap."

Utley contemplated his juice. "Okay," he said. "You've got folks here now. Have them start canvassing."

Excellent. Hank shook his hand again and headed off to find Sheila. That didn't go as well. She gave him a look that turned his bones into her special brand of ice.

"Really? You're participating in the homicide investigation? And why is that, exactly?"

"Because it might be related," he said.

"So? I know they'd be happy to give us whatever information we'd need. We don't need to be involved. Unless you just want something to do so you can stop thinking about the car crash."

He glared at her. He hadn't put the two together. Now the head pounding came back in a rush.

"I'm investigating whether they're connected. That makes me a good investigator, not one who's avoiding something."

He spun on his heel and stomped back up the stairs to the apartment. She was wrong, and he had work to do.

The dude looked like he might be sick. Sam explained again why he was taking everyone's fingerprints. "It's only to eliminate you from the prints collected at the scene," the young deputy said.

Jim the manager stared at him blankly.

"If we don't know which fingerprints are yours, we might think your prints in the apartment are the killer's."

That seemed to wake him up. He stuck out his hands, and Sam started the process, rolling each fingerpad in the ink. He wondered how much the manager had seen upstairs. Sam could sympathize. He remembered his first dead body.

Sam ran his hand over his head, which was covered in stubble. The chief hadn't been happy at all when he'd shaved it. Kept saying it wasn't a healthy reaction to Ted's shooting. But Sam didn't care. He'd barely been able to get out of bed in the weeks afterward, and he certainly couldn't be bothered to comb his hair. It was his fault that a fellow deputy'd been shot and almost killed during a search of some dirtbag's property. Ted Pimental wasn't even back at work yet, and it'd been almost five months.

Sam sighed. He needed to stop thinking about that. Every time he did, the anger and the shame bubbled up. He dragged his thoughts back to the task at hand. He finished with Jim's prints and started to pack up. "Do you live here, too? In the complex?"

Jim nodded.

"Do you get a break on your rent for doing the managing?"

He did. That's the only way he could afford to live here. And since he'd just gotten laid off from his regular job at the big steak house in town, this was even more of a godsend.

Sam put down his equipment and leaned forward. He needed to

start thinking like an investigator. "Can you tell me about the folks who live here? Are they quiet? Noisy? Do you have problems with anything like that? Or any unwanted guests?"

"You mean besides the dead guy in two thirteen?"

It was so unexpected that Sam burst out laughing. Jim seemed to have surprised himself with it, too. He blushed, and then he smiled, a little. And then they had a conversation.

The tenants were generally quiet, Jim said. People pretty much kept to themselves. That was the thing with the nicer apartment complexes. They tended to attract nicer people. He paused. Sam nodded knowingly.

"Yeah. I know what you mean," Sam said. "But I've figured out that murder isn't limited to un-nice people. Bad things happen to good people. A lot."

Chapter 4

UTLEY INTRODUCED THE LEAD detective for Branson PD. Dale Raker was a bullfrog of a man, short and squat with a large down-turned mouth and thinning brown hair. Hank shook his hand and showed him into the bedroom, where crime scene tech Brian Handlesman was already busy photographing the body.

Raker walked around the John Doe, giving the pool of blood a wide berth. "And nobody has any idea who this guy is?"

Hank started in surprise. He'd half expected a voice like a croak. This guy sounded like Michael Jackson. "He's not the man that the manager rented to in July."

Raker faced Hank. "And why are you interested in this?"

"The man who did rent the apartment was using a different ID last night when he was killed in a vehicle accident out near Airport Road. There were five other people in the car. All minors. All fatalities. If this guy really is twenty-two years old and rented this apartment, then I want to know what the hell he was doing with a fake ID and hanging out with Branson Valley High kids."

Raker rubbed his sizable jaw. "So, fine, you've got skin in the game." He went back to his pacing.

"So, what do you think?" Hank asked.

"It's tough. The whole place is so bare, it's hard to pick up any kind of impressions. There's nothing personal anywhere."

Raker pulled on latex gloves just as two guys arrived with the gurney and the body bag. The men maneuvered around until they got the victim up off the floor without stepping in anything. The older paramedic started to zip the bag closed.

"Wait," Hank and Raker said at the same time. Hank bit back the whole list of instructions he wanted to give.

Raker didn't notice Hank's gritted teeth. He started going through the pockets, finding a handful of change in the front right pocket of the man's jeans and a wad of tissues in the left. Hank quickly put on gloves and grabbed a couple of evidence bags from Handlesman. He held them open, and Raker dropped the items in.

Raker gently shifted the body to reach the back. He sighed.

"No wallet. Damn."

That sure would have made things easier. Raker rolled the body a little farther and slid his hand into the last pocket. And froze.

"What do we have here?"

Hank, standing on the other side of the gurney, couldn't see. He peered over the body, and Raker gestured for him to hold the victim. "It's soaked in blood. I need both hands."

He carefully pulled apart the sticky denim and wiggled free a piece of paper. Or rather, a folded brochure.

"I don't have my glasses," Raker said. "Can you read it?"

Hank took the paper. It was a trifold for the *Gunner Spectacular* at the Classic Country Song Theater on Branson's Strip. Hank had never heard of the show. Raker said he hadn't either.

"Yo. Can we take him now?" the younger paramedic said. Raker nodded. Hank slipped the brochure into an evidence bag just as Handlesman beckoned them from over in the corner. He had straightened out and unzipped the sleeping bag. Now he held up a shoe. "This was at the bottom."

A grungy black Nike with gray laces. Men's size 10. Both Hank and Raker swung toward the departing gurney.

Handlesman laughed. "No. That guy had both shoes on. Converse. I don't know what size, though." The tech dropped the shoe into an evidence bag. "That's all I got right now."

Hank and Raker walked back into the living room to find Sheila telling another technician that yes, he did indeed need to book the McNugget into evidence.

"We don't usually analyze old food," he snapped at her.

"When it's the only thing in the apartment, you do," she said evenly. "Oh, hey, Dale."

"Chief Deputy Turley," Raker said, and moved forward to shake Sheila's hand. The BPD tech got the point. He immediately started bagging the fast food and then moved well out of the way. Hank was starting to like Dale Raker.

He and Sheila asked after each other's families, and then Sheila said the paramedics had mentioned the dead man had no wallet.

"I miss the days when Branson was small enough that I'd know the dead guy," Raker said. "Now there're just too many people around."

The grumbling McNugget tech walked outside, and Dale quickly moved to shut the door behind him.

"Okay, let's get down to brass tacks here. We all need to get moving on this thing."

Hank nodded emphatically. "I think—"

Sheila stepped on his foot. "Go on, Dale," she said.

"I'm going to go talk to the folks at the *Gunner Spectacular*, whatever the hell that is. And get on to running the dead guy's prints. And keep tabs on the autopsy."

Hank opened his mouth again, and Sheila ground her heel into his foot again. Dale kept talking.

"Hank, how about you take the Johnny Gall angle, since he's one of your vics. Do you have the personnel to canvass this complex? See if anyone else can ID him as the guy who lived here?"

Hank shot Sheila a quick look before daring to answer. "We do.

Absolutely. I'm also going to talk with the high school. All of the other crash victims were students. I want to know if Johnny Gall was, too. And see if anyone recognizes the John Doe."

Both men froze. Sheila chuckled.

"I know; you forgot to take even a preliminary mug shot of the dead guy." She held up her phone. "Shall I forward it to you?"

"I WASN'T going to get all pushy, you know."

They reached the bottom of the building's staircase, and Sheila put her hands on her hips. She was tired and hungry and not in the mood for finessing her boss right now.

"What you think is low-key isn't necessarily what other people think when you start talking," she said. "You can come across as . . . emphatic. Which occasionally comes across as pushy."

Hank sighed.

"Look," she said, "Dale is a really decent guy, but he's still a cop, and you are on his turf. So put a lid on your everything-interesting-belongs-to-me fixation, and play nicely with others. I know you can do it." She paused. "Besides, I plan on tagging along for his theater interviews."

A grin split Hank's face. "Wait, so *you* get to be pushy?"

"Dale and I've known each other for twenty years. I asked, nicely, if I could observe. And I told him I'd buy him breakfast."

Hank snorted in response and then turned as DeRosia called across the parking lot and waved him over. The two began talking by her Highway Patrol truck. Sam appeared from the other direction and walked over to Sheila.

"You really should warn a person before you text them a mug shot of a corpse," he said.

"Ah. I probably should've," Sheila said. "But now you've got it, so you can show it when you canvass this place."

"I'm the one who has to do the canvassing?"

She knew he was still trying to get back on an even keel after Ted Pimental's shooting, which the poor kid still blamed himself for. But she wished he would hurry up with it. She wanted her old Sammy back. The one who jumped enthusiastically at any

opportunity. The one who was always trying to improve his polic-
ing skills. She missed him.

"Why do I have to do it?"

"Because you're good at it," she said. "And because canvassing is
one of the bedrocks of investigation."

He rolled his eyes and slouched away.

IT WAS easy to track down Bill Narwall, the high school principal, since he was the only one in the phone book. It had been considerably harder to get him to come to the school on a Sunday and
open up the enrollment records. So Hank called Marv Sedstone,
his favorite Branson County Circuit Court judge, who met Hank
on the doorstep of his colonial two-story, pen in hand.

"Son, after what you told me, you can absolutely get into those
school records. If nothing else, you got to notify next of kin." He
signed the search warrant with a flourish.

As Hank drove out to Branson Valley High in Sam's Bronco,
the vise that had been around his chest since the crash started to
loosen. Because he was doing something. Investigating. Not standing on the sidelines, forced to watch impotently while other people
handled what he was responsible for.

On the seat next to him, he had color printouts of the pictures
Sheila had taken of Johnny Gall's driver's license photo and John
Doe's face. And the warrant, which he handed Narwall when he
climbed out of the Ford in the empty school parking lot.

The principal was a small, nebbishy man who seemed to relish
his authority. "I still don't see why this couldn't wait until tomorrow," he said after letting them into the deserted office.

"Johnny Gall is dead," Hank said, exasperated. "All of the students whose names I gave you are dead. There is no waiting in a
death investigation. We need everything immediately."

"Wait. What?" He sank into a chair. "When you called, you said
you were investigating this one kid. Not that he was dead."

The guy started wringing his hands. Then he looked at Hank,
whose glare sent him scurrying for the computer.

Johnny Gall was a senior. He'd enrolled in the school district on the first of August. His school photo showed the same thin-faced, tousle-haired teen Hank had met last night. And all of the information was the same as that listed on his now-bloodied Missouri driver's license. None of this explained how this guy was also John Kalin, renter of apartment 213.

"Where are the documents that he needed to enroll? Birth certificate, proof of residency?"

Narwall pecked at the keyboard and pulled up scanned documents. The residency information was a power bill for the apartment in the name of John Kalin. The birth certificate information had been entered into information fields in the computer system. Johnny Lee Gall was born in Louisville, Kentucky, seventeen years ago in February. Hank wrote down the parents' names.

"Who would have been the one to look at the actual document when it was brought in for enrollment?"

"Somebody at the district office," Narwall said.

"And would the parents have to have been with him?"

Narwall thought a minute. "Not necessarily. Not at that age. It depends, though. You'll have to ask the district office about it."

Hank had Narwall pull up the records of the other five teens. All had been born in Missouri, and enrolled in Branson schools since kindergarten. He asked for everyone's schedules and said he'd be back tomorrow to talk to their teachers. He was almost out the door when he remembered.

"Have you ever seen this man?"

Narwall glanced at the photo and then squinted intently. "What's wrong with him? Is he asleep—oh, God."

"Yes," Hank said. "He's . . . deceased. We think there might be a connection between him and Johnny."

Narwall shook his head. He'd never seen the man before. Hank thanked him and headed back to the Bronco. He was stopped by the ding of his phone.

Where are you? You supposed to make bfast and kick soccer w Maribel. That ball is damn hard. I think I broke my toe.

Hank groaned. He'd completely forgotten his promise of Sunday breakfast with the kids once his patrol shift was over.

And Maggie isn't home yet either. She called at least. Should I go ahead and make bfast?

He started typing. *Yes, make breakfast. Sorry I forgot. Fatal accident. Investigating now.*

He could practically hear Dunc, his father-in-law, grunting in response. *Fine. They're getting choc chips in their pancakes. So there.*

Hank didn't mind. Chocolate chips made up for a lot with a five- and a three-year-old. He wished he were home to eat with them.

No ONE answered the door. Again. Sam moved on to the next one. So far, he had four unanswered doors and one sleepy night shift worker who had never laid eyes on either Gall or John Doe. Sam moved down to apartment 113. He knocked twice and was about to move on when someone called out. "What do you want?"

He yanked the badge off his belt and held it up to the peephole. "Ma'am, I'm with the Branson County Sheriff's Department, and I need to ask you a few questions. Could you open the door?"

The door opened as far as the still-latched chain lock allowed. One very green eye looked out. "What do you want to know?"

"I was wondering if you've ever seen this man around here in the complex." He held up the picture of Gall.

"Lemme see." She stretched two fingers through the crack of open door.

"Ma'am, please. I swear, I'm a sheriff's deputy. This is an emergency investigation—that's why I'm not in a uniform." He held his photo ID up with his badge. "Could you open the door?"

She stared at him, then shut the door. The chain rattled, and then she stepped outside. She was about his age and slim and had long, wavy dark blond hair. Her legs seemed to go on and on . . . Sam could feel himself turning red. He handed her the photo.

"I think so," she said slowly. "Real skinny, right? I think he lives upstairs." She'd only seen him twice. Once coming down the stairs. And the second time getting into a car. A black one.

"Do you remember anything else about the car?"

"Somebody else was driving. He got in the passenger seat. It was a two-door. One of those Trans Am kinda cars. Then they drove away." She thought for a minute. "The other guy didn't get out of the car, so I didn't see him very good. He had black hair. Kinda pale-looking. But that's all I saw of him."

Sam readied the other photo. "So . . . I need to show you another picture. It looks a little weird, but I need to see if you recognize this guy. He, um, he's not alive."

He turned over the Doe photo.

"Oh. Ew. He's dead? Was that why there's been all that noise around here this morning? Did he die here?"

Sam nodded. "So do you recognize him at all?"

"I guess it could be the guy who was driving the skinny dude. But it also might not be. I'm not sure."

There were nonresidents who came and went upstairs, and they could've been heading up to that apartment specifically, but she wasn't sure. She also hadn't heard anything last night in either the parking lot or from the apartment upstairs. She apologized with a smile. Sam assured her that was okay and carefully wrote down her name (Brenna Cassidy, quite a nice one) and contact information. He turned to go but froze when she grabbed his arm.

"Oh, is this important? When the Trans Am car pulled out of the parking lot that time, the old bat from upstairs started yelling at them about making too much noise and sounding like a gang of motorcycles. So maybe she saw them, too?"

Sam beamed at her. She smiled back, and he went all red again. He walked away thinking that his day was finally looking up.

The Country Song Theater looked a lot better than the last time Sheila was there. A bright, new, many-bulbed marquee welcomed theatergoers. The whole place was painted a fresh white, and the parking lot had a new layer of asphalt.

Raker and Sheila walked up to the entrance. There were no other cars in the parking lot, and the large glass doors were locked. Sheila peered into the lobby as Dale pulled out his phone.

"*Country music legend Euford Gunner will make Branson's premier concert theater his home,*" read Dale. "*Shows twice daily at the Classic Country Song Theater.*"

Sheila stepped back from the window.

"Between the glare and the tint, I can't see inside at all," she said. "What else does the brochure say?"

"Not much beyond good ol' Euford's accomplishments, and a promise he'll sing 'Woman, It's You Tonight' at every show."

"Nothing about a production company or anything?"

"Nope. And there's no website for the show. I googled it."

Sheila had her own phone out by now. "It appears that Gunner doesn't have his own website either. That'd be where his manager or whatever would be listed, right?"

Dale nodded. "Yeah. That or a publicist or the actual agent."

They both typed away and came up empty. Dale made a call to someone at his department to start a more in-depth search.

"So what was our victim doing with a brochure for a show that hasn't been publicized at all?" Dale said. "I'm going to make another phone call. There's one other thing we can try."

HANK's children still had chocolate smears on their faces when he walked in the door at noon. They tackled him in the foyer, fueled by delight and sugar. He sat back on the little entryway bench with them both on his lap. And held them.

Maribel almost came up to his chin now. He kissed the top of her head, breathing in the baby shampoo they still used. Dunc must have made her take a bath last night. Benny squirmed closer. He smelled like fresh dirt and wet dog. He'd announced last week that since he was almost three, he no longer needed to take baths.

I'm a very lucky man, Hank thought.

He walked into the living room with a kid in each arm. Dunc was in his recliner with a bag of frozen peas on his elevated foot.

"Really?" Hank said.

"It hurts," Dunc replied.

"Is that what Maggie told you to do?"

"No. I didn't ask her because she's busy. Saving lives."

"She's still at the hospital? I thought she got off at six?"

Dunc shook his head. "Some big emergency came in."

The kids slid through Hank's arms, hit the floor, and took off toward the bedrooms, followed by a suspiciously excited Guapo. Hank watched the dog's ample rump waddle down the hall. Then he sank into the sofa across from his father-in-law's recliner.

"I had a busy night," Hank said. He explained about the accident. He left out the mysterious Johnny Gall and the dead guy in the apartment. He didn't have any idea how to explain those.

Dunc let out a low whistle. "That's worse than anything I could've imagined as to why you were late. I'm sorry, boy-o."

Hank pushed himself to standing. "I think I'll wash up and get something to eat."

Duncan stopped him with a raised hand. "I need to tell you something. Last night, my sister showed up."

"What? Like, here? Now?"

Dunc nodded. Then a happy woof came from the hallway, where the dog and the kids stood next to an elderly woman with hair so gray it was completely white and a jaw so McCleary-ish it always made him do a double take. "Hello, Hank."

"Uh . . . Hi, Aunt Fin."

Finella McCleary Lancaster was five years older than her brother, which meant she'd had more time to hone her irascible Scots demeanor. Hank had always found her bluntness charming.

"What . . . um, what brings you here?"

Her face started to crumple. Hank, alarmed, looked over at Dunc. "Just here for a visit, she is," he said. "That's all."

Well. That wasn't planned. Hank tried to smile. She smiled back, whatever expression there'd been on her face now gone.

Hank went to the kitchen and the leftover pancakes. Once he'd polished off a whole stack, half a bottle of syrup, and most of a pot of coffee, he felt human enough to kick the soccer ball with Maribel. She was determined to score a goal before the end of her first season of rec league. Her skills were coming along nicely. Better, obviously, than her grandfather's.

Once they were finished outside, Hank opened his laptop on the dining table and started plugging into every database he had. He pulled out the information on Gall's parents that he'd gotten from the high school principal. The only Justine Gall he could find had died eight years before Johnny Gall was allegedly born. He tried Justine Drake, the maiden name listed on Johnny's birth certificate. The only one he found was seventy-nine years old.

He started on the father next. Allen John Gall popped right up. Two of them did, actually. A thirty-five-year-old in Louisville and a twenty-six-year-old in a St. Louis suburb. The Louisville one was a petty criminal who'd never had any association with a kid, or with a woman named Justine Drake. The Chesterfield one had three kids, all quite young.

Hank fished through his notes and found the emergency notification phone number that the high school had on file for Johnny. He dialed, and it went straight to voice mail. *Yo, this is Johnny. Leave me a message. If you're lucky, I'll hit you back.*

Hank was not in the mood to think about luck. He shut the laptop just as Maggie came in from the garage. She collapsed in a chair across the table from him. She looked like she could fall asleep right there.

"Babe, good grief," he said. "What happened?"

She laid her head on the table. He knew that sign. She rarely ate when she was on shift, and now—nine hours after she was supposed to be finished—she was crashing. He rushed to the fridge and pulled out the eggs and cheese. Once he got the omelet going, the smell perked her up enough for her to raise her head.

"Ed was late, and then a trauma came in. Teenager. A fall. From at least twenty feet. So many broken bones. We were in surgery for . . . I don't even know."

Hank scooped the omelet onto a plate and set it in front of his wife.

"How is she now?" he asked.

"ICU," Maggie said. "A BVHS kid. Her parents thought she was spending the night at a friend's house. They didn't realize she was missing until the other girl's parents called. The Blenkinships. I had to talk to them when we were done in the OR."

The wringing pressure in Hank's chest was back.

"So, enough about me." Maggie stuffed the last bite in her mouth. "How was your night shift?"

DALE RAKER DUG INTO HIS Cracker Barrel breakfast without answering Sheila's question. Five minutes, two scrambled eggs, and a slice of bacon later, he dabbed at his mouth with a napkin.

"I'd guess there was a fair bit of construction going on inside that theater," he said. "I don't know who did that—companies come in from all over—but when you've got a lot of trash, you get a Dumpster, right? And you're going to use the nearest company. And in this town, there's only one that does it."

Dale's napkin was covered with scribbled information. The construction company that hired Dom's Dumpsters of Branson was out of Kansas City, but Dominic Spignesi always insisted on contact information for the on-site foreman. Dale held up the napkin.

Sheila whipped out her phone. "May I?"

Dale nodded and went back to his eggs. She dialed and waited through ten rings before a woman picked up. Sheila asked for Kyle Hatwick. There was a little yelling and some swearing before Hatwick could be convinced to come to the phone. Sheila introduced herself and was met with silence. "Sir? Are you the foreman on the Country Song Theater remodel?"

"That job's done. Finished last week. Everything's signed off on it. You can't come back at me for nothing."

"Sir, I just need to ask you a few questions about the project. Do you have a list of who worked on it?"

He guessed so. And yes, most of them were young guys. And no one had given him problems.

"Was Euford Gunner there at all?"

A snort. "When was he *not* there? The dude wouldn't leave us alone. He drove everybody crazy."

"Do you have any way to contact him?"

"Uh, no. We're not exactly friends."

"Okay," she said. "I need to come by and show you a photo. I need you to tell me if a person was on your construction crew."

Hatwick sighed and then listed his address in the city of Hollister, just south of Branson. Sheila wrote it down in her pocket notebook and hung up.

When they were getting up to leave, Sheila's phone rang. She listened for a moment and turned to a puzzled Dale. "We've got to get to the hospital."

HANK now understood why Maggie took an enormous thermos of coffee to work every day. The hospital coffee tasted like dirty dishwater run through a sheet of newspaper.

The Blenkinships were in with their unconscious daughter. Hank hadn't talked to them yet. He wandered around the waiting room, sick at the thought that this girl might be another casualty of his horrible bad judgment.

Sheila and Raker arrived, looking confused and excited at the same time. "What the hell? This kid is connected to everything?" she said.

"I don't know about your homicide"—Hank waved his coffee cup toward Raker—"but definitely the car crash. She's the girl that Kayla Anderson told her parents she was going to have a sleepover with. And now she shows up almost dead near the Roark Creek Trail."

"Kayla said she was spending the night at the Blenkinship house?" Sheila said. "Because Hailee Fitch's mother told me that Hailee was spending the night at Kayla Anderson's house."

"And Gabe Schattgen told his parents that he was spending the night at Isaiah Barton's house," Hank said. "Which was news to the Bartons."

"What's not news is teenagers lying to their parents." Raker settled his bulky frame into a chair. "They wanted to go out without having a curfew. There's probably no kid in America who hasn't done the same thing. This one just turned tragic."

"I would agree with that," Hank said, "if one of those kids didn't have a different ID that was used to rent an apartment, which now has a murder victim in it. And if one of their curfew excuses wasn't suddenly critically injured."

The Branson patrolman who'd responded to the initial call, Officer D. Holt, came into the room. He didn't say much. A trail jogger had called in an injured person. Holt arrived at the same time as the ambulance to find the runner sitting with the girl. She was unconscious. It appeared that she had fallen down an incline that was almost a cliff in spots. They didn't know how long she'd been there. She did not have ID. He'd been trying to track down her identity at the station, paging through the PD's collection of local high school yearbooks, when dispatch got a call from Doug Blenkinship reporting that his daughter was missing.

"I found her sophomore photo in last year's BVHS book," Holt said. "Same kid. So I drove out there and notified them."

He looked toward Raker, who nodded an approval. He handed over his notes and left to resume patrol.

"So she fell," Raker said.

"So she landed," Hank countered. "What happened at the top is still unknown."

A middle-aged couple was shuffling toward them. It had to be the Blenkinships—despair weighed down their every step. Raker gently identified himself. He guided them to a pair of the uncomfortably cushioned seats and introduced Hank and Sheila.

"They're working with me on all this," Raker said. "We're trying to figure out what happened, so we need to ask you some questions. But can we get you anything first? Coffee? Water?"

Mr. Blenkinship shook his head. Mrs. Blenkinship needed water. Hank told her he'd be right back with it. It took a minute to find a vending machine, and by the time he got back to the waiting room, everyone had pulled chairs into a circle. He took the last seat.

". . . left the house about six last night," Doug Blenkinship was saying. "She was just walking over to the Andersons' house. It's not far—she does it all the time."

"And you didn't hear anything from the Andersons until this morning?" Raker asked.

Lisa Blenkinship shuddered. "She just kept crying that Kayla was dead, and Lauren wasn't in the car."

Hank leaned forward. "And did Mrs. Anderson tell you that they thought the girls were spending the night at your house?"

They nodded. "That was all we could get out of her," Doug Blenkinship said. "We still don't know what's going on."

"Kayla was killed in a car accident out near Airport Road north of the city," Hank said, looking Mrs. Blenkinship right in the eyes. "That's why Chief Deputy Turley and I are investigating.

She was with five other teenagers. All of them died in the crash."

At the word "five," both Blenkinships gasped. Hank listed off the names. The Blenkinships knew of Alex Danzig—Lauren also was in the high school band—and recognized Isaiah's and Gabe's names. They frowned at Hailee Fitch.

"She was in the car? Lauren and Kayla do *not* hang out with her," Mrs. Blenkinship said.

"We've heard that," Sheila said soothingly. "Would you be able to tell me why?"

"She's a Fitch," Mr. Blenkinship said. "Her family is all sorts of trouble. The girls just kept their distance, that's all."

"Did Lauren ever mention a Johnny Gall?" Sheila asked.

Mrs. Blenkinship shook her head. "I don't think so."

Of course not, Hank thought. Finding someone who knew about that kid was apparently too much to ask. If Johnny Gall was even a kid at all. He still wasn't satisfied that the Kentucky birth certificate was legitimate, and he couldn't call the state Office of Vital Statistics to check until business hours tomorrow.

He pulled his attention back to Raker as the BPD detective reentered the conversation. The Blenkinships listened to him with clasped hands.

"She hasn't been depressed," Lauren's mother said of her daughter. "She's her normal self. She's in the middle of marching band season, so she's very busy, but she loves it. She was going everywhere, talking to herself, making her lists, trying to fit in practicing her flute, and . . . oh, God. Was she overwhelmed?" She stared at the trio of police. "How did I not see it?"

THE concrete stair was cold. And hard. And the only place Sam had to sit as he waited for Mrs. Vandeed, the "old bat" in 207. He couldn't leave and come back later because He. Had. No. Car. The chief had taken his Bronco and was now incommunicado.

"That's no place for a decent person to sit. What're you up to?"

He bounced to his feet. After all that, the lady had snuck up on him. He put on his best friendly young-man face.

She clutched her purse to her chest when he showed his badge.

"Where'd you get that, sonny? Impersonating a cop is a crime."

He forced a smile. "Ma'am, I'm a Branson County sheriff's deputy. I'm investigating an incident in an apartment here in the complex, and I need to ask you some questions."

She harrumphed and tried to move past him.

"Ma'am. There was a murder here last night." Sam crossed his arms and tried to look as official as possible.

She pursed her lips, and her chins wobbled some before she decided she'd give her name. Bitty Jean Vandeed. She'd lived here since four months after the complex opened.

"I need to ask about your neighbors, the ones along the walkway near you."

"All no-accounts. Two oh nine doesn't even work. Two eleven never says hello. And two thirteen—well, rude as the day is long. Always peeling out of the parking lot at all hours. Coming and going too much with friends. Shifty looking."

"About that," Sam said. "What did he look like, exactly?"

"Light brown hair. Needed it cut. Skinny. Probably on drugs."

"How old do you think he was?"

She shrugged. "Twenty, maybe?"

"I do want to ask you about the peeling out in the parking lot," Sam said. "How often did that happen?"

"Off and on, all the time," she said. "It was the same black car every time." It was some kind of sports car, and its back bumper was dented on the left side. She was positive it was the same driver every time, except that she wasn't because she never really got a good look at him. He did have dark hair, long in a hippie kind of way. The man in 213 would go running downstairs, and they would roar off. It was always at night.

There was one thing left. He braced himself and pulled out the John Doe photo. "Have you ever seen this man before?"

Mrs. Vandeed looked carefully and shook her head. And then she swooned and unclenched one hand from her purse long enough to fan herself. "A dead man. I never. Oh, how horrible. I'll never sleep tonight. I feel faint."

Sam sighed and offered his arm. He helped her up the stairs and into her apartment, put on the tea kettle, made sure the cat had water, and left with a splitting headache.

"WE NEED a flowchart," Sheila said. She was pacing in the BPD conference room they'd adjourned to after leaving the Blenkinships at the hospital. The room did not have a whiteboard.

"There is likely no connection between Lauren Blenkinship and the homicide, or Lauren and the car crash," Raker said.

Hank started to respond when his phone buzzed. *Done at apts. Need a ride. Where's my car?*

Damn. He completely forgot he'd left Sam stranded, Hank realized as he looked at his phone for the first time in hours. This was not the first text from the kid he still thought of as the Pup— big-footed, sometimes clumsy, and until a few months ago, eager to please. Another message came in. *Never mind. Lady MSHP here. Will give me ride. Where's my car?*

They needed to know what Sam had found out in his canvass of the apartments. *Have her bring you to BPD. ASAP.*

"The dead John Doe could very well be connected to this Johnny Gall person," Raker said, "but that doesn't mean he's connected to the crash. That was an accident, a bunch of kids lying to their parents so they can stay out past curfew."

"But then what were they going to do?" Sheila countered. "Stay out all night long and not go to sleep?"

"Maybe they all expected to end up back at apartment two thirteen," Hank said. "Somewhere with no parental presence. Where someone had just bled out on the floor."

Raker nodded. "Fair enough. I'll buy the possibility that the kids could be linked somehow to the apartment murder—but I'm not going off on some goose chase that the actual crash was part of it without there being a lot more evidence."

They divvied up tasks as they waited for Sam, who finally walked in and strode up to Hank with his hand out. "I'll take my keys."

Hank pulled out a chair. "How about you give us a rundown of your interviews first?" he said.

The Pup sat. When he finished his briefing, Raker said, "Since the description of this car's driver matches—at least a little—my victim, I'll get my guys going on tracking it down."

"Okay," said Hank. "And we'll keep looking into Gall and the other kids."

Sheila pushed off from the wall she'd been leaning against. "And I'll keep on the theater angle with Dale." She turned toward Sam. "Can you give a copy of your notes to Detective Raker? Then take a break, go get something to eat."

"I would," Sam said. "But I. Don't. Have. My. Car."

"I'll take you to your car," said Hank, who'd driven the family minivan to the BPD station.

They all stood. Dale Raker moved toward the door, pointing at Sam at the same time. "And good job, son, with those interviews. That dented bumper's our most solid lead so far. Well done."

Sam's eyes widened, and he smiled. A little.

"Thank you, sir." He shoved his hands in his pockets and mumbled his way out the door. Hank followed, cursing that he hadn't thought to compliment Sam first.

Chapter 5

HANK WAITED UNTIL THE BELL rang. Then he got out of the car and walked into the school. Crying echoed against the lockers, and whispers came from students clustered together near classroom doors. He wasn't in uniform today, so no one paid him any attention as he walked to the office. Arlene Ostermann, the school secretary, was waiting for him.

"I want to go to Johnny Gall's first period class," Hank said.

"The grief counselor is currently in that class," said Mrs. Ostermann. "I'd suggest speaking with Johnny's English teacher. She's on prep right now. And she also teaches Hailee, Gabriel, and Alex at various times during the day. Oh—taught. She taught them all." She fought back tears. "I'm sorry."

Hank assured her that he understood and asked if she'd be kind enough to show him to Mrs. Rozalski's classroom. Mrs. Ostermann gave him a smile and marched out into the hallway.

They walked down several long corridors before they reached the right door. A petite woman with short brown hair was at a desk in the back. A pile of tissues sat next to a stack of papers. Mrs. Ostermann introduced them and left. Hank took the one other chair in the room that wasn't attached to a slice of desk and introduced himself.

"Arlene said you wanted to talk about Johnny especially. Why is that?" Mrs. Rozalski said.

"Well, Johnny's living situation wasn't . . . typical, really," Hank said. "And we're having trouble tracking down his parents. We think he might have been living on his own."

She sat back. "That does happen. I've had a couple of kids where the parent just took off, disappeared."

"He was able to pay the rent on an apartment in a pretty nice complex. But the ID he used to rent it wasn't in his name."

Mrs. Rozalski's eyes widened in surprise. "I never heard him use another name."

"How did he act? Like a typical high school senior?"

She twirled her pen for a moment. "He was kind of new and shiny, if you know what I mean. Most of these kids have gone to school together since kindergarten. When somebody new comes in, it can be exciting. He gave off this cool, rock-star vibe."

"Who did he hang out with?"

"Lots of different people. No one in particular, though, I think. Wait—I did see him walking around with Hailee Fitch a couple times. Oh, and Matt Chorovich, from the football team."

Hank wrote that name down. Then he asked about Hailee.

"That poor child. No one would go near her. That's why I remember her walking with Johnny Gall. It was unusual for her to be doing that with anyone. She had no friends, because of her sister. I think parents flat out told their kids not to associate with Hailee, too. So she just tried to fade into the background. But she's a very smart kid." Her voice hitched. "She was . . . she was a very smart kid."

"What is it about the sister?"

Mrs. Rozalski shook her head. "Emily was kicked out of school a few years ago. She was arrested for theft, and I heard that there were other things . . . but I don't really know what they are."

Hank leaned forward. "Ma'am, I know that you don't want to spread gossip, but I'm trying to figure out why six young people died and why another one is in critical condition at Branson Valley General. I need to know what Emily might be involved with."

She looked agonizingly at Hank. "There was talk that Emily was involved in drugs. And doing things to get drugs. Like the stealing. And . . . prostitution. But that was just talk. Please don't . . ."

Hank reassured her, then steered the conversation to Gabe Schattgen and Alex Danzig, who were both nice boys with B averages and the typical wandering attention spans of teens in their last year of high school. He stood to leave and was almost to the door when Mrs. Rozalski stopped him.

"Wait—did you say someone was at the hospital? A student?"

He explained how Lauren Blenkinship had been found.

"We didn't know that. This is . . . so horrible. Please . . . if there are answers, Sheriff, please find them."

THE school district office opened at eight. Sam arrived at seven forty, and the superintendent let him in and set him up with a desk. A thin, librarian-looking woman named Joyce was able to find the copy of Gall's birth certificate. It was a black-and-white Xerox.

"Were you the one who made this copy?"

Joyce nodded. "I'm the one who does that with registrations."

"How do you confirm that birth certificates are the real thing?"

"I look at the seal," she said impatiently. "It's embossed."

"What if it's out of state? How do you know that's really what the other state's certificate looks like?" He held up Gall's copy. "Like this one—how are you sure that the seal on here is legit?"

She thought about it. "I don't know. I know it was embossed—I wouldn't have accepted it otherwise. But I don't know what a Kentucky one would look like. Did they give me a forgery?"

That's what he was trying to figure out, Sam explained. He needed to know everything she could recall about the registration.

"I'm trying to remember him, but nobody really sticks out."

"He would've possibly been by himself."

"I'd remember if a kid came in without a parent or guardian. That would have been completely out of the norm."

Sam tapped on his folder and felt the paper clips holding the two photos he still needed to show her. "What about someone with a . . . a different family setup, say? Like a sibling, or something like that? Anybody like that?"

"I guess an older sibling could've come in, but I can't remember if that happened. I'm sorry."

Sam pulled out Johnny's DL picture. Joyce didn't recognize him, but that wasn't to say he didn't come in. Just that she didn't remember. Then he unclipped the murder victim's photo and placed it in front of her, warning her that it might be disturbing.

"Oh, yes. I've seen him before." She contemplated the picture for a minute. "I was running out to my car to go get lunch. And I slammed right into him as I came around the corner on the sidewalk outside, going toward the parking lot. My purse went everywhere. He helped me pick it up."

Sam fought back a grin and tried to stay professional as he asked more questions. She hadn't seen if he was with anyone, or what kind of car he might have been driving. The man never came inside, but he could have been waiting for someone.

Sam took both photos back and thanked Joyce for her time.

HANK walked out to the track, where he'd been told the football player Johnny Gall hung out with was currently in PE class. The kid jogged over. "Yes, sir?"

Hank identified himself. He'd purposefully worn jeans and a button-down shirt—it was easier to talk to teens in street clothes. Hank delicately asked if the boy had heard about the accident. Matt Chorovich nodded and turned a shade of pale that was more the color of guilt than the color of grief. Interesting. Hank gestured toward the bleachers, and the two sat on the bottom bench.

"Were you supposed to be with them?"

A "yes" came out before he could stop himself.

Hank turned to face him full on. He looked the perfect jock. Sandy blond hair that flopped in a disinterested sweep across his face. And right now, sniffling as he stared at the ground.

"Johnny said we'd go have a good time. Nothing big, just hanging out without having parents around."

"Where?"

"An apartment. He said it was a friend's and we could use it."

"Why didn't you end up going?" Hank asked.

Matt let out a long, slow breath. "It was my little sister's birthday. I was going to bail on it, but she was turning thirteen, you know? She thought it was such a big deal. So I stayed."

All the classmates were going to meet up at eight at a park close to Kayla Anderson's house. He'd called Johnny at seven to say he wasn't coming.

"How were seven of you supposed to fit in a little sedan?"

"I have a minivan," Matt said, "my mom's old one. I was supposed to pick everybody up at the park."

That helped explain why Alex Danzig was driving a too-small car belonging to a parent he didn't even live with.

Matt straightened suddenly and pivoted toward Hank. "Was Hailee Fitch really in the car?"

"Yes, she was," Hank said. Matt shook his head.

"I don't know why she was there. That doesn't make any sense." She was not someone who got included in things.

"So who would have asked her?" Hank asked.

"It would've had to have been Johnny. It was his invite."

"Did the rest of the kids in the car . . . make sense?" Hank said.

"I guess. It was kinda a—what's that word, eclectic?—group. I didn't know if any of them really hung out together. And I only really knew Johnny."

Hank asked why Matt thought people wanted to hang out with Johnny Gall in the first place.

"Johnny seemed like he had it all under control. Totally smooth," Matt said. "Like it was all cool and easy."

Sheila banged on the little house's front door again. Finally the door slammed open and a worn-down woman in a bathrobe stood glaring at her. "What the hell do you want?"

Sheila, today in full uniform, identified herself and asked for Kyle Hatwick, the on-site foreman on the theater development.

"It is eight in the damn morning. He do somethin'?"

Sheila decided to be noncommittal.

"Right now, I need to show him some photos. See if he recognizes anybody. So get him out of bed."

The woman sighed and disappeared into the little house. Five minutes and a lot of yelling later, Kyle Hatwick appeared. He leaned against the doorjamb and scratched at his bare chest.

"You the one called yesterday?"

"Yes. I need to show you photos to see if you recognize anybody."

Hatwick grabbed the picture she was holding out.

"Nope, never seen him before."

She took back the driver's license photo of Johnny Gall and took out the other picture. Hatwick started laughing.

"That's Euford's little bitch. What's wrong with him? He looks, like, dead or something."

"He was murdered Saturday night," Sheila said.

"Damn. Really?"

"Yeah," Sheila said, her mind spinning. "What do you mean, 'Euford's little bitch'?"

"He was always with Euford, when he came to the theater. Gettin' him water, findin' him a chair." Hatwick chuckled.

"Do you know his actual name?" Please, please, please.

"Rick, maybe?" A shrug. "I don't know. The guy was a jerk."

"You ever see what kind of car this 'Maybe Rick' drove?"

"I think he always came with Euford. And that was in an old Caddy. Kinda an off-white thing, big as a boat."

She waited on the doorstep while he searched for a list of workers on the Country Song job. He finally found a tattered roster in his pickup. Sheila took it, and he stomped back toward the house. She shook her head and headed toward her squad car.

"Wait!"

She turned back. Hatwick grinned. "Coffee. He'd show up most days with a big ol' coffee. From that new place downtown. With the fancy blue-and-gold cups. Does that help?"

It did. Sheila said so and pointed her cruiser back toward Branson and the new Donorae's Gourmet Coffee on Main Street.

SAM was almost positive the Kentucky birth certificate was a forgery. The clerk of the county where Johnny Gall was supposedly born had emailed him a full color scan of what their birth certificate looked like. The spacing was slightly different. Just to be sure, he scanned Gall's and sent it to the lady. His phone rang two minutes later. "You're right, sir. It's a forgery."

Sam pumped his fist.

"It's just the seal in the corner, really. And one other thing."

The paperwork said the birth occurred at Southern Regional Medical Center. But seventeen years ago, it was called County Hospital and Clinic, so that's what should be on the birth certificate. They changed the name six years ago.

At this, Sam stood up and did a few celebratory dance moves. It was a verified forgery. He dashed off a text to the chief and Sheila. Then sat back down and started thinking.

The next thing on his list was the car from the IMAX parking lot. He headed out.

"WE'VE been open six weeks now."

The owner, a woman named Vicki, smoothed her royal blue apron and shifted in the small space. They were in the storeroom, wedged between boxes of very aromatic coffee beans.

"I need to know if you remember two people coming in for coffee," Sheila said. She held up her phone, where she'd pulled up a Wikipedia photo of the lanky Euford Gunner smiling in a 1980s-era photo. "He'd be a lot older than this."

Vicki considered it. "Maybe? I can't say for sure."

Sheila pulled the next picture out of her notebook.

"Oh, my. He doesn't look good. Is he dead?"

"Yes."

Vicki leaned forward. "There was a guy who'd come in most mornings for the last couple of weeks. It could be him."

Sheila asked to see credit card receipts. Hopefully there would be a "Maybe Rick" in there somewhere.

"Wouldn't you rather see the app? It tracks your purchases and you earn rewards. Hang on." Vicki darted out of the room. She was back in seconds with a laptop. A flurry of keystrokes later, she had a list. "Male, eighteen to twenty-five, purchasing at least a large. I come up with six people."

There was no one named Rick. Sheila frowned. "What if the person ordered two coffees most of the time?" she asked.

Vicki tapped away. There were two. Gavin P. O'Connell and Andrew T. Bennett. One of them could be her guy. Sheila asked for a printout with their names as well as the others and their info. Then she had Vicki do a name search for Euford Gunner, just in case his gofer was using the boss's credit card. No luck.

Vicki disappeared and returned with the printout and a large coffee. "I insist," she said, pressing the to-go cup into Sheila's hands. "It seems like you've got a long day ahead of you. I'd love it if this helps you get through it."

Sheila smiled weakly. She'd love it, too, but a name—not caffeine—was the only thing that would solve her problems.

Jenny Danzig lived in a ramshackle frame house less than a mile from the Anderson place. No one was home. Hank walked slowly down the front path and stopped at the bare patch of yard that was obviously used as a parking space. An oil patch stained the dirt.

He walked to the house across the street. A four-year-old answered the door. He knew this because the boy told him so.

"Is your mom here?"

The kid darted away and returned with a woman in her early twenties. Hank pointed at the badge on his chest. "I'm just trying to find out some information about your neighbor across the street," he said. "Do you know anything about who lives there?"

It was a rental and people came and went, the mom said. Some lady had moved in a few months ago. Never introduced herself. She was older, maybe in her late forties. She came and went, but not regular.

Hank asked whether the woman had a vehicle.

"Yeah. A brown sedan. It's usually parked there in the dirt."

"When was the last time you saw her?" Hank asked.

"It must have been Friday," the mother said. "Because then it was the weekend and Pete was home—that's my husband—and I didn't see her at all then. But she must have been around, because the car was there."

"And when did the car leave?"

She thought for a moment. "It wasn't there when we went to church yesterday morning."

Hank dug out a card and wrote his cell number on the back. "If you see her come home, please call me immediately. She's not in any trouble. I just really need to talk to her."

She held up his card. "If I see her, I'll call."

"Do WE even know if she's heard about the crash?" Sheila said.

Hank shrugged at her. They sat in his office at the Branson substation. They didn't use the space much. There were only a couple of computers, a small lobby, a closet-size interview room, and the office they were sitting in.

Hank gave Sheila a rundown of his search for Jenny Danzig and his morning at the high school. Her boss looked like he'd been used as a punching bag. She'd bet money he hadn't slept at all since the crash. And now he was going on about the possibility that the sedan had been tampered with. That no one anticipated the son would take it. That maybe somebody had been after Jenny Danzig.

She thought about it. Whatever way you looked at it—accident or conspiracy—Alex Danzig's mother did need to be found. She suggested to Hank that he keep at that. She'd track down the list of coffee patrons. Oh, and Emily Fitch.

"What the hell is up with her?" Hank said. "Every person I talked to about Hailee mentioned her sister, too." He repeated every rumor he'd heard, even one about her being the girlfriend of a Colombian drug lord. Sheila snorted.

"Half of those sound ridiculous," she said. "And all of it sounds pretty heavy-duty for a kid who's what, twenty? Twenty-one?"

Hank started banging at the computer's keyboard. "Her DL says she'll be twenty-one next month."

Sheila eyed Hank's sunken cheeks. "Have you eaten?"

"I had something at home this morning."

It was now late afternoon. "You need to get something to eat. Something solid. You're going to pass out otherwise."

He stared at her for a minute. Finally, he nodded and left the room. The black cloud went with him.

SAM headed back to the Branson substation, where he was scheduled to meet Kurt Gatz, the crime scene tech.

He pulled into the parking lot behind the building and saw Kurt circling the little white hatchback, taking pictures. An hour later, they had a fat lot of nothing. Some fingerprints that needed running, although they were probably the two dead boys'. Sam kicked a tire. This was nothing but busy work. He looked over at Kurt with all his gear. "Come on. I got an idea."

Ten minutes later they were looking up at a steep hillside. The Roark Creek Trail was calm and shaded, even right where Lauren Blenkinship had landed.

"I think Branson PD already did this," Kurt said.

Sam began to pace along the paved path. There had to be something they'd missed. Something he could find, and investigate. Something that would get the chief to trust him again. Think.

The dirt at the edge of the path was all torn up, and he could see vehicle tire tracks on the pavement that must've been left by the ambulance yesterday morning. The girl had landed hard, that was for sure. But the theory that she'd jumped didn't make any sense. Throwing yourself down a forested hill, where you'd just as well might end up with a skinned knee instead of fatal injuries . . . He started to climb.

"Oh, man," Kurt said. "You didn't say there'd be hiking. I think I'm just going to wait for you here."

Sam kept going, staring down for any sign of footprints or a scuffle, and up for any sign of broken branches that would indicate this was the exact route Lauren had taken. The vegetation was just starting its autumn die-off, which helped. Things were starting to get more brittle, easier to track.

He hit a spot on the ascent that was clear of underbrush. He knelt, but the indentations were too muddled to tell him much. He carefully stepped five feet to the side and followed them farther up. He smiled, and his breathing slowed. This he could do. This *only* he could do. There were lots of fishermen in the department, but not many hunters.

It became clear that what he was seeing were two sets of tracks. Running. And not side by side for a friendly jog either. One after the other, like a chase. One bigger, one smaller. He went over a little rise in the terrain, and on the other side, the weeds were patchy and many spots had bare dirt. Beautiful, loose dirt. Where he could see the heel of a tennis shoe. That was the bigger foot. The smaller runner had no shoes. Just a set of toes, clearly captured in the Ozark soil.

He dug out his phone and dialed Hank. "Was she wearing shoes? The overpass girl?"

"I have no idea," Hank said. "Why?"

Sam explained where he was. The chief's end of the phone suddenly seemed to crackle with energy. "I'm on my way."

Sam called Kurt, who said he'd move his truck to a better access point and be there shortly.

A half hour later, Sam walked back down to the creek trail to find the chief and one really PO'd Branson detective.

". . . and tear my guys a new one. I can't believe they didn't find this."

The chief caught Sam's eye and winked. Sam fought back a grin. He'd done good. He started to report, but Hank held up a hand. "First, Detective Raker has some information," he said, pointing at the Branson cop.

"She wasn't wearing shoes when she was found."

"Then they've got to be her tracks. Kurt's taking footprint casts now," Sam said. "They start at the edge of the subdivision at the other side of this wooded section. Both participants were running. I think she had a pretty good head start, because the unknown person's stride is significantly longer. If he'd been closer to her, he would have caught up, and the tracks would show that happening. Of course, I can't tell what happened once the really steep section was reached, except that it's clear that's when she started crashing through the vegetation without being able to stop herself. That doesn't mean she wasn't pushed."

Raker pinched the bridge of his nose. "Are you sure it's a he?"

"With the stride length and the size of the shoe, it's pretty likely. Also, I can't say for sure that she was barefoot at any point but that one section. I'd suggest we get some folks and search nearer the subdivision for shoes."

"Oh, my men will be scouring these woods," Raker said.

The detective pulled out his phone and turned away. Sam was glad not to be under his command at the moment. Especially when the guy he did work for slapped him on the back.

"Sammy, you're brilliant. Nobody else would have found this. You might've just saved the whole investigation. We have to be able to link her to the crash and the murder, and now we're a big step closer. Thank you."

Sam hadn't felt this good in months.

THINGS were looking up. Hank was much closer to showing that the car crash was linked to—and the result of—criminal activity. He'd been proven right about Lauren Blenkinship not falling down the hill either by accident or suicidal tendency. Officers had found a pair of ballet flats that Mrs. Blenkinship confirmed were her daughter's. Sheila was closing in on the murder victim's ID. And Johnny Gall was a fake.

And Dunc had actually made a decent enchilada. Hank polished off a third helping and sat back with a sigh.

"I'm going to take that as a compliment," said his father-in-law.

Hank had learned a few things about Dunc in the year they'd lived under the same roof. One was that the older man's relationship with his sister wasn't always civil. He figured it was because they were so much alike. Stubborn, blunt, cantankerous Scots. Which brought him to the question just begging to be answered. What was she doing here?

"She didn't know where else to go," Dunc said once they were alone in the kitchen. "She can't go to her in-laws."

"Why not?"

"Because it's about them. Well, it's about him. About Lew."

Ah, yes. "Mark-down" Lew. He owned a small chain of closeout merchandise outlets. Hank had only seen him a few times, including at his wedding, when the guy managed to corner his dad and talk about clearance sales for an hour.

"She thinks he's having an affair."

Hank's jaw dropped. Lew with the too-shiny loafers and too-loud laugh? That Lew?

"I know." Dunc nodded. "That's what I think, too. Not really plausible. Especially now. Finella's seventy-eight, which means he's eighty-one. They've been married for twenty years."

"So she's here to figure out whether to divorce him?"

"I think so. We haven't really gotten much further than that. She's pretty upset about it. So if you could not bring anything up, well, I'd appreciate it."

"Of course," Hank said.

"You know, I heard they've scheduled the first of the funerals for those kids. It's just such a tragedy."

Hank's breath caught. Dunc peered up at him. He still didn't know the whole story. But he knew enough about Hank to stop talking. He patted Hank on the shoulder and left him alone.

Chapter 6

"YOU SHOULD SEE THEIR facilities, man. They got some nice, new stuff." Kurt Gatz settled into the chair across from Hank's desk. "And they got windows."

Hank chuckled. The sheriff's department forensic lab was famous for its similarity to a closet. "Yeah, well, they've got a good tax base," he said. "All the shows and all the stores are in the city limits. All we've got is back roads, and forests, and little towns."

Kurt pulled what looked like Xeroxes of shoe tread out of a file he'd carried in. "They're consistent," he said. "The print in the woods and the shoe found in the sleeping bag at the homicide scene. Both are a men's Nike cross trainer, approximately size ten." Kurt rattled off the style. "But the woods cast is the right shoe and the scene shoe is the left. I can't tell you if they're the same pair or were worn by the same person."

Hank was pretty sure there weren't two people in the same shoes out there targeting a very specific segment of Branson residents.

"Find out anything else while you were over there?"

The dead guy's prints weren't in the national database, so he didn't have a criminal record, Kurt told him.

"Ah, but I'm closing in on him," said Sheila as she entered Hank's office. "It's got to be either Andrew T. Bennett or Gavin P. O'Connell. I hope."

"How on earth did you even come up with any names at all?"

She explained about the coffee shop app. "Six names fit the age demographic we need. Three are straight-up local boys. None of the DL photos match our guy. And another name is a guy with a St. Louis address. And since his DL photo shows that he's not a white man, he's definitely out, too. I sent Sam over to have Judge Sedstone sign the warrant for the credit card companies so we can figure out these last two names. Neither of them came up in the Missouri DL database."

"Any luck on tracking down Euford Gunner?"

She shook her head. "BPD has somebody searching high and low for Euford's agent or publicist. And they've surveyed all the hotels and such. No Euford. And no big ol' Caddy either."

SAM contemplated the Greater Branson Area. It was the big county 9-1-1 street map that they'd tacked to the wall of Sheila's office opposite her whiteboard.

From what the construction foreman had told Sheila, Euford showed up at the job site every morning. That made it likely he was staying somewhere local. Sam ran his hand across the map. What if Euford was renting a private residence? Something that'd be appropriate for a country music star? He slapped the map and turned toward Sheila's computer. Airbnb netted two possibilities. He wrote them down and headed for his car.

An hour later, he'd met a very nice vacationing family from Duluth and a honeymooning couple from Iowa. So he was back in the cruiser, drumming a Bruno Mars song on the steering wheel and trying to pin down the thing he was missing, which was flitting through his brain like a lightning bug when he caught it.

He pulled off the road and called his mother. She'd been the manager of a doctor's office for the past twenty years, and the professional building where she worked had a tenant who Sam was suddenly very interested in. "That snooty lady who works in your building, is she there today?"

"Huh?"

He explained. His mother told him she'd seen the woman just that morning. Sam sped back to Branson. He walked right past his mom's office and knocked instead on the locked door at the end of the building. Concierge Travel Consulting.

There was no answer. He sighed. There had been no phone listing, so this in-person visit was his only option. He tried again, and now he heard movement.

"This is Deputy Samuel Karnes of the Branson County Sheriff's Department," he said in his loud, authoritative voice. "I'm investigating an urgent matter and need to speak with you immediately. Please answer the door."

He heard the approaching click of high-heeled shoes, and then the door swung open. "You do not have an appointment."

She was mid-fifties. Her makeup and her blond highlights were perfect, and her bucketload of jewelry glittered in the soft light.

"Yes, ma'am," Sam said. "I wasn't able to find your phone number, though. So I'm here in person, and I'd like to come in."

She studied him for a moment and then let him in. He stepped inside. She left the door open and did not offer him a seat.

He explained who he was trying to track down. She looked at him blankly. "I'm afraid I'm not able to comment on whether anyone might or might not be a client or, in fact, on any aspect of my business at all."

Sam put on his official face. "Ma'am, I am conducting an urgent investigation, and I need to find Mr. Euford Gunner. So if you have any information, I need you to tell me."

She folded her hands in front of her. "I am very busy, so I must ask you to leave."

Sam was starting to get angry. "Ms. Gillam, I am a law enforcement officer asking you a direct question, and—"

Her eyebrows shot up. "How do you know my name?"

Sam silently thanked his mother and forced himself to smile. "Knowing who people are and what they do is what law enforcement does, Vivian Gillam. You run a travel agency."

Her face tightened. "I run a service providing individually tailored itineraries and accommodations for people of distinction."

Sam bit back a laugh. So in other words, she made reservations for rich people. "And that's why I'm here. Euford Gunner is a very famous country music star, so I naturally thought he would . . . come to you for his housing needs."

Trying to act casual, she walked to her fancy desk at the back of the small office. She stood behind it and put her hands on the surface. Putting a barrier between them meant he was making her edgy. "I am not able to divulge my client list," she said.

Think. "What, are you a lawyer?"

She looked surprised. "No."

"Are you a priest?"

"Quite obviously not, young man."

"So you have no privilege under the law to keep information from me." He crossed his arms. "Please answer the question."

Her hands started to tremble just a little. But she still shook her head and asked him to leave. He stepped outside, and the door shut behind him with a loud click of the lock.

He made a phone call. Then he sat down to wait.

"I JUST wanted to see how you're doing, ma'am. See if you needed anything."

Nora Rossetto, Hailee Fitch's mother, slumped away from the doorway so Sheila could pass through. They took the same living room seats they'd each used two days earlier. She shook her head and wiped away tears. "My boss is giving me a few days off. Otherwise . . . there's not much to be done, you know?"

Sheila spread five photos out on the little coffee table. They were recently taken school pictures that would go in funeral programs before they made it into the yearbook.

"We're just trying to sort a few things out," Sheila said. "Could you tell me if you recognize any of these kids?"

Nora knew four of them by sight, if not by name.

"You don't recognize him?" Sheila asked, handing her the picture. "His name's Johnny Gall. Did Hailee ever mention him?"

Nora shook her head. And she would've remembered, because it would've been a big deal for her to talk about a boy.

"Do you have any idea where Emily is, ma'am?" Sheila said.

Nora Rossetto hadn't seen or heard from her older daughter in eleven months. That contact had been a quick phone call from Emily to see if any mail had come for her here at the house. The phone number was blocked.

"Why do you think Emily ended up this way?" Sheila asked.

Nora Rossetto looked around the room. Her gaze stopped on the hole in the wall near the front door. "Him. Her father. Hailee's father, too, but she didn't seem to have his blood at all. He's a crook. A con man. Thinks everybody else is just his to use."

"Do you think, ma'am, that Emily is with your ex-husband?"

Nora laughed, a brittle, splintery sound. "Emily hates Mick. Passionately. She hasn't talked to him in years, that I know of. And when Emily cuts you out, that's it. You're done."

HANK grabbed the warrant off the front seat and walked quickly through the open-air office complex. It looked like mostly doctors' offices, with an accountant and an attorney here and there. And the Pup, perched in the middle of a bunch of ferns.

He saw Hank approach. "You got the warrant?"

Hank smiled. "And I figured since she didn't want to just go ahead and answer your questions about one client, we'd ask for a warrant that lets us search the whole office, in order that we might be absolutely sure we get all the information she's got on ol' Euford."

Sam started laughing. "How'd you pull that off?" he asked.

"Judge Sedstone," Hank said. "He's already granted one warrant in this thing, and now he's interested in the whole case. Plus, I don't think he likes people refusing to answer simple questions."

"Me either," the Pup said. "You'll probably have to knock a bunch of times before she'll answer the door."

Hank held out the warrant. "Oh, no. You're the one who's tracked it this far; this is your show."

Sam stared at him, and a smile slowly split his face. He took the paper and marched up to the office. It took three knocks before the door opened. Hank stayed out of sight against the wall. Sam held up the warrant, and after some heated protests from Vivian Gillam, he stepped inside. The door stayed open, and Hank settled against the rough wood siding to listen.

There was some slamming of what sounded like filing cabinet drawers. Eventually, Sam cleared his throat and told Gillam he would need to look through more than just the rental listings.

"There is no way in hell, you little . . . thug."

"Ma'am, the warrant gives me the authority to look through your business records for any and all contracts, correspondence, or indicia relating to Mr. Gunner or anyone linked with him." The Pup was keeping his cool. Hank was delighted.

"I'm going to get you fired," she said. "You won't even be able to write a parking ticket. I'm calling my attorney."

"That's fine, ma'am. But I'm going to go about my search."

Those last few words seemed to be said at a closer distance. Sam backed out of the office, stalked by an aggressively highlighted cosmetics aficionado who froze when she crossed the threshold and saw Hank.

"You weren't trying to force Deputy Karnes out of your office, were you?"

"I'm not doing anything until my attorney gets here. And then I'm calling the sheriff and reporting you both for harassment."

Hank straightened, smoothed his shirt, and stuck out his hand. "By a happy coincidence, I happen to be the sheriff."

He let her stand and stew for a moment. Then he laid it out.

"We're going to come inside, and we're going to go through any file that we feel might contain evidence pertinent to our investigation. Because we have a search warrant. Now, it'll be a lot easier if you cooperate with us. We have no desire to mess up your office, or ruin your filing system, or anything else."

She stared Hank down through heavily mascaraed eyelashes. She blinked first, mincing back inside and sitting primly on a chair by the window. Hank then followed Sam into the office and over to the filing cabinets.

Twenty minutes later, they knew where Euford Gunner was staying and that his show was expected to open in three weeks.

"This seems like a pretty expensive place," Hank said, holding up a glossy photo of the mansion in Gunner's file. "Why is there no record here of a security deposit, or even a credit check?"

Vivian Gillam glared at him. Hank shrugged and started digging through her desk. He got to the locked lower left-hand drawer and reached for a long steel letter opener lying by the desk phone. That led to a stream of muttering. She marched over and unlocked the drawer with a key from her pocket.

There were files for some of the biggest names in town, including copies of rental checks as well as other expenses—housekeeping, transportation, a florist. "So, you're given an amount of money, like, by a record company, and then you pay their expenses out of that?"

She nodded.

"Why wouldn't their companies just do that themselves?" Sam asked. "Why do they need to use you?"

"Because if you come to town and you want to stay somewhere exclusive and secure, you come to me. There are no other options. And everyone who is important knows that."

"Was that your arrangement with Mr. Gunner?" Sam asked as he handed Hank the Euford file. She nodded, but Hank held up his hand as he looked in the file.

"What's Entertainment Enterprises, Inc.? This isn't a record company."

"That's who pays me. For Mr. Gunner's expenses."

Hank asked her for the names, and she said she'd never spoken with anyone at Entertainment Enterprises. It was all done over email, and they'd have to find the address in the file, because she wasn't going to tell them what it was.

Hank straightened, and Sam signaled that he was done. Ms. Gillam rose from her chair. "I'm still calling my attorney."

Hank nodded politely and led Sam out of the office. The door slammed behind them.

SHEILA spent another half hour with Nora Rossetto before it occurred to her that no one had notified Mick Fitch about Hailee's death. His most recent arrest report (for selling stolen cartons of cigarettes out of his car) listed an address out north on Highway 248. It turned out to be a little shack off the road that smelled of beer thirty feet away. Her knock was met with a startled-sounding crash and some swearing. That was promising.

The door opened. A white man with several days' worth of stubble and a tsunami of stench stood there. He was only slightly taller than Sheila, but with broad shoulders and powerful arms.

She said she wanted to ask him some questions. He told her to screw off. She suggested that, seeing as he was on parole, he was not in a position to refuse law enforcement anything. She motioned for him to come out on the sagging porch. Once she was sure he was the only person in the one-room hovel, she patted him down and gave him her undivided attention. She'd get around to notifying him, but first she was very interested in his whereabouts at the time Lauren Blenkinship was chased through the woods.

"Where were you Saturday night?"

That was apparently too far back to remember. Mick eventually narrowed it down to one of two bars. "Don't know which one."

"When was the last time you saw Emily?"

He snorted with laughter. "Emily, my kid? That Emily? You gotta be kidding. I ain't seen her in who knows how long. That little bitch do something again?"

Sheila gave a noncommittal nod.

"She come by here a while back. Don't know exactly when. Was driving a black Dodge Challenger. Looked new. Sweet ride." She'd had someone in the car with her, but Mick didn't get a good look at him. The person had stayed in the car.

"What did she want?"

"She said she wanted to say hi. Which's a bunch of crap. She never did anything without something bein' in it for her." He wiped his nose on his T-shirt. "So she said hi, then left. And that was it. And I don't know where she went. Or where she's now."

He seemed to be telling the truth. Sheila took a breath. "Mr. Fitch, I now need to talk to you about Hailee," she said slowly.

Another blink. "What about her?"

She softened her stance. "Mr. Fitch . . . I need to tell you that Hailee was killed in a car accident Saturday night."

He gaped at her. "What? Damn. I always expected Emily to be the one to go and get herself killed or something. Not Hailee. That's . . ." He trailed off. "I need a drink."

He disappeared into the house, and the door slammed behind him. Sheila headed for her car.

HANK dialed the phone. He hated being an adult. He hated sharing. But he knew that if things were reversed, he'd be furious if he wasn't brought into the loop.

Dale Raker finally picked up.

"We think we found him. Euford." He waited out Raker's Michael Jackson whoop and then recited the address.

Hank let Sam drive. Raker pulled up to the mansion just behind them. It stretched up two stories and out who-knew-how-many rooms, covered in big wooden beams and multihued stone. Raker knocked. After five minutes and several more bangs on the door, he turned and looked around. "Where's the kid?"

Hank backed off the sweeping front steps just as the Pup came trotting around from the left side of the house. He grinned and waved them over. "I think I found him. There's an old dude in a cowboy hat sitting out by the pool in the back."

They found the man noodling around on a guitar. Sightline obscured by a large brown Stetson, he didn't notice them until all three stopped about a dozen feet away. He looked up, and the expression of mild curiosity bled out of his face as he registered Sam's sheriff uniform. In its place, dread.

"Patrick?" Euford whispered.

Raker asked if Patrick's last name was O'Connell.

Euford nodded. "He hasn't come home." The hands holding the guitar, a battered six-string, were trembling now.

Raker pulled another pool chair over and sat down. He said he needed to show Mr. Gunner a photo and that he should prepare himself. Raker handed him the picture of the dead man.

Gunner slumped in the chair, and Raker barely caught the guitar as it fell out of limp hands. Hank moved forward and took it from the detective. He laid it very carefully on the glass-topped patio table, and then he pulled up a chair.

"How . . . how is he dead? What happened?"

"We're still trying to figure that out, sir," Raker said. "That's why we need to ask you some questions."

It took a while, but in fits and bursts and digressions and bouts of sobs, Euford Gunner explained. He met Patrick four years ago in Nashville. It was at a free music class for disadvantaged youngsters. Afterward, some of them came up to ask questions. One of the older ones, who seemed real shy, waited until everybody else was gone and then came up. That was Patrick.

He invited the kid to his show that night, and then he came to the next one, and the next. And then Euford was done with the road for a while, and told him so and thanks for coming out. And Patrick looked like someone just killed his puppy. Turned out he had no place to go. He was eighteen, just graduated from high school, and his folks had said the gravy train was over. He was on his own and couldn't find a job. He'd run out of money and was squatting in an abandoned house.

Euford thought on that and said Patrick could stay in the little cabin on his property in Georgia. The boy made himself useful, and so when Euford went back out on tour, he took Patrick with him. And he'd been with him ever since.

The question hung over them like the sun umbrella swaying on its pole above the patio table. "Sir," Raker began, "I need to ask you a little more about your relationship with Patrick. Were the two of you . . . lovers?"

He barked out a laugh. "There was nothin' like that going on."

"Then why, sir," Hank asked, "has he lived with you for four years? Sure, he's helpful, but . . ."

Euford kneaded his hands together. "He was like Andy."

All three men leaned forward. They could barely hear him.

"I was lonely. And he looked so much like Andy, with that little light in his eyes. All excited about life. He was the best company I could ever ask for."

His son Andy had died ten years ago. Heroin overdose. And Euford had gotten older and older and lonelier and lonelier. But after he met Patrick, the road started to be fun again.

"Then I broke my ankle. Didn't see a curb outside a honky-tonk bar in Fort Worth and ended up flat on my ass. People posted videos of it—can you believe that? Well, that just shot it to hell in that city. And anyplace else somebody cares to type 'old cowboy falls on ass' into Google." He sighed. "The only place it doesn't seem to matter that you're old is Branson. People'll still come to see you here. So we decided to come."

They'd done a show here about a year ago, and they both liked the area. Patrick had been enthusiastic about staying in one place. Euford guessed the younger man had made a few friends.

After a few more questions, Raker asked if they could see Patrick's room. Euford nodded and lifted himself to his feet with his arms. Hank handed him the cane that was sitting by his chair, and they all slowly made their way across the flagstone patio to the mansion's back door.

PATRICK O'CONNELL's room was upstairs. Second on the left, Euford'd said, because he couldn't do the stairs. So Hank and the Pup went on up while Raker stayed below with the musician. The two of them tore the room apart. There was a nice Fender Stratocaster that Hank doubted ol' Patrick had paid for himself. There was a variety of clothing, some name brand and some Walmart. A few battered CDs. A smallish flat-screen TV. Posters from places that Euford must have played shows.

But there wasn't a phone. Or a laptop. Hank stood in the middle of the room and scratched his chin. Then he eyed the heavy wood nightstand next to the bed. That's where he'd put it.

He wiggled the nightstand away from the wall. And there, wedged behind it and half under the bed, were chargers for an iPhone and a Dell laptop. He turned to put them on top of the comforter and stepped on a CD case. It cracked under his weight, and Hank swore. He tossed it on the bed with the cords.

Sam was staring at the bed and scratching his ear. Hank stood quietly—thoughts were happening. Sam picked up the smashed case and pried it open. He slipped out the liner notes, and a folded paper dropped to the floor.

"It's a birth certificate." Sam held it out. A seven-pound, six-ounce boy born in Tennessee just shy of twenty years ago. Named Evelyn Garo Cluth, Junior. "That's one horrible name," Sam said with a whistle. "You think this is Patrick?"

"It could be, even though the age is different from what he told Gunner," Hank said. "We haven't gotten a confirmed ID on any Gavin Patrick O'Connell yet."

"Well, he had it hidden for some kind of reason," Sam said. "Good place, too. Mr. Gunner never would've thought twice about it. A dude that old probably wouldn't think of a CD as obsolete. I'm sure all of this guy's real music is on his phone."

Hank was an idiot. He'd thought nothing of an anachronistic technology in the room of someone that young. He should have.

"There was another one over here." Hank strode around to the nightstand on the other side of the bed and pulled another CD case out of the drawer. He started to open it and then stopped. Sam had figured this out. He handed the case across the bed.

Sam pulled a photo out of the liner notes. It was an old one—shot on film—of an infant. It was impossible to tell if it was a boy or a girl.

Hank stared again at the birth certificate and that horrible name. And then bolted for the stairs.

SAM HUSTLED AFTER THE chief. Mr. Gunner was with the Branson detective in the middle of the two-story-high great room. The big leather couches they were sitting on looked tiny in the huge room.

The chief stopped a little ways from the musician. "Euford Gunner is a pretty good name for a country music star," Hank said. "Seems tailor-made, really. A lot better than Evelyn Cluth."

The color in Mr. Gunner's cheeks drained out.

"Was 'Patrick' your son?"

Damn. Sam fought back a smile. Now that was a piece of detective work right there. The chief stepped forward and held out the birth certificate. Mr. Gunner took it with shaking hands. "I've never seen this before."

Hank pointed. "Is this your name?"

"Yes. Except for the junior part. The rest is my given name."

The chief pointed to the space where the father's name should be. And then to the mother. "Pamela Helbing. Sound familiar?"

He shrugged. "Look, I don't remember this woman. It was a long time ago. But I sure as hell know I'd remember if I'd been told I knocked somebody up. And nobody ever told me that."

The chief took back the birth certificate. "Any recollection of a woman who knew your real name? That narrow it down any?"

Mr. Gunner didn't think anyone knew about Evelyn. He'd worked very hard to keep it that way. Wouldn't you, with a name like that? He started using Euford Gunner when he was sixteen and trying for a record contract. It worked. He "lost" his driver's license at one point, and the folks at the label took care of getting the replacement, saying that their recording star was born in a shack in the Smokey Mountains and had no birth certificate. And "Euford" was official from that point on.

Raker started talking. "I was just about to ask Mr. . . . Gunner, here, about his new show. And where he's gotten the financing for it. Because you seem to have had some money problems in the past few years, Euford, which would make it very difficult to launch that kind of production on your own."

"You read about that, did you? Some of those reporters had a field day with me gettin' taken for a ride like that. My business manager . . . what a bastard."

Mr. Raker raised an eyebrow.

"Okay, okay. That's not all of it. I might've gotten into the gambling a bit. But that's done with now. I'm outta debt. I don't owe nobody nothing."

"Except your financial backers for this show," Raker said.

Euford glowered at him. "That's just ridiculous to sit there and imply that I'm doin' something crooked, just because I—like everyone else in this damn town—need money to mount a show."

"So who's your backer?" Mr. Raker said.

"Entertainment Enterprises, Inc.," Mr. Gunner said.

"Yeah, but who *is* that?" The chief pinned the man down with his laser look. "That name doesn't mean anything."

The old musician admitted that he didn't know. "You done anything to upset them—these mystery backers?" Mr. Raker asked.

"No. What on earth kinda question is that?"

Mr. Raker leaned forward. "It's the kind of question that follows along after a murder. And you have got a murdered companion. Someone who was important to you. So we want to know if there's any reason that somebody would want to get at you?"

Mr. Gunner started to cry. "I don't know. I didn't know he was my son. I didn't know he was dead. I don't know what he was doing . . . I don't know anything anymore."

Chapter 7

THE FIRST BAR SHEILA VISITED was a bust. Yeah, Mick Fitch was a regular. So no, it was near impossible to narrow down which nights he was there, because it was most of them but not all.

The second place Fitch had mentioned was actually more of a restaurant than a bar. Sheila was skeptical that waste of a man had spent Saturday night here with gainfully employed members of society. The bartender, a clean-cut white kid with short brown hair named Austin, confirmed it. "Never seen that dude before. And I worked until close Saturday night. Mizzou game was on."

She pulled something out of her notebook. "You probably get a lot of people coming through here, don't you?"

"Yeah. Tons." He grinned at her. "And I got a great memory for faces. Names, not so good, but faces I remember."

She flipped over a photo and slid it across. He shook his head. She took back Johnny Gall's senior picture and slid across a head-shot of Euford Gunner.

"Oh, heck, yeah. Older than this picture, though. Tall, skinny guy wearing a cowboy hat. He carried himself like a star, you know? Not snooty or anything, but lots of stage presence."

"Anybody with him?" Sheila asked.

"I think so. But I'm not sure. The old guy was kinda dazzling, you know?" So he couldn't say if the purported Patrick O'Connell was with Gunner or not as he looked at the younger man's photo. "But, dude, a dead guy. That's just insane."

Sheila went through the rest of the high schoolers—he recognized the Barton and Schattgen kids as having come with family groups. He pointed to the last one in her pile.

"Her, yeah. She's been in here."

Sheila almost grabbed him by the shirt, she was so excited.

"When? When was she here?" She slid Emily Fitch's most recent mug shot across the gleaming wood.

"She used to come in a fair amount. Not so much anymore."

Sheila asked for every little thing he remembered about her. Austin closed his eyes, like he was replaying scenes in his mind. She was pretty hot. Long blond hair and blue eyes. She hung back, never sat up at the bar with the noisy crowd. Then she began to meet people. She always got here first and picked a table along the far wall. It was always somebody different who joined her. They'd have a conversation and then the other person would leave. She'd stay a bit and then go, too. But she hadn't been in for at least three or four months, he said. "Is she in trouble?"

Sheila didn't have time to list all the things BPD wanted Emily

Fitch for, which now included underage drinking. She wasn't twenty-one yet. Polite Austin insisted that he'd always checked, and she'd had ID. Sheila put the pictures into her notebook, wondering what kind of business Miss Emily Fitch was into.

THE three of them sat and stared at the conference table. And the birth certificate lying on it. Raker disappeared for a minute and returned with a battered laptop and the police chief. He slid the paper toward his boss and started pounding on his keyboard.

"This is Euford Gunner's real name?" Ed Utley, the Branson police chief, said. "And his kid's?"

"That last one's more of a question," Hank said. "Euford confirmed that's his real name. But *we* haven't confirmed this document is legit or that it pertains to Patrick O'Connell."

"Young man," Utley said, turning to Sam, "you're the one who tracked down the mystery high schooler's birth certificate? May I see it?"

The Pup handed it to the Branson chief. Utley pursed his lips as he studied it and then the Cluth document. He slid them both back to Sam and asked him to take the lead on figuring out whether the latter was also forged. Sam nodded emphatically.

Raker suddenly stopped typing, and the silence had everyone turning toward him.

"Searched that name you gave me of Euford's gofer lady," he said. "According to the Missouri Secretary of State, she's the registered agent for Entertainment Enterprises, LLC, a 'foreign entity.' Entertainment Enterprises has a corporate address in Delaware that's listed 'in care of' yet another business, Specialty Inquiries Ltd. It looks like it's nothing but a mailbox." He slammed the laptop closed. "That screams shell corporation and possible money laundering."

"I'd be curious what else Entertainment Enterprises bankrolls," Hank said. "They can't be making an entire business out of funding washed-up musical acts."

"I agree," said Utley. "Why would they bother to fund it, and what deal did Euford make to get it? Did he promise something he couldn't deliver?"

"But the show hasn't opened yet," Sam said. "How could he deliver whatever it is when he hasn't started earning money?"

Raker spun his laptop in a circle as he thought. "What if Patrick was killed to keep Euford in line? As a warning, maybe?"

"Or it's Patrick's involvement with Johnny Gall that put them both in danger. And Euford isn't the focus at all," said Hank.

Raker let out a sigh. "I don't think so. The Cluth birth certificate points to something on that front. Plus, we don't even know for sure he was the one seen hanging out with Gall."

Yet, Hank thought to himself. They didn't know for sure—yet.

SHEILA asked Dale Raker for everything BPD had on a certain young lady. Time to learn the details of one Fitch, Emily Jane.

An hour later, Sheila's head was spinning. This kid was a mobster in the making. She'd started with some shoplifting in her early teens, which resulted in a series of wrist slaps from the county's juvenile court judge. At seventeen, she was picked up with an older boy and four hundred fifty grams of pot—a full pound. She pleaded ignorant of the drugs and embarrassment at her choice in boyfriends. It worked—she got off with another warning. The older boy was convicted of drug trafficking.

After Emily left high school, three years ago, there was one more drug arrest. She once again managed to convince a judge that it was a boyfriend's fault. There was no question why. Sheila stared at the color photo attached to the file. Big, blue, guileless eyes in a heart-shaped face stared back. Golden hair curled around her face and down her shoulders. Sheila chuckled. They never could get over little blond white girls around here.

She opened the next file. Emily was upping her game. She was a suspect in three burglaries, the robbery of an old man walking his dog, and an ongoing fraud investigation. And she was thought to be one of the city's main suppliers of marijuana. But they'd never had enough evidence to charge her with anything. She'd become a ghost, one who'd gotten very, very good at hanging people out to dry. The file was littered with her used linen—the arrest records of people who were quite clearly not the brains behind the crimes.

Associating with Emily Fitch seemed guaranteed to bring nothing but misery.

SHEILA didn't recognize the number.

"Thank goodness you're there. Hank's not picking up. And I don't know how long she's going to be lucid."

"Maggie?"

"Yeah, it's me." Sheila could hear a code blue called over a loud-speaker in the background. "Lauren Blenkinship's awake. I'm headed up there now. She panicked when she saw the male ICU doctor. Hank had said you guys think she was attacked?"

"Yeah. Somebody was chasing her. Wouldn't surprise me if she's afraid of everybody she doesn't know at this point."

"That's what I thought," Hank's wife said. "So I figured maybe it'd be better for a nice, unthreatening woman to interview her."

Sheila couldn't agree more. She told Maggie she'd be there in ten minutes. It took her eight. Maggie was leaning against the wall outside the room, her hands in the pockets of her doctor's coat.

"Her parents are in with her," Maggie said softly. "They know you're coming. They were a little worried about how the question-ing would affect Lauren physically, so I said I'd be there, too. That all right with you?"

Sheila nodded, and the women walked into the room. Maggie stationed herself near the equipment monitoring Lauren's every function and smiled encouragingly at her patient.

"This is Deputy Turley. She needs to ask you some questions. We can take a break at any point. And I'll be here the whole time."

Lauren looked so tiny and ashen in the hospital bed that Sheila wanted to cry. Her left leg had metal pins coming out of it, and both arms were in casts.

Sheila scooted her chair close. "How about you call me Sheila, okay? It's really nice to meet you. Why don't we start with you just telling me what happened. From when you left your house?"

Lauren began to talk. She'd said she was spending the night at Kayla's, but she wasn't really. She was supposed to walk from her place over to the park by Kayla's house instead. And they'd pick her up about 8:30 p.m. in Matt Chorovich's minivan. Then they'd go over to an apartment Johnny knew about and hang out.

Then Lauren got a text from Johnny saying they'd be late. But she'd already left her house, so she'd walked down and back behind some of the houses at the edge of the subdivision where no one would see her and ask what she was doing. Finally, Johnny texted to say they were on their way. So she started for the park. It wasn't her normal route, but she was off in a different direction because of wandering around the creek. About halfway there, she started to feel like she was being followed. She cut over to the next street and then the next, but the man kept coming. By this point, she was terrified. And she could see him now. He was in all black, with a hoodie on so she couldn't see his face. She cut through one more yard, and that was when she heard him running.

She stopped, tears running down her face. Sheila leaned forward. "What happened then, sweetheart?"

"I took off. I was so scared. There weren't any more houses left, and I just started running through the woods . . . so scared. He was getting closer and closer. He almost caught me, but I thought I could make it. Then I fell and slammed down hard on the hill . . ." She trailed off. "That's all I remember."

Sheila gently put her hand on the poor thing's shaky left hand. "You're doing great. This is really important, and you're doing just great. Now, did you know who all was going to be there?"

"Well, Johnny. And Kayla." She smiled and didn't notice that no adult would meet her eyes. "And Matt. Maybe Alex Danzig."

"When Johnny texted you that last time, was it just to you? Or were other people on the text?"

She stared at the metal in her leg and thought. "It was more than me. There were phone numbers I don't have. So I don't know who else was on it. You can check my phone."

They hadn't been able to find her phone. Sheila didn't think she needed to know that. "How well did you know Johnny?"

He was new this year and, like, super cool. She'd said hi to him a couple of times, but that'd been about it until he invited her and Kayla to the thing on Saturday night.

"Do you know why Johnny would've invited Gabe Schattgen and Isaiah Barton?"

"Who? Them? I've got no idea. I never really saw Johnny hanging out with anybody in particular."

"What about Hailee Fitch?"

Lauren's nose wrinkled in distaste. "What about her?"

"She was there, too."

"What? She *was?* You're kidding, right? I would *not* have hung out with her, I swear."

"Did Johnny ever mention Hailee's sister?"

Lauren shook her head and then winced at the pain. "I don't even know if Johnny knew about Emily Fitch, since he was new to town." She paused. "What did Johnny say about it?"

Sheila spoke quickly, before anyone else could chime in.

"We haven't talked to him," she said. She was debating how far to continue the lie when Maggie caught her eye. She needed to end it. She'd gotten more time than she'd expected, considering how broken the poor kid's body was. She hoped they let it heal first, before they broke her heart by telling her about the car crash.

HANK stared at his brand-new Instagram account. He had no idea what he was doing. He tried searching for Johnny Gall and ended up following a Johnny Depp fan's account. Maggie walked into the living room, looked at the screen, and laughed.

"*Fifteen keys?* Your screen name is an Uncle Tupelo song?" she said with a smile.

"I didn't exactly want to be *BransonSheriff1* or something."

"Can't Sam do this? He knows it better, I'm assuming."

"Yeah, but I don't want to overwork him. He's still so fragile from Ted's shooting."

"Have you considered that maybe he's fragile because you've been babying him? If you're not trusting him to do things . . ."

"I trust him. I just worry that . . ."

She gave him her you're-being-obtuse look, just as Benny burst into the room and threw himself at Hank. "It's not just a three-year-old who thinks you're the greatest thing in the world. But Sam doesn't need a father to protect him. He needs a boss to believe in him."

Hank thought about that as Benny climbed all over him, and his wife went into the kitchen to start dinner. He'd never lost faith in the Pup. If anything, the kid seemed to have lost faith in himself. And maybe Hank had been handling him like spun glass.

Benny had managed to make it onto Hank's shoulders and was asking for a ride. They took the long way around the couch and into the kitchen, where Maggie stood over the stove.

"Sam'll be here in about an hour," she said.

"What?"

"I invited him over. For dessert and to help with Instagram."

Hank stared at her in exasperation.

"I'm not going to spend my rare evening off listening to you swear at the computer because you can't figure out anything and then start grousing about how old you're getting."

He wrapped his arms around her and nuzzled her ear. "It's like you don't even know me at all."

He'd just finished the dishes when the doorbell rang. Both kids and the dog stampeded toward the front foyer. Maribel opened the door and Guapo leaped. Sam barely managed to stay on his feet for the waggy, licky greeting. Hank hauled the devil dog away by his collar and apologized.

"That's all right." Sam laughed.

Hank shooed all three family members away and led Sam into the living room. Maggie appeared with two bowls of ice cream, a hug for Sam, and a kiss for Hank. Then she disappeared down the hall. Sam looked around the room. His gaze landed on Hank's laptop on the coffee table, open to the Instagram website. The Pup wiped his hand across his face. Hank suspected he was trying to hide a smile.

"You don't have to sugarcoat anything," he told his deputy. "I know I'm not any good at this stuff. So go ahead and laugh."

Sam grinned and pulled out his smartphone. "You do it on this. The whole point is that you take photos with your phone. Then you post them by using the app."

"Oh." Hank closed his laptop and retrieved his phone from the kitchen. Sam was already busy typing away. Hank downloaded the app, feeling like a very slow dinosaur. Sam looked up.

"Maybe you should just write down the stuff I find?"

Hank thought that was a great idea. He grabbed his notebook.

Alex Danzig's account was public, so they could see everything the high school senior had posted. Lots of band photos. *Star Wars* stuff. No photos had been posted the night of the crash.

Isaiah Barton didn't post many pictures of his own, instead just liking what others had posted. And Gabe Schattgen didn't appear to have an account at all. Johnny Gall had no account, and he didn't show up in photos posted on any of the boys' accounts.

Sam moved on to the girls. He couldn't find one for Hailee Fitch. "I think she's got one though, probably with an obscure username. Just so she could see if anybody posted stuff about her. It's a way to keep an eye out for if you're getting bullied online. Which she might have been."

Hank's heart started to hurt. He could barely stand to think about how miserable her life must have been, and how happy she must have been that night, to be going out with people she thought were friends. He dropped his head in his hands.

"Uh . . . you okay, Chief?"

Hank forced himself to look up. Because here was someone who was miserable, too, for different reasons. Sam'd been by Ted Pimental's side when Ted was shot by a fleeing suspect. Sam blamed himself. Which was completely wrong. "I'm okay. And I want for you to be, too. You're a good cop, and I hope you know that you're appreciated. And"—he pointed at Sam's phone—"also damn near indispensable. I'd still be trying to log in."

He grinned at his deputy, hoping to mitigate the touchy-feeliness of the moment. It worked. Sam grinned back, then logged out of his Instagram account and back in as Kayla Anderson. Her parents had given him their daughter's password and username. That was the only way to see what she shared with the few people for whom she'd approved access.

Hank moved so he could look over Sam's shoulder. Most pictures were of either Lauren Blenkinship or the BVHS marching

band goofing off. There were a few far-off shots of football players.
"Wait . . . stop. Go back." Sam obediently scrolled in reverse.
"There, in the background. Can you zoom in?"

Sam snapped a screenshot and from there, swiped to enlarge the
photo on two figures standing behind Kayla and Lauren as they
took a selfie at the edge of the school parking lot.

Johnny Gall and Patrick O'Connell were leaning insouciantly
against the fender of a black sports car.

HANK didn't recognize the number. And it was six in the morning. He stabbed at the button.

Seven minutes later he was out the door. Jenny Danzig had come
home.

He pulled up to her dilapidated house, blocking the pickup that
was in the dirt parking space. He ran his hands through his hair
on his way to the door. He shouldn't have worried. He still looked
better than the woman who answered the door.

"Who the hell are you? Get off my property. I got a gun."

"So do I, ma'am. And this." He showed his badge. Then he
"asked" her to step outside. She yanked a dangling tank-top strap
back onto her shoulder, and her dollar-store flip-flops slapped the
concrete as she descended the two front steps.

Yes, she was Jenny—Jennifer—Danzig, and yes, there was
someone else in the house. He was a gentleman friend, and he was
asleep. They'd been with friends in Springfield since Saturday.
Hank asked her about the brown sedan.

"Yeah, it's mine. What, did it get stolen? That kid."

Hank made an encouraging noise. "Kid?"

"My son. Alex. He borrowed it. He said it was an emergency.
So I left him the key under the flowerpot." That was about seven
thirty Saturday night, she estimated. "How'd he let it get stolen?"

Hank sidestepped. "Is your son dating anyone? Is that why he
needed the car? Who does he hang out with?"

"I don't know. We . . . aren't that close. He lives with his dad."

"I'm a little curious why your car is registered to your ex-husband's
address. Care to explain that?"

"The rates were lower. And I move around a lot."

"Do you have any mechanical problems with the car?"

"What the hell does that have to do with anything?"

His chest vise started to tighten. "Ms. Danzig, I need to tell you about Saturday night. There was an accident. Alex was driving. And he and his passengers were killed."

She hit him. Just hauled off and swung straight at him, walloping his upper arm and then shoving him smack in the chest with both hands. "Why didn't you tell me that first, you son of a bitch," she yelled. "What kind of monster are you?"

He'd been asking himself that question for the past three days.

SAM sat alone at the table in the sheriff's office crime lab in Forsyth. Staring at the bloody driver's license of one John Gall. The kid's birth certificate was a forgery, so it stood to reason the DL was, too. But he needed confirmation.

He placed the birth certificate for Evelyn Cluth, Jr., next to the license. This was all he had. It would sure help to also have Junior/ O'Connell's license, but his wallet was still missing. Sam'd run both Cluth and O'Connell through the appropriate Missouri, Kentucky, and Tennessee databases and come up empty. If only the guy had a criminal record. That was a quick nationwide search if you had a fingerprint, which they definitely had, seeing as O'Connell was currently lying in the morgue.

He smiled to himself. This might be the first time he'd wished someone was a criminal. Instead, it looked like this guy was doing what a lot of folks in early adulthood did, loafing around and goofing off. It was . . .

Sam stood suddenly. It was a shot so long, it'd be a miracle if it found its target. But if it did . . . He ran out to his squad car and headed toward Branson.

BY THE time Sam pulled into the parking lot, the go-kart track was starting to gear up for the day. It was one of several that dotted Branson's lengthy main drag. This was the only one advanced enough to require a valid driver's license.

Sam strode up to the ticket booth. He had to bang twice on the closed window before someone came. "We're closed, dude. You gotta— Oh, hey, Sammy. Daaaamn." He gave the uniformed Sam a once-over. "I'd heard you was police now, but I didn't believe it. Never woulda thunk it, huh?"

Sam really hated running into people from high school. "Hey, Trevor, how's it going?"

"Man, you ever shot somebody? How about arrested?"

Sam bit back a groan and held up his hand in what he hoped wasn't too rude a way. He explained what he needed, and Trevor let Sam into the little office behind the booth.

"It's a pretty tricky track. So we gotta card everybody. And the boss makes us copy all the licenses. For insurance, maybe? I dunno. Anyway, we keep a couple months back, more or less." He slapped a big box down on the desk.

One hundred and eighty-two sheets of paper later, Sam's long shot hit the mark. The face of his murder victim stared up at him. The name was Gavin Patrick O'Connell. And the license was from Minnesota. This guy really got around.

Sam flipped to the next sheet, just to see if his entire theory was correct. And it was. Because there *he* was—Johnny Gall. They'd come to the track together. He started to pull out the sheet and stopped. It wasn't Johnny Gall. It was John Kalin. A New Mexico license. With an age of twenty-two.

This must be the ID used to rent the apartment. Sam carefully removed the two copies from the stack. He let out a long, slow breath and headed out. Seconds later he was back, grabbing the whole box for "investigatory purposes," he told Trevor sternly. He left his high school past gawking at him as he cruised out of the parking lot, solid gold evidence on the seat beside him.

A woman who looked like she should be selling expensive cosmetics and hollow gold jewelry on a TV shopping network was standing in the otherwise empty parking lot when Sheila and Dale Raker pulled in. She did not look happy to be there. She also didn't look like the stage manager for a country music show.

They both eyed her warily as they sat in Dale's unmarked BPD car.

"We're supposed to meet somebody named Frank Rasmussen," Dale said. "That does not look like a Frank."

Sheila laughed. "I think that's the travel agent who arranged Euford's house. But I've got no idea what she's doing here."

A bland Nissan rental sedan pulled into the lot and parked a few spaces away. A slightly paunchy man of medium height got out. He was wearing black jeans and a Steely Dan T-shirt. Dale shook his head. "He looks almost as out of place as she does."

"Well," Sheila said, "at least he's the right gender."

They climbed out of the car, and the man strode over. "You guys the cops?" He stuck out his hand. "I'm Frank. Just rolled into town. Got an email saying that you'd probably stop by today. How you doin'?"

They introduced themselves, and Dale asked if he had a key. Rasmussen fished out a ring full of them, saying the construction company had sent them along. Dale nodded. The folks at the company were the reason they knew Rasmussen was coming.

"So why you guys here? Was there a break-in or something?"

Dale smoothed down his wrinkled tie. "Someone who was involved in the refurbishment of this theater was murdered over the weekend. So we'd like to just take a look around inside."

"Damn. That's crazy. In this little place?" Rasmussen seemed to notice Vivian Gillam for the first time. "Uh, can we help you? Are you with them?"

Gillam folded her hands primly in front of her.

"I am *not* with them. I am here as a representative of the show's financiers. So I'll be coming inside with you."

Rasmussen shrugged and headed for the door. Dale followed, but Sheila moved aside, forcing Gillam to go in front of her.

The little group made its way into the theater, and Rasmussen disappeared. Seconds later, the house lights came on, and then after a bit, the stage lights.

Rasmussen reappeared, smacking his hands together happily and pointing out features. Sheila surreptitiously gestured for Dale to take the stage manager. She wasn't leaving Gillam's side.

The older woman was trying to disguise the fact that she didn't know where best to stand in order to observe everything the pesky police were doing. Eventually, she walked down the aisle to the stage, with Sheila right behind.

Dale disappeared. Sheila knew he'd be searching Euford's brand-new dressing room.

"Shouldn't you be asking the manager questions?" Gillam said without turning from her inspection of the stage curtains.

"Oh, we'll get to him. Right now, I'm more interested in you."

Gillam pivoted slowly. "I have nothing to say to you."

"Who's your contact person at Entertainment Enterprises?" Sheila said. "How'd they get in touch with you in the first place? Where are they headquartered? How much are they paying you? Do show payments go through you, too? How closely do you monitor Euford Gunner?"

Gillam stepped back in surprise at the barrage. She angrily jabbed a finger at Sheila. "I don't have to answer your questions. I don't have to talk to you at all. This is harassment."

"No. This is obstruction. We are conducting a homicide investigation. That overrides *everything*." Sheila drew out the last word. "So you can answer me now, or you can wait until I come back with an expanded search warrant for all your business records. If you'd rather do the warrant, I get it. It might make it easier for your shadowy bosses to understand why you talked. So that's why I'm going to be nice, stop asking you questions, and allow you to sit yourself down in the front row there until we're done."

Gillam took a seat just as Dale hollered from the back.

Sheila found him just where she thought—Euford's palatial dressing room. Why did one man think he needed a space the size of a racquetball court just to get ready for a show?

"It'll be a lot more crowded in here." Rasmussen popped out from a door on the right, smiling at her expression. "There'll be costume racks, and makeup and hair people, and all the guitars."

He closed the door, which led to a bathroom, and slipped out behind Sheila and back toward the stage. She turned to Dale, who was crawling underneath the brightly lit counter that lined the wall on the left. "What the hell are you doing?"

"I need an evidence bag."

Men. Never carried what they might need. She whipped one out and placed it in his hand. At least he'd remembered gloves. She pulled on a pair of her own as she waited. Finally, he hefted himself to his feet and dangled a bagged cell phone in front of her. The case was sparkly blue paisley. He punched the home button through the bag. The screen lit up with the smiles of Lauren Blenkinship and Kayla Anderson. Sheila let out a whistle.

"I know," Dale said. "What the hell is the phone of a girl chased almost to her death doing in a locked-up-tight theater?"

Dale handed her the bag and dug his own phone out of his pocket. While he called the BPD evidence techs, she poked her head under the counter and then walked its length. When Dale got off the phone, he found her crouched so she was at eye level with its surface. "You evaluating the quality of the granite?"

"Shush," she said. "I'm looking at the dust. There isn't much, but see"—she straightened and moved over, almost to where Dale had found the phone on the floor, and pointed to a faint smear— "it looks like maybe a bag or something was set here. The phone might have fallen out."

Dale nodded. "I can't wait to see what fingerprints are in here. The guys are on their way. And Chief Utley himself is working on getting a search warrant for the whole building. It seemed like it's probably going to be necessary, considering the hassle that fancy lady was giving you."

Sheila grinned. This day was getting better all the time.

THERE was a shuffling sound from the doorway. The Pup. Hank waved him into his office. "So, what's up, Sammy?"

"Um . . . yeah. I found it." He held up a box full of haphazardly stacked papers. He set it on the desk and handed Hank the top two sheets. Then he smiled. For real. Genuine happiness from within.

Hank took the papers and stared. Unbelievable. He looked from the xeroxed faces of Johnny Gall/Kalin and Patrick O'Connell back up to his deputy. "How on earth did you find these?"

Another smile. "Go-karts. You wanna do the big one, you gotta have a license." He patted the box. "It's a pretty popular ride."

"You're a genius," Hank said. "I mean it."

Sam stood a little straighter. "New Mexico has no record of issuing an ID to one John Kalin. Or Johnny Gall, for that matter."

"What about Minnesota?" Hank held up O'Connell's copy.

"Same deal," Sam said. He had also been working on the Cluth Junior birth certificate. The clerk from the issuing county could find no obvious errors, but had no record of it in her archives.

Hank nodded. "Why don't you check with the state vital records department, too, just to be sure there wasn't a mistake on the county end. And I'll get going on trying to track down the woman listed as the mother."

SHEILA was exhausted. It'd taken all day to process Euford's dressing room and the rest of the backstage area. Which had been a whole lot of boring. The only gratification had been hearing that one of the prints in the dressing room was a match for Johnny Gall. So he'd been there. As had Patrick O'Connell, of course.

She flopped down on the bed with a groan. The funerals started tomorrow. They would have to send representatives to all of them. And it couldn't be Hank, with guilt oozing out of him like radioactive waste. It couldn't be Sammy, not with his shaved head and tortured scowl. It would have to be her. Maybe she could distract Hank with his conspiracy investigation. Which, she was reluctantly starting to admit, looked like it might amount to something. The mysterious Johnny Gall was obviously linked to the mysterious Patrick O'Connell. Who was possibly Cluth Junior.

She sat bolt upright. Had they ordered a DNA test on O'Connell's body? If they could answer that damn question once and for all, it would clarify the kid's motivation, and everybody would be happier—including her boss. She'd get him started on that in the morning. It was the perfect diversion from the funerals.

THE argument lasted an hour. There was a significant amount of yelling, a lot of arm waving, and some swearing.

She'd come in prepared. Perfectly calm and professional, probably fortified by a good breakfast of Wheaties or something equally appalling. How was Hank supposed to compete with that when he'd had nothing but half of a frozen waffle and what felt like an accumulated six hours sleep in the past five nights?

And now she was turning to leave. To go to the first funeral. He couldn't find any more words as she walked out his office door. He was glaring at the numerous stacks of paper on his cluttered desk when his cell rang.

"There were no prints on Lauren Blenkinship's phone," Raker said. "Not even hers."

"So it was wiped," Hank said.

"Yep. Which is not an innocent act, as far as I'm concerned."

Hank agreed. "What about what's in the phone? Her texts?"

"There are a few things of value. The text string from Saturday night had five people on it. Alex Danzig, Kayla Anderson, Gabe Schattgen, Johnny Gall, and Lauren. I'll email you a transcript, but basically it's planning the meeting. Various whining about Matt Chorovich not being able to drive, then Alex coming through with his mother's car. They readjust the timeline and agree to meet at that park at eight thirty."

Hank interrupted. "According to Sheila's interview with her, Lauren had already left her house by that point. She killed time by wandering around down by the creek until about eight fifteen."

"Right. During that time period, she sent one text to just Kayla telling her that. *Just walking around.* With a bored emoji."

At eight thirty, Raker continued, Kayla sent a text to the group asking Lauren where she was. There was no response. Just after that message, Johnny texted with a request that they pick him up farther up James Epps Road and 248. Kayla then asked if Lauren was with him. Johnny responded, *It's cool.*

"That," Raker said with an edge to his voice, "makes me think Kayla thought that was a yes—that Lauren was with him."

Hank agreed.

"And this is the kicker," Raker said. "At nine oh two, Kayla sent a text just to Lauren. *I hope you feel better. I'll talk to you tomorrow,* and a kissy-face emoji."

"What?" Hank said. "You're kidding."

"Nope. The only thing I can figure is that someone—say, the one who joined the group last, like Gall—delivered a message that Lauren wasn't feeling well and had gone home."

"You've got to be right. But it doesn't tell us whether Johnny just made that up to get the evening going, or whether he knew Lauren had been chased and forced down a steep hill."

Hank asked if there were any other texts. Not on the group chat, Raker said. He had the phones belonging to the crash victims, but three of them had been damaged too badly to retrieve anything, two of them were working but locked and the parents were pondering what their kids' passcodes could be, and no one had any idea what Gall's code was.

"And we still haven't found Patrick O'Connell's phone."

"No." Raker sighed. "There is a little good news, I guess. We found O'Connell's fingerprints in the theater dressing room, which we expected. But we also found Johnny Gall's."

"More proof those two knew each other," Hank said. And more proof that Johnny Gall was key to this whole thing. He started to say that and then stopped. Before he harped on it with Raker again, there was one thing he wanted to check first.

Chapter 8

Sam was starting to hate identification documents. Especially out-of-state ones. Different seals, different colors, different layouts. He was on day two of combing through every single detail. The conference room table was covered in samples of different counties' birth certificates, scrawled phone messages on sticky notes, two laptops, and cold french fries left from his lunch.

He decided to switch over to tracking down the mother listed on Cluth Junior's Tennessee birth certificate. The chief had tasked him with that this morning. He pecked at his laptop for a minute. Pamela Helbing didn't have a driver's license in Missouri. Which wasn't surprising. Even, on the about two percent chance that she lived in the state, the odds that she still had the same last name as seventeen years ago were infinitesimal.

Sam looked at the paperwork mess in front of him. A groan bubbled up in his throat.

EUFORD was taking forever to answer the door. Hank started to think maybe there was something to him needing a helpmate around the house. The huge oak entry finally swung open. Behind it, the musician leaned heavily on his cane. He settled himself on the same leather sofa he'd used two days before. Hank sat across from him and asked how he was doing.

"Horrible. It's so quiet." He looked like he hadn't slept since Hank was there last. The lean lines of a distinguished old cowboy had withered into gauntness.

"When was the last time you ate?" Hank asked.

Euford couldn't remember. Hank walked over to the kitchen tucked behind an island along the far wall and rummaged through the refrigerator. Vegetables, organic yogurt, cage-free eggs.

He turned toward Euford. "Who did the grocery shopping?"

Euford blinked, puzzled. "That coordinator lady who found us the house. Why the hell does that matter?"

Vivian Gillam. That's what he'd thought. He turned back to the crisper. He stacked together a ham sandwich on gourmet cracked wheat bread and brought it out to the singer, using a paper towel as a plate. Euford thanked him, devoured half of it in about thirty seconds, and then thanked him again. When he was finished, he carefully folded the paper towel and set it on the coffee table before looking at Hank.

"So why else you here, Sheriff? If it was with news, you would've said already."

"True," Hank said. "I don't have any new developments. But I need to ask you something. We need you to take a DNA test."

Euford sat back and sighed. "I had a feeling y'all might come and ask me that," he said. "And I'm going to have to say no."

Hank leaned forward. "And why is that?"

"I don't want to know. If he was my son. He was . . . he was what he was to me, and I don't need to put any label on it."

"Now, Mr. Gunner . . . I respect how you feel, but there's more than just a personal concern involved here. We need to know for the investigation. We're trying to figure out who killed him."

Euford looked him full on. "If he was my kid, and didn't tell me . . . why? Did he decide I wasn't worthy? And if he wasn't my son and was gonna tell me that he was, then it was a con. Either way turns out bad for me, so I don't want to know."

How could someone argue with that? It was time to take a break. "Tell me again about Entertainment Enterprises," Hank said, after getting them both bottles of lemonade out of the fridge.

The company was financing his show. It had paid for the renovation of the Country Song Theater and was footing the bill for the house rental. He would get paid a straight salary—four grand a week, with eight weeks off a year. It was the first steady, guaranteed paycheck he'd had in fifty-two years.

"Did Entertainment Enterprises come to you, or did you go to them?"

"They came to us," Euford said. He swigged at his lemonade. "Patrick said it was the perfect solution. Branson—a town that draws just the kind of folk who'd want to come and see me."

Hank asked who Euford'd met from the company.

"Oh, everything was done through Ms. Gillam."

Of course it was. Her perfectly manicured fingers seemed to touch everything in this case. Hank would have to go back to her. Which made the lemonade in his stomach churn. He cleared away the empty bottles; then he thanked the old singer for his time—and followed it with a warning. "I'm going to have to get a warrant for your DNA, sir. I understand your position, but my investigation has to take precedence."

Euford managed a small, sad smile. He shook Hank's hand and started for the door. Hank watched him carefully as he limped out of the great room. How infirm was he really? Could he have made it up a flight of stairs at an apartment complex? With a knife? Because if it had been a con, and the old man found out . . .

"WELL, my boy, what fresh craziness do you have for me today regarding this case?" Judge Sedstone said as he gestured for Hank to have a seat in his chambers.

Hank explained the DNA and Euford-slash-Evelyn's refusal. Sedstone stared at the ceiling, which was a little worrying.

"That's a big thing, to force a man to turn over the very building blocks of himself. Why do you need to know whether this O'Connell is related to Gunner?"

Hank explained that a DNA test would help to clarify motive in the homicide case. The results could also help with identifying O'Connell.

Sedstone pursed his lips. "Nothing's stopping you from getting O'Connell's DNA. You don't need a warrant for that. But I can't—right now—see that you need Mr. Gunner's. Now, I'm not shutting the door on you completely. If you come up with new evidence, bring it back to me and we'll talk about it."

"I NEED to ask you some questions, Sheriff."

Hank stopped in surprise. The *Daily What's-It* newspaper reporter stood in the parking lot in the rapidly falling darkness. He must have been lying in wait. "Uh, hi, Jadhur. What's up?"

Jadhur cleared his throat and readied his notebook. "I'm working on a follow-up story about the accident out north of the Ozark Mountain Highroad and—"

"You should check in with the Highway Patrol. They're conducting the investigation."

Hank stepped to the side. Jadhur moved with him. "They're not going to be able to comment on the traffic stop that happened before," he said. "Your office stopped the car right before the accident and then let them go with too many kids in the car?"

How did the kid find this stuff out? "I can't comment on an ongoing investigation, Jadhur. I'm sorry, but—"

"Look. I've confirmed that there was a traffic stop and that no ticket was written. And I'm hearing scuttlebutt that you're the one who did it. Is that true?"

Hank drew himself up to his full height. Time to own it.

"Yes. I was the one who conducted the traffic stop on Saturday night. At that point, I judged that the situation would be best handled by sending all of the occupants straight home. They weren't going too far over the limit. They were all sober. They were all respectful and polite. I decided that a good lecture would have the right kind of impact on them. Kids make mistakes."

Jadhur nodded. "The county commissioners are pretty upset, and one of them's saying that you shouldn't keep your job. Sent me a statement and everything. Do you want to respond?"

Hank could feel a flush crawl up his face. "They have no authority over me. I was duly elected by voters this summer."

"Oh, I know," Jadhur said. "I'll point that out. Don't worry."

Hank trudged toward his car. The county commission didn't have any control over him, but it had a whole lot over his budget. He sank into the driver's seat and rested his head on the steering wheel. He needed a minute before he drove home.

SAM could feel the building emptying out, growing quiet. All the documents in front of him on the conference table weren't going anywhere, though. He had at least heard back from Tennessee, which confirmed that it had record of Evelyn Cluth, Jr., being born in Nashville seventeen years ago. He had to laugh. The one document so far that was actually legit might not even belong to one of the people involved in this whole mess.

Tennessee had also confirmed that Pamela Helbing, the mother on Junior's birth certificate, had records that matched her information on her son's birth certificate. She was born in Nashville forty-six years ago. There were no hits on her name and DOB in the national NCIC database. Tennessee and Missouri databases had no state criminal records on her.

He sat back and sighed. And started thinking about the murder. It was the only thing the whole darn county had been talking about for the past five days. Well, that and the crash.

He wondered how the chief was doing. If he'd been the one to stop those kids, he probably would've let them go, too. He didn't know if he could take it if he was in the chief's spot right now. He was barely keeping it together being responsible for Pimental's injuries. He ran his hand over his stubbled head without realizing it. And then he gave up, shut down his computer, and turned out the lights.

THE sun was just starting to split the darkness the next morning when Hank pulled over to the side of the road. The headlights lit up the boulder for a split second before he quickly flipped them off. He climbed out of the car and walked over. No one could miss this curve in the road now.

A half-dozen Mylar balloons bobbed in the air, glowing pink in the sunrise. Stuffed animals sat around the rock two and three deep. A cross fashioned out of fence pickets had been hammered into the ground. And a huge red ribbon wound around the boulder itself. He knelt and stared at the cards, which ran the gamut. Folded construction paper with handwritten messages, fancy Hallmark cards in colored envelopes, scrapbooky things with stamps and raised cutouts. There was even one of those little kid diaries, purple-and-green striped, with a lockable clasp.

Hank sat down in the dirt. He opened a card and blinked the blurriness in his eyes away.

Kayla, I'll always remember being together in band. We had a lot of fun, and it won't be the same without you. Love, Annie

He sat there and kept reading. With the exception of the ones that listed all six names, there wasn't a single one for Hailee. Even Johnny Gall had a few. He put those aside and reached for the little diary. His handcuff key easily popped it open. It was blank except for a drawing on the very last page. Hands from two different people, clasped together like they were walking along. It was done in pencil, slashes and curves in an abstract kind of style. He closed the book and clicked the lock shut, feeling like he'd violated someone's privacy. But whose, he didn't know.

He pulled out the evidence bag he'd brought. He'd originally intended to take every note at the site. But now as he sat in the dirt, he knew. All the evidence collection in the world wasn't going to help him. His guilt wasn't going to magically go away. Nothing was going to save him from this awful black hole.

SHEILA set down the newspaper. She didn't get it at home, so she hadn't seen it until she got into work. Sam had been waiting for her in her office and handed it to her wordlessly.

She rubbed her temples. "Now the whole county knows Hank stopped that car and let them go. Have you heard from him?"

Sam shook his head. "I'm really worried about him. How can we get it through to him that the crash wasn't his fault?"

Sheila nodded. "That's what I've been saying. But he's not listening." Kind of like Sammy hadn't been listening for the past four months since Ted Pimental got shot. She leaned forward. "You know, Sammy, that's a good point. Things happen that we aren't necessarily in control of."

"What're you getting at?"

"You tell me."

He hunkered down in his chair. "We're talking about the chief." She raised an eyebrow.

"C'mon, Sheila. I don't want to talk about this."

"You're as much a mess as Hank. You're letting Ted's shooting destroy you. You've got to stop. You couldn't have prevented it."

"But if I'd run faster, if I—"

She slapped her hand on the desk. "You're not Superman. You—or Ted—weren't going to outrun a bullet." She knew she was pounding at him, but she didn't know what else to do. "And," she continued, "Ted would've died if you hadn't been right there to cinch his leg and stop that artery from bleeding out."

Sam stared at his shoes. Sheila quietly got up and left the room. She'd done what she could. Now it was up to him.

"I FIGURE this time breakfast's on me," Dale said over the phone. "Because you're about to have one awful day."

Sheila agreed on both things and met him at the Cracker Barrel at 76 and Little Pete Road. She passed up her usual scrambled eggs and single slice of bacon and dug straight into the huge fried goodness of a Sunrise Sampler. She was halfway through it before she paused to ask Dale what was new on his end of things.

"You mean aside from the whole world knowing what Hank Worth did? Or didn't do, rather."

She glared at him. "That isn't even your department's problem."

"Thank goodness," he said. "How'd Hank take the news story?"

"I haven't talked to him yet today," she said. It'd be more accurate to say she hadn't been able to get a hold of him, but she wasn't going to admit that. "So, you made any progress yet?"

"Nope. Hoping to soon, though. I've been trying to go through a bunch of financial records. And I think I'm going to bring ol' Euford in for a formal chat here soon."

"Really? What new stuff do you have?"

"Nothing. That's why I want to bring him in. Try to shake him loose. No one else in this town knew O'Connell. So who would kill him? And before you say anything, yes, there's the whole Johnny Gall question. Was the murderer really after Gall and O'Connell just got in the way? I don't know. We got less on Gall than we do on O'Connell. So, Euford's it."

"When are you planning to have this chat?"

"Later today. You can come if you want."

"Hell, yes," she said. "But can you do it real late this afternoon? I've got two funerals before then."

"I know." Dale's look was a mix of sympathy and glad-it's-not-me relief. "Which two?"

"Kayla and Gabriel. Hailee Fitch is tomorrow."

"I wonder if Emily will show," Dale said.

"I'm wondering the same thing. You want to come with me, just in case she does come?"

"I'd love to," he said. "I guess that's one suspect interrogation in exchange for a victim funeral. We're quite the pair, aren't we?"

Sam attacked his paper-strewn conference room with more energy than he'd had in months. He straightened it and then rearranged it, hoping different stacks of things would lead to new inspiration. It didn't work. He needed to go back to the beginning.

What did they know? Nothing about Johnny Gall. Patrick O'Connell was a little better. They did know for sure that four years ago, he'd approached Mr. Gunner at a nightclub in Nashville. His go-cart copy ID listed his current age as twenty-one.

If that was true, he would've been a minor that night he met Mr. Gunner in Nashville. A minor who didn't have anybody who cared about him. Because if he had parents who gave a hoot, they would've reported him as a runaway, and he'd be in the FBI's national database. Which he wasn't.

And if he didn't have parents, he'd be what—up for adoption or in foster care, right? Sam started pounding on a laptop. The state of Tennessee had a searchable list—complete with photos—of children in need of adoption. He entered gender and age search parameters for O'Connell. Nothing, which wasn't too surprising. If he'd aged out, his photo wouldn't still be up. Sam found the contact page and punched a number into his phone.

An hour later, he had a digital file with scores of old photos. Boys who'd been removed from the website because they'd either gotten adopted or aged out before they could be. He ignored the names and concentrated on the faces. Forty minutes in, a younger and very angry Patrick stared back at him from the computer. Sam reached out and touched the screen. He'd found him.

Eric Michael Ganton. Born nineteen years ago this coming December. Which would've made him fifteen when he met Mr. Gunner. No wonder he had a fake ID.

Ganton had entered foster care at age two and bounced around for years. He didn't stay in one place very long until he was about fourteen. Then things seemed to settle down, and he stayed with that foster family until he aged out almost two years ago.

Sam frowned. That wasn't right. Either Mr. Gunner was lying about when he met the kid, or that foster family, which got money from the government every month to care for their charge, had never bothered to report that he'd run away.

He needed to see if Nashville PD would send someone to have

a chat with these foster parents. And while that was in the works, he'd go ask Mr. Gunner a few more questions.

SAM pulled up in front of the massive house. It took Mr. Gunner five minutes to answer the door. Sam politely followed him into the big living room. This time he got to sit on one of the nice leather couches. He hadn't known furniture could be that comfortable.

Mr. Gunner didn't look quite as comfortable as he sank into the opposite sofa. His foot must be acting up. He settled himself, propping the cane next to him and adjusting his legs, then gestured for Sam to speak. Sam started to ask his first question but then stopped. The chief would want to put the old man at his ease.

"Does it bother you more when it's about to rain?" he asked, waving toward the gray sky visible through the wall of windows.

It did, Mr. Gunner said. Could always tell when a storm was coming, ever since he broke it. They talked of that, and arthritis, and the wear and tear that touring caused to a body. And Sam could see the old man relax. So Sam switched gears and asked the first question off the list he'd carefully written out in the car.

"Have you ever heard the name Eric Michael Ganton?"

Mr. Gunner shook his head. "Y'all keep throwing names at me. I don't know. I never heard that one before."

"You never heard anybody call Patrick by the name 'Eric'?"

"Nope. Wait. Are you telling me that's his real name? Why'd he say his name was Patrick then?"

Sam didn't answer. He'd get to that. Had Patrick ever talked about being in foster care? Mr. Gunner didn't seem to understand that one.

"He turned eighteen and his parents tossed him out," Mr. Gunner said. "Happens all the time."

Sam shook his head. Eric Michael had spent almost his entire life in the foster care system. When he was fifteen, he ran away from the Strasburgers' home. "And met you," Sam said.

"He was only fifteen? I never would've let him come with me." He looked at Sam in fright. "I didn't know. I swear."

Sam was pretty sure he was telling the truth. Why would a country music star make trouble for himself by taking in a runaway? More questions didn't turn up any additional information.

Sam offered to see himself out so the old man wouldn't have to get up. Mr. Gunner gratefully nodded. Sam said a mental goodbye to the sofa and rose to his feet.

Once he was out of Gunner's sight, he slowed down. He wanted to look at the amazing house. He couldn't get over the huge back wall of windows. The place was still neat but was starting to show signs of clutter. A sweatshirt draped over the banister, a pair of running shoes over by the back sliding glass door. He supposed it was because Patrick/Eric wasn't around anymore to straighten up.

He let himself out and was halfway across the driveway when his phone buzzed with Sheila's ringtone.

"Where are you?" she asked.

"I'm just leaving Euford Gunner's house."

"What?"

"Yeah. I had some questions for him about O'Connell. Ganton. The murder victim. Did you get my text about his real ID?"

"I just did. I was at Gabriel Schattgen's funeral," she said.

"I tried to call the chief, too," Sam said. "I couldn't get a hold of him. I do have more info on Ganton. Do you want it now?"

"No. What I want you to do is bring Gunner in."

Sam's jaw fell open. "What? You mean arrest him?"

"No. Just tell him we want to interview him down at Branson PD. Just a few more questions."

"I don't think he's going to be real thrilled with that."

"Yeah, well, we hadn't figured that he'd already have been asked a bunch of questions," she said. "So you say whatever you need to say, but get him in here."

She hung up. Sam went and knocked on the door. Again.

SHEILA was halfway through explaining to Dale about Sammy's interview of Gunner when she realized that she hadn't complimented the kid for ID'ing the murder victim. She wasn't sure how he'd done it, but it was brilliant work. Her supervisor work, not so much. She had to pull herself together, because she was the only one left in the department with any damn sense. And now Dale was cranky, thinking that his haul-him-in-for-questioning plan with Gunner might be a failure because who knew what Sammy might have given away about the investigation.

"It'll be fine. Sam won't have ruined anything," she said. "We'll let Gunner cool in an interview room for a bit while we get up to speed on what Sam asked him. It's fine."

Dale frowned. So she told him about the confirmed ID of his homicide victim. That went a long way toward restoring his good humor. When Sammy got there and explained how he'd tracked down O'Connell's real name, Dale was so pleased he only gave a mild lecture about checking in with *all* investigating officers before interviewing a key witness-slash-suspect.

After Dale waddled off to double-check that the sound equipment was working in the interview room, Sheila turned to Sam.

"That was brilliant. And I should've told you so over the phone. You might've broke the whole case open. I'm really impressed."

Sam seemed to grow three inches. She smiled and explained that she needed him to watch the interview from outside the room, because this was Dale's case. It wasn't because Sam wasn't qualified to be in there. Sam nodded and left to go grab a Coke, with a bounce in his step that she hadn't seen in a long time.

Dale returned, straightened his rumpled tie, and entered the interview room. Sheila followed and saw Gunner sitting there, shrunken and nervous. She closed the door firmly behind her.

WHERE was everybody? The halls were empty, and the coffeepot hadn't even been used. It was just as well. Hank didn't want to talk to anyone, anyway. He walked through Sheila's office to get to his own and suddenly stopped. The *Daily What's-It* lay on her desk. He took a deep breath and picked it up.

Jadhur's article was the lead story. It was brutal. He interviewed relatives of the dead teens and talked about Hank's traffic stop. Hank sat down at his desk and tossed the paper aside. It wasn't like he didn't deserve public vilification. He did.

He carefully laid the evidence bag on his blotter. He wasn't sure why he'd taken the diary. He did know why he'd taken the cards addressed to Gall, though. He slid everything out of the bag.

Johnny, I'm glad I got to know you. Love, Simone
Super Cool Johnny, I'm going to miss you. – Paula
Johnny, You were awesome. I wish you'd come to Branson sooner.
Love, Trish

Several more of the same. All girls. None of them said anything actually personal, however. It was like they'd judged him from afar and found him worth wanting to know.

He reached for the last one in the stack. It was a plain white envelope, not addressed to anyone. Inside was a plain white card with no words. Just a drawing. A figure, turned away from the viewer. The head was bowed and no facial features were visible, but the hair fell in a loose and shaggy sweep that resembled a seventies punk rocker. Or Johnny Gall. It was a remarkable rendering for a bunch of slashy lines and abstract shadings.

Hank set it down carefully and opened the diary to the page with the similarly styled drawing of the hands. Then he picked up his desk phone and called the crime lab. Kurt Gatz hustled over immediately and promised a quick result. A half hour later, he returned with nothing. No fingerprints on either item. Hank almost smiled.

Now he just needed to figure out where his staff was. He checked his cell and realized it was turned off. He powered it up and headed out the door.

Chapter 9

SAM SETTLED IN BEHIND the two-way mirror, glad he was here to observe this interview. He hadn't seen Mr. Raker work, and the more styles of police work he observed the better.

Mr. Raker took a seat across the little table from Mr. Gunner. Sheila leaned against the wall and crossed her arms.

Mr. Gunner looked really old under the fluorescent lights. He also did not look happy. "I just talked to that kid. Answered his questions. Why'd you make me come all the way in here?"

Mr. Raker nodded pleasantly and said that he had some additional things to talk about. He opened the file folder lying in front of him. He slid a piece of paper across the table.

"This is a medical record from your doctor in Georgia. The one you went to for follow-up care after you broke your ankle in Fort Worth. It says that the fractures of the 'medial and lateral malleolus' healed pretty much perfectly. The physical therapist you went to gave you a clean bill of health."

"That don't mean I don't have problems with my ligaments and such," Gunner said. "And changes in the weather."

Mr. Raker nodded. "I'm sure it can act up on occasion."

Sam noticed Gunner's bum foot slowly twisting more to the outside. It was the opposite of the Branson detective, who leaned back in his chair, all relaxed.

"Let's talk about Entertainment Enterprises, Inc."

Gunner rolled his eyes. "I already talked to you about them. I told you that I deal with Ms. Gillam, and that's it."

"Yeah, I remember," Mr. Raker said. "But I found out a few interesting things as I was . . . familiarizing myself with the company. For instance, it's registered in Delaware to a front, and Delaware law says we don't get to know who really owns it. Which doesn't make sense to me. If you were helping bring business to Branson, wouldn't you be proud of that? Wouldn't you want folks to know who you are?" The detective leaned forward, very close to Gunner. "So I'm asking you, Euford—do you know who's backing you? Do you know where the money is coming from?"

Mr. Gunner shook his head. Mr. Raker stayed in front of his face and started rattling off numbers. The theater renovations had cost close to two million dollars. His salary for a season of shows was almost two hundred thousand dollars, and that didn't even include the band, or the theater staff. The house rental was four grand a month. All that probably totaled three million. At least.

"You think you're worth that?" Raker said. "I don't."

The old man flinched.

"And," Mr. Raker kept on, "you're not even really advertising. Or whoever's fronting this thing isn't. Which we both know isn't how this whole business works. So who's funneling money through you, Euford? Drug runners? Counterfeiters?"

"You're a lunatic," Gunner said. "I come here to do a show and all a sudden I'm running drugs? I'm leaving. You can't hold me."

Mr. Raker didn't move. "You misunderstand. I'm not saying you're running the drugs. I'm saying you're passing along all that money you're making. I want to know who you're giving it to."

"Nobody's asked me to do anything like that." Gunner was on his feet. Sheila stepped forward. He glared at her. "Unless y'all are arresting me, get the hell outta my way."

He stomped—carefully—out of the room. As the door shut behind him, Sheila smiled. "It's a pleasure to watch you work."

Mr. Raker nodded graciously, then put in a call to patrol to have them follow Gunner when he left the building.

Sheila waved at the mirror. "Sammy, come on in here."

When he got inside, she took a seat in the chair Gunner had just vacated.

"Tell us what you saw," she said. She nodded encouragingly.

"He was moving his foot."

They both looked confused.

"What I mean is," Sam said quickly, "that he kept moving his injured ankle. He was twisting it, in a kind of way that looked really uncomfortable, like he was trying to make it worse."

Mr. Raker was interested. "Was he doing it the whole time?"

"No. Just once you started asking him about the medical records. There was also a pair of running shoes by the back door at his house when I was there. They weren't there the first time we talked to him. Which makes me think they weren't Patrick's."

Raker looked delighted. Sheila looked proud. And Sam wanted to freeze the moment forever.

Then the door burst open, hitting the wall with a boom. Everyone jumped. Hank stood there. Haggard and pale and unshaven. Sam reflexively stepped back. Until he saw the glint in the chief's eyes. That was a sign the old chief was in there somewhere.

"You have a positive ID on O'Connell? Sammy, that's fantastic." Hank clapped Sam on the shoulder. "And Gunner? I missed it, didn't I? You get anything out of it?"

Mr. Raker brought the chief up to speed. The chief asked a few questions, and then Sheila had one for Mr. Raker. "You said the theater cost two mill? How do you figure?"

"I called every contractor on the project, got all their invoices."

"That theater hadn't seemed to be in *that* bad a shape."

"That's why I think they're padding the invoices," Raker said.

They all started talking about the financials, but the chief interrupted. "When's Hailee's funeral?"

Sheila stiffened. "*What?* You're not going. We settled this."

"That wasn't why I was asking," Hank said. He got out his phone and pulled up two photos. They were pictures of two black-and-white sketches. All three of them looked at Hank.

"These were drawn by Emily Fitch."

On his way to the Branson PD, Hank had sent over photos of the drawings to the high school art teacher. They were exactly the style that Emily had been developing when she dropped out of school. Better, more refined now, but definitely the same.

Sheila and the two men stared at him.

"If you look at that card drawing, that's unmistakably Johnny Gall. Which links the two of them together for the first time."

"And you think the diary drawing's in honor of Hailee, don't you?" Sheila asked.

Hank nodded. "I think it's supposed to be the two sisters."

Sam snorted. "A little late for that."

"But I do think there's a chance Emily will show up for Hailee's funeral. That's why I asked. She's our best chance to figure out who Gall really is. How would she know him? By all accounts, she didn't associate with her sister or other high schoolers. So how would she have met Johnny?"

"It's a long shot, but it's the only one we've got where Gall's concerned," Sheila said. "So we definitely should have extra people at that funeral. But you're not going."

He thought about arguing, but he knew his case wasn't a strong one. He looked like a bereaved hobo.

"There's not much else to do right now. Why don't you go home?" she said.

Then the look on her face suddenly changed. She spun around toward Raker. "Did you talk to that Kyle Hatwick guy?"

"Who?" Sam asked.

"The theater construction manager," Sheila answered. "He's the one who complained about Gunner being a pain during the project."

Dale nodded. "Yeah. He's the one who directed me to the subcontractors and everything. He's been quite helpful and very prompt with any documentation he had access to."

Sheila crossed her arms and started tapping her foot. Hank loved it when she did that. It meant something was coming.

"Is that it? Documentation? You talk to him at all?" she asked.

Raker looked at her questioningly. "Should I have?"

"'You can't come back at me for nothing.' That's what he said on the phone before I went to his house on Monday," Sheila said.

All three men's eyebrows shot up; then everyone lunged for Raker's file. They reexamined all the paperwork, but no one could pinpoint any discrepancies. Sure, Raker had a theory that money was getting laundered through those construction costs, but it was going to take a lot more numbers work. Raker started to grumble about the cost of hiring a forensic accountant.

"I'm going back out to talk to Hatwick," Sheila said. "He goes from evasive on Monday to totally helpful on Friday? No way. Not without a reason." She scooped up Raker's paperwork. "I'm going to make copies of all this."

Sam was offering to do it for her when his phone rang. She waved him off and swept out of the room.

Hank watched as the Pup stood very still and then agreed rapidly to what sounded like five different things.

"Nashville PD is making contact with Ganton's foster parents," the Pup said. "They want to set up a call with a detective who's working on a welfare fraud investigation." He grinned at Hank.

"Not only did you figure out something huge on our end, I think you've started something on their end, too," Hank said. "You've done great work, Sammy."

Raker echoed the compliment and suggested that the two of them use the PD conference room.

"I'm going to go with Sheila to talk to this Hatwick guy," Hank said. Raker looked sideways at him. "I know, I know," Hank said. "She told me to go home. I think she'd be more surprised if I did that, though, than if I just show up in her car waiting for her. So that's what I'm going to do."

THEY pulled up in front of Kyle Hatwick's cracker-box house just as his girlfriend got into a beat-up Chevy Malibu and drove off. Sheila headed for the front door, noticing that Hank didn't follow. Instead he drifted silently toward the big Ram pickup that Hatwick had found paperwork in last time.

She rapped on the door. Two minutes later, she pounded. Hank wandered back over to her.

"I can smell pot coming from around the side," he said.

She turned back to the door. "If you don't answer the door, Mr. Hatwick, I will issue a warrant for your arrest." When she wanted to, Sheila had a voice that didn't need a bullhorn.

The door slowly swung open. Hatwick stood there wearing nothing but cargo shorts and a god-awful amount of Axe body spray. Sheila's eyes started to water.

"Nice try, Kyle. We smelled the pot. If you don't start answering my questions with the truth, I'm hauling your ass in on possession charges. So. May we come in?"

Kyle reluctantly stepped back, and they held their breath as they passed through the cloud of cologne and into the living room.

"I gave that other dude all the subcontractor stuff. I don't got anything else."

They both stared at him. Sheila turned to Hank. "We should probably search the house. We have probable cause, and . . ."

"No. No. That's okay. No need to do that." Hatwick slumped down onto the couch. "I added something to the construction."

Sheila gestured for him to continue.

"It was a room in the back. Near the rear loading doors."

It wasn't on the drawings. Hatwick had carved it out of a couple different spaces. It just needed to be hidden, and easily accessible from the back door.

"What's this room for?" said Sheila.

"I don't know. Honest. There was a dude who came in after I did the studwork and he laid in a bunch of wire. Then I skimmed a little bit of drywall from the main order, and I was done."

"Who told you to do this?" Sheila said.

He looked miserable. "I got . . . friends. They asked me to do it." He didn't know their names. "They go by Tom and Jerry."

"And why," said Hank, "would you be 'friends' with people whose names you don't even know?"

"They're my dealers, okay? So I did 'em a favor. There."

"And how much did they pay you for all this?" Sheila said.

"Five grand. And some really good weed," Hatwick said.

Sheila thought for a moment. "Did you tell them that I came by on Monday?"

Hatwick nodded. They'd told him that if any cops came back, he should cooperate, as long as he didn't tell them about the room. He reluctantly recited the phone number he'd called.

"Is that usually how you got hold of them—by phone?" Hank asked.

"Lately that was the only way," Hatwick said. "Before, you could meet at a restaurant to place your order and then there was a rotating set of pickup locations around town."

"What was the restaurant you used to meet at?" said Hank.

One near Wildwood Drive. Sheila froze, then slowly took out her phone. She pulled up a photo and stuck it in Hatwick's face.

"Is this your dealer?"

His jaw sagged open, and he nodded.

"Is there a Tom-and-Jerry 'they' or is it just her?" she asked.

"There's no Tom and Jerry. It's just her."

She handed the phone to Hank. A very slow, very slight smile appeared on his face. "Go get a shirt on," Hank said. "You're going to show us where this room is."

THE Nashville PD detective investigating the adoption case was old and gray and had a Grand Ole Opry accent. Sam had set up the Skype connection—neither the old Tennessean nor Mr. Raker had known what to do with all that, so he'd taken charge.

"Cliff Strasburger last saw Eric Ganton four years ago," the detective said. "Told me the kid ran away in the middle of the night. Said he was a real pain, so they didn't miss him."

Mr. Raker shifted to make sure he was in front of the camera. "They apparently liked his foster payments well enough."

"No kidding. Three years of monthly checks, until Ganton aged out of the system," the detective said. "Strasburger is now a guest of our fine city's jail. DA's going to charge him with fraud."

Sam tugged at his ear. "Sir? You keep talking about Mr. Strasburger. The documentation I saw also had a wife. Tina?"

The detective grinned. "Yeah. She's even more of a piece of work. Cliff says she left him two years ago. She pops up with a DUI arrest six months after that, and then nothing."

Sam was going to ask for a photo, but Mr. Raker got there first. The detective said he'd email over her DL picture and the DUI mug shot. They talked a little more about how to track her down, and then the Tennessee detective signed off.

HANK stared at the photo of Emily Fitch all the way to the theater, with Sheila riding the brakes just enough to make Hatwick's back seat ride bumpy. The pothead said that he'd given his illicitly made set of keys to Emily, so they had to call the new theater manager, Frank Rasmussen, to let them in.

They all walked through the back door and into a large area that looked like it'd be used for loading and equipment. Pothead led them over to a wall that ran perpendicular to the back exterior wall. He stopped near where the two walls met and ran his hand along the surface. One push in the right spot, and a previously invisible door suddenly swung inward. Unbelievable.

The room was long and thin, about eight feet by eighteen feet, and ran along the very back of the theater. The pothead had done a decent job with the drywall, which was still mostly exposed. Only the far back wall had been painted. A half-dozen printers and two desktops with huge monitors sat on long folding tables. Some kind of laminating press sat in the corner.

"Damn," Frank Rasmussen said. "Nobody told me about this."

"That's because nobody's supposed to know," Hank said. He turned to Sheila. "Not everything's hooked up yet. She's still in the process of getting this going."

"What the hell am I supposed to do with this?" Rasmussen said.

"Absolutely nothing," Hank said. "You are not to say a word about this to anyone, do you understand? This is an ongoing investigation. Don't touch anything. Don't come in here. Got it?"

The guy nodded. Hank started pacing the length of the room. "What's she doing with all this?" He waved toward the high-end equipment. "You don't need this to sell some pot. Or even the harder stuff. She's got to be into something else."

He and Sheila stared at the hardware, and then at each other.

"Are you thinking what I'm thinking?" Hank said.

DALE did a jig when they told him. Literally. Sam asked whether they'd found any prints on the equipment.

"There were a couple of distinct sets," Sheila said. "They're running them right now."

"Emily Fitch," Dale said. "I'm going to get her. After all these years." He came back down to earth. "Why didn't you just call us to come out there? Why come back to the station?"

They didn't want to tip her off, Hank said. He'd stationed one of his deputies in a civilian car in the parking lot next door, but they were going to need a lot more manpower to adequately cover all the access points. Dale bolted from the room, yelling for any patrol officers in the building.

Sheila turned to Hank. "So she's been making fake IDs. Which has to be where our foster kid got his. And Johnny Gall. If they're all as good as those, she's got to be making a fortune."

"But where was she doing it before," Sam asked. "Her dad's?"

Sheila shook her head. Hell, no. That place barely had electricity. She told Hank and Sam about Emily's visit to Mick Fitch. "That property was nice and isolated; it just didn't have the power or the internet to support what she needs," Sheila said.

"Could it have been at the apartment?" said Hank.

They both turned to Sam, who'd become the authority on the Bellflower Apartments.

"There were 'a great many too many' comings and goings," he said. "According to that, um, opinionated upstairs neighbor lady. So I'd say it's a possibility."

"Then why'd they quit using it?" Hank said.

Sam thought a minute. "The manager guy did tell me that he'd recently lost his job—his real one, not the managing one. So he might've been starting to be around the complex more. That wouldn't have been good for her business."

Hank slowly sank into one of the big conference room chairs. He leaned his disheveled head back and stared at the ceiling. His deputies knew what that meant. Sheila quietly shut the door, and they took seats on the other side of the table.

"So what does she want? What does she need?" Hank said to the ceiling. "She needs a place where no one will notice people coming and going. But it also needs to be easy for people to find." He lowered his gaze back down to the level of ordinary humans. "People'll be all over that theater all the time. A couple more aren't going to raise any alarms. And it's on a bus route."

"And," Sam chimed in, "they'd just skim whatever power they need. It's got to be a huge utility bill anyway. Nobody's going to notice a little extra."

Dale burst into the room with a bang of the door. "We're on it. I got five guys camped out around all the access points, and another one in the woods behind the theater just in case."

Dale rambled on about logistics, and Sheila's mind wandered back to Emily. Why? Why go into counterfeit IDs? The start-up costs had to be huge—that equipment alone easily hit the mid-five figures. Selling drugs was a hell of a lot easier.

"When's Hailee's funeral?" Dale asked.

"It's tomorrow. Ten a.m. At the Catholic church."

"All right," Dale said. "We're going to need some of your folks for that one. I'm spread thin because of the theater and all."

Hank wasn't bothering to hide his grin. "See, you need me."

Sheila patted at her hair. "Fine. But you have to stay hidden."

"Okay," he said. Deal.

"Good," Sheila said. "Now—will you please go home?"

THE church was empty. Nora Rossetto stood next to Sheila, her shaking hands clutching her purse.

Sheila was about to guide her toward the front pew when there was movement out in the vestibule. They both stared in surprise as three people came in. Then two more. Then another four. Eventually, more than twenty people filed in and took seats. All of them were adults—no teenagers. She recognized one as the high school football coach. The rest must be teachers as well.

Sheila took hold of Nora's hand and settled her into the front row. She saw Dale quietly slip in and position himself in the back. She was about to sit down next to Nora when she saw Sergeant Jenkins slink into the sanctuary and sit in a pew opposite Dale. She couldn't have been more surprised if it'd been Santa Claus.

The priest, a broad-chested Latino, entered, and everyone lowered their heads to pray.

SHEILA had stuck him in the parking lot. Which was smart, actually. Hank knew he still wasn't ready to face an actual funeral service. He'd driven over incognito in Maggie's minivan, and parked close to the exit but in a spot where he had a good view of the church entrance. He leaned the driver's seat back as cars started trickling into the lot.

Kayla Anderson's parents pulled up. They trudged up to the church without speaking. The fortitude it must take to subject themselves to another funeral, and for a child they didn't even know. That was the very definition of classy, Hank thought.

Then DeRosia and Jenkins pulled up in one of their crash unit pickup trucks. The partners got out. DeRosia looked around and spotted him across the broad expanse of pavement. Jenkins pointed toward the church and said something Hank couldn't hear. She responded, and Jenkins marched stiff-backed toward the building. Nina headed toward the minivan.

"Hi."

Hank rolled down his window. "Hi. I didn't expect you guys to come."

She grinned. She hadn't either. It'd been Jenkins's idea. He'd done the initial death notification with Deputy Turley and said yesterday that he wanted to come to the funeral.

"He wouldn't say why. The notification really seemed to affect him." She shrugged. "I decided to come with him because he can be not exactly the most . . . tactful in expressing himself."

That was for damn sure. She turned to go and then stopped.

"Oh, I was going to call you Monday with this, but I'll just tell you now. We have a cause for the crash. Our finding is going to be driver error. There was no mechanical defect. Just excessive speed and failure to negotiate the curve."

Hank managed a "thank-you" and then watched as she walked away to the church. He'd tried to prepare himself for this possibility, but he hadn't done a very good job. He took a deep breath and tried to turn his attention back to the funeral surveillance.

The top of the hour came and went. At 10:05, an old Pontiac rattled into the lot and pulled up in front of the entrance. The passenger got out and the haggard woman behind the wheel drove off. Daddy Fitch paused for a minute and straightened his worn button-down dress shirt. Hank quickly texted Raker, who instantly came into view through the glass doors. There was some talking— by Raker—and some rude gesturing—by Fitch. Then Hank saw Raker take Fitch by the arm, and they disappeared inside. The detective must have "invited" Fitch to sit next to him. Hank smiled. He liked the Branson detective more all the time.

He slouched down lower behind the steering wheel and waited. The parking lot stayed deserted for quite a while. He saw a woman he recognized as the church secretary cross over to the parish hall and go inside. And a plumbing company cargo van pulled in and parked up near the side of the church itself.

Hank sat up a little straighter. The plumber who'd hopped out of Pete's Priority Plumbing van and gone through the side door of the church had a toolbox and was wearing coveralls that looked way too big. A ball cap was pulled way too low over the face.

He started to climb out of the car.

THE priest began the homily, and Nora clasped Sheila's hand. They sat that way as he touched on what a good person Hailee had been. The priest paused, and the sanctuary fell quiet except for the thumbing of hymnal pages. And one soft clank of metal.

Sheila turned. It'd come from the left side of the sanctuary. She caught a glimpse of blue clothing and a flash of blond hair. She rose to her feet, ignored the priest's startled look, and quickly crossed in front of the pews, completely interrupting the service. As she moved, she glanced toward Dale and saw immediately that he couldn't leave Mick Fitch. That guy would bolt at the slightest thing, and they needed him, too.

Almost to the doorway, she saw someone on the opposite end of the back row stand. Jenkins nodded at her and pointed toward the main doors that led to the vestibule. She nodded back and broke into a run.

HANK rounded the car, about to push off in a run when Jenkins burst through the doors. The sergeant waved to the left and started shouting. Hank took off toward the cargo van. He saw the too-little plumber dive inside, and the engine turned over with a roar.

Hank looked at Jenkins, who was closing in on the van by cutting through the landscaping shrubbery, and skidded to a stop. He'd be of more use back in his own vehicle. He scrambled back in and peeled out as he gunned it across the parking lot. He'd block her in. He spun the wheel and fishtailed into position perpendicular to the cargo van. And then slammed into the window as the bigger work van ran full speed into the side of his wife's minivan. His head smacked against the glass, and the air bag followed up with an explosion that felt like a right hook to the face.

The impact had pushed the minivan just enough for Emily to get by. She whipped out of the parking lot going at least sixty.

The minivan was still running. Hank hit the gas and turned the wheel. The whole frame shuddered but managed to move. The entire left side of his face felt flattened and was starting to send shocking tendrils of pain through the rest of his skull.

He fought through the air bag and pulled his seat belt on while the car clattered across the parking lot. He had both hands back on the wheel by the time he turned onto the road. He didn't know how far his battered minivan would be able to go.

SAM was on a side street monitoring traffic for a possible Emily Fitch sighting. He was fighting off a yawn when a plumbing van whipped by so fast he forgot his boredom.

And then the chief's minivan blew by almost as fast. Damn. He fired up the squad car and took off after his boss.

SHEILA spun toward Jenkins. He'd had to throw himself out of the way of the plumbing van and was now picking himself up out of a boxwood shrub. DeRosia was standing on the front steps and calling in the van's description.

"That was the sister, wasn't it?" Jenkins was yelling.

"Oh, yeah," Sheila said. "That was her."

"And your idiot boss is going to catch her in a wrecked minivan?" He rolled his eyes and ran toward his truck at the far end of the lot. Sheila followed. No way in hell was she going to let him go after *her* suspect by himself.

HANK heard the siren, and a quick look in the rearview mirror confirmed that Sammy was behind him. Hallelujah. He switched the minivan to the slow lane, and Sam sped past him in a gloriously functional department cruiser.

Hank wasn't going to stop, though. Not when they were so close to getting answers. Answers that were speeding away in a plumbing van with a broken headlight.

Wow. That van was insane. It had to be Emily Fitch behind the wheel, and she was ignoring every traffic law in existence.

They were getting close to one of the outlet malls. Sam tried to remember his pursuit training. Vehicle traffic. Pedestrians. Weather conditions. He stayed carefully behind her, siren wailing and knuckles white on the steering wheel.

Jenkins was making up ground. The truck flew effortlessly along the Branson streets. Sheila grabbed the car's radio and reported the pursuit in progress. She was told that Deputy Karnes had radioed two minutes earlier that he was in pursuit of a blue Ford cargo van.

His changing locations began getting relayed through various dispatches, and Jenkins followed the updates flawlessly. The jerk actually drove better during a high-speed chase. And had made a point to come to a funeral he knew would attract very few mourners. He had a few more layers than Sheila had thought.

They overtook Sammy and were suddenly directly behind the plumber's van. "Are you taking notes?" Jenkins said. "Because this is how it's done."

And yet, he was still a jerk.

Once they passed Sammy, Sheila took over relaying the pursuit. They were fast approaching the intersection with Gretna.

The brake lights flashed briefly. Then Emily laid on the horn and blew through Gretna Road. There was another major intersection seconds ahead. The light was green. Emily, blasting the horn, raced directly through.

Sheila knew Roark Valley Road dead-ended up ahead, and there was only one way to go. "Go right. Now."

And he did. She braced herself as Jenkins and Emily turned their vehicles simultaneously. The cargo van swung wide and barely managed to stay on the road. Jenkins hugged the inside of the curve like a pro and gained enough on her to end up right alongside.

Sheila got on the radio to Sam and gave him instructions. They heard his siren veer off to the east.

Sᴀᴍ's ᴄʀᴜɪsᴇʀ sᴄʀᴇᴀᴍᴇᴅ north on the expressway, which was thankfully wider, smoother, and better graded than the access road that paralleled it to the west, on the other side of Roark Creek. He reached the spot where the smaller road crossed the bigger one as he listened to Sheila call out their progress.

He parked on the shoulder of the southwest corner and left his lights and siren going as he went around to his trunk. He got out the case and pulled out the accordion-folded strip. He could hear more sirens coming from the north—hopefully BPD officers blocking off traffic from that direction. He flung the spike strip onto the pavement. It wasn't heavy, but man, was it awkward.

Hᴀɴᴋ turned up the expressway and followed the Pup's cruiser at a much slower pace. The minivan's shuddering got worse with every revolution of the tires. And part of the back bumper had fallen off at some point.

He reached the top of the rise and immediately saw what Sammy was doing. He started swerving back and forth across the lanes, trying to stop the traffic coming up behind him. When he laid on the horn, it sounded like the cartoon roadrunner, not the agitated bull blast he was used to in a squad car. But it didn't matter. Turned out that a crazy man in a battered minivan was just as effective as a police car in getting people to back the hell off.

He inched along, steering from side to side. He had no idea when Emily would show up, or how fast she'd be going. It was critical that there be no cross traffic when she hit those spike strips. And it was beyond critical that Sam get far off the roadway before a two-ton vehicle came gunning for him.

Sʜᴇ turned to Jenkins, who was concentrating on staying even with the van. Thank goodness the road was otherwise deserted.

"I told him to set the spike strip on the left side of the road. So we've got to keep her in that lane. And there's a sharp curve right before we'll get there. That should slow her down."

Emily must've known the curve was coming, too, because she

started to decelerate. But Sheila had a feeling that little Emily was out of her depth here. She had no idea what awaited her.

Hank parked the minivan across the northbound lanes and hopped out. He heard sirens behind him now, and he took a few steps to where he could see a BPD unit safeguarding that direction from any civilian motorists. Someone already had stopped the southbound lanes and the road coming from the east.

He took a deep breath, and it rattled around his rib cage painfully as he ran across to Sammy.

"No. Farther back." He pulled on Sam's shirt. "I don't want you getting hurt if that van veers off when it hits that strip."

Before Sam could answer, the whine of an engine reached an unimaginable pitch and the sound of ripping metal echoed through the air.

Jenkins started to slow down. He needed to be able to stop before the van hit the spikes. It would likely keep going straight, but if it didn't, they'd be a lot better off well back from it.

The curve came into view. It was a sharp right turn. They saw the van's brake lights flash, and then Emily must have realized that wasn't going to cut it. The van's back end swung wide and slammed into the paltry outer guardrail along the curve. It tore through the metal, and then the vehicle disappeared over the edge.

Hank and Sam took off running. The Highway Patrol truck screeched to a halt just on the other side of the curve. Sheila was sprinting toward them, and Jenkins wasn't far behind her. They all converged on the gap where the guardrail had been.

The drop-off could have been much worse. The hill only descended about ten or fifteen feet down from the roadway. Pete's plumbing van had carved a path through the trees and now lay on its side in the middle of the fall foliage.

Hank reached out for what was left of the guardrail and got Sam instead. The Pup grabbed him, and Hank tried to concentrate on the feel of the younger man's strong grip on his arm. It wasn't working. His vision blurred. He could hear metal shrieking and smell the blood and the rubber and the motor oil.

Then he felt a hand on his other arm. This one squeezed. Hard. He looked over at Sheila.

"Here and now, Hank. You need to be here and now. This is not that other accident. This is Emily Fitch. We need to get to her. She could be hurt. This isn't those kids. This is different."

Hank stepped off the road and slid down the hill.

It LOOKED like Emily Fitch probably had some bruised or broken ribs. The seat belt had held and saved her from much more severe injuries. Hank eyed her through the window he had to crouch down to see through.

"You're going to be all right," he said. "We're waiting on the ambulance before we move you."

She had a cut above her pretty eye, and blood trickled down her cheek. That didn't stop her from giving him a look that said a couple of things. One, that she was not all right. Two, that Hank was a cop and therefore full of crap.

He tried to ignore the pain in the side of his face. "You're a hard person to find."

She just stared at him.

"But if you were really careful, you wouldn't still be in Branson. You'd be long gone. And yet, here you are."

She tried to blink blood out of her eye, but one arm was pinned.

"It seems you'd be the kind of person to strike out for better pastures. Unless there were business opportunities locally. You know, for the entrepreneurially minded."

He saw her visibly tense. Then Jenkins appeared to say the paramedics were on their way down, and Hank needed to get the hell out of the way. He took a last look at the enigma in the driver's seat and climbed back up the hill.

Chapter 10

SHE SAT IN THE BPD interview room, her arm in a sling. Someone had washed her face and bandaged the cut above her eye.

Hank had lowered himself gingerly into the chair on the opposite side of the table. Sheila suspected his head still hurt from the whack he'd taken when Emily smashed his minivan. Dale, who'd stored Mick Fitch in one of the station's holding cells for the moment, was in the other chair trying not to look giddy. And Sheila was lounging against the wall, staring at Miss Fitch.

"Where were you Saturday night?" said Dale.

Emily stared at him, looking both bored and tired.

"We're going to book you for murder. Because you've given us no alibi. And we're going to book you for accessory to attempted murder. Someone went after your little sister and pushed the wrong kid off a cliff. She's still in the hospital."

"What?" The word exploded involuntarily from her. "That kid who was in the newspaper—that was supposed to be Hailee? How the hell do you know that? They tell you?"

Dale crossed his arms.

"No. They didn't tell you," she said. "'Cause you don't know who did it." She hardened her glare. "I want a lawyer."

"Based on what we've found out," Hank said quietly, "you didn't care about your sister at all. Nobody's parents would let their kids near her. Because of you. Because of all the crimes you commit. Even with all that money you're making, you couldn't be bothered to throw a little her way. She had to be on free lunch at school."

Hank kept at it, pounding her in as dead a monotone as Sheila had ever heard from him. It was brutal. And brilliant. Obviously, she cared about Hailee. Risking the funeral proved it. And now she was starting to shake. Tears rolled down that pretty white face.

"Why would you do that to Hailee?" Hank asked. "What's so important that you would ruin your sister's whole life?"

It was barely a whisper. "I thought she'd be okay. She was so close to graduating and getting out . . ."

"We want to know how you know Patrick O'Connell," Dale said.

Emily was back to acting like a blank wall.

"You know that name," Dale continued. "You gave it to him. He used to be Eric Michael Ganton. Out of Tennessee. Then you changed him into Patrick O'Connell from Minnesota."

There was the barest flicker in her eyes. Hank leaned forward just a little. "Where'd you do it? The apartment?"

No response.

"It doesn't matter," Hank said. "Because we know where you are now. We have everything you'd set up in your secret little hidey-hole in the back of the theater."

She snapped back like she'd been slapped.

"Yeah," Hank said, "it's quite the setup. Did you use your drug profits to buy all the hardware?"

She was so surprised that she nodded before she realized she was doing so. Hank's gaze bored into her relentlessly. He was about to make a very big assumption.

"Why would you go into that line of work? It's risky, and it's a lot more work than dealing pot. Are you helping out felons? Wanted criminals who need to change their identities?" Hank didn't take his eyes off her. "Or," he said very softly, "are you giving kids a fresh start? Are you making minors into adults so they can get out of bad environments and start over? Are you helping foster kids get out of the system?"

Emily buried her head in her arms. Sheila walked over and knelt down next to her. She pressed a tissue into the girl's hand.

"It's important that we get this right," Sheila said to Emily's downturned head. "We need you to talk to us. Before other agencies get involved. Before people have to be taken back. To where they were trying to get away from. So will you talk to us right now? Will you waive Miranda and work with us right now?"

Emily dragged her head up and swiped at the tears on her face. "Yes, I consent. 'Cause it doesn't matter anymore anyway. You're going to shut it all down." She slumped back in her chair. "So yeah. I was helping people, people who been kept down their whole lives. A new birth certificate, a new driver's license, and voila. They're transformed. They're legal age, they're untrackable, they're good to go. Good to go live a life."

O'Connell had found her about a year ago. He said he was already using that name and needed ID to support it. She'd never known his real name.

"I never knew any of their real names. That way, if people came asking, I wouldn't have any information to give."

O'Connell had loved what she was doing and wanted to help—get as many kids out of bad situations and out on their own as he could. When he went on the road with the old singer dude, he spread the word. That was cool. It grew her operation beyond what she'd expected. They were to the point they were drawing in a couple of kids a week. They needed someplace safe to talk to them, take their photos for the IDs. They tried using the apartment, but they stood out too much. Too many eyes watching.

"This wasn't a quick thing. They needed some time—to know that they're not in danger anymore. One girl, we had to wait for the bruises to fade off her face before we could take her picture. Another one still had cigarette burns all over his arms. Fresh ones. So we needed a safe place—a permanent one."

She cased where her dad was living. It was the perfect location, but barely had power, let alone high-speed internet. So she reeled in one of her pot customers who was working on the theater.

"Did you know that O'Connell was linked to the theater? That he was on the road with Euford?" Hank asked.

No. She'd had no idea that Gunner was the one O'Connell traveled with. Not until he showed up with the old dude during the remodel of the theater. O'Connell had been useful, keeping the remodelers' attention away from the area with the hidden room. And he kept putting the word out. Other than that, his time was taken up with lapdog duties for that washed-up Opry star.

She slowly crossed her one good arm over her sling. "I'll tell you the rest of what I know—only if I get a deal."

"You're not getting a deal," Raker said. "You're wanted for about a dozen different crimes in this city. You're going to jail."

Emily nonchalantly started examining her manicure.

"Let's talk about Johnny Gall," Hank said.

She raised a disinterested eyebrow. "Never heard of him."

"That's strange, seeing as you manufactured him out of whole cloth," he said.

She gave him a look that dared him to prove it.

"The birth certificate was a provable forgery. You got the name of the hospital wrong. It wasn't called that until years afterward."

She started laughing. "Damn. Really? I didn't think to check that. So, yeah. I did paperwork for that guy."

"Why two identities, though?"

"I did him the standard one, made him older. Then he comes back and says that he's decided he wants to finish high school here in town. So I made him another one, age seventeen. I charged him full freight for that one."

"How'd he pay for it?"

"I don't know. I figured he talked O'Connell into helping. That one was never hurting for cash."

"So they knew each other."

"Yeah. We were using Johnny's apartment. O'Connell knew that."

"What was their relationship like?"

She rolled her eyes. "How the hell should I know? I'm running a business, not monitoring a bunch of teenagers' social lives. Why do you care about this Gall kid anyway?"

"He pretended to be your sister's friend. He lured her into going out Saturday night. And he was sitting next to her when they were killed," Raker said.

She glared at him. "You're going to bring my sister into this?"

Sheila, from her resumed post on the wall, asked if Emily knew Gall's real name or where he was from. The answer was no.

"You ever heard the name Evelyn Cluth?" she asked.

Emily shook her head. "Nope. Never heard of her."

Raker reached into the file he'd placed on the table and pulled out a photo of the crime scene. He slapped it in front of Emily. She glanced at it and then resumed glaring at Raker.

Hank sat back and considered that as Raker started in with more questions. She hadn't even flinched. And it was the worst picture they had—O'Connell's body in the pool of his own blood.

Emily's answers were getting uncooperative. Hank waited for Raker to pause for breath and spoke. "Where's his wallet?"

She shifted her gaze to Hank. "How would I know?"

"Because you took it, and whatever equipment was left in that apartment." He matched her stare. "I bet you were worried about the ID. Weren't sure it'd hold up under the kind of scrutiny that comes with a murder investigation."

She didn't respond.

"Theft is a whole lot better of a charge than murder. Because this guy right here"—he pointed to Raker—"is about two seconds away from charging you with murder. You're our only suspect."

"Then you're stupid. Because I didn't kill him. And you're never going to know who did kill him if you don't make a deal with me."

When Sam arrived, Mr. Raker was busy yelling at a man Sam recognized from the prosecuting attorney's office. Sheila and the chief stood well clear, on the other side of the room. Emily Fitch was in the interview room. Then a lady in a business suit blew in and closed herself in with Emily. The prosecuting attorney guy and the lady then had a serious discussion in the corner.

The two people in suits finished talking. They all trooped into the interview room. Sam slipped in, too, and stood in the corner.

"We have agreed," the prosecutor said, "that if your information is material to the homicide investigation—as determined by these officers, not you—then my office is prepared to drop any theft charges related to the wallet or obstructing an investigation. We also will reduce the pursuit incident to reckless driving. But the false ID documents, that's a different story and is not included in this deal. Understand?"

Emily and her attorney nodded.

"Talk," Mr. Raker said.

Emily looked from person to person, taking her time. She finally focused on Mr. Raker. "I have the knife."

Mr. Raker looked like he'd been punched. "What?" he croaked.

"You were right," she said, looking at the chief. "I took the wallet. I got to the apartment, and he was dead." She pointed at the file on the table with photos poking out of it. "He had the first Minnesota ID I'd made. I figured there was no reason to leave it there, in case I hadn't gotten it quite right."

So she'd taken the entire wallet, a camera that was the only equipment left in the apartment after the move into the theater room, and the knife. She hadn't seen anyone.

She'd gone there to tell him to cool it. He had been jumpy the last week or so. Had demanded to know what she knew about Johnny Gall, and if she'd made him any other fake birth certificates besides the Kalin and Gall ones. She'd thought the two of them were friends, but suddenly it seemed like an obsession.

"You know anything about O'Connell being Euford Gunner's son?" the chief asked.

"The old geezer singer? No idea. He never said he was. And he wasn't shy about saying how much Euford depended on him, how valuable he was, blah, blah. So I think if he was the old guy's son, he would've said so."

Mr. Raker waved his hand impatiently. "Where's the knife?"

In the woods adjacent to the property her father was living on. She gave directions. Mr. Raker left the room immediately. Sam and Sheila followed the chief down the hallway to the coffee machine in the break room. Sam knew the chief was looking for something in particular. He thought back. It had to do with Mr. Gunner's son. That's what the chief had just asked Emily about.

"O'Connell was asking Emily that," Sam said, thinking it through as he talked, "because he thought Johnny Gall had asked for a fake Evelyn Cluth birth certificate. That Gall was going to pretend to be Mr. Gunner's son. And if Mr. Gunner had a son, why would he need Patrick anymore?"

"Exactly." The chief sipped coffee from a Styrofoam cup.

"But Gall wasn't pretending," Sheila said. "The Evelyn birth

certificate genuinely belonged to him. That *is* his real name. And
O'Connell found the birth certificate. That discovery sent him to
Emily, and then when she said she hadn't made another fake one,
he concluded it was real—which was even worse."

"But then wouldn't Gall be the one who was murdered? Wouldn't
O'Connell kill him to keep his own thing with Gunner?" Sam said.

"They could've gotten in a fight about it," Sheila said. "And
O'Connell lost."

"Then Johnny just went ahead with his Saturday night?" Hank
frowned. "Joined up with friends to have fun? I don't know . . ."

"We're still in the same spot without a DNA warrant, though,"
Sheila said. "We need Gunner to agree."

"If we find Gall's prints, I think we'll have a stronger case with
the judge," Hank said. "So now we wait for the knife."

It didn't take long. Raker seemed to have sent the entire police
force into the woods off Highway 248. They returned in what
looked like a parade line, led by the Branson PD evidence tech,
Brian Handlesman, holding two evidence bags.

"What's in the second one?" Hank asked.

Raker's bullfrog mouth curled upward. "The wallet."

Raker followed his evidence tech into the crime lab. Hank,
Sheila, and Sam crowded in after him. Handlesman removed the
bifold from the bag, photographed it, and opened it. There was no
ID. Hank snorted with laughter. "I'll bet she incinerated it that
night. She wasn't going to take any chances with that."

Handlesman peeled apart the leather, sticky with dried blood,
to get at the currency. After several minutes of careful work, he
extracted three dollar bills and a folded paper. Raker picked it up.
He unfolded it and let out a low whistle. *"Dear Evelyn Cluth . . ."*

Hank leaped forward. Sheila elbowed Handlesman out of the
way. Raker held the letter up for better viewing.

Dear Evelyn Cluth,

   *You may not know it, but you have a son. My name is Evelyn
Cluth, Jr., and I'm 17. My mother was Pamela Helbing. She's dead*

now. I was in foster care in Kentucky for a while, but I ran away. I tried to find you, but I never could. Then I met a private investigator who showed me how to research people. I found your birth certificate in Memphis. Then I found an ad in the old Nashville Banner *newspaper for a show with a guitar player named Evelyn Cluth. The picture looked exactly like Euford Gunner. You must have changed your name. I wanted to find you, but I needed a new ID because the foster people were looking for me. I heard that you could get one in Branson, so I hitched up here. Then I found out that you were going to be starting a show in Branson. So I decided to wait for you. I would really like to meet you. It would be really nice to have a dad.*

Sincerely,

Ev Cluth

They all exhaled at the same time. The kid had just been trying to find his father, and now he was dead.

"This confirms that O'Connell knew Gall was a direct threat to his meal ticket," Sheila said. "And—"

"You all can find somewhere else to talk, right?" Handlesman said. He'd taken the knife, a blood-crusted survival-style fixed blade, out of its bag and was holding it like a platter in front of him. "'Cause I don't really need you while I do this."

They all shuffled out of the room.

"So the question becomes," Sheila continued once they were in exile in the hallway, "did that letter ever get to Euford?"

Raker started to answer, but Hank was already halfway down the hall. He burst into the interview room, making the defense attorney jump. Emily just gave him a slow blink. He pulled up a chair, sat, and put his elbows on the table.

"When you said that O'Connell had been jumpy lately and started to seem obsessed with Johnny Gall, you mentioned that O'Connell had asked you about other fake birth certificates. Did he mention a name?"

"I don't think so. By that point I was tuning him out."

"When was this?"

"A day before he was killed. Why?"

"How did he react when you said you hadn't made Gall any more fake ones?"

"He was pissed. Like he didn't believe me. Like I was in cahoots with Johnny Gall. Puh-leez. In cahoots with a guy who voluntarily went back to high school when he didn't have to? Yeah, right."

Hank studied her. "And that's how he knew your sister."

She straightened slightly. "I guess Johnny did know her. From school. I have no idea if they were friends or not."

"Did Patrick know her?"

"I don't know."

"How did you find out Patrick was angry with you?"

She laughed. "He told me. Loudly. Called me up and cussed me out. Said I'd made Johnny another fake birth certificate and betrayed him. And he said that he'd take something of mine, just like I was taking something from him."

He waited. It took her slightly more than a nanosecond.

"Oh, no. He was going after Hailee. Something of mine."

Hank nodded. "He went after Lauren Blenkinship by mistake."

She sagged back into her chair. "And now that poor kid is in the hospital." She refocused on Hank. "What would I have been taking from him if I made another fake birth certificate?"

"His free ride with Euford Gunner."

Her smile was sad. "There's no such thing as one of those."

Hank rose to his feet. "No, there's not."

SHEILA had seen most of the conversation. She distilled it for Sam and let him extrapolate.

"O'Connell must have found out about Gall's plans for a party at the apartment," Sammy said. "He decided that he needed to get to Hailee before she started socializing with the other teenagers. But he ended up accidentally chasing Lauren instead."

"Yeah," Sheila said. "And what was he planning to do to Hailee? Threaten her? Beat her up? I don't know. I do think he didn't plan beforehand to end up running through the woods. I think that the chase was spur of the moment."

"So then O'Connell ends up back at the apartment. Because he knew Gall and the others were going there."

"But they never showed," Sheila said. "And Gall was with the high schoolers from about eight o'clock on and didn't go back to the apartment. So I don't think he's our killer."

Sam nodded and looked down the hallway. "Do you think he's going to stop at some point?"

Sheila wasn't hopeful. Hank had been pacing back and forth since he came out of the interview room. She should strap her Fitbit on him. He'd shoot her daily step-count over the top.

They loitered for a good half hour before Dale suddenly came hustling around a corner and headed for the crime lab. Sheila and Sam fell in line, and she heard the thudding of Hank's boots as he raced to catch up from the far end of the hall. They all burst in to find Brian Handlesman calmly straightening a pile of papers. He held up a hand in a stop motion, and they all meekly lined up.

"I've dusted the knife," he said. "And I've run all the prints. I had a few comparison prints I needed, so I got a hold of Kurt Gatz at your office." He gestured at Hank. "He's on the line now."

A hearty hello came out of the speakerphone on the table.

"There were three distinct sets, including prints from Emily Fitch's index finger and thumb," Handlesman said.

"Which, since she'd hidden the knife, made sense," Dale said.

Kurt said through the phone that none of the remaining prints matched those of Johnny Gall, which he had in his files courtesy of the medical examiner. While he was at it, Kurt said, he'd also accessed the prints that the medical examiner's office had taken from O'Connell's body. Those matched a thumb and a middle finger print lifted off the knife.

"That could mean he fought for the knife with his killer," Sam said.

"Or that he had the knife in the first place," said Hank. "He brought it to the apartment looking for Johnny Gall."

"Only it wasn't Gall he ended up seeing," Dale said.

The remaining ones, clear prints of the index, middle, and ring fingers, were not in the system. "So I had a thought when Handlesman said he couldn't find a database match for the third set," Kurt said cheerfully. "A couple days ago, the sheriff brought in an empty bottle of organic lemonade and told me to dust it and log it. The prints on the bottle match those three on the knife hilt."

They all turned toward Hank but saw only the door swinging slowly shut. Sheila leaned toward the phone. "Did he say whose prints were on the bottle that he wanted preserved?"

"Yeah," Kurt said. "Euford Gunner's."

Dale spun around. "And Hank took off without us?" He started for the exit.

"Wait," Handlesman said. "There's more. You all need to hear this. There's another print."

"You said three sets," Sam pointed out.

"Three *distinct* sets. There's one smudged partial. I ran that, and got a tentative NCIC database match. Some guy named Franklin John Rasmussen."

Dale paused for a split second on his way out the door and then was gone after Hank. Sheila felt her jaw drop at the same time. She grabbed Sam's arm and hauled him toward the door.

THEY sped toward Euford's stone mansion in Raker's BPD unmarked. Hank had gotten all the way to the parking lot before remembering he'd started his day driving a minivan that was no longer drivable.

The detective turned into the sweeping driveway and pulled up in front of the door. Both men got out and contemplated the enormous house.

"You want to take the front or the back?" Hank asked.

Raker chose the front. Hank reflexively checked his service weapon and jogged around the building. He moved closer to the big glass sliding doors and waited.

Raker's pounding on the front door echoed all the way to where Hank stood. When the reverberations faded, Hank heard faint shuffling coming from his left, over where the kitchen was. He stepped to the side for a better angle but couldn't see much.

Hank stepped forward and tried the handle on the sliding door. The glass slid open easily.

"OKAY, I'M NOT SURE WHAT'S going on," Sammy said as he buckled into the passenger seat. "Who's Franklin Rasmussen?"

Sheila tore out of the parking lot. The stage manager could be any place, but there was only one place to start. On the way, she explained. By the time they pulled up in front of the Classic Country Song Theater, Sam was shaking his head and wondering aloud if this case could possibly get any weirder. Sheila said no.

The front doors were locked. She left Sammy there and went around toward the back door and the loading dock. She was almost all the way around the building when she realized she hadn't called for backup. She grabbed her radio. She issued instructions and then tried the back door. It swung open.

She moved slowly through the jumble of sound equipment stacked everywhere. She didn't like this at all—no good sight lines and way too many nooks and crannies to search effectively. She quickly jabbed at the hidden door and made sure no one was in Emily's secret room. Then she made her way farther in.

One set of stage lights was on. There was a thump, like something had been dropped. She froze, trying to figure out where it'd come from. Damn acoustics.

Another thud. Enough of this. She marched across the back of the stage. If Rasmussen was here, he'd have no idea they'd found his prints on the murder weapon. He'd be going about his duties, not lying in wait so he could pick off law enforcement officers.

She reached stage left and headed toward Euford's palatial dressing room. The door was half open, and she pushed it aside just as something clattered onto the floor of the room.

EUFORD was over by the refrigerator, behind the big, granite-topped island. They stared at each other as Raker continued to bang on the front door. Hank waited him out, standing loosely just inside the sliding door. Finally the old man spoke. "I do need to ask why you're coming at me from both directions."

"I think you know why. I think you've known why all along. Why'd you kill him?"

"I didn't."

"We have the knife. Your fingerprints are all over it."

They had another little staring contest.

"What I don't get is why you didn't just take the knife with you. Unless," Hank said, stepping slowly into the middle of the room, "you panicked. You stood there, in that little bedroom in that empty apartment, and you panicked. And so you ran. Because you move a whole lot better than you let on, don't you?"

Gunner's gaze flitted—just for a second—over to the couches, where his cane leaned against the coffee table.

"What made you so angry that you stabbed to death the person you loved spending time with? The person who kept the loneliness at bay?"

Hank heard movement behind him, which he really hoped was Raker, but he didn't want to take his eyes off Euford to look.

"I need to ask you both to leave," the old man said.

"No. We're placing you under arrest," Raker said. "For the murder of Patrick O'Connell, real name Eric Michael Ganton." Raker moved into Hank's view and readied his handcuffs.

RASMUSSEN was moving around clothing racks. He saw Sheila in the mirror and froze. "Geez, ma'am. I didn't know you were coming. How . . . how'd you get in?"

"Back door. It was unlocked."

"Oh." He hadn't moved, his hands still on the rack and surrounded by glittery cowboy fringe shirts in every color.

"Have you noticed anybody hanging around?" she asked. "In connection with that hidden room we found?"

He relaxed, just an iota. "Ah. No, I haven't," he said. "You need to look at it again?"

"Maybe," Sheila said. "But I have some questions for you first. I need you to come down to the station with me."

Rasmussen didn't seem surprised. He nodded, took one step, and then flung the clothes rack straight at her. Where the hell was he going to go? She was standing at the only door. She fought through the mess of costumes, kicked aside the metal rack, and stopped. He stood there with a gun leveled right at her face.

EUFORD DIDN'T COME forward. His left hand lay on the granite island. Then his right one moved, like it was opening a drawer. He pulled out a large knife. Raker let out an exasperated sigh.

"What're you going to do with that, Euford?" Raker said. "Throw it at us? I didn't know that was part of your act."

The musician's shaky hands grew still. It was the calm of a decision made. Hank tensed and took a step forward.

"We've already talked to Frank Rasmussen," Raker said.

Hank stopped. What?

"He's told us everything," Raker continued, moving toward the kitchen area and readying the handcuffs. "So I suggest you start doing the same."

Who the hell was Frank Rasmussen? Hank suddenly remembered the stage manager guy. Damn, was there anyone who *wasn't* involved in this case?

He refocused on Euford. Hank started around the opposite side of the island from the detective. They both closed in. Euford raised the knife. "Don't." He pointed it at his own throat.

"Euford," Hank said quietly, "what about Patrick? He can't speak for himself anymore. Do you want Rasmussen to be the only one who gets a say in all this? Do you want him to be the one who gets the last word on the kid you loved like a son?"

SHEILA dove behind a clothing rack as a bullet split apart the doorjamb, right at eye level. She crouched on her knees, her Glock in her hand and her heart in her throat.

She was shielded only by a mass of satiny shirts and pressed jeans. She scooted back until she hit up against a wall. The door was to her left and the costumes and the shooter on her right. But she couldn't sit and wait for him to make a break for it. If he decided to keep shooting instead, she was toast. Even as bedazzled as they were, those shirts were not going to block a bullet.

She had to get eyes on him. She started to move a wad of denim aside. A shot ripped through the adjacent outfit. Now he was pissing her off. She shoved at the clothes, caught a glimpse, and fired. There was a yowl, and two more bullets flew at her from the other side of the room. She got as low as she could and fired again. She heard the crack of what had to be the mirror on the far end. She'd aimed too high. She corrected and squeezed the trigger.

A DOT of blood appeared at the tip of the knife. Hank kept talking. "He never had a family. He'd been in foster care since he was two. You were his first true home. You were the first one to treat him like a person, like a son. Don't let that get thrown out the window. Don't abandon him like all those other people did, all his life."

The dot was rolling down the blade. Another joined it.

"Be his family, Euford."

Euford shifted slightly to look at Hank full on. "You think you can guilt me into telling you something?"

Hank took another step forward. "Talk to us, or don't. Either way, Patrick O'Connell lies in the morgue, waiting for family to claim him. Just like he did when he was alive."

He turned away from both men and walked firmly toward the front door. Behind him, he heard a clatter and then a soft thump that sounded like a bag of laundry gently dropping to the floor. He kept going.

ANOTHER yelp. Sheila couldn't see exactly where she'd hit him, but from the whimpers, it must've been someplace pretty good. But as long as he could fire that pistol, she wasn't going to be able to get out of here. Or get him into handcuffs. He fired again. It ripped into her sleeve just above the elbow.

Sheila repositioned, laying herself flat and steadying her Glock with both hands. Another crack split the air. She tensed, but nothing flew by her. Instead, the glass on a framed Euford poster hanging near Rasmussen's position exploded. She looked over her prone shoulder toward the door. Just behind the opening was the most beautiful shaved head she'd ever seen.

Sammy fired one more shot from the cover of the door and then ordered Rasmussen to put down the gun and kick it over. Rasmussen refused in a string of four-letter words.

"You can leave in handcuffs or in a body bag," Sam said. "Those are your only two choices."

Sheila grinned. Then she readied her weapon. There'd need to be one more shot, and she didn't want Sam to take it. His psyche was still too fragile. Rasmussen kept swearing. She could see through the clothing pile that he still had a firm grip on his gun. She fired.

RAKER loaded Euford into the back seat of his unmarked car. Hank moved to join him.

"You're going to sit back there with him?" Raker said. "Why? What's he going to do, escape?"

"It's been known to happen."

Raker shrugged and climbed behind the wheel. Hank slid in next to the musician, who looked like he'd aged twenty years just walking from the house.

They were taking the on-ramp to Highway 65 when Euford shifted from staring at the seat back to looking out the window.

"I never should've trusted him," he said.

Hank just waited.

"I found him. It took me three years, but I found him. And I had him dead to rights. So I thought I could trust him."

That might make a lot more sense if Hank knew who he was talking about.

"But Frank decided to turn the knife over to the cops. Hmm. That means he hates me more than he wants his freedom. Now, that's one to ponder, that is."

Gunner had to be talking about Rasmussen. Hank still had no idea what the man had to do with all of this.

"Why would he hate you, Euford?" he said softly.

"Because I wanted my money back. That he stole from me. And I told him I'd turn him in if I didn't get it. He's got priors, which I didn't know about originally. When I hired him as my business manager. But he's got a record, and he'd get the full-on max in Tennessee if he got convicted on the stealing."

Rasmussen had stolen two-point-three million from Euford

and fled, the singer said quietly as he continued to stare out the window. Tennessee police had not much cared about what'd been Euford's only chance at a decent retirement. So Euford tracked him down on his own. And made him a deal. He wouldn't turn the bastard in if he repaid the money. Because he knew if Rasmussen went to prison, he'd never see any of it.

And so Entertainment Enterprises, Inc., was born. Rasmussen used the company to hire an unsuspecting Vivian Gillam, who thought it was just another concert show promotion entity. Then he funneled money through there to Euford.

"Much more money than I was worth." He let out a weak chuckle and looked Hank full on. "And no, I don't know exactly where the money was coming from. And you know what? I didn't care. I'd earned that money, and I wanted it back. We agreed that he'd be the stage manager so he could keep skimming whatever he was skimming and keep on reimbursing me through the shell company. And then I could also keep an eye on him. That's why I hung around so much during the construction."

Euford sighed and looked out the window again.

"With the shell company, we were almost, what'd you call 'em— accomplices," Euford told the glass. "So he was the one I thought to call that night. After."

The only sound was the hum of the engine. And the rattle of Euford's breath.

"I'd just gone to find Patrick. That's all. I was just worried. He hadn't been home in a few days, and that wasn't like him."

He knew about the apartment. He'd been so pleased Patrick was making friends, since the two of them were going to be settling here and all.

He parked down the street because all the spots in the apartment complex lot were full. He wasn't even sure Patrick would be there that night, but he was. And he was angry. Out of breath and angry. He'd tried to hide it, and he'd told Euford to leave.

"I told him it'd be best if he came home with me. That we could fix whatever it was, and he should just come home. He backed away, and so I followed him into the back room of that apartment.

I think I repeated myself, and that's when he started to cry. Said I wasn't going to want him no more. I thought he might be drunk, and I took hold of his arm."

Euford stopped, and Hank willed himself to stay silent.

"He pushed me. I pushed him back, and he swung at me, and I swatted at him. I thought a drubbing might be what he needed. To clear his head. I swung again, and then he pulled a knife. I was close in, you know, and I pushed at it. Pushed it away from me.

"He fell on the floor, and there was nothing I could do. It happened faster than playing a single chord. He was there, and then he wasn't. And I didn't know what to do. I could barely stand. So I called Rasmussen. It couldn't have been too long before he showed up. He said he'd get rid of the knife. I couldn't stay there one more second." He turned and looked at Hank. "I guess I should've considered that he'd keep it to use against me later."

Hank didn't tell him that what Rasmussen had done was worse. He'd left that knife right where it was, expecting that the police would find it, identify the fingerprints, and immediately arrest Euford. That hadn't happened only because of Emily Fitch.

"Why was Patrick so angry? Why did he have a knife?" Euford contemplated his hands, rubbed at them a bit. "You never really know who people are, I guess."

Chapter 11

"That looks like it's going to take a long time to fix."

Sam stared down at the screaming Rasmussen, whose wrist was no longer in one piece. Sheila holstered her Glock.

"He wouldn't be hurtin' if he'd just come quietly," she said.

They each took a side and hauled the bastard to his feet. There was commotion outside the room, and Sam shouted an all-clear.

Two BPD patrolmen burst in, guns drawn. Sheila told them to put the damn things away, call for an ambulance, and escort Mr. Rasmussen outside because she was about done with his hollering.

Once the cries faded away, Sam turned to her.

"I guess we'll have to wait to find out how his print got on that knife," he said. "I'm super curious about that."

So was she. She dragged herself over to one of the makeup chairs and sank into its leather cushioning. She eyed Sam in the mirror. "I thought I told you to stay put out front."

"Um. Yeah. I heard you radio for backup, so it seemed like the best place for me to be was helping you out."

She smiled. "That turned out to be a good call. Thank you."

He turned the color of a ripe raspberry.

"But how'd you get in?" she asked.

"I picked the lock. Been working on that lately. You know, broadening my skill set."

She was still laughing when Larry Alcoate, the paramedic, showed up and cut the sleeve off her uniform. The track Rasmussen's bullet had carved was deeper than she'd thought, but she didn't care. This damn case was over.

She closed her eyes and let Larry work. Finally the pressure on her bicep eased, and she felt something on her head. Larry adjusted the cowboy hat he'd pulled off a costume rack and grinned at her. Sam doubled over with laughter.

"For our very own gunslinger," Larry said. Both of them tipped imaginary caps at her reflection. "Ma'am."

These men.

They had Euford in the same interview room he'd sat in before. He'd quit talking. Which was fine, because Raker had used his cell phone to record the whole conversation in the car. That was going to make the prosecuting attorney very happy.

Not as happy as Raker, though. The guy came dancing into the break room, positively gleeful at the confession. He explained that Handlesman had called and fully briefed him about Rasmussen's prints while he was outside banging on Euford's front door. Hank nodded and sucked down his second cup of coffee and wondered when the side of his face would stop hurting.

"Come on. Cheer up. This is fantastic. Case closed. On both Gunner and Rasmussen." Raker poured himself a coffee and did a few more two-steps. "Oh, yeah," he said. "Your wife's out in the lobby. Something about her minivan."

"Oh, hell." He'd completely forgotten.

"She also wanted to know if you were here. She looked pretty concerned." Raker pondered that for a second. "Is she more concerned about you or the car?"

"I don't have the strength right now to answer that honestly."

Hank trudged out to the lobby feeling pretty concerned himself, especially when he saw the expression on Maggie's face. He explained, and that didn't help at all.

"What the hell were you thinking? One, you could've been seriously injured. Two, that's the family car. What're we supposed to do now, squeeze all five of us and two car seats into Dad's old Camry? You're going to be the one wedged in the back seat. I'm not going to climb back there and . . ."

HANK changed into a clean T-shirt and jeans, kissed his sleeping children, and wandered into the living room. He sank into the couch and decided he wasn't going to open his eyes again until at least next Tuesday. He tried to doze off, but he kept seeing Johnny Gall's broken body. All week, it'd been the others—the Branson kids robbed of their futures, and their families, now robbed of them. But the skinny outsider who never got the chance for a father . . . Hank wasn't sure how long he'd been sitting like that when he heard it. A sensible squeak.

"Hi, Fin."

He sensed Dunc's sister walking forward until she stood in front of him. He forced his eyes open. She was setting a glass of water on the coffee table. She straightened and clasped her hands in front of her. "Can I get you anything else?"

"No, that's okay. But thank you for the water."

She nodded and looked like she was going to say something else. Instead, she turned away.

"Fin. Why are you here? Really?"

They stared at each other. He was too worn out to dance around it anymore. She slowly sat across from him and tugged at her walking skirt. "I need your help. As a . . . as a policeman."

Hank pulled himself out of his slouch. "What?"

"It's about Lew." She clasped and unclasped her hands several times. "I think he's killed someone."

He chose his words carefully. "What makes you think that?"

"There was blood. And things were missing. His knuckles were bruised, cut up."

"What did he say happened?"

"I didn't ask him. I didn't want to know."

Hank leaned forward. "But what makes you think he killed someone?"

"Because his secretary hasn't been seen in three weeks."

Oh.

They sat there staring at each other.

"Did you call the local police?" he asked.

"No." She looked at him, absolutely transparent. "I don't want to ruin my marriage if I'm just an old fool with an overactive imagination. But I can't keep living with him without knowing. Without an answer. And you were the only help I could think of."

Her voice faded as she spoke, her throat slowly tightening around the words like a vise. Hank knew what that was like. He reached down for the cold pack and again saw the teenage faces that he knew would never leave him. He couldn't help those families. But maybe he could help his own.

"Okay," he said. "Tell me everything."

AfterWords

Claire Booth's career in journalism was the ideal training ground for mystery writing: It exposed her to both the grisly depths of human nature and the inner workings of the criminal justice system. Booth wrote for daily newspapers in Missouri; Washington, DC; South Florida; the Seattle region; and the Bay Area, mainly covering crime. Her last reporting job was on the murder trial beat, which meant, she says, that she "got to watch the story of a crime unspool from beginning to end. Just like a novel."

Booth's first book, a true-crime account of a cult leader who murdered five people, was inspired by a case she covered in California.

Writing about all that crime could give any writer a bleak view of humanity. But Booth purposely made her series character, Sheriff Hank Worth, a man defined by his good heart. According to Booth, Hank is "the result of the influence of the many decent, down-to-earth men in my life." Speaking of which, her husband, who she met while attending the University of Missouri, was also a source of inspiration for *A Deadly Turn*'s setting—his hometown is Branson, Missouri.

Booth is currently working on a stand-alone novel set in California. In addition, she's busy putting together a true-crime project, and fans of the Hank Worth series will be pleased to know that a fourth book is in the works.

ACKNOWLEDGMENTS

Page 147: © Gemma Day Photography. Page 291: © Gary Brown. Page 433: © Berkley (HC) 2019.
Page 575: Sarah Sepe. Jacket and title page image: Crystal Alba/Shutterstock.

The original editions of the books in this volume are published and copyrighted as follows:

The Turn of the Key, published at $27.99 by Scout Press,
an imprint of Simon & Schuster, Inc.
© 2019 by Ruth Ware

A Beach Wish, published at $15.99 by William Morrow,
an imprint of HarperCollins Publishers
© 2019 by Shelley Freydont

Layover, published at $26.00 by Berkley, an imprint of Penguin Publishing Group,
a division of Penguin Random House LLC
© 2019 by David J. Bell

A Deadly Turn, published at $28.99 by Severn House Publishers
© 2018 by Claire Booth

The volumes in this series are issued every two months.
Readers may receive this service by contacting us by mail, email, or company website.

In the United States:
Reader's Digest Select Editions
PO Box 50005, Prescott, AZ 86304-5005
bookservices@rd.com
rd.com

In Canada:
Reader's Digest Select Editions
PO Box 970 Stn Main, Markham, ON L3P 0K2
bookservices@rd.com
rd.ca

Some of the titles in this volume are also available in large-print format.
For information about Select Editions Large Type, contact us at
PO Box 433031, Palm Coast, FL 32143-3031 or selt@emailcustomerservice.com.